THE OBSIDIAN KEY

ALSO BY ELDON THOMPSON

The Crimson Sword

THE OBSIDIAN KEY

BOOK TWO OF THE LEGEND OF ASAHIEL

ELDON THOMPSON

An Imprint of HarperCollins*Publishers*

HarperCollins books may be purchased for educational, business, or sales promotional use. For information please write: Special Markets Department, HarperCollins Publishers, 10 East 53rd Street, New York, NY 10022.

FIRST EDITION

Eos is a federally registered trademark of HarperCollins Publishers.

Based on a design by Iva Hacker-Delany
Yawacor map by Tone Rodriguez
Pentania map by David Cain

Printed on acid-free paper

Library of Congress Cataloging-in-Publication Data

Thompson, Eldon.
    The obsidian key / by Eldon Thompson.—1st ed.
        p. cm.—(The legend of Asahiel ; bk. 2)
    ISBN-13: 978-0-06-074152-5 (acid-free paper)
    ISBN-10: 0-06-074152-X (acid-free paper)
        1. Kings and rulers—Succession—Fiction. 2. Quests (Expeditions)—Fiction.
    3. Demonology—Fiction. I. Title.

PS3620.H658O27 2006

813'.6—dc22
                                                              2006043370

06 07 08 09 10 JTC/CW 10 9 8 7 6 5 4 3 2 1

MATT BIALER

for leading the crusade

when there was nothing but a dream

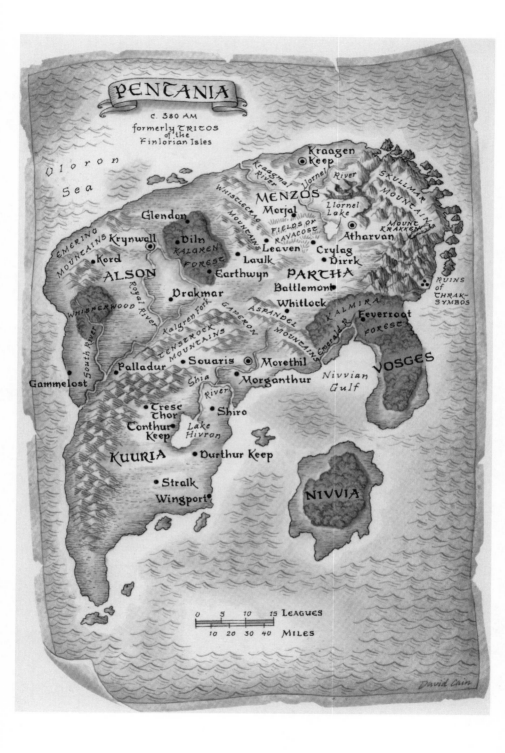

THE OBSIDIAN KEY

CHAPTER ONE

THE WINTER STORM TORE ACROSS THE LAND, ripping and snarling like a caged
beast set free at last. Its howling breath wailed in his ears. Its frigid claws
raked his skin. The darkness of its maw enveloped the earth, rendering deliberate progress a fool's dream.

Grum looked again to his battered compass, scraping at the ice that
shielded its surface. Its needle swung uselessly, drawn in random circles. He
shook the instrument, cursing it to the smelter of Achthium's Forge. To the
west were the Skullmars, the treacherous peaks from which they'd been blown
off course. To the east, the tempest of the sea. Or so he assumed. The world
around him had disappeared, its planes and edges forced together in a hazy
smear. Head bowed, eyes squinting against frenzied gusts of windblown earth,
he could scarcely spy the ground beneath his feet, let alone even the largest of
markers that might guide him home.

He risked a backward glance to check on his companions. He could see
but one, Raegak, tethered to him at the waist in their makeshift line. Beyond
that, the rope stretched into the swirling void of pelting ice and strafing winds.
He could only hope the others were still there, knowing that to become separated now would mean dying alone in these frozen wastes.

Not that remaining together afforded great consolation. Truth was, they
were hopelessly lost, miles from the safety and comfort of their subterranean
home. And even if home lay just around the bend, were they to stumble half a
step to the left or right, they might pass right on by without ever knowing it.

Raegak glanced up, eyes hollow, snow clinging to his beard. Grum looked
quickly away, hiding his compass within a gnarled fist, determined to mask
his dismay. He was *toifeam*, leader of this expedition, and by Achthium, he
would see them through.

To accentuate this silent oath, he crammed the worthless compass deep
into a leather pouch. At that same moment, the earth fell away, and he found
himself scrabbling against a clutching blackness. Chunks of ice and gravel
skittered beneath his feet, while a shower of snow cascaded about him. Everything seemed to be sucking him down, down into some depthless—

A sharp tug caught him about the waist, folding him violently forward and
snatching the wind from his lungs. For a moment he slid downward again,
before coming to a lurching halt. Curtains of snow slid past as his companions

struggled with their footing above. He hung there, twisting in the abyss, before reaching up for the lip of the pit, where Raegak, stout legs braced against the earth, bent down and offered a leather-wrapped hand.

Moments later, Grum huddled with his companions around the rim of the breach, peering into its depths. Should it prove to be the shelter that saved them, he would forgive himself his fright from the fall. Nevertheless, he had lived in these mountains long enough to know not to trust them. Such clefts might become fissures descending hundreds, even thousands of feet—or if not, might open into the den of some surly creature in no mood to share its home. Even the most foolish of his kin knew better than to enter such an opening without knowing what lay within.

Producing a flint and steel with frozen hands, Grum worked to light the pitch-coated head of a thornweed firebrand. But no sooner did the sparks flare to life than they were borne away by shrieking flurries. Grum persisted, ignoring the stiffness setting into his unmoving joints, lips pressed tight in a determined frown. At last, feeling the hopeless stares of his comrades upon him, he slipped his flint back into its pouch and motioned for Raegak to put the torch away.

He regarded each of his companions in turn—Raegak, Durin, Alfrigg, and Eitri. Friends for more than a generation, they held a shared understanding, their faces reflecting hopes and fears that mirrored his own. They would have to risk it. To prolong their exposure any longer would be fatal.

After a few quick signals, each began working loose the knot that bound him to his companions. Grum alone left his intact, for he would be lowered first. Only after assuring himself of the relative safety of this hidden cave would the others follow. With any luck, nature's wrath would expire by morning and allow them to begin the task of finding their way back from this wayward trek.

With the thickness of their gloves—and the fingers within numbed almost beyond use—even this simple task proved arduous. Doubled over, they picked at the iced ropes while quivering lips muttered private oaths. Grum watched them for a moment, until a flicker of motion drew his attention down into the hole. He leaned forward, peering intently, but saw only the void. He was about to shake it off as a trick of the storm when it came again, just a hint of movement, of something even darker than the ink in which it swam, shriveled and twisted, almost like—

He fell back as the thing shot forward, blinding in its swiftness. There was a flap of wings, a splash of blood, and a terrible cry that just barely resounded in the din of the gale. By the time Grum had regained his balance, Raegak knelt in the snow, his empty shoulder socket gushing. Already, the thing had moved on. An ebony claw seized Alfrigg by the face. He screamed as barbed nails gouged his flesh, tearing free chunks of skin and even an eyeball. Before he, too, had fallen to his knees, a silent Durin lay gasping, his throat flayed wide.

Grum brought his pick-axe up just in time to deflect a strike from the whirlwind that pressed him. It hit him like a sack of gravel, and off he flew into the blizzard, the pick-axe sailing from his grasp. He caught a glimpse of red-bearded Eitri, battle-axe drawn, peering up at a shapeless mass of whipping black tendrils—like a shredded pennant snapping in the breeze. Raegak, the iron bear, was rising to his feet. Then the battle scene vanished, devoured by a roaring curtain of ice.

Down an invisible slope he flew, skidding headfirst on his backside. His fingers clawed desperately, leather gauntlets plowing the frozen earth. As before, however, he jerked to a halt almost before he realized what was happening. This time, the rope bit into his skin, wedged into a seam of his woolen garments. He grimaced sharply, then reached immediately for his own battle-axe, his first and only thought that his companions needed him.

That changed when the rope about his waist gave a sharp tug. He sat up, seeking to find his feet, when another yank threw him down once more. He knew straightaway by the strength of the force that it was not his companions who were at the other end, hauling him back.

Panic seized him. Instinctively, he gave up trying to free the unwieldy battle-axe and reached instead for his smaller hand-axe.

It slipped from his belt as the creature snatched his ankle with a crushing grip. Grum felt his bones splinter, and he arched his back in agony, letting loose an involuntary wail. His enemy pulled, dragging him up toward the lip of the hole that moments before had tempted him with salvation. Summoning his strength, Grum bucked at the waist and brought the blade of his weapon down hard. A shriek rang out, and, as the creature recoiled, Grum aimed a second strike at the length of rope that served as his tether. It split at once, curled up against the edge of a stone and cleaved by the diamond-edged sharpness of his blade. As his enemy leaned in, more carefully this time, Grum gave a shout and hurled himself out of harm's way.

The fire in his ankle erupted as he bounced and rolled down the mountainside. The slope wasn't steep, but the icy conditions would not allow him to slow. Nor did he try. Using gravity as his ally, he clenched his jaw and rolled onward, as far and fast as his god would allow. He gave no thought to where he was going. His only prayer was that whatever he had uncovered would not give chase.

He should have known better. The Skullmar Mountains, even at low elevation, comprised some of the most unforgiving terrain found above or below the earth. Though impossible to gauge, he doubted he had covered even a hundred paces before the ground beneath him once again gave way. This time, there was nothing to halt his descent as first the fall, and then frigid darkness claimed him.

IT WAS THE LIGHT THAT WOKE HIM, illuminating a world both foreign and familiar. A world without color, sound, or smell. Yet it remained, somehow, a world of pain.

Numbed, yes, though not so fully that he was dead to its touch. It coursed through him in shallow waves, radiating from one area in particular. Drawn down the length of his body, his gaze fell upon the region of his lower left leg.

Understanding, creeping along a pace or two behind, leapt forth like a thief from the bushes. Although packed loosely in fallen snow, his shattered anklebone lay exposed enough to reveal the truth. His memory flashed back in an instant to the secret cave, the sudden struggle, his rolling flight from the savage creature that had ambushed them all.

And after? He opened his eyes, realizing only then that he had closed them against the onrush of mental imagery. His colorless prison he now recognized as a crevasse, a scar in the surface-earth whose floor was filled with a mattress of snow. This bedding had saved him, unless he missed his guess, for the rift's opening stood at least two dozen feet above where he now lay. The breach itself had been plugged by a wedge of ice and boulders, sent skidding after him as part of the small avalanche he had no doubt triggered. A fortunate turn, really, for the natural barrier had sheltered him from both beast and storm—the only explanation as to why he still drew breath.

Any joy wrought by this discovery quickly faded, however, as he thought of his friends. He had to assume they had perished, far from their homes in the shadow-earth, made to face death out of doors like a pack of wild dogs. He shut his eyes in pained remembrance: Raegak, bairn of Raethor; Durin, bairn of Nethrim; Alfrigg, bairn of Adwan; Eitri, bairn of Yarro.

And Tyrungrum, bairn of Garungum, he added harshly, tacking his own name to the list. For if he did not haul himself from this hole quickly, it would become his cairn. Dwarven flesh or no, he could not survive these elements forever. If the cold did not claim him, his hunger would. As it was, he ran the risk of being buried alive if he could not dig free before the next layer of snow fell.

Tentatively, Grum lifted an arm from where it lay half-buried in powdery snowfall. He reached first for his face and then his head, feeling along its growths and protuberances, tracing the signature collection of bone spurs that marked him unique among his people. At least a handful of those spurs—along with his nose—were frostbitten, he was sure. But that was the least of his concerns.

Somewhat encouraged, he shook free his other arm and worked now to pat along his chest and each of his gnarled limbs, making sure all was intact. It took more than a steep fall to damage a Hrothgari, he thought heartily. His brightening mood, however, lasted only as long as it took to haul himself into a sitting position, at which point the pain in his crushed ankle flared to agony. He gritted his teeth, waiting for the body-stiffening waves to subside. Eventually they did, though he shuddered to think of how it would feel once he had thawed.

First things first, he reminded himself, forcing his eyes open and his head back. At least the storm had passed. The sun shone brightly through cracks in the ceiling of his shelter—and through those covered areas where the ice and snow was thinnest. Water dripped here and there, mostly to catch along cavern walls already wet with moisture. It occurred to him that his roof might melt suddenly and dump upon him. But then, that would be almost too easy.

He cast about for his hand-axe, remembering belatedly that he had let it go early on after making his escape, so as not to carve his own hide during his frantic tumble. His pick-axe was gone as well. All that remained to him was the hefty battle-axe—strapped to his pack—that he had been unable to free in the fight above. A poor climbing tool, but it would have to suffice.

As he reached around to grip the weapon's familiar haft, he recalled his final vision of Eitri, axe in hand to face certain death. In another time and place, the image might have brought tears to his eyes. But time now was his enemy. He would pay tribute to his comrades and beg their families' forgiveness later.

Biting down against a pain made worse by the slightest of movements, he shifted his pack from his knotted shoulders. When at last he had shrugged free, he paused to catch his breath. He then brought the pack around in front of him, careful to set it to the side and not on his lap. He paused momentarily to admire the bag's straps and buckles, not one of which had failed him.

Then he went to work.

Like it or not, he had to do something about his leg. He didn't need to see beneath his boot to know that his toes would be purple with blood loss. Judging by its mashed appearance, the limb was lost to him, if not now, then by the time he dragged it back to Ungarveld. But fresh wounds were often deceiving, and he preferred that a surgeon make the final determination—not to mention any amputation. Still, he could not have it flinging about, threatening his climb at every pull.

After some quick rummaging, he pulled free an unguent, then changed his mind and took three long draughts from his mead cask. Only then did he dip his fingers in the salve with grim intent. Rather than cut away his boot and leave his foot exposed, he reached carefully inside the padded interior . . .

A mere brush against the damaged area was like bathing it in molten metal. His resulting bellow echoed in the confines of the narrow cavern and within the canyons of his throbbing ears.

The noise, as much as the pain, gave him pause. He bit off his own scream—nearly taking his tongue off in the bargain—and shook his head, which swelled with the unreleased pressure. As spasms wracked his body, he listened intently, fearful of what monsters the outburst might bring down upon him.

But as the moments passed, and the only sounds remained those muffled by the closeness of his icy tomb, he began to relax and think clearly once more. Had the creature from above wanted him, it would have sniffed him out the night before. His trek had taken him into the southern reaches of the Skullmars along the eastern coastline. His friends were dead. Just who did he suspect might hear him?

He'd spent just a short time alone, and already he was raving. He needed to get moving before madness set in.

He decided against further use of the unguent. As of this moment, he'd be lucky to die of infection. And its numbing properties wouldn't do much more than the snow already had.

Seeing no way around it, he doubled up a length of leather and placed it in his mouth to guard against further screams. He then unstoppered his scroll tube, set aside the rolled maps of tanned goatskin, and used a diamond-edged dirk to split the hard leather canister down its center. After carving out the base, he had himself the makings of an excellent splint.

Lashing the guard into place was another matter. By his estimation, it took more than fifty drips from Achthium's Spear, though the great stalactite by which his kinsmen gauged the passing of time was far away from here. Still, he only lost consciousness once, and completed the task with no more than a dozen swallows of mead. When finished, he felt immeasurably better about his prospects.

He fastened his climbing spikes next, to the foot of his good leg. He sure as stone wouldn't be putting any weight on the injured one. His hammer and anchors hung in a pouch about his waist. The rest of his belongings, those not needed for the actual climb, he left in his pack, to which he measured and tied a long length of rope. He secured the other end to a rear loop in his belt, making sure to leave plenty of slack. He could not have the pack weighing him down, and yet he wanted to be sure he would be able to retrieve it once he'd reached the top.

As a final precaution, he gathered as much loose snow as possible into the center of the chamber, so as to more deeply cushion any fall. After that, he attached his hand spikes, mapped his desired path, and began to climb.

It seemed impossible at first. Just rolling over and levering himself from the floor was a test of will unlike any he could recall. As soon as he stood, the blood began returning to his feet, causing him to swoon with agony. But the mead helped, and the thought of having to start all over again kept him upright. Reaching up, he set his first anchor, buckled tight his safety rope, and, with one leg, lunged for his first mark.

He made it, and clung there for some time, grimacing in pain, wondering how in the world he could make himself do this. It would be so much easier to simply lie down and let the ice take him. Yet he was determined that if Achthium were to come for him, here and now, He would not find him lying down.

It grew easier after that, though his pace was methodical at best. From shelf to shelf he hauled himself, doing most of the work with his hands, while using his good foot as his base. Where there wasn't a handhold, he used his axe to chip away at the earthen skin. He set his anchors dutifully, at least every third pull. Despite his best efforts to protect it, his wounded leg bounced and swayed, clipping the stone every now and then, causing him to grind his teeth into nubs. But the splint shielded him from the worst of these minor collisions, allowing him to continue.

Hours passed. Hunger and thirst assailed him. Grum ignored these aches as he did all the others, drawing himself ever higher, until at last the doorway to his freedom came within reach.

Perched beneath the lip of the crevasse, he paused to gather his strength. Above the sound of his own labored breathing, he heard what he believed to be more than just the wind. There was that, to be sure, whistling through the cracks of his ceiling, but there was something else, deeper and angrier, the unmistakable restlessness of the sea. Had he and his team strayed so far?

When ready, he set a final anchor and pulled forth his axe. The daylight was fading, its red glow through the ice dimmed. The sooner he emerged, the better, especially if he wished to find new, suitable shelter before nightfall.

He stopped short, however, before making his first cut. Once again, fear gripped him, the dread possibility that that creature might still be out there, waiting for him. Hack through this blanket of packed snow, and he might bring his own death down upon him.

Grum growled the notion away as he had before. If that was his fate, so be it. He deserved no better than his friends.

The snow was thicker than it appeared, and more solid. Sun melt throughout the day had helped turn it to ice. Grum braced himself as well as he could and continued to chip away, forced to hit harder than he would have liked. After all, he had to be careful not to dislodge the entire pack, for if he were to do so, he might end up right back at the bottom.

As if made manifest by his concern, the wedge of ice and stone gave a shudder before cracking and shearing away. A jagged boulder struck his wrist, and his axe went spinning into the chasm below. Grum closed his eyes and clung to the rock face, doing his best to ride out the sudden storm. Had he glanced up, he might have seen the larger boulder that slipped in after, skidding down from somewhere higher up the escarpment. When it struck him, his world exploded, and amid the telltale song of snapping anchors, he felt himself bouncing, flailing, plummeting once again, down into darkness.

WHEN CONSCIOUSNESS NEXT GREETED HIM, Grum knew right away that he was in worse shape than before. His head rang, and his vision would not seem to clear. The snow around his head was colored pink with blood, and the pain in his crushed ankle reached now through both legs, clear to his waist.

He lay this time upon his stomach, his arms sprawled out in pinwheel fashion. When he brought them in and tried to push up, a piercing agony in his lower region left him whimpering. He tried again, having no other choice, and twisted his head around to survey the damage. A boulder had landed atop him, sandwiching both legs, and now held him pinned.

Turning back, he cast about for his axe. A couple of his teeth lay in the bloody snow before him, and a hand went to his swollen jaw. His weapon was nowhere to be seen, buried, in all likelihood, on the other side of the cavern. If only he might have fallen on its edge, so as to end his suffering quickly.

Instead, he kept himself alive for two more days. Foolish hope, perhaps, or sheer stubbornness. He had no right to expect a rescue, and there was no longer any way to set himself free. He ate the snow, though it chilled him from within, while his shelter continued to ward him from the storms that swept overhead. He became ill, and was set upon by delirium, to the point that he was not surprised when the voices of his slain comrades began to call down to him.

"Grum! Grum!"

Grum moaned and stirred, but was unable to escape the haunting echoes.

"Grum, we're coming for you."

He dreamt then that they were there, surrounding him. Durin and Alfrigg, even Raegak, with his missing arm, lowered down in a leather sling. They inspected him, and let him sip mead. He mumbled his apologies, but still the wayward spirits would not let him be. They dismissed his concerns and whispered reassurances that all would be well.

The throbbing pain had for the most part died away, but it wracked him anew as the boulder was shifted aside. There was more discussion, and then he felt himself being hoisted skyward, no doubt lifting free of his mortal coil so as to join the bellows winds of the Great Smithy in His everlasting Earthforge.

The Forge itself was scintillating in its brightness. Grum squinted against its glare as he was brought up from the fissure and hauled from the sling. There was much more jostling than he had imagined might be found in the afterlife. And no release from the pain. He felt himself being set down again in the snow, the way it crunched beneath his weight. But if he was now a spirit . . .

His eyes flickered open. The glare was gone, blocked by the shadows of his friends, who encircled him. They were all there now, even Eitri, who grinned broadly.

"Thought we might have smelled the last of you," the red-bearded dwarf said.

Only then, as he heard the other's voice crisp and clear in the brine-filled wind, did Grum realize the truth. He was not dead, but very much alive. More importantly, so were his friends. Impossible, he knew, but he could no longer deny the physical evidence.

"You're—" he tried to say, but his voice cracked, lending further proof to his realization. "You're alive."

His companions glanced at one another, their smiles cold.

"And so shall you be, my *athair*," Raegak offered. "So shall you be."

The others laughed, grunting harshly. Grum's own mirth began to fade as his gaze shifted from face to face. Something wasn't right. It was clear his friends all bore the wounds from their final battle. What *wasn't* clear was how they had survived them. Raegak's bloody stump was unbound. Alfrigg's face remained a mangled mask of torn flesh. Durin's laugh hissed weirdly through shredded vocal cords.

He turned to Eitri, inspecting the other more closely. A great gash was revealed in his side. Grum saw a hint of internal organs. Like those of the others, the open wound did not seem to trouble him.

Grum felt his pulse quicken, yet wondered anew if he might be dreaming.

Then the dagger struck his chest, biting his lung, so that his scream was choked short by a mouthful of blood.

He looked over, gaping first at the familiar bone handle protruding from his chest, then at the gloved hand of he who held it. Raegak smiled and hissed in his ear, although Grum was no longer certain *who* his friend was speaking to.

"Taste, my *athair*. Taste this realm of flesh."

IT WAS A WORLD UNGLIMPSED BY MAN, a world of mystery and wonder, uninhabitable by his standards of life. Yet there it flourished in the lightless depths, a veritable jungle of exotic plants, animals, and organisms—forms of life that were not troubled by the frigid cold and impossible pressures, or that needed sunlight to thrive. Creatures here milked the earth of its thermal energies, or fed upon those that did. They saw in ways that beings of light could not, and dwelled their entire lives in isolation from the world above—a world as separate and foreign to them as they to it.

Except for him.

He alone among his deep-sea brethren had seen that world and others, he who bore an awareness and experience unmatched by any mortal being. But this was his home now, and he had learned to cherish the isolation of his surroundings, the tranquility of his final resting spot. Untroubled by even the harshest elements of his environment, he had long ago come to terms with his fate, even learned to take comfort in it. It was as good a place as any in which to while away his eternity.

And yet, he could ignore the waking summons no more. After weeks of restlessness, he had at last stirred to life, allowing his barnacle-encrusted eyelid to slide slowly open. After so many centuries, so many mortal ages, it had taken him but a moment to orient himself, lying upon the bottom of the Oloron Sea, countless fathoms below the world above.

A world to which he must soon return.

He shifted his gargantuan body, and the millions of creatures that had made his coral-covered hide their home scattered. The tides themselves recoiled, and beyond, the seeds of quests were sown—those of the witch . . . the avatar . . . the one who had unleashed this storm . . . He could feel their reactions, even if they as yet could not. For nothing so great had ever lived—or ever would again.

Still, even he could not resist the call, that which beckoned him to emerge, to make known his wrath upon the world. So be it. For despite the passing of centuries, it felt as though he had just barely settled down to rest, and his anger was indeed kindled. He would answer the call. He would resume his timeless hunt.

And he would feed.

CHAPTER TWO

TORIN DUCKED BENEATH THE SWINGING SWORD, close enough to feel the breeze of its passing against his sweating brow. He followed up with a roundhouse kick, separating himself from his assailant, clearing space in the battleground for the approach of the other two.

They came without hesitation, and he met them head-on. As anticipated, one went low, the other high. Torin spun from the trap, engaging with the fighter on his left so as to guard his flank. Doing so also enabled him to avoid the blade of the first, whose return charge carried him now headlong into his own companions, rather than into Torin's back.

As they took a moment to disentangle themselves and catch their wind, Torin crouched low, measuring what he had learned so far. Brown-beard was clearly the strongest of the three, but also the slowest, with a fondness for great, cleaving strikes meant to finish an opponent in one fell swoop. Scar-cheek was fast, with rapid thrusts of a rapier whose pricks stung, but had yet to do any real damage. Fish-eyes . . . Fish-eyes seldom did anything more than parry, as if afraid of taking a hit.

Truth be told, their individual skills complemented one another well—if coordinated properly, they might make a formidable trio. Fortunately for him, it seemed as though this was the first time these ruffians had ever fought side by side.

With a growl, Brown-beard took up the charge, his comrades following. They were determined; Torin would give them that. Heart pounding, he raised his broadsword to meet them.

Lunging past another of Brown-beard's windmill strikes, he took aim at the smaller Scar-cheek. The larger man was already tiring, and Torin wanted to waste as few swings as necessary clashing with the giant until it was time to bring him down. It was Scar-cheek for whom he had to conserve his energy. That might best be done by getting rid of Fish-eyes, but he first had to goad the mouse into a more offensive stance. Otherwise, he might spend all day railing away at the other's perfect defenses.

Across the floor they danced in fiercest harmony. Torin slipped around and through their chops and thrusts, dodging or parrying a flurry of blows. He continued to focus on Scar-cheek, pressing the man at every available juncture. At long last, Fish-eyes took the bait. No doubt thinking himself forgot-

ten, he made a lunge for Torin's exposed flank. In an instant, Torin disengaged
from Scar-cheek, driving the other's rapier up high while *he* spun low. Fish-
eyes had overextended himself. Torin saw it in the man's eyes, which widened
further in dismay. Hack, slash, twist—just as he'd been taught—and Torin
watched the other's weapon go flying. Another well-placed kick sent the little
man himself sailing after.

Torin smirked with satisfaction as he spun back to intercept Scar-cheek's
renewed assault. Brown-beard was huffing heavily now, all but standing aside.
The day was Torin's. One on one, he'd met only a handful who could outduel
him. His strength and energy actually increased as he beat his enemy back,
driven from within by the sureness of his victory. With his heavier broadsword, he continued to slap the rapier out in ever-widening circles until at last
he saw the opening he needed.

But as he was about to deliver the final blow, a burning pain sheared
across his back. The hit was accompanied by a mighty crack, and snatched the
wind from his lungs. Releasing his sword, Torin crumpled.

He managed to catch himself, but only on hands and knees, where he
clenched his teeth in anticipation of the next strike.

"My lord . . . my lord, I'm sorry," Fish-eyes offered, bending to help his
king.

Torin reached forth an arm to ward the little man off, then at last drew a
giant gulp of air into his starving lungs. He rocked back on his heels, grimacing
in relief as his breathing was restored and the worst of the pain dispersed.

"My lord, I didn't mean . . ."

Fish-eyes didn't seem to know how to finish, but instead looked at his
blunt-edged iron practice weapon and cast it aside as if it had become a
snake.

"All part of the training," Torin wheezed, brushing aside the other's concern. He glanced to where the discarded weapon clanged upon the arena floor.
"What's your name, soldier?"

"Cordan, my lord. Of the City Shield."

Even now the lad appeared horrified at what he'd done. Torin gave him a
reassuring grin.

"Well played." He extended a hand so that the other could help him up.
Cordan did so, and seemed to finally relax once they were both standing.

Torin turned to Scar-cheek. He always saved the introductions until afterward, preferring to know nothing about his opponents going in. "And you?"

"Evhan. First Rank. Also of the City Shield."

"Bullrum," Brown-beard managed between breaths. "Legion of the Sword.
Friends call me Bull, Your Majesty."

"I can see why," Torin said.

"Shall we again?"

Torin turned. It was Evhan who spoke, still holding his rapier at the
ready.

For a moment, he considered granting the bold lad another go. But then
he looked to Bull, huffing still, leaning on his greatsword, and to Cordan,

whom he doubted he could convince to cough in his direction, let alone take up arms—even practice ones—once more.

"I think that will be all for today, Lieutenant." On the young man's crestfallen look, he added, "We'll spar again, I grant you."

It was a promise seldom given. Torin much preferred to exercise with those whose tendencies had to be learned on the spot. But he liked the other's heart, and the fact that Evhan had yet to address him with any form of royal endearment.

The young lieutenant at last lowered his sword and gave a perfunctory bow. "As you wish," he said, though neither his voice nor his countenance hid his disappointment.

With the decision made, Pagus came forward from the edge of the chamber to help Torin from his lightly padded leather armor. Upon his promotion to chief herald, Pagus had become more like a personal attendant from whom Torin could seldom escape. He was young, having not yet completed twelve full years. But in the short time Torin had spent here in Krynwall, he'd found none other who could match the boy's enthusiasm. Besides that, he continued to reserve a special significance for this lad who had hailed Allion and Kylac's long-awaited return from Mount Krakken, as well as Torin's own betrothal.

"This is a savage welt, my lord," Pagus chided.

Torin winced as the boy's fingers poked at the streak of inflamed skin that he could feel stretched across his naked back.

"Leave it be, then," he hissed, spinning around to face the spiky-haired youth. The words left his mouth more sharply than he'd intended, and so he chased them away with a laugh.

"Sorry, my lord," Pagus replied, hanging his head. The leather vest in his other hand drooped toward the floor.

"No harm done," Torin assured him. "May I have the Sword?"

Pagus grinned before setting down the vest and shrugging out from under Torin's sword belt, which hung over his small shoulder like a baldric.

The Sword of Asahiel.

The boy presented the divine talisman proudly, his hands low on the scabbard so that Torin could take hold of it by the throat. With his other hand, Torin clutched the weapon's hilt, that intricately carved crutch of silver with its nine flaming heartstones—those principal, rubylike gems in which swirled the same tendrils of crimson fire found in the blade. At a mere brush, the Sword's strength coursed through him, dulling the pain and soothing his wounded pride.

While using the weapon in sparring sessions, he'd been able to carve through as many as two dozen men while taking nary a scratch—not only because he had yet to find an armor or weapon the Sword could not slice through like hot butter, and not only because of the endless reserves of stamina it granted him. Mostly, it was due to the miraculous way in which he was able to anticipate attacks before they happened, as though the Sword understood his will and knew better than he how to execute it.

Pagus, as always, beamed at having served as the artifact's temporary bearer. And, as always, Torin smiled in understanding. Forged by the Ha'Rasha and made vessel to the power of the Ceilhigh, it was a wondrous weapon from which he seldom parted. But in an effort to avoid becoming too reliant on its divine nature, he exercised most often without it, choosing to test his own burgeoning skills. And while these sessions often ended in painful lessons such as this one—not to underestimate a downed enemy—Torin inevitably felt better for the knowledge and talent gained.

After all, as he watched his fellow fighters Evhan and Bull and Cordan limp from the arena clutching bruises of their own, he could see that he'd administered at least as many hits as he'd received.

"Perhaps you should see Lady Marisha for a salve," Pagus suggested.

"Ah, let it bruise," Torin decided, buckling the Sword into place around his waist. "The lady is likely not yet risen."

With Pagus's help, he returned his practice gear to the storage racks before donning an open shirt and setting forth from the sanctum of the training hall. Despite the fresh lumps and bruises, he did so with a spring in his step. He always felt invigorated having taken his exercise first thing in the morning; he found it gave him much-needed strength in confronting his duties of the day.

No sooner had he exited the hall and turned the corner than those duties found him.

"King Torin! King Torin, my lord!"

The urge to ignore the voice flared within him, but Torin forced it down. It had been roughly twelve weeks since the death of the Demon Queen, eight since his shattered world had been made whole by the triumphant return of Allion and Kylac and Marisha's acceptance of his abrupt marriage proposal. In that time, he had made numerous concessions, not the least of which was the adoption of his birth name. He was Jarom of Diln no longer, but Torin, king of Alson.

Not that he relished the title. On the contrary, it had been the cause of more bother than he'd expected—and he'd expected a great deal. But there were too many battles to be waged on too many fronts to allow for continued, futile resistance of rank and moniker.

"Good morning, Master Stephan," he greeted, turning on his heel to meet the aging steward.

Stephan continued to jog toward him with that strangely feminine gait—knees high, toes pointed, hands gripping his fancy skirts so as to keep from tripping on his own robes. He held his breath in his plump cheeks, so that the only sound was the rasp of his slippers on the stone flooring. When at last he reached a bemused Torin, he let that breath out in a great puff along with small flecks of spittle.

"My lord, General Rogun seeks audience with you."

Torin resisted the urge to wipe clean his own face, not wishing to offend. Stephan had been chief seneschal of Krynwall since the time of Torin's father, King Sorl, before falling out of favor with his former lord and ending up in Sorl's dungeon. A merciful fate, it had turned out, for as a prisoner, he had escaped the wrath of Soric, Torin's elder brother, during the wizard's occupation of the city. For all his hate-driven behavior, Soric had a soft spot, it seemed, for those branded as criminals—perhaps because he had once been branded one himself.

"Can the general not wait until after breakfast?" Torin asked.

Stephan shook his head. With those fatty cheeks and his prominent front teeth, he looked rather like a chipmunk. "My first question as well, my lord. The general felt the matter too urgent to postpone."

Torin frowned, though he was not surprised. Seldom was the day in which he did not have to face down Rogun on some issue, usually when it was least convenient. The general, he believed, liked to keep him off guard. Just one of the many games his new rank called upon him to play.

"Very well, you may tell the general . . ."

Torin hesitated. In addition to his many functions and titles, Stephan often served as crier for any matter involving the royal household—a task to which he was ill suited. As the seneschal continued to catch his breath, sweat beaded on his brow and ran down his reddened cheeks, carrying the oils with which he kept his hair dyed black with false youth. Torin hated seeing the man used as a runner. But then, they'd spoken of this before, and it seemed there was no dissuading the proud steward from personally fulfilling each and every one of his self-assumed duties.

"My lord?" Stephan asked, waiting expectantly.

"I was just thinking of where the general might meet with me."

"Right here should suffice," came the rugged response.

Torin felt a weary weight settle about his shoulders. The hard clop of boiled-leather boots and the jangle of spurs rang against the stone walls as Rogun himself turned the corner.

"I thought I might catch you at play," the general announced, having emerged from the passage that led back to Torin's private sparring arena. "A short session today?"

"Long enough to get the blood flowing," Torin replied.

"Your wounds aren't too grievous, I trust?"

Torin bristled at both the assumption and the other's condescending stare.

"My lord," Stephan cut in, "shall I have the cooks begin breakfast?"

Torin nodded. "I'll take it in my chambers. If you would be so kind as to draw my bath?" Among everything else, Stephan was pleased to serve as master chamberlain.

"Of course, my lord," he replied with a bow.

"Go with him," Torin said to Pagus.

Stephan scowled, but stopped short of refusing the younger one's assistance. That also was a conversation they'd already had.

With both seneschal and herald slipping away, Torin turned his full attention back to Rogun. "What can I do for you, General?"

Rogun stepped forward. With the others gone, his imposing bulk filled the narrow corridor. If he was an imperious man, he had every right to be. Tall, powerfully built, he projected rugged manliness in every way. Even in his face—from the wide jaw to the broad forehead to the thick mustache hanging down over thin and weathered lips—all seemed as durable and unyielding as mountain stone.

But with Rogun, looks did not begin to tell the story. He was a fourth-generation soldier whose great-grandfather, Caruth, it was said, once saved the life of the king in battle. As a reward, Caruth was offered a lordship. Caruth refused, asking instead for a promotion within the ranks of the military. His wish was granted, as he was made a lieutenant general. Both his son and grandson had served likewise, in ceremonial fashion if nothing else.

There was nothing ceremonial with Rogun. Exceeding even his forebears, he had become chief commander of Krynwall's armies, both the Legion of the Arrow and the more recently instituted Legion of the Sword. Like Stephan, he was a holdover from the days of Sorl and a survivor of Soric's conquest. During the wizard's occupation, Rogun alone among Sorl's chief military officers had been spared, for Soric had seen something in the other worth turning to his advantage. The general had resisted these overtures, unmoved by bribery and uncowed by torture. He had thus been left behind in Krynwall's dungeons—to be dealt with later—when the wizard had taken the bulk of his mercenary army and gone off to join the Demon Queen.

The man's fire was admirable. But once freed, he had quickly become Torin's staunchest opponent and rival. Alson was a land in chaos—understandable, given all that she'd so recently endured. Rogun had very specific ideas about how to set things aright, and Torin, despite having been accepted as the son of Sorl—or maybe because of this—had been treated from the beginning like no more than an obstacle in the general's way.

"I received word this morning of one of our aid caravans being attacked," the general snapped.

Perhaps it was only his own insecurities, but to Torin, the man's tone always seemed rife with accusation, as if he himself were responsible for all of Alson's ills—this one included.

"Last I heard, one in five of our missions to the outlying areas has been beset. Unfortunate, yes, but hardly the most pressing matter of state." Torin did not care for the callousness of his own words, but with Rogun, he knew he must sound stronger than he felt.

"These were not ordinary bandits," the general growled. "These were ogres."

Torin blinked. "Ogres?"

"Accompanied by trolls. But the ogres did the most damage."

"And you're sure the reports are accurate?" To Torin's knowledge, it had been more than a century since either of the creatures now mentioned had been spotted in Alson—or anywhere else in Pentania, for that matter. Naturally there was the occasional sighting by a hunter or trapper come from the high mountains or deep forests—often shared for the price of a drink—but unsurprisingly, none of these claims could ever be confirmed.

"I would not have troubled Your Highness otherwise."

Rogun seldom stooped to mockery. It did not suit his blunt nature. But Torin believed the general would bleed wine before addressing him with genuine respect. He therefore scowled away the royal appellation as he formulated his retort.

"I assume you've already dispatched a patrol, or you would not be wasting your time with me."

"As surely as I breathe," the general affirmed. "But a single patrol will not suffice. You've got us chasing around putting out fires, while the rogues lighting them remain free to set more. To put an end to these attacks, we must strike at the source . . ."

Torin knew where this was headed, and so let his attention slip to the throbbing welt across his back. Despite the wounds of his physical training, he much preferred these to the mental toil of dealing with such issues of state. Although never prone to headaches, he found he had them often these days. Listening to Rogun rail on, he could feel another coming on now.

"Grant me the authorization to marshal the legions for a full sweep of the countryside. Let me stop these rogues and restore order to our lands once and for all."

As was often the case, Torin was not entirely at odds with the general's way of thinking. However, given his inexperience, he did not wish to make any unilateral decisions. That was why he had established a ruling council—the Circle of Elders, named for that which had once governed his home village of Diln. Despite differences of opinion, it was the members of this council—young and old, male and female—who would come together to shape the lives of all.

And on this matter, at least, the Circle had already taken a stance, deciding that a sweeping military force such as Rogun suggested would face a road of perception too narrow and dangerous to tread. The people of Alson craved protection, but did not want to feel threatened or restricted. They'd had enough of that in recent months. And while this made Rogun's job of defending them that much more difficult, who was Torin to go against the will of the council?

"General, can we not save this matter for debate within the Circle?"

Rogun spat. "Damn the Circle. You're the king. All it takes is an order."

Torin decided he could take the man looming over him in that cramped corridor no longer. "General, walk with me."

He did not wait for a response, but turned and began making his way toward the royal quarters. Glaring heatedly over his shoulder, Rogun fell into step behind him.

"Believe it or not, General, I am on your side in this."

"Then grant me my request."

"As Third Elder, you have the right—"

"That title means nothing to me."

Torin glanced back at the other's disgust. "Well, it should. Because the Elders speak for the people, and so *they* are the ones you must convince. I'm sure that with this new report—"

"Perhaps I should convince your precious Elders of our need for a new monarch. A man who does not require the crutch of a council in order to lead us against that which threatens."

Torin had to bite his tongue to keep from laughing aloud. What would Rogun claim he'd been doing before this? As best as Torin could tell, the general had been campaigning actively for his crown almost from the beginning.

Truth be known, he was often inclined to simply hand it over to the man. Nothing would please him more than to take Marisha and run back to the Kalgren Forest to live a quiet life of peace and contentment, far from the bustle of the city and the exigencies of the throne. Perhaps they would resurrect Diln, as some of his former villagers were contemplating. But even if they were to do so, they would remain under the thumb of whoever was chosen to rule in his stead. Until he found a person to whom he would willingly entrust the lives and well-being of his dearest loved ones, he would cling to the mantle himself.

"Should the Circle wish to entertain that notion, you'll hear scant argument from me," he agreed, struggling to keep the weariness from his tone. "Until then, I am king, and will conduct the affairs of this land as I see fit."

Rogun snarled. "You have no idea what it takes to rule this kingdom. You are a forest peasant, nothing more."

"Which is why I depend so greatly on your counsel, my good general." Rogun may have been above mockery, but Torin was not. "If you would but—"

"Torin, my sweet."

He stopped at the sound, and there she was, the light on a frosty morning, Marisha Valour. Or Marisha Lewellyn, as she preferred to be called now. *Valour* was the designation applied to an apprentice healer of her former order, while *Lewellyn* was reserved for those who had attained the rank of master. And although none other remained of that sect to bestow the coveted mantle, she had taken it upon herself so as to honor her former people.

His bride-to-be was framed by the doorway of an embroidery chamber. Within the chamber, she stood upon a pedestal, flanked by a pair of handmaidens. She wore the framework of a breathtaking gown, which the maidens were fussing over with all the determined focus of master craftsmen—measuring, cutting, folding.

"Hold still, my lady," one of them said through gritted teeth. She removed from those teeth a pin that she used to hold an unstitched hem in place.

Marisha froze, though her candid smile remained ever bright, untroubled by the rebuke. Torin found himself drawn to it like a drowning man to the water's surface.

A gruff snort from behind reminded him of Rogun's presence.

"General, will you excuse me?"

Not without protest, it seemed. "We've not yet—"

"I thank you for bringing this to my immediate attention. We shall discuss it at length this afternoon."

"I've no doubt we will," Rogun grumbled. "Without action whatsoever."

He spun and marched away, the jangle of his spurs echoing down the corridor.

"What was that about?" Marisha asked as Torin approached.

"Nothing new." He reached up to clasp her outstretched hands. "You look radiant this morning."

The woman freed one hand to paw at her hair in a self-conscious fashion. The golden tresses hung free, unbound by ribbon or braid, to steal light from the sun streaming in through an open window.

"I've not yet had a chance to prepare for Your Lordship's greeting," she teased in apology.

"None is required, given such natural beauty."

Marisha pushed him away with a laugh. Torin smiled in return.

"I expected you'd still be sleeping," he said.

"On the day of first rehearsal for my lord's coronation?"

Torin's smile slipped.

"Or had you forgotten?"

"No, of course not," he assured her. Why had Stephan not reminded him?

"What do you think?" Marisha asked, twisting back and forth so as to cast a ripple through her garment. This of course drew sharp glances and even a cough from the seamstresses fighting to hold her steady. A coronation dress, yes, but also that which she would wear for their wedding, scheduled just two weeks hence.

"Does it not bear ill fortune for the bridegroom to see his lady in her gown before the ceremony?"

"As you can see, the gown is not yet finished. Besides, there is no ill fortune that we cannot overcome."

Torin flinched. Though he had come to believe that destiny was what one made of it, he saw little need for tempting fate. Still, no small sense of foreboding was safe in Marisha's presence, and he found the chill sensation melting quickly away. All things considered, he had much to be grateful for. The responsibilities, the headaches, the enemies—a small price to pay for that which his fortunes had granted him.

Marisha sniffed twice in exaggerated fashion. "Someone needs a bath," she remarked.

Torin stepped back, bowing humbly. "With your leave, my lady."

The woman tossed a piece of fabric at him. "Get out of here, you knave." She then smiled. "I'll see you at the rehearsal."

Torin held his bow until he reached the doorway, then flashed her a grin of his own and stole from the room.

Amazingly enough, he was able to reach his chambers almost without interruption. The entire palace had awoken early, it seemed, no doubt in preparation for the midmorning rehearsal. The halls were filled with decorators, designers, organizers of all form and fashion. Fortunately, most were too busy to spare him more than a nod in greeting. Those who sought more seemed understanding enough when he politely excused himself, and went about their business.

The coronation. His fate, such as it was, made formal and sealed at last. He'd escaped it as long as he could—longer, in fact, than he had any right to expect. He saw no need for it. But then, this celebration wasn't for him. It was for the people.

With a quick word of hello to the sentinel posted outside, he ducked into his personal living quarters. As the door closed, a temporary relief settled in. An undisturbed peace so seldom to be found these days. Freedom from retainers, courtiers, and supplicants of every variety. Upon second thought, perhaps this rehearsal wasn't such a bad idea. At least it offered a break from the usual routine, a respite from the long days of giving audience to everyone from city planners to local guildmasters to simple well-wishers—an endless menagerie of those in need, those with grievances, and those who sought to form alliances or otherwise sway him to their particular cause.

He glanced around the sitting room with its hearth and overstuffed chairs. Breakfast had not yet arrived. Likely, Stephan had ordered the cooks to delay until after he'd bathed, so that his food wouldn't grow cold. As if royalty had softened him to the point of being damaged by dried bacon grease or lukewarm eggs.

With a sigh of resignation, he moved toward the bedchamber, unbuckling his Sword belt as he went. Setting the weapon aside in the doorway, he went straight for the wardrobe closet, surprised not to find old Scar—the one-eyed cat inherited from the father he'd never known—blocking the doors as usual. For once, the beast had found something better to do than make his life difficult.

He pulled forth his bathrobe and slung it over an adjacent chair. The bath itself would be waiting by now across the hall. He stripped off his boots first, then his shirt. He wore no jewelry; save for the Sword, he eschewed adornments of any kind. He was about to unlace his breeches when he twisted instead to examine his most recent welt in the mirror. Pulling one arm over at the elbow, he reached around to test the line of swollen flesh.

Only then did he spy the intruder.

Torin's heart skipped. The reflection showed a figure stood on the opposite side of the room, wedged in a corner beside the shuttered window. He blinked, thinking it was Rogun, come to renew their unfinished debate. It took only a moment to determine otherwise. This figure was tall like Rogun, yet thin, wrapped tight in a cocoon of dark robes. Its face, if there was one, was mostly hidden behind damp strands of hair hanging loose about the forehead, as well as a black beard that jutted from its chin. In color and stance, it was something less than human, like a scarecrow come to life.

Instinct drove him where rational thought could not. With legs slow and leaden, he lunged for the inner doorway between sitting room and bedchamber—and the weapon he'd left there. In the corner of his eye he spied the scarecrow, uncoiling, charging to intercept him. It moved faster than he would have imagined possible, as though its size aided rather than impeded its motion. More wraith than substance, its outline billowed and swam. He felt its shadow descend upon him, and sensed in that moment the chill of imminent death.

Then the Sword was in his hands, its warmth burning through his palms and coursing through his veins. With a lightning motion, he reached with one hand to tear the scabbard free. As he cast aside the sheath, the weapon's glow filled the room, revealing to Torin the face of his enemy.

A man after all, or so he seemed. The billowing was that of his robes, dark in hue and soaked darker with rain. He had come to a stop mere inches away, throat perched upon the tip of the Sword, features twisting in its crimson light. Emotions swept across his skin like the colors of a chameleon—rage and frustration, contempt and loathing, pity and sorrow, until at last they settled into a derisive sneer.

"Behold, the instrument of our doom."

Before Torin could respond, there came a swift knock from the outer doorway as the posted guardsman stuck his head in.

"My lord? I thought I heard . . ." He stopped as he took in the scene.

"Kien, call the Shield."

Torin kept his eyes on the intruder, but heard the other fumbling for his sword.

"Kien! The Shield. I will hold our friend here."

At last he heard Kien scamper from the room, leaving the door to his chambers open. With the other gone, Torin refocused on the stranger before him, at a sallow face bathed in sweat. He looked like a man staving off some form of illness.

"You will raise a panic," the scarecrow intruder observed, his jaw clenched in checked fury.

Torin coiled, resisting the urge to shuffle back a step. The man's breath reeked of decay, rushing down over the cliffs of his craggy beard. His blue eyes reflected the light of the Sword, so that the same flames that swirled within the polished blade seemed to smolder beneath the surface of his orbs.

Questions skittered through Torin's mind. Despite the stranger's menacing stance and sudden, unwanted appearance, there was something about him, some sense of familiarity that Torin could not quite place.

"Who are you?" he asked, the Sword lending strength to his quavering voice.

The man seemed to swell in size, even as he withdrew slowly from the radiant blade. "You have no idea. Even now."

If Rogun's tone had been accusatory, then this one's was downright incriminating. Torin felt himself laid bare by its assault. Again the feeling that he knew this man—or should—dug like a splinter at his mind. And yet he refused to lower his guard for an instant, for the haunting notion did nothing to allay his fears.

"My lord, your bath—"

"Stephan, stay where you are," Torin commanded as the other's shadow filled the outer doorway. He could hear his master chamberlain sputtering in alarm as they each focused on the unwelcome visitor.

"You've not answered my question," Torin growled, using anger to steady himself. He took a step toward the intruder, putting him back within range of the Sword's gleaming tip.

The man's sneer remained, even as his eyes narrowed. "Kill me," he cautioned, "and you condemn us all."

"And don't think I lack the will to do so," Torin snapped.

"My lord—"

"The Shield is coming, Stephan. Just stay back."

The stranger was shaking his head. "A reckless response from a reckless whelp." He lifted his hands in mock surrender, revealing sun-baked skin and open lacerations as his sleeves fell away. The wounds looked as if they should be bleeding, but were not, and only then did Torin notice that the man's dripping robes hung in tatters, as though shredded by some wild beast.

"I am your past and your future," he answered finally, smirking at Torin's sudden doubt. "I am living proof of the horror your foolishness has unleashed upon us all."

Again the man's stench washed over him. Only this time, Torin recognized it. It drew him back to the defining moment of his young life, the moment during which he had drawn the Crimson Sword from the orb and altar into which it had been embedded, deep within the bowels of Thrak-Symbos. Again he watched the shattered pieces of that edifice crumble into the pit that had lain concealed beneath. And again, he felt the stagnant wind that had escaped that pit, the frigid gust that had driven away the lizards by which he and his companions had been surrounded. Its chill ripped through him now as it had then, and abruptly he wondered: What else had escaped from that pit?

His thoughts reeling, Torin was ill prepared for the sweet sound of Marisha's voice as she came upon Stephan, still frozen in the doorway.

"I just ran into Kien. He said—" Her words ended in a gasp, and Torin turned to find her staring into the room.

"Stephan, get her out of here," Torin moaned, glancing back and forth between the woman and the intruder.

The chief seneschal, Torin noted, was already doing his best, blocking Marisha with his ample body, an arm and a leg thrust up against the opposite side of the jamb. Surprisingly, Marisha was not fighting him, but continued to stare at the two men without speaking, without blinking. Her face was as pale as Torin had ever seen it.

All of a sudden, she slumped to the floor, sliding just inside the chamber. Torin had to fight the urge to drop his guard and rush to her aid. There she sat, openmouthed, until he feared she was the victim of some sort of wizard's spell. He didn't know whether to go to her, or to throttle the stranger.

He chose neither when at last her lips came together to whisper a single word that echoed throughout his chambers.

"Father."

CHAPTER THREE

Torin blinked in the tomblike stillness that followed. He gaped at Marisha, waiting for her to say something more, to explain. When she did not, and tears began to brim in her eyes, he turned back to the stranger. The man's wrath had dissipated, it seemed, as he stared back at Marisha in respectful silence.

"What is this?" Torin asked. Confusion reigned, forcing him to grope for words. "Are you . . . are you her . . . her fath—"

He stopped abruptly, realizing suddenly why this man seemed so familiar. He squinted, peering not so much at the stranger but into the past at his own memories. The recollection only intensified his bewilderment. For he had been eight years old at the time of their brief encounter, while the other's appearance had not changed in over a decade.

"Darinor." He mouthed the name, yet, like Marisha's quiet exclamation, it seemed to reverberate in the taut air.

"Yes," Darinor huffed, though his gruffness now seemed forced. "On both counts."

Torin found his sword arm lowering. Darinor came forward, but moved past him, staring all the while at Marisha. He approached slowly, reverently, this towering, cadaverous man who was at the same time as hale as any Torin had ever encountered. In the outer doorway, Stephan shrank back, his eyes like full moons. Darinor ignored the seneschal as he had Torin, focused still on the young woman whose lip was now quivering. The great man knelt calmly before her, reaching out in a manner both soothing and supplicating. Torin did nothing to stop him, but watched as one great hand cupped her cheek. As it did, she reached forth both of her own hands to catch hold and press it more tightly against her. The dam burst, and she wept.

Torin continued to stare, suddenly feeling as if *he* were the one intruding. He glanced up as Stephan did the same. As their eyes met, the sound of booted feet came tramping near at a hurried pace.

Led by Kien, a team of Fasor—the City Shield—had arrived. Known before as the palace guard, Torin had changed the name to sound less elitist and more inclusive of the general populace. And once again, he'd paid homage to those of his home village by naming them after the position of guardianship that he himself had once held—that of Fason, captain of the City Shield.

After shouldering Stephan aside, they too crowded in the doorway like a clutch of awestruck children. They might have been watching a flame-swallower rather than the reunion of a father and daughter separated for more than a dozen years.

Torin caught Kien's questioning eye, and shook his head. He was struggling to recall all that Marisha had told him about her father. There wasn't much. The man had left both her and her mother when she was but a child—at her mother's request. Upon his departure, he had bestowed upon her the secret pendant she wore, the pendant that had saved her life—and Torin's—but that now, with her mother gone, only the young king knew of. Sacred blazes, she hadn't even shared with him the man's name. Although even if she had, he never would have assumed it to be the same Darinor he himself had met as a child, the same Darinor whose night of storytelling had inadvertently spawned in him the lifelong desire to one day seek out and recover—

"Whoever is in command here, I don't think we require an audience," Darinor said. He made no effort to keep the edge from his voice, although as soon as he had spoken, he went back to consoling his daughter by resting his forehead against hers.

Torin studied Marisha carefully. She continued to be wracked by sobs, but they appeared to be sobs of disbelief, maybe even joy. Though she had never said so, the one thing he had gathered from their sparse conversations on the subject was that she loved her father deeply, reserving for his memory a sacred regard such that she could not even share it with him, her husband-to-be.

"Kien, that will be all."

To a man, the Fasor hesitated, as if seeking some further confirmation.

"All of you, you are dismissed. I bid thanks for your prompt response." As they began to disperse, he added, "Kien, resume post, please. See to it that we are not disturbed."

Kien nodded before remembering his salute.

"Uh, my lord," Stephan intervened, "the rehearsal?"

"The rehearsal is postponed. See to it, Master Stephan."

"Canceled would be better," Darinor remarked.

The seneschal's jaw dropped, and he looked to Torin in protest.

"As he says," Torin agreed.

"My lord—"

"Kien, if you please?"

Kien saluted again before drawing the red-faced Stephan from the doorway. The door closed—carefully, so as not to disturb the pair kneeling just inside the threshold. An ensuing silence persisted until Torin wondered if he should excuse himself as well. He was about to do so when Marisha finally withdrew from the apparition before her.

"Father, is it really you?"

Darinor did not respond, but gently reached toward the silver chain barely visible around the neckline of her unfinished wedding gown. Marisha did not resist, but let him pull forth the flaming heartstone that hung from clasp and chain—the Pendant of Asahiel.

From the angle at which he stood, Torin could not quite see the other man's face. But he guessed that the look Darinor gave was somehow lacking in approval, based on the guilt that flashed across Marisha's features.

"I kept it secret, Father. As you warned."

Darinor turned, just enough to frown at Torin. "And here I half expected to find *him* wearing it."

Torin scowled, a renewal of both his uncertainty and anger. This was not the kindly storyteller of whom he held such fond remembrances from his youth. What had he done to so fuel the man's ire? He chewed up any number of retorts, seeking instead to set a tone of civility. "If you *are* Darinor," he said, "you know that you are welcome here."

"And yet you still brandish your stolen blade."

Torin glanced down to where he held the Crimson Sword, half lowered at his side. With another scowl, he set its tip to the floor in front of him and folded his hands upon the pommel. "Will you tell us now why you've come?"

Darinor lowered the Pendant softly to Marisha's chest, then stood, pulling her up after him. "If you've composed yourself well enough to listen."

Despite the calming influence of the Sword, Torin felt his frustration building in waves. "You will forgive me, I'm sure. I am not accustomed to being ambushed in my own quarters."

Darinor guided Marisha to one of the worn velvet chairs beside the hearth, turned so that she faced Torin. "Is that how you would describe my patient vigil here?"

Torin thought back to their encounter moments ago. "If you intended no harm, why lunge at me like some rabid animal?"

"You appeared to be fleeing," Darinor replied as he folded Marisha's own delicate hands in her lap. All the while, she continued to gaze up at him as if worried he might disappear before her eyes. "And I've come a long way to see you."

Torin opened his mouth to object, but realized he could not disprove the other's account. That it might be true caught him off guard. "Me?"

"But I thought . . ." Marisha squeaked, eyes glinting with hurt and confusion.

Darinor sandwiched her hands in his and crouched low, gazing deep into her eyes. He said nothing, but held that pose for another long moment. When finally he arose, he kept one hand gripped reassuringly upon her shoulder.

At long last, he turned to face Torin, and at once, the bearded face curdled in accusation. "You are Torin, are you not? King of Alson, savior of Pentania, wielder of the last known Sword of Asahiel." His lip curled in mockery—and in satisfaction, Torin thought, at his listener's helplessness. "Thus, it is you I seek."

Torin's tongue felt thick in his mouth. Nevertheless, he felt he had to say something in order to deflect the other's penetrating gaze. "You seem to know a great deal about me," he admitted. "Once again, you have me at the disadvantage."

"Perhaps. I know your story, for your countrymen speak of little else.

Then again, I dare not believe this common account by half. Despite certain evidence, there are details of which I am skeptical, and many others that are altogether missing."

Torin peered past the speaker to Marisha, who still looked betrayed.

"But we've not the time needed to explore them," Darinor went on, his tone made sharper by Torin's inattention. "Your foolishness has seen to that."

"Am I to unravel these riddles?" Torin responded crossly. "Or should I but stand here and remain their target?"

Marisha turned in his direction. "Torin, please . . ."

This time, however, Torin remained focused on Darinor. For a moment, he felt the other meant to strike, and as one hand slipped down from the Sword's pommel to clasp its hilt, the weapon flared slightly, revealing his anticipation. A slow smirk drew tight the elder man's thin lips, as he appeared to come to a decision.

"Save your strength," he chuckled mirthlessly. "You will need it for your journey."

"And just where is it you think I'm going?"

"To restore that which you have destroyed. Else to the grave, here and now, before you take the rest of us with you."

"Enough!" Marisha shouted, springing from her chair and seizing her father's arm in restraint. "I'll listen to no more of this from either of you. Torin, if you would have your answers, sit and be silent. As for you, Father . . ." Her voice cracked, yet remained authoritative. "You will explain your presence here, or you will leave at once."

Torin fumed a moment longer, then dipped his head in apology to his lady love. With a hawk's eye upon Darinor, he moved to the nearest available chair, across the hearth from Marisha, and sat, laying the Crimson Sword across his lap.

"Then listen closely," Darinor admonished them, when Marisha had retaken her seat and he alone stood so as to face the pair. "For our enemies multiply as we speak."

"What enemies?" Torin urged, glancing sidelong at Marisha.

Darinor ignored him, brow twisting as if considering where to begin his narrative. "You must know something of the Swords of Asahiel," the sallow-faced man determined, "else you would not be holding one now."

Torin merely nodded, but Darinor's look prompted him to elaborate. "Forged by the Ha'Rasha and imbued with the divine power of the Ceilhigh, to be used in the shaping of this earth and the shepherding of those who lived upon it."

"And the Dragon Wars?"

"That's when the Swords passed from these avatars into mortal hands, given to the Finlorian elves that they might withstand the armies of the Dragon God."

It was clear that Darinor did not recognize him, nor recall that he himself had once related to Torin much of this mythology. Torin was emboldened by the fact that he knew something the other did not. In any case, he was always proud to share with others the knowledge of his favorite study. With even this brief overview, his enthusiasm for the topic fortified his voice.

"In the millennia that followed the defeat of the Dragon God's minions, the Swords were lost, one by one, save that which was passed down along the lines of Finlorian royalty to the high king Sabaoth, some three thousand years ago. Finally, even that blade disappeared, when Sabaoth and the entire city of Thrak-Symbos were buried by an earth-shattering cataclysm."

Torin waited, silently daring the other to contradict his account. For a long moment, Darinor made no attempt to do so. He stood with that brooding glare, waiting, it seemed, for Torin to say something more. As the weight of his pause increased, a determined Torin held his gaze.

"In other words, you know nothing but what you've been given to know." A menacing smile tugged at one corner of Darinor's mouth.

Torin frowned, but guarded any further reaction to the man's theatrics.

Darinor crouched close to Marisha once more. "That is not Sabaoth's Sword," he said, indicating the weapon in Torin's lap. He reached up once again to finger the heartstone Pendant on its silver chain—the Crimson Stone, as they had nicknamed it.

"This is."

Torin did well to hide his interest. But he was undeniably excited by what he was about to learn. What little Marisha knew of the secret talisman had been revealed to him only guardedly—and only after Torin had discovered for himself the Stone's existence. Even then she had kept him at arm's length, clinging to her childhood oath to a man who had deserted her, honoring his memory, fearing for her own safety and that of the artifact. Pretending to understand, he had respected her wishes, allowing the matter to remain a quiet source of bitterness. For he could not help but wonder if she knew much more than had been revealed.

"My daughter was granted no knowledge of the Pendant's true history or purpose," Darinor remarked, as if to dispel Torin's unspoken suspicions. "She knew only a father's stern command that the talisman never be revealed to anyone."

Once again, father and daughter shared a quiet moment. And yet Torin noted that Marisha's features had taken on a stern and demanding cast, as though her own understandable anger was beginning to win over her shock and adoration.

"A charm by which to remember me," Darinor added, echoing his words of long ago. "A talisman to keep her safe." While addressing Torin, he continued to stare into Marisha's eyes, the slightest tremor weakening his voice. "But most importantly, the means by which we might one day be reunited. That I might share with her the truth of her family's legacy."

Like the lull in a storm, the moment of tenderness passed. Darinor turned his head, a mask of dark clouds once more.

"Sabaoth was a fool. Like you, a seeker of glories he was not meant to attain. The Finlorian Empire had reached the height of its majesty. Its people believed that all manner of art and industry conceivable to mortal minds had already been achieved. Thus, their thoughts moved beyond the mortal toward the immortal. They thought to ascend to the heavens, to connect this world with that of the Ceilhigh."

A strange excitement began to bubble up within Torin at the realization that tragic secrets, centuries old, were about to be revealed. Despite the circumstances, he felt himself leaning forward, unable to deny his growing fervor.

"In their arrogance, a sect of Finlorian magi, commissioned by Sabaoth himself, created a rift beneath the city of Thrak-Symbos within the tunnels of their dead, at a point where the veil between this realm and what they believed to be the realm of departed spirits was at its thinnest. Thinking to open a doorway to their gods, they instead breached a realm of chaos such as never before had been imagined. From this rift poured the Illysp."

Torin blinked. He had never heard of an Illysp. He had no notion of what they were. But he was fairly certain that he had no desire to learn.

This sentiment must have been scrawled across his face, for Darinor addressed it almost immediately. "Do not bother to envision these denizens," he said, raising his lacerated hands, "for they are unlike anything you may have encountered before."

Torin was not sure whether to be relieved by this, or horrified. It was decided a moment later as Darinor finished his pronouncement.

"They're far worse."

The young king's stomach growled with hunger—or perhaps in response to the slow dread boring its way through the pit of his belly. He didn't bother trying to hide his unease from Darinor, but waited for the other to take delight in it.

But Darinor, it seemed, was past any hope of delight, even at Torin's obvious discomfiture. "In their natural state, the Illysp can best be described as spirits, lacking bodies material to our plane. When first unleashed, they had only limited mobility, like a foul scent in dead air."

"Then how . . . ?" Torin began, before Darinor waved him off.

"They quickly overcame this limitation by clinging to the mind of a host creature—whatever crossed their path—where they lingered like a thought unbidden. Slipping from mind to mind, they learned to travel as might a swarm of flies among a herd of cattle, dancing from host to host. They even learned to influence their hosts through the power of suggestion, with silent promptings to lie, thieve, and kill, thereby carrying out their innate desire to spread mayhem and violence. As with any undesired thought, these urgings were not easy to dispel."

"I don't understand," Marisha admitted, stealing the words from Torin's lips. "Mortal beings have always been tempted. Were these so much harder to resist?"

"They were," Darinor assured her. "But what the Illysp really craved were bodies of their own, that they might touch the physical world and sample for themselves the sensations of flesh, in order to participate fully in the hateful activities for which they were bred and to exercise dominion over others. It was not until they learned how to obtain these bodies that their true horror was exposed."

Torin's heart slipped into the chasm that his stomach had become. "Possession," he presumed grimly.

"A suitable term. Although still not quite what you think. For it required a dead body, a mortal housing from which the living essence had already departed. Presented with a coil thus abandoned, an Illysp could infuse itself therein. After a brief incubation period, the original essence returned, but as a prisoner in his own mortal shell, subject to the whims of the controlling Illysp. A collection of memories, a consciousness, and nothing more. Upon waking, the Illysp consumed this former consciousness, laid bare its knowledge and experiences while retaining its own, and made this the vessel of its destruction."

Torin glanced at Marisha and wondered right away if his eyes were as wide as hers. "Could they be killed?"

"In a manner of speaking. For an Illychar—as it was known once it had taken physical form—did not live in the traditional sense. It did not require nerves, a brain, or vital organs. It functioned via a form of innate memory. Like the phantom pain of an amputated limb, an Illychar retained whatever abilities were inherent to its chosen vessel in life. It breathed, though its lungs needed no air. It moved, provided the muscles and ligaments required to do so had not completely rotted away. Its body may have contained blood, but it sat stagnant in its veins. Since it did not require the functioning of organs, it did not have to feed, and was subject only superficially to the ravages of time. Left alone, an Illychar would live forever."

The harsh words resonated from his chest as if from the grave. Torin gripped tighter the Sword's hilt, reflexively seeking its placating warmth, and saw that Marisha's hand was clasped firmly about the Stone.

"But this innate memory worked both ways, making an Illysp-possessed creature as susceptible to injury in death as in life. Even an eviscerated carcass, if pierced by an arrow where a vital organ had once been, might fall over dead. Not due to visible injury, but to what that injury would be if the creature were still alive. It was as though the mind understood—not the physical mind, but that of the deepest body or soul. For even a headless corpse could be resurrected to stumble around again; the same rules applied when the brain wasn't there. It was all about perception, the primordial sense within."

"And the Illysp?" Marisha croaked. "What happened to the Illysp when its body was slain? Could it not simply inhabit another?"

"No. Once an Illysp selected a coil, it was bound to it, inheriting its weaknesses along with its strengths. Convince an Illychar of its death, and the Illysp within was dispelled and could no longer sustain itself."

Torin found it odd that they continued to speak of these creatures in the past tense, as if their threat were far removed. For if that were so, he would not be here listening to this.

"Then they can be fought," he said, seeking assurance.

"They can, and they were," the gaunt-faced speaker rumbled. "Seizing the carefully preserved bodies of Finlorian dead, they rose up against Sabaoth and his people. With the influence of his Crimson Sword, the high king held them back for a time. But an Illychar was generally swifter and stronger than its host was in life, its physical attributes heightened by its savagery. They sensed pain, but ignored it, and were thus difficult to bring down. Furthermore, it was soon learned that a slain Illychar, while freed forever of one Illysp, could be possessed by another and reanimated again. And again, and again—forever, as long as an Illysp remained to claim it. And the number of Illysp in pure, spirit form was without end."

As he went on, the great figure seemed to lose some of his bluster, as if bent with resignation beneath the weight of his own account.

"Had Sabaoth known how to command the Sword's full fury, catastrophe might yet have been averted. But he did not, and pressed by the ever-increasing numbers of his parasitic enemy, he was overcome, killed, and possessed himself."

The man stared at Torin pointedly, as if the words alone were not enough to impress upon him the horror of this threat.

"After that, the Illysp spread far and fast across the land of Tritos, as this island continent was named at the time. Many fled across the seas, counting themselves fortunate in that it seemed the Illysp did not care to follow. But many more stayed to fight a violent struggle for dominion of these shores. The Illychar ranks swelled with orcs and goblins, trolls and ogres—no creature was safe."

Trolls and ogres. The names resonated clearly in Torin's mind, shedding grim light on his morning's encounter with Rogun.

"The Finlorians were without hope. But at least one group refused to surrender, a warrior sect made up of a handful of those descended from the first mortal wielders of the Swords of Asahiel during the Dragon Wars. It was this sacred company, the Vandari, who had been responsible for the preservation of the blades ever since, and who could not abide that their king and captain—along with one of the divine talismans—remained in the clutches of the enemy.

"They journeyed far to the south, farther than almost any other had dared by sea, to reach the distant shores of Sekulon, the birthing grounds of man. For there dwelled the order of the Entients, self-proclaimed shepherds of mankind, who possessed the only other known Sword of Asahiel. The Vandari made their pleas for assistance, or at the very least, for the loan of the talisman. But the Entients refused. Man was a fledgling race struggling for survival, and the Entients, as overseers, were too obsessed with matters of their own to lend aid to outsiders.

"Only Algorath, a prominent member of the order, took pity, urging his fellow Entients to reconsider. But they continued to vote against him. Unless the threat spread to their lands, it was none of their concern. That by then it might be too late was an argument that fell on deaf ears.

"In response, Algorath left the order, stealing the Sword and traveling with the Vandari back to Tritos. While evading pursuit, Algorath led a renewed resistance against the Illychar swarm. In a desperate attempt to turn the tide of war to their favor, Algorath confronted Sabaoth himself. During a battle that pitted Crimson Sword against Crimson Sword, the true power of Algorath's blade was somehow released, shattering Sabaoth's Sword and immolating the high king himself.

"In the aftermath of this conflagration, Illysp and Illychar alike were driven back into the tunnels from whence they had emerged. But the rift remained. The best Algorath could do was to trap them there, deep beneath the surface. With the aid of Finlorian magi, the Vandari fashioned an altar over the exit and set upon it the Dragon Orb, a talisman of great power. Through it all they thrust Algorath's Sword—now the last Sword of Asahiel—the key to a lock meant to contain the Illysp forever."

Torin was consumed by a dire fascination. It was all so real to him. For he had seen the Sword unleash its flaming fury more than once, and could imagine easily enough the titanic struggle between Sabaoth and Algorath. Not only that, but he had viewed and felt the magic of the lock that had kept these Illysp from his world, there in the catacombs of Thrak-Symbos. He even understood now, at least in part, the blade's curious appearance as it held that lock together: its crimson radiance masked in gleaming obsidian while its inner fires were diverted through this "Dragon Orb" and its altar. Only after being drawn had the obsidian key been fully revealed as the Crimson Sword. By then, the lock was no more. A construct of divine majesty designed for a single purpose. Reduced in an instant to shards and rubble—by his own hand.

Marisha sensed his torment, coming over to crouch beside him. One hand slipped around his stooped shoulders, while the other took comforting hold on his arm.

"Why?" he murmured, staring at the Sword. "Why would the Entients have assisted me in—"

"The Entients?" Darinor snorted. "Doddering fools. Did they have a hand in this?"

"They spurred me on my quest," Torin said, feeling no less responsible, "planting dreams and suggestions in my head, even sending me a map so that I would know where to begin. I didn't know it at the time, but afterward—after I retrieved the Sword—they met with me. They wanted to witness the blade for themselves and to learn all about the manner in which it was found. In return, they told us—"

Darinor was shaking his head. "I might have known. How a mere lad such as you could even begin to seek out the Sword was a mystery I could not fathom. That the Entients spurred you on explains a great deal."

"But how could they have done so?" Torin replied, ignoring the inherent insult. "How could they have succored me in this, knowing the truth?"

"Because they did *not* know the truth," Darinor snapped. His eyes were wide, his brows raked, his chin tucked into his beard, giving him the stern and ruffled look of a great owl. "Like all others, they knew only what they were meant to know."

"How can that be?" Marisha asked, coming to Torin's defense. "Are they not avatars of the human race?"

"Self-proclaimed," Darinor scoffed. "The true avatars were the Ha'Rasha. The Entients are descendent only, the progeny of those demimortals who bred with mortals and have been doing so for ages since. Each is more human than avatar, though together they have long played at being more than what they are."

The truth hit Torin's lungs like a ball of flaming pitch hurled through a ship's sails—first piercing, then devouring. Although it made sense, it shocked him to have to relinquish such a long-standing belief.

"Still," Marisha insisted, "they knew of the Sword, the Vandari, the Illysp—everything. How could they have forgotten?"

"First off, even by the standards of the Entients, this all took place roughly ten generations ago."

"But older legends persist today," Torin argued, cutting the other short. "Even among the mortal races, there would be myths, memorials, festivals of remembrance."

"Second," Darinor continued unabated, "no sooner had the war ended than the cover-up began. So terrible had been the struggle, so widespread the devastation, that the Finlorians elected to continue the exodus that most had already begun. Few cared to wager their lives against the odds of an Illysp escape. So the Vandari warded with magical snares the catacombs in which the sealed pit lay, then unleashed a series of earthquakes and landslides that buried the entire city. After that, they took flight with the rest of their people, leaving their ravaged lands to those who would emerge eventually from the high mountains or from deep within the earth—or later, from across the tempest seas.

"But even this was not enough. Algorath and the Vandari agreed that no one should learn what had happened, lest some fool brave the dangers set for him, unearth the seal, and draw the Sword, destroying the lock. So they changed the stories, misleading those who would pass the legend down to their descendants. Elven historians left formal records of a great and natural cataclysm of the earth. Bards and minstrels helped to spread this false word. Few knew the truth to begin with, and over the course of centuries, this revisionist history replaced that of actual events—even among those whose forebears had lived through it. Only the Vandari, along with Algorath, preserved the knowledge of what had really transpired, as a necessary safeguard should it ever happen again."

"And what of the Entients?" Marisha reminded him. "Surely they kept records of their own."

Darinor sneered. "For his betrayal, the Entients struck all records of Algorath's existence. His studies remained, but in altered form, his deeds and learnings attributed to another. To hide the further embarrassment of having the Sword stolen from them, they modified their writs and journals in such a way as to obscure the fact that they ever actually possessed one of the talismans. Since Algorath had obtained the blade and brought it to the order, and had also removed it again, it was easy enough to do this. All that was kept were general writings and images concerning its legendary powers and ancient history.

"There was of course some opposition," Darinor proceeded, heading off Torin's next question. "One among them, who had spent years studying the Sword with Algorath, decided to give chase, and was permitted to do so. It was agreed that if he retrieved the talisman, he would be allowed to return and take the place of Algorath in their records. If not, then he would be exiled and erased along with his former mentor. The rest would continue to devote their time and energies to matters of their own race and their own lands."

Something wasn't right, and Torin knew it. When he shook his head, Darinor went on with the frustrated sigh of someone instructing a dullard. "The order was in its infancy at that time, its focus narrowed, its attention drawn by man's own wars. They had neither the inclination nor the resources to expend recording the trials and history of faraway lands. It was therefore left to the hunter to capture these events, if any record was to be made."

"And how did Algorath learn of this?" Torin asked, brushing this last bit aside as he realized why the explanation didn't work. "Or did he just take for granted their response?"

Darinor leaned forward, a haunting black shadow. "He learned it from the hunter's own lips, before making sure that the other failed in his endeavor."

Torin swallowed thickly.

"The Entients were left to assume that both had perished in this Finlorian war of which they kept no record. Most likely, it was not until their descendants began colonizing these lands, more than two thousand years later, that they began digging into its past—too late to have any recollection of what had actually occurred. For by that time, the only surviving history was that which had been altered by the Vandari. Clearly, their support of your quest indicates an effort to uncover at least part of this missing truth—as blind as any to the consequences."

Though sitting forward, Torin felt as if he were sinking into his chair. His mind was a maelstrom, thoughts and emotions swirling ever faster in a sucking spiral that threatened to pull him under. Questions gathered at its edge like mosquito swarms on the shore of a lake.

"If everyone forgot, then how do *you* know all of this?"

Darinor relaxed, if only slightly, from the aggressiveness of his stance. "Have you not already guessed? After the war, the remnants of Sabaoth's shattered Sword were buried by the Vandari in a sacred shrine. Except for one small piece, a heartstone from the ruined hilt, seated in a clasp and fastened to a silver chain. It was presented to Algorath as a token of appreciation. But more than that, it was a tool with which to monitor the integrity of the Illysp seal. An enchantment woven upon its links connected Pendant and seal, so that if the magic of the seal were to fail, that failure would resonate with the bearer of the Pendant."

Darinor's expression softened predictably as once again he turned his focus to Marisha.

"Like the Finlorians, so too did Algorath abandon the shores of Tritos, departing for a secluded island far to the southeast. As the seventh great-grandson of the renegade Entient, I came eventually to serve as guardian of the Pendant and gatekeeper of the Illysp seal. I refused the charge at first, rebelling against my father and all that he expected of me. I left his island to journey far and wide, eventually settling upon these shores, where I met your mother." He paused with open mouth, looking as if he were about to say more, before shaking his head.

"When later I accepted my calling, your mother refused to accompany me or permit me to stay. As a pure mortal, she felt it best to say our farewells then and there, before suffering the indignity of growing old long before I."

Indeed, that would explain the man's unchanged appearance, Torin thought. A life measured in centuries, rather than decades—whether by mystical or divine embrace. He glanced at Marisha with fresh wonderment and a twinge of fear.

"She understood, however, that you, my daughter, might one day come to question the unique nature of your own existence, and that I would be the one to best explain it to you. She permitted me, therefore, to leave the Pendant with you, knowing little more than what I had shared with you, that it was a sacred talisman that would protect you as long as you protected it."

He reached into the tatters of his robes and, from a hidden pouch, pulled forth a small length of silver chain. "Only she and I knew of this, the token I kept, links from the chain you now wear. Without the attached heartstone, the power of the enchantment is latent, but can be called upon by one who knows how. Thus I could not only check on the status of the seal, but could use it to track you down when the time came."

His eyes shifted back to Torin. Sure enough, their gaze hardened.

"Never did I imagine my return would come under these circumstances. Even after I discerned that something had gone wrong with the linking magic, I rejected the notion that the seal itself might be broken. Nonetheless, I came with all haste to inspect it for myself. As you can see, that decision nearly cost me my life."

Marisha gripped Torin's arm with reflexive concern. "The Illychar?"

Darinor nodded. "The first had emerged and scattered weeks before. But in the ruined depths, a large brood lay in ambush for those they knew must come. I escaped only narrowly before coming for the Pendant in search of answers—many of which I found along the way."

"Hold on," Torin said. "You mean to suggest that the same Illychar who were trapped three thousand years ago are still alive today?"

The other flared with impatience. "Have you heard nothing I've said? They do not feed. They do not age. They kill among themselves, certainly, but for every coil that is felled, innumerable are the legions of Illysp just waiting to raise it up again. As long as the seal held, they could do no further harm. But you, my young fool, have single-handedly let loose their horror upon all of us."

Torin felt Marisha's restraining hand as he tensed in bitter frustration.

"What about you?" he demanded. "If the secret of the Sword was to be so closely guarded, why did you go around telling of it?"

It was Darinor's turn to betray uncertainty, and Torin relished it.

"Or do you not remember? Twelve years ago. Not long, I'm guessing, after you abandoned your daughter. You came to my village, Diln, in the Kalgren Forest west of here, where you spent the night telling stories of the Dragon Wars, the ancient Finlorians, the Swords of Asahiel . . ."

A squinting Darinor waggled a crooked finger at him. "You. You're the youth who asked me afterward if the Swords remained, or if they were merely legend."

It was a small triumph, but Torin took it. "Had you told me then that the blades did not exist, this might never have happened."

Darinor chuckled, a subtle, scoffing sound that barely carried past his own beard. "Then cast upon me a measure of your blame," he agreed. "Although I daresay such common myths have been shared countless times and by many others besides me. With you alone did it result in the plundering of the Sword."

Torin's scowl deepened. He considered pressing the attack, but decided against it. His gaze slipped to the proof of his guilt, resting in his lap, and he lost himself in its flaming depths. The Sword's crimson radiance bathed him as he studied the eternal fire that swirled within the polished blade.

"You seem to have all the answers," he said, "so tell me this. In the fight against Sabaoth, how did Algorath trigger the Sword's wrath?"

Darinor shook his head. "My ancestors and others have spent centuries pondering that question. None have found an answer. The first Vandari, those who served as generals during the Dragon Wars, are the last to have commanded the full force and fury of the blades. They did not share that knowledge, even among those who followed in their footsteps, for fear of the destruction to be wrought by their misuse. As they died out and disappeared, their secrets vanished with them."

Torin sagged. He should have expected as much. For it was the one riddle he most wanted answered. Still, there were plenty more where that had come from. "Well then, what of—"

"No more questions!" Darinor barked, with such sudden force as to startle his listeners. "I have told you already more than you need know. The Illysp are upon us. The only question that matters now is this: What do you intend to do about it?"

CHAPTER FOUR

*T*HE ANSWER TO THAT HAD SEEMED OBVIOUS ENOUGH.

Between the two of them, Torin and Marisha uttered only a handful of protests to the plan that Darinor laid out for them. Despite a host of unreconciled concerns, Torin saw little room to argue. For he believed the man's account. Despite a great many details which they had not the time to discuss, the renegade Entient's story fell into place so snugly with what he already knew, filled in so many of the gaps that had long existed in this land's history, that he dared not doubt it. There were at least as many questions as answers, but this much he understood instinctively: Though he had yet to meet his enemy face-to-face, he could not wait to do so before taking action against it.

He had begun his preparations straightaway, as soon as their clandestine meeting had come to a close. Breakfast was forgotten; he had no appetite for food. Taking Stephan aside, he instructed the chief seneschal to lay out provisions as quietly as possible for an expedition party scheduled to leave on the morrow. Torin wanted no word to be leaked of any of this until he'd had a chance to meet with the Circle. He gave a rough estimate of numbers and emphasized the need for swiftness. He tried not to be cross, but Stephan plied him with questions he did not then care to answer, forcing him to send the steward off with his tail between his legs.

By then, Allion had returned from his morning rounds. Torin went to his Fason at once, skipping over the daily report on the welfare of the city in order to relay all that Darinor had told him. He did so in search of the man's counsel, but at the same time, worked to impress upon his friend the need to do as the mystic suggested—much as he had months earlier, following his surprise reunion with Queen Ellebe and the charge he'd been given then.

As before, Allion was not easily convinced.

"He looks and smells like a corpse himself," his friend complained.

The pair had been briefly introduced just before Marisha had whisked her estranged father into a private council, allowing king and captain to do the same.

"He nearly was, to hear him tell it."

"Then how can we trust him? How do we know he's not one of these Illychar himself?"

Torin motioned for the other to keep his voice down, even though they had found their way into a private audience chamber and posted a pair of guardsmen outside.

"Because," the king replied, his own voice lowered, "if he were Illychar, why would he have come to warn us like this?"

"To get you out of the way, it seems," Allion snapped.

"Why? Why not just kill me and take the Sword for himself?"

"Perhaps he means to do just that."

Torin shook his head. "I already offered him the blade."

"What?"

"You think I want any part of this? I bade him take it before I make things any worse. I'm merely a foolish human, after all, while he's an Entient—or at least, close enough that I don't know what else to call him. He turned me down."

Allion hesitated. "Why would he do that?"

"He said mine is the greater need. The Sword is vital to this quest, not only as a matter of survival, but to convince those who must be found. He, on the other hand, must stay here in order to marshal the land's defenses."

"He's not going with you?"

"He alone knows how best to direct our armies so as to contain our enemy's numbers."

"That may be, but how does he expect you to accomplish this other task without him to guide you?"

"I asked him that very question." Torin sighed. "He said that since I am the only living man to wield the Crimson Sword, I am the most qualified person to do so. It's my mess, he said. I should be the one to clean it up."

"And what if you or the Sword are lost? If any of what he says is true, it seems to me that's the best weapon we have. He's not concerned about that?"

"I—" Torin stopped himself. He was about to say that he would be wearing Marisha's Pendant as well. Darinor was indeed concerned about tracking his whereabouts during his journey, and more especially, those of the Sword. The mystic assumed that should one of the artifacts fall into a thief's possession, both would. By exercising his control over the enchantment that connected his links of silver chain to the necklace from which they'd been taken, the Entient should be able to give chase and retrieve the talismans, should it become necessary.

However, Torin had not yet told Allion about the existence of the Pendant, omitting any such references from his narrative. He assumed it was only a matter of time now before others found out about it, but he preferred not to be the one to violate Marisha's long-held secret.

"*He*, I mean." Torin coughed, covering his misstep. "He claims to have some means of tracking me, as he tracked Marisha. Some form of magic, I would guess."

Allion's brow wrinkled in distrust. "And is it by magic that he expects you to find these so-called Vandari?"

The Vandari. Those who lay at the heart of his quest. For Darinor had reiterated that as gatekeeper of the Illysp seal, he was but a lookout. It was the Finlorians, and more specifically the Vandari, who had so long ago served as its architects. If any could rebuild what Torin had destroyed, it was they.

And yet, by Darinor's own admission, the Finlorians had abandoned these lands ages ago at the conclusion of the Illysp War. The only elves known to still exist upon these shores were the Mookla'ayans, those savage tribespeople secreted away in the jungle marshes of Vosges. When Torin, against his better judgment, had suggested he go first to them, Darinor had quashed the notion as he might an insect. Only the Finlorians could help them—and among these, only the Vandari.

"I wish that were so," Torin admitted. But it would not be that easy. Not even Darinor possessed a charm or cantrip that would reveal the whereabouts of the missing elven nation. He knew only what he had learned from his forebears, that most had fled westward across the Oloron Sea, there to tame the lands of Yawacor while leaving their own to be reclaimed by wilderness.

"This is preposterous. How long does he expect you to search?"

"As long as it takes, would be my guess."

Allion's brown eyes fixed him with a glare that was every bit as immutable as the earth they resembled. "And if they no longer exist?"

A shiver traced the edges of Torin's spine. He did not want to consider that possibility. For if Darinor was to be believed, the Vandari alone might hold the key to salvation for the peoples now occupying their former lands. If not—if their light had been extinguished, or if Torin could not find them, or if they had not the knowledge or powers with which his people could arm themselves against this scourge—then, as the renegade Entient had promised in that ominous manner of his, both Torin and those he loved were about to face a gloom and misery such as his mortal mind could not fathom.

But they did exist, Torin assured himself, and would not be told otherwise. The empire of Finloria was no more. But the Mookla'ayans had survived, despite centuries of effort on the part of man to drive them to extinction. And Yawacor, it was told, was yet home to many of the older races, those deemed undesirable by Pentanian standards and long since swept from her lands. While such reports were largely disregarded as superstitious hearsay, Torin refused to presume that the Finlorians no longer lived simply because he had never met one.

"You wondered the same thing about the Sword, remember?" Torin said. "Whether I could find it. Whether it existed at all."

"Exactly my concern." Allion, whose attention—like his—had been drifting inward, came back suddenly. "Don't you see? It's your quest for the Sword all over again."

"I was successful, wasn't I?"

"Were you?" his friend challenged, pinning him again with those eyes. "And what of the cost? What of Diln? How will you feel if something like that were to happen again, here at Krynwall?"

Torin tensed. Allion had assured him over and over again that he did not blame Torin for what had befallen their home village while he had led them off in search of the one weapon that might allow them to defend it. But it hardly mattered what his friend said. Despite every attempt to rationalize the decision—then and now—Torin blamed himself, and was tortured every day with thoughts of what might have been had he acted differently. His Fason and others could say what they wished, but deep down, they all held him accountable.

Allion must have recognized his darkening mood. "All I'm saying is, are you honestly willing to take that risk?"

"Aren't you the one who likes to trumpet duty over desire? I'd only be doing what has been asked of me."

Allion shook his head. "Too much is unknown. About this Darinor. About these Vandari." Torin sighed, for his friend was already repeating his arguments, but Allion pressed on. "I have a bad feeling, a viper in my gut. Don't do this."

Torin glared. "I guess I don't see where I have a choice."

"Of course you do. It's one we all have. Stop risking everything to change the world in one fell swoop, and work instead little by little, day by day, like everyone else. You were raised a cultivator, not a monarch, remember? Stay, and we'll face together whatever dangers arise."

It was difficult to argue. Even if he found the Vandari, he had no guarantee they could or would agree to help. But there were times when one had to be guided by instinct rather than logic. Despite his own reservations, the gnawing sense was that he had to do this.

"I don't think Darinor will see it that way," he said.

"Then make him see it that way. Your duty is to your people, not some raving madman wandered in from the rain. And he'd have to be mad," Allion hurried before Torin could cut him short, "not to see that there are too many responsibilities for you to leave behind."

"Those can be handled by someone else," the king muttered.

"And they will. Mark my words, if you leave now, Rogun will have usurped your throne by the time you return."

In this, at least, his Fason was probably correct. Allion had constantly chided him for giving the general too strong a voice on the ruling council. Torin had done so in an effort to placate the overbearing commander and quiet his objections. Instead, it had made him all the louder, giving him a platform from which to shout his agenda, allowing him to drive a wedge of dissent into the foundation of all that Torin hoped to accomplish. With Torin away, Rogun would move swiftly to wrest control of the kingdom from the Circle and its speaker.

"Rogun will come around," Torin replied, feigning confidence. "In the meantime, that's why I need you to stay here as regent in my stead."

His friend's eyes widened in shock. "Hah! There's a fanciful dream, even for you."

"Come, Allion, you said it yourself. My mission means nothing if this city and its inhabitants are not kept safe until my return."

But Allion was shaking his head emphatically. "This is madness. Complete and unwarranted. But if you insist on leaving, you know I'll follow, with or without your commission."

Torin scowled. He knew. It had happened before, hadn't it? But Allion understood as well as he the challenges this land faced. Torin's honeymoon as king was over. Expansionists from neighboring Partha, as well as nationalists within Alson, had already begun to question his authority. Few did so as openly as Rogun, unwilling to risk their political futures in debate against a man who was still deemed a hero by a majority of the populace. But the rumblings were there, and pressure had begun to build as the more powerful guilds and factions made their demands known, probing for weaknesses like ivy upon the wall. Rogun, a popular figure, was a spearhead for many of these efforts. But without a strong counterpresence to keep them in check, the audacity of all was likely to grow.

"Allion—"

"Call upon Nevik, if you must. Just don't think for a moment that you can weaken my resolve in this."

Torin's jaw locked with frustration. Of course he would like to call upon Nevik. When first they had arrived at Krynwall, the loyal baron had spent weeks lending him invaluable assistance, aiding in every way his assumption of royal duties. He was, in truth, the one noble thus far to whom Torin would happily entrust his own welfare and that of Alson. Time and again he had tried to abdicate to the more-qualified baron, but Nevik had refused him just as often, focused as he was on healing his own lands to the south. The young man was in much the same position as Torin, and the king knew that it would be unfair to ask of the baron more than he had already given.

"I'll send word to Drakmar at once. But there isn't time to await Nevik's response, let alone his arrival. And I would feel terrible about forcing this upon him in any case."

Allion threw his hands up in mock surrender. "But you care nothing about forcing it upon me."

Torin's chest tightened with regret. They had both been forced to grow up so quickly. Not yet twenty, Allion, formerly a village huntsman, was now captain of the City Shield, chief defender of the capital city of Alson. Was that any less of a leap than Torin himself had taken from village guardian to king? But circumstances were what they were, and any control he or his friend might have was limited to their response.

"You're the one, Allion. The one I most depend upon. The best man I know to defend this kingdom against its enemies—both within and without. Most of all, you're the only person I trust to watch after Marisha while I'm away."

Allion, who had been rolling his eyes and preparing any number of retorts, halted wordlessly. For a moment, he seemed uncertain of himself, and Torin figured the argument was won. Then a slow, smug smile spread across the other's face.

"You've no greater chance of keeping her here than you do me," he declared.

Torin looked to the closed door of the audience chamber, as if his gaze might somehow track the corridor beyond and settle upon the room in which Marisha was even now beginning to reacquaint herself with her long-lost father.

"Part of me would like to believe that," he admitted. "But something tells me she will remain here with Darinor. I can't see him permitting her to accompany me, and I don't see her challenging him on it."

Allion's confidence slipped. Torin knew that his friend cared for Marisha with a brotherly devotion. All three had been hard-pressed of late by their newfound endeavors—those of king, captain, and in Marisha's case, master and founder of a new order of healers here within the city. But Torin remained far and away the busiest, and Allion had taken it upon himself to keep company at Marisha's side when Torin could not. The pair had become close, for which the young king was grateful. Especially now, as he sensed his friend's dilemma in refusing him this request.

For a moment, Allion shifted from foot to foot. One hand twisted the tasseled ends of his ropes of office, then reached up to rub the back of his neck beneath his ponytail. Finally, it came around to pick at the hilt of his hunting knife. "When would you leave?" he asked reluctantly.

Torin kept his own arms folded across his chest. "As soon as the expedition force is assembled. No later than dawn tomorrow."

"Tomorrow? You can't raise an army in that time!"

"We're not taking an army."

"You'd better," Allion advised.

Torin disagreed. "Speed is of the essence. Summoning and outfitting a full force would require time we do not have. Nor could such a team move as swiftly as a smaller party of, say, half a dozen."

"Half a dozen? How do you expect to find anything," Allion demanded, "combing an entire land with but a handful of men?"

"Darinor claims that the Finlorians, if they still exist, are most likely in hiding, and will be far less likely to reveal themselves if made to feel threatened. The smaller the number, the less threatening we'll seem."

"And what of safety? From what little I know, this Yawacor is nothing more than a frontier wilderness overrun by cutthroats and warlords. And that's assuming you manage somehow to survive the sea crossing."

"That's why I've come to you." Torin grinned. Silently, he wished his friend would stop reminding him of all the obstacles that he himself feared. "Stephan is already handling the preparations. But since I can take only a few men to accompany me, I'd like you to handpick those who will see me safely home."

Allion did not share his attempt at enthusiasm. "And what makes you think I know anyone mad enough to join in this?"

"I was thinking City Shield. You're their captain. I'd hoped you could persuade them."

The Fason started to object, but Torin could see that his friend was already beginning to consider whom to select. "This is madness," he repeated finally.

"So you've indicated. Unfortunately, that doesn't change matters."

Allion glowered, then brightened as if struck with a sudden thought. "What about the Entients?"

"What about them?"

"Maybe you should pay a return visit to Whitlock, see if the meddling codgers can at least confirm Darinor's story."

Torin rejected the notion with a shake of his head. "And how would they do that, given that most of it is supposed to be unknown to them? Besides, we failed to find them the last time we searched, remember? If these creatures are already prowling our lands, we haven't time to hike those mountains again, hoping that the Entients sense our need and agree to grant us an audience—especially when I see no reason to trust them any more than we do Darinor."

Allion's jaw worked from side to side as he searched desperately for some other suggestion. At last he yielded, heaving a sigh of exasperation. "I'll introduce you to a few guardsmen—and let *you* explain to their mothers why it is you intend to drag them off on this fool's adventure. Maybe then you'll reconsider."

"As enticing as that sounds," said Torin, glancing at the clock that stood in its mahogany cabinet against the near wall, "I have to meet with the Circle to set things in place for the new regent."

"I never said—"

"And please, keep it quiet. If word is spilled too soon, every guildsman and supplicant and courtier will be demanding that his license be signed or grievance heard or dispute settled before I leave. I can't afford to be waylaid."

"I make no promises," Allion said.

"Nor do I require any," replied Torin, clapping his friend's shoulder. "As always, I trust you will do everything in your power to see that the needs of this issue are met."

Allion frowned at the compliment as Torin released him and headed for the door.

"How did Evhan fare in this morning's session?" the Fason called after him.

"Very well," Torin admitted, recalling an event just hours old but which seemed to him a lifetime removed. "He held his own to the last. Had me promise him another row."

Allion smirked with barely concealed pride.

"They made a good team," Torin acknowledged. "I should think they'd be excellent travel companions."

"Oh no, you're not getting Evhan. If there's even a chance I'll be remaining here to look after your job, I'll need someone to watch over mine."

Torin suppressed a grim yet satisfied smile of his own. "I leave it to your good judgment," he said, before flinging open the hardwood door and striding from the room.

ALTHOUGH HE COULD BARELY CONTAIN HIS EXCITEMENT, Pagus held himself in check, waiting until Allion had followed Torin from the chamber before daring to breathe normally again. Even when he was alone, he kept still for several moments longer, tucked away in his place of concealment, waiting to make sure that none of them—the king, the Fason, or the sentries—would return. He made himself measure ten full minutes before replacing the tiny viewing slat and reaching through with his knife to trigger the outer latch.

He emerged slowly at first, a crack at a time. Once assured that the way was clear, he swung wide the door of the cabinet in which the pendulum and other clockworks were housed, and leapt free. His knees were only slightly cramped at having been pinned open for so long, and he ignored the uncomfortable tingling sensation as he reached back to latch the closet shut.

Wiping the sweat from his brow, he tiptoed toward the exit. That had been close. The herald had been tracking his king ever since the commotion of that morning, fighting to get near enough to give ear to these furtive goings-on. It wasn't like Torin to brush him and so many others aside, and he had been all the more determined for it. When the king had found Allion, Pagus knew they would be meeting here, in Torin's favorite audience chamber. Still, the halls were abuzz with activity, and the pair had moved with uncommon urgency. Pagus had just barely managed to squeeze into his regular hiding spot before the private council had begun.

And what a council it had been. Even now, his ears hummed, and he had to struggle to retain all that he'd heard. He didn't want to forget a word of it, knowing that to do so would cost him dear. A miner took greater caution when carrying diamonds than coal.

By the time he reached the doorway, his heart had settled somewhat, skipping rather than pounding. The organ had nearly failed him when Torin had looked in his direction toward the end of the meeting. That had happened before, and under normal circumstances, it didn't bother him. But given this newfound treasure, his every fiber was drawn taut, as he just waited to be discovered.

He peeked around the edge of the doorframe, glanced in both directions, then slipped into the hallway beyond. By the time he reached the stairs, his skin had cooled, and he allowed a spring into his step. It wasn't until he reached the landing below that he met his first guardsman. Kien greeted him with a quick hello, and Pagus responded with his typically bright and eager smile.

"On my horse," he said, making his standard apology without slowing.

He made sure of Kien's nod before scooting down a side passage that would lead eventually to his quarters. A quick stop, then on to the stables. All the while, his smile remained, as he blithely considered just what his news might be worth.

CHAPTER FIVE

A SHOWER OF SPARKS CASCADED OVER HIS NAKED ARM, covering him from chest to foot, to dance like silent hailstones on the earthen floor. Faldron disregarded them, protected as he was by his leather smock and by a hearty layer of soot and sweat. Ropes of muscle bunched and corded as he gripped the iron with a pair of tongs, while with the other arm he continued to rain blows from above.

After forty years of shaping metal in this armory that he'd inherited from his father, the smith's hearing was not what it had once been. Nevertheless, he could still detect the ringing tones of the service request bell strung from the storefront to this, the back of his workshop—even over the clangor of hammer and anvil. He ignored its summons all the same, waiting for his loafer of a shop boy to answer the call. When after several moments the ringing continued unabated, he responded with a growl. Laying his tools and gloves beside the unfinished piece, he stanched the airflow from his bellows and closed the damper to his forge, then stomped forth to greet his uninvited guest.

By the time he reached the front, he had stowed the worst of his anger and donned the mask of geniality reserved for customer interactions. All of that changed when he caught sight of the spiky-haired youth hanging from his bellpull.

"Leave off," he snarled, slapping at the boy's hand. "I ain't deaf, you know."

The youth gave one last, accidental tug as he jerked away, just barely avoiding the smith's meaty swipe.

Faldron looked daggers upon the scamp, who was not fazed in the least. The lad was covered in grime and dressed as a street urchin. But even this could not hide the bright eyes and even brighter smile that shone through the meager disguise.

"What did I tell you about coming to me during hours?" the smith scolded, glancing out at the busy roadway.

"Sorry." The boy beamed without the slightest hint of apology. "This couldn't wait."

"Well, it's going to," Faldron rumbled. "I've told you before, even out of uniform you're too recognizable. Come back after dark."

"But—"

"Sorry, lad. Price you pay for becoming the king's favorite." He was about to withdraw when the slow clop of approaching hoofbeats drew him back.

"Master Faldron," the newcomer hailed. "Good afternoon."

Faldron glanced at the boy, hoping the lad had the good sense to make a swift and discreet exit. But it was already too late.

"And young master Pagus, is that you?"

Pagus coughed, cast about as if to flee, then nodded.

"Why, I can hardly recognize you. What would your king say if he saw you looking like that?"

"He's just here to pick up a pair of heavy boots for His Majesty," Faldron covered swiftly.

Commander Zain was a weasel of a man, with an ermine's face to match. The thinnest tracing of a beard hugged his jawline, highlighting its sharp angles and the upturned corners of his mouth. Black eyes glittered like marbles in their sockets.

"I wasn't aware His Majesty ever wore heavy boots," Zain observed, peering down from his mount with a reptilian smile.

"What can I do for you, Commander?"

"Just come to check on our order," Zain answered, his gaze bearing down upon Pagus. The young lad, to his credit, had ceased to squirm, but faced the other squarely now that he'd been found out.

"Your order will be ready in two days as promised. I might finish sooner," Faldron added, "if you and your men would cease coming by to measure my progress."

Zain's horse tossed its head and gave a flick of its tail. The steed of one of his two soldiers behind him snorted.

"I do beg your pardon," the commander offered with that infuriating tone of mock civility. "We'll be on our way, then, and leave the two of you to talk."

Faldron glared. "Come, lad, let's fetch you those boots."

Zain's soldiers pulled aside to let their commander by, then fell into line behind him. Faldron, meanwhile, came around to grip Pagus by the shoulder. The trio looked back only once before falling in with the traffic upon the roadway.

The armorer breathed a sigh of relief. As commander-in-waiting of Krynwall's armies and the right hand of General Rogun himself, Zain was not one to be trifled with. No doubt, Rogun would hear of this before the day was out.

"Well, then," Faldron snarled, shaking the boy so that his pretty teeth chattered. "The damage is done. Let's hear what you have to say."

He shifted his hold to the scruff of the youth's neck and hauled him around the counter, leaving the boy's disinterested roan tethered to one side. With a stern pace, he propelled the other forward, past the front awning under which display racks showcased samples of his wares, and into the dark opening of his smithy. He did not stop there, but marched deeper, back through storerooms filled with armor and weapons in various stages of creation or repair, stowed upon shelves and racks or in assorted piles. There they came upon Tam—his useless bum of a shop boy who hoped one day to be an apprentice—hanging gorgets upon the wall.

"Where were you?" the smith roared, kicking a battered helmet in the boy's direction.

Tam started and fell back into a rack of halberds that threatened to tumble around him. "I . . . I was replacing the well rope, as you requested."

Faldron felt Pagus twisting for a look at the other, and so jerked the herald away to keep his face hidden. "And you didn't hear the bell from there?"

"N-no, sir," Tam stammered, eyes affright.

Of course he hadn't, the smith realized. Nor could anyone. "Bah," he grumbled, and hauled Pagus onward.

The smell of fire and molten metal and singed hair replaced that of oil and leather as at last they reached the forge. They kept going until they came to a far corner where slumped a pile of coal. There they stopped, with Faldron flinging Pagus toward the mound of crushed ore and jabbing a beefy finger in his face.

"This had better be good," he warned.

For a moment, the herald did not respond, his young eyes fixed upon Faldron's blunted nose—an ancient injury that had never healed quite properly. Then, Pagus seemed to remember himself, and in an instant, his smile returned.

Faldron worked hard to mask his own delight as the news was delivered. The stranger named Darinor, the Illysp, and most critical to him, the report of the king's planned departure. This last part was something for which he'd been waiting a long time, an opportunity that would surely fetch him a handsome sum.

Nevertheless, he squelched his enthusiasm, guarding his emotions behind a stern frown as he considered the eager face of his youthful informant and pretended to deliberate on what this knowledge was worth.

"You did well in bringing this to my attention at once," he allowed. He uncrossed his arms and reached beneath his smock, pulling forth a small key. "Wait here."

Leaving Pagus to do as told, he retreated briefly to an adjacent office, where he removed a small wooden chest from a hidden drawer. Using the key, he triggered the lock and withdrew from the chest a smaller leather pouch, which he carried forth with him.

At the sight of the pouch, Pagus's keen young eyes widened to the size of a breastplate whose outer edges had yet to be hammered round. Faldron smirked inwardly and jingled the pouch before producing two coppers and a three-piece of silver.

As the coins fell into Pagus's outstretched hand, his hopeful visage crumbled. He seemed at first unable to speak, then screwed his courage into place. "I thought all of that should fetch at least a gildron."

"A gildron?" the smith balked, though he knew the value to be ten times the suggested amount. "Where would a young lad like you spend a gildron? Least of all without raising suspicion."

"You said—"

"Bah, this news would have come to me—as to everyone—soon enough. Bring me something secret, something I can use, and the reward will be much greater."

Pagus was unmollified. "But—"

"Keep it or return it." He loosened the purse strings suggestively.

The herald gave him a dirty look before thrusting the coins into his pocket.

"I'll lead you out," Faldron offered, as if that might ease the lad's pain.

"I can manage," Pagus muttered. He turned and shuffled away.

The smith called after. "Wait!"

Pagus rounded, even now, with a glimmer of hope. That hope faded when the armorer handed him a pair of heavy boots.

"Consider that part of your payment," said the smith. "You may return them to me for a copper. Next time, be more careful, or wait until dark."

The herald slunk back the way they'd come, looking as though his horse had ridden over him.

Faldron followed him out, scanning the roadway for any sign of Zain or his men. Seeing none, he disappeared back into his workshop, there to stare at the abandoned blade whose angry red folds had chilled to burnt umber. His sudden urge was to leave it be and set forth at once to meet with his client, for by the sound of it, the man would need this word as soon as possible if he wished to organize a pursuit.

But no, he decided. Better that he follow the structure of their agreement. He did not wish to fan the man's ire as Pagus had fanned his.

After replacing his coin purse within its chest, and the chest within his desk, he squared himself before his anvil and roared for Tam.

"Yes, sir?" the boy answered, skittering near.

"Run down to Orru's with a full brace of butcher's knives. Tell him to raise the red."

"Sir?"

"Just do as I say." He flipped the other an ivory half-piece withheld from his purse. "Make haste."

"Yes, sir."

When the boy had gone, leather-wrapped bundle in hand, Faldron returned to his forgotten task, suppressing the rash of anticipation that prickled beneath his skin. Firing his forge, he snatched up hammer and tongs and went back to work.

AT DUSK, THE ARMORER RODE FROM HIS SHOP on the back of a well-worn bay. He was an easy man to recognize, what with that twisted spade of a broken nose. His giant body was practically hairless; that which wasn't shaved had long ago been singed to the roots. Closer up, one could see that his fire-tanned skin was mottled with burn scars, the signature of an ancient blacksmith.

"Good work, Lieutenant," Zain said, lowering the spyglass and handing it back to his junior officer. Perched in a clouded window on the second floor of an abandoned masonry storehouse across the way, the soldier had been ordered to keep a sharp lookout, and to alert him of this very moment. "Follow me."

The lieutenant accepted the spyglass and saluted sharply before pivoting on his heel and heading with his commander for the stairs.

Moments later, the pair mounted their steeds and urged them into the crowded street. Night fell early during these winter months, coinciding with the end of the workday. Traffic was therefore at its evening peak, allowing Zain and his man to hide themselves among the grinding throng. They kept to the far edges of the brick-laid avenue some twenty lengths back, shielded by a wagoner and the near darkness, wrapped in riding cloaks. Within the hoods of those cloaks, they pinned an eye to their quarry at all times.

Zain recognized a rat when he saw one, especially a royal rat stripped of his tabard and masked in soiled woolens. And it was well known to him that despite his considerable skills with hammer and tongs, Faldron specialized in intrigues. To find the king's own brat meeting with the renowned armorer on the very day in which an unknown stir had interrupted a long-planned coronation rehearsal was a matter that needed to be explored.

A choking layer of dust coated his throat and scratched at his eyes. Zain would have preferred to be lying as usual within his chambers at this time, being bathed in oils by a pair of palace wenches. But in order to retain such favors granted him by General Rogun, he had to be willing to focus on his duties whenever an opportunity such as this arose.

Time slipped by with slow monotony as they fought their way along the congested maggot trail. Behind his turned shoulder, the sun spewed a final, desperate burst of color over the city's curtain wall before being dragged helplessly away by the night. Stars glimmered against a charcoal sky, twinkling like dying embers, as the day's fire cooled.

All the while, Zain and his lieutenant clung to their man as surely as if they had him leashed, giving slow chase through the city streets. Faldron glanced around from time to time as if sensing he was being followed, but never came close to spying the guilty pair.

At last, after forging a circuitous route along the city's main avenues, the smith doubled back along a zigzag path of quiet lanes and deserted alleys. Continuing the pursuit at this point was more of a challenge, but that only heightened Zain's thrill. Working as a team, the bundled soldiers kept pace.

They came finally to an inn of some repute—and none of it good. Years ago, Zain had been a regular, and enjoyed himself well enough during those times. But over the years, his tastes had become more refined, until this place had grown too coarse for his liking. A tattered pennant flew upon a flagstaff in the small picket courtyard, fluttering restlessly in a cold evening breeze. It teased and waved, then unfurled at last to reveal the embroidered symbol of a honeycomb. The pennant was scarlet in color, Zain noted, rather than jade. The Queen's Hive was full.

So why did it appear deserted? From his position of hiding, the commander-in-waiting breathed forth clouds as his narrowed gaze scraped over the beaten woodwork. It seemed far too early in the evening for the Hive to have filled itself to capacity. Certainly, it was odd that none of the upstairs lights were on, rooms from which Zain would have expected to hear the sounds of drunken laughter and lecherous cajoling. By all appearances, the Hive was closed.

This did not stop Faldron, who vanished temporarily into an adjacent stable to tether his mount. Emerging a moment later, the armorer came around to rap at the Hive's front door. Zain crouched lower, wary of being seen. He had left his lieutenant with the horses in a dilapidated shack two streets over— just a short dash to safety, without risking that the animals would give him away. Still, he bated his breath as he awaited the Hive's response.

As the moments passed, it appeared there would not be any. Perhaps Zain had guessed wrong in what the armorer was about. Perhaps Faldron was here for sport, and just didn't understand the sign of the red. Perhaps, despite the dim light that glowed through the shuttered windows of the inn's lower level, the place was deserted.

Then the door cracked, and that light spilled briefly onto the threshold. When the light disappeared, Faldron was gone.

Zain waited awhile longer, attuning his eyes and ears to the night around him. No new sounds came from within the Hive; no new flames were lit.

When confident that the vanished smith would not be coming out directly, Zain dashed forward from his cover, clutching his scabbard to keep the blade from rattling. In a crouch, he scurried across the empty street and up to the side of the Hive's slatted exterior. The drumming of his heart echoed in his ears with accelerated rhythm. The thrill of the hunt.

Skulking along a bed of withered flowers, the commander crept toward the nearest window from which a muted light shone. The paned glass was in need of cleaning, but was clear enough to show him the inn's common room. Peering closer, he caught his first sign of movement—there, behind a counter against the far wall. A man appeared, fetched an oil lamp from a sagging shelf, and was gone.

Zain smirked. Orru. He'd heard that the butcher had taken over management of the Hive, but had forgotten it until now. He didn't bother trying to track the dealings of all the various whoremasters in this city, just those with whom he had direct business.

Was it Orru with whom the armorer was trading? Zain didn't think so. More likely, the butcher was merely facilitating some other meeting. That might explain why the Hive had been shut down for the evening.

He was about to surrender this rather limited vantage point and seek another when Orru returned, his lamp alight, and headed upstairs.

Zain looked around, eyeing the balcony that skirted the second floor outside. Every inn of this nature worth its coin was equipped with at least one means of hasty egress, and if memory served, the Hive was no exception.

The commander left his window and went searching for the hidden ladder. He found it behind a rotted woodpile. Obvious, to anyone in the know, since the Hive had no hearth. Each room contained a small coal stove, but relied for the most part on the flush of drink and activity to keep its patrons warm.

Zain's soft-soled leathers made scarcely a sound as he ascended the weathered rungs to reach the platform above. Just as he did so, the light of an oil lamp filled the window nearest him. Zain started and flattened himself against the wall. His heart beat frantically now as he waited for the alarm. But there were no cries, no hustle. Just the quiet rustle of windblown leaves.

He realized, however, that he could not stay in this position. The lamp was most likely a beacon, a signal for someone who might or might not be entering through the front door. Remain here much longer, and he would certainly be exposed.

He skittered like a roach from the revealing signal light, until he reached the corner of the building and had followed the balcony in wrapping around its side.

The commander paused. He needed to get closer to that room, yet dared not do so by sneaking inside. But the Hive had two kinds of rooms. Those that offered absolute privacy were located in the cellar. These lacked windows of any sort, and no doubt had an escape route of their own. Zain, however, had always preferred the upstairs rooms, which had windows in the walls *and* in the ceiling.

Leaping from the rail to catch the edge of the gabled roof, Zain hoisted himself as quickly and noiselessly as he could manage atop the slanted bed of shingles. Keeping to the front side of the building, opposite the slope on which the lighted window was found, he rolled patiently and quietly toward the far end. Leaves and needles clung to his clothes, and, along with a layer of moss, helped to cushion his approach. The boards beneath creaked, but not so loudly as to be a concern, especially when he believed the rooms below to be empty. Once he'd gone about two-thirds of the way over, and had aligned himself with where he thought his target on the other side to be, he settled onto his stomach and crawled carefully toward the peak.

He missed his target by a dozen paces, and was glad that he did. For just before he crested the roof's peak, a dark shape alighted at the very spot for which he'd been heading. It did so almost like a bird: weightless, soundless. Zain froze, chilled from the inside out. A window entry he had anticipated. But what manner of unsavory character descended upon his cohorts through the roof?

The commander held his breath as the cloaked shadow figure turned its cowled head from side to side. Then it held perfectly still, and Zain feared he'd been spotted. An unnatural dread filled his gut, coring him like an apple. Had he not lost his capacity to move, he might have fled.

With a muffled crunch of shattering glass and splintering wood, the shadow thing disappeared. As soon as it had gone, Zain's terror lifted, and he scrambled forward to see what had become of it. In truth, he already knew, else he'd not have dared to pursue.

Along the rear side of the building, one for each room, were a line of eyebrow arches in the roof plane. Faint light spilled from only one of these—the one in which the window had been broken and the shadow had gone.

There was a deep, flustered cry—Faldron's, he was sure—before the light flicked out. What could explain that? Perhaps they'd gone to another room. But no, the light had died suddenly, as if extinguished. Besides, he could still hear Faldron's voice, quieter now, but there just the same. Perhaps the shadowy newcomer insisted upon absolute darkness in which to conduct its affairs.

Zain's dread fascination grew.

That fascination, however, did not warrant a potentially bloody encounter with whatever creature—man, woman, or beast—Faldron had called upon this night. While inching closer to the open dormer window, Zain made sure to shield his body behind the adjacent arch, avoiding the area beneath which the conspirators held their council—so that the crunch of his movements would not be heard. As a consequence, their gossip escaped him. But he could pry that from Faldron later, if necessary. Some things weren't worth the risk.

A cold wind probed the folds of his cloak, seeking to slow the pulse that kept him warm. Hunkered against its chill touch, Zain waited for the secret meeting to draw to a close. Once it did, he had every intention of following this shadow figure—from a distance, of course—to see what he might learn.

Faldron's hushed account went on for quite some time without interruption, more recitation than conversation. Not once did Zain detect the voice of the other, if indeed it had one. From the night without came the occasional clop of a distant horse or the echo of a drunkard's merriment. In this far-removed quarter, at least, the city slept.

His level of attention was starting to sag, his sharp mind drifting, when he heard the scooting of a chair. He perked at once and ducked lower against the protective dormer. There was the sound of footsteps, the closing of a door, and silence.

Zain waited. Had the shadow exited by a different route? He started to look, then stopped himself. That was exactly what a hunter did, outlast his prey, wait for it to show itself. The parallel almost made him laugh. Which of the two was he?

It was not until he heard the slamming of the Hive's front door that he craned his neck to peer around. There was no sign of the shadow. Quickly he scampered across the roof's peak and down the other side. Faldron was shuffling toward the stable. Orru, when finished locking up, did the same. The pair stopped briefly to share a grumbling exchange, then disappeared within. A moment later, each was on his separate steed, and headed off in separate ways.

Zain sank back on his haunches, feeling a slight twinge of regret. He'd missed his chance to gather anything more this night. He should have known that anyone who would go through as much trouble as the shadow had to enter a place unnoticed would not leave the same way. Or maybe he had just flown away on the wind like smoke.

Either way, the commander's disappointment was assuaged by an even stronger sense of relief. There were safer ways to study strangers than to track them through the city streets. With Faldron, he knew what he'd been up against, but this other had caught him completely by surprise.

No matter, he assured himself, delaying for good measure a few moments longer before dropping from the roof and heading for the balcony ladder. He could still rely on Faldron. Maybe even Orru. One way or another, there was clearly more to uncover here, and he intended to do so—just in case it was something he might twist to his own advantage.

As he made off to retrieve his waiting mount, he felt the stars, like the eyes of a bird of prey, watch him go.

CHAPTER SIX

MORE OFTEN THAN HE COULD REMEMBER, Xarius Talyzar had killed a man as a matter of precaution. Every now and then, he let one live for the same reason.

The spy on the roof of the Queen's Hive was not Faldron's. The assassin could see that just by watching the man's furtive movements around the building's exterior. More likely a flea picked up by the armorer somewhere along the way. A nuisance rather than a threat. But Xarius tolerated neither.

He went straight for the roof, cutting off the spy's approach to the lighted window. His purpose was not to confront it, but to startle it, then gauge its reaction. Had it scampered off in fright, it was probably of no concern. Instead, the insect had held its ground.

It had come no closer, however. The assassin's abrupt appearance had made sure of that. He'd marked its skittering movements even while listening to Faldron's account, making sure it did not venture near enough to see or hear anything. He'd made no mention of it to the armorer. For all his subtlety, the mistrustful smith might have ended their meeting then and there.

One thing at a time.

Afterward, given Faldron's report, the insect's presence became much more meaningful—or utterly inconsequential, depending on its identity. If a stray rat seeking crumbs, it was of no concern. If someone who might alert the king of the assassin's presence, it would have to be exterminated.

For that reason, Xarius had lingered until the spy departed, watching to see if it had friends—potential witnesses—before he questioned and then killed it. When it flashed by in the lighted pool of a street lamp, the assassin took a long, studied look. What he saw surprised him, and justified his decision against rash action. He knew this man, this Commander Zain, if only by repute, which complicated his decision.

Zain was Rogun's man, and Rogun was no friend of the king. There was scant chance, therefore, that he was rushing back to the palace to warn Torin of suspected danger. However, he was powerful enough and devious enough to have spun this entire web, or to have designs that might otherwise conflict with the assassin's own.

After all this time, Xarius was not about to take that chance. He could already guess what his employer's reaction to this news would be. This was the opportunity they had long been waiting for. Best to confirm the truth and remove any potential complications here and now.

He was still mulling over his options when the skulking commander dashed in through the rear of a confectioner's shack whose walls and roof listed dangerously. As swift and silent as the man's own shadow, Xarius slipped up to the leeward side.

"Sir. Did you learn what you needed?"

"Not near what I'd hoped. That fool armorer is plotting something, and with dangerous company, but I know not what."

"Shall we report to General Rogun now, sir?"

"No." A saddle creaked, and a horse tamped and whickered. "Not yet. Let me work on the matter until we have something worth bringing to the general's attention."

They rode swiftly through the door, Zain and his lone companion. The assassin could have felled them both, but let them go. Zain was an outsider in this, and Xarius's own identity remained a mystery. Better that he let the commander live and avoid the undue attention his death might bring.

The decision weighed on the assassin for some time, though his doubts were alleviated by the expectation of what this all meant. A strange turn, but one that worked in his favor. For nine weeks he'd been stuck in this ruin of a city, relegated to the role of lookout, commanded by his employer to sit and observe and do nothing but mark the movements of the young King Torin—a test of patience such as he had never before endured. All of a sudden, it would seem that was about to change.

He blew forward on a billowing wind, a vessel slipped from its moorings to sail the dark, placid waters of night. None saw him as he passed by the few rabble who crossed his path at this late hour and in this quiet sector. Within moments, he had returned to the district in which he'd made his home, an area that had unofficially been cordoned off for the pariahs of even this society—the deaf and dumb, blind and maimed, disease-stricken and mentally infirm. To Xarius, these shunned vermin were no more or less disgusting than the rest of those who rotted within the walls of this city. He lived among them as a matter of convenience, having found that such individuals tended to be isolated and withdrawn, with far more respect for one's private business than those of rank or basic privilege.

When he came upon the sewage duct, he reached out with all his trained senses, searching for anyone nearby. Only then did he pick the lock of the grate and duck inside. Without a torch, he ran along the narrow ledge that rimmed the enclosed channel, keeping clear of the sluggish and foul-smelling river current, kicking aside squealing rats and bits of debris. Every now and then, moonlight slipped through another gated service portal. Judging by the cracked and festering condition of the tunnel, most had gone too long unused.

At last he came to a break in the tunnel that opened into a spacious alcove. He had no idea what the area had originally been used for. A staging ground for crews or their equipment, perhaps. More recently, it had been home to a flock of lepers whose only other choice had been exile from the city. When one after another of their companions had started to die off—not as a result of their ailment, but due to severed windpipes—the rest had decided that life in the country might not be so bad.

It was but one of many temporary shelters in which the assassin lived. His needs were small. He had no possessions and needed no comforts. He found that he kept a sharper edge by denying himself even the most basic luxuries. His only companions were his blades and quarrels, his only friend the darkness.

Squatting in the center of the dust-covered alcove, he scraped about until he'd lit a small fire within a ring of stones. It didn't take much; even a candle's flame would do. He then pulled a pouch from his belt and reached for a pinch of the dried-skin powder inside. Xarius did not pretend to understand how it all worked; nor did he care to. As a result of their devastating nature, the arcane arts had been abandoned by man centuries ago. They certainly held no interest for him.

A sprinkle was all it took. The fire hissed and guttered, and its smoke turned black. Xarius recoiled slightly from the stench of burning flesh.

Within moments, an image took shape within the vile curtain of smoke. The image of a man. Elder brother to Torin and son of Sorl. The onetime crown prince and then king of Alson.

Xarius Talyzar, the wizard greeted.

He did so without voice, using instead the assassin's sign language. And though his image was but a sixth of his true size and made of wavering smoke, his motions were clear.

Good news, Xarius signed in reply. *Our little bird prepares to leave the nest.*

When? Even through the smoky image, Soric's eagerness was manifest.

At dawn. Better still, he is heading your way.

The assassin proceeded to relate all that he had gleaned this evening from their hired mole. He skimmed briefly over that which did not matter—the rumors of bestial races on the prowl, ancient spirits unleashed, and the unknown history of the Crimson Sword. He focused instead on the result. Torin, he who had usurped Soric's throne in the wake of the Demon Queen's failed conquest, would be setting forth at once with only a small party, boarding a vessel, and sailing westward across the ocean.

Directly into their hands.

The wizard's initial reaction was even more gleeful than Xarius had anticipated. Understandable, given Soric's obsession, and that they might have waited months or even years for a lesser opportunity.

Xarius's own enthusiasm was quickly quelled, however, by the wizard's secondary response.

Give chase, my midnight falcon. But make no move to sink your talons unless I signal otherwise.

What?

I wish you to observe only. Alert me to any changes in his progress. You will not seek to capture him, is that understood?

The wizard's signals had become rigid and harsh. Xarius replied in kind. *I've been waiting for this as long as you have. You'll not deny me now.*

You had your chance, remember? You failed to bring him to me then—and that when he traveled with but a single companion and without the weapon he now carries.

Soric's reminder was a slap in the face. All of a sudden, the dancing flames felt cold compared to those that scorched his cheeks.

I will arrange for another to handle delivery. You will follow from the rear to help guide my hand.

Then you will find another, Xarius fumed. *I am a hunter, not a lapdog.*

You will do as I say.

Or I will kill him myself, here and now, and end this pointless charade.

You will not! Or I swear by all my powers, Talyzar, you'll be next.

The assassin felt his nostrils flare. Had the wizard been standing before him, he might have taken his chances and unleashed his hand. As it was, there was little he could do.

You cannot run far or fast enough to escape me, the wizard warned. *Do not think to try.*

Too late for that, Xarius thought, but kept it to himself.

It will all be over soon, the other continued, seeking now to smooth his raised hackles. *And your sacrifices will be well rewarded.*

Indeed, it was these rewards, more than any of the wizard's threats, that had kept the assassin chained so long. Until recently, Soric had been the perfect master, with deep pockets and a long leash. The only thing Xarius enjoyed more were the tasks themselves, tasks that challenged him, and which were free of moral restraint. From the outset, theirs had been an ideal arrangement.

But all of that had changed—overnight, it seemed—with the ill-fated hunt for the wizard's younger brother. For it was then that each had become distracted by his own obsession. Soric, of course, was consumed with his need to exact revenge upon the upstart king, for reasons to which even the assassin was not fully privy. Xarius, meanwhile, cared nothing for the whelp one way or the other, except in how he might be used to gain access to his own bitter rival. Had he not believed Torin might make for the perfect lure, he never would have agreed to this otherwise wasteful expenditure of his time and talents.

Our agreement stands, the wizard promised. *When Torin is mine, I shall lend whatever assistance you may need in hunting down Kronus. Do not unravel on me now, so near the end.*

The youth's name, even unspoken, rankled Xarius to his core. He resisted the urge to reach for the scar the other had left with him as a result of their last encounter, to trace its raised length and swear death to he who had placed it there. An obsession that was every bit as unhealthy as the wizard's, he knew. But like the wizard, he didn't care.

Am I to sever loose strands? the assassin prompted.

Soric's image smiled. *Our work here is finished for now. Do as you deem necessary.*

Xarius bowed in acknowledgment. A small concession, but at least it was something. A residual twinge of regret swept through him at having allowed Zain and his companion to escape, now that he knew for certain his time here was coming to a close. If nothing else, their deaths might have lent him some small measure of satisfaction on this most inauspicious night.

But that was too dire an outlook, the assassin realized, as the oily black smoke burned away and the wizard's summoned image drifted into the ether. One way or another, he was ready to move on. He'd been idle for too long, constrained to gathering gossip while his skills eroded from lack of use—a hobbled raptor left with only its sight. Although he was not yet free of the wizard's tether, this next exercise would at least allow him to stretch his wings.

Nevertheless, he squatted before the dying flames for some time, simmering in frustration. Dissatisfied with having sat around for as long as he had while his ultimate quarry escaped him. Aggravated by the wizard's negative assessment of his abilities. Xarius Talyzar, the Shadow, was a patient man. But that patience had worn thin, leaving him exposed, as naked as a soldier without his armor. It was a discomfiting feeling, and he knew of only one way to resolve it.

Kicking aside the failing embers, he took hold of the hilt of his saber and made his way back out into the night.

"CONGRATULATIONS, FASON."

The young Evhan let slip a crooked smirk of pride and gratification. To hide it, he looked down, fingering the ropes of office that had just now been bestowed upon him.

But Allion would not deny him this pleasure, even under these grim circumstances. The lad had made it known from the first day of training that this was his goal, and had ever since labored tirelessly—and with an infectious intensity—to make that dream a reality. He had been a wonderful influence, not only on his fellow guardsmen, but upon his leaders as well. Allion could think of no one more deserving, and he clapped the young man's shoulder in approval.

"The promotion is well earned," the former captain assured him. "I've no doubts that you are ready."

Nor did Evhan, he noted. The new Fason grinned fully this time, although the scar upon his cheek caused his face to retain its lopsided appearance.

"I will fulfill the duties of my office with the utmost faith and fidelity," the young man swore.

Young man. The lad was two years older than himself. "I'm confident you will."

One of the double doors to the assembly hall lurched open. Both men turned at Marisha's approach.

"Sir?"

"Dismissed, Captain," Allion agreed.

Evhan saluted, right fist covering his heart, before taking his leave. On the way out, he bowed to Marisha, who dipped in curtsy.

When the doors had closed, Allion offered a weary smile. "Best sight I've seen all day."

Marisha blushed. "I'd thought you would assemble the Shield and hold ceremony for Evhan's promotion."

Allion sighed. "I would, if I knew for certain I'd be here in a day or two to conduct it." Marisha came forward to take his hands, and a measure of the weariness drained away. "Please tell me you've talked him out of this."

"I haven't tried," she admitted. She touched his hands to her cheek in fond greeting before releasing them.

"How can you not?" The words sounded more cross than he'd intended, resounding in the empty hall.

"Because I believe he must do this. For all of us."

Allion was taken aback by her commitment. "And what makes you so certain?"

"Because I believe in my father."

"Your father." Allion snorted, and again made a note to have these stark stone walls softened with flags or tapestries. "You don't even know the man. How can you trust him?"

Marisha took his hand and led him over to a bench beneath an arched alcove. When both were seated, she stared intently into his eyes.

"Because he is the only one we *can* trust. The only one who can guide us in this." She hurried on to cut short his protest. "There is much to learn about him, yes. With all the time we've lost, much that I may never know. But of what I remember, my father is a kind and devoted man, self-sacrificing and honest.

"Much like you," she added, and Allion squirmed in his seat. He turned away, but she squeezed his hands, then forced his chin back around to face her.

"He may seem impatient and headstrong," she continued, "and with no tolerance for foolishness. But that is only because he is unconcerned with what others think of him. He is concerned only with what needs to be done. My mother used to tell me as much. It was the reason he left us. To see to the greater good of mankind, no matter his personal desires."

Her eyes fell, and her hands withdrew into her own lap. Allion wasn't sure whether to reach for them, or to let her be.

"I will not yet say that I understand," she said, her voice unusually timid. "Perhaps I never will. But I've always known this much. He left us out of respect for my mother's wishes, not his own. He did what he had to then, and I've no reason to believe he'll do otherwise now."

Allion gulped. The argument, in and of itself, was not enough to allay his fears. But the way in which she made it, the conviction in her posture and in her eyes, was much more difficult to discount.

"And you'll not leave him," he presumed, "even if it means letting Torin go off alone on this dangerous venture."

"Especially because Torin is going off on this venture," she replied. She quieted for a moment, during which Allion thought he detected the briefest tremble. "I deserve an opportunity to learn who my father is. I deserve to learn who *I* am. This may be my only chance. And Torin will be safe in the hands of those you've selected, will he not?"

Allion let loose a long, slow breath. "I don't know." How could he? He'd done his best to assemble what he thought would be a good mix. Men like Cordan, of the City Shield, whose cunning and loyalty were without question. Men like Bullrum, of the Legion of the Sword, whose strength and determination put to shame those of an ox. But when it came right down to it, he'd only known these men for a few months. "The only way to be sure would be to accompany him myself."

"And you're still considering doing just that."

He gave her a sullen look, but did not bother denying it. Even without his comment regarding the hasty manner of Evhan's promotion, she knew him well enough to sense the truth.

"You gave him your oath."

"I most specifically did not."

"Then you would leave me here alone, under my own care and that of a man you do not trust?"

Allion measured carefully his response. "I believe you're quite capable of defending yourself," he said, smiling bravely.

"I appreciate that. And yet you do not believe your best friend can do the same?"

"I . . . It's different. Jarom—" He caught himself, having accidentally referred to the man by his childhood name. "Torin and I have been looking after each other for as long as I can remember."

"I understand," she said, and he believed her. "But I think you must, just this once. I think you should respect his wishes. Do not set aside your natural impulse, only follow it in a different way. He needs you here. I need you here. The entire kingdom needs you here."

Allion held his breath as he gazed into her pleading eyes. It was difficult to see her like this, lacking her customary playfulness and confidence. Something about her father's return had scarred her more deeply than he yet realized, leaving her—leaving all of them—dazed and uncertain. Always the first to lend aid, she now seemed to require it. Or maybe she was merely challenging him to find his own strength, as she so often did with others. Either way, he could deny her nothing, and ached with the truth of it.

"In any case, if you were to leave, you would be putting me in the awkward position of abandoning my father or breaking my oath."

"What oath?"

"The oath I made to my betrothed, our lord the king, to keep you safe while he is away."

Allion choked on a sputtering retort. He did not know whether to cry out in indignation or to laugh. Marisha's charming expression decided it.

"I suppose I should have seen that coming," he chuckled in defeat.

"Then it is agreed. Each of us will have the other to look after them."

Allion shook his head. It was the inevitable decision. As badly as he wanted to refuse this forced regency, the sense of duty instilled in him by his parents and others would never allow it. He was too well versed in doing what was expected of him to simply abandon his appointed role. Toss an obligation to Marisha into the mix, and he no longer had a prayer.

"Where *is* the conniving scoundrel?" he asked.

"Still in council, last I checked."

"It's late. Think we should attempt to rescue him?"

Marisha leaned her head upon his shoulder. "I warned him not to expect a quick briefing. I think at this point, Torin is best able to rescue himself."

With the scent of her hair in his nostrils, Allion was less inclined than he might normally have been to disagree. "I hope you're right," he said instead, closing his eyes against the absurdity of it all. "I hope you're right."

CHAPTER SEVEN

*F*ALDRON AWOKE TO THE DIM LIGHT OF A GUTTERING CANDLE. The assassin watched him squint and squirm, then finally lurch up to lean upon a powerful elbow.

"You," the armorer acknowledged, peering across the bedside table to the black form of the visitor seated there. "Have you brought my payment, then?"

Xarius was impressed. Any normal man would have pissed his breeches to find himself so intruded upon. Especially in these hours of waning night, when a man's strength was at its furthest ebb.

In response to Faldron's question, the assassin shook the heavy contents of a leather purse. The sound had a remarkable effect on the other's wakefulness.

"First, we must discuss your trail," Xarius whispered.

The armorer scowled. Xarius could almost see the other's senses at work, testing the air of this unexpected meeting. It was unlike the assassin to reveal himself so openly. Even though his hooded face was kept clear of the candle's aura, the fact that he'd lit one at all, in addition to the time and manner of his coming, was unusual enough to elicit concern.

"What trail?"

"The trail of your spies," Xarius explained. "Those who delivered this information to you. And any others with whom you may have shared it."

Faldron growled. "My sources are my own business. You agreed to that going in."

"And you're certain they know nothing of me?"

"*I* know nothing of you." The armorer snorted. "Save for your unnatural interest in the king."

Xarius set the coin purse upon the table, massaging its contents with his gloved fingers. "And what of your spy on the roof?"

"What spy?"

"You were not to include any observers. That also was part of our deal, was it not?"

Faldron was indignant. "What game are you playing? I know nothing of this."

An honest response, of course. Xarius already knew the truth about Zain. But he was enjoying watching the armorer sweat. "Then you are not as adept as your reputation would indicate."

The burn-scarred smith was running out of patience. "If you don't like the way I do business, why don't you find someone else from now on, eh? Why not deliver that payment and be on your way?"

"One problem." Xarius twisted at the pouch's drawstrings as if distracted by his thoughts. "If I can't silence your informants, I'll have to silence you."

The other laughed. "You think you're the first to threaten old Faldron here? I've been around a long time, lad. Watch yourself, and you might live to say the same."

"Your source," the assassin repeated. "I'll give you a count of three."

Faldron laughed again, nervously this time. His eyes flicked momentarily to the far side of his bed.

"One . . ."

The laughter persisted.

"Two . . ."

With a practiced lunge, the armorer reached down with a quick swipe and produced a crossbow, cranked and loaded, that hung from the outer bed-frame. With a fluidity that belied his size, he leveled the weapon and sent its bolt screaming toward the assassin, all within two beats of a steady heart.

But Xarius was already gone. Two steps up and along the cornering wall dropped him atop the oblivious armorer, where the shorter of his two sabers slipped easily through the center of the man's windpipe and pinned him to his headboard.

The assassin knelt there for a moment as the powerful smith coughed and sputtered, rage flashing in his eyes. "A fine blade indeed. Rest assured, I will put it to good use."

Faldron tried to spit, but succeeded only in dribbling more blood down his chin. Before long, his eyes lost focus, and his helpless struggles ceased.

Xarius waited a moment before freeing his weapon with a single smooth tug. His switch to the heavier sabers was yet another consequence of that last confrontation with his former guildmate, Kylac Kronus—a duel the other had won only as the result of a broken blade. In response, the assassin had sought out the best swordmaker Alson had to offer to forge him a new set—he who now slumped lifelessly in his own bed.

A small cloth was used to wipe the blade clean, then discarded over the body of the victim. After that, Xarius stepped away. Although the night was failing, there was time yet to track down Zain—maybe even one or two more who might know of him. But that would be an unnecessary risk. The deaths of Orru and Faldron would likely serve as warning enough to their lesser informants. And by the time Zain or someone else discovered these bodies, the assassin's quarry would be beyond help, and Xarius himself long gone in pursuit.

He did not intend that either of them should ever return.

Besides, he still had preparations of his own to make. Horse, provisions—nothing drastic, but neither was he one to wait until the last minute.

Retrieving his abandoned coin purse, he blew out the lone candle, then slipped outside like a stray breeze that had found its way at last.

◆   ◆   ◆

THE SUN HAD NOT YET RISEN—its faint promise a mere blush in the eastern sky—when it came time for Torin to say good-bye.

They met beside a rear gate of the palace grounds, at the edge of a hill-top cemetery overlooking the city below. Stephan and Pagus joined Allion, Marisha, and Darinor as those who would be remaining behind, come to bid farewell to Torin and his six-member expedition team. A ring of distant guardsmen, led by Evhan, the newly appointed captain of the City Shield, saw to it that they were otherwise undisturbed.

"Before the thaw, would be nice."

It was Darinor who prodded, but Torin was slow to react. In the frosted gray mist of predawn, the world had taken on a ghostly quality, causing him to wonder if the entire episode were naught but a dream staged somewhere in his mind. Given the whirlwind of these events, he found it difficult to think clearly. There had been no sleep, for when finished with the Circle, he had gone to his most trusted servants, Stephan and Pagus, and explained all with his apologies. After that, he had met with both Marisha and Darinor and accepted from them the Pendant. When finally he had completed these preparations and thought to lie down to rest, the dawn—and this moment—was virtually upon him.

Now that it was here, it felt as though all the hours of explanation and debate had never taken place. Had he truly given thought to this course?

"I wish you would reconsider, my lord," a sullen-faced Stephan pleaded. Torin did not recall having approached the man, and yet stood before him, watching the breath that clouded from his chipmunk face while impish breezes rouged his already reddened cheeks.

"I leave the palace in your good hands," Torin said, giving his devoted seneschal a warm embrace about the shoulders. "See to it that you treat your regent as well as you've treated me."

Stephan nodded, then lowered his eyes and tucked his chin into the high collar of his fur coat.

"And you, Master Pagus," said Torin, moving on. "I trust you will be the first to give me a full report upon my return."

The boy herald also looked glum—angry even. Nor did he brighten when Torin tousled his hair.

"Stephan is right," Allion asserted, ignoring the throat-clearing cough of the renegade Entient behind him. "You don't have to do this."

The sky had begun to roil overhead. Ashen clouds billowed, and the mist thickened. Flitting breezes coalesced, converging in larger streams to form a blustery wind, and a distant clap of thunder echoed across the land.

"Let's hope you are both right," Torin agreed. Allion's frown deepened, but he accepted Torin's hand and allowed himself to be pulled into a one-armed hug. "If not, remember to look after her, and yourself," the king added quietly.

And then, suddenly, it was Marisha's turn.

"Don't worry." She smiled. "I'll keep them all in line. And anyone else who needs it."

Torin laughed. "I know you will." He was serious then, and saw that she was too. For a moment, he did not know what to do. He might have kissed her, but he was keenly aware of the presence of the others—most notably her stern father looming over him from behind her shoulder. Despite all that they had been through, all the time they had spent together, it would have been their first. And while this would seem the perfect time for it, it also seemed the worst.

Behind her encouraging smile, Torin saw a similar strain within his lady's eyes, but could only imagine what she was thinking. At last, feelings overcame confusion, and they fell together in a clinching embrace.

"You can do this," she whispered in his ear. "Have faith."

Yours will be enough, Torin thought, and held her tighter. Ultimately, he was doing this for her—like everything else, with an eye to their shared future. Although torn to be leaving, he swore silently to achieve his goal, rectify the error of his ways, and return to the newfound glory of his life. A glory that did not exist without her.

"I'll be back before you realize I've gone."

Marisha sniffed and pulled away. "Too late." She placed her hand upon his chest where her Pendant hung, safely buried beneath the layers of wool and leather. "You carry my heart with you."

At his daughter's request, Darinor had explained better how the linking magic worked. Ripples, he had said, caused by the rhythmic squeezing and heating of the intense aura of divine pressure surrounding both seal and Pendant—fueled in both cases by the power of Asahiel. These pressure ripples were like waves of sound attuned to the same frequency, and formed a specific pattern between the two nodes. When the Sword had been removed and the seal broken, the shift in that pattern had caused a resonance in the Pendant, much as matching sound waves generated by marching soldiers might cause a bridge to collapse.

Of course, these vibrations existed on a scale that were beyond untrained senses. Had Darinor been wearing the Pendant, he would have sensed the trouble at once. Instead, he had relied upon the latent enchantment of his piece of the Pendant's chain, which, while lacking the constant power of Asahiel, could be used much like a musician's fork and tuned to the same magical frequency. It was this that would enable the renegade Entient to track Torin's movements, just as it had enabled him to locate his daughter. And it was for this reason that he would not allow Torin to leave the heartstone Pendant behind to protect its rightful bearer.

Nevertheless, Torin considered again doing that very thing before he surrendered the idea and forced a confident smile. "I will safeguard it more dearly than my own," he swore, squeezing her hand.

Marisha nodded and stepped back, reaching for Allion's arm. They would be fine, Torin assured himself. They would protect one another as he had made them promise.

"May fortune favor you," Darinor offered.

Torin ignored the man. Was that meant to be encouraging? All it did was remind him that not even the mystic could be sure as to whether or not the Finlorians still existed, or in what state. How could he possibly be expected to succeed in this?

"It's not too late to join me," he challenged at last, his eyes never shifting from Marisha.

"It is you who sought the glory enjoyed by heroes of old. Now's your chance."

"I sought no such thing," Torin snapped, wrenching free to glare at the other. "I'd have much preferred to remain nameless in all of this."

Darinor's smile was slow and sardonic. "Those who wish to remain nameless do not fetch a Sword of Asahiel from the ruin of time. In any case, it is too late for regrets. And if I were to guide you, who would stand guard against this scourge you've unleashed?"

Torin looked morosely away, his attention drawn by an aged cemetery groundskeeper who had come forth at this early hour to collect dead leaves from beneath a skeletal tree. The swirling breezes continued to strengthen, and the old man, wrapped in his coat and scarf and fingerless gloves, was having a difficult time. If he had noticed their gathering, he did not seem interested by it.

Torin, however, was struck by the correlation. His world was like that pile of dry leaves caught in a gust of wind—just when he had gathered up its pieces, they'd been scattered once more. And yet there was no help for it. It was his job, and he would see it done.

Squaring his shoulders, he faced Darinor directly, his features somber but resolute.

He turned then to the members of his expedition team, those few brave souls who had agreed to see him through this madman's venture. Sacred blazes, he wasn't even certain of their names. Trustworthy and capable, he was sure, else Allion would not have selected them. Men to whom he could entrust his life.

A sudden pang gripped him. He would trade them all, he realized, for the one who wasn't there. Kylac Kronus, the boy who had been raised an assassin but had become his friend and mentor—who had saved his life more than once—would not be with him this time around. Never one to sit idle, the warrior youth had been gone for two months already, having wandered off to parts unknown within days of his and Allion's triumphant arrival. Were he here, Kylac would be leading the charge—in which case Torin would feel much better about their prospects.

As it was, he was on his own.

"Give my regards to Nevik," he said to Allion. He hoisted himself into his saddle, there to join his waiting men. "And to Kylac, should the rogue show up again."

The regent dipped his head. Of course he would do those things, Torin thought, and realized abruptly that they had moved beyond words that needed to be said.

Still, he sat astride his mount, staring at those gathered—at Marisha in particular—until another thunderclap shook the cathedral of the heavens. As he looked up, the first rains of the new day began to fall. He glanced over to where the groundskeeper had been raking leaves a moment ago, only to see that the old man had gone.

Drawing his gaze from the grave-covered hillside, Torin gave a final wave of farewell, then pushed through the open palace gate and started away through the mist and the rain.

ROGUN'S WAR ROOM WAS CHILL AND DANK, pinned deep enough beneath the city that it might have been used as a cold cellar. The general liked it that way. The frigid temperatures kept him alert, his mind sharp and focused.

Even so, he was finding it difficult to concentrate at this particular moment. An array of plans and diagrams papered the tabletop beneath his white-knuckled fists. Everything from troop registries to proposals for shoring up damaged areas of the curtain wall to maps of the city's aqueducts and irrigation lines. Ordinarily, he was able to conduct such reviews with an artisan's flair, attacking even the most mundane report with the same lust that he carried into battle. For it was all part of defending his city and her surrounding lands, doing the work that needed to be done.

But on this evening, his thoughts were elsewhere. An opportunity long anticipated had come to him at last. Not in the manner he had expected, but that was the way of such things. Torin was gone. The city was in the hands of the Circle of Elders and its regent, Allion. All had been agreed to the night before, when the young king had shared with them the ill tidings delivered by the savage-looking Darinor.

His time had come.

Although he urged himself to remain focused on the business at hand, the thought would not stay banished for long. His great-grandfather had been a fool to decline becoming a member of the nobility, and that poor decision had cost his progeny dear. Especially now, with Alson in such dire need of a strong-willed person who could make things happen. Had Rogun had a noble title and not just a military one, he would have found it much easier to assume the reins of this runaway steed his land had become.

The general did not consider himself—as others whispered—to be power-hungry. He already had more notoriety and respect than he required. The simple truth was, he did not trust the son of Sorl to rule this kingdom. Torin may have proven to be more responsible than his father, but the youth was weak, too easily distracted. By his own admission, he did not want to be king. He should therefore leave it to someone who did.

That he had not stormed in, seeking to direct matters over which he had no experience, had endeared him to the general, initially. But any leader, even an unseasoned one, needed at some point to plant a standard, a point around which others might rally. Unwilling to enforce his own will or surrender to another's, Torin instead wasted time listening to everyone, giving all a fair and equal voice. What he refused to realize was that such politics were impractical at best. Few people knew what it was they really wanted, and those who did could never be made to agree on a singular course. As a result, nothing was ever accomplished.

Just thinking about it caused the muscles in Rogun's neck to tighten. Action. Action was paramount. Even poor actions could be undone by assessing the negative results and taking further measures to offset them. Mistakes were to be expected. But the key was to move forward at all times, not to stagnate while every man, woman, and child with a voice expressed feelings and opinions, too obsessed with one's own needs to give ear to another's. Torin's Circle was a romantic notion, but it needed a man of strength, a leader who could unite its members in their thinking. Rogun had long argued that if Torin would not take action to do so, then he should step aside so that someone like himself could.

"General, Commander Zain to see you."

Rogun looked up from where his vision foundered in the depths of a weaponry supply listing. "Send him in, Corporal."

The stern-faced sentry saluted, then beckoned to another guardsman posted farther down the hall. A moment later, Zain's rasping footsteps carried him into view.

"You're late," Rogun noted.

"My apologies, sir. There has been a development."

The general pushed himself from the table. He obviously wasn't going to get anything done this evening anyway. "You've got my attention, Commander. Proceed."

Zain did, telling Rogun all about his activities of the previous night, during which he had tracked Faldron to the Queen's Hive. He did so without fanfare or embellishment, delivering straight fact as the general required. Rogun did not interrupt, but waited for the other to finish.

". . . I was unable, therefore, to discern the identity of this shadow figure with whom the armorer met."

"I assume there is more to this," Rogun replied.

"This morning, sir, I was as distracted as everyone else by news of our king's departure. It was not until this afternoon that I went to follow up with Faldron. I found him dead, sir."

"Dead? Faldron?" As a matter of point, the general was not often surprised. But this surprised him.

"Orru as well, sir. Both in the middle of the night, it would seem, in their own beds. And Orru's wife alongside him. I questioned their children. None of them heard a thing."

Rogun settled into a hardwood chair, his brow furrowed. "What does it mean?"

"I've been working on that, sir. I cannot say for certain, but it would be too great a coincidence if any but this shadow were our killer."

"Agreed."

"I can only assume, then, that his actions were prompted by last night's news, which I imagine to have been leaked from your briefing with the Circle—perhaps before."

"Torin's voyage."

Zain nodded, his ermine mouth twitching. "I suspect, sir, that our young king is in danger, although from whom, I dare not guess."

Rogun's chin slipped into his hand as he considered the possibility.

"Shall we send warning, sir?"

The general did not respond right away. "I think not," he determined finally. "Even if our riders could catch up to him, such warning as we might send would be vague and indirect—and therefore of little use."

Zain's features twisted in mild astonishment. "Then we're to do nothing?"

Rogun glared to keep his smirk from showing. "If the son of Sorl doesn't return, so much the better."

CHAPTER EIGHT

Despite the foul weather, muddied roads, and host of doubts that dragged after him like an anchor, Torin and his company reached the seaport town of Gammelost on just the second day out from Krynwall. They had spent the night at the edge of the Whisperwood, disguised as vagabonds. At dawn, they had traded their horses to a sharp-eyed rancher for a set of remounts. These, along with the widespread rumors of savage races marauding the countryside, hastened their progress. As did the enthusiasm of his men, Torin noted, each of whom seemed far more eager about this adventure than he.

He had learned their names, at least. Bull and Cordan he already knew from their recent sparring session. Two others, Ashwin and Ulric, he had sparred with before, although too many weeks and too many faces had passed since then for him to recall without a friendly reminder. The last two, Silas and Kallen, were a pair of brothers he'd never met, whose ceaseless, almost comical ridicule of each other helped to keep Torin from dwelling too deeply on more distressing matters.

The town greeted them all with a cold shoulder, its face turned to the west and the boundless ocean that gave it life. The sea itself was not immediately visible, blocked by hills and shrouded by a stone-gray curtain of mist, but Torin could smell its distinctive breath.

Soaked through by a blustery rain that had fought them the entire way, he led his mount down the principal roadway and into town. He kept his head low and his hood up, clinging to his hidden identity. Buildings and storefronts in varying degrees of disrepair leaned down from either side with sagging roofs and drooping eaves. Street gutters overflowed, clogged with natural refuse from winter's storms. Torin had never before visited Gammelost, and though it may have been just the dreariness of the season or the somber circumstances, he could not imagine ever wanting to do so again.

He continued without pause, ignoring the various side streets and alleys that angled off at random junctures, trusting in his nose and in this principal thoroughfare to lead him to the harbor. Sure enough, as he emerged from the town's backside and crested a small rise that bent like an elbow around a craggy bluff, he spotted it through the fog, a collection of docks that sprawled below like threads protruding from a frayed cloth.

They reached tentatively into the iron expanse of the cold sea, these jutting piers and curving jetties, and Torin almost laughed at the absurdity. From this vantage, it seemed as if the slumbering oceans, with a single restless heave, might sweep them all away to reclaim its littered shoreline. It made him think of man's efforts as hopeless and inconsequential. It reminded him of how small he was.

"Suppose we can find you a woman down there?" Silas asked his brother. "I've heard those who comfort these sailor types ain't choosy."

"I've heard the men ain't either," Kallen retorted. "So maybe we'll both get lucky."

"Business first, lads," Bull reminded them before Torin had to. Already, Brown-beard had become an unofficial leader on this expedition, a captain who kept an eye on the little issues so that his king could focus on the larger.

Of which there were many. Torin's grandfather, Sirrus, had once owned an entire fleet of merchant ships. But Sorl had long since sold those vessels off for short-term profit, leaving the crown without a single schooner to call its own. As a result, they were facing the prospect of paying for transport—and secrecy.

"How long will it take to book us passage?" asked Torin. The question was directed toward Ulric, who'd been raised upon the wharves of this town—one of the principal reasons for his selection.

Ulric breathed deeply of the salty air, savoring it as one might the scent of fresh-baked bread. "Could be awhile," he admitted, "given the lack of ships at sea this time of year. Longer still, given our destination. We may have to hop vessels more than once before boarding one that will carry us clear to Yawacor. Either that, or wait a few weeks."

"We don't have a few weeks," Torin replied, although deep down, he felt a willing flutter at the possibility of being forced to return home for a time. Long enough, perhaps, to reconsider this entire course.

"I'll dredge us up something," vowed Ulric, misreading Torin's thoughts.

Ulric took the lead, guiding them through a twisted maze of streets, each more lively than the last, as they worked their way down to the harbor, then quayside along the town's face. Much of what they saw had been battened down for the winter, from vendor booths to fishmonger stalls—even some of the giant shipyards. When he saw the harbor up close, Torin had to admit that it seemed much more impressive than from afar, an expansive network of labor and commerce that bustled with gruff workmen and steadfast activity even in these slow months.

They stopped first at the office of the harbormaster to view the public log of ships in port, as well as general postings of those seeking to hire help. In both areas, the pickings were slim. A sprinkle of coins and a couple of names gave them access to the private logs, including a schedule of incoming vessels, but still yielded little hope.

"Not to worry," Ulric assured them. "These lists are seldom accurate, and never complete. Just gives us our bearings, is all."

From there, they visited the offices of every maritime merchant, builder, and recruiter they could find along the wharf, before moving onto the docks themselves. In most every case, the answer was the same. It was the low season. Some of the most skilled sailors in the land were out of work. If they were lucky, they might find themselves scrubbing barnacles or painting hulls in dry dock, mending sails or repairing rigging. But considering that most of these jobs were taken up by those normally at sea, even this was probably asking too much.

They fared no better when inquiring about straight charter. Once again, the few vessels that dared head out to the deep waters this time of year were already booked to capacity.

It came to the point where Torin feared they might have to reveal their true identities and purpose. They had agreed early on that to do so would bring them no great advantage. Though they might be able to bump a voyaging band of lesser importance, the price for their passage would likely double. Alson was a poor kingdom, its resources bled dry by hedonism and then war. Torin had taken very little from its coffers for this voyage, deciding they could earn their keep and forage their food as they went along.

For even if they *were* to spend the necessary coin, they would not be able to do so without drawing unwanted notice, and above all, Torin did not wish to add to the panic already sweeping this nation. That he'd embarked on this journey was a secret that would not long be limited to the esteemed members of the governing council. Allion and the Circle would then have their hands full—as if they didn't already—coming up with excuses for his absence and reassurances that all would be well. As it was, he worried that he might be recognized by some prominent townsman who had visited the royal court. For that reason, he'd sullied his appearance and used leather wraps to conceal the jeweled hilt of the Sword. Having taken such precautions, he remained reluctant to simply give himself away.

With the gray afternoon passing swiftly toward night, they split into pairs to widen the search. When that didn't work, they fanned out as individuals, with the agreement that they meet back at the harbormaster's at sunset. It was not long before Torin began stopping men he passed in the street. One knew of a local fisherman in need of a hand or two. Another had a cousin aboard a merchant vessel that often made the full crossing, though as best he knew, she had dry-docked in Yawacor for the winter. Everyone knew someone, it seemed, who worked in one capacity or another as loaders or ferrymen upon the pier.

Tired and thirsty, Torin found himself drawn at last to one of many taverns that lined the waterfront, where most of the action seemed to be. A clamor echoed from within—the drone of voices, the creak of chairs and tables, the clack of wooden cups and leather tankards. An occasional shout of anger or laughter punctuated the din and gave him pause. Probably not the best place to seek out those serious about offering employment. Then again, he was wet and shivering and had had no better luck elsewhere.

After tethering his mount, he entered through the open door, dodging swiftly to avoid another who was staggering roughly out. The place was poorly lit, and even more poorly ventilated. Shadows and smoke filled the musty room, enough to cover the rank odor of fish and brine that clung to this town as tightly as the fog that filled its streets. The bar was centrally located, an island amid the milling throngs. A thin carpet of sand covered the floor.

Everywhere he looked, men and women seemed to be caught up in games and challenges or boisterous conversation. While his eyes adjusted to the dimness, Torin searched the quiet corners, seeking those who were not so fully engaged. At last he spotted his first target, a single man brooding over a tankard at a booth along the far wall. With a deep breath that nearly choked him, he started in that direction, careful not to push or shove too crossly at the jostling patrons who blocked his way. The last thing he needed was to trap himself in a barroom brawl.

He reached the table and stood over it, waiting for the stranger to acknowledge his presence. A moment passed, however, in which the other did not stir. At last, Torin seated himself across from the man, whose eyes were riveted upon his untouched tankard.

"Begging your pardon, this place is packed. May I join you?"

The man never flinched, staring blankly into nothingness. His eyes were shot through with streaks of red and underscored by charcoal rings. His arms lay on the table, gangly in shape and white in color.

"I don't mean to disturb you," Torin pressed. "I was just wondering if you knew someone I could speak with about securing passage overseas."

The man's cracked lips parted as if to speak, then hung open uselessly. A string of drool dripped from the corner of his mouth.

"Thank you for your time," Torin muttered, slipping from the booth.

He scanned the room again before pushing toward the counter. Perhaps the barkeep could direct him to someone who was at least coherent.

But that was assuming he could catch the other's attention. Three times he signaled the man eye to eye. Only on the third attempt did he garner a response. The bustling barkeep nodded curtly, then scurried off to attend a customer on the far side.

"Here then, lad. Share mine."

Torin lowered his hand and looked to the patron beside him, a swarthy-faced individual with a gold tooth in the middle of his black smile. The stranger nudged a bottle in Torin's direction.

"Actually, I'm not . . ." He stopped as he noticed the stranger's naked arms, mottled with tattoos. And not just any tattoos, but images of sea creatures—both real and mythical—and of flags and symbols, all of a nautical nature.

"Go on. Have a drink," the seaman insisted, reaching for an abandoned cup. He dumped the dregs of its former contents and gave it a sniff, then poured from his bottle.

Torin eyed the dark brew warily. He'd not been raised on strong drink, and had yet to develop a taste for it. A refill of his empty waterskin would have sufficed. But he didn't dare refuse this gesture and alienate any potential help.

"Most kind of you," he said, raising the liquid in salute. Its scent went clear to the top of his head. With a concerted effort, he tossed it back, grimacing as it scorched his throat.

The seaman grinned, amused by his discomfort. "You look familiar, lad. Do I know you?"

"I have a common face," Torin replied. He opened his mouth to let in some cooling air, and wiped his lips with his sleeve.

"Perhaps I've met someone in your family then. A father or brother." His grin widened. "A sister, perchance?"

Torin glared. "Not likely."

The seaman chuckled. "A joke, lad. Meant nothing by it."

"I've never had a sister," Torin explained. "A father and brother, once upon a time. But I no longer have either." That was truthful enough, he decided.

"Sorry to hear it, lad."

"Anyway, I'm not from around here."

"No, you don't look it. That's what had me confused." He quaffed another draught of his own, straight from the bottle. "Where you from?"

Torin hesitated. Despite a grisly voice, the man seemed affable enough. Only far too prying. "Glendon," he lied.

"Northern Alson, right? Edge of the Kalgren."

"You've heard of it." Torin was impressed. Though many times the size of his real home village, Glendon was a small town, out of the way by most respects.

"Been there myself. Been all over. Name's Malus."

The man had an unforgiving grip. "Jarom."

"Well then, Jarom, how can I be of service to you?"

His wink caught Torin off guard. "What makes you think I'm in need of service?"

"Saw you pestering that rooter over there. Then you come to the bar, not looking for drink. The sun ain't baked *all* the clams in this shell."

Torin wasn't sure yet whether he liked this Malus or not. Perceptive, yes, but with an abruptness that set his nerves on edge. There was a wicked gleam to the man's eye, though that was probably just the lighting.

"Clearly not," he responded at last. "You're a seafaring man, are you not?"

Malus smirked. "What gave it away?"

"It so happens, I'm looking for passage to the west."

"The west? Yawacor? Ain't too many vessels making that crossing this time of year, lad."

"So I've discovered. I'm willing to work my way, or pay for the privilege."

Malus looked him up and down, as if measuring him for some task. "Pay with what? That's an expensive trip you're talking there."

"I've a horse and supplies to sell. Why? Do you know someone who might help me?"

The man took another drink, seeming to consider. One eye squinted as he swallowed. "Perhaps," he said finally. "I've a friend setting sail tomorrow, if that's not too soon."

"Not at all," Torin agreed, a bit too hastily.

"He ain't got plans to go all the way to Yawacor, mind you. But sometimes, ships from either land meet to exchange goods halfway. Might be you can hitch a ride that way."

"I have companions."

Malus scowled. "I didn't see any come in with you."

"They're out searching, same as me. There would be seven of us altogether."

"When are you meeting these companions?"

"At dusk. Outside the harbormaster's office."

"And what about home? Ain't you got anyone back in Glendon going to miss you?"

"We're on our own," Torin admitted, fighting down a fresh wave of nervousness. Or maybe it was the drink, settling about as smoothly as it had gone down.

"Tell you what. Why don't we go meet with my friend now, let you have a chat with him? That way, you'll know better if it's an option for you and your companions."

"I'd be most grateful."

Malus nodded then and drained his bottle. As he rose from his stool, the barkeep came scampering over at last.

"Can I get anything else for you gentlemen?"

"Gentlemen? How do you like that?" said Malus, flashing Torin a conspiratorial grin. "Too late, my good sir. We're on our way out."

The fresh air was greeted by Torin with welcome relief; this time, even the fish didn't smell so bad. A damp gust swept past with a warbling sigh. He paused for a cleansing breath, then went for his horse.

Malus emerged a moment later, clothed in only the leather vest and breeches he'd been wearing at the bar. A brace of knives hung across his torso. He too inhaled deeply of the smokeless air, causing his chest to swell.

"Where's your cloak?" Torin asked him.

"Didn't bring one."

"You're not cold?"

"Wait'll you're at sea, lad, soaked to the gills while she rails at you with her frozen breath. Then you'll know what cold is."

Malus had no horse, so Torin followed afoot, guiding his mount by its lead rope. The seaman spoke incessantly as they went, asking all manner of questions. It felt as if the man were fishing for something, though his disarming nature made it all come across as innocent banter. Torin answered as openly as he could, guarding details, but not wanting to seem evasive. Every now and then, he tried to squeeze a question in edgewise, just to stem the tide, but always the focus ended up back on him.

One topic they hadn't discussed yet was that of money. Or more specifically, what Malus's cut would be for doing him this favor. This, more than anything, raised Torin's suspicions, and kept his free hand resting casually on the disguised hilt of his weapon.

"What manner of trade did you say your friend was involved in?" he asked, mimicking the other's offhand tone.

"I didn't," Malus replied without turning. A sheen of water clung to his bald head, so that it reflected the waning daylight. "The answer is, all kinds. Whatever will fetch a coin. He's been a merchant, a fisherman, even a pirate, from time to time. Not to worry," he added, as if sensing Torin's unease. "He's no brigand. Just lacking in focus. At the moment, he runs supplies—fresh water and such—to some of the deep-sea fishing vessels. Comes back with some of their catch. Allows them to follow the schools without making any unscheduled stops."

Torin forced a smile to match the other's own.

"This way," Malus beckoned, indicating a narrow, rancid-smelling alley.

Torin eyed the garbage-strewn path with obvious distaste. "How much farther is it?"

"Back door to his place is just around the corner. What's wrong?"

"The docks are that way."

"So they are. But my friend doesn't spend his time on ship when in port. This is his chance to get away, you know?"

"You said he sets sail tomorrow. Should he not be loading his cargo?"

"He has a crew does that for him. This here's personal time. Spend a few weeks at sea, you'll understand."

It made sense, but still Torin didn't move.

"What're you afraid of? Strong lad like you has nothing to fear from an old sea dog like me."

"Perhaps your friend would be willing to meet me out here, where the air is fresher."

Malus shrugged as if it made no difference to him. "Don't know why you'd want to stand out in this slop when you could be sitting by a warm hearth, but I'll ask. Wait here, then."

He ducked into the alley, disappearing quickly behind a pile of broken crates. Torin waited only a moment longer before shaking his head in private disdain. What *was* he afraid of? The man had done nothing to earn his mistrust. Why offend him with misguided suspicions?

He started down the alley. "Malus?"

He'd taken just a few steps, passing the mound of crates, when his horse whickered and his own senses, heightened by the Sword, screamed in warning. Had the blade been in hand, his assailant would have met with quite a surprise. As it was, Torin was unable to draw before darkness stole his vision.

The scent of burlap smothered him. He kicked and shouted, thrashing against the suffocating hood, but a string drew tight around his throat, further strangling his wind and weakening his protests. Powerful hands pinned his arms behind his back before a knee or elbow shoved him face-first to the ground. A leather thong lashed his wrists.

"Easy, lad," came the muffled sound of Malus's voice. "The more you fight, the worse it'll be."

The voice came from in front of him, which meant that the odds against him were at least two to one.

"His weapon," Malus ordered.

Torin gave another stifled shout as the Sword slid free. He bucked, but a booted foot held him down. Aside from his own struggles, an awed silence ensued. Even his horse grew quiet.

"Sweet pearls of the mother sea," Malus whispered. "This ain't the blade of a farmer—is it, lad."

Torin's stomach churned, but it was all he could do to keep breathing.

"Looks like we snagged ourselves a royal, eh, Dahl? And not just any royal at that." The voice drew closer. "But what would you be doing so far from the nest, royal?"

"I say he's a thief," said the one called Dahl.

Malus snickered. "Which is it, lad? You a thief? Or are you the one they call Torin, one and only wielder of the Crimson Sword, and this land's very king?"

"Those is just stories," said Dahl.

"Then how do you explain that blade in your hands?"

The other didn't have an answer for that.

"Come, let's have a look," said Malus.

Although he couldn't see what was going on, Torin sensed Dahl's hesitation.

"Dahl, you lumbering oaf. Do you want to stand in this alley all night? Give it here."

Torin could feel himself edging toward unconsciousness. The reassuring pressure of the Pendant dug into his chest, but he couldn't see how the talisman would be of any use. His heart fluttered. His mind raced. Despair washed over him.

"Give it . . . Let go, Dahl. Let go!"

The pair were tugging back and forth. Their scuffle reverberated in Torin's back, where Dahl's foot was planted for leverage. He squirmed, trying to throw off his assailant's balance.

Then came a sickening crunch, and the tussle came to an abrupt end. The pressure on his back released as Dahl pitched over, splintering crates. It sounded as though Malus hit the ground as well.

"Something tells me that doesn't belong to you."

Torin's ears perked at the sound of the new voice. Malus hissed in response, then was heard scampering away. The whoosh of a heavy object hurtled after him, followed by another crunch. A weapon skittered on gravel. A body slapped down on the same. Then silence.

His first thought was that one or more of his companions had found him. But that wouldn't explain the newcomer's quiet, measured march down the alley. For a moment, Torin wondered if he'd not been rescued from one set of thieves only to be robbed by another. The footsteps returned, and a presence loomed over him. A knife rasped from its sheath. Torin's breathing, rapid and shallow, came to a bracing halt.

Hands worked around his neck. There was a rough sawing motion before the hood came free. Torin rolled to his side for a desperate gulp of air, and came face-to-face with his savior.

The man wore a gray cloak with the hood drawn back. Pale blue eyes softened an otherwise stony visage dotted with sharp fields of stubble. Matching blond hair was trimmed short except at the neck, where a tuft of curls billowed like mist at the base of a falls.

The stranger held up his dagger. "I'll cut your hands loose, if you'll hold still."

Torin blinked, taking in the scene. The Sword lay beside him, next to a spiked war hammer. Blood and hair were matted against the hammer's uneven surface. Dahl's body lay twitching, draped over his feet. Down the alley, Malus was a motionless heap.

A series of ragged breaths pumped through Torin's lungs. Finally he looked again to his rescuer, and nodded.

He rolled back over to show his hands. When the bonds were severed, the stranger helped him to his feet.

"I'm indebted to you, friend."

"Arn." The man was short, not much taller than five feet. But his shoulders seemed almost as broad, and his handshake was like a stretched noose. He bent to pick up their weapons. "This your blade?"

Torin resisted the urge to lunge for the Sword, waiting for Arn to hand it to him. The man did, after a moment in which he hefted it in admiration.

"Never seen its like."

Torin did not sheathe the talisman right away, but held it at the ready. "You're not from around here, are you?"

"I come from Yawacor, to the west."

"Yawacor?"

"Been in port for the past seven days."

"You're not a sailor," Torin observed, as Arn bent to wipe his hammer on Dahl's jerkin. He tried not to look too closely at the mashed hole in the back of the fallen man's head.

"More of a mercenary," Arn admitted. When finished cleaning his weapon, he hung it from a sling on his belt. "A mercenary with a grudge."

"Grudge?"

Arn spat upon the lifeless form at their feet. "I don't care for these kind of men."

"Thieves?"

"Slavers," the other replied, as if surprised Torin didn't know. "Were it not for me, you'd have been shipped overseas and shackled to a trading block within weeks."

A warm sense of dread flushed down Torin's throat. "Again, I don't know how to thank you."

"That weapon, I think, would even the scales between us."

Torin felt the remaining color drain from his face.

"I'm jesting," said Arn. A sneering grin flashed across his face. "You can probably put it away now."

Torin did so, double-checking the fastenings of the leather wraps around the hilt. His would-be abductors had not had time to remove them, but their struggle had tugged them out of place.

"Blade like that has a story goes along with it. Would go well with a solid meal, no?"

Torin smiled. "Supper and a tale? It's the least I could do. Though I'll be surprised if you've not heard rumor of it already."

"Haven't spent much time at the local watering holes. And like I said, I'm not from around here."

"Yawacor," Torin said, regaining focus. "Any chance you'll be heading back there soon?"

"Tomorrow, actually. Would've been today, but one of our primary suppliers was behind schedule. Lucky for you, I'd say."

"I thought we agreed you were no sailor."

"Swordhand," Arn clarified. "Hired guard for a merchant vessel. Not the most exciting work, which is why I've been stretching my legs ever since we got into port, hunting thugs like these. Been stalking the big one here for days, waiting to catch him in the act."

"Any room for a few more? Hired swords, I mean?"

"You looking for work?"

"I'm looking to hitch a ride. And my companions, if possible. Whatever it takes."

Arn shook his head. "Our roster is full. Though it can't hurt to talk with the captain. How many in your party?"

"Seven. But I'll go it alone, if necessary."

"Running from trouble, are we?"

"Toward it, more likely."

Arn continued to regard him with a discerning eye. "Let's talk it over with the captain. With that blade of yours, might be you'll fetch me a recruiting bonus."

Torin smiled with newfound hope and relief. He moved out of the alley, giving chase to his restless steed. Arn fell into step beside him, leaving the bodies where they lay.

"What's the name of your ship?" Torin asked. Even now, it would not hurt to be cautious.

"*Pirate's Folly.*"

Torin's pace faltered. "I don't recall seeing that name on the harbormaster's list."

"Of course you didn't." Arn snorted. "Captain Jorkin has money and influence. Not to mention common sense."

Although he hid his frown, Torin's silence gave voice to his doubts.

"It's not near as shady as it sounds," Arn assured him. "Best way to avoid a thief is to hide your business from him altogether."

"I suppose."

"Come now," said Arn, slapping him on the back with a brawny hand. "If I intended you harm, I'd have left you in that alley. You want to meet Jorkin? Then tell me your story."

It was hard not to be reminded of Kylac. Although he had yet to break a real smile, Arn had that same roguish style, the same unassuming air.

And he *had* saved Torin's life.

Finally, as they turned toward the docks, Torin relented, and did as he was asked.

WHEN THE PAIR HAD GONE, Xarius emerged from the shadows. Perched upon his roost, he watched them trail away through the sordid city streets, his mind clenched around a single notion.

So close.

For a moment there, he'd thought he would have to intervene if he wished to preserve the wizard's prize. Were it not for this mercenary, Arn, he might have done so, and the whelp would now be in his hands. Soric had been explicit in his commands, but would have forgiven his actions upon learning the circumstances for them.

They were exactly the kind of circumstances for which the assassin had hoped. Despite the wizard's instructions, he had no intention of allowing Torin to be delivered by any but himself. Perhaps Soric would grant him his release to hunt down his nemesis as promised, once Torin was handed over. Perhaps not. The best way to be sure was to put himself in the position of dictating the terms of the young king's release.

If nothing else, he had to get close enough to Torin to extract the information he needed as to Kylac's whereabouts. His city informant, Faldron, had failed him miserably on that count. According to the late armorer, none in the palace had any idea as to the youth's destination. Xarius had to believe otherwise, had to believe that Torin, of all people, could provide him with a stronger lead.

Upon the moss-grown rooftop overlooking the alley, Xarius hissed a private oath. All of that had been within reach, but was now slipping away through the soggy brume. Perhaps he should have risked killing this Arn. It would have been a simpler matter to secure passage for himself and his prisoner aboard a slaver's vessel than that of a wealthy and well-armed merchant. Thieves were so much easier to barter with.

A temporary setback, the assassin assured himself. The journey was young. His opportunity would come.

Keeping to the crowded rooftops, he set off in pursuit.

CHAPTER NINE

No sooner had Torin stepped aboard the *Pirate's Folly* than he began to question his decision in doing so. Even in port, the great ship lurched and swayed, rocked gently by windswept harbor swells. Like a living creature, it tossed restlessly, heaving and then settling to an unsteady cadence.

But it was not the motions that troubled him. Rather, it was the roiling doubts, the fears and suspicions with which he'd been plagued since the night of Darinor's coming. Why was he doing this? What had possessed him to give such credence to what could only be considered a madman's account? Surely he'd not been told enough to merit this hazardous journey, undertaken at a moment's notice. Were it not for Marisha, would he have believed a word of what the renegade Entient had told him? Or would he have listened to Allion and turned a deaf ear?

And Allion, faithful Allion, upon whom Torin had thrust the burden of a ruined kingdom, a land and monarchy in disarray. In all likelihood, General Rogun was already breathing down his neck. Allion, who had always supported his endeavors, both sane and otherwise. Left behind with a mountain of responsibility and scarcely a word of farewell.

His friend deserved better. So convinced was Torin of this that he very nearly spun around and headed for the gangplank. It was not too late to turn back, to relieve the man of this burden, to take Marisha in his arms and refuse to leave her, to face the consequences of his actions head-on. For in some respects, it felt as if he were running away. Should he take too long, or fail in his quest altogether, who would pay the price? His closest friends. His dearest loved ones. While he was half a world away.

"Are you all right, sir?"

Torin looked up to find fish-eyed Cordan peering back at him, wondering why he had stopped. The others marched on ahead, boots thudding on the wooden planking, oblivious to their lord's reservations as they followed Brand, a freckled ship's boy, to their cabins belowdecks.

"Just fine, Bearer," Torin lied, addressing the other by his rank within the City Shield.

"Is it the ship, sir?" Cordan pressed. "I'm told not all adapt well to life at sea."

Torin saw past the other's concern to the nervousness haunting his young eyes.

"You'll do well, my friend. Of that much I'm certain."

He hefted the strap of his leather pack and forced a smile. Cordan smiled bravely in return. He was doing what he had to, Torin reminded himself. His misgivings were only natural, brought on by a sense of upheaval, of venturing into the unknown.

Only, no amount of rationalization could change the way he felt.

Together, they hurried after the others in their party, ducking aside as sailors bustled about, carrying out duties in preparation for their departure. The ship was like a nest of spiders, teeming with activity. Men scurried about the decks, clung to the rigging, even swung about the outer hull on lines and harnesses. Measurements were being taken, gear stowed, crates lashed into place. It was a good thing they'd been accepted aboard as guardsmen, because Torin wouldn't have had the first idea as to how he might contribute any other way.

Captain Jorkin, it had turned out, *had* heard of Torin and his recent adventures. As such, he'd been thrilled to welcome the other aboard his vessel, even leaving behind half a dozen of his own men to make room. The only price was that he should get to glimpse this talisman of divine creation up close, and to hear the truth of the rumors of this so-called War of the Demon Queen. This made Torin more than a little nervous, and he could not help but wonder what Jorkin's plans might be for him and his company once they were trapped aboard the other's ship.

Another disadvantage was that he'd been forced to divulge to both the captain and Arn the true purpose for his voyage. He hadn't done so in any great detail, but it was made clear up front that his was a quest to find the Finlorians, to enlist their aid in a struggle against a dark threat emerged from their time upon these shores. A threat brought about by the retrieval of the Sword.

His candor had seemed to win him favor with the ship's captain, and the decision had been made before he'd left the other's office that space would be made before they embarked at dawn.

Of course, dawn had come and gone hours ago. Having been delayed already an entire day, Jorkin was in a fire to get under way. An assortment of officers, from the first mate to the master deckhand, were bellowing commands with thunder in their voices. Threats of docked wages, lashings, even an occasional keel haul kept the men hopping, but with the way things looked to Torin, they'd be lucky if the ship was ready to cast off on the morrow.

Somehow dodging the worst of the commotion, he and Cordan caught up to Bull and the others just as they reached the stairs leading down to their berths. Against Torin's protest, Jorkin had afforded them a pair of apartments among the officers' quarters. They needed no special treatment, Torin argued, but Jorkin had insisted. Taking it as a minor victory that he was not sleeping in the captain's own billet, Torin had been the first to relent.

Now that he saw the truth of things, he was glad that he had. Ducking below was like crawling into an animal's burrow. The halls were tight, the ceilings low, the air moldy and close. The cabins themselves were closets, smaller than some of those he'd seen used as wardrobes in the royal palace. If these were officers' accommodations, he shuddered to think of those in which he would find the crew.

"Will you require anything else then, sir?" Brand asked him upon showing him his room.

"Not a thing." As he set his bag of provisions upon a feather-thin mattress, the frame beneath creaked and a rat was sent scurrying across the floorboards. "Please give my regards to the captain."

"The captain requests that you and your men dine with him tonight in the officers' lounge."

"Again your captain is most gracious. We'll be pleased to join him."

Brand nodded without once making eye contact, and ducked from the room.

As soon as he'd left, Silas entered. "Can you believe this?"

"Could be worse." Ulric's voice echoed through the thin walls from across the corridor. "It's better than being stuffed with the rest of the crew like rats in the hold."

"Small difference. I just heard one scampering underfoot. And I've yet to see a woman on board."

"That's why the rats," Kallen taunted. "You won't need a woman with them to nibble on your ear."

"Be quiet, all of you," said Torin. "Any man wants to leave can do so now. Otherwise, be grateful for what we have."

"Just wondering aloud, sir. Wondering how a man's supposed to keep his wits together while buried in a floating coffin."

"Well, do it silently from now on. We spoke of this before. Until we know we can trust these men, it'd be best not to show any sign of weakness."

"As you say, sir," Silas mumbled, making his way back to his room.

When their gear had been stowed, Torin led them back on deck to see if they couldn't help make the ship ready. But after Ashwin was nearly decapitated by a swinging boom and Silas almost crushed by an incoming cargo crate, the prevalent opinion was that they could best serve by staying out of the way. Arn led them back to their quarters, and asked that they wait patiently until he came to retrieve them—which he promised to do as soon as they were ready to shove off.

It seemed as if that might never happen. With all that was going on, and all that had yet to be done, Torin feared they might be trapped in their stale cabins for days before the voyage even began. But the estimate proved grossly unfounded as Arn reappeared within the hour. The final boxes and barrels were loaded, calls of departure were made, and their vessel set sail from the pier, headed toward the open sea.

He could only hope that time would transpire as mercifully in the days ahead.

◆　◆　◆

EVHAN, CAPTAIN OF THE CITY SHIELD, strode quietly down the abandoned tunnel. A thick layer of dust stirred beneath his feet, while cobwebs tickled his arms and face. He brushed these aside as best he could and moved onward, using a torch to light his way. The air was stale, unused save by the rats and insects that scurried along the gutters and walls.

It had become a nightly ritual, the last step of his daily routine, to walk this tunnel and ensure that it remained clear. In actuality, it wasn't a single tunnel, but a long string of interconnected passages, storerooms, and workshops that together comprised an emergency egress route for the royal inhabitants of the palace—those who knew of it, anyway. Not many did. Rumor had it, this was the route Queen Ellebe had used to escape the siege of the unknown wizard who had so briefly occupied the city before throwing in with the Demon Queen and disappearing when her armies had been vanquished. It had served its purpose then, and Evhan wanted to make sure that, if necessary, it could serve its purpose again.

As the eyewitness accounts of savage races continued to tighten around the city, that grim likelihood seemed an ever greater possibility. And Evhan had taken it upon himself, as Krynwall's chief defender, to sweep these grounds to keep them free. If the worst came to pass, he would be able to lead his king, his regent, and any number of men out through these tunnels, so that even if the city fell, they might live to fight another day.

The odds of that happening were still remote, but Evhan took his newfound responsibilities seriously, and preferred to be prepared. As of yet, only he and a select few knew these scattered bands for what they were: Illychar, mortal creatures who owed their unnatural lives to the Illysp, parasitic souls that preyed on the bodies of men. Or at least, that's how it had been described to him. Whether or not this was true, he would not have enemy creatures skulking the streets of his city or clogging its escape routes.

He'd told Allion that it all sounded a bit far-fetched to him. But deep down, he hoped the stories would prove real. Not that he wanted any great harm to befall the citizens of this nation, but he'd not enlisted in the City Shield just to wear down with measured paces the stones fronting some nobleman's manor house—not even the king's. He'd enlisted to make a difference, that he might defend the lives of others, even at the cost of his own. To live his life on the edge of a blade for the sense of excitement and satisfaction it would bring.

Even when alone, he found it difficult to contain his zeal. As he marched these deserted corridors, his imagination took hold, conjuring a gang of creatures just around the bend. A family of orcs, perhaps. Maybe even an ogre. A company of intruders to fall before his sword. He would raise the alarm, and disaster would be averted. He would make himself a hero.

Alas, on this night, nothing seemed different from the previous nights in which he had made this trek. The same fetid smells filled his nose; the same gentle squeaks raked his ears. It would not be long before this duty grew stale, and he passed it on to one of his subordinates. It was the idea, he supposed, more than anything. A route of secret escape. Every city was rumored to have them, like ghosts in the bell towers. But to have learned that it was actually there, to have been charged with keeping it secure, had provided a thrill not easily dispelled.

He arrived at what appeared to be a dead end, where the tunnel emptied of mortar and bricks and ran aground of an earthen wall. Tools and materials lay stacked about as if the workers might return at any moment to finish what they'd begun. Except of course the tools were rusted, the masonry stones blanketed in dust and webs. Whoever had begun this task had not been back in awhile.

Evhan ducked left, into one of many niches that lined the unfinished walls. There he fished around until he found what he was looking for: in a hole in one of the rough-shaped blocks, behind a collection of loose stones, a rusted chain. He tugged, coughing against a light cloud of dust. A counterweight mechanism shifted, and an area of the floor within the niche fell away, lowered like a drawbridge on creaking chains.

On hands and knees, Evhan ducked through the opening, doing his best not to dislodge the dirt caked atop the lowered board. Below, he found himself in an earthen crawl space, tucked away beneath the rotting floorboards of an ancient charnel house. He pulled another chain to raise the concealed bridge, then peered ahead through the gloomy expanse. It was the worst stretch of the entire course, wide and flat, foul and confining. He held his breath as he scurried through, scooting awkwardly along beneath the waist-high ceiling in the manner of a trundling insect. At the other end lay a trapdoor, this one set in the wall. After using a dagger to pick at the inner latch, he flung it open, then pulled his body through.

He closed the door securely behind him. From this side, it looked to be a part of the walls that surrounded him, with the keyhole hidden inside the empty knot of a pinewood board. He was able to stand now, at least, hunched over within the square confines of a wooden crate. Without hesitation, he rose up, pushing open the top of the box. Finding the footholds, he stepped up and clear, lowering the lid once more.

The cellar was stacked high with barrels and crates, which helped to disguise the false one. Evhan strode quickly down the uneven aisles, following the trail of prints in the dust. He exited not through the door, but through another empty crate and wall gate. There was another tunnel, followed by another storeroom. This time, he took the main door and cut a sharp angle down the hall to another portal, this one shaped of metal, in the rock wall.

Passing through this door was like stepping into an oven—which was not altogether inaccurate. The cavern into which he'd emerged was that of a smelter, an underground area belonging to the larger complex of an ore refinery. The smelter was still used, along with the rest of the refinery, and was awash with the superheated temperatures required to melt stone and separate the metals from within. Fires burned within towering blast furnaces, controlled blazes that were never fully extinguished, even after the workers had gone home. Their deep glow gave off a sulfurous stench and painted the cavern eerie shades of blood.

The Fason did not linger in this fiendish pit, but moved quickly down one of the large, tunneling exit corridors. Just a little farther and he would begin an ascent into fresh air once more. With sweat dripping down his brow, he looked forward to the cool, refreshing temperatures of the winter night. After that, he would return to the palace by a more direct route, his sweep concluded. He had already logged a false exit from the city gates, so his return by the same would not be questioned.

For a time, his path followed that of a railway track for mine carts. Conscious of his step, he kept his eyes mostly on his feet, wary of tripping on one of the ties. Gravel crunched beneath his hard leather soles, a steady munching sound that—along with his huffing breath—might have been the noise of a predator feasting in its lair.

It was then, as his attention began to slip, that the ambush was sprung. They appeared seemingly out of nowhere, but must have been lurking in the side tunnels and caves. He barely looked up in time to free his blade, but in the process, dropped his torch. It hissed and sparked as it struck the ground, lighting the tip of a sword that flashed across his wrist. He recoiled as if from a snakebite, clutching the wounded member to him, lashing out with his rapier to beat his assailant back.

His enemy retreated, a quick spring back to the edge of the guttering light. Evhan risked a glance at his damaged wrist and wished immediately that he hadn't. The skin was flayed in a wide arc, and blood spilled forth. He tucked it back again, just as another blow came, this one from his flank. He parried the thrust with a desperate shout, sending the other back as he had the first. This brought the other forward again, as if the pair were on opposite ends of a pendulum's swing. With himself caught in the middle.

His superior swordcraft kept them both at bay. But for how long? Theirs were exploratory strikes, he could tell, meant more to test his reactions than cause him harm. His opponents were fast and precise. Outnumbered and losing blood with every beat of his racing heart, he knew it was but a matter of time.

He fought anyway, like a caged animal. His shouts echoed down the lengths of these tunnels. Perhaps someone—a stray miner—would hear his pleas and come to his aid. He scarcely had time to hope. He'd not yet even figured out who his enemies were.

To change that, he went to one knee, a dangerous ruse to bring one or both in close. It worked only too well. He slapped one blade aside as the other took him in the shoulder. His scream frightened both off, but not before he saw the face of each.

A chill dread swept his spine, at odds with the warm waves of dizziness that coursed through him. They were not human. They looked like elves—as he'd seen in illustrations and murals and tapestries, anyway. But how could that be? The last of the ancient Finlorians had long since fled these shores, and the Mookla'ayans seldom strayed from their jungles—and never this far. How had one or the other come to this place, here and now?

He knew the answer even before he was forced to fend off another attack. Illychar. Moments ago, it had been some vague, imaginary term. Just another name for a child's ghoul. Now, almost too swiftly to comprehend, that night-mare had come to life.

Evhan gritted his teeth. He might have charged, seized the offensive, but could ill afford to leave his diminishing circle of light. His assailants' eyes glittered. For all he knew, they could see in the dark. And yet if he did not take drastic action, his struggles would soon be ended.

He had to break their rhythm, catch them by surprise. Once again, he went down low, drawing in the enemy at his back. Instead of turning to face the attack, he came up flinging a fistful of gravel. A sword bit into his leg, but he howled away the pain and used it to fuel his fury against the suddenly un-certain companion. Moves practiced a thousand times were executed almost without thought. As he forced his enemy wide to draw blood along his arm, his own rapier found the creature's throat.

Evhan rounded at once, but was already too late. He was hit yet again, this time in the soft side of his belly. The elf sneered at him, a skeletal mask with shriveled, leathery skin. Nothing like the romanticized depictions of ancient legend, Evhan realized, though quite healthy for a creature three thousand years dead.

The blade twisted in his gut. Without thinking, Evhan reached down with his free hand to grasp it. The edges dug into his clasped palm, slicing fingers to the bone. But in the same movement, he sent his sword through the other's stomach. They held like that for a moment, locked in a grisly embrace. Then Evhan yanked free and, while the other tottered in confused shock, struck deep through its chin.

With the tip of his blade protruding through its skull, the elf's eyes wid-ened, then narrowed in defiance. It spat and clawed, but Evhan clenched his teeth and held firm. His strength won out, and a moment later, his enemy pitched to the earth.

Evhan followed it down, slumping to his knees. He looked to his wounds, but couldn't tell which was the most grievous. He doubted he had the strength to bandage them, but would never stumble out of here without doing so. Waves of fire and ice collided beneath his skin. A dizzying darkness closed in.

He snarled it off like a wolf defending its kill. He felt himself sway, but refused to shut his eyes, refused to fall. If he did, there would be no getting up. For strength, he focused on his slain attackers, then looked to his own tabard and the strips of binding cloth it might provide.

But before he could begin, a soft rustle closed round, echoing strangely in his ringing ears. He looked up, his head heavy and rolling to one side. They were all around him now—four, five, half a dozen more. They studied with interest the bodies of their fallen companions, then focused their attention on him. Although each had its own distinct features, they all appeared more or less the same to Evhan. Enemies. He had to sound the alarm. If only he could hold his head in place. If only he could find his sword.

Then his torch failed, and the stabbing blades closed in.

◆   ◆   ◆

TORIN LEANED AGAINST THE SALTY RAIL, peering out at the vast ocean with a faint smile upon his lips. It was his first experience at sea, and he'd never felt anything like it: the crisp air, the gentle swells, the invigorating spray. As he gazed out upon the endless waves, he lost himself in the rhythm of their motion. He closed his eyes then, and listened to the murmuring surge. The sense of freedom, both exhilarating and frightening, buoyed his spirits, filling him like the wind in the ship's sails and carrying him along on the endless flow.

Out here, nothing seemed to matter. Not his lingering questions about Darinor, his regrets at having left Allion to tend to his duties, or his doubts as to whether he had made the right decision. Out here, where the dome of the sky stretched unbroken from horizon to horizon, he knew only peace, a divine tranquility. His only regret was that Marisha was not here to share it with him.

"Hey, if you're just going to stand around, why not lend a hand with this rigging?"

Torin turned from his fantasy to find Iigo, the ship's boatswain, glaring up at him.

"Just taking a moment to admire the scenery."

Iigo snorted. "You'll grow tired of that soon enough. It ain't going anywhere for awhile, trust me. Now grab a hold."

"Master boatswain," a new voice interrupted. Both men turned as Captain Jorkin sauntered near. "Is there a problem?"

Iigo snapped to attention. "No problem, sir. Just putting a layabout to task, sir."

"Just because Master Torin here has offered to lend a hand doesn't mean he was hired to do your duties. Unless, of course, you wish to surrender your pay to him as well?"

"Yes, sir. I mean, no, sir."

"It's no trouble," Torin assured the captain.

"As you are, swordhand. Master boatswain, carry on."

"Yes, sir," said Iigo, hefting his load of heavy lines and dragging it off across the deck.

"May I join you at the rail, swordhand?"

Torin nodded. He still wasn't sure whether to accept this man at face value or beware some secret agenda. Whatever the captain's emotions, he hid them behind kind eyes and a pleasant smile. Or maybe he was genuinely that way.

"You were made for the sea," Jorkin observed. Standing beside Torin, he stared out at the wind-tossed swells, seeming to admire their sparkling beauty as the sun edged toward the horizon.

"What makes you say that?"

"Where are your shipmates?"

"In their cabins below. Wishing they were dead."

Jorkin smiled. "As I said. You were made for the sea."

From the corner of his eye, Torin studied the man, his pocked face and balding pate, tanned and blistered by countless years beneath the sun. But ever more obvious was his heartfelt respect and love for the ocean itself, and this way of life. Difficult, yes, and not for everyone. Regardless, there was something satisfying in seeing someone who lived his true calling every single day. Swept up in the moment, Torin couldn't help but wonder if the captain was right, and he had missed his.

"The name, *Pirate's Folly*. Is that meant to discourage marauders?"

"The reputation came first," Jorkin replied. His gaze remained lost among the sun-dappled waves, like a drunk given in to his stupor. "She was christened the *Shark's Fin*, for she cuts through the waves like no other. But over the course of her maiden sailing season, she staved off no fewer than seven pirate attacks. Sank one vessel, crippled two others, chased off the rest. Word like that spreads, even among pirates. Such a name by itself would do nothing, but she's got the deeds to back it up."

"I must say again, it was good of you to welcome my men and me aboard."

Jorkin looked to him at last. "A stroke of luck for both of us, it seems. Two days now and not a hint of a storm."

"Should we be expecting one, then?"

"Always, lad. Always. The moment you turn your back to her is the moment she'll remind you of her deadly grace."

The captain left him then, walking off with the loose, rolling gait of an experienced sailor. Torin shook his head as he watched the other go. Every time Jorkin approached him, he expected to be hounded further about his business, asked to divulge more concerning his mission. But the captain continued to show complete trust in him, a trust he had yet to earn, just as Jorkin had yet to earn his. Whatever the reason for this undue respect, perhaps it was time to put aside his suspicions and offer the man the same courtesy.

A stiff gust pushed Torin back to the rail. It seemed the sun was melting into the ocean, spilling molten gold into its endless troughs. Sails billowed overhead, straining to hold the wind that blew them swiftly toward that glittering treasure. They were making wonderful time, as the captain had indicated. But the realization brought to Torin an unexpected twinge of doubt. On the one hand, the sooner they reached their destination, the sooner he could return home. On the other, he didn't want this leg of the journey to end.

He let his mind wander, setting thoughts adrift like foam upon the seas. It felt good to relax, to put aside the many concerns that at this moment could not be helped. He wondered fleetingly if this was what death might be like, this welcome release of worldly cares. If so, then there was little he had to fear.

At last, the sun disappeared, so that all that remained was a dim glow of heat to mark its passing. In the gathering dark, stars began to emerge, and the sky grew deeper, more vast. Torin considered them with a distracted air, searching absently for any familiar constellations.

All of a sudden, a call came from the crow's nest, a sort of strangled yelp. Torin scarcely had time to register the warning before the ocean erupted, dousing him in salty spray. He turned his head, crouching low, and gripped the rail. The ship lurched beneath him, feeling as if it might capsize. He wiped his eyes and, blinking against the stinging bite of seawater, looked up as a shadow fell over him like an eclipse.

The thing surged forth with a power and majesty unlike any Torin had ever witnessed. It hovered off the starboard bow, a mile or more away, yet was large enough to swallow up his entire field of vision. It appeared to be a great pinnacle of rock—a sliver of the earth itself. Then it turned to face him.

Shouts went up, but Torin held his breath, bolted like a capstan to the deck of the ship. Above him, the beast loomed, higher than the ship, its snout raking the heavens. Coral and barnacles grew in reefs along the spine-studded length of its silver, eel-shaped torso. Forests of seaweed clung to it like hair. An obsidian orb rotated in a crusted socket, gleaming in the moonlight. An eye, Torin realized, far too small for its gargantuan body. It seemed to peer down at him. Seemed to pierce his soul.

Though he could not recall reaching for it, the Crimson Sword appeared in his hand. The monster leaned closer. Its lips parted, revealing a cavernous maw ringed with mountainous teeth. Men screamed in fear.

But the leviathan remained nearly motionless, reared up as if to challenge the very sky. Gills opened and closed, while a pair of nostrils flared, altering the course of the winds. Torin gripped the Sword and stared up at the thing, unable to flee, unable to look away.

Then, as suddenly as it had surfaced, the unfathomable creature slid slowly back into the depths of the sea. As it slipped away, a mournful groan filled the night, reverberating long after the immense head had vanished beneath the dark waves. When it finally died away, not a trace of the creature remained. Only the churning waters, an awestruck silence, and a shivering sense of dread.

CHAPTER TEN

*F*OR THE BETTER PART OF A WEEK, the *Pirate's Folly* continued westward, un-challenged by wind or weather. In all that time, no mention was made of the unknown creature of the deep, though Torin could tell it was on everyone's mind. With haunted looks, guarded movements, or the anxious stare with which he swept the sea, each man revealed clearly enough the same fear. But none dared give it voice, as if to do so might make it real.

Routine alone saved them from going mad. While some among the crew whispered at night of ill omens and the desire to turn back, most knuckled down and found escape in their daily duties. Torin was among the latter. Al-though he had yet to learn much about sailing, he was only too happy to serve in a menial capacity: hauling, swabbing, sanding, painting—whatever was required. He took his instructions from deckhands and cabin boys, Iigo the boatswain and Hocker the helmsman. Here and there, he picked up a thing or two about the craft, but mostly he just kept himself busy, fixing his thoughts on matters above the waves so they would not slip down to dwell on what lurked below.

That they continued to make blessed time was an unexpected boon to everyone's spirits. The winds, said to be especially volatile this time of year, remained steadfastly in their favor. The sun, so often held hostage to storm clouds and rain, blazed unchecked across a gentle sky. Such perfect condi-tions—and the fact that they were ahead of schedule—made it difficult to focus on less positive matters. Some, like Torin, began to question privately whether the unlikely encounter had been anything more than a hallucina-tion.

"What was that thing, do you suppose?" Arn asked finally.

It was dawn, the sixth since the encounter, and the first that showed signs of a gathering squall. Torin stood on the poop deck, looking down at the blond-haired mercenary, who rested upon one knee following the latest round of their daily sparring session. The shorter man was stripped to the waist, huffing for breath, his torso rippling.

Torin shook his head, casting a fearful glance toward the sea. "You mean I wasn't the only one to imagine it?"

He recalled with a shudder how he had felt in that moment, and in the moments that followed. Even with the Sword in hand, an insect to be crushed, a candle to be snuffed, shivering and wet and wondering why he was not dead.

"A beast like that surfaces either to breathe or to feed," Arn declared. "But that thing had gills."

"As well as lungs," Torin noted, "to have made that sound."

"So why didn't it swallow us whole?"

Torin shifted nervously. "I've never encountered a sea monster before. Why don't you tell me?"

"Sea monster?" Arn's pale blue eyes had been staring into space, but swung about now to fix Torin with a chilling stare. "I spoke with Captain Jorkin. He's battled sea monsters—from great whales to giant serpents to the ten-legged kraken. That, he says, was no sea monster."

Torin started to respond, then realized he had nothing to say.

"Something caused it to breach. You're sure it wasn't that Sword?"

Their gazes flew across the deck to where Cordan and Bull stood at the rail, guarding the Crimson Sword while observing the mock combatants.

"I couldn't tell you," Torin admitted. "There is far more about the blade that is unknown to me than is known. That it might have summoned the creature or discouraged it—or both—seems a possibility. Either way, I'm at a loss to say."

Arn continued to study him, or perhaps just his words. He was looking for some form of reassurance, as they all were. Torin had none to give.

"Fair enough," Arn said finally. "But I'd be careful around the men. Sailors are a superstitious lot. That thing shows up again, I'd not be surprised if they tried to throw you overboard."

Torin nodded, unsure how to take that warning. Was Arn himself one of those who intended to do so? He had certainly noticed the looks, the cautious distance afforded him by many of Jorkin's crew since that day—even those he had toiled alongside. But he had thought it merely a part of the uneasiness they all shared. He hadn't considered that they might blame him.

They completed a few more turns of spirited fencing, spiked war hammer versus borrowed longsword, as a dense fog rolled in. Normally by this time, the sun had begun to burn away the thick tendrils of dawn's blanket. On this morning, however, the soup roiled and darkened, leaving night's chill heavy and moist. Though long expected, the foul signs marked a definite shift, a clear indication that their luck was about to change.

Even so, none could have predicted the cry that shrieked down from above.

"Pirate vessel! Port astern!"

Together, Torin and Arn raced to the aft railing, where they were met by Bull and Cordan. At first, Torin saw nothing through the swirling fog. Then Arn thrust forth a muscled arm.

"There!"

"I see it," said Cordan.

Torin squinted. Suddenly, there it was, a black beetle on the horizon, its raked masts and taut lines like horns and pincers in the gloom.

"Where did it come from?" he asked.

"And how do they know it's a pirate vessel?" Bull grunted.

"They know," was Arn's only explanation. He turned, scooped up his leather jerkin, and dashed across the deck toward the wheelhouse. Torin exchanged weapons with Cordan, then led his companions in pursuit.

Hocker was in the pilot box, his mane of sandy hair tossed by filtering breezes. Arn stood beside Captain Jorkin, who was peering through an expensive-looking spyglass.

"By the looks of them, they're built for speed," Jorkin observed.

"They'd have to be," Hocker spat, "to have stolen upon us like this."

"What say you, Captain?" There was no mistaking the gleam in Arn's eye. "Shall we come about and meet them head-on?"

Before Jorkin could respond, a relay of new calls came from the lookouts.

"Two more! Starboard bow!"

The company in the wheelhouse spun about. The brume was thicker ahead of them, and even with the spyglass, it took Jorkin a moment to pinpoint the enemy vessels and confirm the report.

"Sangho's Tempest," he swore. "What is this?"

Hocker's gaze narrowed. "A pirate *fleet*?"

"What does that mean?" Torin asked.

Jorkin lowered his spyglass. "It means the time has come for you and your mates to earn your passage."

The captain stepped from the wheelhouse, where he was met by a cadre of senior officers. "To arms!"

That set off a blur of activity. Crewmen scurried about as if the sky were falling. Orders were executed, responses relayed. Torin didn't understand the half of it. Sails were lowered, while others were raised. There were shouts regarding course and heading, given in response to the maneuvers of the enemy vessels. At the same time, deck catapults were unhooded and ballistae wheeled into place. Missiles and bows and polearms were produced, taken up by almost every member of the crew.

Arn led them out to the bow rail, where Clave, the master swordhand, was assembling the troops. As Torin's group joined the muster, Silas and Kallen, Ashwin and Ulric, came running up.

"You men ready for this?" Clave called back to them.

Ashwin, the last to recover from his seasickness, still looked a little pale. But he nodded fiercely alongside his fellow fighters.

"We'll be the first defense against any boarding parties," Arn explained calmly. In addition to Torin's seven, there were half a dozen others, seasoned veterans, huddled in front of the stout mercenary, taking orders from Clave. "Rarely does it come to that. But with three ships—"

"Arn, does your team know its assignments?" Clave demanded.

"Yes, sir!" Arn replied.

The huddle broke, and the defenders hustled to their stations. Torin and his men followed after Arn, who took them down one level to the main deck.

There they braced themselves amidships, toward the bow on the starboard side, waiting for the battle to begin.

An unnatural quiet settled over the ship's passengers, as raucous preparation gave way to breathless anticipation. The most prevalent sounds were the sloshing of the waves and the creaking of the vessel that rode them. All hunkered in their posts, awaiting that first, terrible volley.

"What's taking so long?" Arn wondered aloud. His spiked war hammer slapped against the opposite palm, while his thick muscles bunched and corded with expectation. "They should be upon us by now."

Torin had been thinking the same. As a show of strength, Jorkin had raced the *Pirate's Folly* under full sail directly toward the pair of heavy galleons that lay ahead, as though he intended to brush right past them. The great warships, however, had called his bluff and stood their ground, swinging broadside to present the widest possible barrage. The captain had then had little choice but to tack south. With the third ship coming up from behind, he could ill afford to be caught between the three. In response, the forward vessels had moved to cut him off, while the smaller, faster ship gave chase along a tight intercept course. Oddly enough, the forward attackers had yet to close in, as if waiting for their weaker comrade.

When Jorkin realized this, he spun his bark about, pointing her toward her own wake. Better to confront and dispatch the large schooner coming up on their tail. It would be an easier contest than taking on the two ahead, a strike both swift and sure. With any luck, they would put on such a display of power as to give the others pause.

But the trailing schooner was not as swift as she had first seemed. Weighed down with men and weapons, perhaps, or with stolen loot. Though she showed no signs of furling sails, it took a long time for her to catch up. Were it not for the ships ahead, they might have outrun her after all.

Now it appeared as though they would in fact be trapped. The three attackers were equidistant from them, forcing Jorkin to order Hocker hard about once more, maneuvering to protect their rudder. The brunt of the assault would come from the heavy warships ahead of them, and they had no choice but to position themselves accordingly.

That was where they now stood, almost still in the water, awaiting the first strike. The twin galleons were nearly on top of them, dark and ghostly, shimmering in the fog.

"Perhaps they mean for us to surrender without a fight," Torin suggested.

Arn grunted. "They'd have fired a warning shot, at least. Something here is ghastly strange."

They continued to stare at the looming ships, which, despite their closeness, remained hazy and indistinct. Torin measured the time with the beats of his racing heart, as he searched for men upon the rigging. They were almost within hailing distance. Any moment now, something had to give.

Then they vanished.

It happened so suddenly that Torin blinked and rubbed his eyes. One moment, the black and bulky shapes were gliding soundlessly ahead through curtains of brume. The next, all that remained was empty fog.

"Incoming!"

The shout was followed by a terrible rending and cracking sound an instant before a great crash rocked the ship to its core. Men screamed, wood splintered. The entire vessel shuddered with the impact of falling timbers and broken spars.

Torin got to his feet and tore across the uneven decking, a burr on Arn's heels. On the port side, the unmistakable hum and twang of arrows being fired sang through the air. A powerful whoosh signaled the release of a catapult, and Torin turned the corner as its load splashed into the churning sea.

Another blast rocked the ship, and again Torin was thrown. He recovered just in time to dodge the whipping descent of a severed stay. Despite the chaos, it was easy enough to see what was going on. Unlike its companions, the enemy schooner, the first they had seen, was still out there, pelting them from afar with a long-range catapult. The *Folly* was frantically returning fire, but had yet to gain proper position. Not only had she been caught off balance by the phantom galleons, but it seemed her own weaponry had the shorter range.

The pirates had the element of surprise. And given the accuracy of their initial volleys, Jorkin was dealing now with a wounded vessel. Shouts continued to fly—damage reports, cries of alarm, commands meant to right the sluggishness of the ship's responses. Torin clung helplessly to the rail, Sword in hand, awaiting an opportunity he feared would never come.

Another projectile came flying in from the enemy's deck catapult. This time, it sailed long, taking a bite out of the far rail. Jorkin shouted in triumph as the *Pirate's Folly* swung around at last. The order to shoot went up, and three catapults returned fire. Two fell short of their target once again. The third, however, scored a direct hit on the enemy's hull, only to be deflected aside by an iron plate, exposed beneath the smashed and splintered wood.

"She's armored, sir!"

Torin was close enough to see the shock on his captain's features. But Jorkin wasn't interested in excuses. He continued to order a raking assault with ballistae, arrows, and catapults. The onslaught was intense—piercing sails, cracking masts, and punching holes in the hull and planking. But the smaller schooner weathered the storm, shielded in iron where she was most vulnerable, making her deceptively resilient. A cunning ruse, Torin realized, to disguise a lumbering warship as a fleet schooner, to convince its enemies to fight rather than flee, luring them close with a false sense of strength.

Not that it would matter in the end. With the extent of the damage being taken on both sides, Torin could not see how this conflict would end with anything less than both ships at the bottom of the ocean. Perhaps it was only his untrained eye, but he felt certain the time was fast approaching when neither vessel would be able to stay afloat.

"We're being pulverized!" Iigo shouted in despair. Torin turned to find the master boatswain at his shoulder, anger and fear reflected in his eyes.

"They don't want to sink us," Jorkin growled. The captain spat blood as Arn helped him from beneath the debris of a fallen sail. "If they want our cargo, they have to come aboard to get it."

A series of impacts rocked the blasted vessel, seeming to argue this point. But as the air cleared of splinters, Torin found the enemy sidling up close. Hooked lines were thrown forth, tethers to hold her in place, while bloodthirsty shouts echoed in the morning gloom.

As the ships ground together, a swarm of arrows cut through the air in either direction. Torin ducked and closed his eyes, listening to the splashes of men pitching overboard, and to the sharp thud of those bolts that missed their mark. Then a cry welled up from the enemy horde, and the takeover began.

Torin rose up to meet it, the Sword's radiance a beacon in the mist. He followed Arn, who rushed forward to confront the first wave. Clave was beside him, but went down almost at once, a thrown dagger sticking from his eye. He had a vague sense of those at his heels—Cordan and Bull, Ashwin and Ulric, Silas and Kallen. Somehow, they had remained with him through the initial assault. Only to rise up and join him now within a whirlwind of death.

But it was too late to consider their safety or order them back. A fever had overtaken him—the calculated frenzy wrought by possession of the Sword. As always, it seemed an extension of his own will, only with a heightened awareness of the threat, a clearer understanding of his goal. It guided his hand as much as obeyed it, though he never felt in danger of losing control. His passion fueled it, and the Sword responded in turn, filling him with limitless energy, unbridled strength, an alert fervor that was nothing short of divine.

It did not take long to make a spectacle of himself. With each stroke, the radiant blade tore through whatever it came in contact with, be it armor or wood or bone. Each time, it did so wreathed in crimson flames—a protective sheath burst forth from within. When the stroke was finished, the flames vanished, retreating back within the depths of the polished blade, leaving it as perfect and pristine as before. Its glow undimmed, its beauty unmarred, it bathed him in an aura of ruby light, an unmistakable brilliance that lent strength to his companions and filled his enemies with awe.

But they kept coming, brandishing their weapons of iron and steel, feinting and dodging and drawing him on. Torin did not hesitate. He was being baited, he knew, even as he danced across the boarding plank that lay stretched between the ships, high above the black seas below. Nevertheless, their insolence troubled him. Surely, in just a few short moments, they had seen enough of his flaming blade to tuck tail and scurry away. And yet they refused to do so. Insulted by their lack of deference, Torin lunged ahead, determined to make them regret that decision.

Before he knew it, he was aboard the enemy schooner, his onslaught gone virtually unchallenged. But then, who could challenge him? Who could withstand the Crimson Sword, this talisman of gods and avatars, whose holy might had been used to shape the very earth? Even with just this small measure of its power, who could oppose his will? Certainly not a boatload of criminals, men who knew nothing of honor, only murder and greed.

The tumult enveloped him. There were cheers now, from both sides. Pressed from every quarter, Torin was too busy to give the matter more than a passing thought. Perhaps his foes thought him cornered. Perhaps they supposed he must eventually tire. Little did they know that he could dance like this forever, with flawless aim and lethal proficiency, turning aside his enemies' blades while gradually using their own weariness against them.

Too late, Torin realized his mistake. It had happened to him before, and he cursed his foolishness for allowing it to happen again. During the Battle of Kraagen Keep, the first time he had wielded the Sword against an enemy, he had gone too far, allowed himself to be swept up in the undulating rush of power and forged too far afield of those he was fighting beside. As a result, he'd been cut off from his company, and only the Sword—and the warrior skills of Kylac Kronus—had saved him from a quick defeat.

His first indication were the warning shouts from the *Pirate's Folly*. As he shifted focus just enough to see what had caused this fresh alarm, he heard and spied the sawing of ropes and the tossing aside of planks. The pirates were cutting loose, shoving off from their intended target. It would appear they'd had enough, and were leaving their spoils behind.

Or perhaps they already had what they had come for.

Despite the rapture of the Sword, worry bloomed in the pit of Torin's stomach. Already the vessels had disengaged, with the armored schooner beginning to pull away. Only a handful of fellow fighters had crossed over; most had been more concerned with holding the pirates at bay. He saw Arn and Cordan and a pair of unknown swordhands nearly buried amid the throng. Bull was at the rail of the *Folly*, bellowing and snorting, trying to draw the pirate ship back but finding little help from Jorkin's crew. Beside the big man, Ashwin made a reckless leap, only to catch an arrow in the chest and go pinwheeling into the breach, where his body slapped down against the roiling waves.

Torin cried out and surged across the deck, scattering enemies in his haste to free Arn and Cordan and get them all back to where they belonged. If nothing else, perhaps they could sweep this vessel clean, or near enough to take control. Whichever, they needed to do so quickly, for whether as a result of her wounds or the will of her officers and crew, the *Pirate's Folly* seemed content to let them go.

His enemies laughed at his urgency, rising against him with rattling blades and sneering faces. A few scored minor hits, as Torin sacrificed a measure of his own defense in order to rush to the aid of his comrades. Even so, he was too slow. Before he could cut the intended swath, the pair of unknown swordhands went down. Arn and Cordan followed, swarmed over by the enemy crush.

Torin roared a denial. At that same moment, the nets began to fly.

He sensed the first coming behind him, and whirled to meet it, slashing it in midair. The Sword ripped easily down its center, opening it wide. But the severed strands were weighted at the corners and coated in pitch, and thus clung to him like a spider's webbing. He might have extricated himself, but then a second and third blanketed him, followed by a fourth. His own thrashings tripped him up, and he succumbed in a tangled heap.

A beating followed, a pounding of clubs and staves and weapon hafts from every direction. He gritted away the worst of it, shielded by the thick strands of netting, clutching the Sword for all he was worth. But ensnared as he was, he was unable to mount a defense. A battering assault on his arm loosened his grip before burly hands pried the hilt from his fingers. He grasped after it, feeling as though someone had snatched the heart from his chest, but a barrage to the skull left his mind dazed and his vision clouded.

"Enough!"

A few last-ditch blows landed. Through a haze of grogginess, Torin recognized the whistle of arrows and the *thunk* and clatter of spears, as the ships made their parting salvos. The pirates cheered. Somehow, he pushed himself to his hands and knees, weighed down by the sticky nets. An enemy spat upon him.

"I said enough!" a cool voice reprimanded.

"Aye, Cap'n."

Torin peered from beneath the ridge of a swollen eye to see a swarthy, dark-bearded brute lower his head and step back. The Sword was in his hands, but even with the strengthening caress of the concealed Pendant, Torin was too dizzy to reach for it.

Then the other came forward. A tarred mop of greasy black hair hung straight to his shoulders. Beady brown eyes glanced at the Sword, then locked upon Torin.

"Take him below."

A flurry of hands reached for him, seizing hold of his hair, his limbs, and the netting of his cage. When he tried to resist, they punched or shook him, knocking him down again and dragging him across the deck.

"This one's still alive, sir."

Sweat and pitch stung his eyes, but Torin forced them open. Nearby, Arn was on his knees, head lolling. A straddling enemy clenched his tuft of curls and put a dagger to his throat. His blue eyes were clouded, his blond hair matted with blood.

"Feed him to the sharks," the man with the tarred head ordered. "His mates too."

A lump filled Torin's throat as the semiconscious mercenary was tossed overboard. Cordan's limp form went after, as soon as a pair of laughing pirates had plucked their bloodstained blades from his back.

Torin forced his gaze away, over the rail and beyond, to where the *Pirate's Folly* lay crippled, abandoned in the middle of the ocean, midway between continents. He thought he could make out the somber forms of Silas and Kallen, standing now with Bull, staring after the pirate vessel as it slunk away. Kallen leaned upon his brother, one hand covering a wounded eye.

Then he was being dragged once more, like a haul of netted fish, leaving his companions to fade in the mist.

CHAPTER ELEVEN

Allion gaped at the severed heads, his stomach churning with revulsion. Amid the gasps and shouts of his comrades, bile rose to his throat. He willed himself to look away, but his gaze refused to be drawn from their open-mouthed stares, their lolling tongues, their rolled-back eyes.

When the furor had calmed, Thaddreus spoke. "And what point do you wish to make with this display, General?"

Rogun snarled, tossing the bloody sack—from which he had dumped the three heads—onto the table beside them. "That it is time, once and for all, to address this threat in the manner that I, as chief commander of Krynwall's forces, see fit."

Thaddreus, speaker of the Circle of City Elders, did not appear impressed. "Which would be what? To sweep this land like a team of plow horses, raking everything underfoot?"

"Are you blind, old man? Do those look like human heads to you?"

They did not, which was part of the reason for Allion's dismay. The skin of their faces was dark and wrinkled, sucked tight against high cheekbones, stretched to a point at the eyes and ears. Though ravaged, their features reminded him of those of Cwingen U'uyen, chieftain of the Powaii, of the Mookla'ayan elves.

"We've all heard the evidence to suggest the old races have returned to roam our lands," Thaddreus persisted, refusing to be riled. "Your exhibition, while striking, tells us nothing we do not already know."

"These were not found roaming our distant lands," Rogun growled, "but the woods beyond our very city."

A fresh clamor went up among those assembled, with fourteen of the sixteen Elders all fighting to be heard and Rogun, a fifteenth, trying to quiet them. Of their ranks, only Thaddreus kept his tongue, along with Allion beside him.

"The three here represent only a small portion of their band," Rogun went on, his powerful voice drowning out those of the others. "The remainder of their party escaped into the trees. The patrol that happened upon them was not large enough to root them out."

Again the general paused, and again the shouting ensued. Allion at last pried his eyes from the trio of heads, holding back his nausea, and found

Rogun staring at him. The general appeared both pleased and disgusted by the row he had caused. It had been some time since he had joined them in council, having no stomach for their pointless deliberations. Allion had been grateful for the respite, had even begun to hope that he'd heard the last of the man's grumbling. He should have known the general was merely biding his time, and would intervene when certain that his presence might make the greatest impact.

Allion did his best not to flinch beneath the general's withering gaze. He had caught them off guard was all, storming in unannounced, grisly baggage in tow. The din was rife with fear and anger, accusation and loathing—just the kinds of emotions to play when seeking to manipulate men along a desired course. Though Allion was as moved as any of them, as regent, he had a responsibility not to show it.

Thaddreus waved his arms in a slow flapping motion. At first, this only heightened the uproar. Gradually, however, his patience won out, and the furor abated.

"Please, General," the old man bade. "Take your seat with us here in the Circle."

Rogun refused, leaning down to plant his fists on the great marble-topped table. "I did not come to join your ceaseless debate. I came to end it. Declare martial law. Grant me charter to combat this enemy before it is too late."

A chorus of cheers lauded the general's plan, while a smattering of grunts opposed it. Before long, the discussion had deteriorated into a shouting match once more.

Allion rubbed his temples to ward off an encroaching headache. Less than two weeks had passed since Torin's departure, and already he'd had enough. Each day, he considered seriously abandoning his oaths and responsibilities and chasing after Torin as he had before. Were it not for his vow to watch over Marisha, he might well have done so. The city was a crumbling pile of stone, the land around it barren and worthless. Citizens within and without waged an endless war against poverty and starvation, still working to rebuild their lives following the taxing reign of King Sorl and the invasion of the wizard. Everywhere he went, people looked to him for relief.

Small wonder that Torin had been so willing to leave it all behind, to accept even this wild charge as an avenue of escape. As Fason, Allion had been painfully aware of the challenges his friend faced, but had been a step removed from the politics of them. As regent, he had stepped squarely into their midst.

"Where is our Fason?" someone demanded, as if attuned to his thoughts. "Any word yet from our captain of the guard?"

Allion perked up. Evhan had been missing for a week now, having vanished without a trace just days after his promotion. Despite a sweep by the City Shield and Allion himself, there had been no sign of the young captain, leaving the regent deeply saddened and suspicious.

"Deserted," Rogun replied, shaking his head. "Or slain, perhaps, by one of the enemy. It matters not, except as another sign that we have sat on our hands too long."

Allion narrowed his gaze at how quickly the general dismissed the issue. The prevalent opinion was in fact that Evhan had deserted them. But Allion knew better. Until this very moment, he hadn't considered that Rogun might be behind the young captain's disappearance. Such a move would be just the sort of inexplicable, off-balancing maneuver used to generate the chaos and confusion on which Rogun was now feeding. Even so, he felt surprise that the other could be so bold, and found himself wondering who might be next if the general did not soon get his way.

"We cannot continue to fight in this manner," Rogun pressed, "allowing our enemies to strike and disperse as they see fit. If we are to win this war, we must force them to engage us in direct confrontation. The only way to do so is to assemble a force that will sweep across these lands and flush the cowards into the open."

"And how will you control the widespread panic to ensue among the populace as the result of such an extreme course?" Thaddreus challenged.

"Extreme?" Rogun gestured toward the rotting heads upon the tabletop. "Perhaps I should have brought you the heads of the innocent victims, rather than those of our enemy—though it would have required a team of men to carry them."

A blistering outcry commenced, and lasted for several moments. Still Allion remained silent, praying the storm would pass. While it scarcely seemed possible, the gathered councilors were growing ever more agitated. When Rogun spoke, most everyone listened. Other than that, it was becoming increasingly difficult to make out one argument from the next.

Although the governing council was yet in its infant stages, Allion had begun to think its creation may have been a mistake. Hoping to iron out differences through a fair and equitable discourse, Torin had given its strongest voices to members of those factions who opposed both him and one another. As such, it had settled into little more than a forum for the airing of grievances, each presented more loudly than the last. Some saw the entire Circle as a sign of weakness, an indication that the young king—and now his regent—was unable to rule. Perhaps so. Nevertheless, it grated on Allion that their bickering had become second nature, so that even when presented with a common problem, the councilors found the pursuit of deep-seated rivalries and prejudices more important than resolution.

He was about to holler a desperate appeal for silence when once again the chamber doors burst open without call or warning, and a startling figure strode in.

A deep hush fell over the room, brought on by perhaps the one man capable of silencing this brood. He was tall and gaunt, with a sallow face and the tattered robes of a scarecrow. A gust of wind accompanied his entrance, stirring the stench of decay that clung to the severed Illychar heads.

Sickened anew, Allion covered his mouth.

"Well, now, if it isn't our guardian and protector," Rogun muttered. "Where have you been?"

"The same as you." Darinor glared, stepping forward with the swish of heavy fabric. "Scouting the movements of our enemy." He paused as he eyed the heads of the elven dead. "I see you have made some progress."

"And you?" Despite surrendering half a head to the thinner man in height, Rogun showed no signs of standing down.

"The Illychar spread more quickly than I had imagined," Darinor confessed, his deep voice rumbling from that cavernous hollow within his craggy beard. "Their overall movements bespeak caution, as if testing our waters, but by packs and individuals, they grow bolder by the day."

"Again, you tell us nothing we've not discerned ourselves," Rogun complained. "You claim to be our leader in this. Do you have a plan?"

Darinor gave the other a scornful glance before turning his attention to Allion and the seated members of the Circle. "The plan is this, and the time to execute it is now. If you let them, the Illychar will fight like owls in the night, swift and silent before winging away. They will do so forever, or at least until their numbers are so much greater than ours that we will be overrun."

"Go on," Rogun said, his interest piqued.

"The key is to draw them out, and the only way to do this is to assemble a singular force around which—"

"I've already suggested that," Rogun grumbled. "Time and again. It is these fools before you who cannot see the truth."

Darinor fixed him with a stern eye. "Your plan does not go far enough, General. You speak of an army that stomps across this land, beating the tall grasses as if hunting snakes. What I am proposing is much more radical. Empty this city of soldiers. Leave only the young and the elderly, the immature and the infirm—coils that will do little to tempt the Illysp spirits come to haunt these grounds. Since each Illysp can claim only one mortal shell with which to wreak havoc and mayhem in the physical world, they crave the bodies of soldiers, not nursemaids. Put the land's men-at-arms in one place and the Illysp—and the Illychar who support them—will gather like flies to a corpse."

Rogun frowned. "You say they will come to us?"

"If the temptation is great enough. Which is why you cannot afford to divide your forces into wandering patrols as they are now. In fact, Krynwall's army alone is not sufficient—I speak not only of Alson but of all Pentania. You must unite your strength with that of your neighbors, with Partha and Kuuria. Only then, when all are marshaled, will your enemy have no choice but to combat you openly."

"Then we could at best defend a single city. You would have us leave all others defenseless?"

"To defend your cities, you must lure the Illysp away from them. Leave a token garrison if you must, but the greater their numbers, the greater the temptation will be for the Illychar to ransack those stores for the sake of their Illysp brethren and the swelling of their own ranks."

Allion didn't have Rogun's sharp mind for military tactics, nor his experience and training. But he, too, was uncomfortable with what Darinor seemed to be suggesting. On the surface, it made sense. At the same time, Allion's stomach knotted in warning.

"No," Rogun said flatly.

"What you suggest would require a terrific leap of faith on our part," Thaddreus agreed. "Both on those sallying forth, and on those left behind."

Darinor nodded. "Then a leap of faith it shall take."

"No," Rogun repeated. "What you suggest flies in the face of any convention of war known to man, and I won't allow it."

"In case you haven't noticed, General, we are not fighting a conventional enemy."

But Rogun was emphatic. "We build walls and cities for a reason. It is the same strategy by which our forefathers came to dominate these shores—and against many of the same creatures it would appear we must battle now."

"Yes," Darinor allowed. "But in the past, when one of your ancestors slew a troll or ogre or elf or goblin, that creature did not rise up to battle you again. And again. And again."

With that, the bickering began anew. Once more, Allion refrained from participating, choosing to think the matter through before he offered an opinion. Unfortunately, it seemed to boil down, as before, to a matter of trust. As some were shouting, if Darinor was wrong, then the soldiers risked coming home to find their wives and children and grandparents slaughtered. But, as others argued, if he was right, what choice did they have?

Through the jumble of loud voices and flailing bodies and gesturing limbs, Allion peered across the table at the grim figure standing at its far head. Just who was this Darinor? What motives might lie behind his latest scheme? Despite Marisha's pleas, Allion was not yet ready to trust the man. If he was as honorable as his daughter claimed, why send Torin off on such a foolhardy mission?

But try as he might, the regent could discern nothing of Darinor's thoughts by studying the man's visage. Only the eyes conveyed anything at all—a wealth of secrets that Allion meant to uncover.

As those eyes turned to him, Allion looked away. Without the swell of his fury, the mystic seemed less threatening than before, like an adder at rest. And yet his stripping gaze was still too terrible to face.

"And what does our regent say?" the renegade Entient asked.

The roar of voices died away, and all eyes shifted toward the reluctant Allion. He fought to meet those stares evenly, to conceal the trembling weakness he felt. Though he did not want this burden, he refused to crumble beneath its pressure.

It was Rogun, in a roundabout way, who came to his rescue.

"Who is he that we should take his advice in a matter of such critical importance?" the general challenged before Allion had opened his mouth. "This is a military issue. Since when does a woodsman know anything about war?"

Allion had heard this argument before. Only, this time he was grateful for it. Upon coming to Krynwall, his true desire had been to become a commander in the Legion of the Arrow, the city's legendary troop of archers. Decimated by the wizard's invasion, the legion had to be rebuilt almost from the ground up, a task to which Allion felt eminently suited. But Rogun would not allow it, decrying his lack of military experience—never mind his unrivaled skill with a bow. Rather than force the issue, Torin had made him captain of the City Shield, over which the king was the ultimate authority. For while the same might have been said of the army, Torin and Allion had agreed as a matter of appeasement not to tell Rogun his business.

"If I'm not mistaken, he is your acting ruler," Darinor snapped. "It is his vote that carries the greatest weight."

So much for dodging that arrow, Allion thought. In truth, part of him was glad to see Rogun put in his place. On this particular occasion, however, he'd have rather the general won.

Fortunately, the commander was not yet finished. "My plan is not only one of experience, but would seem now to be a fair alternative to the madness this one suggests." He glared at Thaddreus, as if knowing that were he to sway the First Elder, the other dissenters would fall into place. "Put it to a vote, if you must. But I demand to know where the Circle stands before I leave this room."

Thaddreus stroked at the arms of his moustache, which hung down over a pointed chin. A beam of sunlight from one of the room's vaulted windows lit the table before him and shone upon the braids of his silver mane. The light held for but a moment before a winter cloud stole it away.

"I for one would continue to argue against either action as reckless and rash"—the First Elder held up his hands to quiet the ensuing murmurs. "But it seems neither proponent is willing to allow for more prudent deliberation. If we *must* come to a conclusion now, without full understanding of the risks involved, then I shall file formal objection and surrender my vote to the king—or in his absence, the king's regent."

A few groused at this notion, or hollered outright protest. But little by little, the sentiment took hold. It was their way of ducking the responsibility, plain and simple, and of heaping any subsequent blame or consequences onto Allion's shoulders alone. Allion could see it happening, like the flames of a wildfire leaping out of control, but was powerless to stop it.

When he looked to the far end of the table, he found Rogun and Darinor standing side by side, staring at him expectantly.

A warm flush crept through his cheeks as he considered the choices—not the plans themselves, but the men who offered them. On the one hand, there was Rogun, a warmonger of the first order and an unforgiving adversary. On the other, there was Darinor, who, with his Illychar-infected wounds and the pallor that hung over him, appeared as if he might be the very enemy they were fighting. To which should he listen?

He wished he could defy them both. If his heart wasn't so heavy, his mind so full, perhaps he might formulate a more reasonable alternative. As it was, he felt as if the only choice he had was to select the manner of his own execution.

"This is useless," Rogun hissed in exasperation.

Allion ignored the man, shifting his focus squarely to Darinor, this descendant of a renegade Entient who claimed to be the keeper of this buried history. Should he, or should he not, put his faith in the man? If so, then he—like Torin—had little choice but to do as the other said, regardless of what Rogun or anyone else might think.

But why should he believe even half of what he'd been told? What proof had he that this petulant mystic was who and what he claimed to be? Again he stared into those smoldering blue eyes, seeking but a glimpse of the truth behind them, like searching shadows with a dying light.

And then it hit him, the unexpected memory of another from his recent past, another whose gruff mannerisms had belied a noble intent. It was the Entient Ranunculus who had carried the tome that would start them on their quest for the Sword, and later had guided them to the secret stronghold of Whitlock, where they had learned how they might overcome the dragonspawn of Killangrathor. That man, also, had possessed an irascible, almost threatening nature, acting on the will of his peers and against his own better judgment. But had it not been for his help, the Illysp would now be fighting the Demon Queen rather than mankind for dominion over these lands.

A cruel irony, actually. For if Torin had not reclaimed the Crimson Sword, none of them would be alive today, save as slaves to Spithaera and her minions. And yet, what had he truly won them? Instead of dying at the hands of the Demon Queen, they would now be consumed by the Illysp, an enemy from which not even the grave would grant relief. Torin's actions had delivered them from one scourge, only to serve them up to another. So was he a champion of mankind, or a harvester of doom?

Allion brushed the wayward thought aside. All that mattered was the present, in which they still had a fighting chance. At least Torin had given them that much.

"I cannot speak for King Thelin or King Galdric," he said slowly. He addressed Darinor, but his voice echoed in the grim silence of the room. "We would have to send forth emissaries to advise them of your plan."

"Then do so at once," Darinor commanded. Allion searched the other's face for a hint of triumph at the apparent choice, but the grave mask he wore may as well have been chiseled from stone.

Rogun, on the other hand, was incensed. Without another word, he removed his fists from the table and stormed toward the exit, spurs rattling like the horned tail of a sistrum viper. As the doors slammed shut behind him, the arguments started up once more.

"Silence!" Darinor shouted, robes billowing in a windless air. "I'll say it once more. You must put aside your petty differences—among one another, and among your neighbors on these shores—if you are to combat this enemy. For I assure you, it will smother all without any such discrimination."

"We've tried this before," Allion noted, thinking back to their previous attempt to unite the kingdoms of Pentania under a single banner. "It will not be easy."

"Nor will surviving this threat. The more time we waste with words, the more difficult it becomes."

Many of the Elders wore sullen faces, like children denied, but none seemed prepared to dispute the mystic outright.

"Do as I tell you now," he urged in final rebuke, "or regret it later."

His glare swept aside all challenges before piercing Allion to the core, as if to pin ultimate accountability on him. Turning his back on any further protests, he then slipped like a dark cloud from the room.

No sooner had he gone than Allion slumped in his high-backed chair, caught between waves of relief and defeat while the Circle's grumbling filled his ears like an ocean's dull roar.

CHAPTER TWELVE

A STEADY DRIP FROM THE CEILING hammered against the top of Torin's skull. At first, it hadn't troubled him, but after he'd been alone in the darkness for several hours, it had become like a spike being slowly driven into his brain.

There was no escaping it, lashed as he was—even at the neck—to an upright beam in the tiny storeroom. He'd caught only glimpses of his prison while his captors hauled him down and roped him in place. Then the hatch was closed. There were no windows, no light, leaving him in damp, inky blackness.

They posted no guard, and so he had wriggled at his bonds for awhile, thinking to wrench free. But if there was one thing sailors knew best, it was their knots. The more he pulled, the more his bindings seemed to tighten. As their bite deepened, he surrendered his struggle.

After that, darkness and solitude laid claim. A coppery taste filled his mouth, from the cuts sustained during his beating. His entire body throbbed and stung, as bruises formed and lacerations filled with sweat and pitch. The nets used to capture him were gone, but the sticky coating remained. Its scent dominated a potpourri of damp wood, of must and mold, of the ever-present brine of the sea.

In his blindness, he listened to the thunder of rain on the decking above, and to the trample of men hustling to and fro. He could hear their shouts, but could not make out the words. The walls of his hold creaked like an old wagon wheel over rocky terrain. The nail in his head drove deeper.

He wished they had left him the Pendant at least. With it, he would have been able to better tolerate the aches and pains. Alas, if there was one thing *pirates* knew best, it was how to loot their victims.

But his own ignorance troubled him most, more than his physical condition. Why the pirates had abducted him remained a mystery, as did their reasons for keeping him alive. The only thing clear to him was that he had lost his friends, his freedom, and any hope of accomplishing his mission, all in one fell swoop.

A cunning adversary, this team of seafaring brigands, with their skills of illusion and the manner in which they had lured the *Pirate's Folly* to her fate. He might even have been impressed, had he not been on the receiving end of it. Instead, all he could think of were his slain comrades—Ashwin and Cordan and Arn—whose deaths resonated with every drop of rain. Even without understanding how, or why, he knew the blame for their sacrifice was his to bear.

He never should have boarded Jorkin's ship. He should have turned around when he'd had the chance. As usual, he had made the wrong choice, and now there was no going back.

He wondered idly if the merchant captain might chance an attempt to rescue him. Not likely, he conceded. The *Folly* and her crew had suffered enough at his expense already.

These thoughts circled like vultures in his mind, winging around again and again, waiting to finish him. But just when he thought they might settle, another raindrop would strike his skull, and they would scatter once more. Over and over, until he was certain he'd gone mad.

Finally, after what seemed like days though was probably no more than hours, there was a scrabbling sound and the hatch to his prison lifted. The muted drum of rain and voices sharpened. Gray dusk poured through on the shoulders of a gusting wind, which whistled through the crack. The light of a flame followed. Torin squinted as its yellow glare pushed back the darkness, accompanied by the thud of booted feet. He heard a mutter of instructions to someone stationed above, then the hatch slammed shut.

The footsteps continued, heavy on the stairs, then across the warped flooring. Torin blinked slowly, painfully, until his eyes had adjusted enough to force them open. A lantern bobbed into view, illuminating the stark face of the pirate captain, whose tarred hair hung thick about his face and shoulders. He stood there dripping for a moment, then shook himself, hurling beads of water in every direction.

"Vicious storm brewing up there."

Torin ignored the comment, uncertain he could respond had he wanted to. The cold had numbed his aches, but had left him shivering, and he strained instinctively toward the meager warmth of the pirate's lantern. Its weak light revealed the shape and contents of a leaky storage hold, stuffed with ropes and barrels and all manner of nautical equipment.

"Your name is Torin, is it not?"

Despite everything, Torin's brow lifted in surprise.

"Things will go better for you if you answer my questions," the other added, producing a long, ivory-handled dagger.

Torin scowled. When he tried to respond, he found it difficult. His wind was impeded by the cords around his chest and neck. His lips were cracked, his tongue like a cured strip of rawhide. The first few attempts caught in his throat.

"What is it you want from me?" he managed finally.

The pirate was silent for a moment, his beady eyes and his grim face contemplative. "Someone wants you dead."

Torin was too confused and too angry to show alarm. His best guess as to why the pirates had nabbed him and no other was for the Sword—which didn't explain why they hadn't killed him, since the blade was already theirs.

Likely, they suspected the weapon held a power that only he could teach them. Or else they wanted to know more of where and how he had come upon such a treasure.

But this now suggested something else, not an accidental encounter, but a manhunt commissioned by yet another, outside party.

"Whatever this person has offered," Torin croaked, "I will pay you that and more."

The pirate sneered. "I'm not interested in your money, any more than I'm interested in his."

"Then why not let me go?" The leak in the roof persisted, faster now, as the roar of rainfall above grew louder.

"As I said, someone wants you dead. To start with, I want to know why."

"It might help if I knew who this person was."

"Are there so many people with cause to kill you?"

Torin seized the offensive. "Those who have dared present themselves as enemies are vanquished. The rest hide in shadows, too afraid to make themselves known."

It was a bold statement, and not entirely true. From the other's perspective, Torin realized, he must have sounded ridiculous.

"And how many of these foes practice magic?"

Soric. The name rose like bile in Torin's throat, warm and nauseating. It had to be. The use of magic was a forsaken art. Those who practiced it today did so in dark corners, feared and reviled—and in regions governed by law, under threat of arrest. Even in these few rumored cases, the power in question was often of a simple, benign nature, little more than the tricks and illusions practiced by court entertainers and street magicians. All other forms had long ago been set aside or stamped out.

Then the wizard had come along, with a command of natural energies not seen in ages. It was his conquest that had led to the revelation of Torin's true identity, and ultimately his quest for the Sword. Later, he had learned the wizard to be none other than Soric, the elder brother he had never known, returned from more than two decades of banishment to lay claim to the throne. Where and how the man had uncovered such arcane knowledge remained a mystery, as did his whereabouts. For when the Demon Queen had usurped Soric's conquest with her own, only to be defeated, the wizard had scurried away like a roach into the night.

Torin had known all along that he hadn't seen the end of his brother. But he had never imagined this.

"Judging by your silence, and the pallor of your face, you know who I'm referring to."

Torin blinked at the pirate captain, unable to respond.

"A ruthless man, is he not?"

The accusation sounded strange, coming from a man such as this. Nevertheless, Torin grunted, after a failed attempt to nod.

"And tell me, what is his grievance with you?"

Torin's gaze fell. Where to begin? He only scarcely understood the enmity his brother bore him. And he certainly was in no condition to relay his entire story to the cutthroat before him; nor was he inclined to do so. Still, it appeared he must say something.

"The man laid siege to my nation, the kingdom of Alson on the island of Pentania. Doubtless, he holds me responsible for his defeat."

"I've heard of the land, though I've never visited it. And you are?"

Torin frowned in confusion. "I thought you already knew."

"I know your name, your point of departure, and the route along which your vessel was headed. I was given a description of both you and the flaming weapon wielded against my crew."

Torin gritted his teeth at the memory of the battle and their ignominious failure. Once again, he heard the slap of Cordan's body being cast to the waves.

"I know nothing else," the pirate continued. "One of the many reasons for which I refused to become involved."

"Yet here you are," Torin spat, "doing a madman's bidding."

"Here I am," the captain corrected, "trying to rescue the woman I love."

Of all the surprises he had endured so far, this was the greatest. For a moment, Torin stared blankly. When his wits returned, he studied the ruffian's features, looking to unravel this absurd riddle. At first, the pirate appeared as shocked as Torin by his own admission. Then, as if to prove he was unashamed, he went on to explain.

"Hard to believe, no? Harder if you knew anything about me. Red Raven, they call me—and not for my windburned cheeks. For nearly ten years, my ship, the *Raven's Squall*, has hunted the seas of Yawacor, living a life of opportunity. I've sent ships like yours to the bottom of the ocean, and for no better reason than to fill my own coffers. My mates and I have killed men, women, and children, in numbers I dare not recount."

He glanced down to his dagger, which he spun on its tip, pointed into the crate on which he sat.

"But that was before I met Autumn of the Rain. Only months ago, following the sinking of a merchant vessel, a fell wind blew us westward. We drifted into a cove on the northern coast, where we happened upon a castaway from that very same vessel. She convinced one of my men to take her aboard. Almost immediately, she went from being my prisoner to my companion. We have sailed together since."

"Let me guess," Torin scoffed. "In her arms, you've sworn to become a new man, to settle down and atone for your past."

Raven's eyes narrowed sharply. "Bilge rot. I've done only what was necessary to survive. I make no apologies for the life I've led. Nor has Autumn asked it of me." His eyes lowered again, and his voice quieted. "But while she has done nothing to discourage my pirating, I find myself losing my taste for it. Her mere presence has turned my thoughts for the first time toward a life of peace."

Had speaking not required such effort, Torin might have declared his skepticism. Instead, he kept his suspicions to himself, waiting to hear what more the pirate might reveal.

"We were in port for the winter when your wizard's man came calling—Madrach, a man I know, and my first clue that this was something in which I wished to have no part. He bade me to an isle he called Shattercove to meet with his master, with an overview of what would be expected. A kidnapping, he said, worth a year's supply of plunder. Though I've committed worse for less, I refused. Nothing that man could offer was going to pry me from my season's den."

The dagger stopped spinning, its ivory handle clutched now in a savage grip. Its owner's eyes found Torin's and, in the flickering lamplight, seemed to flash with dangerous fury.

"To persuade me, his mercenaries paid Autumn a visit. By the time I reached our cottage, she was gone. How they found her, I know not. When I discover who it was betrayed me, I shall see him boiled and the flesh peeled from his bones. All that remained was a note from Madrach. He had taken Autumn hostage, to be ransomed in exchange for the one his master sought.

"So I gathered my crew and followed Madrach to this Shattercove, where I met with the wizard who calls it home. There I learned of the ship you were sailing, and the course along which it could be found. I was given your description, and told you served as a swordhand. I was to deliver you alive, should I wish Autumn to be returned the same. Thus, here I am."

Torin started to shake his head, but stopped as the coarse ropes chafed his skin. "How could he have known where to find me?"

"One of many questions I'd thought to ask you," Raven admitted. "The wizard declined to tell me; nor was it the heaviest of my concerns. Sorcery, perhaps."

That answer did not begin to satisfy Torin, but he brushed it aside in order to ask a more pertinent one. "Why are you telling me this? You've all but completed your task. Why not deliver me in irons and be done with it?"

The other fixed him with a discerning eye. "Because I know better than to trust this wizard to comply. More likely, he will kill me—and Autumn—the moment he has what he wants."

"And what cause have you to believe that?" Torin snorted dryly.

"Because that's what I would do."

Torin swallowed thickly. Clearly, the pirate was unwilling to make light of the situation. Perhaps there was something to all of this lost-love nonsense after all.

"Are you saying you don't intend to turn me over?"

"I'm saying that this wizard picked the wrong pirate. I did not become one of the most feared men on the high seas by allowing others to get the better of me. I'm saying I would much prefer to punish the man for his insolence, and that your interests might best be served by helping me."

"Helping you?"

"Though he demanded you be delivered alive, it seemed clear the creature does not intend to long keep you that way."

"I would think not," Torin agreed. "But I'm not sure how it is you imagine I might be of assistance."

"I've visited the wizard's isle," Raven reminded him. "I know something of its perils. Alone, I do not believe they can be overcome."

"What of your own magic?"

The pirate raised a puzzled eyebrow.

"When you attacked my vessel," Torin replied with renewed bitterness, "there appeared two phantom ships, in addition to your own. Was that not magic?"

Raven smirked, but waved dismissively. "Illusion, as you saw. A minor contrivance. Nothing that would hold sway against the powers I saw your wizard to possess."

"And what makes you think I have any?"

"He is your adversary. And a vanquished one at that, to hear you tell it. There must be something you can share with me, some knowledge I can put to use."

So that was the purpose behind this meeting, Torin realized. The ruffian sought to gauge him as a potential ally, to use him against Soric in whatever manner might befit his own designs.

"And if I refuse?"

"Then I take my chances, and leave you to the wizard's mercies."

"You killed my friends."

"As you killed mine. Unless you wish to join them, I suggest we put that behind us and do what we can to aid each other."

Torin considered his limited options. He would deny the pirate if he could, but as he'd already recognized, there was no going back. The best he could do was press onward and see where matters took him.

"All I want is to rescue Autumn and offer her a life of contentment," Raven continued. "Some might say I'm reaping the seeds of my own villainy, but I won't accept that. You can either benefit from what I mean to accomplish, or fall victim to it."

Torin studied the man anew. His professed goals were easy enough to relate to. And despite a lingering skepticism, it was hard not to be won over by the other's scathing honesty.

"I assure you I have every reason to hate this wizard," he replied at last. "My mother, my father, and countless friends lie dead at his hands. Unfortunately, I know nothing that might aid you. The wizard fled my lands as a matter of circumstance. I wouldn't begin to know how you might face him."

Raven considered this with a dubious expression. "Can you at least tell me who he is? Why he's so desperate to claim you?"

"He—" It was Torin's turn to hesitate. He hadn't told anyone, not even Marisha, the truth about the wizard's identity. As far as he was aware, no one knew of their blood tie, and he preferred to keep it that way.

"As I said," he began again, clearing his throat. "He blames me for usurping his throne, for I am Alson's recognized king."

The pirate skewered him with that beady gaze, as if detecting the omitted falsehood. "That sword of yours. Has it no power that might be used against him?"

"It is the last Sword of Asahiel," Torin confessed, seeing no reason to deny it. "Are you familiar with the legends?"

"None that I would believe. The wizard warned me to beware its strength, lest you single-handedly decimate my crew. I didn't believe that, either, though I'm glad I made preparations to the contrary."

He was speaking of the nets, Torin realized, designed especially for his capture. "The Sword may grant you some protection against the wizard's magic," he allowed. "My pendant as well, assuming your men handed it over to you." He paused, seeking some sign of confirmation. The pirate captain didn't blink. "But as I say, I've never confronted him directly, so I cannot promise how much use either may be. What I *can* promise, should you set me free, is to do what I can to secure Autumn's release."

Raven shook his dripping head. "I had not intended on storming his keep. From what I've seen, he might dash us against a reef before we come within a league of his isle, should he suspect such an attack."

"Then what do you offer me, if not my freedom?"

"Your freedom comes later, when the wizard is dead. What I must know now, if nothing else, is whether or not I can count on your support when the time comes."

In spite of the circumstances, Torin snickered, which in turn caused him to cough and choke against the suffocating ropes. "You offer precious little inducement," he rasped, once he had recovered. "Do you mean to tell me nothing of your plan? Only that I am to trust blindly in the word of a brigand?"

"The lesser of two evils, am I not? Think of me as you will, but in this matter, we both want the same thing."

Torin's smile faded. "Then how about this? You say the wizard informed you of my destination. What he may or may not know is that I did not set forth for this foreign land in the dead of winter in search of salt air. I don't care to explain to you my business, and doubt you'd care to hear it. Suffice to say, your future, and that of your precious maiden, may be short indeed if I do not succeed in what it is I've come to do."

The ruffian regarded him evenly, unimpressed. "What would you have of me?"

"When this is over, if any of us are still alive, you will give me back my possessions and return me to my ship, that I may resume my journey as before."

Raven hefted his dagger, eyeing its gleaming edge in the murky light. "Seems to me, you are not in any position to set the terms of our bargain."

"I will have your oath, such as it is," Torin demanded. "On Autumn's life, if I am to aid you, you will find me a way back to my companions."

"On Autumn's life," the pirate agreed finally, "if you are to aid me, *and* see to it that Autumn is returned to me unharmed, then I will deliver you to Yawacor myself—at any landing you desire."

Torin considered the careful phrasing, turning the words over in his mind in search of any hidden meaning or loopholes.

"Fair enough?" Raven pressed.

Torin continued to ponder. "Fair enough."

"Good," the pirate said, sheathing his dagger with a sharp rasp. He turned then, snatched up his lantern, and headed for the hatch.

As he reached the base of the steps leading upward into the storm, he paused and looked back. "But understand," he said, "king or no, if it means Autumn's life—or my own—I will gladly slit your throat myself."

Before Torin could respond, the hatch opened and closed, and he was abandoned yet again to leaking darkness, in which the rhythm of raindrops etched away at his aching skull.

CHAPTER THIRTEEN

*T*HE OLD MAN SHUFFLED as quickly as his ancient bones would carry him down the rough-hewn corridor. At this depth within the buried keep, only the floor was paved, and unevenly at that. Jagged walls curled up along either side, joined in a ceiling supported by arching ribs of iron at regular intervals. Beyond that, the weight of the mountain bore down on him like the stones of a cairn.

He carried no torch, nor did any burn along the walls. Rather, he made his way by tuning his vision to the spectrum of the shadow-earth. Veins of minerals glowed blue before his sapphire eyes, casting all the light he needed to navigate the rocky tunnel. His sandals scraped along the rugged flooring, a rasping echo in the otherwise oppressive silence.

But it was the burden he carried that oppressed him most—and paradoxically forced his pace. He had lived for nearly three centuries, a time during which he had witnessed wars and treaties, seen bloodlines come and go, observed the erosion of the land and the buckling of nations. Consequently, few events in the natural order of things gave him cause for alarm.

This did.

Perhaps because this particular chain was not entirely nature-formed. It had begun that way, its initial links forged by the curiosity of two children— Garett and Elwonyssa Culmaril, of the ruling family of Souaris—whose intrepid explorations had led into the dank lair of a demon avatar and given her new life. But he could have prevented it, he and those of his order. He could have persuaded the youngsters by any number of subtle means to turn down a different path, to carry their journeys elsewhere so that Spithaera—whose secret presence the Entients had long ago discovered—might continue slumbering undisturbed, of no threat to the races of man.

He had argued that very course all along. But his brethren, especially Maventhrowe, had sensed an opportunity, and convinced the others of it. That opportunity was twofold: to present a quarrelsome mankind with a common enemy that would compel them to unite, and to give one man of faith desperate cause to seek out the last known Sword of Asahiel—whereby their order might at long last shed light on a missing chapter in the history of this land.

The plan had worked only too well. Despite a plethora of unforeseen incidents, the young Torin had retrieved the Sword from its centuries-old resting place and put an abrupt end to Spithaera's conquest. However, as was always the danger when going beyond the study of man's affairs to active involvement, they had unwittingly helped to unleash an even greater menace. Htomah had learned all about it when scrying upon Torin during the king's meetings with the renegade Entient who called himself Darinor. Darinor was correct in his assumptions concerning the Entients' fragmented knowledge of the history of these lands. It had been fascinating to hear how this blot of ig-norance had come about—among those who for millennia had chronicled so much. At the same time, the truth had filled him with an unease that bordered on dread.

If only he could convince his brethren to share his sense of urgency. He should have gone to them right away when first he had scryed the creatures known as Illychar emerging from the well beneath the Sword. But he had not understood at that time the extent of their peril, and had feared to cry wolf. Instead, he had continued to keep watch as much as he could, night and day, waiting for the right moment in which to share his fears.

He had missed seeing Darinor's fight with the Illychar within the ruins, and the renegade Entient's narrow escape. But that only made sense now that he knew the truth about the man, having heard it while scrying upon Torin during the pair's conversations. For while a fellow avatar was generally the easiest form of life on which to focus his third sight, they also had the ability to cloud themselves from view. Why Darinor would do such a thing had at first aroused in him a deep suspicion, but once he had heard the other's account of willing exile, the curtains of isolation were easy enough to understand.

It was then, of course, that Htomah had hastened to meet with his breth-ren and tell all of what he had learned. Like Torin, he had no cause to dis-believe the tale Darinor shared. Nor could they afford to stand idly by if it were true. This catastrophe was their fault—in part, at least. They had to take action at once.

He might have received greater reaction had he addressed a wall of moun-tain stone. As usual, where he saw fire, the others barely smelled smoke. Ma-venthrowe, their leader, was the worst. Though the average life of an Entient spanned three or four centuries, Maventhrowe had lived already more than five. Too long, perhaps. For such years taught patience of an uncommon va-riety, filling one with an assuredness that while the earth and its inhabitants might crumble away, he would go on. When older than the founding of the first human city on these shores, one tended to lose sight of the potential sig-nificance of daily events.

Or maybe the others were right, the old man thought as he continued down the empty corridor. Maybe it was *he* who lacked perspective. Maybe he did just enjoy the seeds of excitement blown on the winds of calamity. It was entirely possible, he admitted privately, that he was making canyons of wallows.

The air in the tunnel thickened, growing warm and damp. Its wetness gleamed on the rough surface of the granite walls. Moments later, he reached what ap-peared to be a dead end, with the cave closing about a portal of solid stone.

Almost without stopping, he waved a hand before the marble slab. The barrier shimmered and disappeared, and he stepped through it as if it were smoke.

Across the threshold, a vast cavern was revealed, filled with ledges and outcroppings whose many tiers were connected by winding stairs chiseled from stone. Earth-warmed mineral pools dotted the many shelves and spilled over the ridgelines, forming a dazzling array of falls. Steam rose in curtains from each of the bubbling hot springs, filling the great underground chamber with a sultry mist.

"Ah, welcome, Htomah. You are late."

Htomah scowled in the direction of the voice. Though it was nearly swallowed by the immensity of the cavern, he knew where to find it. Several of the pools were occupied, filled with the bodies of his brethren, who came here often to bathe and relax, to revitalize tender muscles and aching joints. Many of the Entients had their favorites among the springs, and Maventhrowe was no exception. He had long ago laid unofficial claim to the largest in the complex, a bean-shaped pond up two levels and only slightly right of center, directly beneath the shadow of a giant amethyst that jutted from the ceiling above. The pool was of a size to hold twenty men or more, but seldom did it host even half that.

On rare occasion, Maventhrowe held council here with his inner circle, those Entients who served as representatives of the order. Today was such a time. In addition to the unmistakable white mane of the head Entient, Htomah spotted the bald pates of Barwn and Sovenson, the hunched shoulders of Uthan and Alganov, the toothy grin of Quinlan, the necklace worn by Prather, the earrings of Oreshand, the tattoos of Merreseth, and the peppered beard and chiseled frown of Ranunculus.

Htomah stalked toward them, taking his time so as to catch his breath. Beads of sweat cut across the furrows of his brow and the lines of his cheeks, to catch in the coarse grass of his beard. His nose wrinkled in the sulfurous air.

"Where are the others?" he huffed, once he had reached the side of the pool.

"Wislome is trying to cage a rather nasty craggobite, and Jedua is working to plug a breach in the primary celestial chamber." Maventhrowe beckoned with a dripping hand. "Please, join us."

Htomah crossed his arms before him. "He has been captured."

"Who?"

"Torin. By pirates, a week out from his destination."

"Htomah, please—"

"They deliver him now to his brother the wizard."

Maventhrowe's next words were lost to the same silence that stilled the others. For a moment, all that could be heard was the bubbling of the waters and the rippling of others in their distant pools. Htomah gritted his teeth to hide his satisfaction. At last, he had their attention.

"And what would you have us do about that?"

"I fear it's too late already," Htomah complained. "I see not how Torin can escape his brother's vengeance, unless we conjure a storm to blow his ship off course—which would but leave him in the hands of brigands."

"Now, now," Maventhrowe droned with intractable calm. "I do not think we need do anything so dramatic."

"We need not do anything at all," said Uthan. "Come, Htomah, we have been over and over this."

"And yet done nothing!" Htomah snapped, glaring at the other.

"Htomah, soak with us," Maventhrowe urged. "Your emotions carry off with you."

"How can all of you be so blind?"

"Maventhrowe," Ranunculus grumbled, "must we listen to this?"

The head Entient raised his hands in a placating gesture. "Please, everyone, have patience. Let us hear what our senior brother has to say."

Indeed, Htomah thought. For other than Maventhrowe, he was eldest among those present. Even in some of the most barbarous societies, that meant he should be accorded some respect.

"I say again," he began, glaring at Uthan, "the time for action is long past. Whether any here will admit it or not, we are the ones who prompted Torin to seek the Sword of Asahiel in the first place—"

"Not I," Ranunculus snarled. "I was against this from the first."

"As was I," Htomah reminded him. "And Merreseth, as I recall. And the absent Jedua. But that does not erase the part we all played. The responsibility for Torin's retrieval of the Sword and this ensuing madness must be ours to share."

Oreshand's earrings jingled as he shook his head. "Torin's actions were and continue to be his own. I will accept no blame for them."

"Nor I," agreed Prather.

A murmur went up as each of the others echoed this sentiment. Only Quinlan remained silent, his smile slipping. And Maventhrowe, who, as always, sat back with an air of mild amusement, as if none of this were of any concern.

"Our influence was minimal," Alganov claimed. "You cannot possibly hold us accountable."

"For the decision you make now, which may lead to the end of mankind, I most certainly will."

The murmurs grew louder. Many scoffed. Some were angry. All appealed to Maventhrowe to end this.

"My friend," the head Entient cautioned, "we must not make a habit of affecting the lives of those we were born to study."

"Not even to rectify that which we have already affected for the worse?"

"Our purpose is to observe and chronicle, not dictate."

"They are only mortals," Ranunculus muttered.

Htomah snorted. "Darinor was right. We are not Ha'Rasha. We may expect to outlive these mortals, but we share their world, and will in fact, each of us, come to our own end. I fear that if we ignore this blight any longer, our end, and that of our human flock, may be one and the same."

"Then I ask again," Maventhrowe offered calmly, "what role would you have us take?"

"That is what we must discuss."

But Maventhrowe shook his head, the ends of his great mane floating in the waters around him. "The truth is, we have no knowledge with which to combat this threat. Though there may come a time when we must act, we must not do so in haste."

"Haste? Haste would have been for me to take measures the moment I learned of what Torin had set free. Or upon the return of this renegade Entient. Long before Ravar's awakening and certainly before Torin's capture. Already, any action we take may be too late.

"And do not speak to me again of forbearance," he added hastily, heading off Uthan's next protest. "Had we done so in the beginning, as I and others insisted, none of this would have happened."

Uthan smirked. "I was only going to remind everyone that Torin has surprised us with his resourcefulness in the past. I say we let him do so again."

Several of the council members softly hailed their assent.

"You may be right," Maventhrowe conceded, "in suggesting we were wrong in our prior endeavors. I will not be so foolish as to defend a decision born of foresight against an attack based on hindsight. I might argue, however, that we would have come to this crossroads sooner or later. Knowledge is preferable to ignorance, is it not? We have uncovered an unexpected danger, but at least now we realize it exists, and will not, therefore, be caught off guard. I encourage you to observe these matters closely, since they trouble you so, and to keep us abreast of the situation. Should cause and opportunity coincide, we shall decide then if action on our part is warranted."

"That is not good enough," Htomah growled.

Maventhrowe raised a bushy eyebrow. "No? Remember, according to the tale this Darinor tells, our forebears did not act when begged by the ancient Finlorians to do so. And yet, here we are. We survived, as did the Finlorians, who managed to contain the threat on their own."

"Only with the help of Algorath," Htomah pointed out.

"I submit," Maventhrowe continued, "that we not so readily accuse our ancestors of blindness. Rather, we should respect them enough to trust that they acted in wisdom, and that we, therefore, should be slow to overrule their decision—which is what it would mean for us to behave now in a contrary fashion."

Htomah held his tongue, considering carefully what his response should be. His brethren already thought him an overanxious fool. No reason to lend additional weight to those accusations.

"I would like to know more," Maventhrowe assured him. "Especially with regard to this Darinor."

Htomah grunted. "He continues to shield himself from scrying eyes. I can mark his comings and goings only in the presence of another."

"Then so it shall be. Do your best, and it shall be more than we require.

Now please, join our council. Let us engage your mind with less-worrisome matters."

"If it pleases you, my brothers, I think I shall return to see if the Sword of Asahiel has yet fallen into the clutches of the wizard Soric." He bowed, then turned toward the chamber exit.

"Htomah."

The retreating Entient paused.

"Lest you be tempted to follow in the footsteps of Algorath and defy your brethren, know that you will share his fate."

Htomah cocked his head. Despite his frustration, he could not help but be surprised, for never had Maventhrowe spoken so sternly to him. "Meaning what, precisely?"

"Unless those here disagree, you are hereby forbidden any unauthorized human contact. Should you choose to intervene on your own, you will be stricken from the order."

The head Entient glanced around, seeking the concurrence of the others, and received it in their gruff nods.

"Such as it is," Htomah groused.

Maventhrowe smiled that benevolent smile. "Such as it is."

"I have been warned," Htomah acknowledged, then exited the cavern, sealing the portal behind him.

As he left the sweltering air behind for the relative cool of the outer tunnel, a terrible weariness overcame him. For nigh upon three hundred years had he dedicated himself to his calling—a charge handed down to his progenitors by the Ceilhigh themselves. He had done so with faith and diligence, never once questioning what his role as servant to the gods should be. He cared not for vain glories; not for recognition or prestige. He sought only to do the work asked of him, to carry on the legacy of those who had come before, to play his part and no other in the unfathomable scheme of the great creators.

Now, as he dragged back down the stale corridor toward the upper levels of the keep, he found himself wondering which was more important: his divinely inspired studies, or the endangered welfare of his earthly flock.

CHAPTER FOURTEEN

With the colored sands burning in his nostrils, Soric inhaled deeply of the winds that blew through his tower window. The potent mixture worked swiftly, clearing his upper passages and heightening the sensory vessels within. He closed his eyes, focusing his thoughts. There, beyond the leather and stone and dust of his chambers, beyond the salted sea, he found what he was looking for: the mildew of sails, the pitch of watertight timbers, the oil and sweat of men.

"Seems our Madrach chose well," the wizard said. He opened his eyes and turned to his captive. "Your champion draws nigh."

She sat upon a pile of cushions, chained to a corner of the castle wall, farthest from the window before which he stood.

"And does he carry what you seek?" the woman asked.

"We shall know soon enough. Let us hope so, my flower, lest your delicate beauty be made to wilt before his eyes."

As always, his threat had no apparent effect on her. But then, that was what drew him to her, the key to her mysterious charm—the principal reason for which he had moved her here, to his tower, from where Madrach had stashed her in the dungeons below. Autumn of the Rain, she called herself. She professed to be a common girl, the daughter of a shipwright recently slain. And yet she possessed uncommon courage, an air of unflappable confidence that did far more to attract him than did the shimmer of her hair, the color of her eyes, the softness of her skin. Soric was not easily enchanted, but this pirate's concubine mesmerized him in strange and wondrous ways. A fortnight had she been his prisoner, yet there were moments when he wondered who the true captor was.

He banished his predatory smile and turned back to his window. Time enough for that later. For now, he had far more immediate concerns. His brother, delivered unto him at last. The very notion caused him to shiver with anticipation. Nearly four moons had come and gone since the fall of Spithaera and his withdrawal from the lands of his birth, but those months felt more like years. Like decades, even—longer than those he had spent marooned here before, alone upon this isle, following the wreck of the ship that had carried him forth into a life of slavery. For this time it was not his parents who had sent him away, but a young upstart, a whelp of a brother whose only authority was that of a stolen crown—*his* crown—wrested not by strength but by cruel chance, and given to another less worthy.

As before, he meant to have his revenge.

Further maddening was that he had been compelled to retreat, to leave behind all that after years of planning he had finally achieved. His adversary hid behind an army, while his own had been stripped from him by Spithaera—an obligatory barter in order to spare his life from the wrath and hunger of the demon avatar. Even so, following the rout of her dragonborn at Souaris, he might have ambushed Torin at Krynwall, waiting for his brother to stake his false claim before striking him down in that very moment. But death, Soric had decided, was not enough. Not after the agonies and indignities he had endured, both before and after he had learned of Torin's birth. No, he meant for his brother to suffer, to experience a touch of the despair and loneliness he himself had suffered, to teach the last of his kin—those who had cheated him throughout his life—the true measure of pain.

It was for this reason he had elected the path of patience, leaving Xarius Talyzar and a private network of spies behind. Not to assassinate the lad, but to keep a close watch on his movements, to seek a window of opportunity, the chance to snatch him from his nest of pilfered comforts and to bring him to the wizard's den—here, where Soric could exact upon him the fate he deserved.

"What will you do to this man," Autumn asked, "should Raven deliver him to you?"

Soric grinned. The woman spoke as if he had been uttering his thoughts aloud.

"A fate most befitting," he assured her, as he set aside the mortar and pestle in which he had mixed his scent-enhancing powder. Already, its effects were beginning to fade. "One that will ensure he will not trouble me again."

"And will that somehow comfort your own pain?"

Her melodic voice sounded out of place within the constricting confines of his quarters, like a songbird in a rusty cage. Her words, however, brought his blood to a boil.

"What know you of my pain?" he demanded. He did not face her, but continued to stare out the open window, his hands white as they gripped the edge of his worktable.

"Only that you seek to allay it. But inflicting pain on others is no way to heal one's own."

Soric just barely smothered a laugh. His pain was what fueled him, his hatred what gave him strength. This was not about healing, but retribution.

"I will have what's mine, what has been taken from me."

"What has been taken is lost," she said. "Yet you stand to lose even more, should you continue on this path of vengeance."

He turned to face her. "I suppose you would have us become friends, allies, like you and he who sent your father and shipmates to a watery grave."

"It is not too late," she agreed. "Put aside your bitter past. Look instead to paving your future."

Again the wizard smiled cruelly. "With every breath I take."

He continued to stare, fascinated by her unblinking gaze, as a violent rapping caused his chamber door to shudder. With a gesture, he threw back the locking bolt from a dozen paces away.

"Come."

The portal opened, and Madrach entered, short of breath. He stopped upon the threshold, where he quickly removed his helm and bowed low. "My lord, the *Raven's Squall* approaches."

"Excellent news, Captain," Soric acknowledged, smiling still at Autumn. "Assemble the guard. We'll greet them in the courtyard. Take our prisoner with you, but see to it that she remains unharmed. Am I understood?"

Madrach saluted. "Understood, my lord. Will you be joining us, my lord?"

"Once I have seen to their landing. Go."

"Aye, my lord."

The wizard moved back to his window, listening to the clank and rattle of chains as Madrach produced a key and unlocked the iron wall clasp to which Autumn had been anchored. From the woman herself, he detected not a hint of loathing or struggle.

As they left the room, however, her voice sang out once more, echoing an old refrain. "It is not too late."

Soric ignored her, waiting for Madrach to close the door before throwing the bolt back in place. Upon its dull slap, he peered into the gray mix of cloud and sky, searching the horizon for the vessel carrying his brother. He spied it straightaway, a black speck in the afternoon gloom, like a flea on the pelt of an old hound. He imagined what Torin might be feeling—the desperation, the terror. That thought, along with Autumn's parting words, brought a fresh smirk to his taut lips.

For you, my brother, it is.

TORIN CLENCHED HIS EYES AGAINST THE SUN'S HARSH GLARE. Though it was swathed in misty cloud cover, its brightness was more than he could bear. He tried to recoil, leaning back and raising his arms—bound before him—as a shield. But his escorts shoved him forward without mercy, up the wooden stair, through the hatch, and into the light.

It had been five days since he'd felt the brush of daylight, five miserable, wet, chill-wracked days since his arrest on the high seas. For the duration of his journey aboard the *Raven's Squall*, his jailors had kept him locked away within that dank storage hold. He hadn't seen the captain, Red Raven, since his interrogation on the evening of his capture. The only allowances had been food and drink—though he could barely call them that—and a loosening of his bonds. That, and he had been moved to a different corner, so as to be spared the torturous drip of leaking water. All in all, the rats—some of whom had kept him company—had had it better.

That he was being brought above deck was hardly cause for relief. Not only did he have the sun to contend with, but he hadn't moved, and had scarcely slept, in nearly a week. His joints were stiff, his muscles seized by cramps, and he had lost the sense of balance with which to stand on his own. Moreover, being sprung meant something had happened, or was about to—and most likely *not* something to anticipate.

Half blind, he stumbled across the unfamiliar planking, dragged from the front and prodded from behind. As his eyes adjusted, he took note of his surroundings. Men in smelly rags hustled about their business. Few bothered to notice him. Those who did, did so with sullen stares, yellow-toothed sneers, or animal snarls.

"Come along," someone growled, as his attendants passed him off to another set. Peering out of the corner of his eye, Torin recognized the man. It was the one called Keel Haul, perhaps the friendliest of those who had tended to him over the past several days. The man smelled of cheap ale and vinegar, but had been the one to accommodate Torin's requests where possible, and had even spent some time talking with him. The others, Torin sensed, would just as soon have flogged him as fed him.

"Time to look sharp," Keel Haul added with a grin full of dead teeth, as Torin tripped over a coil of rope.

The man's real name was Kell. All aboard went by an assumed name, the pirate had told him, given by the captain when welcomed into service. Torin had wondered whether "Keel Haul" meant the other had survived one . . . or if he enjoyed performing the savage deed. He hadn't felt comfortable enough to ask.

He *had* asked whether Kell knew the *captain's* real name. At that, the pirate had laughed and shaken his mangy head. As he understood it, no one did.

Torin tripped again at the next stair, which led to the top of a forecastle. While Kell tried to help him keep his feet, the man on his other flank jerked him pitilessly, leaving his knee to crack against the wooden step. Torin refused to cry out, but swung his head to glare at the ruffian, another he knew. Flambard, of the flaming red hair, sightless eye, and scathing disposition. As if sensing his anger, the pirate stared back at him with his one good eye, and snarled.

When at last they reached the bow rail, they found Raven stood beside the swarthy, dark-bearded brute who had first taken the Sword upon Torin's netting. Together, the pair stared forward into a rapidly thickening mist, pierced by the vessel's bowsprit. Beneath the jutting spar, Torin saw the figurehead that clung to the prow: a blood-colored raven, its wings outspread as if it might catch the wind and fly from its perch.

The pirate captain glanced over as Torin lurched to a halt. "Shattercove," he murmured.

Torin squinted through the gathering haze, which helped to smother the sun. A rocky isle loomed in the distance, on which they were closing apace. Even so, he could see little more than its silhouette, stark and jagged, bristling with stunted jungle growth. A promontory raked sharply to the east like the horn of an anvil, atop which a lone tower rose up among a walled compound of outbuildings. He was allowed only a brief study of its rugged contours before a curtain of brume shrouded it from view.

"Grimhold, Madrach called it," said Raven. "The wizard's fortress."

An unnecessary clarification, Torin thought, but a fitting name. A fresh chill rattled his bones, and not from wind or spray. Having glimpsed the wizard's home, it was as if he could feel his brother's baleful eyes upon him.

An eerie disquiet closed round with the fog. There were no voices, just the crash of the cutwater as it split the waves, the creak and groan of planks and fastenings, the whip and flutter of stay and sail. Torin craned his neck toward the stern of the ship, and saw pirates clinging to their ratlines, staring forward with dour faces. In the gauzy stillness, they looked like wraiths.

"We'll not be able to navigate the shoal in this," Raven observed.

Then the wind died. The sails went limp, and the ship's momentum slowed. Several of the crewmen groaned or muttered, but otherwise held their ground, as if uncertain how to react.

"Drop anchor," Raven ordered.

Torin looked to the pirate captain as the brutish companion relayed his command.

"That there's Black Spar," Kell whispered. "First mate."

"Shut your hole," Flambard snapped, wrenching Torin's arm as if to send a shock wave through to his comrade.

"That will be all," Raven said sternly. "Prepare three skiffs. Put four men in each. Marauders only. Flambard, I want you and Pike as my oarsmen. See to it."

"Aye, Cap'n," Kell replied quickly. Flambard grumbled the same.

When they let him go, Torin only barely managed to keep his feet. He was alone now with Raven and Black Spar, both of whom continued to stare into the fog as if seeing something Torin couldn't.

"Do we have a plan?" he asked.

Spar glared at him with curled lip, raising a fist as if to clout him on the ear, until Raven turned. "Keep quiet, or I'll have you gagged."

Torin responded with brooding silence. So much for their partnership. It would seem he was to have no knowledge of what was expected of him, no inkling of Raven's plot for penetrating the wizard's tower and freeing Autumn. He understood only that the pirate was not going to do anything to jeopardize his lady love. In all likelihood, Raven intended to go along with the parlay until such time as the wizard tried to back out of their deal. It was a poor bargain Torin had struck. But what choice did he have?

Moments later, Kell returned. "Shore boats are ready, Cap'n."

Raven grunted. "You know what to do?" he asked of Black Spar.

The first mate nodded. "Aye."

"Remind Mackerel he is to set forth at the first sign of trouble."

"As you say, Captain." Spar's voice was like thunder on the wind, Torin thought, then peered up at the motionless sails. Had there been any.

"Move."

This time, Raven's order was directed toward him. Torin gave the brigand a sour glance, then turned and shuffled after Kell, who led him astern. Though his movements remained slow and painful, he was pleased that he managed not to fall, even on the stairs.

When he reached the skiffs, suspended in their rigging over the starboard side, he was shoved aboard by Flambard and caught by a lanky pirate whose skin was chafed and mottled as if ridden with fever. He ignored this as best he could, just as he did the size of the man's nose—a hooked wedge on a face so angled it might have been shaped with a carpenter's plane. Pike, Torin supposed.

Flambard climbed in, then Raven after him. Pulleys on either side screeched as the tiny boat was lowered to touch down upon the dark waters. All of a sudden, swells that had seemed mere wavelets from above loomed large, lifting and lowering like the chest of a slumbering giant, tossing them like cork. Were the wind to return, Torin thought the waves might swallow them whole.

Nevertheless, cables were unhooked and oars set to motion, grinding within their locks. Raven crouched in the bow, peering into the drizzly, low-hanging cloud cover. Pike and Flambard sat center with their backs to the captain, each bent over an oar, while Torin lay in the stern like a sack of provisions. Behind them, barely visible across a foggy stretch of maybe twelve oar-strokes, trailed the other two skiffs, filled like theirs with glum, shadowy forms.

They had not gone far before the waves turned to surf, breaking against a jagged reef. A few strong pulls left them in the calmer waters of a coral shallows. Every now and then, Torin thought he saw fish darting through the inky depths, though the only ones he glimpsed for certain were those scooped up by hunting cranes and diving herons. Even these were but a flash of pale color and a glitter of scale.

Perhaps it was because he was watching the waters so closely that he was the first to spy the unexpected disturbance.

At the edge of the reef, just before the break line, there was a guttering light, as though a torch had been set to burning beneath the sea. It lasted only a moment. When it passed, the ripples began, swirling outward in widening circles. Over a slow series of heartbeats, the rate of their spiral quickened, until the waters in the middle started to drop, as if being sucked down through a submerged funnel.

"Look!" Torin shouted, pointing with his bound hands.

Flambard reached over and cuffed his ear with a studded bracer. Glowering, Torin peered past the ruffian to Raven, who had turned to check on the alarm. The pirate captain's face was a mask of irritation until his gaze slipped from the mist to the ocean's suddenly churning surface.

"Whirlpool!" he cried out.

By now, the lookouts on the other boats had seen it for themselves, and were barking frantically at their oarsmen. But their warning came too late. The vortex had grown so far and so fast that already both skiffs were upon its outer edge, with no chance to swing about. Oars became useless as the pair of skiffs were pulled round and round, steadily toward the roiling center. The crewmen in each dove and clambered, tripping over themselves and one another in a mad panic. Their helpless pleas sounded to Torin like the shrieking of gulls.

The waters around his own vessel were darkened further by billowing clouds of silt. Pike and Flambard continued to row, turning their paddles at an urgent pace. From this position of relative safety, Torin gaped as the first of the trapped skiffs reached the mouth of the maelstrom. The small craft lurched suddenly, torn from beneath its occupants by the incredible pull. He felt their horror as both skiff and men were ripped to splinters by an unnatural force, then sucked into the abyss. By the time the second craft overcame the first, he closed his eyes, unable to watch.

When the screams had died, and only their echo remained in his ears, Torin looked back to see that the whirlpool's spin was already slowing, its fury dissipating. Scraps of wood floated to the surface, along with other bits he tried not to recognize. When the last of the ripples had drifted away, a gathering flock of birds swooped down to make their own inspection.

For several moments, the only sound was the violent chorus of these birds, pecking and flapping at one another over the remains. Torin was the first to pry his gaze from the grisly sight in order to study his boatmates. Pike and Flambard gripped their oars above the waterline, as if preparing to wield them against an unseen attacker. Raven sat stock-still in the bow, his own hands clenching the gunwale. All aboard the lone skiff stared in stunned silence, unwilling to believe what they had just witnessed.

Finally, Raven swallowed as if choking down a lump of meat. "Carry on, mates."

Torin looked at Pike, who blinked.

"Carry on!"

"But sir—"

"If the dog had wanted us among them, we'd have been so. Carry on, I say!"

Pike continued to hesitate, while Flambard scowled so that his red eyebrows curled up like flames. With Pike beside him, he began working his oar, squeezing its haft and looking for all the world like he wished it to be his captain's throat. In this case, Torin could not bring himself to fault the man. The more he saw of this Red Raven, the more he questioned the pirate's sanity. Well and good that he should risk his life for that of his woman, but did he have to take the rest of them with him?

Still, Torin could not help but admire the glimmer he saw in the other's eye as Raven turned to face the hidden isle once more. Such focus and determination was infectious, even when misplaced. The captain was entrusting his life to them as surely as he was demanding theirs be entrusted to him. Like it or not, the four of them were now in this together.

Pike's eyes roamed anxiously now, Torin saw, across both misty sky and murky water. Flambard, he noted, had refocused his glare upon his hated prisoner, leaving Torin to wonder whose throat it was the rogue truly meant to strangle. With nothing to win in a contest of stares, Torin looked away.

After several nervous moments, their craft slid aground on a glistening shore. Raven leapt out and helped to pull the skiff up onto the rocks, then dragged a rope and anchor out after.

"Bring him."

The pair of marauders stowed their oars and moved to join their captain, yanking Torin along. He twisted his ankle as he exited the boat, slipping with a splash into the small waves that lapped at his feet and flooded his boots. But his captors simply dragged him forward, across the sharp, weed-slicked stones.

They stopped when they had caught up with Raven, who held a loaded crossbow.

"From this point hence," the captain said gravely, "I need each of you to keep your wits about you. Take no action without my signal. If I detect so much as a whimper, I will personally bury this bolt in the back of your skull, then leave you to the wizard. Is that understood?"

He waited for their reluctant nods.

"Trust in my lead, and I'll do what I can to see us all through this." Raven then dropped a purposeful gaze upon Torin, though what reassurance he was to take from this, Torin wasn't certain. "On your feet."

Torin obeyed, wrenching free of the clutching hands of Pike and Flambard and drawing himself to full height. Freezing saltwater scratched at his wounds, but he hid his discomfort behind a glare of defiance. He had survived worse, he reminded himself silently. If only he knew how that might help him here.

Raven smirked as if reading his thoughts. "We make for the wizard's tower," he said, gesturing with the crossbow for Torin to take the lead. He then added, "Your Majesty."

Again Torin did as he was bid, turning his back to the pirate and allowing Raven to nudge him with the crossbow toward a distant, fog-shrouded scrub line. Already, the haze was beginning to diminish, making clear the desired path at the base of a cleft leading up through the isle's deadwood forest. Raven pointed him toward it, and without complaint, Torin started their trek across the rocky beach.

CHAPTER FIFTEEN

THE CLIMB TO THE WIZARD'S STRONGHOLD took longer than expected, so that darkness was virtually upon them by the time they reached its face. The curtain wall was a sad, crumbling thing, its black stone pitted and ravaged by untold centuries of coastal storms. The merlons atop the gatehouse had eroded into nubs, filed by wind and rain—such as that which had picked up during their trek. A haunting glow hovered beyond, seeping through crenellations, arrow slits, and the crack of its iron gates.

They had not quite come to a stop when the great doors, emblazoned with mysterious glyphs, began to open, yawning wide on groaning pins. Chains squealed in the background; through the widening breach, Torin could see the rusted links being taken in.

It took forever. When at last the portal was clear, the eyes of the company flicked about uneasily, looking through the opening and at one another. Save for a roiling black mist and a ring of torches ensconced in iron wall brackets, the courtyard appeared deserted. At last, Raven nudged Torin with the tip of his loaded crossbow. The point pricked Torin's neck, but still he did not step forward. It was not a conscious decision, but instinctive, as if he knew that should he set foot within this Grimhold, he would not step out again.

The immediacy of Raven's threat won out, however, causing him to stagger onward. Glancing back, he could see that Pike and Flambard were just as tentative; despite the blades they carried, their legs quivered like those of a foal taking its first steps. He could not see whether Raven was as frightened as the rest of them, but supposed it wouldn't matter if he was.

The empty yard was filled with broken paving stones that had been shoved aside by weeds and grasses grown up beneath. Torin strode as bravely as he could across this cobbled terrain of rock and sand and vegetation, while raindrops struck like icicles upon his neck. The haunting scene reminded him of the graveyard from which he had bidden his friends farewell, and the chill he felt deepened within.

They had gone no more than twenty paces when the black mist drew aside like a curtain. As suddenly as that, his elder brother, erstwhile crown prince and king of Alson, was revealed.

The man wore neither the supplicant's robes in which Torin had first met him, nor his studded battle leathers, but a belted tunic not unlike Torin's own.

Black in color, only with longer sleeves and a stitched pattern of scales. In one hand he gripped his ebony staff, carved to resemble a hooded serpent, while from his neck hung the iron skull pendant with its rictus grin. Yellow eyes beamed like lanterns in the near darkness, matching well the sickly pallor of torchlight upon his ghostly skin.

Torin's breath lodged in his throat. He had forgotten what it felt like to gaze upon his brother, a creature poisoned by the use of powers mankind wasn't meant to harness. Without the Sword, he was utterly helpless beneath that gaze, a mouse at the mercy of a hawk.

The wizard's lips compressed in a tight smile. "Welcome, brother."

The words hissed like steam from a kettle, raking Torin's already over-wracked spine.

"What do you think of my home?" Soric asked, gesturing with his staff. Torin glanced around as a ring of soldiers armed with crossbows were exposed by the retreating mist, perched atop the bailey. "An uncharted isle. Well off the regular sea lanes. Only a rare southeasterly wind, coupled with an even rarer tide flow, will deliver the uninitiated to its shores." His smile widened with gleeful menace. "I'm so pleased you were able to come."

"Where's Autumn?" Raven croaked, jabbing Torin with his crossbow.

The wizard's glee seemed to dissipate as he inspected Torin from head to toe with an unblinking gaze. His eyes shifted then to the pirate, whom he addressed rather sternly. "He was to be delivered unharmed."

"Unkilled, you said."

The wizard's smile returned, seeping slowly to the corners of his mouth. "So I did." He paused. "You made good time, given the damage you sustained."

Torin could feel Pike and Flambard shifting to glance at one another, wondering like he how the wizard could know this. Or perhaps Soric was only guessing, seeking to put them off guard. The cold sneer told them nothing. "Come inside then. Let us see to the condition of your flower."

"If it's all the same," Raven said through clenched teeth, "I think we'll make our exchange right here."

Soric inclined his head, then tamped the butt of his staff against the ground. From a stone-framed doorway behind him, a soldier stepped forward, bearing at knife-point a woman draped in heavy manacles. Again, Raven's bolt dug into the back of Torin's neck, betraying the pirate's sudden fervor. Other than that, the ruffian held himself in check.

As the pair continued forward, beyond the wizard to within a few paces of where the visitors stood, Torin found himself breathless once more. Autumn, he decided, should have been named for the spring. She was a modest beauty, the kind whose fair looks would draw eye in a seedy tavern, but might go unnoticed among the fancy maidens at a town festival. Her smooth skin was lightly freckled, her shoulder-length hair thick and lustrous. But it was her bearing that captivated him, some quality he could sense but not quite see. Her eyes, perhaps, which glimmered with a hint of amethyst as they seemed to stare at him alone. Or perhaps the way in which she smiled, as if considering some private, warmhearted jape at his expense. Whatever it was, she caused him to feel detached in a soothing, comfortable way, as if his cares should belong to someone else, and nothing should matter beyond the connection they now shared.

"As you can see," Soric said, "she has been well tended."

"Then let us be finished here," Raven snapped. "Tell your dog to release her."

Torin continued to match Autumn's stare, which he found both curious and enticing. Her hair, he now noted, was neither light nor dark, but a blend of shifting hues in the uncertain light. At last he grew self-conscious and looked away—though not far—to the soldier beside her, who hadn't moved.

"Release her, Madrach," Raven demanded again, "else I drain this man's skull here and now and let your master do what he will with the corpse."

The soldier, Madrach, was almost as striking as his prisoner, given the resemblance he bore to the ill-tempered pirate captain. He was clad in tight-fitting armor, leather mostly, but with greaves and bracers and cuirass of hammered plate. His helm fit close against what appeared to be a shorn head. He was a stretch larger than Raven, in height and in girth, but the features—the flat nose, the beady eyes, the crooked mouth and cleft chin—might have been etched from the same mold.

"Careful, Captain," the other teased, pressing a stubbled cheek close to Autumn's, "lest I start and cause her pale throat to sprout a pretty red smile."

"Madrach!" The wizard's voice cracked like the bite of a whip, a clear reminder as to who was truly in charge. "Turn her loose."

The mercenary stiffened, but did as he was bid, sheathing his dagger and producing a key that he used to remove Autumn's shackles. He let them drop to the earth, then shoved her forward.

Somehow, despite the rough treatment, Autumn lost not a trace of dignity. She stepped forward, eyes gleaming in Torin's direction, as she came to stand next to Raven. Quickly she gave the pirate a kiss upon the cheek, before slipping her arm around his waist.

Raven leaned into her, but kept his attentions focused on the wizard, on Madrach, on the circle of crossbows above. One last time he prodded Torin with the crossbow, and only then did the young king realize he had turned his head almost fully around in order to watch the reunion. With a wink from Autumn, he faced ahead once more, and, at Raven's urging, took a pair of uncertain strides.

Madrach stepped forward to meet him. Before the image of Autumn's wink had faded from his mind, Torin, still bound, found himself given over to the enemy.

"The Sword," Soric prompted. "Where is it?"

"The Sword remains aboard my ship," Raven announced. Wood and leather creaked as the soldiers upon the bailey leaned in and tightened pressure upon their triggers. "There it remains until my men and I are returned safely, else cast into the sea."

Torin's gaze flitted from Raven, to the wizard, to the soldiers looming above. He glanced at Autumn, then back to his brother, whose response he awaited.

"You play games with your men's lives," Soric said. He appeared bemused, but his words bore an unmistakable chill. "Theirs I can see, but Autumn's—"

"Do you want your trinket or not?" Raven squawked.

The wizard grinned, no doubt to hide his calculating thoughts. Everyone but Raven himself—and Autumn, of course—seemed surprised by the pirate's boldness.

"Very well," Soric agreed. "Madrach, take a score of men and accompany our good captain to the beach. Deliver them to their ship, and procure the Sword. From there, each will allow the other to be on his way."

"Yes, my lord," Madrach said, scowling at Raven.

Raven smirked in return. Upon seeing this, Soric's own smile slipped like a spider into its hole. "If you cross me," he warned, "I shall command the winds and waves to shatter your vessel upon my reef, where gulls will pick clean your remains. Are we agreed, Captain?"

Raven matched the other's glare. "Let's get moving."

At a snap of Madrach's fingers, the soldiers standing watch atop the bailey shuffled down the steps on either side, filing to order within the murky courtyard. Their numbers appeared to ease the mercenary's malcontent. "After you," he sneered.

Raven wheeled about, signaling Pike and Flambard to keep eye on those who followed.

"Take the prisoner," Soric added, when Madrach had stepped past Torin as though to leave him behind. "Have him identify the talisman our friend hands over. I leave his life in your hands, Madrach."

The mercenary nodded, refusing to be cowed by the implied threat. He seized Torin by the arm and propelled him forward.

Torin's thoughts raced as though he were a badger caught in an iron trap. Clearly, he had no allies here. He had only himself to turn to if he wished to survive—or at the very least, to prevent the Sword from falling into his brother's hands, where doubtless it would be used in future conquests against his land and others. Better that it should remain in the possession of pirates.

Or was it? With the Sword might go the Pendant. Either way, there would come a time during which Darinor would have no choice but to come in search. Had that not been the reason for taking the Pendant in the first place? It might make sense to see that Raven surrendered both, to make sure the two artifacts remained together, and close at hand.

But that was foolishness. What reason had he to believe the wizard would keep him alive long enough for Darinor to attempt a rescue? Likely, he would be long gone, and would have only made it harder for the renegade Entient to retrieve the divine talismans, in that he would have to pry them from the wizard rather than a mere pirate—or whomever Raven sold them to.

He was still wrestling with these choices when he reached the gates to the courtyard, where everyone came to a startled halt.

A trio of men filled the narrow path fronting the keep, on the last leg of their winding journey from the rainswept beach. In the lead was Kell, his hands lashed to an oar that he wore across his back, his bloody face smeared with mud and leaves from multiple falls. Behind him was Raven's first mate, Black Spar, unbound, and carrying a long, wooden box. A handheld crossbow tickled his jeweled ear, wielded, it seemed at first, by the man's own shadow.

Then the shadow came into focus, taking on a form of its own. Torin blanched.

Xarius Talyzar.

The assassin halted at the head of the trail, in the shadow of the open gates. Kell's eyes flicked back and forth like those of a deer surrounded by hunters. Black Spar's gaze found Raven, and the two shared an unreadable look. But it was Talyzar Torin focused on, the man who had come nearer than any other to ending his life, months ago, during his quest for the Sword. He hadn't seen the man since the other had plunged a dagger in his back. To face his would-be executioner now, so unexpectedly, filled him with shock and residual dread.

"Have we missed the festivities?" Talyzar hissed, his voice masked in whisper.

Soric came forward, parting the sea of soldiers that stood between him and the new arrivals, breezing past Torin like an icy gust. "What have we now?" he asked, in a manner that suggested both amusement and irritation at the surprise.

Talyzar gave a slight bow. "You bade me leave delivery of the whelp to these pirates," he observed, with a clear measure of distaste. "But I thought you might like to take possession of his blade."

Torin's reeling thoughts came sharply into focus. The assassin's presence explained much. It was Talyzar who had followed him to Gammelost, supplying the information ultimately used by Raven to locate him. Talyzar who had stowed aboard first the *Pirate's Folly* and then the *Raven's Squall*, sending messages as to Torin's progress, and the results of the sea battle between the two. It all made sense—save for the means by which the man was able to go undetected and relay messages to his master over so great a distance. But those were details, trade secrets of assassins and wizards and perhaps beyond his understanding. What pained him was to learn that he'd been so blind as to carry along his own doom, right from the beginning.

"You've brought me the Sword?" Soric asked, delight gaining sway over displeasure.

The assassin nudged Black Spar with his weapon. "Show him."

The pirate grunted.

A knife appeared in Talyzar's free hand, so quickly that it might have been there all along. Its edge fell upon the seam between the gruff pirate's head and ear. "With or without your ability to hear."

Spar looked to Raven, who nodded.

With a bolt at one ear and a dagger on the other, the first mate hefted the wooden box he carried and flicked free the latch. He turned its facing outward, so that those before him could see, before flipping back the lid. In a shallow tray, pillowed among velvet folds, lay the Sword, its crimson radiance muted but still drawing gasps of astonishment. Its silver hilt gleamed in the twilight; its blade and heartstones swirled with inner flame.

Hung around the hilt was the Pendant.

Soric smiled. "Well done, my assassin. Well done indeed." He turned to Raven, who swallowed thickly. "So, my good captain. It would seem you have nothing else with which to barter."

The pirate looked to his own crossbow, leveled before him, aimed now at the wizard. But the air went out of him, as even he seemed to realize how pointless was his stance. His arm tightened protectively around Autumn's shoulders.

"No?" Soric asked. "Then perhaps you and your men would be good enough to remain as my guests, until you have had such time as to reconsider my previous offer."

The wizard raised a finger, and his soldiers took action, quickly disarming both Pike and Flambard and pinning their arms behind them. Madrach himself took Raven's crossbow with a laugh.

"The box," Soric said.

Spar glared as if to tear the wizard asunder, but closed the hinged lid and latched it shut. He posed no struggle as Soric stepped forward and slid the container from his grasp.

"Madrach."

"Yes, my lord?"

"The lady, I'm sure, will be more comfortable in my tower. Find quarter for the rest within our dungeon."

"Yes, my lord."

There was a jostling from Flambard, and another growl from Black Spar, as the soldiers closed ranks. Raven tightened his grip on Autumn.

"My brother is to remain unharmed," Soric clarified. "As to the others, gut whoever resists."

That ended the lingering protests. Even Raven remained still as Autumn was jerked from his embrace.

"Welcome, all of you." The wizard smiled, clapping Talyzar on the shoulder.

"My lord," said Madrach, when all had been gathered. "Permission to sack the *Squall*?"

Soric considered. "To what end?"

Madrach blinked as if confused. "To safeguard against a rescue, my lord. We would gain additional prisoners, and loot. There might be treasures—"

"I see no reason to risk the lives of my guardsmen for the price of a few trinkets," the wizard replied, waving the request aside. "Let those who remain keep their plunder. There will be no rescue. My guess is they will not wait long before hoisting anchor and setting forth like whipped pups."

"Indeed," Talyzar whispered, turning a heated stare in the mercenary's direction. "They have done so already. The moment I brought these others ashore."

"There, you see?" Soric snickered. "Such is the valor of thieves. Away now, Captain. See to my orders."

Madrach cast a wary eye in Talyzar's direction, trying hard to appear neither cowed nor crestfallen. His flagging spirits lifted when he turned to find Raven his captive. "Carry out," he barked, and the procession started forward, back into the wizard's keep.

Though he received a rough shove for doing so, Torin twice glanced back at those just behind him. One was for Autumn, who met his look with a faint smile devoid of concern—a simpleton, perhaps, lacking the capacity to understand. The other was for a stooped Raven, and the headstrong pirate's masterful plan.

CHAPTER SIXTEEN

Sᴏʀɪᴄ's ɢᴀᴢᴇ sᴡᴇᴘᴛ ᴛʜᴇ sᴛᴏɴᴇ ᴛᴀʙʟᴇᴛ, marking carefully each dusty rune, though he had all but committed its verse to memory. Too long had he waited for this. This very night, he meant to finish it. He would not risk that anything should go awry.

Twenty-one years had he prepared, through exploration and study. Closer now to twenty-two. For this was merely a continuation of what had begun decades ago, when he had been escorted from the court of his father like a common brigand. Once Torin was gone, he might finally lay to rest the demons that plagued him, and give thought to the renewal of his rightful conquest.

It would be easy enough to assemble another army and to repeat the strategy and troop movement that had met with such success the last time he had invaded Alson's shores. This time, there would be no upstart rivals—no secret heirs, no army of dragonborn, no demon avatars—with which to contend for his throne. Not only would his resistance be weakened, but his own powers would be even more formidable, given these added months during which he had honed his craft—and that he would soon be adding a Sword of Asahiel to his arsenal. And the pirate, Red Raven, should he be properly persuaded, might make a noteworthy ally, capable of rallying a fleet of ships to plunder the coastline and pave the way for a more direct landing.

But all of that remained open to planning and debate. Eggs before fowl, the wizard thought with a shake of his head. Banish his usurper. Torment him with isolation and exile. Serve unto him a dose of the bitter loneliness and unimaginable suffering that had shaped his own life. Should he never lay claim to his birthright, this alone might bring him peace.

Strange it was: the depth of his feelings, the strength of his resentment. He had thought himself evolved beyond such pettiness. But returning to his homeland, seeing how life had progressed without him, had stirred emotions long since buried. And there was nothing petty about survival. Let others label him evil, should they so choose. Nature did not distinguish between right and wrong, good and evil—only strong from weak, predator from prey. With the perception of evil came fear. With fear, respect. That was all he demanded from his fellow man.

He eased away from the tablet and closed his eyes. His victories this day had made him heady, sapping his focus. He would have to settle his churning thoughts and emotions if he meant to do this. What he intended was no simple cantrip or dweomer, but a channeling of mental energies through all ten sephiroth, clear to the ascending plane of the Carafix of Life. To do so was well within the range of his abilities, but not an exercise to be taken lightly. The slightest misstep or uncertainty could wreak havoc upon him, both mentally and physically. He would have to be ready.

He stepped back, seating himself upon an altar of granite, carved from the floor of the chamber. Discipline. It had served him so well—saved him, really. He would not let it desert him now.

Before he could begin a deeper meditation, there came a tug at one of the lines of magic with which he warded his keep. Moments later, Xarius Talyzar stepped through the open portal to this subterranean chamber, and bowed his head in greeting.

"I pray I'm not interrupting," the assassin remarked with unusual courtesy.

Soric sighed. "I welcome the diversion. Come," he said, waving the other forward.

Talyzar strode to within a pace before stopping and bowing again. He glanced down at the tablet on its broken, lichen-covered pedestal. "An incantation?"

"Which I'm preparing especially for our guests," the wizard confirmed. "One of them, anyway."

"Do I even wish to know?"

"Why ruin the surprise?" Soric smiled. When the assassin smiled with him, concealed as he was within the shadow of his cowl, the wizard knew for certain something was amiss. "What can I do for you, Talyzar?"

"My actions. They have met with your approval?"

"You know they have. Since when does that concern you?"

"I was thinking of our arrangement."

"Ah yes," the wizard said. He should have known at once. "The Kronus boy. Your young rival."

Talyzar tensed. "The whelp you requested is yours. His blade as well."

"And so you seek your leave to hunt down this rogue and repay his insult."

"For a time only," the assassin assured him.

"But how much time, Talyzar? That is my concern."

"If you would allow me to question your brother—"

"You believe he can tell you something our spies did not already uncover? As I recall, there was no great secret to the youth's departure. None knew his destination because he himself did not."

The assassin clenched his teeth. "I will find him."

"Of that I've no doubt, my raptorial nightbird. But at what profit to me? Should you find the youth, will you be able to defeat him this time? Either death—his or yours—merits me nothing."

"It would assure you a faithful servant," Talyzar hissed.

"I have that already, do I not?" Soric glared into the other's hood, daring contradiction.

"I've done all you asked, and more."

"Indeed you have. But the time is not yet right. After this night, we resume measures for our return to the east. I may have need of you."

"A man such as you thrives on making enemies. Until that changes, there will always be a need for me."

Soric chuckled. "That may be. Though let us not confuse *use* with necessity. Bear with me, Talyzar, awhile longer. Your vagabond pup is most likely to show up once he learns of the fate we shall bring to his friend's kingdom. You need not waste your time—and mine—giving chase."

The assassin did not respond, but stood there simmering. Soric hoped he had not pushed the other too far. He would hate to have to destroy him.

Still, it would not do to have one of his dogs testing its leash, lest the rest follow. His vaults—those of this ancient stronghold he had discovered—were filled with more wealth than he might spend in a lifetime. But coin went only so far toward keeping men like Talyzar and Madrach in check. As with all men, it was more important that they know and accept their place.

"Have you another task in mind then?" the assassin asked finally.

"Yes. Take some rest. Seek comfort, whatever you may find within these walls. You have earned it."

Talyzar bowed once more, his deepest yet, before gliding from the room like the wraith for which he was named.

When the other had gone, Soric took a deep breath of the stale air here in the bowels of his keep. Time was wasting. After all this, he would not risk that anything should go wrong. To make certain, he intended to lay forth the entire procedure ahead of time, so that he would have only to trigger it later. It was the best way, he assured himself, yet it meant he had that many more preparations to make.

Sharpening his focus, he took to his feet and set about his tasks.

THE DOOR TO THEIR PRISON SLAMMED SHUT with a resounding thud that sent shivers through the cavern stone. When it faded, all that could be heard was the scrape and clank of men dangling in their metal cuffs. Six of them, all told. From the corner of his eye, Torin watched the others huff and grunt, twisting uncomfortably. Raven and Black Spar, Pike and Flambard, and a battered Keel Haul—all swaying like suspended candle holders in a storm-wracked house.

The reverberations of their guards' departure had barely expired when Raven broke the near-silence. "Why didn't you tell me this wizard was your brother?"

Torin lifted his head. "Why didn't you tell me Madrach was yours?"

Raven's features soured, then broke in a snorting laugh. "I suppose that's only fair."

Nothing about this was fair, Torin thought, but offered instead, "It makes no difference now, does it?"

The cast of their surroundings was gray and damp, permeated like all else by the chill of the sea that cradled this mountain rock. Once inside the wizard's stronghold, they had been led through a series of tunnels that burrowed downward through the isle's heart. They had ended up in this mostly natural cavern, a rugged hollow shaped with clefts and ridges and broken bits of crumbling stone.

"Perhaps not," Raven agreed, glancing up into darkness, to where his chains were anchored to the cavern ceiling. "Though perhaps we should share our stories now, just in case."

Before he could object, Torin coughed, his lungs rejecting the oily black smoke that drifted from a loose array of pole-mounted cressets sheltering them from absolute darkness. By the time he'd overcome his fit, he lacked the will to deny the pirate his meaningless request.

"I've nothing more to reveal," he sighed. "He was exiled before my birth, sold into slavery at the age of twelve for attempting to poison his father the king. I don't know how he escaped, or how he learned the craft he now wields. I never knew him at all until our paths crossed during his invasion of Alson."

"Where he found you sitting his throne."

"In a manner of speaking," Torin allowed, having no desire to delve further simply to explain the truth of things.

Raven was quiet for a moment before responding. "Madrach is my younger. We used to sail together, up until four years ago, when he led a failed mutiny against me. Because he's my brother, I would not have him killed, but turned him out to fend for himself."

For some reason, the pirate captain was swaying a great deal more than the others as he squirmed against his restraints, though Torin paid this little heed.

"Since then," Raven continued, panting from his efforts, "I'd heard only rumors of his dealings. Most had him roaming the coastal lands of Yawacor as the leader of his own mercenary band. I'm assuming that's how your wizard found him."

And why, Torin realized, when the wizard needed someone to carry out his abduction, Madrach had gone to Raven. He scoffed at the irony. In effect, they were both here because of grudges held against them by their siblings. "Perhaps *they* should have been brothers, and left us out of it."

"Perhaps." Raven laughed. "It's been my experience that siblings make for the closest companions, or the fiercest rivals." As he twisted around on his chain, he fixed Torin with a knowing stare. "I suspected there was something more to your relationship, to have fostered in the wizard such a deep feeling of insult."

"Yes, well, now you know."

"Then let us strike a bargain, here and now," Raven proposed. "Whatever else happens, we will trust in one another to see the other delivered from his brother's menace."

Torin bit his lip to keep from laughing aloud. Just what was the man thinking? They were trapped, strung up like sides of beef in a butcher's salthouse. Buried in a hive of rock in the middle of the ocean, secluded from the outside world. Even if they could escape their bonds, even if they could fight their way past Madrach's soldiers and the wizard himself, their ship had fled, leaving them no way off this reef.

No, their only hope was for Darinor to come for them, to follow the emanations of the Pendant's chain to these misbegotten shores. Which, as he'd already decided, could only happen too late.

Still, the very idea of an angry Darinor showing up on Soric's doorstep was cause for a grim smile, such that, for a moment, he forgot his predicament altogether.

He came to at the sound of a sharp click, followed by the quick and sudden descent of Raven dropping free to the floor.

For the span of several heartbeats, Torin merely gaped, while the captain rubbed his wrists and got to his feet. Only when he moved away did Torin begin to stammer, glancing back and forth between the pirate and his empty manacles. "How . . . how did you—"

"A minor talent," Raven assured him, brushing his escape aside as casually as he had the matter of his phantom ships. He fetched the stool used moments ago to hang each of them in place from the ceiling chains. "Do we have our bargain?"

Torin checked the reactions of the other pirates. Pike and Kell were shaking their heads in wonderment, more relieved than surprised, as if they should never have doubted their captain. Flambard flashed Torin a cruel grin. Black Spar, to whom Raven went first with a pair of lock picks, grunted for the other to hurry.

"I apologize," Raven said, more to his men than to Torin, "for not taking each of you into my confidence. I felt where the wizard was concerned, it was best to keep things quiet. A man can't reveal what he doesn't know."

Torin did not bother trying to hide his astonishment. "You planned this?"

"Me and my relief captains—Black Spar and Mackerel," Raven admitted. Spar's cuffs came free, and together the pair moved stool and lock picks over to Pike. "Of course, I hadn't counted on the wizard shredding two of my skiffs and leaving me eight men short. Nor did I foresee our stowaway. Sneaky one, that. But old Spar was to come ashore with your blade anyway, under pretense of selling it—and me—out to the wizard."

Torin's mind worked frantically. "But why? Once you turned me over, the Sword was your only leverage."

"Even had we made it back to our ship," Raven replied, working ceaselessly, "the wizard wasn't going to let us off this isle. We're inside, lad. We'd never have gotten this far had we tried to force our way."

A scrape, and Pike joined the ranks of the free. The whole operation shifted to Flambard, gaining momentum, like a snowball rolling downhill.

Could it be? Torin wondered, hesitant to take anything from this group at face value. He had supposed the pirate's latest overtures to be those of a desperate man forced into collusion with any possible ally. Since Raven's plan had failed, he was perhaps hoping Torin would have another. But if it was true that all of this had been but a ruse intended to help infiltrate the wizard's keep . . .

"So what now?" Torin snickered. "We fight our way free? We're weapon-less, outnumbered, and with no way off this rock, thanks to your shipmates having deserted us."

This brought scowls and snarls from both Black Spar and Flambard as the group worked now on Kell.

But Raven would not be troubled. "The wizard holds all the advantages, right? Good. That's what I want him to think. The numbers I didn't count on, but we'll have to make do. And we've not been deserted. As for weapons, that was why we smuggled your blade inside—not quite as planned, but I won't argue results."

"Except that you gave it to the wizard." In the echo of his own voice, Torin could hear his conviction slipping.

"The wizard doesn't have your sword. Not yet, anyway. Although it prob-ably won't take him long to find it."

"What does that mean?"

"I'll explain along the way," said Raven, turning at last to face him. "But first I must know, are you with us, or against us?"

Torin let his gaze slip briefly over the others before fixing on their captain. "I'm with you, of course—though I feel like a blind man."

Raven nodded to his mates, who slid the stool—grudgingly, it seemed—beneath his feet. The captain climbed up next to him to have at the slackened cuffs.

"Wait," Torin said. "How could you have known the wizard wouldn't kill you—kill all of us—right there on the beach?"

"Hold still," Raven chided him. "I visited the man before, remember? As cocksure as they come. Only cowards go about killing foes recklessly, so as not to risk facing them again. Men who believe themselves impervious think first as to how they might profit by keeping others—even enemies—alive. If I'm no threat to him, why not use me?"

Torin shook his head. "But—"

"That offer he spoke of was to retain my services on an ongoing basis. I refused, of course. And I've done nothing since that he wouldn't expect, giv-ing him no reason to raise his guard, and certainly no reason to dispose of me out of hand."

The pirate uttered a brief exclamation a heartbeat before Torin's shackles opened up. The young king lowered his arms to his side, massaging his wrists as he'd seen the others do, while mulling through Raven's reasoning.

"Seems to me a rather dangerous maneuver," he decided.

The pirate nodded. "A gallows wager. But with better odds than that he would turn Autumn over to me and let us leave." He stepped from the stool onto solid ground, beckoning Torin to do the same.

"I still think you might have warned me as to your plans."

"And risk letting you set them awry?" Raven asked, askance. He clicked his tongue disapprovingly, slipping his lock picks into the greasy mop of his hair and turning his attention toward the door. "There were already more wild cards than I normally care to deal with," he said, shuffling ahead of the others. "The less you knew, the less likely you could betray me—willingly or otherwise." He reached the door of studded iron and leaned an ear against its surface. "Besides, would knowing my plans have given you any greater sense of peace?"

Torin considered this, a step back from the others, and determined the pirate was right. Still, he wasn't ready to give the other the satisfaction. "Depends on what else you have in mind," he muttered. He added gravely, "Especially since I doubt he'll spare any of you a second time."

Raven offered him a wink. "I wouldn't."

Torin wasn't sure which he preferred: the glowering, uncompromising brigand he had met aboard the *Raven's Squall,* or this new, almost playful rogue crouched before him. Nor did he get the chance to decide; for as quickly as the mood had come, it seemed to wash past the pirate, who placed his hand upon the door's pull ring, all business once more.

His shipmates fanned out to either side, arming themselves with stones. Torin hadn't been paying close attention, but he believed the door to their prison contained a locking bar on the outside. Sure enough, it refused to open when Raven yanked upon the ring. He half expected a sentry to come barging in at the attempt, but there was no noise from without. It seemed they had truly been abandoned.

While his mates and so-called marauders continued to stand guard, Raven slipped from under his belt a long, waving piece of metal that had been looped around his waist. It looked like a shortsword, only hammered to a mirror finish, thin as parchment. It fit between door and frame as if made for just that purpose, and while Torin immediately doubted it would be sturdy enough to unseat the locking bar on the other side, he kept the comment to himself.

"These tools of yours," he wondered instead. "Why didn't Madrach take them?"

"I've only acquired these skills over the past few years," Raven confessed. "Had he not betrayed me when he did, my brother, too, might have learned them."

Torin thought to ask a follow-up question, but a growl from Black Spar persuaded him against it. With nothing else to do, he watched the captain work in silence. For several moments, Raven struggled with both the weight and position of the unseen bar. More than once, he retracted his slip of metal through the lightless gap to begin again from a new angle. In that time, Torin matched eyes with Keel Haul, and thought back to his mistreatment aboard the *Squall.* As it had turned out, Raven had been right not to show him any kindness, due to Talyzar's presence onboard. The pirate had disavowed any knowledge of the assassin, but Torin wondered if he had not at least suspected the wizard of prying eyes, and if that—and not cruel-hearted malice—had been the cause of his actions.

Before his thoughts could wander any further afield, there was a dull clattering from beyond the door and a whispered cry of exuberance from the man leading their escape. Raven jumped back, whipping his metal serpent back through the tiny fissure. The others held their positions, adjusting their grips on their stones. All was quiet as they listened intently for a reaction from without. For several moments, Torin heard nothing over the drumming of his own pulse.

At last, Raven reached again for the pull ring, leaving the giant Black Spar to guard the crack. As the door groaned open, Spar nodded. He lowered his rock and thrust his bulk through the opening, first his head, then his shoulders. After a quick look to either side, he ducked back in.

"All clear," he rumbled.

Raven smiled at Torin, signaling silence before he scooted out into the rough-hewn corridor. The others followed on his heels. Beyond, the captain paused just long enough to close the door and replace the locking bar before herding them all down the tunnel and into the first available alcove.

When all were tucked aside, Raven produced yet another hidden device, this one resembling a compass. He studied it for a moment, glancing down the corridor in the direction its needle pointed. Apparently satisfied, he then snapped its lid shut and drew his mates close in a tight huddle.

"Time now to find where Autumn is being held, retrieve the Sword, kill the wizard, and escape. Does anyone have a problem with that?"

In these close quarters, Torin was more concerned with the smell, an offensive musk of breath and sweat that made him long for a bath. When he realized that Raven's question was directed primarily at him, he shook his head fiercely.

"How do we do it, Cap'n?" asked Kell.

"The wizard must keep a ship or two upon this isle. Spar, I need you to find it. The rest of you will go with him. Seize it, and send signal to the *Squall*. She's to be hiding off the north coast, out of view of this tower."

Flambard scowled; his features seemed incapable of anything else. "What about you?"

"Torin and I will start by tracking down the Sword. I'm guessing that will lead us to Autumn, and to the wizard."

"Just the two of you?" Flambard's scowl deepened, and Torin, as always, seemed to be the target of his ire. "You should let one of us come with you."

"You'll do as commanded," Raven snapped. "When he learns of our escape, the wizard will expect us to flee. The theft of his vessel will confirm this, and draw his attention. He won't then be expecting our attack." He turned to Torin, who was shaking his head. "Better that we be rid of him now," Raven insisted. "We won't get a better opportunity."

"I'm not opposed to that," Torin clarified. "I'm only wondering how you mean to find him, and to lay hands on the Sword before he does."

Raven explained. "This compass is attracted to the box in which your blade is hidden. The box itself is a smuggler's device. There is a switch, near the bottom on the back, disguised as a knot of wood. This switch must be triggered when the lid is opened. Otherwise, the box will reveal a secondary chamber and the weapon inside—that of an ordinary broadsword."

Torin's brow furrowed in suspicion. He looked to Black Spar, who nodded.

"Clearly," Raven continued, "I don't expect to fool the wizard for long.

But it should buy us some time. Time enough for the *Squall* to return and launch a diversion assault. Time enough for us to lay hands on the real Sword and rescue Autumn."

If he understood the plan correctly, Torin could spot a dozen holes before they'd even begun. It was like setting sail in a leaky skiff. Impressed by the manner in which Raven had won them entrance into the keep and then set them free, he had dared hope the pirate captain would have some brilliant scheme for carrying out their escape. Still, even this was probably more than he could rightfully have hoped for, and wasting time in further debate could only hurt their chances.

"So be it," he agreed.

Not to be outdone, the other pirates nodded or grunted or slapped their fists in accord.

They shuffled from the alcove and back into the corridor, where Raven double-checked his strange compass. The needle held its direction, and the captain bade them all follow. At the next fork, a sloping tunnel, he consulted the compass again. It led upward, which caused him to pull Spar aside.

"We split here. Look for a hidden harbor, somewhere within the cliff. When in doubt, go down."

Spar grunted, and clasped the captain's outstretched arm.

"Full sail," Raven tendered. "Oh, and Spar, I'd prefer to deal with Madrach myself, but should he get in the way, do not feel obliged to spare him on my account."

Spar grunted again and turned to the others. "Mates."

With that, the brute took off down the tunnel, drawing the others after like a shark leading scavenging minnows. Each of them—Pike, Flambard, and Keel Haul—shared a nod and handclasp with his captain before departing, and even glanced or glared in Torin's direction. The young king met those looks until a chill weight settled upon his shoulders. At once, he turned his gaze back down the passage from which they had come, where for half a heartbeat he thought he spied a flicker of movement.

"What is it?" Raven asked him when the others had gone.

Torin squinted, but could detect nothing unordinary about the shadows that skulked amid the staggered line of torches.

"Bats in my vision," he mumbled, shaking the heavy feeling aside.

"Shall we do this?"

"I'll be right beside you."

Raven flashed him a roguish grin—meant to be reassuring, Torin supposed—before squaring his jaw in determination. "For Autumn."

For Marisha, Torin amended silently, then had to hurry to catch up.

CHAPTER SEVENTEEN

"*I* ASSUME YOU'RE PERMITTING THIS," Xarius hissed, perched again in the doorway of the chamber in which the wizard busied himself.

Soric did not deign to look his way as he tapped fluid from a vial over the flat head of a statue on the far side of the room. "Of course I'm permitting it. Within this keep, I sense their movements as clearly as I sense yours."

"And you would have them roam free?"

"For a time," the wizard said, wringing his hands above the statue as if warming them over a flame. "Madrach has been told not to let them off the isle."

Xarius withheld a snide remark regarding his faith in the mercenary's abilities—he who had become Soric's right hand while the assassin was left to linger in Alson. "They do not seek escape," he said instead. "They seek a reckoning."

"Do they now?" The wizard added a few more drops of his arcane solution. "For that is what they shall find."

"They are tracking the Sword as we speak. With a compass drawn to some manner of lodestone, it seems."

"Good. Then it will not take them long to find their way to me." The wizard stoppered his vial and returned it to a pouch on his belt. He turned toward the center of the room, where the box containing the Sword rested upon a plinth at the edge of a swirled pattern etched into the granite floor.

It occurred to Xarius to mention the secret of the box and its trigger, but, for now, he preferred to keep that information to himself. "Might it be you're underestimating this rogue?"

Soric laughed, a mirthless hacking sound. "Madrach already suggested as much, when I ordered their prison unguarded." He stared at the assassin with a gimlet gaze. "Your concerns are touching, Talyzar, but unnecessary."

Xarius wondered if the shadows were sufficient to hide his true heart from the wizard's vaunted insight. For it would seem Soric had it wrong. He had indeed come to warn the other of the prisoners' escape, but only to mask his own intentions on the wizard's life.

"I don't understand these games," he said.

Soric drew sand from a small leather pouch and sprinkled it over the floor near the Sword. "That surprises me. For I've always admired your artistry.

Poetic, is it not, that an enemy choose his own fate, rather than having it forced upon him?" He paused to stare again at the assassin. "Rest assured, I take no chances with my life in doing so, and misery unto those who think to catch me unawares."

The wizard's words echoed with grim warning. Given his own treacherous thoughts, Xarius dared not move, blink, or breathe, lest something in his manner betray him.

"Power is born of perception," Soric added. "And nothing is more demoralizing than to believe you have an advantage over your enemy, only to find that you were playing into his hands all along."

"You still mean for the pirate to join you," Xarius reasoned. It seemed to him a poor excuse for the risks being taken, however minuscule they might be.

"If possible." The wizard smirked. "But come. Should it soothe your worries, stand guard as I grant our guests their final choice, and watch how easily I dispatch those who oppose me."

Xarius bowed. "I think that might be best."

Soric's smirk became more of a grimace as he stowed his powder. "Bring the woman then, from my chambers. By the time you return, I shall be ready."

"How many guard the keep?"

"Twoscore, not counting the servant staff, which is more protection than I require."

Xarius nodded in obeisance. "The pirates mean to signal their vessel, which is waiting to attack."

Soric waved dismissively. "Madrach will see to that. A boat full of brigands is of no threat to us. If need be, I will deal with them when this other matter is finished."

"As you will," the Shadow whispered, and bled into those of the hallway behind him.

As he padded silently down its length, an itch of readiness went with him. For one of his trade, the sensation was never far off, like the buzzing of a persistent bee. But its presence was heightened by what seemed to Xarius an opportunity. A dangerous one, to be sure, but it might be the only chance he would get.

If the wizard seemed overconfident, he had every reason to be. Despite such reckless talk—poetry for Torin, a lesson in power for Raven—Xarius was not about to presume his master on the verge of a mistake. But the assassin was determined to reclaim his freedom, and it had become clear that the only way to achieve this was to see Soric slain. If he could find a way to turn the upcoming showdown to his advantage, he might rid himself of the wizard and extract the information he so needed from Torin on Kylac's whereabouts—all in one fell swoop.

He had done his part, Xarius brooded silently. He had resisted the urge to abduct the young king himself and had instead followed him across the seas, sending messages to Soric by sign language over dim flame, making certain the bounty was delivered in accordance with the wizard's every request. He had then foiled the pirates' bid to keep the Sword aboard ship as a bargaining tool, imparting both the weapon and its handlers as additional gifts. All had been done so as to win the wizard's favor and that which had been promised in return.

Soric had betrayed him, sure and simple. And while the assassin would never allow his pride to overrule caution, it was in fact the core of who he was—the reason he was compelled to hunt down Kylac, and something that no one would take from him, not even one as formidable as this wizard.

He knew not how he would manage it; he need only be ready to exploit the possibilities. There would be no plan, no scheme whose hitch or failure might leave him paralyzed. Though he preferred to know every potential outcome to a situation beforehand, such was not always feasible. No matter. He was ultimately a creature of instinct, trained to react with serpentine reflexes to each situation as it arose. So it would be this night, and given the opening, he would strike.

Coiling in preparation, he pressed onward, upward, toward the wizard's tower. To fetch this pirate's woman, and the final piece of bait.

"HOLD, YOU FOOL!" SPAR RASPED, seizing Flambard's shoulder with a muscled paw.

Flambard scowled, but could not break the other's grasp. "The way is clear," he protested. "All is quiet."

Spar drew his mate roughly back. "Too quiet," he whispered with a frown of his own.

Kell, hunkered along with Pike a pace back from his mates, agreed. His eyes scoured the near-darkness, searching for sign of that which crawled like an army of insects along his spine. Beyond the mouth of the tunnel in which they crouched, ocean waters heaved restlessly against rock and piling. In the closed quarters of the cavern, its quiet murmur, like that of a slumbering dragon, echoed a dull roar.

Raven had been right about the harbor. Although the reef that warded the shores of Shattercove seemed to skirt the entire isle, there was a break here on the eastern side, in the shadow of the cliff upon which the wizard's tower was planted. They had traversed a maze of tunnels from their dungeon to find it, aiming ever downward, trailing Spar as they might a bloodhound. At last they had arrived at the edge of this hollowed, sea-filled cavern, where now they considered their next move.

"Where are all the men?" Pike asked, suggesting that he, too, shared the reservations that held his shipmates, Kell and Spar, in check.

"Sleeping," Flambard insisted. The flame-haired pirate peered hungrily through the tunnel opening, staring out at the giant carrack lying in berth beside a wooden dock. Its handful of longboats were tied off alongside. All rested upon the black waters, limned by fog-shrouded moonlight pouring through a cleft in the cliff face off to their right. "We're wasting time."

Kell wondered at his mate's anxiousness. Likely, the man was simply eager to be away from this place. The overwhelming temptation, this close to freedom, was to make a dash for it. So thought the mouse with the cat waiting to pounce outside its hole.

"We'd be hard-pressed to set sail on that thing with just the four of us," Spar muttered grimly. "They're like to catch us before we've unfurled the course sails."

"What then? Sit around here till dawn? Cap'n wanted a diversion."

"The diversion comes when we signal the *Squall*," said Pike. "We'd do better shoving off in one of those longboats."

Kell nodded quickly. Silent sounded safer than swift.

Spar's eyes glittered black in the darkness. "Too long," he decided. "We don't know how far out the *Squall* might be. Besides, in this murk, she may not see us."

What did that leave them? Kell wondered. There were no mid-sized craft that they might rig quickly to carry them on their way. For such smaller vessels, it would be a difficult voyage indeed from the mainland to this treacherous isle. All they had to choose from was that which floated before them.

"Flambard is right," Spar agreed at last. "We've no choice but to launch the carrack."

A hole opened in Kell's stomach, and any protest he might have uttered was sucked into it. He stared again at the imposing ship, then swept the harbor for sign of sentries. Their view here was partially obscured. They might very well be spotted the moment they stepped from the tunnel.

"Follow my lead," Spar growled at Flambard, who was itching again to get moving.

Once again, the marauders fell into line behind their giant first mate—Flambard, then Pike, then Kell—moving ahead in a crouch and glancing to either side. Setting foot within the main cavern felt to Kell like emerging naked onto a frigid snowscape. The eyes of imagined enemies dug like slivers of ice into his skin. Every hair stood on end.

But there were no sounds, no sudden movements. It seemed Madrach's mercenaries were indeed tucked away in their billets, wherever those might be. Difficult to believe, but since they'd not felt need to post dungeon guards, why should they post any here?

Still, Kell gripped his rocks in his sweating palms, ready to hurl them at the slightest skittering. Odds were, he'd end up braining a rat or cracking the shell of a rock crab—assuming his throw was true—and give them all away.

For this reason, he tried to steady himself as they crept from stony ground onto the planks of the makeshift wharf. Ocean waves growled, surging in and out of the cavern breach. While listening, Kell scanned the many caves and alcoves lining the subterranean walls, searching their yawning depths for anything that might justify his alarm.

At last they reached the carrack, rising and falling in its berth. The gangplank was raised, but a series of rope ladders hung over her sides. The members of their company took turns peering over one another's shoulders, taking one last look around. They listened, but all they heard were the waves.

Spar let Flambard go first. The marauder scurried nimbly up the rungs and rolled over the edge. After a tense moment, his head popped back into view and he gave a signal. All clear.

Pike went next. Then Kell, tucking his rocks into his shirt. Spar remained below, his back to the hull, searching. Only after Kell had clambered over and onto the main deck did their first mate make move to join them.

They waited for him, though by now Kell was as antsy as Flambard. It was too late to do anything but go forward. Should they be discovered, they might scatter, but where could they run?

"Haul," Spar grunted quietly, "find us some weapons. Pike, Flambard, make ready to sail."

The pirates nodded, then scrambled in opposite directions, running low and on the balls of their feet. Flambard claimed the foremast, Pike the mizzenmast, and Spar the mainmast. Kell went in search of the nearest weapons closet. He didn't have to go far. The main deck was lined with them, chests filled with hooks and pikes, hand-axes and shortswords. He claimed a couple for himself, then scooped up an armful and wheeled toward the pilothouse.

"Hello, Keel Haul."

Kell nearly soiled his breeches to hear Madrach's voice, and to see the mutineer standing so suddenly before him. As it was, he dropped his load of arms and stumbled backward, pitching over the rail. There was a rush of cold air, then the plunge into what might as well have been a bucket of ice, so frigid was the winter sea.

When finally he righted himself in that depthless void, he kicked toward the surface, where his attempt to draw one big breath resulted instead in a staggered series of small ones, fractured by the cold. Over the sound of his own splashing and wheezing, he could hear an odd mix of shouts and laughter from above.

"Fish him out," Madrach hollered. Men barked and crossbows hummed, and Kell knew his comrades were under fire.

His first instinct was to pull himself from that water as quickly as possible. It clutched at him like fingers from the grave, chill and sharp, and with a dying man's insistence. Had Madrach's mercenaries tossed him a rope then and there, he might have seized it, heedless of the consequences.

But it took them a moment to gather themselves, and to overcome their merriment at his expense. In that time, Kell's thoughts cleared. Not for anything he might consider actual reasoning, but enough that one urgent need overcame the other. The need to reach the longboats. The need to warn the *Squall.*

His frantic effort to tread water became an equally frantic swim. He did not stop to calculate the odds, or even to worry about his mates. They would cover for him, if they could. Perhaps one or more would escape on his own. It all depended on whether Madrach's orders were to kill or recapture. He could let neither happen to him.

And so he strained against the cold, against the darkness. He slipped under, carving his strokes beneath the surface, hoping to hide his intent. He did not pause to look back, and came up to breathe only when his lungs demanded it. Every now and then, he opened his eyes to confirm his path and direction. Otherwise, he simply swam.

He nearly rammed the skiff before he saw it—a collision that could have knocked him senseless. Kicking and pulling, he tumbled aboard, grateful to be free of the sucking sea.

"To the boats!" he heard someone shout.

Kell lunged for the mooring lines, fore, then aft. Each was a simple slip-knot, which he yanked free. His frozen hands grappled with a pair of oars, struggling to fit them in their locks, while the gangplank hit the dock with a thud and a cadre of mercenaries came scampering out.

At last his uncooperative oars fell into place. Even then he flailed uselessly for a moment, too anxious to be away. The paddles slapped and spun, resisting his unsteady control. He forced himself to take a deep, shivering breath in order to gain his balance, then thrust deep, and pulled.

A shredded cry sounded from aboard the ship, reverberating along the jagged walls of the cavern. Flambard, Kell thought, grimacing.

"Fools!" Madrach roared. "I want them taken alive!"

That was of small consolation to Kell as a half-dozen men leapt into a trio of longboats, snarling with a huntsman's glee. Even if they'd heard and decided to obey their leader's command, Kell knew this was his one best chance to get off the isle. He didn't know what sort of game the wizard and his underlings were playing, letting them escape their cage only to round them up again. But he wanted no part of it.

He'd gone maybe a dozen strokes, and already his back and shoulders burned. With no idea as to how long he might have to keep this up, and with the first of his pursuers shoving off with not one man but two at the oars, his prospects seemed grim.

The shadow of the cavern slipped away like a blanket as he reached the mouth of the underground harbor. Misty starlight fell upon him, funneled down between giant pinnacles of limestone that flanked the opening like tusks. A wave swelled beneath as if to carry him back through the cleft, but he dug deep and slid over its backside, into the retreating trough.

Gritting his teeth to still their chattering, he tucked his chin and rowed on.

TORIN DROPPED TO A SUDDEN CROUCH, shoved back against the wall of the tunnel by a sweating Raven.

"What is it?" he asked.

The pirate silenced him, then looked to his compass. The needle was dancing, as if closing upon its goal and excited by the prospect. The unlikely companions had come a long way from their dungeon, traveling what seemed to Torin more than a mile of rough and winding corridors—an entire warren of chambers and passageways that cored through Grimhold's rock foundation. Clinging to the shadows and to each other, the pair had run a labyrinthine course through these hidden levels, and, as best as Torin could tell, were hopelessly lost. He wondered if Raven had any better sense of their location, but was afraid to ask.

"Just ahead now," the pirate whispered, confirming Torin's hopes and suspicions.

Even now, Torin wasn't sure what to make of this man. Throughout their trek, he had continued to wonder what reason the pirate would have to return his weapons and set him free when this was over—to say nothing of their bargain to deliver him to Yawacor. The only scenario in which he could imagine that happening was one in which he somehow gained the upper hand, able to turn the tables on the other. But could he do so? Could he perhaps threaten Autumn's life as Raven had his and thus force the pirate to do his bidding? He didn't think so. He didn't think he could turn cutthroat, even with the greater good at stake.

Nor would he get the chance, he berated himself silently, if they started scheming already against each other. Their only hope of surviving this was if they trusted each other, as the pirate suggested, focusing their full faith and efforts against their common enemy. He had little choice but to assume Raven believed the same.

Shrugging aside his lingering doubts, he peered with the pirate around the corners of this newest intersection. Their tunnel had run headlong into another, which forked off to the left and right at rounded angles. To the right, low-burning torches flickered in their sconces, illuminating an open portal in the far side of the curving hall a few paces down. To the left was blackness.

Raven pointed, indicating the empty doorway. They had encountered a dubious lack of guardsmen in their travels; those whom they had spied had been easy to avoid. The same was true here, which caused Torin's skin to prickle. By the look on Raven's face, the man shared his discomfort. *This is it*, the eyes seemed to say. A warning, a plea, a question. Torin took a deep breath, and nodded.

They turned the corner as they had most others, back to back, to guard against ambush. Raven scooted ahead, Torin watching the rear. Even so, he knew when they had reached the doorway, for his companion stopped and coiled, as if braced for attack.

Torin spun quickly to get his own look of the room. It was a windowless chamber, round and spacious, lit by a scattered array of braziers. Like most of what they had seen, its construction appeared both natural and man-made. While the floor was paved, the walls and ceiling were of raw stone. A swirling pattern dominated the center, four or five paces in diameter, gouged into the earth. Around it was gathered a brood of crumbled statuary, overgrown with lichen.

He couldn't be sure how much of this Raven saw, for the pirate's attention was drawn at once to one of the statues to their left, an altar in the shape of a spitting gargoyle. A woman, blindfolded and gagged, was pilloried to this sculpture, locked at the wrists, her hands jutting from the creature's empty eye sockets. Despite being unable to see, she turned her head in their direction.

Autumn.

Raven spared a quick glance to either side before rushing to her. Torin was more thorough in his search, bending his knees and casting about as if the roof were threatening to collapse. He half expected Soric to materialize before his eyes, but the wizard was nowhere in sight.

"The Sword," Raven said as he reached the strange altar. Autumn remained inexplicably calm, making no effort to speak through her gag or to squirm against her stocks. Then Torin saw what he had missed before. Before him was a pedestal, at the edge of the circular floor pattern, almost directly across from Autumn's position. The pedestal faced out over the circle like a lectern. Midway up, on a ledge of the plinth at the base of the pedestal, on the side opposite the would-be speaker, lay the box containing the Sword.

A caterpillar of warning inched across Torin's neck, and he renewed his desperate scan for hidden occupants. It was clear enough what was happening. He was a wild animal sniffing at the bait of a hunter's trap. The smart thing would be to turn tail and scamper as quickly as he could from this place.

Or was it? They were in the wizard's house, and would have to play this by his rules. Torin had known that much coming in. And all of their feeble posturing had done nothing to change it.

"What are you waiting for?" Raven snapped, fumbling with the statue, searching for a trigger or latch that would spring the clap-piece holding Autumn in place.

Torin shook his head. Ignoring for lack of options his own better judgment, he stepped toward the pedestal, eyes darting. Raven, meanwhile, had given up on figuring out the statue, and reached instead for the gag roped around Autumn's mouth. Whatever the knot, it melted beneath the rogue's skilled fingers.

"Close your eyes," the woman said at once.

"What?" The pirate blinked in bewilderment. "Autumn, how do we get you out of this?"

He slipped off her blindfold. Doing so sparked an explosive pop, as a scintillating flameburst erupted from the flat head of the statue. Autumn's exposed lids were already clenched, but Raven scarcely had time to cry out. Torin, who had been watching the pair as he crept toward Sword and pedestal, threw an arm up to shield himself from the blast. An intense glare flashed across the chamber, consuming gloom and shadow, then flickered and was gone.

Torin let his arm down slowly. Raven was staggering about, arms flailing as if warding off a swarm of locusts. Then the pirate's legs failed him completely, and he crumpled to a seat on the stone floor.

A flutter of movement from the opposite edge of the room stole Torin's attention, and he whirled in its direction. From the depths of a hidden alcove stepped Soric, yellow eyes agleam.

Torin's own eyes snapped back to the Sword box, and before he could rethink his decision, he lunged. A crack echoed as the wizard's staff butted the earth, causing the ground around the box to glitter. Torin saw it, but by then was a slave to his own momentum. As his foot came in contact with the suddenly glowing sands that lay sprinkled about, once-solid rock became as mud, swallowing his leg halfway to the knee.

It hardened as quickly, clamping down and causing him to pitch forward with an agonizing wrench of muscle and bone. He was able to recover, thrusting out with his hands and shoving himself mostly upright, but he found himself trapped within the outer rings of the circle, stuck at a sprinter's angle, with the box mere inches from his extended reach. He yanked and twisted, but the sands' glow had faded, and the stone held fast.

The wizard laughed. "Gnaw through it, if you wish, dear brother. The mount will sooner crumble than release its hold."

Torin spat and wheezed, desperation overcoming him in waves. He strained again for the Sword, tugging at his anchor, but the weapon remained out of reach. His eyes flew then to the exit, a reflexive response, to find it blocked by the familiar form of an assassin's shadow.

"So let it end between us," Soric hissed, "once and for all."

CHAPTER EIGHTEEN

Kᴇʟʟ's ᴍᴜsᴄʟᴇs ʙᴜʀɴᴇᴅ. Though strong winds and a misty rain numbed his already sodden skin, they couldn't reach the flames that consumed him from within.

Still he rowed, driven by his fear. The pain of weary muscles would heal, but not if he failed to make his escape. The trio of longboats that had flushed him from the secret harbor maintained their pursuit. Unable to close distance with their oars, they had taken to firing upon him with their crossbows. Kell ducked and twisted to avoid the attacks, but had refused to slow, trusting to the shield of his boat's stern and the protection of whatever gods he hadn't alienated long ago.

The wind and weather aided him in this regard. His foes were shooting while standing in a boat, with both bowmen and target being tossed by the swells. In addition, when one man decided to fire, that left the other to take up his oar, so even when Kell was forced to drop his, the enemy gained no ground. Best of all, his hunters seemed to be treating it all mostly as sport, pausing to laugh and jeer whenever they came close.

Nevertheless, it was but a matter of time before his luck ran dry and a quarrel found its mark. This much Kell understood clearly, and it spurred him on with desperate strokes.

But even desperation had its limits. He'd been edging north along the eastern shore of the isle for better than ten minutes, he guessed, and still no sign of the *Squall*. Worse, his pursuers appeared at last to be showing signs of competence, coordinating their chase so that while one or two boats kept him pinned with fire, the others concentrated on moving in. And the closer they came, the more tenuous his predicament grew.

At last he realized that he could go no farther under these circumstances. He cast about frantically, wondering what he might do to alter his fortunes. The sea was of no help. Were he to lunge overboard, as tired as he was, it would swallow him with scarcely a gulp. Yet if he were to stop and throw his hands in the air, he might only be filled with crossbow quarrels before ending up the same.

A crash of waves against rock triggered a desperate hope. Looking over his right shoulder, he spied a smattering of clifflike formations jutting from the water, broken apart from the main isle. They reminded him of tombstones in a poorly tended graveyard. The ocean slapped and churned around their base, spewing foam with an angry roar. To approach would be to risk being splintered against their jagged sides. And yet, if he could slide his craft among them, he just might be able to lose himself in their mammoth shadows.

When a crossbow bolt slammed into the haft of his oar just above his hand, Kell decided it was worth the risk. Dragging the right, he pulled hard with the left, digging a tight turn toward the isle's surf. Once again, he managed to catch a wave just right, its surging crest helping to speed him away from his would-be captors. Another bolt whistled wide. Kell glanced back to check his markers, biting down on a muttered oath.

More than once, his arms threatened to give out on him, like flaming driftwood on the verge of crumbling into embers. He bent at the waist, redistributing the weight of each pull as best he could among back, shoulders, and limbs. Though he yearned to succumb, he denied his muscles' dire need, fearing that to take even a moment's rest would make it his last.

His breath was sawing in and out by the time he reached the shadow of the first rock. Its craggy skin glistened with spray, obsidian in the moonlit darkness. For a moment, as its sharp mass loomed menacingly above him, he was convinced he'd made a mistake.

Then he glanced up and saw that the others had eased off, betraying their hesitation. Kell savored a reckless sneer, even as he fought against waves that threatened now to dash him against the fortified shoreline. He had just about cleared the corner. Already, two of the pursuing longboats were blocked from view by the giant rock's rugged outline.

Before the same could be said of the third, the vessel's crossbowman loosed a final shot, catching Kell square in the shoulder. His cry was lost to the wind as his left arm went limp as wet sea grass. His oar dropped, an eddy seized him, and he spun wildly out of control.

He tried to recover, but his wounded arm would not respond, lifeless save for the stabbing waves of pain. Nor was there any use, he soon realized, in trying to steer his vessel with one oar. He was at the mercy of the ocean or that of his tormenters—whichever claimed him first.

Up and down the tide took him, twisting him this way and that. Sneaker waves crashed in over the gunwale, sweeping him from his seat and into the bottom of the boat. Freezing water sloshed and roiled around him. When he tried to breathe, he coughed and sputtered on a mouthful of brackish foam. Roving seabirds screamed overhead. Among this garden of cliffs, this close to the jagged shore, he was as good as dead.

He managed to right himself, clinging to a bench and using it for leverage. Peering over his prow, he saw those of the other boats, headed straight for him. They had lit their lanterns, which bobbed and flickered, but glowed brightly enough in the coastal brume. Kell's eyes, however, had begun to lose focus. He couldn't tell how far off they might be.

Then the lanterns began to flash—a series of signals that Kell recognized. He squinted, shivering uncontrollably, as the signal was taken up farther away and relayed once again. A moment later he stiffened, as the silhouette of a large vessel cleared the edge of another of the tombstone rock formations. At first he thought it to be the nose of Madrach's carrack, set sail from its underground lair. But then a shaft of starlight spilled through the cloud cover to illuminate the figurehead of a bloody raven, its wings outspread in flight.

Kell smiled against thickening waves of pain. Not even another sneaker wave could wipe it from his face. When he came up this time, his boat had been turned around once more, to face the direction from which he'd come, where the first of his pursuers were only now coming around the rock. He twisted the other way. The *Squall* and her lookouts remained, the most blessed sight he'd ever seen, emerging from their place of hiding and bearing toward him on a swift wind. Without thinking, he reached up with his one good arm and gave his mates an emphatic wave.

Then the ocean surged up beneath him, catching his hapless vessel at an odd angle, flipping him over and into the sea.

TORIN'S GAZE SWEPT LIKE AN ANIMAL'S around the chamber. From her altar, Autumn studied him in silence, while behind the mysterious woman, Raven blinked and rubbed his eyes in obvious dismay. Talyzar's dark form hovered in the doorway, blocking any hope of escape—even if Torin were to break free from where his leg was rooted to the floor. And then there was Soric, who stepped forward to loom over him like a hooded executioner.

He struggled until the wizard's shadow covered him, then forced himself to return the other's gaze boldly. A tight smirk strained the corners of Soric's mouth, seeming to mock his struggles, while the gimlet eyes shone with anything but mirth.

His brother surprised him by stepping past without a word toward the disoriented Raven. The pirate had come to his hands and knees, but was groping about like a blind man. As if sensing the wizard's approach, he froze suddenly.

"Our games are ended, Captain," Soric said. "Time now to make your choice."

Raven spat in the direction of the voice, striking the ground at the wizard's feet.

"Your fire is admirable, but misguided. We need not be adversaries."

"Then free her," Raven growled. "And let you and I be rid of each other."

"Too late for that, I'm afraid." Soric turned to Autumn, who, to Torin's continuing wonderment, did not shy as he cupped her chin in his hand. "Like you, she has sparked my interest. I will make use of her as I will of you, one way or another."

Raven made a lunge from his knees, reaching out as if to wrap the wizard by the legs and tackle him to the ground. But while his aim was true, Soric calmly stepped aside, leaving the pirate to bash himself against the stone of Autumn's gargoyle statue, where he crumpled at its base.

"You *will* serve me," the wizard declared. "Willingly or otherwise. The only difference will be your reward. Be it unbridled wealth and freedom," he said, gesturing toward the assassin in the doorway, "or pain."

With that, he reached down to snag the pirate by the chin, using thumb and forefinger like a barbed hook. Raven fought with clenched teeth, but was drawn steadily to his feet. When he reached forth to grapple against the hold, Soric merely twitched, sending an invisible jolt through the captain's body that snapped his arms out wide.

Rigid with pain and defiance, Raven was nevertheless helpless as Soric led him to a sculpture much like Autumn's. There the wizard raised the hand holding his staff. As if attached by strings, the crest of the statue's head lifted straight up with a dull scrape, exposing the deep prongs on either end that rooted it like a tooth into position. With another jolt, Soric forced Raven's wrists out straight and into the cups of the empty eye sockets, then dropped the lid of the pillory shut once more.

With the pirate secured, the wizard drew a gleaming knife from his belt. "As proof, you will first help me to dispose of this, the last thorn of betrayal in the circle of my crown."

"Let them go, Soric," Torin snarled, addressing his brother by name for the first time. "They've nothing to do with us."

"My preference as well," the wizard replied, scowling at the blind Raven, who flapped at his stocks. "I had hoped to use their shipmates for this purpose, or soldiers of my own. But a horse must be broken before it can be ridden."

With deft swiftness, he slid his blade across the bottom of Raven's wrists, forced downward before him. The pirate thrashed and wailed, more in fury than in pain. Blood pulsed from the wounds, catching in a trough of the gargoyle's snout. A moment later, it emptied in a trickle through the creature's mouth, a tiny rivulet beginning to flow.

"Yes," Soric hissed in Raven's ear. "Fight it. The more you struggle, the greater my strength and control."

Raven turned purple with strain, veins bulging from neck and face as he twisted and clenched as if to tear the wizard to pieces. As he did so, Torin watched the flow of blood drip from the altar and into the grooves of the swirled pattern carved upon the floor. His eyes widened as the entire design began to emit a faint glow.

"Your stubborn refusal condemns not only yourself," the wizard reminded the flailing pirate, "but your flower as well." He stepped toward Autumn, presenting the knife and the trace of blood along its edge.

Torin felt his own fury rising, and jerked again at the mountain rock that held him trapped. He leaned out for the box containing the Sword, but was no closer to reaching it than before. Forced to admit defeat on a physical front, he looked back to Autumn, whose calm gaze seemed to sap a measure of the wizard's thunder.

Then the dagger found its mark.

"No!" Torin shouted, as the blood slipped from her wrists. The woman herself uttered not so much as a whimper. "Damn you, Soric! What do you want of me?"

The wizard was held captive a moment longer by Autumn's glittering, amethyst gaze, then turned toward Torin, wiping the blood from his knife.

"Want?" he echoed. "Desire is for the weak, a craving by those who have not. Look around you, brother, at this keep that has become my home. Rough it may appear, but within its vaults lie treasures beyond compare—not only the metals and gems used to purchase men's allegiance, but ancient knowledge, a limitless store of tomes and scrolls and artifacts of unspeakable power. I alone was chosen to unravel their secrets, to inherit command of natural energies one like you can scarcely begin to fathom. There is nothing for which I want. Nothing I cannot have."

Torin looked to where Autumn's blood now met Raven's upon the floor. The glow of the strange pattern deepened.

"But there is a stark difference," the wizard continued, striding over to leer down at him, "a chasm between desire and demand. Destiny grants us opportunities, nothing more. The rest is up to us, to claim or leave behind for one of stronger will. I have sacrificed half my life in pursuit of a legacy to which I was born. And I shall be damned indeed before I watch the fruits of my labors be enjoyed by one to whom everything has been so freely given."

"And what is it you think I've been given?"

"Everything!" Soric gnashed. "Everything that by natural order should have been mine."

"Love," said Autumn suddenly, and both men turned. "Nurturing. I pity you, wizard, the envy you bear."

Soric's eyes narrowed. "Envy?"

"Had you received the attention and support your brother did, everything he has achieved—the joy and recognition—might instead be yours. Worse, he does not enjoy what fame and glory are his, while you crave it. Is that not what this is about?"

The wizard sneered. "He is the younger son, is he not? What right has he to the blessings of the first?" When Autumn did not respond, he scoffed. "Either way, you may keep your pity. Were it not for my actions against our father, this whelp would never have been born. Everything he has is due to me."

Though his mind remained addled with hopeless thoughts of escape, Torin could not help but acknowledge the truth of his brother's words. Queen Ellebe had told him as much, that he'd been conceived only after Soric's banishment, to secure a monarchy bereft of an heir. Whatever else the wizard chose to believe, Torin did, in essence, owe the man for his very existence.

He looked up, feeling the heat of his brother's glare.

"In return, he would take that which remains to me, that which I have earned by right of birth and toil. Speak all you will of envy and desire. I speak only of demand. Demand for the fealty owed me. Demand that a thief be punished. *That*, my dear flower, is what this is about."

Torin waited for Autumn to raise another argument, as he was out of his own. But the woman only stared at him, her head tilted to one side, her expression unreadable.

As if their silence marked a grim victory, Soric snorted and walked away, coming to a stop on the other side of the pedestal. There he peered down at a disc-shaped tablet Torin hadn't noticed before. With a crooked finger, he began tracing spherical patterns upon its stone surface. Suddenly, the circle beneath Torin started to vent, trailers of mist wafting from its furrows.

At the same time, the air within the chamber began to hum and crackle, alive with mystical energy. Torin's gaze flicked to Talyzar, to Autumn, to Raven—all of whom appeared to be at the mercy of the wizard.

"And now, my brother, we see to your fate."

KELL COUGHED, SPEWING SEAWATER from his lungs. The salty fluid tasted like bile and burned like acid, but then air—wondrous air—filled his chest once more. He sucked it down in ragged gulps, while a powerful hand slapped his back in encouragement.

"Spit it out, mate. There's a good lad."

Kell reached up to ward off the enthusiastic pounding, which sent waves of agony through a stinging shoulder. He glanced about, his eyes slowly regaining focus. He was in a skiff—not that stolen from the wizard's harbor, but one of those belonging to the *Raven's Squall*.

"Welcome back, my friend," said another of his mates, at whom he could only manage to stare.

"Boy doesn't know head from tail," replied a third, and a snicker passed through the boat.

"Cap'n!" Kell wheezed, clutching at the bolt lodged in his shoulder. "Black Spar! They need help."

"Settle down, mate. Let's catch your breath first."

But it was all coming back now. Amid painful coughs and the bucking of their little vessel on the choppy waves, Kell righted himself. "We've got to get to the *Squall*. Raven's orders."

"She's a mite busy just now, mate. Take a look."

Kell squinted along the line of the other's outstretched arm. The longboats that had pursued him were rowing desperately toward shore, seeking the shelter of the reef. Closing fast was the *Squall*, her deck firing away with ballistae and catapults. Though trapped at the edge of the shoal, she was not letting them get away.

The half-drowned pirate found his smile as the first of the boats was struck by an iron ball that bit off its stern and launched the mercenary in its prow screaming into the air. While pulling frantically away from its doomed comrade, another of the enemy boats was seized by a wave and dashed against a coastal outcrop, where it crumbled into splinters.

The last looked for a moment like it might actually get away, but then a volley of spears caught its oarsmen through the chest and stomach. It carried on, dead men aboard, steered by the sea.

As her firing ceased, the *Squall* heaved to, waiting for her longboats to return. Kell turned to Brack, the burly boatswain who had slapped the breath back into his lungs, and shared with him a roguish grin.

"Hurry, mate," he said through chattering teeth. "We've a bigger fish to reel in."

"Yeah?" Brack asked. "What might that be?"

"One of the largest carracks I ever saw, nested in the wizard's harbor, captained by one Madrach."

Brack's grin vanished. The man had lost his favorite tooth and three fingers from his left hand during Madrach's attempted mutiny four years earlier. To Kell's knowledge, not a day had since passed in which he had not grumbled about a chance to even the score.

"Captain gave us permission to take him down," he added.

"You heard the man!" Brack roared to his oarsmen. "Back to the *Squall*! Faster!"

Kell shivered as the wind whipped through his soaked body. Brack tossed him a blanket of coarse wool, fetched from the storage locker beneath his bench seat. Clutching its folds about his neck in a blue-fingered fist, Kell sat facing out over the prow. Perhaps he should have lied to save his own skin—told them he was the last and urged them away with due haste. The *Squall* was still hurting from her fight a week ago, and Madrach's ship posed a much more lethal challenge than a handful of longboats. He hadn't gone through all that he had just so narrowly survived to plunge headlong into a serpent's hollow.

Then again, he hadn't come so far in his duty only to fail his beleaguered mates now.

The winds blew and the boat rocked, and Kell hoped he was not already too late.

CHAPTER NINETEEN

"*I* KNEW EARLY ON," Soric said, "what was to become of you."

Torin was only half listening. Whatever his brother had planned for him, he wanted no part of it. His mind raced, trying to come up with something, anything, to extricate himself from this before it was too late. But strive as he might, dipping over and again into his well of ideas, the bucket kept coming back empty.

The wizard droned on, leaning upon his lectern like a magistrate passing sentence. "Almost from the beginning, when I learned of my mother's betrayal and her plans for you. I knew it would be something special, a response worthy of the risk and planning she underwent to prepare you for taking my role.

"As if to erase me," he snarled. "Like some failed experiment."

His only hope, Torin decided, was to reason with the wizard somehow. He couldn't tell if the man was gloating or venting. Either way, it seemed clear that what he truly wished for was some form of acknowledgment—an admission of guilt, perhaps. Otherwise, there would have been no need for such theatrics.

"I, too, was betrayed," Torin blurted. "Lied to from the beginning. The crimes of which you speak—we are victims, one and the same."

Soric scowled. "Dare you compare your idyllic village to the bowels of a slave ship? The embrace of a foster father to the whips of those who barter in human flesh?"

Torin shrank from those flashing eyes, down into the runner's stance forced by his foot being buried in the stone floor. The mist from the circle swirled higher, brushing at his ears.

"The same? Hardly, my brother. Though you shall taste soon enough what it means to be tormented, made outcast, while your world goes on without you. While those who knew you speak your name only in guarded whispers, as if it were better had you never been born. You would usurp my existence? Then let you suffer for it, as I have. And let us see if you prove strong enough, as I did, to return."

There were whispers in fact now, a voiceless susurration rising out of the mists, swirling at the edge of the circle—like the wind through the forest in the moments before a storm.

"Would you know how it happened?" Soric taunted. "How I escaped our father's decree? Fate would not have it that I live my life as a slave. I knew that much even while being led away in shackles— Stay where you are, assassin."

Torin's gaze flew to the doorway, where Xarius Talyzar had eased across the threshold and into the chamber. Although the wizard had not even glanced in his direction, the assassin stopped in his tracks, pinned in place by his master's outstretched hand.

"But destiny has a way of testing us," Soric continued, "of preparing us for what is to come. So I realized when the storm overtook us, and I washed ashore this lost isle. So I learned when I crawled through the depths of this keep to discover the crypt of those who had built it, those who had conducted their study of magic within.

"They were gone, but their treasure—and their secrets—remained. Secrets I would one day reintroduce to this world. For years I labored just to interpret the language in which the knowledge was recorded. After that came the pain, of a kind you cannot comprehend, as I made their findings my own and experimented with my newfound power. It shaped me as much as I shaped it. But in the end, it was the magic that saved me, that made possible my rebirth."

It was becoming more difficult to hear, let alone focus on, the wizard's words. The whispers had given way to low, sinister growls, and the thickening mist had begun to spin more rapidly. He looked to Raven, slumped now against his altar—whether alive or dead, Torin couldn't tell. Autumn was still alert, but was focused upon Soric, as if it were her attention alone that kept him talking. Perhaps it was, Torin thought, for the wizard was speaking to her as much as to him, almost as if caught in some sort of trance. If only he could figure out what all this time might buy him.

"Strange, the truth of magic," Soric said, his yellow gaze clouding. "For it is no great secret, really. We are, each of us, fashioned from the same universal energies. Such energy can be broken into separate spheres, each a state of being, through which man can attune himself to the natural flow of the universe and thereby manipulate its component forces."

He closed his eyes, drawing a deep breath. When he opened them again, he stared directly at Torin, like a tutor addressing a difficult student.

"Energy follows thought. To practice magic, one must imagine it, feel it, make it real in his own mind. Focus hard enough, and that which the wielder desires will become manifest. In the days when magic was strong, some did so with words or tunes, some with artifacts or charms, some with gestures or an absolute stillness of form. All are trappings, a means by which to draw and aim one's focus in order to cast the desired manipulation of energy."

Torin had heard enough. The growls had given way to screams, a cacophony of agonized wails. The mist had become a vortex beneath him, completely obscuring the circle at his feet. Its winds whipped about him, scratching his flesh with dust and grit. Atop it all, he had to endure this tirade from his brother, like something out of a poorly conceived mummer's tale.

"Why are you telling me all of this?" he shouted over the mounting gale.

The wizard smiled. "All? Dear brother, I might as well give you a blade and tell you to put the sharp end in my belly. There's a bit more to it than that, is there not?"

"Why don't we find out?" Torin snapped, his eyes falling again to the Sword box, so painfully close to his grasp.

His brother's smile vanished. "I tell you this so you know, brother, that your fate is nothing more, and nothing less, than what I demand. A spell I have been perfecting ever since I returned to this keep. A banishment, like that decreed for me. Only, I send you not to sea in the belly of a ship, but into the Great Maelstrom, that churning tempest from which all worlds are born. Within its fiery winds, you will be stripped of your mortal shell, but your essence will remain, with an eternal understanding of your punishment and a perfect recollection of he who cast you hither. Pain, my brother, is all that shall stand between you and oblivion."

In response, Autumn's voice carried above the shrieking tumult. "A dangerous game, wizard. To give vent to the Maelstrom is to open a rift not easily contained."

The words were lost on Torin. He had never heard of this Great Maelstrom. An old-world mythology, perhaps, pagan in its roots, from before the enlightened age of the Ceilhigh. Even if it were true, as this vortex might suggest, he was focused solely on what he knew: that if he did not soon find a way to the Sword, he would not be long for this earth.

"The Sword!" he blurted. "It can still be yours!"

Soric wrested his gaze from Autumn and fixed it on Torin. "Do you think to bait me, brother? The energy is in motion. You cannot stop it."

"But *you* can," Torin said. "And you will, if you wish to lay claim to the true Sword of Asahiel."

The look the wizard gave him fell somewhere between fury and amusement. "Are you telling me, then, that the weapon I saw is not in this box?" He stepped around to the other side of the pedestal and lifted the container from its perch.

"Look for yourself," Torin urged, clutching a final shield of hope.

The wizard scowled in warning, but what more might the man possibly do to him? Even so, Torin held his breath as Soric slid aside the latch and opened the box.

Revealing, as Raven had claimed, the ordinary broadsword within.

Fury was the clear winner now, flashing across the wizard's face amid a terrific flickering of shadows cast by the whirling mists. "What trickery is this?"

"Release these prisoners," Torin said, nodding toward Raven and Autumn, "and perhaps I'll tell you what I did with the real Sword."

Soric seemed on the verge of erupting, but, with an obvious effort, regained control of his seething emotions. "It matters not," he hissed through clenched teeth. "A trophy, and little more. Like all else to which you've laid claim, the Sword was never yours to begin with. It cannot save you now."

Torin's feeble shield shattered and fell away.

"A look, perhaps?" Talyzar suggested.

Torin wasn't even certain he'd heard the man, but Soric snapped a hard gaze upon the other.

"Know you something of this?" the wizard demanded. "As I recall, it was you who brought me the blade."

The assassin shook his head. "A suspicion. If I may?"

Soric glared at his servant, then at Torin, then back and forth between the two, as if attempting to discern some form of subterfuge. Torin, meanwhile, could only frown uncertainly. If Talyzar was working a ploy, it didn't include him.

Finally, the wizard held out the box, and the assassin came forward. Under his master's watchful eye, Talyzar closed the lid and began feeling around the outside with one hand. Again Torin held his breath, wondering what the assassin was up to.

After a moment of inspection, Talyzar froze, the searching hand positioned near the bottom of the box. He tilted the box in presentation, then opened the lid.

The Sword of Asahiel, along with the Pendant, gleamed red in the darkness.

"Marvelous," Soric crowed. He turned to Torin and his smile became cruel. "Although what I am about to show you is no illusion."

Torin studied the assassin. Had Talyzar known, or simply figured it out? But of course he knew, Torin fumed. He'd been spying on them the entire time, betraying him to the wizard more than once already. Why should this be any different?

"Step back, my shadow," the wizard bade his servant. "You'll not want to stand too close."

Talyzar followed him around to the other side of the pedestal, leaving Torin alone within his circle. It was like staring through glass at an inverted funnel cloud, which waited to drag him in.

"Give my regards to the Great Fiend," Soric said, "if ever you find the mercy of the Abyss."

He raised his palms out wide, then slapped them together. The noise they made was like a thunderclap, and the roaring wind shrilled suddenly louder.

Then it happened. One moment, the wizard was closing his eyes, chin lowering as he muttered some sort of incantation. The earth shuddered, and Torin glanced at the ground beneath him. When he looked up again, the wizard's mouth was agape, his gaze fixed and staring.

The tip of the Crimson Sword extended from his chest.

Torin could barely see, his eyes squeezed tight against the clawing winds. But he knew the telltale glow of the Sword, could almost see the flames that licked along the part of the blade that was stuck in his brother's body, illuminating the edges of the wound. Those within the tip shone brightly.

Soric slowly turned, and the blade turned with him, so that the hilt was now in Torin's view. Beyond stood Talyzar, the box tossed aside, a pair of sabers at the ready.

"Traitor," the wizard croaked, choking on a mouthful of blood.

The assassin stared back coldly. "We had a bargain."

"You think you can kill me?"

"I already have," Talyzar assured him, eyes narrowing like those of a viper.

But it was Soric who showed a viper's speed, lashing out with one hand to seize the assassin by the throat. Talyzar put one blade in the wizard's gut, while the other hacked at the arm that grabbed him. But neither loosened the spellcaster's inhuman grip. The assassin's eyes bulged as Soric shook him like a child's doll, breaking his hold on his blades.

A great fissure opened suddenly, cracking the chamber down its center. An astonished Torin found his leg released by the earth, and he flung himself to one side as the entire vortex shifted away from him with a deafening rumble. Like shears through wool, it carved a path through the pedestal that separated him from the unexpected combatants, causing its sides to split and crumble away.

Soric pulled Talyzar's body close as the funnel settled under them. "For an eternity shall I repay your treachery."

The invisible barrier shattered, and the storm was upon them. Torin was scarcely able to overcome his shock, but did so to lunge after the Sword. He could feel the winds engulf him. But when he clutched the gleaming hilt protruding from his brother's back, and the Sword's warmth swept through him, their tug slackened. After yanking the blade free, he tottered upon a raging precipice as the vortex sucked and swirled, stripping cloth and armor and flesh from the bones of those who vanished within.

But the storm did not disappear with the one to unleash it; rather, it sent forth lightning streams that rent the earth and widened at the edges, the threads of a great web that devoured all in a void of whirring darkness. Clinging to the Sword, Torin found himself trapped on all sides, with that darkness closing in.

Then a scream pierced the tumult. Autumn. Still alive, doubtless horrified by what she saw.

But in the next few heartbeats, the storm seemed to run out of breath and collapse under its own weight. Inch by inch, the earth reclaimed its hold, like water rushing toward low ground. The black threads withdrew; the snaking rifts closed. In a moment, the maelstrom had drained into a tiny hole at the center of where Soric and Talyzar had stood, then evaporated in a puff of mist. All that remained was the quaking and rolling of the mountain beneath Torin's feet. Finally that, too, ceased.

When it was over, Torin blinked in stunned disbelief. A few of the braziers remained, shedding meager light over what looked like a charred landscape, with the last trailers of mist drifting upward from a floor of black stone. His ears rang in the sudden stillness.

"Torin."

He spun at the sound, alarmed by the weakness in the voice. Autumn, once again, draped upon the head of her altar.

His bounding steps carried him quickly to her side. He set down the Sword, and, with both hands, heaved upward upon the head of the altar the way he'd seen Soric raise the lid of Raven's stocks.

It wouldn't budge.

"Autumn," he said, picking up the Sword. "Autumn, I'm going to cut you free. Will you trust me?"

She peered up at him with a half-formed smile. Even now, her eyes sparkled.

"Keep your wrists down."

Pale-faced, she nodded. It would be amazing, he thought, if she still had the strength to raise them. He stared at the line between the altar's lid and base, visualizing his stroke. He then struck with the Sword, ripping a path of fire along that line, just above her wrists. Cut from its tusklike prongs, the sculpted slab of granite offered little resistance as he shoved it aside, which enabled him then to assist the woman in wriggling her hands from the cups.

He knew they would be unscathed by the blade, even before he inspected them. What he did not anticipate was seeing that, somehow, the blood spilling from her wrists had already begun to clot.

"Raven," she said.

Torin gave her hands a squeeze, to be sure she was all right, before rushing to the pirate captain, who lay upon his altar like crumpled linen. With a deep breath, Torin freed him as he had Autumn, then helped the woman to lay him gently upon the ground.

"He's alive," Torin noted, though the other's breathing was shallow. Nor had his blood congealed nearly as well as Autumn's. Torin gave her a concerned look.

"Let me tend to him," she said.

"You're hurt too," he reminded her. "Lie down. Let me help."

She refused the first part of his request, but made no attempt to interfere as he cut strips from his shirt and used them to stanch Raven's bleeding. Before he could complete his work, however, his attention was stolen by the sound of booted feet stamping near.

"Stay here," he said, snatching up the Sword and running to guard the chamber entry.

He nearly cut the first newcomer in half before he realized who it was. Looking like a drowned rat, with a crazed gleam in his eyes and a crossbow bolt sticking from his shoulder, was the pirate Kell.

The man's eyes went wide as he caught sight of Torin, and he skidded to such a sudden halt that he fell flat on his back to avoid the glowing blade.

"Keel Haul!"

He reached quickly to help the other up, careful of the rogue's shoulder.

"The captain?"

Torin nodded toward the chamber. "In there, with Autumn. They're safe now, but badly hurt."

"Here! Over here!" Kell shouted back down the corridor.

Torin ducked back inside. Within a few moments, Black Spar, Pike, and others Torin didn't recognize had piled into the room. Spar, he noticed, had taken two bolts in the chest, and suffered a gash that bled freely down one arm. The first mate pushed past his comrades and glared down at Torin, who warded Autumn as she tended to the unconscious Raven.

"The wizard?" the big man asked.

Torin shook his head. "Gone. As is the assassin. What of Madrach? Is the keep secured?"

"It will be soon," Spar growled. "Just rooting the last of the buggers out. Haul here brought in the *Squall* just in time."

Torin glanced at Kell, then back to Autumn and Raven. They had both lost so much blood. Too much, perhaps. "Can we get them to the ship?"

"Pike, Sloop, see to the captain. Conger, Jib, the lady. Everyone else, grab your blades and follow me."

Torin was the last to leave, pausing in the doorway to look back on the scene of his brother's demise. He didn't believe for a moment that Talyzar had intended to rescue him—any more than *he* had meant to help arm the assassin with the killing blade. But whatever the villain's true motives, Talyzar had saved his life. He might even have felt grateful, were it not for his horror at the overall result.

Only after stepping away did he remember the Pendant. With a lurch in his stomach, he spun back, searching for the box, fearing that it had been swallowed by the mystical maelstrom.

But no, there it lay, overturned upon the stone floor. Torin rushed up to it and flipped it over. Concealed beneath its edges was the flaming heartstone, aglow at the end of its silver chain.

He picked it up and dropped it over his neck, breathing a sigh of relief. He then tucked the Stone beneath his shirt so that its warmth touched his skin, and raced after the departing pack of pirates.

This time, he did not look back.

WITHIN THE HOUR, he was back aboard the *Raven's Squall*—moored in an underground harbor next to the crippled, half-sunk remains of a giant carrack. Given the condition of their own ship, it would be some time before they were able to set sail. The wizard's mercenaries had all been rounded up—the dead, the wounded, and those who had surrendered—along with the members of his servant staff. The pirates not engaged in this were licking their own wounds, or looting the keep. Torin wasn't certain that was wise, prying through the vaults and cupboards of a wizard—even a slain one. But he kept his reservations to himself.

He was helping Pike to bring down a tattered sail when a hulking shadow fell over them. Torin looked up to find a moonlit Spar glaring down at him.

"Captain wants to see you."

The first mate was bandaged but still bloody, his face sweaty and drawn.

"Shouldn't you be resting?" Torin asked.

Spar grunted. "This way."

Torin trailed the other amidships, marching past the hold in which he'd been locked away on his journey to this isle. A sinking feeling accompanied him. Should Raven die now, it was Spar's mercy he would be forced to rely upon.

The brutish first mate led him belowdecks to rap at a cabin door. A husky voice bade them enter.

Spar held the door as Torin stepped inside. Raven lay abed within, slurping at a flask that Autumn held to his lips.

"Torin!" Autumn squealed, and set the flask aside. With a burst of energy, she flew across the cabin and gripped him in a tight embrace. "Let us wed and have a thousand children!"

Torin stood rooted in place, his arms at his sides, a flush of embarrassment warming his cheeks. He peered over the woman's shoulder at Raven, who drew himself to a sitting position.

"Forgive my love's exuberance," the pirate laughed. His blindness, it would seem, had passed. "What she means to say is, thank you."

Autumn withdrew a step, her smile radiant. Amazingly, her color had all but returned.

"I can't say as I did very much," Torin admitted.

The woman arched a single delicate eyebrow. "You came for me, didn't you?"

Torin grimaced. "Your man didn't give me a great deal of choice in the matter."

"No, but you might have left us there," Raven said. The skin of his face was ashen, with a waxlike sheen in the light of an oil lamp hung from the ceiling.

"I suppose. But then, it would be a long swim to get to where I need to go."

Autumn beamed. Raven snorted with laughter.

"We've been discussing that," said the captain. "Autumn says that if it's the Finlorians you're looking for, your best bet is to find and question Lord Lorre."

"Lord Lorre?" Torin asked, then stopped abruptly. "Wait. How did you learn of—"

"Autumn heard it from the wizard."

Torin nodded slowly, peeking at the woman with quiet suspicion. Autumn winked at him.

"Is this not so?" Raven asked.

Before Torin could answer, there was a commotion in the hall. Spar, who still blocked the doorway, glanced out, then back to his captain.

"Madrach, sir."

"Ah," Raven said. "Show him in."

Spar stepped aside and allowed a pair of captors to drag a bound Madrach into the room. The mutineer-turned-mercenary was bleeding at the mouth—where he was missing a front tooth—and from the stumps of three severed fingers on his left hand.

"Well, well," Raven said, once he had looked his brother over. "It would appear Brack got to him first."

"Not first, sir," Spar confessed. "But he had his go."

The sagging mercenary drooled blood upon the floor.

Raven turned to Torin. "I wonder if we might continue this later. I summoned both of you, but now that I've seen him, I'd like to have a few words with my brother in private."

Torin nodded, and with a lingering glance at Autumn, headed for the exit.

"Torin," Raven called.

"Yes, Captain?"

"Autumn filled me in on what happened in there. If you're upset about your brother, I'm sorry."

Torin considered. He still had a lot of questions, many of which, it now seemed, would never be answered. Aside from that, he wasn't sure what to feel. "He fashioned his own noose."

"As do we all," Raven replied. He took another drink and stared at Madrach. "As do we all."

Torin bowed and took his leave, heading above deck to see where he might be needed.

Spar closed the door behind him.

CHAPTER TWENTY

"W<small>ELL?</small>"

Allion's eyes lifted from the freshly delivered parchment long enough to take in the stern angle of Rogun's brow. He would have preferred to have read the message first in private, without the weight of the other's demanding gaze. But Rogun's right hand, Commander Zain, had intercepted King Thelin's emissary on the way in, and had seen to it that his general found Allion at the same time as the Souari courier. At Rogun's urging, Alson's regent hadn't even exited the hallway before unstoppering the scroll tube.

"It appears that Thelin has agreed to Darinor's proposal for combating the Illysp," Allion replied, his eyes still scanning the page.

"Impossible," Rogun said, looming closer.

For a moment, Allion thought the other meant to snatch the scroll away and read it for himself. Had the regent any place to retreat, he might have done so. As it was, he was backed against the wall of the stone corridor, with a sudden understanding of how Torin must have felt all those times the general had cornered him for one of these forced meetings.

"It remains for the Imperial Council to ratify the decision," Allion continued, hiding his nervousness. "But nowhere do I see objection from the king himself."

"Thelin would not be so foolish. Let me see."

Allion whipped the paper aside, out of reach of the general's grasping fist. "His list of concerns is as long as yours. But it reads here that he has trust enough to follow Torin's lead."

"Torin is not here," growled Rogun.

"He acknowledges that," Allion went on, pointing to a specific passage as he continued his hasty scan. In earlier correspondence, he'd done the best he could to explain to the Souari king—as well as to King Galdric of Atharvan and Nevik, baron of Drakmar—Torin's absence. Nevik had already sent return word, expressing no small measure of dismay. If Allion was reading correctly, Thelin's response was more muted, but no less heartfelt in its expression of both faith and concern. "He says that if Torin chose to submit to Darinor's judgment in this, and that our governing council has done the same, then he sees no reason as yet to suggest his countrymen do otherwise."

"Madness!" Rogun roared. "Is that not reason enough? Who is this man—this Darinor—that we should risk everything on his word alone?"

Allion had no answer. Not a night had passed in which he hadn't wondered the very same thing. He had half hoped that Thelin would in fact devise an alternative to the renegade Entient's radical proposal. Alas, with Thelin's acceptance, it seemed too late now to stem the other's tide of reasoning.

"I am the only one who understands the enemy you face," came the startling response.

Both Allion and Rogun looked up as the grim cloud that was Darinor scudded toward them on the corridor's stale wind.

"You may heed my counsel and live," the mystic said, his smoldering eyes boring holes in the rigid general, "or ignore it and meet a fate worse than death. The more I hear of this ignorance, the less I care."

Rogun's hand gripped the hilt of his sword. A reflex, it seemed, more than anything else. Still, Allion did not want to risk being caught between the two men in these tight quarters.

"Are you not the one, General, who has been urging action in this matter?" he asked.

Rogun continued to glare at Darinor until the other came to a stop—much too close for Allion's liking.

"As I've plainly stated," Rogun spat, "the action this one suggests flies in the face of any military tactics I've known. Leave our homes defenseless and trust the enemy to follow? I'd as soon march into combat naked and trust my foe to strike only my shield and not my exposed flesh."

"Then imagine you bear not a shield," Darinor countered, "but a haunch of beef, and that your enemy is a starving predator. Imagine further that your cities are filled with but scraps of leaf and root. As the enemy, which would you go after first?"

"As a mindless predator, I would go after whichever I came across."

A corner of Darinor's mouth turned up in a cruel smirk. "Then you have yet to understand the nature of your enemy. These are rational creatures. To believe otherwise is to seal your fate."

"This is madness," Rogun repeated.

Once again, Allion tried to intervene. "General—"

"Are you hearing this?" the chief commander ripped into him. "I speak of shielding lives. He speaks of satisfying hunger. Are we discussing war, or famine?"

"Both," Allion snapped, "if I understand correctly." He met the gaze of each of his listeners in turn, the pair of whom were caught off guard by his commanding tone.

It was Darinor who recovered first. "Is that a response to one of your emissaries?" he asked, looking to the parchment clutched in Allion's hands.

"It is," the regent acknowledged. "King Thelin has agreed to your course, and proposes we assemble our singular force south of the Gaperon."

"Naturally," Rogun scoffed. "Where it will shield his lands entire, and ours not at all."

"He also indicates," Allion added with a stern glare of his own, "that any and all refugees from our lands are welcome at Souaris, and that if necessary, room will be made within other Kuurian cities as well."

That seemed to disrupt Rogun's forthcoming outburst, giving Allion a surge of confidence until Darinor assailed him from the other side.

"There is no need to send civilians south," he argued, his tone dismissive. "Doing so would waste time we do not have, and expose many to unnecessary risk."

"You've assured us repeatedly that there's no such danger to our civilian populace," Allion replied hastily, before Rogun could formulate what he was sure would be a far less civil response.

"In their homes, beyond thought and sight, yes," Darinor explained. "But to march them across the countryside . . ." He shook his head. "You may as well herd a flock of sheep through a pack of wolves."

"That's not what you would have had us believe up until now," Rogun snarled.

Allion raised a hand to bid silence from the general, but made no effort to mask his own frown.

"Never before has that suggestion been raised," Darinor replied with ease. "Thus far, we have discussed troop movement only, not that of those we must protect."

"It's a fair suggestion," Allion maintained, not quite satisfied. "A reasonable option for those who wish it."

Again, Darinor shook his head. "Ordinarily, perhaps. But in this instance, it is a fool's course."

Allion glanced at Rogun, who continued to glower.

"Is that not why I am here?" the Entient demanded tersely. "To guide your actions against this enemy of which you know so little? To warn of mistakes that could cost innocent lives? Either way, I am through explaining myself to those who can scarcely comprehend the most basic tasks assigned to them."

Allion pressed his ground. "I think we are owed—"

"You forget yourself, young mortal," Darinor interrupted, hissing through clenched teeth. Allion froze as the towering man leaned over him. "My ancestors were beholden to an authority higher than any you can understand. Do not presume to know what I owe, or to whom. Nor should you mistake my charity for anything other than what it is."

Allion gulped. Even Rogun, he noticed, had eased down a bit.

"I'm telling you now, and for the last time, if you wish to buy Torin the time he needs to repair the damage he has caused, you must deploy now—to whatever location you desire. Your choice is not *whether* you will face the Illychar, but *where*. Stall much longer, and you will find yourself battling within the streets of this very city, among your homes and your families. Is that what you desire?"

"What of Galdric?" Rogun asked. The fire had gone out of him, leaving him to pout like a scolded child. "You claim that for your plan to work, all must participate. Yet we've no word from he who commands Pentania's second-largest army. Should we not wait a few days longer?"

"The sooner we light our beacon, the sooner we can draw our enemy—and allies to our cause."

For the first time since Allion had known the man, Rogun seemed at a loss. It was clear he was not yet convinced. But it seemed equally clear that this was not a debate they could win.

"I must still bring the matter before Thaddreus and the Circle," Allion cautioned, seeking to salvage a measure of pride for him and his general.

But Rogun, he realized, put no more stock in the Circle than he did in this renegade Entient. Maybe less.

"The fools will do as you tell them," the general muttered in disgust. His imperious gaze never left that of Darinor. "If this is truly the course you would set for us, we may as well carry it out."

"The army is ready then?" the Entient asked.

It was, Allion knew. Despite his opposing stance, Rogun had been preparing his troops for several days, ever since the council session during which Darinor's proposal had first come to light.

"Unless by miracle our regent here can talk sense into our so-called Elders," the general rumbled, "we march at dawn." He turned to Allion. "I'll not be holding my breath."

With that, he spun on a booted heel and spurred himself down the corridor.

"I'm not sure he trusts you," Allion dared a moment later, if only to break the uncomfortable silence left in the general's wake.

Darinor snorted. "I don't need him to trust me. Only to do as he's told."

"I'm not sure that I trust you."

The mystic regarded him without insult. "We'll learn in the end, won't we?" He leaned forward, eyes glinting with captured torchlight. "Until then, you defy me at your own peril."

Then he, too, headed down the hall, opposite the direction Rogun had taken, and Allion was able to breathe once more.

"Inform your precious Circle," the Entient called back without slowing. "By tomorrow, your city shall be empty of soldiers. Your citizens will want to know why."

So will I, thought Allion. As Darinor turned a corner, the regent looked back to the parchment in his hands, rolling it shut with a heavy sigh. So will I.

THE VERY NEXT DAY, ROGUN SAT ASTRIDE HIS FAVORITE STEED, watching the road being churned to mud by the hooves and feet and wagon wheels of his passing army. Ordinarily, it filled him with a grim sense of pride to be on the march, to see those under his training and command venture forth on campaign. To test his will and savvy against that of an enemy. It had been a long time since he had done so beyond the walls of his city, and never with his entire force arrayed before him.

He was anything but pleased.

How could he be? He had been all but stripped of his command, made puppet to another's will. It was one thing to ask a man to risk his life in a maneuver the general believed in so strongly that he would wager his own on its success. But to ask them to take that same risk on a course of utter folly . . .

It went against his every instinct, every bit of learning to which he had dedicated his life. Yet here he was, on the road south to assemble at the gateway of another's lands, while his own were under siege. Trusting blindly that the enemy would not ransack what he'd left behind, but would instead give chase—eschewing unguarded spoils for the fight itself.

He looked up as a company of pikemen trooped by in loose formation. Each man saluted as he passed, and Rogun did so in turn. Stout lads, these. Most were new recruits, pressed into service following the slaughter that had befallen the regular army at the hands of the usurping wizard. How long ago it all seemed, the general thought, as a windswept rain beat upon his helm. A period that felt like years, but had in fact been a matter of months. Scarcely enough time to rally a new defense force, let alone offer its members proper training. What they lacked in skill, they accounted for with pride, courage, and faith in he who led them.

Their trusting smiles cut Rogun to the bone.

To say nothing of those back home, many of whom would be incapable of defending themselves at all should the attack he feared come. The only word they'd been given was that the army was venturing forth to flush the recent scourge from their lands. Unsuspecting fools, they had bidden their men-at-arms farewell with roses and banners and sweetmeats for the road. Rogun had wanted to scream at them the truth.

They had not, of course, been left entirely unprotected. Even the doe-eyed Allion and lackwit City Elders had insisted on that. But the City Shield alone remained to them, less than a thousand in number, barely enough to control their own populace should it choose to rise against its rulers. A more fitting end to this mess, Rogun could not imagine, though it would remain to him to go through and sweep up afterward.

There had to be another way, the general told himself through gritted teeth, as he continued to survey and acknowledge those who marched past in their various regiments. He had half a mind to impose his own will, to ignore Darinor and use this force instead to march through and cleanse his lands of these so-called Illychar. But doing so would make him an outlaw in the eyes of Alson's rulers—pretenders though they might be. Thereafter, the only way to escape a charge of treason would be to take the crown by force. He was not yet prepared to do so. Not while Torin remained in such favor with King Thelin, who, despite his losses in the War of the Demon Queen, was capable of marshaling a force no less than twice—and up to six times greater than—Rogun's own. And comprised of seasoned warriors, at that.

He felt his stallion fidget restlessly beneath him, and gave it rein. The animal began working its way north, opposite the flow of soldiers and supply carts, brushing aside the tall grasses atop the embankment on which it strode. Krynwall's army carried on like a river, hemmed in by the near slope and a forested ridge on the other side. Rogun continued to monitor its rush, absently searching for the answer to his ongoing riddle.

When at last his horse stopped, tugging against its reins in order to sniff at a patch of wet clover, the general's gaze fell upon a rotted trunk that lay to one flank. Its sodden skin was in an advanced stage of decay. An army of beetles swarmed its flesh, scuttling over and under the softened edges. At least a score within, Rogun guessed, for every one without, working their devastation from the inside, unseen by the birds and rodents that might otherwise feast upon them.

And then it hit him. As suddenly as that, it became clear what he must do. An idea only, still vague around the edges, but he knew at once that it was the answer he'd been searching for, the best means by which to execute his sworn duty. Carry it out, and he might yet earn the label of traitor. But for the sake of his land and its people, that was a risk he would have to take.

"Runner!" he barked.

The obedient herald, who had been shadowing him some thirty paces off, galloped near. "Sir!" He saluted sharply, fist to chest, water dripping from his elbow in streams.

"Vanguard relay. They are to set a new course."

"Heading, sir?"

"South. We make for Drakmar."

The runner did not question the order, but gave another salute. "Sir!" he acknowledged, then wheeled his horse about.

"And fetch me Commander Zain!"

"Yes, sir!"

Rogun glanced once more at the fallen log and its nest of hidden beetles before gripping his reins. His headstrong mount resisted, but only until his spurs bit into its flanks. Pulling about, he started forward, gazing down again upon his troops. Despite the midday gloom, a smile lit his face, as that grim sense of pride he'd been missing began to fill him at last.

A CHARCOAL SUNSET FILLED THE WESTERN SKIES as Nevik fixed his gaze on the northern horizon. A chill dread continued to stir within the pit of his stomach, a sense that all was not right in the world. He tried to dismiss it, but like a nagging child, it refused to go away.

He should have been used to it by now. Things had not been right in his world for some time. Not since the wizard's invasion and the death of his father, Baron Nohr, followed hard upon by the conquest of the Demon Queen and her hordes of dragonspawn. Even after these enemies had been vanquished and he had returned home to his father's lands, his life had seemed a lonely and unfamiliar thing.

Only now, after months of working to repair what had been ruined, to gather what had been scattered, had he begun to feel comfortable once more. Like his king and friend, Torin, he was at last learning to accept his fate and to move on, filling his father's boots as best he could.

The timing, then, could not have been worse. First, the marauding packs of creatures from ages past, growing bolder by the day in these, the southern lands of Alson, as reports suggested they were everywhere else. Second, the news of Torin's departure on a voyage of startling scope and design, coupled with the story of what it was they were fighting. According to Allion, of the many barons and liege lords and city governors throughout Pentania, only he, King Thelin, and King Galdric had been given to know the full truth of the Illysp threat. They who could be trusted to remain discreet, and who would be relied upon most heavily to combat it. But how could he be expected to wage war against a foe he wasn't even sure he believed in, with just the sad remnants of his father's once proud army, while still protecting that which he had been working so diligently to restore?

And now, word from his northern watchriders that General Rogun was on his way, the entire army of Krynwall in tow.

His father, he knew, had always borne a grudging admiration for the chief commander of Alson's principal military force. But Nevik himself had spent weeks at Krynwall following the War of the Demon Queen, having accompanied Torin there to help start the rebuilding process from his nation's capital. There, he had seen for himself the animosity Rogun bore for their king, the long-lost son of Sorl. Heard with his own ears the general's demands that the crown be worn by someone better suited to the task. Despite his father's opinion, Nevik wasn't certain Rogun had the country's best interests at heart.

At last, the vanguard of Rogun's army crested the hills fronting his castle home. Nevik tensed, but stood his ground, his retinue at his sides. Against the protests of his advisors, the young baron had insisted on greeting Rogun himself, before the general was even welcomed into Drakmar's halls. He wondered now if he had made a mistake, for with the force at his back, the chief commander need beg no such welcome. Should he desire, he could simply trample the keep and its occupants into the ground.

Nevertheless, the baron remained where he was, more than fifty paces out from the shadow of his gatehouse, whose portcullis he had commanded remain open. He had no cause as of yet to expect hostility from his guests— though it was possible Rogun had already overthrown Allion and the Circle and come now to demand fealty from him.

With thunder beneath their hooves, a detachment of horse came down from the main force, while the rest maintained their steady march. Thirty in all, Nevik counted quickly. More than double his own numbers. A spreading blot of ink against the rain-smeared backdrop. At their head, flanked by a pair of standard-bearers, was Rogun himself, unmistakable in full armor of blackest night. Its color matched that of his horse, a wild stallion it was said no other could ride. Together they came, huffing and snorting like something out of a youth's nightmare.

When it seemed their pace must surely carry them through Nevik's line, and those who formed it had begun to fidget on either side of him, the baron held his breath and watched the party skid to a grinding halt in the wet earth. Horses tossed their heads, chomped at their bits, and shook their dripping manes. At last, when all had settled, Rogun reached up and raised his visored helm.

"Greetings, young baron."

Like his bladebreaker armor, the general's face was full of deep clefts and sharp ridges, as rugged as mountain stone. With gloved fingers, he combed the arms of his moustache, frowning as if a smile might cause it all to crumble.

"And you, General," Nevik replied with a dip of his head. "To Drakmar, I bid you welcome."

Nevik himself was a stout man—bearlike, some said, though not so much as his father. He was not particularly tall, however, and felt even shorter as his guests remained on horseback. When he had finished his bow, he looked to Rogun's right, where Commander Zain flashed him a weasel's smile.

"To what do I owe this honor?" the baron asked.

"I am bid deploy to Kuuria," the general replied.

"A straighter road to which lies to the east, unless I'm mistaken."

Rogun smirked briefly. His harsh features held. "I am compelled to reject that order."

Nevik's stomach knotted. "On whose authority?"

"My own, as chief commander of Krynwall's armies, and guardian of these lands."

As he had feared. The general turned rogue at last. Nevik did well not to panic, and could only hope that his guard would obey his earlier command to stand fast no matter what. Clearly, they could ill afford to react with aggression.

"I have plans for Alson and its capital city," Rogun admitted. "And those plans require your involvement."

"Come inside then, and let us discuss—"

"I've had enough of discussion," the general snapped. "I will have my way in this, by one means or another."

The hands of Nevik's soldiers went to the hafts of their weapons.

"And should I refuse?" Nevik asked, his heart hammering against its cage.

"Refusals are for requests, which this is not."

"And yet you have rescinded, it seems, your own orders."

Rogun regarded him silently for a moment, as if taking measure of some quality hidden within.

"How fares Palladur?" the general asked.

The abrupt shift of focus caught Nevik off guard, and those in his entourage glanced at one another uncertainly.

"As well as can be hoped, at last word," the baron answered, while guarding his suspicions.

Before the wizard's invasion, Palladur and Drakmar, Alson's two major baronies to the south, had been bitter rivals. Nevik's father, Nohr, and Satallion, baron and self-proclaimed high lord of Palladur, had long viewed each other as opponents for what had been believed to be an heirless throne. This rivalry had come to a head when Nohr led a siege against Krynwall to recapture it from the wizard, and Satallion had joined the battle on the side of the enemy, in a gesture of supplication to the invading wizard. The ensuing struggle had seen Nevik's father slain, and Drakmar's people driven south to beg the protection of Kuuria.

Satallion, it was rumored, had been rewarded by the wizard with a painful death.

Whatever the truth, the high lord had not been seen again. Because of this, and due to the former baron's act of treason, Palladur's lands had been offered to Drakmar once Torin had come to power. Nevik had declined. Lording over his father's lands presented challenge enough. He had no desire to complicate matters by trying to govern a people trained to dislike any wearing the boar's head sigil. As a result, the southwestern barony had fallen into the hands of one of Satallion's cousins—with the crown keeping stern and watchful eye against any hint of fresh treason. Despite these and other pressures, Palladur's new lord and Drakmar's had become friends and compatriots, sharing plans and resources in a combined effort to restore their broken lands and make the enmity of their father and cousin a thing of the past.

So what was Rogun hinting at by making mention of it now?

"You're a good man, Nevik," the general offered at length. "You have your father's strength, and an uncommon forbearance. I would make you my ally in this, rather than my enemy. But I must know now, before I set foot within your walls, if I am to do so as friend or conqueror."

A gusting wind rustled the curtains of rain between them. Nevik suffered its chill within his joints and felt old beyond his years. The last traces of daylight slipped away, leaving the world muted and gray. In that drab, depthless void, he matched Rogun's unyielding gaze, before glancing over to catch Zain's smirk.

The baron of Drakmar suppressed a heavy sigh, responding instead with one of his father's scowls. "Then perhaps you should tell me what it is you require."

CHAPTER TWENTY-ONE

A STIFF WIND FILLED THE SAILS of the *Raven's Squall*, pushing the vessel steadily south along the rugged shoreline. Standing amidships, Torin watched the landscape slide by, a mist-shrouded procession of cliffs, coves, and rocky beaches. The night before, there had been only the endless expanse of the sea. But upon awaking that morning, there it was, as if risen with the sun, his crossing of the great ocean come to an end.

They had been at sea only a day after setting forth from the wizard's isle of Shattercove, with much deliberation as to their course. Given Autumn's suggestion that he seek the one called Lord Lorre with regard to the missing Finlorians, they had considered first dropping him off in the northern port of Kasseri—the closest on the eastern coast to Lorre's homeland. But that would mean a westward trek through the passes of Serpent Reach, said to be impenetrable this time of year. The only way across the Dragontail Mountains so late in the season was farther south, through the Dragonscale Cleft—and even that would pose a challenge. Still, it would be faster than trying to sail all the way around the treacherous horn of the Southland, a six-day voyage with favorable winds, meaning more likely ten. And the *Squall* itself was damaged and ill equipped, which would cost them another day or two at least. On the other hand, they could drop him off quickly and easily at Razorport, where with any luck he could reach Neak-Thur—the gateway city between territories north and south—in half the time by cutting across land, even if he had to do most of his traveling afoot.

Besides, Raven had assured him, he would be more likely to find a guide in Razorport than Kasseri. The latter was known primarily as a shipbuilding town. Land tradesmen to be found there seldom traveled farther west than the Splinterwood. Razorport, however, was home to all sorts of crazy rogues—maybe even someone mad enough to lead him to Lorre.

Torin was at the mercy of their word. Even after studying their maps, he knew nothing as to the nature of this land's cities and inhabitants. Nothing more substantial than rumor, anyway, and he was reluctant to put much faith in that. After all, those same rumors held that the Finlorians had long since disappeared, thus dooming his mission from the start.

So he listened to what the pirates had to tell him, having no idea how much of it would prove useful, and wary of any preconceived notions even their judgments might impart.

"Ready?" asked Raven, his approach marked by the advance of confident footsteps upon the ship's decking.

Torin half turned to greet the other, amazed again at how quickly blood had returned to the pirate captain's cheeks. His gaze lingered only a moment, however, before shifting to the marauder's companion, Autumn of the Rain. Even on this cloudy morn, her amethyst eyes shone round as radiant moons, made all the brighter by that perpetual smile of private amusement.

"Still a ways off, aren't we?" Torin asked.

Raven shook his head. "Aren't too many harbors where this ship is welcome. Got a place farther south, but we'd be overshooting your destination. Pike and Jib, they're prepping a boat to take you ashore. Be a short hike, about half a league, to Razorport. If you hurry, might beat the rains."

Torin looked back to where a ridge of dark clouds peeked over the mountains like froth bubbling over a kettle's rim.

"Are you sure you wish to do this?" Raven asked. "Not too late to change your mind."

"And do what?"

The pirate shrugged. "Go home to refit. Else stay with us. We've always room for another lad such as yourself."

Torin surprised himself by not snorting at the offer. At the moment, staring up at those looming peaks of an unfamiliar land, with but a glimpse of the darkness awaiting him on the other side, he was more than a little inclined to accept.

"Had I a choice, I would not have come this far," he said. Again he found Autumn's smile, and was awed at what lay beyond its mysterious depths: a warm mix of both innocence and wisdom—the wonder of a child for whom the entire world was a toy.

"I'm sorry I cannot tell you more that might aid you in your quest," Autumn said in that melodic voice of hers. "But if any can tell you the fate of your missing elves, it is Lorre."

Torin nodded. In the time the pair had allowed him, he had shared a rough account of that which threatened his homeland, and learned a bit about the conflict that marred theirs. Though each claimed to have lived outside that conflict, both knew enough to understand that it was the ambitions of Lord Lorre, self-proclaimed overlord of Yawacor, that had come to divide their lands north from south.

Autumn reiterated this now.

"Approach him carefully, for many would accuse him of a vicious temperament."

"He's a tyrant," Raven added, "who will accord you no more than a tyrant's mercy. Beware."

"I will," Torin promised them. He took a deep breath of the cold ocean air. "What about you? Where will you go next?"

"Back to Grimhold," Raven admitted, "to finish looting the wizard's keep."

"And Madrach? What will you do with him?"

"I've not decided. But I'm inclined to leave him there, as master of his own isle. Not until I've gutted the place, mind you. I've no desire to see him follow in your own brother's footsteps."

Torin winced at the notion, but held his feelings in check.

"After that," the captain continued, "perhaps I'll look to settle down as you suggested. Find me a life more suitable for this maiden of mine."

"I wish you the best," Torin said.

"And you," Raven replied. "I owe you everything."

"If ever you have need," added Autumn, "of anything, call upon me, and I shall see it granted."

Torin nearly chuckled, but given the luster of the woman's countenance, found that he did not disbelieve her promise. His stifled laughter gave way to a bewildered smile. "I just may do that."

Autumn winked.

"Captain," a burly voice interrupted. All three looked up as Black Spar tromped near. The first mate's wounds had been dressed, but bled through their bandages, as he refused to take any unscheduled rest. "Pike and Jib are ready."

"Thank you, mate," Raven responded, dismissing the brutish sailor. Then to Torin, "Are you sure you'll have no escort to Razorport? I hate to send you off alone. This is a dangerous land."

"I'll manage," Torin assured him.

The pirate smirked. "I've no doubt you will," he said, offering his hand.

Torin looked at it, reminded of the risk in petting a strange dog. He'd not forgotten that it was Raven's orders that had killed his comrades. Then again, the marauder might have sent all aboard the *Pirate's Folly* to a watery grave, and had instead let them be. So too, last night, might he have taken back the Sword and Pendant and killed Torin in his sleep.

"I'll not soon forget you," Torin said, eyeing Autumn as he gripped the other's outstretched hand.

The pirate clapped his shoulder. "Farewell, King Torin."

"Farewell . . ." Torin hesitated, raising an eyebrow. "Red Raven?"

The captain glanced around. "Karulos," he confessed.

Torin grinned.

"When you get into town, visit the Gilded Tankard. Ask the barkeep about a trapper named Hargenfeld. If *he* can't guide you through the Cleft, he'll know who can."

"Hargenfeld," Torin repeated, then shifted to accept Autumn's embrace. "You're certain this is what you want?"

The woman nodded, beaming. "Remember," she whispered, "anything you wish. I am but a longing away."

Once more, Torin peered into her eyes, both captivated and mystified all over again.

In the next moment, their vessel began to slow, and he was led away. En route to his skiff, he accepted parting wishes from Keel Haul, Mackerel, and a dozen others whom he didn't really know. Even Black Spar grumbled a forced good-bye. Torin wasn't sure how to react to these unexpected supporters, but did the best he could to acknowledge them with due grace.

The valor of thieves, he thought, recalling his brother's words.

Minutes later, he found himself alone upon a narrow beach, waving back at Pike and Jib, and at those aboard the anchored *Squall*. He then double-checked his possessions, most particularly the Sword and Pendant, before turning his attention to the south, where a thin trail cut a meandering swath between black waves to the east and wild, cliffside forest to the west. A lone raindrop struck his nose, and he looked up to the dark clouds that threatened now to escape the clutching peaks that held them back.

With a determined breath, he started down the sandy path.

Gusting winds and an uneven terrain sought to knock him from his course. Gnarled roots and lunging growth, along with swirling sands and roaring spray, made an easy hike much less so. At times, he found his path completely eroded away, and was forced up into the brush or down into the shallow surf. He crept across rockslides, ducked beneath low-hanging branches, and clambered over fallen trunks wet with moss. Only once did he check to see if the *Squall* was still there, out in the deep waters. All he saw was a curtain of fog.

At last his trail cut through the forest to join an actual roadway. Torin followed. By that time, he was already soaked through by a driving rain. The woods offered moderate protection going forward, but the damage had been done. Despite the warmth of Sword and Pendant, he was shivering beneath his cloak when finally he came upon the outskirts of Razorport.

He was less than encouraged by the sight.

The forest fell away, receding up the mountain slopes to the west. What remained was a collection of buildings loosely scattered or tightly packed, each in all the wrong places. Everything had a sagging, dilapidated look to it, drained of color—even the warm, earthen hues—leaving behind a world of gray. Those he could see traveling the unpaved road ahead did so beneath hooded robes, their faceless forms made ethereal by the rain and mists, like battlefield ghosts trying to make their way home.

Burying himself deeper within the folds of his cloak, Torin lowered his head and trudged forward, into the gloom.

Upon closer inspection, his surroundings fared no better. Peeling layers of paint made a poor shield against the elements. Wherever his gaze fell, there waited another sign of disrepair—rusting metals, woods swollen and split, mortar seams grown over with lichen and moss. All, it seemed, was dusted with sea salt. A battle against nature, he decided, and nature was winning.

He paid scant attention to those he passed, except to seek directions to the Gilded Tankard. The first ignored him, while the second grunted and shook his head. A third crossed to the other side of the street. Finally, a woman smelling of ale gave the name of a crossroad. Torin thanked her and continued on his way.

The ocean's roar was ever present. That and the hammer of rain drowned out any bustle. Torin scarcely heard the creak and rattle of a cart that drove right past him. As he neared the area the woman had indicated, he became distracted by his search for signs. The Wounded Gull. The Black Heron. There seemed to be any number of inns and taverns, interspersed among dealers offering the anticipated array of food, clothing, and trinkets. What he hadn't anticipated was the limited number of patrons, causing him to wonder how any of these shops managed to stay in business. By the looks of things, many didn't.

He was peering through the cracked remains of an actual glass window, into what appeared to be an abandoned furrier shack, when he was caught off guard by a sudden grunt and a pair of hands that shoved him roughly to the muddy earth. As he reached back to halt his skid, he looked up to see the man who sneered down at him.

"Out of my way, boy," the stranger snarled, with a face like a dented hatchet.

Torin swallowed his anger. It was a bit early, he thought, to be making enemies.

"My apologies," he mumbled, turning to pick himself up.

A booted foot sent him down once more. "Keep them apologies. Just watch where you're going."

Fighting the urge to straighten the ruffian's nose with a driving fist, Torin kept an eye on his assailant this time as he arose from the mud.

"Learned your lesson?" the man asked.

Torin glowered, but remained silent, avoiding the other's gaze as he started past.

"Boy, I'm talking to you."

Torin spun as a powerful hand gripped his shoulder. A knee came hard and fast toward his midsection. This time, he didn't hesitate, but kicked out twice as fast to sweep the man from his remaining leg. The stranger buckled, falling with a splash into a deep puddle.

The young king saw the rage in his opponent's eyes, and braced himself for the man's charge. But rather than fling forward recklessly, the ruffian surprised him by scrambling to his feet with a sputter and putting greater distance between them.

"You'd best pray our paths don't cross again," the man growled, gnashing his teeth in warning. He then turned and hobbled off, down the dripping roadway.

Torin marked the coward's flight with a shake of his head. Fine start he was off to. Would everyone he met in this land be as civil? After watching to make sure the other did not spin around to put an arrow in his back, Torin adjusted the fit of his cloak, shrugged into place the sack of provisions Raven had supplied, and found his stride.

He focused on the touch of the Pendant against his chest, and gripped the hilt of the Sword, trusting each to warn him of danger. Even so, he tried not to be so easily distracted as he moved ahead, for as he'd learned, their power could not protect him from his own inattentions. Wary and watchful, he resumed his search along the mostly empty street.

He had just about given up in favor of the nearest shelter when he came at last upon the Gilded Tankard, its weather-beaten sign all but unreadable.

Its boisterous clamor gave him pause, reminding him of the alehouse he had visited back home in Gammelost. Then again, at least this one had a promising name.

Yet the Gilded Tankard was anything but—dimly lit, poorly ventilated, reeking of smoke and drink and sweat. Less crowded than he would have guessed, though, if judging by its noise. Most seemed to come from a single table, off to the right, where more than a dozen men knotted round a pair engaged in some manner of contest. He couldn't tell whether it was drink, dice, or strength of arms. None held any interest for him.

Instead, he made his way toward the bar, built at an angle in the northeast corner of the room. It was decorated primarily with articles from the sea—nets and buoys, shells and driftwood, and the like—some of which, Torin noticed, would make for excellent weapons in a brawl, such as fish clubs and gaff hooks. Most were stained with use, though whether in a former life at sea or right here in this room, he couldn't discern. He wondered how often a man came here to drink only to leave blood—his or another's—on the floor.

He sighted an empty stool, wedged between a bare-armed figure with skeletal limbs and another so draped in heavy furs as to appear an animal himself. Torin looked for another, but it seemed to be his only option. Groaning inwardly, he moved to claim it.

No sooner had he sat down than the first man—the scrawny one—turned on him with a sneer.

"Who told you to sit your dripping ass there?"

Torin regarded the other through the corner of one eye. A pimpled face hid behind an oily veil of long black hair, while curled lips revealed a crooked set of browning teeth. Hoping the man might leave off if his challenge were ignored, Torin turned away, motioning to the barkeep.

"Water, please."

The barkeep scowled.

"If it's water you want," said the larger man to Torin's left, "try ordering an ale."

The barkeep snatched up the nearest tankard, but paused to jab a meaty finger in the other's face. "Eat your slop 'fore I shove it up your dunghole," he snapped, then turned to one of several barrels lining his racks.

"I asked you a question," the scrawny man spat, his fetid breath on Torin's cheek. "Or do I need to break that stool over your head to get your attention?"

Torin gritted his teeth. He was beginning to think he'd be better off seeking his answers from the orcs and trolls said to roam these untamed lands.

"Ah, let him be, Tahnos," the fur-wearer mumbled through a mouthful of food. Torin glanced over as the speaker's gaze came away from the Sword's hilt, freshly disguised in leather wrappings and tucked inside his cloak. "It's obvious he ain't interested in your advances. Find yourself some other lass."

Tahnos sneered and took a drink.

"That was an insult to you," the big man explained, giving Torin a nudge.

"I'll be offended in a moment," Torin muttered, eyes forward as he accepted his drink. "My thanks," he told the barkeep.

As he lifted the cup to his lips, the barkeep's massive hand slapped down upon the counter. "Hey, your thanks don't pay my debts."

"You charge for water?" Torin asked, with a half-turn to the open doorway and the sheets of rain cascading outside.

"Don't get smart, lad. There's only one drink comes free 'round here, and that's to be found in my privy."

Again Tahnos snickered. Torin glared, unsure yet if he was being had, before deciding his pride was of small issue here. Reaching into the coin purse given him by Raven, he withdrew a silver half-piece and watched the barkeep's eyes light up.

"I could do with some information as well," he said, holding back at the last instant.

An outburst of hails and jeers arose from those competing in the corner. Money exchanged hands, a fresh contestant was brought forth, and the process began anew.

The barkeep's scowl returned. "You pay for the drink, then ask me what you want to know."

Torin started to withdraw, then dropped his coin to the counter. The barkeep snatched it up on the second bounce. He examined it under a lantern's flame before pocketing it in his apron with a smirk.

"Make it quick."

"Hargenfeld," Torin replied.

"Old Rags?" It was not the barkeep, but the fur-wearer who responded, drawing Torin's attention.

"What about him?" the barkeep asked.

"I was told you'd know where I might find him."

"And who told you that?"

Torin started to answer, but thought better of it. Raven had neglected to mention how word of his name might be received around here. He'd led Torin to believe this was a lawless land, making slim the possibility of arrest. Still, pirates had a way of making enemies, and he had no intention of drawing Raven's to him.

"An acquaintance," he said finally. "Do you know him or not?"

"Well as anyone, I'd guess," replied the furs man. "And better than most."

Again Torin glanced the other's way, unsure now who he should be speaking to. "Rumor is, he runs expeditions through the mountains west."

The barkeep snorted, his smile cruel. "Interesting rumor."

A man farther down the bar shouted for a refill. That same request was taken up by the gang across the room. Sniffing out the greater profit, the barkeep pushed himself away.

"Talk to this one then," he said, gesturing toward the furs man. "I've customers to attend."

Perhaps I should give him my silver as well, Torin thought snidely, but elected to forgo that argument.

As the barkeep trundled off, so too did the sneering Tahnos, as if seeking better entertainment. That left Torin more or less alone with the furs man, who licked his greasy fingers before offering Torin his hand.

"Name's Gavrin," he offered with a grin. "Friends call me Moss."

Though it was difficult to tell beneath that mountain of furs, he appeared a portly man, only slightly less hunched than his garments made him look. His hair was sandy in color, and ruffled as such. A cropped beard, patchy below the ears, clung to his chin. The gleam in his cobalt eyes hinted of a past steeped in mischief.

"Gavrin," Torin acknowledged, declining the saliva-smeared hand. "I'm not looking to make friends."

"Too bad." The big man shrugged, without offense. "'Round here, friends can be useful."

"How's that?"

"Well," Gavrin said, scraping up a final mouthful of what looked like mutton and potatoes, "first off, they can watch your back."

"Or stab you in it."

Gavrin chuckled. "For a newcomer to these parts, you seem to have grasped hold of things pretty quick." He swallowed his bite with a swig from his mug. "It ain't companionship you're here for. So what is it you want?"

Torin's response was automatic. "To conduct my business and return home as soon as possible."

"Business, is it?" Gavrin looked him over. "What kind?"

"The kind I'd rather not discuss with the first drunken stranger I meet."

"Well, that there would be Tahnos," Gavrin replied, leaning back and pushing aside his empty plate. "So I guess you ain't got nothing to worry about."

The man was disarming. Torin would give him that. But the young king was not about to be taken in so easily.

"You're looking for something," Gavrin surmised.

"Some*one*," Torin amended. "I thought I'd made that plain."

"Rags," the other recalled, picking at his teeth and giving a contemplative squint. "Was it *him* you needed? Or a guide in general you're looking for?"

"A guide. But I was told he's the one to ask."

"And where is it you're going?"

Another outburst from the corner. Some form of dice, Torin now realized, as he watched one skitter to the floor, dancing away from those who gave chase.

"If it's all the same, Gavrin, I think I'd prefer to talk to Hargenfeld."

"Call me Moss. Gavrin was my father's name." Upon Torin's look, he added quickly, "It don't have to make us friends."

"Fine. Moss. Any chance you could take me to him?"

Moss seemed to consider. "It would be my great pleasure. Only, I don't think he can help you."

"No? And why is that?"

"Because the man's a ghost; that's why."

"What?" Torin frowned. "You're sure?"

Moss snorted with laughter. "Now, boy, I may look like a mule, and smell about the same, but I ain't dumb as one. Don't take no sage to recognize a dead man."

"That's not what I meant."

"Buried him myself just last winter. Yep, I'm sure."

Moss took a drink. Uncertain he should believe what he was being told, Torin searched his own tankard as if the truth might be found within.

"But me and Rags," Moss went on, "we was associates. If it's a guide you need, look no further."

Torin studied the man, searching for any sign of a lie. "You've crossed the Dragontails?"

"Crossed 'em? Shades of mercy, from east to west, north to south, I've been all over."

"And what is it, exactly, that you do?"

"Hmm, now there's a question. I'm not one to limit myself to any single talent, you see. I've been me a trapper, hunter, merchant, scout, tracker, miner, explorer—"

"In other words, a rogue."

Moss flashed a toothy grin. "Born and raised, right here in the Southland."

It was as Raven and Autumn had warned him. Wylddeor, the Southland of Yawacor, had also been dubbed Land of the Rogues, having long been home to a lawless rabble of independent, free-roving men and women whose only common interest was a life free of moral and governmental restraint. There were no rulers, and few towns—most of which were little more than trading camps grown up around a handful of brave merchants, and which served the basic needs of those who trekked this savage wilderness as packs and individuals. As a whole, these people despised authority, using their freedom to cheat, steal, and kill—whatever it took to get by. A man had to be fit, savvy, or downright lucky to survive.

"Although," Moss added, lowering his voice and leaning near, "I wouldn't go 'round calling everyone a rogue. Doesn't bother me, you see, but these days, most prefer to be called Wylddeans."

"Wyl-what?"

"Wylddeans, the people of the Southland. Rogues is what the Northlanders call us—among other things."

And then there was Lorrehaim, the Northland, domain of Lord Lorre, who had been carving up the land for nearly two decades and bringing it under his personal control. The man's armies were said to consist not only of men, but of orcs, trolls, and giants—the dregs of these ancient races. By all accounts, Lorre was a slave master. Those who lived under his thumb believed in law and order, because to believe otherwise was to defy their ruler. As a result, his people looked down upon their southern neighbors as barbaric, uncivilized. Though such views might, Raven had suggested, have more to do with envy of the freedoms these so-called rogues enjoyed.

"It don't make us a people, you see, in terms of a nation, because we Wylddeans reject all such notions. Fundamental code of our existence. But then, I can tell you all about that. If it's the Resistance you're interested in, or—"

"I'm not interested in your resistance," Torin assured him. "Or your theories on how a people should or shouldn't be ruled."

"Well, what *are* you interested in?"

Torin glanced toward the door as another troop of angry-looking men entered the room, heading directly for the bar.

"I don't suppose we could finish this someplace a little less public?"

"Sure. I keep me a cabin on the outskirts of town. Buy me supper, and I'll answer any questions you have."

"You just finished eating."

Moss gripped his teeming waistline. "There's always room for more."

Torin did not return the other's grin. The man appeared harmless enough, but that was part of the problem. And yet, of those he'd encountered, this was his most promising lead by far. When the leader of the new pack shoved his way onto the stool vacated by Tahnos and claimed his spot by stabbing a dagger into the top of the bar, Torin made up his mind.

After waiting for the new arrivals to receive their first round, he gave Moss the go-ahead to order. A rack of seasoned beef, a wedge of cheese, some day-old vegetables, a loaf of hard-baked bread, and a cask of the barkeep's darkest ale were added to the tab. On top of that, the proprietor demanded from Torin a finder's fee for having introduced him to Moss. Torin balked, but paid the requested amount, careful to do so in small coins. He was quite conscious of those at the bar who looked on. Most, thankfully, were more interested in the gaming going on across the room.

When finally the order had been put together, Moss wrapped it up, bade those nearest him a pleasant and entertaining evening, and swaggered from the room. Doing his best to ignore an array of feral stares and crooked smiles, Torin followed after, into the rain.

CHAPTER TWENTY-TWO

*T*HOSE RAINS CONTINUED WITHOUT SLACKENING as Torin trudged westward along rutted avenues of mud in the wake of the rogue named Moss. The weather alone was enough to make him second-guess his decision to leave the tavern, but the big man's pace brooked no hesitation. He could only hope that the damp and the chills would be the extent of his distress.

Moss, he noticed, wore no hood, and did not seem bothered in the least.

"Does it always rain around here?" Torin asked.

"Always," Moss replied, his lower lip bulging with a wad of ground to-bacco leaf. "You'll never see it snow though. Not at these lower elevations anyway."

At last, Torin groaned inwardly, *something positive to look forward to.*

"As I was saying," Moss added, resuming their conversation from the tav-ern once they had left the last of the ramshackle booths and buildings behind them and started up along a narrow forest trail, "these days, anyone found roaming the Southland is considered Wylddean—even an outlander such as yourself. Means 'Wild Ones.' Name was first brought about by those who banded together at Neak-Thur to defend against invaders from the north, but has since been adopted by everyone south of the Bastion, since they prefer this to being called rogues, barbarians, or outlaws—as they're known to North-landers like Lorre."

"Lorre. Can you tell me about him?"

"Dragon's furrows, anyone could tell you about Lorre."

"I'm asking you."

Moss turned to smirk at his surliness. "So you are. But it don't do a man good to talk about him. Riles the blood. A villain, sure as the rain. His subjects live only to serve him. The farther south he gets, the less resistance he finds. Tough to organize a collective force among those who care only about them-selves. Rumors are, he's turned eye at last to Neak-Thur, which has finally got folks down here startled enough that some are suggesting action to slow his advance. As if the northern recruiters ain't been preaching it for years."

The big man spat and shook his head. "But you ain't interested in any of that, you said."

"He can have it all," Torin agreed. "What I need to know is, how does one get in to see him?"

Moss laughed. "There's a notion!" But when Torin failed to return his laughter, the big man stopped. "Now hold on. You saying what I think you're saying?"

"My business is with Lord Lorre. I'm on my way to see him."

Moss's ruddy face pinched with suspicion. "Who are you?"

"Who I am is of no concern. But you owe me for that food. So answer my question. Can you help me or not?"

The man looked to the bundle he carried as if considering handing it back over. "You don't trust me."

"I don't know you," Torin clarified.

"And yet, you expect me to trust you."

"Your trust I'll have to earn. As you will mine. That's how it works, in this land or any other."

Moss chewed as if his tobacco had gone tasteless. "Wise words. But if you're half as wise as you let on, you won't go anywhere near Lord Lorre."

"You said if I needed a guide, to look no further."

"That was before you made mention of the most ruthless warlord in all of Yawacor."

"Are you saying now you can't help me?"

Moss turned to spit. "I'm already helping you, by telling you it would mean your death and mine if we was to go anywhere near that man."

Torin spun around and started back into town.

"Where are you going?"

"To start all over, it seems."

"If you and Lorre are allies—"

"We're not allies," Torin snapped. "We're not enemies. The man is said to have information I need, information that could save the lives of those back in my homeland, maybe even your own. I've come a long way already, but I need someone who can take me north, near enough to beg an audience with him. If that man isn't you, then my search continues."

Moss considered him carefully. "You've got quite a critter gnawing at your withers, don't you?"

Torin frowned and turned away.

"Wait," Moss called. When finally Torin rounded again, he found the big man shaking his head. "By grace, you may be the least sociable fellow I've ever met. But at the moment, you're the only company I've got."

"You'll take me north, then?"

"Now, I didn't say that. But I can get you through the mountains, at least."

"Fair enough," Torin agreed, taking a few return strides.

"For a price," Moss qualified, raising a hand in due caution.

Torin returned the warning. "I don't have much."

Moss chuckled. "If I believed that, we wouldn't be here now."

This time, Torin shared the man's amusement. "I have no horse, and no possessions save those that fit in a single sack. What makes you think I have money?"

Moss's smile turned predatory. "You came from overseas, for one. That takes means. Your face is bruised and I've seen you limp, so you've been in a scuffle of late. You come creeping into a tavern, speaking the name of a guide known to peddle stolen wares, and seeking passage west. That makes you a thief, I'm guessing. But then, that there's always a safe bet, with or without the evidence. Then there's your sword."

Torin felt his own gaze narrow, recalling suddenly how he had caught the other stealing a glimpse of the hidden blade back in the tavern. "What about it?"

Again his companion chuckled. "That trick with the leather bindings might fool thieves where you come from, but 'round here, you might as well be carrying a golden scepter in plain view."

"So you think a leather-wrapped hilt makes me wealthy."

Moss shrugged. "Men with nothing ain't got nothing to hide. Stolen, or maybe not. Makes no difference to me."

"And were you planning on setting a price in advance, or just looting me while I slept?"

"Now, now, ain't no cause for that. I won't say the thought never crossed my mind, but if Lord Lorre's in any way mixed up in this, I'm keeping my hands to myself. I just want you to know that I ain't fooled, and that if you want my help, it'll cost you a fair and reasonable sum."

Torin smiled wryly. "All right, Gavrin. Name your price."

"Twenty gildrons, plus rations and supplies."

"I can pay you half that to take me clear to the border. Neak-Thur."

The big man scoffed. "That there's a five-day journey, and ten gildrons don't pay for that *and* the return trip."

"We'll discuss my return if and when I make it that far."

Moss snickered. "I wasn't talking about *your* return. I was talking about mine. Fifteen."

"Ten. Take it or leave it," Torin said firmly.

His companion scowled, rivers of rainwater washing down his face.

"I'd offer more, but it would seem I spent too much on supper."

The big man cracked a smile, but remained silent.

"Perhaps I should try my offer back in town?" Torin suggested, with a half-turn down the trail.

"Oh, all right," Moss groaned. "I'll do it for the ten."

"To Neak-Thur."

"Yes, yes, to Neak-Thur. But I want half up front."

"You'll get two now, and another for every day of completed travel."

Moss's jaw worked back and forth, sawing and sluicing on his tobacco. "Deal. When would you want to leave?"

"How about now?"

But the rogue shook his head. "Would be tomorrow at the earliest. I gather speed is of the essence?"

"It is."

"Won't nobody be following us, will there? Looking to take back their property?" He cast about for the imagined pursuers.

"No," Torin assured him. "Of that you have my promise."

Moss squinted, as if determining what that might be worth. "Bah, have to risk it, I guess. Even so, we'll need to equip for the road, particularly the Cleft. If we wait to do so until we reach Latymir, we'll end up paying twice as much, and will save no time either way. Might as well do so here and now."

"What about horses?" Torin wanted to know.

"We can get those here, trade 'em in at Latymir. That'll buy us a day. But ain't nothing but mules and mountain goats going to make it through the pass this time of year."

"So we prepare tonight, set forth at dawn?"

"Dawn comes awful early," Moss grumbled, then smirked at Torin's frown. "But dawn it is."

A fair compromise, Torin decided. Although he chafed at the idea of spending one more moment than he had to on this forsaken continent, he saw little to gain in questioning his new guide's every opinion.

"We'll be spending the night in town, then?" he asked.

Moss snorted. "Only if you care to lose half the night fighting off rats and brigands." He grinned jovially. Torin did not. "Come," the rogue offered. "I'll show you my cabin. If it don't look safe to you, we'll find you someplace else when we come back to make fit for tomorrow."

Torin agreed, and so fell back into step alongside the other.

A good half-mile farther on, they reached what Moss claimed was one of several temporary shelters he kept throughout the Southland. More shack than cabin, it was all but overgrown by the surrounding forest, with a caving roof and walls that leaned dangerously down the slope to which it clung. Before they reached its rotted stoop, Moss dashed ahead with a growl. Torin's hand flew to the hilt of his weapon as the rogue bashed in the front door, roaring like a wild bear. The young king realized why a moment later, when a family of five went racing out into the rain-slicked woods, scattering in separate directions.

"Filthy buggers," Moss vented, reappearing in the drooping doorway. "Can't turn my back but what they fill the place like roaches. And stay out!" he shouted after the fleeing squatters.

It occurred to Torin to ask whose home this really was, but it seemed already too late for that. Its former occupants might as well have been startled deer. And Moss had already gone back inside.

Stepping in after, Torin made a quick and cautious survey. The place appeared even smaller within than it had without, a single-room affair consisting of a single large bed, closet, heating stove, and a line of cupboards above and beneath a nicked counter. A stepstool was the only other furniture, and creaked now beneath Moss's weight as the rogue inspected the upper shelves. If it wasn't his place, then he had borrowed it before, Torin decided, for he seemed to know his way around. Then again, Torin thought with a second survey, how long might that take?

His host came down from the cupboard with a clay jar from which he shook forth a small leather pouch. Finding it empty, he muttered in angry disappointment. "Damn buggers." The rogue spied Torin looking at him and shrugged. "Made off with my reserve coin stash."

"What of your travel supplies?" Torin asked. "Surely you don't go around with just the furs on your back."

"I don't carry much. Keep places like this so I don't have to." Moss sighed. "But yeah, I got me some of what you're talking about. Stow it with my mule there in town at a livery stable. Costs to have it held, but it's safer than leaving it to the vermin out here."

Torin nodded, withholding judgment.

"What do you think? Closet full of blankets here—spun wool and fur. You'll be plenty warm, and more or less dry," Moss said, taking a rusted kettle from the counter and moving it beneath a drip in the ceiling. "We'd have to share the bed, but she's plenty big enough. You ain't got lice, do you?"

Torin looked glumly at the arrangements.

"That be a yes or a no?"

"This will be fine," Torin said. "I'm your guest, Gavrin."

"Moss," the big man reminded him. "Well then, if you don't mind, I'll leave you here to guard the food while I head back into town to set a few provisions for tomorrow. Any of them vermin come skulking back, just shoo 'em off, you hear?"

Torin started to decline, preferring that he be there for any "provisions" Moss intended to set, then decided otherwise. He could use some time to himself, to rest comfortably, before standing guard all night against whatever violent designs his host might have for him.

"Go on," he said to the rogue. "I'll be here when you get back."

"Make yourself cozy. Be gone an hour or so. After that, don't be shy about preparing some of that grub so it's ready when I get back." Moss snickered. "Damn, it's like I went and found myself a housewife." Then, before shutting the door, he added, "Don't fret. You're safe with me. You'll see."

Surprisingly, the man proved good on his word. No one troubled Torin while Moss was in town. Upon his return, they spent the evening talking mostly of their plans for the westward trek. Torin did not sleep, but that had more to do with his anxieties concerning those he'd left behind—Marisha, Allion, Nevik, and others—than any he had for himself. With the Sword in hand as he lay there, tucked in at the edge of the bed, listening to the endless thrumming of rainfall, he feared no threat to his own well-being. Only the strangeness of a land to which he did not belong, and the dread uncertainty of a dark and clouded future.

He arose at the first hint of a brightening sky, weary of listening to Moss's resonating snore. He woke the big man, who grumbled and snorted and then finally rolled to his feet. Belching and scratching, the rogue headed outdoors to attend his morning's business. Torin, meanwhile, checked his outer garments, which had been left overnight on a line above the heating stove to dry. They remained damp and chill, but he had no others, and so gritted his teeth and slipped them back on.

The rains had slowed to a drizzle, making room for moments of sunshine beneath a patchy gray sky as they headed back into town. But the light would not be coaxed from its cocoon, and the gloom would not be dispelled. By the time they had paid for and collected the possessions that would carry them through the mountains, the gaps in the clouds had filled, and the rain had summoned reinforcements on a westerly wind.

Despite pushing headlong into this mix, Torin and his guide made good time on their rented mounts. They reached the town of Latymir, on the eastern edge of the Dragonscale Cleft, just before midday. As Moss had warned, Latymir was smaller than Razorport, an outpost serving as the eastern gateway to the true wilderness that was Wylddeor, the Southland of Yawacor. Its denizens appeared even less friendly than those Torin had encountered on the coast, but restrained themselves to wicked sneers and guarded looks. Strength in numbers, Moss explained. Had Torin elected to travel here alone, he might have received a much different welcome.

Passing through a gauntlet of hawkish vendors, they came to the desired livery outfit, where Moss traded back their mounts and selected a new mule for himself. They haggled for some time over price, a shouting match that seemed to Torin unnecessarily vicious. Once an agreement was reached, however, both men calmed and spoke then as if not a cruel word had passed between them.

"What news of the Cleft?" Moss asked, flipping the man an extra copper.

"As of yesterday, conditions were good," the stableman replied as he worked. "Only a handful of minor landslides reported. Trapper come through this morning, though, with a storm on his heels. Nasty business, by his word."

"And was this a man knows what he's talking about?"

The stableman shrugged. "Never seen him before. But sounds about right, this time of year. *I* wouldn't risk it."

Torin soured as Moss turned to him with a grim expression. "How much time would we lose?" the young king asked.

"No telling. Good squall might close things up for weeks. Better that, though, than being caught in the middle of it."

Torin shook his head. He'd already lost half a day in preparing to come this far. Another day or so, he might be able to surrender to caution. But weeks?

"Best yet would be to outrace it," he determined.

The stableman chuckled. "Outlander, is he?" he asked of Moss. The big man nodded. "Do yourself a favor, boy. Listen to your guide here. Ain't no good can come of challenging the Dragontails."

He held up his fingers, the majority of which, Torin now saw, were missing their tips, trimmed at the second knuckle. Only his thumbs remained intact.

"Toes look about the same," the man continued. "She don't just nip up there. She bites."

Torin swallowed his discomfort. "I appreciate the warning, friend." He turned to Moss. "This won't wait."

Moss chewed broodingly, juice from his tobacco grounds dribbling down his chin. "No, I didn't figure it would."

"I'll go it alone if I have to."

The stableman snickered, but made no further comment, shuffling back to his storeroom with an armload of tack.

"We'd best find you a heavier coat," Moss replied at last. "Because I sure as rain ain't going to lend you mine."

Soon after, they were headed up the trail leading west from town, where a smattering of folk were found moving in either direction, mostly in small herds. None, however, claimed to be making their way to or from the pass, only outlying dwellings. Thankfully, Moss shrugged aside their looks of derision, his focus now on getting the job done. Without grunt or murmur, he led Torin and his mule dutifully along the switchback forest trail. Before long, the settlement at their backs was lost in haze and a screen of brush, leaving naught but the road ahead.

By then, they had that road to themselves. It was an eerie feeling, especially given the black wall of clouds looming above the treeline before them. Torin hunkered within the hood of his new fur cloak and tried not to let his anxiety show.

Moss remained an amiable companion. As they pressed onward at a steady pace, the rogue entertained both himself and his charge with stories from his adventurous past. To hear him tell it, the man had been everywhere and done everything, making him a font of experience from which to learn. Assuming, of course, that even half of the tales were true.

Hoping to learn something about the Finlorians—yet without arousing suspicion—Torin inquired as to the history of these lands and its races. Which could still be found? Mostly orcs and trolls and giants, Moss had replied, all three of which he had encountered at one time or another—though always in the wild. He'd seen the prints of an ogre, but had been lucky enough not to cross the beast itself. And he'd heard rumors of gnomes, but none that he could ever confirm. The latter were said to be deep-cave dwellers, and the big man spent as little time as possible in those dark, cramped spaces.

"What about elves?" Torin finally pressed.

"Heard a tale or two, but only from the far north. Same as goblins. If they exist, might as well be ghosts."

The big man went on to confirm what Raven and Autumn had suggested, that as part of his conquest, Lorre had done away with most of the so-called savage races, rooting them out of their forests and caves and mountain lairs, driving them deeper into the annals of history. Some were said to have joined the ranks of his army as fodder or slaves. Most were butchered for sport.

The forest changed as they drew higher, the less resilient vegetation falling away and leaving only that which had adapted to the greater altitudes. Landslides became a constant threat, slopes weakened by the incessant rains. But thus far, they had come across only one large and treacherous enough to cause them to reroute. Moss's breathing became labored as the air thinned, yet he trooped on without complaint, leading their mule with an expert hand. Torin himself was unfazed.

That all changed when they reached the snowline. A light powder at first, it piled quickly before them with the climb in elevation. Less than an hour after the initial dusting, Torin found himself slogging through an ankle-deep crust and knee-high drifts. The lightweight flurries offered relief from the rain, at least, but that was of small consolation when speed—not comfort—was of primary concern. Torin was tempted to ask how much farther they had to go, but didn't want to give his guide a chance to suggest they turn around.

In any case, the big man hardly seemed to notice. He went right along, prattling now about the pleasures of women and strong drink. Although the winds were picking up and visibility diminishing, he assured Torin that he knew their path well—well enough to walk it blind, if necessary.

A meager reassurance, but Torin was not really troubled. He was beginning to warm to this rogue. Although a bit crass in speech and behavior, he projected an overall reliability. A false air, perhaps, but Moss exuded a self-confidence that bordered on arrogance. It was something Torin felt he could use a shade more of himself, to be so comfortable in his own skin as to put others at ease as well.

Despite the harsh elements, Torin found a certain peace in the midst of that snowswept wilderness. In addition to carpeting the earth beneath their feet, the virgin powder lay piled on the limbs of trees, floated as ice in nearby streams, and continued to swirl silently upon the wind. Though he was a world removed from where he wished to be, and the snow itself was but an obstacle to his return, there was a rugged majesty not to be denied—much like that which he had been surprised to find at sea.

As before, he wished Marisha was there to experience it.

Their pace slowed after that, weakening as the trail steepened and the oncoming storm gathered in strength. Individual snowflakes fell harder and faster, no longer the delicate shavings that had kissed Torin's cheeks, but great, meaty slices that slapped at his exposed skin and refused to melt. The trees had grown tall and scraggly, offering scant protection. Once or twice, he thought he heard thunder overhead.

"We'd do well to find shelter now," Moss urged finally. "Seems the old trapper was right. We're marching into a wailer of a squall, and cover will become scarce once we near the teeth of the pass."

"We haven't even hit the pass yet?" Torin asked in dismay.

"Not by a fair margin. Once we clear the treeline, we've a good two, three hours out in the open, with nothing but granite outcroppings, narrow trails, and steep drops to shield us."

Torin peered into the wind, studying the churning skies. "I can't afford to be trapped. Any chance we can push through, find shelter on the other side?"

"Always a chance," Moss granted him. "But only a fool would wager his life on it."

"Surest way to fail," Torin reasoned, "is to not try."

The dark cast that shadowed Moss's features told Torin what the other thought of his empty platitude.

"We make it through," the rogue countered, stopping dead in his tracks, "I want the remainder of my payment. All of it."

"After just one full day?"

"If I feel like it, I'll continue on with you to Neak-Thur. If not, you'll be on your own."

Torin glowered. "Scant inducement, if you ask me."

"Otherwise, we camp here, and hope the pass ain't buried on the morrow. You decide."

They pressed on, as much to show Moss he wouldn't be cowed as out of necessity or consideration of the facts. It would take more than a snowstorm to keep him from completing his task.

That conviction faded somewhat with the failing of the light. Dusk arrived early, dimming the sky and leaving the pair stranded in a lonely world of bleak shadows. The storm intensified, almost as if the meager sunlight had been holding it back before. As they emerged from the trees, gusting winds shrieked in fiendish greeting, clawing at their faces. Torin buried himself against their sting, focusing his squinted vision upon his guide's snow-encrusted heels. The crests of the mountains rose up on either side of him, reserved and immutable.

In defense, his thoughts drifted, in search of a more comfortable time and place. Not surprisingly, he found himself returned home—not to Krynwall, but to Diln, his village as a youth. There, he passed like a ghost among those of a former life, drawing strength as he touched upon friends and locations of a warm and familiar past.

And yet, something about his reveries startled him. The scenery was unchanged—a perfect vision of the forest village in its prime, before its desecration at the hands of the wizard's soldiers. The townspeople were kind and inviting. But the entire setting seemed somehow foreign and remote, as if he were looking at memories belonging to someone else.

He shrugged the feeling aside as weather-driven dementia, and spat its bitter taste from his mouth. The heavens darkened further. He could no longer recall how long they had been traveling. He started to ask Moss, but quickly decided to save his breath.

Then the true brunt of the storm hit them—like an endless wave, heavy enough to knock Torin briefly from his feet. Hail mixed with snow, pelting him like gravel. He leaned into it like a spear. Moss's stark silhouette struggled before him, outlined against a sea of frothing white. Slipping and sliding on the icy trail, they flattened their backs against the cliff face and fought forward, staring out at a chasm on the other side.

Though rogue winds threatened to rip them from their perch, and minor avalanches forced them twice to deviate from the safer path, they managed to hold their ground and press raggedly ahead by fits and starts. Somehow, they made it through. As soon as they crossed the summit—a narrow, winding defile between shivering peaks—Moss drew near and roared in his ear.

"There's a small cave not far from here! The path is difficult! Stay close!"

Torin could scarcely make out the other's words over the howl of the tempest, which wailed and moaned as if comprised of vengeful spirits. He nodded stiffly, then left Moss to concentrate upon navigating the path before them. Under assault from a barrage of icy shards, Torin followed with clenched eyes, while the wind maintained its tormented caterwaul.

As if a predator that could sense its quarry slipping away, the storm took aim, narrowing its attack with a fury that caused even the mountains to rumble their displeasure. More than once, Torin was knocked aside by a pummeling gust, while ducking low against a continual volley of hailstones. The mule shrieked and brayed. Torin knew not how Moss kept the animal from breaking its own neck.

Its struggles, however, were not without consequence. All of a sudden, a portion of the trail gave way, chipped loose by the panicked mule's thrashing hooves. It happened while he and his companion skirted a yawning chasm, into which the broken pieces fell.

Torin watched the fissure appear before him, yet was too slow to react. He had just barely registered that he was going to have to jump the gap when it widened abruptly, causing his stomach to heave as the earth beneath his feet slid away.

He did not have time to draw breath, and so did not get a chance to cry out. Flailing arms sought desperately to halt his descent. Moss reached for him, but was too late. In a billowing cloud of icy powder, Torin fell, sliding and bouncing, all the while scrambling for his life. He battled to retain consciousness, but a blanket of snow went with him, enveloped him, and he knew no more.

CHAPTER TWENTY-THREE

ALLION'S HEAD HUNG LOW as he slouched over his work desk. His eyes squinted, stung by the smoke of low-burning candles, strained by the long hours of reading beneath their meager light. A stack of parchment lay piled before him and on all sides, scrolls and tomes of varying length and subject, but all needing to be addressed. Were he a battlefield commander, and these the armies of his enemy, Allion would have surrendered long ago.

But he couldn't. He was not at war. Not yet, anyway. And there was no one else. Stephan, the ever loyal seneschal, did what he could to help, as did Pagus and a host of clerks. But the final burden was his to bear, the bulk of these tasks his to complete. Unlike Torin, he would not shirk his responsibilities and leave them to someone else.

The regent stopped, dismayed by his harsh thoughts. Like all of them, Torin was serving as he believed he must.

Then again, Allion couldn't help how he felt.

He wondered often how the other was faring. A sealed note from Gammelost had indicated that Torin and his expedition team were setting forth from the coastal town aboard a merchant vessel as hired swordhands. Since then, more than two weeks had passed without so much as a whisper of rumor. Not altogether bad, Allion supposed, since sending word overseas would be difficult, and any word come this soon would most likely be bad. But that left those of them here at home in the dark as to the company's progress, trusting blindly that all they needed would come to pass.

A demanding test of patience, when what precisely they needed had yet to be made clear.

Even so, supposing Torin could find these Vandari, and supposing they lent him what knowledge or talents were required to subdue the Illysp, how long would Allion have to wait? How long before he could relinquish these duties and return to his own? How long before this madness came to an end?

The regent leaned back and rubbed his eyes. Such thoughts clouded his mind constantly, depriving him of sleep at night, robbing him during the day of hours and focus better directed toward the mountain of unfinished tasks before him.

With a determined grimace, he scooped up his quill and bent low once more. But before his bleary eyes could make sense of the characters scrawled across this particular page, there came a rap at his open chamber door.

"A message, sir," announced Kien, who stood post just outside.

Allion did not bother to turn. "Put it with the rest," he said, gesturing vaguely toward a pile of neglected scrolls.

"Beg pardon, sir. It bears the seal of His Majesty, King Galdric of Partha."

That drew the regent's attention. Allion twisted in his chair. Though he did not recognize the courier standing beside his guardsman, he identified quickly enough the red-on-black falcon's sigil of Parthan royalty embroidered on the man's tabard. Most messages sent across the lands went by a shared network of staged riders. But many of the noble lords and rulers kept their own string of carriers for the passing of royal documents, to mitigate the chances of tampering. This indeed appeared to be one of Galdric's.

"Forgive me," Allion said, beckoning the other forward. He accepted the scroll tube, which the other presented crisply, and reached at once to remove its cap.

"Your mark, sir," the messenger reminded him.

Allion murmured another apology, and quickly scribbled a note of receipt for the other to return to his superiors. He sealed it with a wax impression of his own signet, then handed it over with a nod of dismissal. The echo of the courier's footsteps had not yet receded by the time Allion had retrieved the message from its sleeve and torn through its seal.

He hesitated then, half expecting General Rogun to barge in on him before recalling that the chief commander was no longer there within the city, let alone the palace. Except for the faithful Kien, he was alone.

As he read, his already disconsolate mood soured. He had known this would never work. It had been a foolish plan to begin with, made more so by Darinor's insistence that they execute it before securing the necessary agreements. Now, it would appear his fears and Rogun's had come to pass.

Allion struck the table in disgust, then cursed as a pile of scrolls tumbled about him. In trying to catch them all, he managed to knock over a pair of candles and send another stack of papers to the floor, followed by a river of ink from his upturned well.

"Is everything all right, sir?" Kien asked.

"As you were, Kien," he sighed, scooting from his chair and dropping to a crouch upon his heels. "Everything is in order."

"There's a refreshing thought," came a woman's voice, startlingly close.

Allion looked up as Kien did the same, the guardsman fumbling for his weapon before he realized who it was.

"Although," Marisha continued, "if this is your idea of order, I'd hate to see what you might consider a mess." She smiled and placed a steadying hand upon Kien's arm.

The guardsman bowed and stepped from the room, resuming his watch outside the open door.

Allion scowled. Ever since Torin's departure, Marisha had been spending more and more time with her father. In doing so, she was beginning to adopt some of his poor habits, such as stealing upon people without notice.

"Looks like you could use some help," she observed.

Allion grunted, bending to his task with gritted teeth, forcing himself to think beyond the fact that he was doing Torin's work.

Despite the rude welcome, Marisha stepped near, stooping to collect some of the rogue articles papering the study floor. "You should get some rest," she suggested.

"I haven't time," he grumbled. "This work should have been completed weeks ago."

"The work is without end. A man's strength is not."

"Yes, well, I'm not so quick as some to pass his charge on to others."

Marisha's smile became crooked. "Is that a tone of self-pity I hear?"

Allion tried to glare at the woman, then laughed at himself and shook his head.

"Are you going to tell me what's troubling you?"

"Unfortunate news, is all," Allion replied, sifting through the clutter. "Nothing unexpected."

"About Rogun?"

Allion stopped. "Haven't you heard? I received and passed word to Thaddreus on the general's progress perhaps an hour ago. Surprisingly enough, he has obeyed orders and arrived at the Gaperon, almost on schedule."

"Almost?"

"Poor roads to the south. Nothing major."

"Then why the heavy heart?"

Allion cast about for the scroll delivered him by Galdric's courier. When he found it, he handed it to her. "Here, read for yourself."

Marisha did. Allion watched her for a moment, awaiting her reaction. He couldn't seem to look away.

"My father will not like this," she said at last.

"No," Allion agreed, clearing his throat, "I don't suspect he will. And it makes my duty that much more difficult."

Marisha stared at him. He met her gaze until it became awkward. "It's not fair, is it," she said.

"What?"

"That you should be burdened with all of this."

He searched her bright face for any sign of ridicule. "Someone has to carry the load."

"But must it always be you?"

She did not appear to be mocking him, though Allion might have preferred *that* to her sympathies.

"We do as we must," he said, "with what comes our way. As best I can tell, fairness has little to do with it."

"No, but many are those who would rather bemoan their fate than accept it. I've never seen you do that."

"Nor will you," Allion vowed, a fresh determination sweeping through him. "There are too many challenges in life to bother facing down those I can't win. I don't know how Torin does it."

The air between them changed abruptly, as if he had said the wrong thing. Marisha blinked and went back to gathering papers.

"You should show this to my father at once," Marisha said, remembering the scroll in her hand.

Allion nodded. Odd, he thought, that they had forgotten it, even for a moment. "I suppose you're right." Still, his stomach knotted at the thought of sharing this news with the renegade Entient face-to-face on his own. "I don't suppose you'd be willing to accompany me."

Marisha's smile returned. "Of course. I left him not long ago in the library of the east wing. He should still be there."

"Sir, you have another visitor—"

Kien's warning came but a moment before Darinor brushed him aside and entered the study, his looming shadow eclipsing the dim light like an ocean squall.

"Father," Marisha greeted. She rose hurriedly, a clutch of papers in one hand, Galdric's message in the other.

"We have received word from Partha?" the other demanded without preamble.

Allion stood, depositing an armload of papers and scrolls on the desktop. Marisha glanced back at him.

"I have it here," she offered.

"And when were you planning on sharing it with me?" the Entient asked, his disapproving glare leveled at Allion.

"You just missed its carrier," the regent replied, wondering what he had done this time to merit the other's anger.

"Then how did I know word had arrived?" Darinor asked, a scornful edge to his already hardened voice. He continued to stare at them in strange accusation.

Marisha presented the scroll. "If you wish to read it—"

"I don't need to read it," Darinor snapped, barely taking his eyes off Allion. "Just tell me what it says."

"It says they have taken the matter under advisement," Allion sighed. As always, he tried to exude civility where he himself would wish to receive it. But he was tired, and whatever strength he had gained from Marisha's visit had seeped away with the appearance of her father. "However, the Parthan Legion is heavily engaged, and cannot agree to our proposed course at this time."

Darinor's gaze narrowed further. "Amazing that it should take so long to draft such a quick refusal."

"Would you care to have a hand, then, in crafting our response?" Allion asked.

Darinor snorted. "And how long will that take?"

"I can assemble the Circle and send for the scribes straightaway."

"And then what? Wait yet another week for but another refusal?"

"Have you a better idea?"

"I will waste no more time," Darinor declared, shaking his head, "but will go to visit with this King Galdric myself, to impress upon him the realities of our situation."

"I'll go with you," Marisha offered.

"You will not," her father replied sternly. "As reluctant as I am to leave you unattended," he said, casting another swift glare in Allion's direction, "it is far too dangerous for you to travel at this time."

"Two are safer than one," Marisha insisted. "I would be there to watch your back—"

"You would be a distraction I don't need. No."

"But—"

"Child! You have my response. Do not make me repeat it."

Allion's gaze slipped back and forth between the pair, and he found himself holding his breath as the air thickened around them. Marisha's eyes were pleading, but her features were taut, indignant. She would not allow herself to beg.

"I will return to you when this business is finished," her father added, his own visage softening. "You have my word."

Marisha hung her head. Rather than seek to comfort her, Darinor looked to Allion.

"I leave her safety in your hands," the Entient said. "I pray you give me no cause to regret it."

Allion met the other's stare without flinching. "Safe journey then. We'll be awaiting word." *Once again,* he groused inwardly.

Darinor gave a curt nod before turning to his daughter, who refused to look at him. He raised his hood and, in a swish of dark robes, ducked through the doorway.

Allion was about to return to his cleanup when Marisha made a slight curtsy.

"By your leave, my lord regent, I think I shall take some rest of my own."

Allion nodded, feeling awkward at her formal tone. "Please, my lady, don't let me keep you."

She managed a weak smile, for him, and then for Kien on her way out.

When her perfume was all that remained, Allion addressed his guardsman. "Kien, if you would be so kind as to send for Elder Thaddreus? I'll be in my chambers."

Kien saluted. "At once, sir. Shall I have the attendants straighten up, sir?"

Allion considered again the mess of documents still strewn upon the study floor. "That might be best."

He took a moment after the other had departed to pick up the felled candles and right the upended inkwell. By that time, his decision, loosely wrought, was made. With a final appraisal of the study and its contents, the regent of Krynwall collected his personal articles and strode from the room.

A MURKY WASH OF FILTERED STARLIGHT seeped through the seams of the stable's outer wall. The windows had been left closed. Though Marisha had paid the head groom a handsome sum to keep quiet and to deliver her note on the morrow, she did not want to take any unnecessary chances.

She worked through her inspection of horse and tack, thoroughly double-checking the groom's work. While she was no expert at handling steeds, she knew enough not to trust blindly in another's preparations. A long journey lay ahead of her. She had to make sure nothing was forgotten, and that both animal and equipment were up to the task.

"Is my lady certain about this?"

Marisha nodded without so much as a glance at the nervous stablemaster. Her father should have known better. As should Allion, had they become half as close as she thought they had. Though conflicted about a great many things these days, she would not let her father disappear again from her life. There were still too many secrets between them, too many questions needing to be resolved. The young woman meant for that to change—to learn, once and for all, the full truth of who she was, and who she was meant to be. All her life she had lived with uncertainty, her sense of purpose derived from the aid she gave to others. And while she still took pride in her chosen calling, it no longer seemed enough, not if it was possible to affect the world and its many sufferings in some larger fashion.

Either way, she intended to find out.

Her fingers ran gently over the head and mane of her mount, beneath its chin and down the bridge of its nose. She whispered all the while to the young gelding, letting the animal familiarize itself with her as she did with him. She inspected straps, buckles, and pouches, and verified the contents within. All that she had asked for had been provided.

"He is a fine animal, my lady," the groom assured her. "The finest I can offer at this time."

"So he seems," she agreed.

"Is there anything else I can provide, my lady?"

"You will see that the regent gets my note?"

The groom bowed. "As per my lady's instructions."

"Good," Marisha replied, taking hold of her mount's lead rope. "I thank you, good sir, for assisting me on such short notice. Your reward shall be doubled upon my return."

The groom bowed again. "Your gracious thanks are enough, my lady. Just please, return to us unharmed. Else His Majesty will have my head."

Marisha smiled reassuringly and headed toward the exit, her steed in willing tow. The groom scurried ahead of her, to slide free the locking bar and crack open the heavy door.

A surprise awaited them both. A man dressed in travel leathers stood just outside beside a saddled mare. Marisha's heart leapt to her throat. She looked to the groom for an explanation, but the poor soul seemed even more startled than she, stumbling backward into a small stack of hay.

"A bit late for a ride, isn't it?" Allion asked.

"I might ask you the same thing."

"You might," Allion agreed, "although I asked first. Where is it you're off to?"

Marisha glanced at her own tunic and riding cloak, suddenly self-conscious. She then squared her jaw, eyeing her friend evenly. "Don't try to stop me, Allion."

The man laughed. "Does it look like I came here to stop you?"

She looked again to the groom, who had picked himself up but stood frozen in place, staring at Allion as if fearing reprisal for his role in all this. The regent, however, ignored the man completely, his gaze fixed on Marisha.

"Your duty is here," she reminded him.

"Yes, well, I'm tired of being the one to sit around while everyone else takes action in this."

"What of your oath to Torin?"

"My oath was to look after you, remember? If I'm not mistaken, yours was much the same."

"I meant the one concerning your defense of the crown. Will you leave this city to the wolves just to chase after me?"

Allion shook his head. "I've already made arrangements with Thaddreus. He has agreed, as First Elder and speaker of the Circle, to serve as regent in my stead."

"But Torin wished—"

"Now that Rogun is gone, the danger to the monarchy is lessened. In any case, neither Torin nor I fear that threat half as much as we do the danger to you."

Marisha was grateful for the cold breeze blowing through from outdoors, for it helped to control her flush. Admittedly, this scenario was even better than that for which she had hoped when deciding to set forth. Since Torin had left—and in some ways, before then—Allion had been her closest companion. In truth, she had *wanted* him to try to stop her. But she hadn't dreamed he might offer to go with her, allowing them both to keep their oaths, one to the other, while yet doing what she must to be with her father.

Her eyes slipped to the bow slung across his back, and from there to the quiver of arrows nestled among his saddlebags. She would indeed feel better protected against the many dangers of the wild with Allion at her side. Except for Torin himself, and maybe Kylac Kronus, she could think of no one with whom she would feel safer.

Still, she forced a frown, letting him know that this was *her* journey, not his, and would take place according to the rules *she* set forth.

"I journey east," she confirmed, "to join my father in his petition to King Galdric. If you mean to accompany me, I'll have your oath that we'll not deviate from that course unless we both agree."

"If I intended to interfere," Allion pointed out, "I'd have brought the Shield."

"Your oath," she insisted.

"Is given, my lady."

Marisha failed to conceal her smirk. It felt good to see him like this, the hunter once more, no longer weighed down by the duties and trappings of an office for which he had no use. Even in the pale light, he looked fresher, more alive, than she had seen him in weeks.

"And you," Allion said, addressing the mute stablemaster at last. "While it should come as no surprise, see to it that the Circle of Elders is apprised on the morrow of events here tonight."

The groom bowed. "Yes, my lord."

"And next time you agree to do the lady here a favor, take care not to do so behind my back."

"Yes, my lord. Your forgiveness, my lord."

"Carry on."

The groom bowed again, then turned to Marisha and presented the open door. Marisha nodded and slipped through, then mounted her steed and brought it quickly under control. Allion watched her before doing the same.

"Are we ready then?" he asked, as the stable door closed behind them.

"We'll want to keep some distance," she advised. "If my father senses us too soon, he'll send us right back."

Allion looked at her and chuckled. "Stubborn as you are, I'd like to see him try."

"What's that supposed to mean?"

"Never mind. Trust me, the less time we spend in that man's company, the more comfortable I'll feel."

Marisha thought to offer a rebuke, but saw from his sly grin that he was expecting just that. "Then I should warn you," she said instead, "his wrath is nothing compared to mine."

"Is that so?"

She winked, then kicked her heels and started ahead toward the moonlit roadway. Allion followed, and together they set course for the gates of the city, their thoughts already on the journey beyond.

CHAPTER TWENTY-FOUR

A SHARP STING, FOLLOWED QUICKLY BY ANOTHER, jolted him from his co-coon of darkness. His eyes opened, and he found himself in the middle of a dream—a memory. He recognized it at once as one of the defining moments of his life, in which he had first set eyes on his future wife. She regarded him now as she had then, hovered near as he lay upon his back, a reassuring look on her unblemished face. Her blue eyes were bright and inquisitive, her blond hair full of captured light.

"He's coming to," she said.

Another sting, followed by light waves of pain that receded quickly. His gaze shifted to find another woman, this one with tanned skin and freckled cheeks, who crouched beside a gaping tear in the left leg of his breeches, through which the skin of his thigh was visible.

"I told you that would work," the second woman boasted, rubbing her fingers to brush away a sheaf of hairs plucked from his leg.

He looked away, quickly back to the first.

"Your name," she prompted.

"Torin," he recalled. He was aware now of the seasoned smells of earth and woodland, and of a heavy mist that clung to his sodden skin and clothes. This was not the Lewellyn village of Feverroot, he realized. And the woman kneeling over him was not Marisha. "Where am I?"

"Among the dead, I should think, were you not speaking to me."

Torin blinked, then gathered his elbows beneath him. The world spun as he propped himself upon them, and he squeezed his eyes against the unsettling motion. When he felt it safe to do so, he opened them again, and cast about in swift survey. He found himself at the base of a wooded slope. Snow was piled about, save for the melted hollow in which he lay, littered with gravel and boulders and the deadwood of fallen trees. Beneath him, the ground was clear of all but needles and moss—wet, but soft, and warmer than he would have expected. It was cooling rapidly, however, its chill and that of the wind seeping through him in the form of a wracking shudder.

A suspicion gripped him, and he reached toward his breast. The Pendant was gone, as was the chain that held it. His eyes flew to his weapons belt—it, too, was missing.

"Is something wrong?"

Torin looked back to the first woman, surprised again at how remarkably similar she appeared to Marisha. Her face was leaner, her lips thinner, pressed firmly between smile and frown. Her hair hung straighter, though that might have been the weather. The most telling difference was in her eyes, dimmer than Marisha's, and ringed ever so slightly with reddened circles. The gleam they reflected was almost feral, bespeaking an animal wariness he had never seen in those of his lady love.

"I—I wore a pendant," he stammered.

"Hmm," the second woman murmured thoughtfully. "Did it look anything like this?"

Torin shifted to find the freckled companion with the chain of the Pendant around her neck. She hooked a thumb around its length to pull the Stone itself free of her forest tunic and into view.

"Lovely, isn't it?" She beamed.

Torin reached out reflexively.

"Only, this one is mine," she said, tucking it away again.

"Stop it, Jess," bade her companion. To Torin she said, "Your effects are safe. Those we found on you, anyway."

"My sword?"

Jess shifted, reaching behind her to produce his weapons belt. She planted the tip of the scabbard like a standard into the ground, one hand resting upon the Sword's gemstone hilt—its leather wrappings removed—and gave him a wink.

Torin glanced back and forth between the pair, trying to hide a rising sense of panic. It occurred to him that they were most likely bandits, to have stripped him of his possessions before reviving him. But if that were so, why revive him at all? Why not slit his throat and be on their way?

"A precaution is all," Marisha's doppelganger claimed. "For your protection."

"*My* protection?"

"So that we wouldn't necessarily have to kill you."

Her earnest manner smothered the smile that might otherwise have formed on Torin's lips. He regarded her evenly, more curious than afraid, yet uncertain that it would be safe to disbelieve her.

"If that's the case," he said, and coughed, finding his throat dry despite the damp, "may I have them back?"

"Not before you've answered my questions."

Torin looked to Jess, who grinned roguishly, then back to the other. On the surface, her voice was smooth and pleasant, laced with a tone of sympathy and the hint of ready laughter. And yet, there was an unmistakable edge to it as well, as if she might turn on him at any moment.

"Fair enough," he agreed. "What is it you care to know?"

"How you came to be here, for one."

He stole a fresh glimpse of his surroundings. "I'm still not even certain where *here* is."

Soulful eyes regarded him as they might a wounded animal. "This will go better if you do not play games with us."

Torin's features soured, letting slip his irritation.

"If true," she allowed, "then tell me where you've come *from*."

"Alson," he replied, "a land of the island continent Pentania, from across the Oloron Sea."

The woman nodded. "I've heard of it. Go on."

"I was headed west through the Dragonscale Cleft when an avalanche took me. That's all there is to tell."

"An avalanche, was it? Then why were you not buried amid all this snow? Why aren't you dead?"

Torin didn't know. He had no recollection of anything that might have occurred between this moment and that in which he had tumbled from the mountain trail above. Although an involuntary glance toward Jess and the talismans she now wore betrayed his best guess.

He looked back hurriedly, but the gesture was not missed.

"I see."

"Come, Fawn," Jess urged, "let's take him to the Nest." Her own voice was steady and strong, wild eyes agleam with mischief.

Again Torin's gaze darted back and forth between these two, Jess and Fawn. "The Nest?"

"Our home," Fawn admitted. "We are Fenwa. Nymphs, to the rogues of these lands. Have you heard of us?"

Torin frowned and shook his head.

"This is our forest. All who enter unbidden are deemed trespassers."

Jess's broad grin seemed suddenly predatory. Torin looked back to Fawn.

"As I told you," Torin said, "I arrived quite by accident. If you would be kind enough to show me the nearest road, I'll be on my way."

Fawn considered. "I think our Granmarch should be the one to make that decision."

"Granmarch?" His frown deepened.

"The leader of our clan. We can't report your effects without reporting you. Unless we claim to have found you dead. And I'd not do that without making it so, for risk of another finding you later."

Torin scowled. "Then why not return them to me? You need never have found me at all."

"Because there's more to this than what you're telling me," Fawn said solemnly. "But it's not my place to judge, except to determine whether or not you may be worthy as a Catch."

"And what does that mean?"

"It means we're inviting you to accompany us, back to the Nest."

"As your prisoner?"

"As our guest."

"How long will this trip take?"

"Have you somewhere else to be?" Jess laughed, raising an eyebrow.

"I have business to the north. The shorter my delay, the safer we'll all be."

"Ooo," Jess purred, "he's good."

Fawn nodded. "I'm sorry, but coming with us is the only way you'll leave this forest alive. Yes?"

He didn't seem to have much of a choice, and so accepted their offer, such as it was. It was either that or make a grab for his weapons, hoping their threats were a bluff. A foolish move, given his condition and what little he knew of them. Better, he thought, to journey with them for a time and see what more he could learn—not only about these Fenwa, but also about where he had ended up. After all, now that he had lost Moss, he had only the faintest idea as to where he was going.

He could only hope he wasn't swimming into even deeper waters.

Fawn offered him her hands. After a wary glance, Torin accepted them. Though delicate in appearance, their sinewy strength was unmistakable as she rose and pulled him easily to his feet. As they came to, Jess leapt back, quick as thought, keeping her distance. The reaction seemed to Torin not so much a precaution as a warning.

For a moment he stood where he was, head spinning anew. He grimaced against an assault of aches and bruises made more sensitive by the biting cold. Even a moment's brush of the Sword's strengthening warmth would have been most welcome, but he wasn't going to ask again.

"Can you walk?" Fawn asked.

Torin nodded. "Lead the way."

Jess smirked as she turned her back to him, then climbed the snowbank on its shallow, downhill side. Torin waited for Fawn, until she waved him forward with a nod. He didn't argue, but fell into step behind her companion, marching up and out of the melted hollow, leaving the other to take up the rear.

He found it difficult to tell fresh wounds from old. His body was a wreck, and any chance he might get to rest seemed a long way off. Nevertheless, he hid his discomfort as best he could, trying hard not to look or feel a victim.

"You're lucky we found you," Fawn said after those first brief moments of silence. "We don't often patrol these higher elevations."

Torin grunted, not quite ready to share her assessment. He glanced back, peering through a break in the trees to trace the line of slopes and bluffs from which he'd made his sudden descent, clear up to the peak that loomed invisibly now above a stone-gray ceiling of clouds. It was indeed remarkable that he hadn't suffocated, or been pummeled by the tons of icy debris with which he had barreled down the mountainside. He looked again at the crater in which he'd been discovered, then to the Sword, slung in its scabbard over Jess's back. It was either that or the Pendant that had saved him—or both. But how had their power been triggered? He had seen each defend its wielder against magical assault, but that didn't seem to apply here. Before that, there had been the incident at the jailhouse in the city of Leaven, where he had seen the Sword defend itself against physical assault. That must be it, he decided. Though he knew not how, it must have done so again here.

If only he could understand how it had happened, perhaps he could unlock the mystery of how to summon those inner fires at will. He would wield then not just an invincible blade, but power of a kind to bring down a dragon from the sky, raise or level mountains . . .

Perhaps even prevent him from falling captive to a pair of forest-dwelling girls.

His attention shifted from the Sword itself to she who carried it. Jess's frame was lean and sinuous, with limbs much the same. She was the taller of the two, with chestnut hair hanging down like a veil. She trod lightly upon a thin crust of snow that became thinner as they headed downslope, following no discernible trail, but weaving confidently between the slender boles of evergreen trees and the scraggly brush grown up around them.

"Nymphs," Torin recalled aloud. "Imaginary fairy creatures, are they not?"

"It's just a nickname," Fawn admitted. "Given us by those who've spread rumor of our ways."

"Oh? And what rumors are those?"

"They say we are seducers of men, that we lure them to their deaths after taking what we wish."

Torin nearly tripped on a snow-covered root broken free of the earth. "Any truth to these rumors?"

"Some," Jess said, turning to grant him another wink.

"Mind you," Fawn added quickly, "the usefulness of such rumors. This is the Fenwood—or Widowwood, as some have come to call it. As I said, it is our forest. Stories like that serve to dissuade many from entering, granting us a measure of peace from those rogues who might otherwise defile our lands."

Torin held back his response, trying to decide whether he should feel more—or less—at ease. They certainly had made no effort to seduce *him*. Then again, was he not traipsing blindly alongside them into whatever fate they held in store?

"I seldom give stock to rumor myself," he replied finally. "So who are you really?"

Jess gave Fawn a cautionary glance.

"It might be best if we allowed our Granmarch to answer those questions," Fawn said, seeming to agree. "Such knowledge now might jeopardize any chance of your release."

The phrasing of her words was not lost on him. Nor did he miss Jess's snickering laugh. Though this abduction was far more civil than that suffered at the hands of Raven's pirates, he remained a prisoner unlikely to be freed. At least Raven had been willing to divulge the expectations and demands under which he was to be held. These "Nymphs" offered only blithe smiles and left him to guess.

They traveled in silence after that. The girls surrendered nothing more as to who they were or where they were going, and Torin didn't ask. His thoughts had turned wholly toward making his own escape. He wondered how quickly Jess would react if he were to rush her from behind. He wondered if he might hold one or the other hostage against her companion. But neither option seemed any more likely than it had upon starting out. He was not bound. He was not gagged. And yet he was as powerless as if he were.

They continued on through the dripping boughs and the sopping mist. Eventually, the snows disappeared and the brush began to thicken. The earth leveled out as they left the foothills, but remained rugged and misshapen, cut through by meltwater streams and bramble walls. Unless Torin misread the signs, they were headed north, which pleased him. Should he have to suffer this detour, at least it wasn't taking him completely off course.

Midday came and went. He thought constantly about asking how much farther they had to go, but did not want to betray any sign of nervousness. His body was stiff and battered; his wet clothes, heavy and torn, chafed his skin. Though his stomach growled, he did not ask for food. Twice, Fawn shared water with him from her own skin. He thanked her, and pretended this was enough, doing his best to appear at ease.

It was midafternoon before they came upon anyone else. When they did, it was another pair of women. These were somewhat older, and judging by their interaction with Fawn and Jess, served as some form of sentry. They inspected his articles as Jess presented them, gasping and whispering to themselves when catching glimpse of the swirling flames and crimson glow of Sword and Pendant. With wide-eyed interest in his marvelous talismans, they looked him up and down, then waved his party on.

Soon after, they followed a switchback trail down the side of a steep embankment, coming at last upon what looked to be an ancient riverbed. Within its sloping basin lay a tumbledown series of shallow caves, roofed over by humpbacked piles of boulders left behind by the missing waters. Dozens of figures passed in and out of the gap-mouthed openings. Female all, he quickly realized. Nymphs, young and old, of various shapes and sizes—but all in pairs. A nervous prickle began to take root in the nape of his neck as he descended into their midst, where most stopped what they were doing to study the new arrival.

He wasn't sure what to think of the looks they gave him, for there was a wide range. Anger and disgust appeared in equal measure to the welcoming smiles and suggestive poses, making it difficult to determine if the territory he had entered was hostile or friendly. Quite obviously, he could expect a bit of both.

A few called or whistled, both to him and his companions, as he entered the throat of the riverbed and was herded upstream amid the uneven carpet of stones. Like the silent faces, these verbal responses varied in their level of approval.

"You're out of season, Fawn," one might grumble. While across the way, another would purr, "Hey, Jess, when you're finished, bring him to me."

Torin did what he could to take it in stride, which meant ignoring the many inferences—both positive and negative—while yet glancing about with grim intensity so as not to miss any scrap of sensory information that might prove valuable later on.

Like an animal sniffing out a strange home, when it would prefer to return to its own.

They ushered him on toward what was perhaps the largest of the boulder clusters, picking their way over and between natural fortifications of rock and elevation to reach its yawning cave mouth. The forming stones were smooth-faced, worn so by untold centuries of water flow. Still, this and its fellow structures reminded Torin of cairns more than anything else, an association he found more than a little discomforting.

The space within was remarkably dry, the overhanging boulders sealed together with thick layers of moss and grass—as strong and tight as any pitch or mortar. Flaming braziers lit the cavernous foyer and lined a series of corridors passing back into darkness. In addition to their smoky haze, the cave was filled with a pleasant musk that reminded him of his own one-time forest home, spawning a gentle pang of fond remembrance.

When their eyes had adjusted to the dimness, they continued on, rounding a corner to the left, where not one, but two pairs of guards came forward to meet them. These provided additional escort as he delved deeper into the cave tunnel, coming at last to an opening beside which had been rigged a lever contraption of wood and leather used to open and close a stone door. It was here that Fawn and Jess said their good-byes.

"Anything else you would wish the Granmarch to know now?"

"Only that I'm looking forward to her visit," Torin replied, hoping he sounded respectful and not just aggravated.

Fawn gave a slight nod, Jess another smirk and a wink, and the pair turned back the way they had come, his possessions in tow, one pair of guardswomen setting their pace.

The remaining guards nudged him forward through the cleft in the cavern wall. Beyond lay what appeared to be an immense holding area, wide-ringed yet low-roofed. Sets of bindings lay empty throughout—leather cuffs roped to anchors that had been hammered into the stone walls. With each set of cuffs went a belt and collar. A fresh rush of alarm swept through him when they marched him across the chamber and demanded that he kneel beside a group of these opposite the cavern door.

"Is this necessary?" he asked, his words muted by the weight of the cavern.

"Kneel," one woman repeated, while the other leveled an artistically designed but cruel-bladed halberd at his throat. Torin obeyed, resisting the urge to make a break for it, and, while held at blade-point, allowed the other to buckle collar, belt, and cuffs into place.

"It may be awhile," his binder warned before turning to leave. The halberd-bearer withdrew her weapon and spun away with a snort.

A moment later, the slab of stone serving as the door to his prison slid into place with a heavy grinding sound, and except for a lone brazier set to burn near the sealed exit across from him, Torin found himself left alone in deep, musty darkness.

He spent the next few moments testing his bonds, more in reflex than in any concerted effort to slip free. Though it had the potential of becoming the worst decision he'd ever made, his sense was that he had a better chance of surviving this in submitting to their will than in fighting to impose his own. In any case, he remained in a poor position to choose otherwise. His cuffs were roped behind his back, attached to the belt in such a way as to deny him the maneuverability required to remove tongue from catch. The ropes themselves were coarse, and stronger than they appeared, seeming to be made of interwoven strips of bark that gave them the feel of a thick and healthy bramble stalk. And of course, even if he were to break free, there was little possibility of his remaining that way for long.

So he waited, with no idea how long it might be, only his jailor's brief warning to go by. He wondered if Moss might be tracking him, hunting him down in order to earn out the rest of his payment. More likely, the rogue had moved on in order to seek out a safer charter. Which meant there was no one who could know where he had ended up. Until such time as Darinor decided to come in search of the Pendant, he was yet again on his own.

He sat down, slumped against the boulder to which he was chained, and marked the flickering patterns of light and shadow at play upon the cavern walls. He must have dozed for a time, for before he knew it, he was alerted by the grinding of rock as the entry door was levered aside. His head came up swiftly, eyes heavy with grit as he blinked in the darkness. A torch and materials were brought in by one of the guardswomen and used to light the now extinguished brazier. With its flame crackling once more, the halberd-bearer from before marched up to him.

"On your knees before the Granmarch," she said.

Torin did as he was told, rising awkwardly from his seated position, ropes and collar chafing. He blinked some more as the woman and her partner stepped aside and bowed as if presenting him to another.

He looked past them as yet another pair of Nymphs came forward. All of a sudden, his blinking stopped. So too did his breathing, which he held in an attempt to mask his own surprise. For of all the striking young women he had seen that day, this one put them all to shame. Though she wore no adornment that he could discern, he knew her at once as the leader of this band. It was in her bearing, in her face and in her eyes: a confidence of the sort possessed by generals and kings. Rarer still, it radiated outward without bluster or fanfare, which somehow made it all the more evident.

"I am Dynara," she said, in a silky voice both smooth and authoritative. "Granmarch of the Fenwa."

Torin realized he was staring, but could not seem to recall what a more proper etiquette might be. Though oft enchanted by a woman's beauty, he felt something here beyond simple appreciation. Perhaps because he had expected someone older, a grand matriarch with wrinkled skin and shriveled frame, wise yet weather-beaten from having lived a life out-of-doors. But like Fawn and Jess, Dynara looked almost exactly his own age, with a silken shirt and leather tunic cinched tight about her slim waist. Auburn hair hung free, clear to her beltline. The cavern's shadows could find no purchase on her face, so smooth and evenly formed and hollow-free. Despite the dim lighting, her maple eyes gleamed.

She snapped her fingers, and for a moment, Torin worried his obvious attentions had given offense. He was much relieved, therefore, when the Granmarch's partner stepped forward, his divine talismans in hand. This other had a roundish pixie face with hair not unlike a mushroom cap, individual locks full of spring and body as they fountained down so as to barely tickle the nape of her neck. There was a rouge to her cheeks—her skin much whiter than Dynara's—and a pleasant smile upon her lips.

"I'm told these were taken from your possession," Dynara said, gesturing toward Sword and Pendant.

A frog in his throat, Torin managed a polite nod.

Dynara took the Pendant from her companion. With one hand holding the silver chain, she used the other to cup and admire the flaming heartstone.

"A marvelous enchantment," she said, congratulating him. "Are you a warlock of some sort?"

Torin shook his head.

"And yet it is clear you are no ordinary rogue. So tell me, Torin of Alson, what were you doing in our woods?"

Torin did so. He told her everything, from the moment of his brother's invasion to now. He had decided even before he had fallen asleep that he would, if given the chance. Perhaps in being utterly revealing he might win this Granmarch's trust. Or if not, perhaps he might be able to impress upon her how dire was his situation, spawning in her a fear that would earn him his freedom. He'd been able to think of no reason not to, since there was nothing he could tell her that would make him any more vulnerable than he already was.

That had been his reasoning going in. Now, however, he felt an additional motivation, a subtle urge that went hand in hand with the rest. Seldom did he feel the need to tout his own achievements, to use them to build himself up in another's eyes. But he did so now, speaking freely about who he had been, and who he had become. He assured himself privately that it was only for the benefit of his mission, to help convince his captors of its importance. He told himself it was this and nothing more, that it mattered not what she thought of him as an individual.

Even though it might have been a lie.

The narration took some time. His listeners didn't seem to mind, doing nothing to rush him, bidding him continue whenever he took pause. By the time he had finished, his knees were screaming at having been pinned against the cavern bedrock for so long. Dynara and her companions, however, remained where they stood, showing no sign of discomfort and making no mention of having noticed his. Both the Granmarch and her partner appeared stolid in their reactions, as if wary of being taken in by some charlatan. Nor did the pair of unnamed guardswomen, flanked to either side of him, reveal anything in their bluff expressions.

As their silence lengthened, Torin began to wonder if he should not say something more. But his story spoke for itself; he had nothing else with which to plead for clemency.

At last, Dynara spoke.

"That may be the most unlikely tale I've ever heard," she said. "For you to tell it means either you truly believe it, or else you presume me a fool."

Torin played through half a dozen potential responses, but not one that might win him favor, and so kept his mouth shut.

"I'll assume for a moment it's the former, and not the latter," she continued. Her gleaming eyes held him fast. "The question then becomes, what do *I* presume of *you*?"

Torin worked hard to match her gaze, careful not to let his own slip or roam.

"What do you think, Naia?"

Her pixie-faced partner puckered her lips in consideration. "I see little risk to us, either way."

Dynara smiled, supple skin drawing back without creasing, the teeth beyond like whitewashed marble. "Naia," she said to him, indicating the other. "My kinmate." The smile diminished. "She's right, of course. So let us agree for now that neither of us is a fool. What would you have of me?"

"Only to be set free to resume course, with my deepest apologies for having trespassed upon your lands."

"That's all?" Dynara asked, arching a single brow. "You are an outlander. You claim to know nothing of these lands. You ask me to set you free so that you may find your way into the hands of the warlord Lorre. Perhaps one of us is a fool after all."

Torin frowned. What sort of game was this woman playing?

"We are rangers," she explained. "To care for this forest and its inhabitants is our solemn duty. If I am to believe your story, it might be said that the best way to serve that duty would be to see that your quest—mad as it seems—succeeds. Otherwise, it might be that I should keep this so-called Sword of Asahiel for myself, using it to strengthen our defense against unwelcome outsiders."

Torin thought he saw now what she was hinting at. "Perhaps we can do something to aid each other," he suggested. "An arrangement that would benefit both of us?"

Dynara's smile returned. "Now *that* at last is a sensible idea."

"And does my lady have something in mind?"

"What would you say, I wonder, to having a pair of Hunters of my choosing sent to escort you on this journey—to Lorre and beyond, if necessary—with the understanding that if at any time it seems you are about to fail, or they decide you have not been utterly forthright with me, their instructions would be to kill you on the spot and return these talismans to me."

Torin scowled. "You *could* just kill me now."

"But you might be telling the truth—as you see it anyway. In which case I would be doing neither of us a great favor. Besides, we are not brigands, merely a band of women determined to resist the oppression of men, offering both refuge and purpose to freedom-loving souls throughout the land."

"*Female* souls," Torin noted. "Making men like myself the enemy." It was dangerous territory, he knew, but ground that needed to be tested if he was to have any true sense of where he stood.

Dynara responded without anger or apology. "Tell me, how are women regarded in your land?" Before he could answer, she continued. "Here, we are treated much like mules and horses, animals of service and little more."

Torin opened his mouth to press the issue, before thinking suddenly of a better way around it. "Suppose I were to accept this gracious offer," he began, his skepticism plain. "What would be in it for you—should I find the Finlorians, prove my claim, and return home with my talismans in hand?"

"You mean, in addition to knowing that I've helped save the lives of your countrymen and perhaps a few of my own?"

"Yes, in addition to that."

Dynara grinned. "It so happens that in the journey itself, you would be doing me a favor. Certain"—she paused, as if searching for the right word—"elements within my clan have become a source of disruption. I have a sister, in particular, who has become dissatisfied with some of the principles of my leadership. I've done what I can to tolerate her opposing views, but I will not have her sowing seeds of dissension among the ranks. Were she not my sister, I would have silenced her voice long ago. I'm afraid that if I wait much longer, I may have a civil uprising on my hands."

"You want her to be among those who accompany me."

"I'm certain she would be among the first to volunteer. Of primary issue between us is what role we Fenwa should play in the ongoing struggle between Lorre's armies and the rogues of Wylddeor. Our position has long been one of neutrality: Let them grind one another's bones to dust. My sister does not agree. She feels that if the Southland falls, our freedoms, too, will be threatened."

"And what do *you* think?"

Dynara's expression darkened. "I need not explain myself to you. Only, rest assured that I have the best interests of my fellow Fenwa at heart. Should my sister join you, even for a time, it will grant her the opportunity to satisfy her wild cravings, and give me a chance to mend the rifts she has caused. All three of us will have what we want."

Or so it would seem. Torin would have a fresh set of guides, Dynara would be rid of a malcontent, and this sister might get her chance to take action against Lorre's threat. If the Granmarch was being as honest with him as he'd been with her, it struck him as a fair arrangement. Skewed toward Dynara, of course. For if he failed, the Sword and Pendant would fall to her—unless her sister also was unable to return, which might be exactly what the Granmarch was hoping for. But Dynara held all the advantages. It only made sense that they should have to play by her rules.

"The lady's proposal is most gracious," he reiterated with a low bow. "Should it please her, I would be happy to accept her offer."

"Good. Then I shall send for and have word with my sister. In the meantime, you will be set free in order to prepare as you see fit—under armed protection, of course." She turned to the guard who had locked Torin in his leather shackles. "Amber."

Amber nodded and stepped forward. As she worked to release his bonds, Torin again bowed his thanks.

"One more thing," Dynara said, her face pensive. "If it's elves you're looking for, you might do well to visit first with a woman I know. Her name is Necanicum. She used to live among us, but resides now in a region of the Fenwood all her own. She is among Yawacor's eldest known citizens, and must be approached with utmost caution. But it seems to me that her wisdom may be of use to you in this matter. And better that than to seek audience with Lorre, who is as likely as not to kill you before you come within a dozen paces."

Torin nodded, though he wasn't so sure. Would Autumn have suggested he visit with Lorre if the man was truly as ruthless and implacable as everyone seemed to believe? Of all those he had encountered upon this voyage, he still trusted Autumn the most. Then again, Lorre's was the only name she and Raven had mentioned, and even they had done so in fair warning. They may not have known this Necanicum. As long as it was en route, what could be the harm?

Moreover, he dared not dismiss any advice the Granmarch had to offer, for as of yet it was her aid or none at all.

"Any counsel my lady would give would be most helpful," he replied.

Dynara's smooth face was expressionless. "Rise."

Torin did so, wincing at the pain in his cramped knees.

"I will keep these for now," the Granmarch stated, handing the Pendant back over to Naia. "You will have them again when all other preparations have been made."

He forced himself to nod. "As you wish, my lady."

With that, Dynara smiled, just a hint, before making her exit. Naia went with her, while the jailor Amber and her halberd-wielding counterpart held him back in what he supposed was a show of proper respect. Only, they forgot to arrest his gaze, which clung with a will of its own to the Nymph leader's retreating form. It found its focus in the hypnotic swish of the woman's hair, the supple sway of her rounded hips, and the seductive twitch of her heart-shaped buttocks—which traded kisses with every confident stride.

CHAPTER TWENTY-FIVE

EVHAN, CAPTAIN OF THE CITY SHIELD, stood at attention before the Circle of Elders, doing his best not to sway with the exhaustion that gripped him. It had been a long day, from the moment of his arrival upon the perimeter gates of the palace, to this one, in which the Circle had gathered to hear his tale. It was a story he had told at least a dozen times that day, and to a dozen different people—from the perimeter sentries to First Elder Thaddreus himself.

He told it now as he had before. Of how, after completing a sweep one night of the secret route of escape reserved for the city's royals, he had happened upon a band of ruffians, members of a particularly notorious gang of thieves known to operate within and without Krynwall. Recognizing him by his ropes of office, the thieves had taken him hostage. For the past two weeks and more—the entire time during which he had gone missing—he had been held against his will in one of their hideouts right here within the city walls. It had been a harrowing ordeal, surviving on little water and even less food, while his captors plotted as to how to make best use of their unexpected find. Taking advantage of the dissension among them, he had managed at last to free himself, dispatch his abductors, and make his escape.

It was an incredible tale, but measured out with a perfect mix of grandeur and aplomb that held his listeners spellbound. On top of that, there was the physical evidence—the hideout itself and those left behind. A team of City Shield led by Jovanek, the acting Fason, had been sent forth earlier to inspect the location and confirm his account. Among the slain bodies, all of whom were recognized as known criminals, the team had found various materials—ropes, gags, instruments of torture, drafts of ransom notes, and the like—which would seem to support the missing man's story.

"You should not have been out alone, Captain," Thaddreus observed when all relevant testimony had been delivered. "You are lucky to be alive."

Evhan nodded with due deference. "A foolish mistake, which I do not intend to repeat."

The First Elder did not respond right away, but fixed him with a calculating gaze. "With respect for all that he has been through, I move that Evhan be relieved of duty until such time as he has made a full recovery," he determined at last.

"With respect to *you*, First Elder," Evhan replied firmly, "and to the esteemed members of the Circle, I think my recovery may be served best by being allowed to return to my duties at once."

Several of the Elders nodded, while others shook their heads in wonder, all applauding the young man's courage.

But Thaddreus was unconvinced. "At this time, with the legions away, we must be doubly vigilant against any hint of a threat. We cannot afford a chief defender who is prone to lapses of judgment such as that which led to your capture."

"Elder Thaddreus—"

"I am lord regent," the older man corrected. "Until the return of our lord king or his appointed caretaker, you may address me as such."

Evhan bowed in apology. "Forgive me, lord regent. Much has happened in my absence, and I am only now coming to terms with it. But it seems to me that with the legions away, this city needs every able-bodied defender who is willing to serve. And I am willing. Your own physicians have pronounced me well. If a demotion is in order, I will gladly accept it. Jovanek," he added, with a glance across the chamber at his fellow City Guardsman, "has served capably in my absence. I would not see him stripped of his interim title. Only, do not ask me to sit around like a wounded hen, as I have done these past two weeks, but let me offer my life in defense of yours and the citizens of Krynwall as I am sworn to do."

It was an expressive speech, if not quite eloquent, one that roused the spirits of his fellow guardsmen within the hall and drew shouts of approval from the majority of Elders giving ear. Their people needed passion such as his, the Fourth Elder said. Was he to be punished for being a victim? asked the Sixth. What of his resourcefulness and bravery in setting himself loose and dispatching his assailants? added the Ninth.

It was not often the voices in this chamber were given cause to unite, but they seemed to do so in this instance. Their vote of solidarity spoke volumes to the young Evhan, revealing just how fearful and desperate they had become. It was something not even he had counted on.

"Very well," Thaddreus agreed at last, as if accepting it as the only way to quiet the mounting furor. "Let the record show that the Circle has completed its review of this matter and voted to reinstate Guardsman Evhan to the position of Fason, captain of the City Shield, with full rights and privileges thereof. Guardsman Jovanek is thus relieved of his temporary duty in order to rejoin the First Rank. Lieutenant?"

Jovanek saluted, first to the speaker of the Circle, then to his captain, returned from the dead.

Thaddreus sighed. "This session is adjourned."

BEFORE DAWN THE NEXT MORNING, Evhan strode the palace halls, still amazed at how easily his ruse had succeeded. He had taken a calculated risk in returning like this, one that might have exposed not only himself, but his entire brood—that which he had joined within the secret tunnels beneath the city. But with both Darinor and Allion away—they who were least likely to be fooled—the time had come to execute the next phase of attack. In the end, none had dared disagree with he who insisted it to be a risk worth taking.

"Sir!" Kien greeted, snapping to attention before the door to the chambers he was guarding.

"At ease, Bearer," Evhan replied, returning the other's salute. "You are well this morning?"

"Yes, sir. And you, sir?"

"Immeasurably better than this time a day ago," Evhan admitted. "Scrapes and bruises. Nothing that won't heal."

"Glad to hear it, sir."

And he was, Evhan could tell. Like most of the others, Kien was genuinely elated to see him again, and find him well. It was this, more than anything, that had made them all so easy to deceive. The people of this city were on edge as only frightened humans—so keenly aware of their own mortality—could be. With all of the uncertainty that surrounded them, they were in dire need of good news, and the unexpected return of their chief guardian served that purpose, leading most to welcome him with open arms.

"Is our lord regent occupied within?" Evhan asked.

"He is not yet risen, sir."

Evhan frowned with disappointment. "It is important that I speak to him at once. Would his loyal guard permit me a brief audience?"

Kien hesitated. An instinct, perhaps, born of training. "If the captain can wait but a spell, the master chamberlain should be along with breakfast within the hour."

"I would rather not be delayed, but neither will I command the bearer to put aside his sworn duty."

The guardsman fidgeted. "Let it not be said I denied my chief commander," he said finally, stepping aside. "Only, bear that in mind should our lord regent recommend I be put to task scrubbing privies."

Evhan shook his head. "That will never happen on my watch. You've been a faithful guardsman, Kien. First Torin, then Allion, now old man Thaddreus. If only your royal charges were as dependable as you," he said with a wink.

Kien responded with a wry grin, covered up quickly with a cough and a salute. "You're an inspiration to us all, Captain."

Evhan bowed, smirking inwardly at the usefulness of this newfound hero status. It would make that which he intended to accomplish so much easier.

"Please see to it that we're not disturbed," he said, as he opened and then closed behind him the chamber door.

Inside, the speaker's sitting room was layered in the gray shadows of pre-dawn. Coals burned dimly in his hearth beneath a blanket of ash. A hint of morning brightness limned a pair of shuttered windows.

In the unbroken silence, Evhan could hear clearly the old man's breathing, deep and even. Glancing about once more, he made his way toward the adjacent bedchamber. It, too, was empty, save for the sleeping regent. Even in slumber, Thaddreus's aged forehead was furrowed, his thick brows knotted.

He wore a pinched, discerning look, such as that which he had been wearing the night before, during Evhan's review before the Circle.

The captain paused, thinking back. Thaddreus had been listening closely, Evhan knew, though that review had marked the third time the Elder had been audience to his tale. Searching for inconsistencies, perhaps, for any sense that the Fason's prolonged disappearance was part of something more sinister than the abduction of a high-ranking city official. There were none to be found—Evhan had made certain of that.

Avoiding examination by the physicians and healers sent to look him over had been the biggest challenge, but he had done so by assuring them that he only needed rest—and by giving each a ten-piece of silver to simply deliver their reports and leave him be. Together, they had agreed. None would speak out now, for the risk of censure all would face.

And yet, judging by Thaddreus's reaction the night before, Evhan's work was not yet finished. Despite his unerring testimony and the supporting evidence, despite the favorable analysis given by the physicians, despite the eager embrace of his fellow guardsmen and the general populace, the Fason could see that Thaddreus required additional persuasion.

Hence this morning's visit.

Of course, bringing the city's acting ruler over to their side was imperative in any case. Start at the front, and the rest would follow. Were he not so wary, Evhan might have taken this step against the previous regent, Allion. But he hadn't dared. Not with Darinor around—he who held them all in check.

He reached down almost idly to pick up a pillow fallen from the speaker's bed during the night. It was heavy, stuffed with down. Almost gently, he laid it upon the old man's face. He then leaned over and, with both arms, pinned it in place.

Thaddreus tossed fitfully in natural response before coming awake. At that point, he thrashed and squirmed, crying out in muffled denial. Evhan felt the speaker's terror as it radiated outward through the smothering material in waves. He bore quite a kick for an old man, but Evhan was young and strong—stronger now than ever before. The regent's frantic desperation was not enough to overcome the Illychar's own savage resolve. Soon, the struggles ceased, and the twitching began. Evhan held fast a few moments longer before letting go.

The old man's eyes stared up at him, frozen wide with fear and surprise. His mouth gaped within the frame of his pronged moustache. Evhan tucked the extra pillow back into place. He then smoothed over the man's lids and pushed up on the pointed chin. After that, the regent looked at peace, his normally plaited hair freed from its braids to lie across his bedding like strands of woven silver.

The Fason went out after that, drawing shut the bed curtains and returning to the speaker's sitting chamber. There, he stoked the remaining coals in the hearth, coaxing forth a crackling fire because it would be the expected thing to do. He then removed himself a safe distance, to a chair that he carried to the far side of the room, and waited for the sun to rise.

Some time later, the knock he had been anticipating sounded on the outer door.

"My lord?"

Evhan made them wait.

"My lord, the master chamberlain begs entry."

At last Evhan stood and moved to open the chamber door.

"Ah, sir," Kien greeted, and stepped aside. Beside the guardsman, a breathless Stephan bowed his head in surprised greeting over a breakfast food tray.

"Captain Evhan, sir, I've brought my lord's breakfast."

"Thank you, Master Stephan," Evhan replied, taking the tray of breads and fruits. "If you will please pass the word, His Lordship is not feeling well this morning, and asks that the Second Elder assume charge of his duties."

"Sir?" Stephan mouthed with some dismay, craning his head for a look.

"He prefers not to be disturbed," the Fason reiterated, holding forth his free arm to ward against the other's entry.

"I shall fetch the physicians at once," the chamberlain assured him.

Evhan shook his head. "That won't be necessary. I will sit vigil with him myself, and will send for attendants as needed. As it turns out, I, too, am not without need for rest, and the regent and I have much to discuss."

The chief seneschal frowned his staunch displeasure. "Sir, it is my duty—"

"Your duty is to serve as commanded," Evhan reminded him crisply. "I speak for His Lordship on this. Anyone wishing to question me will also answer to him later."

Stephan pouted, but made no further attempt to enter.

"Kien," Evhan continued, "assure our chamberlain here that everything is under control, and that his assistance is not required at this time."

Kien saluted and reached forward to pull the other away.

"I can bring the captain another food tray, if he wishes," Stephan offered.

"Make it dinner. His Lordship and I will share this for now."

Before the seneschal could utter further protest, Evhan closed the door and tripped the latch.

He went back to his chair, setting the unneeded food—which he would consume later for the sake of disposal—on a side table. Unusual behavior, certainly. Enough to raise eyebrows, perhaps, and spawn a few new suspicions. But he was chief guardian, after all, and three days was not such a long time for which to stall. After the required incubation period, all would be forgiven and forgotten, as the Illysp assumed full control of its host and the newly risen speaker walked among them once more. He need only keep any from discovering the truth until then.

After that, while the others of his brood remained in hiding, the regent, too, would be among them, giving the Illysp a sympathetic ear at the highest level of city government. Nor would it end there. Like most illnesses of the winter season, this one was certain to spread.

Of course, even this was only part of the plan. The numbers he gathered within were but a shadow of the legions being positioned without. When the time was right, all would be unreined, and their enemies crushed in the resulting stampede.

So Evhan settled in, readying his excuses, preparing himself against any and all challenges, determined to make sure that when the man known as Darinor returned, the Illychar would be ready.

CHAPTER TWENTY-SIX

CLOUDS WRAPPED THE SKY, a blanket tucked round the heavens so that only a sliver of the sun peeked through. From these fell a light rain, a swirling mist like that found at the base of a waterfall. Trees and stones glistened amid the morning mix of haze and shadow, their soaked and ragged forms suggesting an inner chill that would not be dispelled.

His cloak wrapped loosely about him, Torin sat upon an outcropping at the edge of the entrance to the Granmarch's cave, watching Nymphs of all ages at work and at play. As they had upon his arrival, some returned his observation with looks of disdain, while others teased him with smiles and gestures both coy and inviting. Most, however, ignored him. Being the only male around, he was surprised they didn't treat him more as an oddity. Clearly, men had no place in this society. Or did they?

He resisted the urge to ask Amber or Mirren—his constant companions since being freed from his restraints the night before—for their surliness toward him made it seem a dangerous topic. Instead, he peered past their looming shadows and into the cave mouth behind him. Though he'd been allowed barely more than a glimpse of the deeper areas, he was inarguably impressed by these formations beneath which the Fenwa had tunneled in order to make their homes. Were it not for the braziers used for light and warmth, he might never have guessed he would find anyone living within. Animals, perhaps. Wolves and bears and the like. Or maybe one of the ancient races—orcs or gnomes or dwarves—said to have inhabited such burrows in untold numbers before the coming to prominence of man. But not humans. And certainly not a rogue band of women, out here in the wild.

Seeing no sign of movement among the cave's shadows, he shifted his attentions outward once more. Despite the various activities, the land itself remained virtually unmarked and undisturbed. Against all odds, these Nymphs appeared to have forged a rare balance between their needs and those of nature, resulting in a simple, harmonious co-existence.

It struck him as so very primitive, and he wondered how they managed it. At the same time, it all spoke of a plainness and serenity that was somehow appealing. If given the choice, he wondered which he would truly prefer: the comforts and responsibilities of a progressive society, or the rugged freedom of being removed from it all.

He was still pondering this when he heard the light scrape of footsteps approaching from behind. By the time he turned, Dynara and another he did not recognize were already upon him. As Amber and Mirren parted to either side of him, Torin rose quickly to his feet. Surprised to see the Granmarch so clearly outfitted for travel—and with another besides her kinmate—he glanced about for the missing Naia while offering a confused greeting.

"Dynara," he welcomed with a polite bow. "I thought you were sending another."

Her brow tightened, but the smile she gave him was utterly beguiling. Before he knew what she intended, she snapped forward with serpentine swiftness. He found himself stumbling backward, tripped at the heels. An instant later, he was on the ground, facing the sky and a sneering visage that remained somehow beautiful. A booted foot pinned his empty sword arm, while her opposite knee drove into his stomach. When all had settled, he could feel his pulse against the edge of a dagger held to his throat.

Helpless to do otherwise, he stared at his assailant with astonishment, and watched her sneer transform into a tenacious grin.

"You must be Torin."

He held his tongue this time, along with his breath, waiting for the other to relax. She did so finally, leaning back and taking her dagger with her.

"My name is Dyanne," she declared matter-of-factly. "Dynara is my sister. I would encourage you to remember that."

He wasn't likely to forget, Torin thought, fixating on the girl's features—most specifically her breath as it clouded the surface of her blade.

When he realized that she was awaiting confirmation, he nodded.

"My kinmate's name is Holly. Say hello."

Torin glanced at the other, who regarded him with a devilish smirk. The best he could manage in return was an amiable grunt.

"Well then, I see my sister has already introduced herself," came a familiar voice.

Dyanne's bluff expression never changed as she slid her weapon into its sheath and offered him her hand. Torin accepted it, and she sprang back, helping him to his feet. From behind her came Dynara and Naia, the latter bearing the Sword and Pendant.

Once upright, Torin was able to get a better look at the newest pair of Nymphs to make his acquaintance. He could see now that Dyanne did in fact possess a handful of physical characteristics that set her apart from her twin. But the differences were subtle—a freckle here compared to a mole there, a slightly shorter length of hair, minor variations in shape and stance. Aside from that, she might have been a mirror's reflection of the Granmarch, and every bit as stunning. He doubted their own mother had ever had an easy time distinguishing between the two.

Holly looked a child by comparison, with sable hair and beady black eyes. Given her plaintive cast and petite frame, she might have been a lonely waif with no more strength than a sapling of her namesake. But Torin remembered clearly that flash of a devil's smile, and had been caught off guard more than once already by these Nymphs' deceptive ways. He would not be fooled by this one.

"Your effects," Dynara said, as Naia extended his talismans. Torin accepted them eagerly, trying not to appear so, keeping one eye on Holly and Dyanne.

The Sword's hilt, he noted, had been rewrapped with leather covering and thongs. It was amazing handiwork, much tighter and cleaner than his own. He considered inspecting the blade to make sure it was in fact his weapon and not a fake, but he didn't need to, for even while sheathed and bound in its disguise, its soothing aura was unmistakable.

"I trust I do not have to remind you of the terms of our arrangement?"

Torin hung the Crimson Stone in place around his neck. "I'll give you no cause to regret it."

"Dyanne and Holly have agreed to accompany you. They have been instructed to aid you in whatever manner you require, but to utilize their own judgment in doing so. If you intend to do something foolish, do not expect them to follow. It will be up to them to decide at what point, if any, those precious artifacts are taken from you and returned here."

They can try, Torin thought, with a wary glance at the pair of Nymph Hunters. Now that he had the divine talismans back in his possession, he was determined not to lose them again. "I'm in your debt," he said.

Dynara nodded, first to him, then to her sister and Holly. "Then I bid you all farewell."

With that, she turned on a heel and headed back into her den. Naia went with her, as did Amber and Mirren, wheeling about one after the other. The next thing he knew, he was alone with Holly and Dyanne.

"Have you all the supplies you need?" Dyanne asked him.

Torin hefted his leather rucksack. Meager as they were, its contents appeared to be twice those contained in the various bags and pouches slung or cinched into place on the girls' slender frames.

"I was instructed to prepare only for myself," he admitted. "It's not much."

"It's likely more than you'll need," Dyanne assured him, dismissing his concern with a toss of her head. "The forest will provide for us."

Torin did not challenge the claim. Although he wanted to be sore with her for her unforgiving welcome, he found that as they stood there contemplating one another, he felt guilty instead.

"I'm sorry for my confusion," he said, surrendering the apology he felt he was owed. "No one told me you were twins."

"An honest mistake," she replied evenly. "I'm sure it won't happen again."

Torin couldn't decide whether her words constituted an acceptance or a warning. Finally, he looked to the sopping gray skies, seeking escape from her level gaze and the awkwardness he was feeling.

"Shall we set forth then?" he urged.

Dyanne studied him a moment longer, then turned to Holly. The two shared a brief, unreadable look that yet spoke volumes between them. When it ended, both wore what seemed to Torin a knowing smirk.

"This way," Dyanne said.

They worked their way west, following the downhill flow of the river-bed past the various boulder clusters that comprised the Nest. Several of the Nymphs stopped what they were doing or emerged from their dens to wave or whistle or call out wishes for a safe journey—mostly to Dyanne and Holly, Torin noted, rather than to him. He searched among them for Fawn and Jess, but saw no sign of the pair who had brought him here. The rest of those he did see barely marked the trio's progress. He counted more than twoscore, all told, a fraction of the number he was certain were busy elsewhere, in their cairn-houses or the surrounding woods.

He would've liked to have met more of them, he realized, which surprised him. His brief visit to their private community had thus far provided him little more than scrapes and bruises to both body and mind. But it had been memo-rable to say the least, repaying in the hint of hidden wonders what it had cost him in self-esteem. He knew not what sort of spell these Fenwa had woven, but it intrigued him enough to make him want to learn more.

When they had passed below what appeared to be the last of the inhab-ited boulder caves, his guides veered northward, up along a switchback trail similar to that which he had descended upon entering from the south bank. Dyanne and Holly strode side by side ahead of him. It was difficult to keep his eyes on the path and off their strutting forms. Each carried herself with an unflappable air of self-assurance, as if fully aware of her own strengths and charms. Neither bothered to glance back at him, seemingly unconcerned with whether he followed at all. He watched their unbraided curtains of hair swish back and forth to the rhythm of their stride—particularly Dyanne's, whose silken strands ended just above the small of her back, as if to draw focus to her hourglass shape. Once he was caught, it became that much harder to look away, for one contour led to another, trapping his gaze in an endless flow across her supple physique. Twin sister notwithstanding, never had Torin seen such a fine array of arcs and bends in a single individual, each and every curve right where he would have placed it himself. If the woman had been a sculpture or painting, he would have considered her a flawless work of art.

A sight so rare, it almost made his trials in coming here seem worthwhile.

He shook his head at his own fascination, and averted his eyes. Time and duty did not permit for such fancies. Nor was it fair to Marisha. Wriggling free of Dyanne's enchantment, he turned focus to the many questions that would need answering before he traveled much farther along this new road.

The first was on his lips as they reached the top of the Nest's embankment and started into the surrounding trees. But no sooner had the forest swal-lowed them than Dyanne headed him off with a question of her own.

"Did my sister tell you why she was letting you go?"

Her head only half turned as she asked him this, so that for a moment, he wasn't certain she was speaking to him at all. He started to answer, then hesitated, unsure what all Dynara might have said, and thinking it unwise as of yet to reveal the Granmarch's desire to be rid of her own sister.

Dyanne took measure of his silence with a lighthearted snort. "Don't worry, I'm no fool. You're clearly a viable Catch. Worth keeping until next Season. Maybe longer. She must have really wanted me out of her way."

Torin cleared his throat. "She made it sound as if you were itching to leave."

She went on as if she hadn't heard him. "Visiting Necanicum. I'm guessing that was her idea, not yours."

"Did Dynara say otherwise?"

"No, but I didn't want to confirm by asking her. To do so would've been a sign of weakness."

Siblings and their power struggles, Torin thought. He shook his head. "I was told to seek Lorre. We don't have to make this other stop if you think it's too dangerous."

Dyanne laughed. "Same thing my sister said. A dare if you ask me, making a suggestion and then telling me to follow my own judgment."

"Seems a poor reason to go marching into trouble."

The woman shrugged, still keeping her back to him, her pace unrelenting. "It's the right thing to do, if I understand your mission correctly. The Finlorians have not roamed these lands for our lifetimes and longer. Despite how unpredictable she is, we've a better chance learning something from Necanicum than from Lorre. Just wanted to clarify your knowledge of the situation."

Torin suppressed a groan. "I'm at your mercy."

At that, Holly laughed. "He's a fast study, at least," she said to her companion. She glanced back at him with impish delight. "What shall we do with him, I wonder."

Torin frowned at the amusement all of these Nymphs seemed to be enjoying at his expense. His frustration emboldened him to ask a question that had been gnawing at him. "Tell me, what does it mean, all this talk of *catches* and *seasons?*"

Dyanne spared him another half-turn. "Many of those who form our ranks come from the lands abroad, seeking escape from various circumstances. The rest are the result of controlled breeding. Our Hunters capture men from the wild and deliver them to the Nest, where the best specimens are given over to those chosen to be Mothers for the Season."

"And that's all that's required of them?" He couldn't help but scoff at what was surely many a man's fantasy. "I can think of worse methods of servitude."

The pair looked at each other, Dyanne with an innocent smile, Holly with a wicked grin.

"Our breeding periods are strictly observed," Dyanne explained. "The men are leashed, and disposed of at Season's end. Rarely is it worthwhile to keep one alive throughout the rest of the year. Men are plentiful. For each new cycle, a fresh crop is brought in."

Torin's tongue grew thick in his mouth. Perhaps the Nest would not have been such a magical place to remain after all.

"The last Season ended months ago, and the next remains several months off. Otherwise, my sister would have been far less likely to set you free. Of course, most trespassers caught out of Season are required to pay the toll."

"The toll?"

"Stripped of their possessions and executed straightaway."

Torin swallowed his growing discomfort. "That doesn't strike you as barbaric?"

Dyanne considered him with a raised eyebrow. "We've a long way to go to repay men for their crimes."

Torin couldn't argue that, and would have resisted any inclination to do so. "So the two of you aren't Mothers?"

"Next Season, perhaps. Although neither one of us will be volunteering."

He wasn't certain what to make of her obvious distaste. "Are the two of you . . . joined?"

"*Joined?*" Holly mimicked, with another laugh.

"Sworn to each other."

"We are," Dyanne admitted, "but not in the manner you're thinking of. All among our clan are matched at birth, or paired with another of near age upon arrival. An act of survival. It's not intended as an amorous partnership, although those do develop sometimes."

"Then why resist becoming a Mother?"

"Because Holl and I mean to impact things in a larger way. We love the freedoms provided by our way of life, but in order to keep those freedoms, we're at some point going to have to take action to defend them. Though babes are taken from their Mothers and raised by Nurses, even just a few months is too long a time to be trapped in a birthing den."

Torin's first response was shoved aside by another thought, one which he was immediately afraid to ask. But he made himself do so. "What happens to the children born male?"

"That never happens. Our Mothers are given an elixir that ensures all our children are born female."

The answer was completely unexpected, and seemed to head off any moral debate over infanticide. He wondered if it was truly possible to predetermine a child's gender in such a fashion. He wouldn't have thought so, but then, there was a lot he didn't know. Some things, he wasn't sure he wanted to know.

His thoughts turned. The questions he had actually meant to ask had been scattered and forgotten the moment Dyanne had spoken. He sifted now through those that remained, and latched upon that which seemed most pressing.

"This Necanicum. Who is she?"

"She's one of us," Dyanne replied. "Or was, I should say. One of the founding sisters of our clan. It was she, in fact, who developed the elixir I just told you about."

"So what happened that she is no longer with you?"

"The way Holl and I heard it, the elixir was just the beginning. Necanicum was fascinated with the dark arts and their effect on nature."

"Dark arts? You mean magic?"

"Witchcraft, as it's known to us. The manipulation of life and its natural order. I don't know how else to explain it."

Torin nodded. "Go on."

"Some say it was this that brought about the disease that overcame her, causing her to go insane. But in all honesty, no one can prove the two were related. The fact remains that she became more and more withdrawn, retreating into a world of dark practices and secret experiments. A world frowned upon by the other Fenwa. A world in which no others dared go."

"She murdered her kinmate," Holly interjected, turning to fix him with a glittering gaze.

Dyanne glared at the other's impatience, though there was no real anger in the expression. "We don't know that either," she argued. "It is said the woman perished under mysterious circumstances. No one seems to know how, exactly. But the other Fenwa had had enough. Rather than seek another with which to pair her, as is normally the custom, they asked her to leave. They were afraid of her; they wouldn't dare try to threaten her outright. But it was only a matter of time before their fear and mistrust would have led them to it. Some say Necanicum recognized this. Others say she left much more willingly, seeking isolation in which to continue her studies. Still others say she was already mad, if not from her disease, then from grief at the death of her kinmate, Granmarch at the time. Whichever story you choose to believe, she left the Nest, venturing north into the older, more wild regions of the forest. Few claim to have seen her since."

Torin mulled it through. He didn't care for tales that left so much to interpretation, for they raised as many questions as answers. "When did all of this take place?"

"Some twenty years ago, just before Holly and I were born. Necanicum was an old woman even then." She glanced back at him briefly, her stride unbroken on the narrow forest trail, maple eyes agleam. "You're wondering if she's even still alive."

Torin nodded. "You say few claim to have seen her."

"Few are foolish enough to try. We leave her to her woods; she leaves us to ours. An unspoken agreement we dare not violate. But the rogues of this land accord no such respect. They tread where they will, and pay the price. More than once have we ensnared men gone mad with raving about the dark things come to life in the northern Widowwood. Necanicum may well be gone, but her influence remains."

"And yet, you believe it wise to trespass now?"

Dyanne slipped him a patronizing look. "I never said it was wise. I only agreed it to be a risk worth taking—at least in comparison to visiting with Lorre. In either case, this is a challenge that every Fenwa born in the last twenty years has considered facing, and one my sister should never have dared us to undertake. If Holly and I succeed, our influence among our clan will grow stronger than ever before."

A sense of disquiet began to form in the pit of Torin's stomach. He didn't

like the idea of wandering unbidden into the domain of a mad witch, especially for the reasons they were suggesting. Whatever petty struggle Dynara
and Dyanne wished to wage between themselves over the direction of their
people had nothing to do with him. Nor could he afford to risk his own mission over it. At the same time, he was relatively certain that with the Sword in
his possession, he was well armed against any sorceries this Necanicum might
possess. And if there was even a glimmer of chance she might know something
of the fate of the Finlorians, he owed it to those for whom he was fighting to
find out. Besides, he could take heart in knowing that all of it was most likely
little more than folklore and hearsay.

"Where I come from," he submitted hopefully, "men tell stories of all
kinds of ghouls, but rarely does that make them true."

Both Dyanne and Holly turned to regard him as one, their faces an odd
mix of scorn and amusement. "We'll find out soon enough, won't we?"

They did not wait for his reaction, but tossed their heads and sauntered
on ahead. Like spoiled princesses, he imagined, with he a palace servant left
to follow behind. If that was indeed their attitude, he saw no need to let it
trouble him.

He allowed his focus to drift for a time, to be taken in by his surroundings.
For all its drab color and dour weather, the land had a life to it, a vitality in the
air. It was not something he could see or hear. It was not something he could
quite smell, taste, or touch. But he could feel it nonetheless, like a tingling in
his bones. He was better attuned to such emanations of natural energy—had
been ever since he had claimed the Sword. But having been locked away for
what had seemed ages within the stifling walls of Krynwall, he noted that it
had been a long time since the environment itself had seemed so enchanted, so
filled with hope and promise.

It was a refreshing feeling.

Up ahead, the girls began speaking to each other, though he could not
quite hear their words over the rustle of his movements through the underbrush. He tried to listen for a time, before surrendering it as a useless and
unnecessary venture. Unless they should invite him to participate, he would
cling to his thoughts as they clung to theirs.

They proceeded in this fashion for several hours, Torin trailing while his
forward guides shared plans and observations and whatever other private
merriments served to pass the time, all the while matching each other stride
for stride. Though he had a great deal to be troubled with, Torin pretended
otherwise. It was easy to do, strolling through that captivating woodland. He
marked all manner of small detail: the tenacious bloom of winter flowers, the
silver sparkle of brooks and streams, the unswerving dedication of a mother
fox foraging for her young. In these and other minor distractions, he was able
to lose himself, allowing his burdens to drift away like puffs of smoke. There
were no Illysp, no Vandari, no quest to find the latter in order to banish the
former. There was only the simple serenity of this virgin realm, unspoiled by
man and his concerns.

They stopped twice to rest and eat, snacking on roots and bulbs provided by the forest as Dyanne had promised. Torin nibbled courteously if halfheart-edly, wishing for some form of meat or cheese and thinking that if this was all they ate, it was of small wonder that most of the Nymphs he'd seen were so thin. At least the water was refreshing, sweetened and taken from a skin given him back at the Nest. As with his other thoughts, he kept these to himself. Even during these periods of rest, the girls made scarcely an effort to involve him in their conversations, inquiring politely as to his tastes and opinions, but expressing no real interest in his answers. What little there was worth know-ing about him, he supposed, had been relayed already by Dynara. He might have taken offense, but again decided not to. This fellowship had been all but forced upon each of them, and was unlikely to last long. There seemed little point in trying to become friends.

He thought of Marisha frequently throughout the day, but was discom-fited because it required an almost conscious effort to do so. Once, not long ago, he'd had to expend such effort to keep her *from* his thoughts, so that he could concentrate on matters of the crown. He still envisioned her easily enough, but each time that vision seemed farther away and less distinct, as if reluctant to answer his summons. It felt almost as if something more than time and distance had come between them, but there was no imagining what that might be. Eventually he ceased his attempts and let the feeling go, finding it too frustrating to contemplate.

His shifting mood affected his view of the woods as well. They seemed colder than before, and darker, a maze without beginning or end, the only trails those forged by his guides in front of him. He soon realized, however, that it was not just him. Dyanne and Holly spoke sparingly now, in hushed and solemn tones. The forest *had* changed, grown shadowed and crooked, like a living creature shaped by a heart full of menace.

It grew worse as the afternoon lengthened. Black trees, many of them stripped of leaves and needles, offered scant protection from rains become thick and heavy. While the thinning cover should have allowed more light to filter through as well, Torin found this was not the case. The sun, already on its downward arc, was being drug away like a mewling animal into a nest of snakes. Gusts of wind rattled the trees, flinging fallen raindrops in new directions. The Sword's fires burned low, as if in measure of Torin's flagging courage.

His guides, he noticed, had stopped speaking, and stood waiting for him to catch up. Torin hastened to do so, more than a little concerned by the grim look on Dyanne's face.

"Her domain has grown," the Nymph Hunter remarked, sounding strangely distant.

Torin stood rooted, transfixed by her gaze. It took him a moment to find his voice. "What do you mean?"

"Look around. We're just now entering the buffer between her woods and ours. What do you see?"

She gestured. Torin did not have to follow the sweep of her arm to know what he would find. Gone were the nesting ferns and winter trilliums, withered into dust. Broken was the stately majesty of the ancient granitewood, as well as the bold arrogance of the juvenile alder. What grew here was a grotesque array of blackened boles, many twisted and splintered beyond recognition. Between the toes of these gnarled giants grew only mold and fungus. Not a single squirrel could be found darting upon their trunks, nor a single bird perched upon their barren limbs. The air, unnaturally silent save for the endless thrumming of rain, smelled of rot and decay.

"Stay close," she commanded him. "Keep your mouth shut and your eyes open. If you sense trouble, alert me or Holly, but do not draw weapon unless I give you leave. We mean her no harm."

Were it not for the oppressive stillness, Torin might have laughed. For he had intended no harm to Fawn or Jess or any of their clan, and yet had somehow ended up their plaything. He was about to remind Dyanne of this, but saw in her eyes what little hope there was for any argument he might raise. Opting to save his strength, he wrapped his cloak more tightly about him and nodded.

Dyanne regarded him silently for a moment, as if sensing he had something more to say and welcoming the challenge. Torin let his gaze drift about the dripping woodland before bringing it back to her. The diminishing twinkle in her eyes seemed to betray a sense of disappointment. It caused in him such a sudden and unexpected sting of compunction that he very nearly obliged her with the struggle she was seeking. But before he could open his mouth, she shrugged him aside and started forward once more.

A bewildered Torin shook his head, and followed.

CHAPTER TWENTY-SEVEN

An actual trio now, Torin and his companions eased their way through the gathering dark. The girls still strode ahead of him, but only by a pace, one each to a side. The earth they trod upon was soft and sodden, a mix of wet leaves and rotting deadwood that sucked at the soles of their boots as if reluctant to let go. With each step, Torin wondered if that might not be true.

The land's sickness became ever more apparent the deeper they delved into the northern wood. He would have scoffed at the possibility were he not seeing it for himself. Whatever poison gripped these lands did so with a will that was frightening. Nothing wholesome prevailed here, and only ants and beetles and spiders made it their home. As many trees lay fallen as were standing, the latter of which leaned upon or curled round one another in support. No, not support, Torin realized, but battle. Locked in a struggle for survival, each sought to strangle or otherwise bear down upon its neighbors, as if blinded by desperation to the fate that awaited them all.

The last of the daylight succumbed to the darkness, and only the smothered gleam of moon and stars was left to light the way. Torin looked up to find skeletal branches stretching across the dome of the sky like knives, carving up the clouds and the moon's dim radiance. So eerie was the withered landscape that, were it not for the familiar drumming of rain upon the meshed ceiling of mottled tree limbs and his own shoulders, he might have thought himself trapped in a nightmare from which he must eventually awake.

They pressed ahead with heavy hearts and wrinkled noses, subdued by the devastation wrought upon this diseased woodland. Though he didn't say so, Torin began to worry that this blasted region might stretch on forever—or at the very least, beyond the limits of the girls' endurance. His own was bolstered by the Sword and Pendant, and he was determined that if he must, he would march all week to get clear. He wondered what he might do should his guides elect to stop for the night: camp with them here in this forsaken wildwood, or abandon them to its ghosts?

Before he could decide, a mist began to form about them as if risen from the ground. Within moments, its dark layers had grown so dense that he could not see his own feet. Molding leaves, fallen trees, and wilting underbrush all drowned beneath its curdled depths, while islands were formed out of small rises that dotted the landscape. Still the vapor rose, past their waists, their chests, until its veil threatened to obscure all from view.

Dyanne drew them both close.

"We can't travel much farther without risk of wandering in circles or becoming lost," she said, her words soft and urgent. "It may be best to camp here until dawn."

Torin checked the pale faces of his companions, and saw that each was about as excited by the prospect as he. "The Sword might be enough to light our way," he offered.

"No weapons," Dyanne insisted. "Not unless they become absolutely necessary."

"Then we could light torches—"

"I'm thinking a campfire. For warmth and protection, yes, but also to send signal to Necanicum that we're here."

"If she doesn't know already," muttered Holly.

"And what else might we be sending signal to?" Torin asked, peering about guardedly and seeing nothing but the fog.

Dyanne's grin seemed cruel. "What, now you believe in our stories of ghouls?"

"I believe in hoping for the best, but planning for the worst."

"Very well," the woman agreed, "then I leave it up to you. Either we continue forward blindly, drawing whatever you fear might live out here to the torches we'll be forced to use, or we set for ourselves a position of defense atop one of these mounds and meet whatever may find us head-on."

Neither option was appealing, but the Nymph Hunter was right. Should they continue, they would still be drawing attention to themselves, and deep within the bowels of the fog, would be even more vulnerable to attack. Nor would they catch sign of Necanicum's dwelling should it lie more than a pace or two to either side. The choice reminded him of that made with Moss while crossing the Cleft, and the consequences thereof. And that had not been the first time his impetuousness had cost him. With Dyanne watching him carefully, he finally relented. Better that they seek high ground and wait out this foul night than hurry forward and accomplish nothing.

They settled on a rise of Dyanne's choosing, a mostly bare knoll walled to the east by a tangled stand of what might once have been fir or spruce. The mist swirled about its banks like an incoming tide, but stopped just below its lip and climbed no higher. Torin kept watch with one eye while helping his guides gather wood for the fire. Most of that which littered the ground was so wet and rotted that it crumbled at his touch, and he was forced instead to snap dead branches from standing trees. By that time, his imagination was running amok, for the crack of each limb sounded to him like an indignant shriek uttered by the disfigured giant from which it was broken.

Somehow, his guides coaxed a flame from that soaking pile, sending out a thick tail of smoke that bled into the unbroken fog. Their little company gathered round, shifting as needed to clear the smoke's path, eyes darting about while they listened to the hiss and pop of rain upon their meager fire.

Despite their elevated position, they could see little of the forest beyond the crest of their own hill. Night had descended like a phial of spilled ink, forming a black backdrop beyond the flickering aura cast by the flames. Beyond that, the Widowwood had become an insidious void that sensed Torin's fears and granted them life. He saw faces in the air and in the mist, wraiths that seemed to pass through heavens and earth as though they were one and the same. They were in the flames and in the trees, tormented spirits come to share their anguish with those settled upon this cursed ground. He wondered if his companions saw them, but felt foolish enough without asking. He closed his eyes, blinking them away, only to find that those which fled invariably returned, larger and more loathsome than before.

Perhaps he needed some rest. He was about to suggest as much, that they take turns sleeping and standing watch, when he found Dyanne squinting at him curiously from across the fire, as if seeing something she hadn't noticed before. Then her eyes widened suddenly.

"Behind you!"

At the same time, he felt the flaming rush of Sword and Pendant, burning in warning, and the whoosh of heavy shadows dropping about him. He spun, lost his footing, and reached back to catch himself. He very nearly scrabbled into the flames to escape what he spied—a face made of bark, locked in a rictus grin.

A whirling knife struck the thing in the chest, and though it seemed unable to scream, its face stretched, as if to hiss in silent fury. Torin did not wait for Dyanne's order, but rolled to his feet and drew his weapon. In the talisman's glow, his attacker hesitated, and Torin saw what it was they faced.

Despite the warmth of the Sword pulsing through him, Torin froze. The creature looked more than anything like a sapling tree, humanoid in form, but horribly misshapen. It was lean and skeletal, comprised of a trunk of sinuous wetwood. Its legs and arms were branches, its fingers and claws no more than twigs. Atop its head and from its chin grew scraggly tufts of thin, branching roots. Vinelike strands kept it all sewn together, along with a barklike skin wrapped tightly about its gnarled frame. Fathomless eye sockets burned yellow with unnatural light, reflecting feral hunger and madness.

Torin brandished his blade and again the tree-demon shied away. He saw now that there were others, on the ground and in the trees, similarly assembled, yet each shape unique. Several were even now detaching themselves, tearing their emaciated bodies from the interwoven stand that had earlier served the companions as a windbreak but appeared now to be one of the demons' nests. They dropped from their perches like falling seed cones to gather around the edge of the knoll, hiding just within the shelter of the mists. Torin could still see their faces, though, each a leering mask of death.

He glanced back at his companions and wondered if his visage was as horror-filled as theirs. Each of them was armed now, Holly with a pair of throwing knives from a brace he'd not seen before, and Dyanne with a dagger in one hand, rapier in the other. As of yet, he saw nothing beyond them to suggest they had been surrounded.

He spun forward again, sensing motion. The first of the tree-demons was advancing, Holly's knife still stuck in its chest. Its lipless mouth stretched further, pulled open by roots that acted like tendons, revealing a tongueless maw lined top and bottom with jagged rows of toothlike stakes. Torin retreated a step in spite of himself. The thing's movements were not stiff or awkward, but quick and graceful. The only sounds it made were the snap and scrape of its limbs and bindings, along with the wind whistling through narrow gaps in the creature's bundled form. An eerie rustle signaled the approach of its fog-shrouded comrades below.

The demon pawed the air before him with a series of exploratory swipes. Torin wasn't yet certain how he should respond. If this was some kind of pet in service to the witch—

It lunged then, moving twice as fast as it had before, and Torin had no choice. Up came the Sword, sheathed in flames as it cleaved the beast in two. The lopsided halves went sliding through the muck to lie twitching in the darkness.

For a moment, he thought that might drive the others away. But they came on, groping and with silent hisses as they emerged from the skirting mists. He realized then that the other did not seem to have perished, but lay there in its ruined state, flailing at the air with frantic swipes of its arms and legs, refusing death. Torin allowed himself to study it for a moment, then looked back to the scores of others. Only then did he realize the trouble they were actually in.

"We have to run!" he yelled, hoping his companions would simply agree, and not make him explain himself.

"In this murk?" Dyanne asked. "Are you mad?"

She was right, of course. For all they knew, these things could see in the dark, and give chase without need for rest. Could *he* say the same? Even if his strength held out, this was their domain, not his. He may as well attempt to outswim a shark.

But how long could they remain on this drowning crest?

They came for him then, in a concerted rush. He had only a vague sense of numbers, but feared at once they were more than he could handle. Crimson flames ripped along the Sword's blade as it carved through two, three, four of the things, almost faster than he could count. A fifth lunged from his left, just as his stroke swept out to the right. Holly's knives hammered at it like the beak of a woodpecker. Although they barely slowed its momentum, the blades turned it aside so that it lost its balance and went crashing through their fire pit, scattering flaming brands in every direction.

Again its brethren recoiled, swiping hatefully while their comrade steamed and burned. Dyanne was on it in a heartbeat, hacking at it with sword and dagger, then twisting her blades in such a way as to fling it forward over the edge of the knoll while tripping it with her heel. The smoking creature pitched and sailed out into darkness, illuminating for a moment the inkwell mists and the packs of angry faces hidden within. Almost instantly, the small fires that had sprouted on its limbs were extinguished, and the threat became all but invisible once more.

"They're surrounding us!" Dyanne shouted, sounding alarmed but determined.

Torin snorted, trying to clear the burning stench from his nostrils. He kicked at a firebrand so that it lay as a barrier between him and his enemies. "Backs to the fire!" he hollered. "Use the brands to keep them at bay!"

They did so, arranging the burning pieces in a loose perimeter, brandishing torches or weapons whenever one of the demons came near. But this, too, Torin saw, was unlikely to buy them much time. Alone on the damp earth and in the incessant rain, the scattered pieces were fast smoldering and going out. And each piece taken weakened the primary flame of their signal fire. Nor did the creatures appear truly cowed, as even the scorched one reemerged, shoving forward among its brethren. It was almost as if they recognized fire as a natural enemy, but understood that what flame their quarry wielded could do little damage to them here.

Torin tightened his grip upon the Sword, watching the tree-demons draw about in a tightly knitted ring of hunched backs, twisted limbs, and gnashing stake-teeth. It was a pathetic schilltron he and Dyanne and Holly formed, gazing outward, encircled shoulder to shoulder with too much space between in order to provide for the fire in the middle. He wished for even one or two more fighters to help plug those gaps. Even better, he wished Kylac Kronus were here, and not out seeking whatever purpose the youth felt to be lacking in his life. Perhaps then he might have liked their chances.

After several moments of tentative approach, the tree-demons launched a fresh charge, leaping over or kicking aside the gap-toothed wall of firebrands. Torin stepped forward to meet them. He let the Sword take him now, no longer searching for an easy way out, but resigned to do battle until injury—and then death—lay claim. He gritted his teeth in a savage euphoria, thrusting and sweeping in precise lines and arcs. The creatures came in waves and bounds, diving at face and flanks, above and below. He could feel them scoring hits, their claws raking his flesh with furrows of blood. But it was nothing compared to the damage he inflicted, as he sent them away in bits and pieces.

And yet they came on.

He couldn't see how his companions fared. Every now and then, while ducking or spinning, he caught sight of one or the other in the corner of his vision. His sense was that they were holding their own, coordinating their defenses and attacks as only a pair trained to complement one another all their lives could manage. Not only that, but it seemed the bulk of the demon charge was directed at him, as if the creatures understood his talisman to pose the greater threat. Bring him down, and the others would follow.

Torin fought on to make sure that didn't happen. But not since Spithaera's dragonspawn had he faced creatures so driven. Whatever fueled their hunger, these tree-demons fought now without any trace of self-preservation, as if guided by a pack mentality that seemed to encourage individual sacrifice. As stubborn and determined as he considered himself to be, Torin realized full well that this battle would not be won by force of will alone.

Just when it seemed the enemy's numbers were endless, the unexpected happened. It began with an anguished cry—Holly's, he thought. Her pain startled him, and drew him about. The clutch of demons he was fighting refused him pause, looming over his back like a cresting wave. He felt their darkening shadow, and then their claws upon his back, shoulders, and arms.

Then what remained of their campfire erupted in an explosive gout of green-tinged flame. Torin's view of Holly was obscured as he stumbled backward, arm raised to shield his eyes. In the same instant, smaller fires began springing to life all around him, from each of the smoking brands scattered about. Together, they lit the woods for dozens of paces in all directions, revealing a swarm of tree-demons milling about in startled chaos.

Those nearest him and the fires were scrambling away as if suddenly afraid for their own lives. Small wonder, for wherever one of the creatures came into contact with even a spark of green flame, its entire body lit up like an oil-soaked funeral pyre. There were no screams, but the stench was horrendous. Torin remained where he was, crouched on one knee. He searched for his comrades, but could not find them through the haze of smoke and light and flaming bodies.

Within moments, those demons who had not been reduced to cinders scuttled from the knoll in bitter retreat. Torin watched them go, his guard up, casting about should any return. He found himself squinting, blinded by the sudden radiance, wary lest the fires spread.

Then his eyes happened upon a lone shadow ambling from the south, out of the dark, bearing a globe of dim light. It was neither large, nor threatening, and yet the tree-demons, he noticed, gave it a wide berth, like waters split by a river's fork. For a moment, Torin had no idea what it might be.

"Necanicum," Dyanne whispered.

He glanced over as the Nymph and her kinmate stepped round the fire to join him. Each was breathless and glistening from her exertions, spattered with mud and sporting any number of welts and bruises. But neither appeared to have suffered any serious harm. Turning back, Torin joined them in marking the shadow-thing's approach—up the side of the knoll, edging through the mists and picking its way past the twitching debris of battle. He saw it clearly now—a woman, hunched and knotted, draped in the hides of animals that had not been properly skinned. Legs and tails, still attached, swayed back and forth, withered by rot, while bouncing skulls stared at him with shriveled eye sockets.

She came to a stop directly before them, lifting her lamp as if to have herself a closer look. The lantern itself was odd, its battered casing aswirl with shifting lights, as though filled with twitching glowworms and dancing fireflies. As she raised it high, the surrounding flames lost their greenish tinge, dying into weak, yellow-orange curls that were once again at the mercy of the rain. Beneath their feet, the mists swirled round.

Torin joined Dyanne and Holly in lowering his weapon, waiting to be addressed.

"Ah, the young sisters, they looked affright. They did not understand the gnats were but children."

The witch's voice was wispy and ragged, and as soon as she had finished speaking, she tucked her chin into her shoulder and mumbled something Torin couldn't hear.

"Mother Necanicum," Dyanne said again, bowing deeply. "You saved us."

The old woman ceased muttering to whatever dead thing it was that hung there and cast about the flaming rise. The others followed her sweeping gaze to find dismembered tree-demons lying everywhere, wriggling and flailing in the firelight.

"Did she now?" the witch asked, as if only then becoming aware of what had taken place. "The earth's blood burned hot that night. But was it not they who brought the Immortal One to shield them?"

Sweat dripped from Torin's forehead and trailed down his limbs, stinging rivers that carried salt and grime across the field of claw marks that criss-crossed his skin. He glanced at Dyanne to see what she might be making of this.

"We did bring one to speak with you," the Nymph admitted quickly. "A man who seeks your wisdom."

"Men seek not wisdom," the witch groused, "but the power that comes with it." She muttered again to herself before turning to Torin with a birdlike thrust of her head. "Ah," she said, peering close. "Here stood the one the Teldara spoke of."

Torin held his tongue as he returned the witch's gaze. Her lumpish face was twisted and grotesque, with patches of hair that sprouted from more moles and growths than he could count in one sitting. And her eyes looked more like those of a cat, with multi-colored facets to both catch and reflect the light. They stared right through him as she spoke.

"This way then, yes?" They followed Necanicum before the gnats did return.

Torin's own eyes lifted reflexively to search again the night-shaded wood-land. He saw only the helpless struggles of those tree-demons already severed and destroyed, their teeth and claws digging piteously at the earth.

By the time he looked back, Necanicum had turned, and with a final word to the carcass hanging from her shoulder, shuffled on down the slope.

"What now?" he hissed at his companions.

"It's your quest," Holly offered rather pointedly.

"The woman is witless."

"She saved us," Dyanne reminded him. "I'd rather not wait here to see if she'll do so again." She cast about, gripping tight her sword and dagger. "Care to disagree?"

He didn't. Not after what had quickly become the longest day yet of this ill-fated voyage. He knew not where this witch intended to lead them, nor even that it was Necanicum they had found. But at that moment, surrounded by the scrape and scuttle of those dismembered tree-demons, anything seemed better than remaining where they were.

"Fine, but I'm not putting away my sword."

"You'd be a fool otherwise," Dyanne agreed. "Keep watch of our guide."

Torin did so, eyeing the bob of the witch's lantern while Dyanne and Holly retrieved what knives they could find and selected a pair of firebrands to use as torches. After that, the three of them hurried down the rise, following the sound of the witch's voice as she continued to mumble in the darkness.

CHAPTER TWENTY-EIGHT

A GEYSER OF SPARKS BILLOWED SKYWARD as Allion poked and twisted at the crackling fire, rearranging its pieces in order to stoke the struggling flames. Although it hadn't rained for hours, the elements were stacked against the little blaze he had built, the land around him wet and cold and swept by gusting winds. But he had decided against one the night before, and had nearly frozen in his sleep.

He stopped for a moment, allowing the fire to respond to his efforts, warming his hands over the flames. Through the shimmering veil of their heat, he peered over at Marisha, who sat upon a downed log before a line of trees they had selected as a windbreak.

"Warm enough?" he asked her.

Marisha nodded, a pleasant smile come to her face. Allion couldn't help but stare at her, bundled there in a fur-lined hood and cloak, coiled tight against the cold. Her breath clouded before her, her nose and cheeks made ruddy by the frosty night. So helpless and dependent she appeared, when nothing could be further from the truth.

"Come sit down," she said, patting the log beside her.

Allion hesitated, reluctant to abandon his position by the fire.

"Leave it be," Marisha insisted. "It's fine."

The hunter blew a slow breath and climbed to his feet. Circling around the fire's pit, he took a seat at the edge of the fallen tree.

"Do I smell like horse or something?"

Allion looked at her. "Of course not."

"Then come closer. You're wasting body heat, sitting all the way out there."

He started to argue with her, but didn't want to appear uncomfortable, and so shuffled nearer. What room he left between them disappeared when she moved over to close the gap.

"Much better," she said when pressed against him.

Allion grunted, peering out over the edge of the plateau serving as their campsite. On the plains below, he could just make out the shadowed ruins of the Parthan city of Dirrk, one of those that had been razed by Spithaera's army of dragonspawn weeks before. Like many of the devastated holdfasts and settlements, the city was to be rebuilt. But those plans had been slowed, first by a lack of manpower and the season itself, and now by the threat of wandering creatures that had all but the most stalwart—or foolish—hunkering close to home.

"A beautiful night, is it not?" Marisha asked.

Allion turned his gaze from the husk of broken walls to the celestial ceiling above. Despite a nest of dark clouds strung across the sky to the east, both moon and stars were out in force, casting a silver light that lent a crystalline quality to the land below.

"Think it'll rain again tonight?" she pressed.

"Snow, more likely," Allion replied finally, glancing again at the looming cloud bank.

It was their second night out from Krynwall in pursuit of Darinor. The first had been spent in the shadow of the Aspandel Mountains on the eastern fringe of the Gaperon. They had ridden hard, because as best as they could tell, the man they chased did so as well. At this pace, they would likely reach Atharvan, the capital of Partha, on the morrow.

As far as Allion was concerned, the trip couldn't end too soon. It had started out well enough, a welcome relief after too many weeks of being cooped up behind Krynwall's stifling walls. Nor had they encountered anything but cold trails of the various bands of enemies said to be plaguing their lands. But a threat of a different sort had arisen, one that Allion might have seen coming had he been paying better attention to the signs. Or maybe he *had* seen them and simply chosen to ignore them.

He leaned forward, hands reaching for the halo of warmth given off by the fire.

"Your hands must be freezing," Marisha observed. "I don't know why you insist on wearing fingerless gloves."

Allion wiggled and stretched the digits she was referring to. "I need a full sense of touch when it comes to my arrows," he admitted. "What full gloves grant in comfort, they sacrifice in sensitivity."

"Yes, well, fine protector you'll be when your fingers fall off altogether. Here, let me warm them."

The hunter's chest fluttered in minor panic. "I'm fine, Marisha, really."

"Don't be a stubborn child. Give them here."

"Marisha—"

"It's the least I can do for having you here with me."

He ceased struggling and, with an exaggerated sigh, allowed her to take his hands in her own, where she pressed them between thick leather gloves lined with wool.

"As I recall," he said, "you didn't exactly invite me."

"No, but here you are anyway, and I'm grateful for it."

Allion scoffed.

"I mean it, Allion," she said, pulling at him so that his gaze found hers. Her sapphire eyes had never glowed so bright and blue. "Thank you for coming, for not leaving me to face these wilds alone. For being so dedicated to me—to Torin."

She stopped, leaving the man's name to twist awkwardly in the wind. Silently, Allion cursed himself for ever leaving his place by the fire. He'd been much safer sitting with the tiny blaze between them.

He cleared his throat and forced himself to look away, back to the flames. "Yes, well, friends do that for one another."

"And I've known no truer friends than the two of you," Marisha confessed quietly. She looked to his hands as if she might release them, then started gently rubbing them instead. "How do you suppose he's faring?"

"Torin? Well enough, I imagine. Hip-deep in trouble, no doubt, and probably of his own making. But if there's one thing I know about him, it's that he doesn't know when to quit."

"It just seems so impossible, what my father has asked of him. I can't help but wonder sometimes if he's ever coming back."

Allion turned to her. "You must never stop believing that he will."

"And what do you believe?"

She could read the doubt in his eyes, Allion knew. Doubt as to whether his friend could survive in that savage land long enough to find the Vandari. Doubt as to whether it was all part of some horrible ruse orchestrated by her own father, Darinor. He hid these doubts as best he could in order to answer her.

"He has you to return to, remember? If it were me, there's nothing that would stop me. Nothing."

Marisha leaned her head upon his shoulder. Allion closed his eyes and wondered what he had gotten himself into.

"In any case," he added, "I suppose only your father can tell us for sure what progress Torin is making."

His bitter tone made the words sound harsher than intended, but it was too late to take them back. She pulled away immediately.

"You still don't trust him."

"He's keeping secrets, even from us. How can you trust someone like that?"

"We all have secrets. Is that not so?"

He started to argue, to explain to her that with Darinor, it was different. The Entient was hiding something—a great many things, probably—but something in particular that had nothing to do with personal shame, and that was vital to their struggle. Allion could sense it, gnawing at his mind like a rodent trying to escape its cage. But he scarcely understood these suspicions himself, much less knew how to explain them to the man's doting daughter. So he shook his head instead.

"I suppose I'd feel a lot better if I could place my faith in someone I knew a little better, someone other than just him."

"Then trust me," Marisha bade him. "Or do you fear me to be an enemy as well?"

Allion snorted. "Of course not."

"Even if I told you that I, too, have a secret? A secret I've kept from you all along, from the time we met in Feverroot until now?"

He knew better than to dismiss the matter when he saw the earnestness in her eyes. "Marisha, what are you talking about?"

He listened then as she told him about the Pendant of Asahiel, worn since her childhood. She told him of how the talisman had given her the strength needed to survive her enslavement at the hands of the dragonspawn when all others of her village had perished. She told him of how Torin had discovered it, and of the role it had played in their final confrontation with the Demon Queen. She told him finally of how it had been given over to Torin—that it was this artifact by which Darinor was purportedly able to track him.

Allion was not entirely surprised. He had long suspected there was something they hadn't shared with him about the battle that had taken place in Spithaera's lair. The details given him had never quite added up. He hadn't pressed the issue, because he felt perhaps it had to do with horrors too great to relive. Hearing it now, though, he couldn't understand why he'd been left in the dark.

"Why didn't you tell me this before?" he demanded.

"Were you not listening? I told no one. Not even Torin. He discovered it for himself."

"And why didn't Torin say something?"

"Torin's silence was in respect for my wishes. If you need to blame someone, blame me."

Allion blew into his hands, which he had withdrawn from Marisha during her narration, then wrung them in frustration. "It's not that anyone needs blaming. It's just . . . If it was meant to be such a secret, why are you telling me now?"

"Because you're right. You deserve to know. Do you think less of me now, knowing I kept this from you?"

He scowled for a moment to delay giving her his only honest response. "No."

"Then do not begrudge my father the secrets he keeps. Sometimes, to defend an oath, those closest to us must suffer—just as you put aside your responsibilities to family and friends at Krynwall in order to defend the oath you made to protect me. Is that not so?"

Allion fidgeted, but refused to answer.

"And does your presence here mean you care for them any less?" Marisha asked.

At last he met her entreating gaze. "Perhaps you're right. In any case, thank you for telling me."

"I should think you'd feel privileged." She smiled. "Being the first person I've ever told."

Allion didn't know what to feel. His emotions were running like deer in flight, leaving him but scattered glimpses until he knew not which way to turn. Fear, resentment, guilt—taken individually, any one of these was difficult to comprehend. Viewed together, they were a roiling mess.

Marisha studied him as if sharing in some measure his torment. She was good at that, he knew, always commiserating, regarding people as if by look alone she might draw their suffering and ease their pain. Torin had told him once that it was this compassion, more than anything, for which he loved her. Allion could see why.

He realized suddenly that too much time had passed since her last comment. He should have responded by now, rather than simply stare at her. They had gone beyond awkward. Each was transfixed, lost in the other's eyes. Marisha leaned into him, and before he could think of what to do, she kissed his cheek.

As she pulled away, their eyes remained locked. Allion's pulse raced, and while the heat from their little campfire washed over him, a deep chill wracked his body. The moment had taken on a will of its own, and like an eddy in a river's current, there was nothing he could do to stop the flow.

Then the horses screamed, with such pain and terror that Allion nearly pitched over backward. Upon recovery, he lunged for his bow and his quiver of arrows, left leaning nearby with their sacks of provisions. He strung the supple wood reflexively, and came up with an arrow nocked and ready, aimed toward the trees where their horses were picketed.

By that time, one of the animals was already down. The other, Marisha's gelding, reared up, flailing at the darkness. What Allion saw made his blood run cold. For it seemed the darkness itself had come alive, like a whirling funnel cloud. It ripped at spruce needles and branches and the low-lying brush indiscriminately, whipping up a fog of debris. Great gashes appeared in the horse's hide as stroke by stroke it was flayed alive. Blood spattered and sprayed, coloring the mist red.

When the second animal had fallen, the cloud-thing held its place, huffing and growling. Then it moved outward, toward the camp. Allion fired his arrow, but the storm parted to let it pass. The attacker slowed its approach, but widened and split again—no longer a single funnel cloud, but three, emerging from the trees and into the moonlight.

Allion glanced at Marisha, who crouched low behind their fallen log and stared outward with horrified eyes, a dagger clutched in her hand. An acute terror sucked at him, gutting his insides. It was a fear greater than any he had ever felt for himself—the certain dread that he was about to watch Marisha die.

His numbness was forgotten, cold fingers dipping into his quiver and strumming his bowstring as never before. He didn't pause to see what became of his shots, for he already knew. As one after another sailed harmlessly into the backdrop of trees, he worked all the faster, his desperation driving him. The trio of storm-creatures came on, black and twisted, their shredded forms billowing.

Marisha squealed in warning, and Allion, reaching for another arrow, sensed the creatures breaking forward now in a sudden rush. He let go the arrow and reached instead for his hunting knife. With the knife in one hand and his bow in the other, he leapt atop the log.

"Run!"

In that final moment, the heavens opened, and a great, scintillating light surrounded him. The accompanying boom was so loud that Allion felt the earth rumble. He lost his footing and tumbled backward to lie upon the chilled ground, eyes clenched against the radiant light and scorching heat.

It was the screams that forced him to respond, for he had to make sure they were not his own. He lurched up, squinting. Marisha was atop him by then, having abandoned her shelter to cover his body with her own. Riddled with shock, he peered past at their woodland shield. A leap away on the other side burned a steady pillar of brilliant white lightning, its crackling streams splitting and grinding in a dance about the three creatures, pinning them in place upon the earth.

The stench of their burning forms nearly knocked him back down as Allion wrestled Marisha aside and forced himself to his knees. He cast about, sweeping the ground for his bow or knife. It was then he saw the other, at the northern edge of their campsite, a towering scarecrow of a man whose gaunt frame buckled with strain against an invisible burden. His cupped hands were raised skyward, and Allion flashed back to a different fight not long ago, when the Entient Ranunculus had joined them in battle against a pair of Spithaera's demons on the shores of Llornel Lake.

Darinor!

But this fight was not yet over. A horrible screeching sound pierced the rumble of thunder, driving into his ears like rusty knives. Whatever these creatures were, they refused to die, though their flesh was steaming and melting away beneath the lightning's onslaught. Allion wanted to help, but all he could think of was gathering Marisha and fleeing.

Within the dancing streams, the creatures clawed at one another in rage and frustration. But the lightning shower appeared to be weakening. Allion turned back to Darinor, whose legs were trembling. The renegade Entient could barely stand, and yet their enemies struggled.

At last Allion spotted his bow, lying beside the campfire, and managed to haul himself to his feet. Marisha tugged at him, but he ran for his quiver first. A moment later, he dashed back toward the fire, where Marisha had already retrieved his bow. She understood without words what he intended, and so traded items with him before feeding the first of his arrowheads into the flames. One after another, she then handed him the burning shafts, which he sent whistling through the air and into the midst of their enemies. Slowed by the deadly lightning, the things within were unable this time to dodge his strikes, and Allion carried out his assault with grim determination as their continued shrieks rent the night.

Two were almost fully aflame when the jagged streams of energy flickered suddenly and died out. Released from their stinging cage, these two fled into the woods, flapping away in the manner of grounded birds. Allion's eyes widened when the third turned in a direct line toward Darinor, who hunched forward now on one knee, shuddering breathlessly.

"Allion!" Marisha yelled, clutching his arm.

The hunter turned, accepting the final arrow. Allion looked at the single bolt in dismay before stealing a glimpse of her pleading eyes. Shaking free of her grip, he took the arrow and nocked it to his bowstring, then peered down its shaft at his intended target. Through the wisps of smoke and curling flames, he could just make out its starlit outline, like ink swishing about in a clear bottle. It seemed without set shape or form, but his earlier strikes had told him otherwise. With practiced aim, he stared down that swirling cloud, narrowed gaze digging deep with focus, and fired.

With a meaty thwack, the arrowhead sliced deep through what he had guessed to be the monster's throat. He must have guessed right, for it collapsed to the earth, where it spun and writhed but made only rasping noises. With a final, choking screech, it arched stiffly along its crooked spine, then went still.

Mere paces away from where the thing had fallen, Darinor fell back raggedly. Marisha raced toward him. Allion followed with a loping stride, favoring a twisted hip. He held up when he reached the smoldering creature, shielding his nose with a raised forearm.

While Marisha pawed at her father in search of wounds, Allion studied the thing they had killed—shriveled limbs and barbed nails, black hair and leathery skin. Though burned and mangled beyond recognition, it reminded him of a bat as much as anything else, with its folded wings and hooked teeth and pointed ears. Only, this "bat" had been taller than him, and humanoid in its stance.

"Are you hurt, Father?" he heard Marisha ask.

"Leave me be, child," Darinor wheezed, shoving his daughter away.

Allion looked over as the mystic muscled himself unsteadily to his feet.

"What *were* those things?" the archer asked.

The renegade Entient limped near, blue eyes still glowing from his magical summons of nature's energy. The look he gave held such fury that for a moment, Allion thought the other meant to strangle him.

"Illychar," Darinor snarled, as if the answer could not have been more clear.

Allion pointed at the smoking corpse. "No. I mean, what manner of creature is that?"

Darinor looked at it. "In life? A goblin. King of the Eldrakkar family. Cousin to the elves. Illysp-possessed and strengthened throughout centuries of serving host to the fell spirits." His fierce gaze shifted to Allion. "Were it not for me, you would both be dead."

As would you, were it not for us, Allion wanted to say. He settled for matching the other's gaze, refusing to turn away.

Darinor snorted and turned to Marisha. "You disobeyed me."

Marisha appeared sullen, but refused to apologize.

"And you," the mystic growled, rounding upon Allion once more. "Is this what you consider looking after her safety?"

Before the hunter could think of an excuse, a mournful whinny came from the area of the downed horses.

"You will need to finish them off," Darinor spat. "Goblins prefer their meals to struggle while being consumed."

Allion found his horror reflected in Marisha's face. "I thought Illychar did not eat."

"They obey the natural instincts of the creature they once were. Behaviors such as killing methods often remain the same."

The hunter gulped down a wave of nausea.

"And this one," the mystic continued, kicking at the charred carcass at their feet. "This one must be destroyed utterly, unless you wish to face it again later."

The hunter looked at the Entient with doubt. In its present condition, the goblin appeared a useless rag. Allion could not imagine it ever rising again, no matter how many Illysp might come to possess it.

"Those that fled . . . Will they return?" Marisha asked.

"They will," Darinor assured her. "Though it is unlikely they will do so tonight. Still, there are others who will come sooner. We must complete our tasks and be away from this place at once."

Neither Allion nor Marisha felt like arguing, and so went about doing as the Entient instructed them. They put the horses down first. Although a hunter all his life, never had Allion seen so much blood, nor an animal whose eyes shone with such helpless pain and fear. When that was finished, he helped Marisha carry brands from their fire in order to rebuild it over the corpse of the Illychar. It took a considerable effort to set it alight, and in the end required that Darinor use his powers to enhance the heat of the flames. Only when the Entient was satisfied did he lead the pair in the retrieval of his own mount, the gathering of their possessions, and on down the trail.

For the longest time, no one spoke, until the silence began to drive Allion mad. They'd not heard the last from Darinor on their actions in coming here; that much was certain. And waiting around for it, he thought, was worse than any punishment the other might actually impose.

"The pyre back there," he began, as they continued to wind their way down from the plateau. "Why was that necessary?"

The Entient, walking with them alongside his steed, glared back at the hunter disapprovingly. Allion had really only meant to trigger a revelation of what it was the mystic intended to do with them. Darinor surprised him, however, by answering his question.

"Is it not obvious?" he fumed. "Fire is the only way to ensure the destruction of a host's functionality. It does so not only by consuming the components of motor skill—muscles and tendons and ligaments—but more importantly, by destroying the marrow within, where it is believed that the Illysp takes root at a granular level. Anything short of cremation leaves open the possibility of reanimation, since even a skeleton, if held together by the necessary connective tissues, can be made to rise again."

It was a conversation, Allion realized, that they should have had a long time ago—and would have, he was certain, had he or anyone else believed the half of what Darinor had told them. Only now, after a personal encounter, did the hunter feel the need to understand fully that which he'd heard tell of these Illysp.

"I should think that by cutting off one's head, or removing one's heart," he said, struggling to make it all fit with what he knew to be true in nature, "that that would be enough."

"Then you have not listened at all since the moment of my arrival. When it comes to the functioning of an Illychar, the physical condition is less important than the mental condition—that which exists deep within a creature's smallest, most fundamental living particles. To eliminate the potential for infestation, both must be destroyed."

Allion still wasn't sure that he believed, but this might have been because he didn't want to. If he accepted that what Darinor suggested was true, then they really were in the middle of a struggle that most likely could not be won. For if the skirmish they had just waged was any indication, given a full-fledged war, he doubted they would be able to destroy the corpses on either side fast enough to keep them from rejoining the conflict.

"What about . . ." Marisha began, before stopping to collect herself. "What about the horses? Are they not subject to this possession?"

"Only those of a humanoid intellect or greater have shown themselves susceptible to Illysp conquest—though I find even human rationality to be suspect at times."

A clear reprimand, Allion thought, and he wondered again what the renegade Entient intended to do with them.

He didn't have to wait much longer. As they neared the base of the plateau, Darinor steered them into a cave worn by earthquake and erosion into the face of the sandstone bluff. After guiding them through its shadows, to a cavern lit by faint streamers of starlight filtered through a cracked ceiling, he turned them against a jagged wall and pinned them with his gaze.

"Listen closely. Come morning—"

"Don't ask me to go back," Marisha said immediately.

Darinor leaned forward, glaring. "That's precisely what I *should* do, isn't it? What I *would* do if circumstances were any different." He settled back, though his frown was no less severe. "Sending you home now would be a death sentence. Atharvan is two days away on foot; Krynwall is closer to eight. What I was going to say is, come morning, we make for Atharvan together. Your childish disobedience has cost us dear," he added, waving a finger before their faces as if it were a blade that might be used to cut away any smiles. "Because I must now remain with you, rather than ride on ahead. But that damage is already done. Besides, there seems to be no sense in leaving you with instruction when the only way I can trust you will comply is to keep you under my own watchful eye."

Marisha swallowed the rebuke bravely, no doubt emboldened by the fact that, ultimately, she now had what she'd wanted all along.

But Allion's focus was on Darinor himself. For as he stared into the mystic's eyes, he saw something he hadn't noticed before. Pain. As clear as that which he'd seen in the eyes of their slaughtered mounts. It confused him momentarily, and he wondered at its source. Concern for Marisha, maybe? The realization humbled him. For despite the man's belligerent behavior, it seemed he was in fact subject to the same emotions of love and fear and sorrow that gripped the rest of them. A deep-seated anguish was driving him, sparked surely by the feelings of uncertainty they all faced. The man could speak and act however he wished, but those eyes betrayed the truth of his torment.

"I extend this proposal with one condition," the Entient continued, his eyes fixed now on those of his daughter. "From here on out, you do as I say, when I say it. I must have your oath that you will not disobey me again."

Allion sensed Marisha's hesitation. "Father—"

"Now, child. No matter what. Else we leave your protector behind and ride ahead to Atharvan alone, where I will have King Galdric lock you in the safety of irons."

Marisha's gaze slipped toward Allion.

"Look at me, child, not him, and swear."

The young woman shifted uneasily as she studied her father. Her response was barely audible. "I swear."

"Should she break this oath," Darinor rumbled, addressing Allion, "I shall hold *you* accountable. Do not disappoint me again."

The hunter gulped and nodded. Given the fiery look aimed his way, he did not need to ask what the consequences of failure might be.

"Very well. Sleep now. Tomorrow will be a long day."

With that, the Entient retreated back down the tunnel toward the cave's opening, drawing his horse with him.

"Where are you going?" Marisha called after.

"To stand watch. Get some sleep."

The tone in which he spoke was the softest and kindest Allion had yet heard from the man, and it triggered a fresh wash of guilt within.

"Good night, Marisha," the hunter muttered when the other had gone, then marched to the far side of the cavern, fighting hard not to look back.

"Good night," he heard her whisper, before he unfurled his bedroll and settled upon the stone floor, prepared to wrestle with his demons in his dreams.

CHAPTER TWENTY-NINE

Catching up with the madwoman they believed to be Necanicum did not prove difficult. The witch limped along as if wounded in both legs, her gait slow and ragged. Torin hoped they didn't have far to travel, for if so, it might take them months to get there.

Dyanne must have been having similar thoughts. "Forgive me, Mother," the Nymph intruded, "but to where do we accompany you?"

The witch did not answer, except to mumble again to one of the desiccated creatures hanging over her hunchbacked shoulder. Dyanne glanced back at Torin and shrugged.

"Are you certain you know your way in this gloom?" he asked the elderly woman himself.

"No harm came to Necanicum in her travels. Were it otherwise, the world of Eddaron would be a much different place."

She began humming to herself after that—like a dying frog, Torin thought, croaking its final lament. All further attempts at communicating with her proved useless.

So Torin settled in alongside, flanked by his Fenwa companions, grinding his teeth at the slowness of their pace and the helplessness of their situation. They were clearly at the witch's mercy—at least until dawn, when they might feel better about navigating these woods on their own. It had been a mistake to come here, he was sure. But then, might not the same be said of this entire voyage?

He studied the darkness as they went, peering past the mix of light cast by the Crimson Sword, the witch's lantern, and the Nymphs' torches. Though he could not see them, he could sense the sinister things that waited just beyond, rasping and skittering at the farthest edge of his senses. It left him to play games in his own mind: Were they real, or simply madness setting in?

The exasperating trek, however, turned out to be mercifully brief when measured against his fears and expectations. They had been traveling less than an hour in a meandering line to the south and east, hugging nearer the Dragontail Mountains, when they came upon a great, interwoven stand of trees whose branches dropped forth thick streamers of vines like roots into the earth. Varying in thickness from the tiniest tendril to strands that might have been their own trunks, these shoots formed a series of veils and curtains that reminded Torin of frozen waterfalls spilling out over a series of cliffs.

The closer they got to it, the larger this tree nest loomed, its girth large enough to swallow some of the bigger courtyards back home, its uppermost reaches soaring well beyond the limits of his sight. Torin was wondering what in nature could have caused such an unusual eruption of growth, when his shifting gaze fell upon Necanicum. Perhaps in this case, nature had been moved by a guiding hand.

Eventually they came to an opening in the base of the gnarled structure, into which the limping Necanicum led them. A warren awaited them within, shoot-lined corridors crawling with all manner of tree-dwelling insect, many of which glowed. The members of the trio kept close, forced together by the narrow walls and low-hanging ceiling, dodging knots and protuberances that sprouted forth at odd angles. The pungent smell of decay that had ruled the surrounding woodland was less prevalent here, overtaken by a strangely pleasant musk.

He stole frequent glimpses of his companions as they went along, watching them for signs of unease. Holly's face reflected a sheen of sweat, but her eyes remained bright and eager. Dyanne had long since sheathed her blades, and no longer did her free hand rest upon the hilt of her dagger. They were each captivated, it seemed, with these new surroundings, as if children come to marvel at a new playground. A charming response, Torin thought, though he might have felt better had either displayed even a hint of his own wariness.

Their journey ended abruptly. After cutting through a string of alcoves crammed with articles of fur and leather, wood and clay, the passage emptied into a wide burrow that loosely resembled a central living area. Or a workshop, Torin amended privately, for what had at first glance appeared to be a pile of sleeping rugs looked now to be a stack of unfinished weaves, heaped beside a broken loom. Tables and shelves had been hollowed out of the interior walls, which were pitted, overgrown with mold and fungus, and swarming with beetles. The many surfaces were littered with bowls and phials, fluid-skins and herb-sheaths, as well as numerous implements of mysterious function, and pouches filled with ingredients unknown. Like the structure itself, dug deep within the heart of the enfolding nest, everything was fashioned from natural materials—tanned, carved, fired, stitched, or otherwise molded into useful form.

As his gaze slipped about the chamber, exploring its many crags and niches, it snagged upon a curious-looking altar with rounded edges and tunneling hollows, almost like a honeycomb. Crooked seams ran throughout the uneven surface. It wasn't until he looked away and came back to it that he recognized it for what it was—a mound of rotted skulls, piled high, sealed to one another with pitch the way a mason might assemble bricks.

The skulls were human.

His stomach churned, and bile rose to his throat. He hefted the Sword in reflex, his tongue lashing out like a whip beyond his control. "What do you want with us, woman?"

Both Dyanne and Holly gawked at him, alarmed at his disrespect. Necanicum, however, showed nary an interest in either his words or his blade. She had set down her strange glow lamp, and was busy rooting around her tables, gathering items he could not see, and for reasons he could not discern.

"It was not Necanicum," she rasped, "but the Immortal One who sought, when he entered her woods."

Torin wasn't sure which was more infuriating: the gibberish itself or the unruffled manner in which she spoke it. Before he could react, Dyanne motioned him to keep silent, then turned to address the old woman herself.

"And did this 'Immortal One' find what he was seeking?"

They had to wait, as expected, for the witch to finish grumbling to herself before she could respond. "The Immortal One found less than he was seeking"—she wheezed—"and more. Not enough to save him from his fall, but enough to rise again from it."

Torin scowled. "What sort of riddle is that?" he demanded.

Again the private conversation with her own shoulder, like an involuntary twitch. Torin wondered if the weasellike animal slung there, with its dried-out eyes and gaping mouth, ever spoke back.

"In the end," she replied, "the riddle was solved. But the answer was again both less and more than that for which he yearned."

Torin was still trying to unravel the words in his own mind when the witch rounded slowly, a cracked mortar and bloodstained knife in hand.

"Few remember it was Necanicum who turned the tide."

He might have been troubled by the appearance of the knife, but found that he wasn't. He was too confused by what he was hearing, wary now of dismissing the other too quickly. She might well have been nothing more than a raving madwoman, but she spoke as if in prophecy—albeit one that in her mind, it seemed, had already occurred. Torin was not one to believe in such things, but he saw now what Dyanne was thinking: Perhaps there was something useful to be gleaned from all this madness.

"Turned the tide," Torin said, echoing the witch's words. "And how did she do that?"

"By bearing his sacrifice, given the Teldara. That which would preserve and make him whole again."

While Necanicum muttered to herself in follow-up, Holly whispered at him from where she stood, near the altar of skulls.

"I've heard of these *Teldara,*" the Nymph said. "Spirits of divination called upon in ancient tradition. I believe she intends to foretell the results of your quest."

"An orcish rite," Dyanne confirmed, her supple features pinched with distaste. "Requiring a sacrifice of hair and blood."

Torin was prepared to pull his hair out by the roots, if that's what was required to make sense of all this. "How much blood?"

"A trickle, and it was done," Necanicum assured him, though her grating voice was anything but soothing.

Torin studied the old woman as if seeing her for the first time. Her twisted frame was so gnarled and bent that he could not seem to separate joint from limb. She carried a mountain of knobs upon her back and a jutting nose upon her face. The face itself drew out toward the center, as if stretched by her crusty snout. Her skin was infested with warts and ravaged by lesions, and her hair, tousled and matted, brought to mind an image of wilting leaves.

And yet, despite her horrid appearance and the knife in her hand, he felt no threat from her. Perhaps it was the eyes, those multifaceted orbs that seemed to stare right through him. Perhaps it was the fact that she had saved them once already when she hadn't had any obvious cause to do so. Whatever this old woman was or wasn't, he had no sense that she intended him any harm.

Much good that would do him when he lowered his guard and allowed her to slit his throat.

He looked to Holly, who nodded almost imperceptibly, and to Dyanne, who merely shrugged. The decision was his. There was no one, he supposed, who could guess any better than he as to what she might do. Only the ghosts of this place could tell him for sure.

At last he lowered the Sword, though he refused to sheathe it.

"Take what you need."

Necanicum hunched forward, reaching for his left hand. Torin let her have it, disgusted by the gritty feeling of her flesh on his, repulsed by the filth caked beneath her yellow, clawlike nails. He held himself steady, though, even when she used her bone-handled knife to cut three vertical lines in his wrist. She murmured to herself while doing so—what sounded like an invocation. She then set aside her blade and turned his arm over, positioning her mortar to catch the blood that poured from the wounds.

It was more than a trickle, but Torin clenched his jaw and waited patiently, only once looking up to glare at Holly. When the mortar was full, the witch set it aside, then reached again for her knife. Torin was acutely aware of his own heartbeat as he let her reach up with the blade while pinching a finger full of hair. A quick sawing motion and the short strands came free. When she looked at them, Necanicum chuckled, a splintering sound like the snapping of deadwood.

The old woman turned away then, veering toward the altar with her ingredients in hand. The trio repositioned themselves, granting her room to work, while craning their necks to see what exactly she was doing. Though he, too, was curious, Torin made no effort to hide his skepticism while wrapping a cloth around his wrist.

The young king had met a fortune-teller or two in his day. From what he recalled, their routine depended greatly on their presentation—gaudy dress and extravagant movements, coupled with sly speech and meretricious mannerisms. Intended to be entertaining, if not truthfully fulfilling, and requiring more than a little imagination on the part of the audience.

Necanicum's ritual bore none of that. Once again, she acted as if she were the only one present—she and whatever fell spirits she was talking to. Little by little, she poured his blood into a clay dish set atop the altar, and stirred it round with her knife. Then she diced up his stolen hairs and added them to the mix, stirring some more. When that was finished, she scooped up a strange-looking jar and dumped its contents into the dish. Beetles, Torin saw, and watched them squirm and scuttle throughout. All the while, Necanicum crowed in archaic verse—or else more gibberish—even then mumbling intermittently to herself. Torin's eyes shifted from the witch, to each of his Nymph guides, and then back again, marking each of the shadows that painted their faces in the smoky light of torch and lamp, on guard should something change.

"He went in search of Eldrakkar," Necanicum said suddenly. Her face was lowered to the dish, mere inches from where the beetles skittered and swam, studying their movements. "Not the lesser, nor the greater, but the middling variety—the elf, as it was known."

Torin started. Though he could not remember for certain, he was confident he'd made no mention to the witch of what it was that had brought him here. Holly flashed him a triumphant grimace.

"The Finlorians," he granted. "You know where they are?"

The room's shadows seemed to deepen. "He was told to seek the Overlord. But the Overlord did not lead him to the elves. He led the Overlord to them."

Torin's mind raced. The Overlord. Lorre? A flicker of excitement burned through him. But what did it mean? "How do I find them," he asked, "if not with the Overlord's aid?"

The witch dipped a fingernail now into the dish, nudging one beetle after another this way and that, then tasted his blood on the tip of her tongue. "The many he did not discover without the one."

"The one?"

"He of the shadow-earth, made to walk the surface. Alone, like the Immortal One."

Torin was no longer certain he was getting anywhere. "Who is this 'Immortal One'?" he growled impatiently. "Is that supposed to be me? What of the other, the one I must find? Where do I look for him?"

"He drifted from place to place, his friends no more, the last of his brood. Chained to this land by the blindness of those around him."

Torin repeated the words to himself, but still they meant nothing. He looked to his companions, searching their faces, but both women just shook their heads.

"Is the Immortal One lonely?" Necanicum asked. It would seem she had finished with her reading of the blood-soaked beetles, for she turned from the altar to face him. "Does he, too, long for his friends?"

Again Torin was forced to guess as to whether she was actually addressing him, or referring to someone else. Her gaze remained distant, as if peering beyond him, beyond this bizarre scene, into a world he could not see. He hadn't missed the shift in her inflection of time, from past to present. And yet, as a potential clue, it wasn't enough to help him.

"My friends, are they all right?"

The question seemed to jar the old woman, whose visage shriveled in confusion. "He lost the first so long ago, before she was ever truly his. She took to another, and so he let her go. Or was it that *his* heart wandered first?"

Her moment of clarity, such as it might have been, was gone. She was out of time again, speaking of the past. But whose past? His or another's? And had this past already taken place? Or was it but a glimpse of what might be?

He fought to clear his thoughts. "Necanicum—"

"What matters is the Immortal One found his way, as all children must. So that when next he came to a fork in life's path, the choice was his to make."

Torin was about to ask another question, then hesitated. It seemed the longer this went on, the more perplexed he was becoming.

"The Immortal One left then," the witch bade in her husky voice, turning away, "and the young sisters with him."

"What?" He blinked. "But you haven't told us—"

"They hurried, while the way was clear, for the heavens did open up to them, and the youthful gnats had been warned to leave them be."

The old woman looked to be storing the unused portions of his blood, pouring them from the mortar and into a wooden phial. An unused pinch of his hair followed.

"Mother Necanicum," Dyanne interrupted, sensing Torin's frustration. "Is there any more you can tell us? Which way should we go?"

"The sisters were right to guide him through Necanicum's woods, though it did not change the course the Immortal One had to take."

Dyanne turned toward him like an interpreter. "Our course is the same as it was?"

Necanicum nodded. "They left her quickly, for they did not wish to delay Necanicum in her journey. Down the tunnel," she added, indicating with a deformed finger the corridor through which they had entered, "and into the night."

There seemed little point in pressing for more. Necanicum had started humming again, the same tune she had used to shut them out during the hike between their camp and her abode. And even if they were to get something else out of her, it was likely to be more of the same nonsensical rubbish as before.

It certainly wasn't worth challenging the witch's intent that they depart—about the only thing that had been made clear. His guides seemed to agree.

"Thank you, Mother," Dyanne said with a courteous bow.

"Thank you, Mother," echoed Holly.

Necanicum did not respond to either woman, leaving Torin to take one last look around before rolling his eyes and heading for the exit.

They moved quickly back the way they had come, down the winding passage crawling with grubs and insects, led by the light of those that glowed and of the Sword and torches they carried with them. They could not escape that stifling place quickly enough, Torin decided. The witch's words haunted his thoughts—those that he could remember. He wished now that he'd written them down, then realized that it probably wouldn't have mattered. A madwoman's ravings; that's all they were. It would have been easy to become angry, but best just to be grateful the encounter hadn't cost them any more than it had.

When they reached the outer threshold of the witch's giant tree hut, he hesitated. The land without looked different than when they had entered. The dark clouds had drifted on, setting free the light of moon and stars, which washed down through blackened limbs. The mist that had trapped them had dissipated, opening up the forest's lanes. The air remained foul, the shapes of the trees stark and menacing, but their way appeared clear.

"Just like she said," Holly whispered with evident wonder.

Torin wasn't so readily convinced, as he peered about for sign of the tree-demons or anything else that might threaten. "Those creatures might still be out there. Are you sure you want to chance it?"

"She said they'd been warned," Holly insisted.

"Either we move on while we can," Dyanne agreed, "or we wait here. Which would you prefer?"

That settled it. With his guides slipping ahead to retake the lead, Torin was on the move once more through the witch's domain. The Nymphs set a mean pace this time, one that Torin—practiced though he was at racing through woods—found difficult to match. He ran with the Sword in hand, drawing upon its endless reserve of strength and stamina, its pulse at rhythm with the beating of his own heart. Dyanne and Holly, he noticed, kept guard as well, each with a blade in one hand and a torch in the other, casting wary glances every which way. Torin smirked to see that even they had their doubts.

Those doubts proved well founded when, more than once, one or the other of them caught sight of Necanicum's "gnats" leering at them from amid the trees. After a time, the things became easier to spot, and appeared more and more frequently. But the creatures threatened only from afar, swiping at the air, hissing silently, and making death's faces at them as they passed. Nor did the company hold up, refusing the demons the opportunity to mass. They jogged on, sprinting occasionally, sometimes slowing to a walk, but always moving forward.

The night waned. When the torches burned low, new ones were found. They headed north, with the tacit understanding that for now, at least, nothing had changed. A visit with Lord Lorre remained their primary objective. While Torin placed no faith in the witch's riddles, even these seemed to suggest that it was the overlord of Yawacor who held the key to his search. Perhaps that would change come morning, and they would recognize the need for a fresh plan.

Assuming, of course, that a new day ever arrived.

Their stumbles grew more frequent as the hours wore on. Enemies both real and imagined closed in. But the company endured, by turns hurtling or staggering through the near-dark, scanning the wooded labyrinth and using their blades and torches to keep the more sinister shadows at bay. After a time, their diligence was rewarded, as, leaf by leaf, needle by needle, life returned to the forest. Trees straightened, scars healed, mold and rot shrank and with-drew. The underbrush burgeoned about them, thick and hearty, filled with the rustling of nocturnal animals. The air smelled fresh and clean once more.

At the sound of a night owl, the guiding Fenwa slowed their pace, and Torin followed them to a lurching halt. They looked about, at their surround-ings and at one another, chests heaving in welcome relief.

Dyanne was the first to speak. "I think we're safe," she observed.

Torin nodded, though his thoughts were not yet ready to move on. "So, can anyone tell me what we learned back there?"

Dyanne looked at Holly, and the pair of them shook their heads.

"Likely nothing you haven't already determined for yourself," the smaller Nymph said.

Torin stared at the flames swirling within the depths of the Sword. "So it all comes back to Lorre."

"It was worth the effort," Dyanne maintained. "I for one feel better about this trek than I did before."

Holly nodded. "As do I."

A host of antagonistic responses came to mind, as Torin returned the looks aimed his way. They viewed him differently now than before; that much was obvious. As to why—or how it might affect their journey—was much less clear.

"Simple for you to say," he huffed finally. "I see no cuts on you that won't easily heal."

"We should clean that," Dyanne suggested, glancing at the bandage wrapped about his left wrist. "Before it has a chance to sicken and fester."

She sheathed her dagger and handed her torch to Holly. A slight chill swept through him as she approached.

"Sit down," she said.

Torin did so, sheathing his own weapon and settling against a massive fir. While Holly built them a small campfire, Dyanne removed his blood-soaked wrap and set about washing it with a clean cloth and some of that sweetened water. She was firm and gentle at the same time, scrubbing when necessary, dabbing at the more sensitive regions. Torin winced once or twice, but withheld any complaint. Though for the most part he watched her work, he couldn't help but sneak an occasional glance at her studious face, so smooth and focused. He kept waiting for her maple eyes to find him, but they never did.

When satisfied with the cleansing, the woman prepared a quick poultice of herbs and wrapped it in place over the jagged lacerations. Its prickling coolness sent a fresh shiver through Torin's body.

"Keep that in place," she instructed, "until I tell you to remove it."

Torin nodded as the Nymph rose, still without looking at him. "Thank you," he said, as she turned away.

Dyanne stopped in her tracks to peer back at him. For a brief moment, she frisked suddenly in place, rocking back and forth as if in tune with a frolicsome melody only she could hear. Her hair swished with the movement, and an unabashed smile lit her face. "The pleasure was mine, Immortal One," she teased.

She stepped away from him then, to where Holly had arranged her blankets by the fire. Torin was left behind, momentarily breathless. He couldn't shake the image, so unexpected, so revealing, a mere peek at the depthless, freedom-loving spirit this girl possessed. His eyes flew after her, hungry for another glimpse, but Dyanne was already curled up in her bed of moss, with night's curtain come between them.

"I'll take first watch," Holly offered.

Torin nodded, though he should have refused. It should have been he who had taken that watch. For despite the long hours and the many trials of that day, he found himself refreshed, invigorated, unable to close his eyes and even pretend at sleep. Whenever he did, Dyanne was there to greet him with that smile . . . that dance . . .

A vision he could not have dispelled had he wanted to.

NECANICUM SIGHED AS SHE FIT THE LID to its jar and tied it in place. It had taken her some time to wipe clean each Tongue of the Teldara. So many grooves within their hard-shelled bodies. So many jointed legs. She hadn't even needed them for the telling, for on this matter, the Teldara spoke willingly. But in order to draw his blood, she'd had to play at performing the ritual of forced communion.

Do not forget the phial, they told her, those who lived within.

She looked at it, the tiny container she had filled with his blood. Preserved by the necessary incantation. Stoppered and secured for the journey that lay ahead. Such a little item, upon which rested the fates of so many.

Hurry, they urged.

"Don't rush me," she muttered back. "There is still time."

But none to waste. The Leviathan stirs. We must act before He does.

They were right, of course. They always were. She had learned that lesson long ago, though not a day went by that they didn't remind her of it. Still, better to take her time, check her inventories, ensure that nothing that would be needed was forgotten.

If the Immortal One learns what he is up against, he might simply turn away.

"I should think so. But we didn't tell him now, did we?"

That cannot happen.

"It most certainly can," she warned, "if what you've told me is correct." And she knew that it was.

That must *not happen,* they amended.

"I suspect it won't."

Did you see the way he looked at her?

"I'm not blind," she mumbled. "Sometimes I think I see these things more clearly than you."

She couldn't remember now how it had happened, whether they had chosen her or she had chosen them. It no longer seemed to matter. Regardless, the time they had long predicted had come, and she would not let it be for naught.

Hurry.

She gritted her teeth, resisting the urge to snap back at them. She almost wished she could leave them behind. It might have made this entire trek more palatable.

Before long, she had gathered up her things. She didn't require much. A few horns, skins, and pouches. An extra fur. And of course the phial, tied to a string and hung around her neck, so that it lay against her breast. Where she could almost feel his heartbeat against hers.

Are we ready, then?

Necanicum nodded, more to herself than to them, and picked up her light globe. She would refill it on the way out, though even that would not last her long. Once beyond the borders of her woods, these woods to which she had given such magnificent life, she would have to find another source. She had no doubts but that they would help her do so.

When she reached the exit to her home, she stopped to peer up at the dawning sky. The sun had not yet risen, but she could taste its yearning, and smell her destiny in the wind.

You know the way, do you not?

"You'll not let me forget, I'm sure," she griped, her chin digging at her shoulder.

For once, they remained silent, and she did nothing to discourage them. They could sense it as well as she, the significance of what she must do. A mystical moment, setting forth, like that in which she had given birth to the first of her forest children. They would recall it as she did. And in the end, if no one else remembered, they would.

That when the Immortal One walked her woods, and this world as they knew it hung in the balance, Necanicum answered.

She hesitated a moment longer, drawing a deep breath to absorb what she could, then stepped off her gnarled stoop and took her first strides toward the mountains along the narrow path. She moved quickly, but comfortably, refusing to rush. The road before her was long indeed, and these but the initial steps. She would carry on as well as her old bones would let her, and trust that it would be enough.

Limping along, hunched and crooked, Necanicum settled in on her great journey to the north.

CHAPTER THIRTY

WHEN TORIN FINALLY SLEPT, HE DREAMT OF MARISHA.

She spun toward him out of the darkness in a pale azure gown—the one she'd been wearing when he had asked her to be his queen. He did so again now, to which the woman responded with a kind laugh. Smiling, she welcomed him into her arms, where she pursed her lips as if to grant him a kiss. When he closed his eyes to receive it, however, she laughed again—differently this time, sharp and rasping. He looked to find not her face, but Necanicum's, mere inches from his own. He recoiled, and she danced away in a whirl of nimble grace, Marisha once more. Rather than give chase, he waited for her to stop. Only, she never did, trapped in an endless spin that carried her farther and farther away . . .

He awoke to a shaft of sunlight that knifed its way through the canopy of trees. For a moment, he knew not where he was. Home, it would seem, in the woods outside of Diln. A comforting revelation, to learn that all of his trials and travails were but ghosts of his imagination. He leaned up, casting about, eager to confirm his suspicions.

He found instead Holly's slumbering form beside the coals of their fire. Farther off, on a stump overlooking the game trail that cut through their little glade, sat Dyanne, her back to her companions as she filed her dagger against an oiled whetstone. In a flood of imagery, Torin recalled where he was and why. Only, for some reason, he felt no real disappointment upon learning the truth.

Sensing his movement, Dyanne turned, greeting him with a polite smile. "Sleep well, did you?"

Her sly tone suggested she already knew the answer to that question, so he chose to ignore it, glancing again toward the brightness of the midmorning sky. "You didn't wake me for my watch."

Dyanne's blade rasped down the length of the sharpening stone. "You've been thrashing about all night. I checked on you once or twice and decided you needed the rest."

Torin rubbed his aching neck. No use in denying it. He felt as if he hadn't slept at all.

"How is *anyone* supposed to rest," Holly groused suddenly, "with all of the chattering around here?"

Torin shifted back to the smaller of his two guides.

"Why should *you* complain?" Dyanne asked her. "You've been awake for hours."

"Precisely," Holly muttered, sitting up with a groan. Her sleek, sable hair was littered with moss and leaves, which she brushed at irritably.

Dyanne, Torin noted, appeared exactly as she had the evening before, her carefree beauty undiminished by their late-night run through Necanicum's woods, or her few hours of sleep. Her face actually seemed to shine in the unexpected light of this new day as she put away her dagger and stone and sprang to her feet. "Shall we be on our way, then?"

They prepared a quick meal, cleaned up their campsite, and exited to the north. There was little discussion, and nothing at all regarding their encounters of the previous night. Torin wondered if that was because the girls had made as little sense as he of what they had seen and heard in the witch's burrow. He came near to asking more than once, but preferred not to relive any part of it. Whether or not the girls had learned anything that might help their status back home, he had gained nothing but nightmares from the experience. To speak of it out loud could only make them more real.

Except for the cuts and bruises that proved otherwise, it seemed as if the entire episode might never have happened. For there was no hint of a survival bond between him and his guides. Once under way, they traveled as they had when first setting out from the Nest, with Dyanne and Holly locked in persistent chatter between themselves while Torin trailed behind like a child forgotten by his parents. Despite what the three of them had been through, the Nymphs did not seem any more inclined than before to include him in their conversations. Put to it, he might never have convinced a casual observer that he had faced death with these women, and won.

Of course, that was looking at it from an outsider's perspective. From his vantage, things were decidedly different. Most notable was the way in which he saw Dyanne. There was no denying he was smitten with her; her little jig following last night's escape had erased any doubt of that. But that didn't mean it was anything he intended to act upon. Left alone, such feelings were certain to wither away.

To encourage them along that path, he worked as before at keeping Marisha in the forefront of his mind. It was easy to do at first, troubled as he was by the dream from which he had awakened that morning. But it wasn't long before that image faded, replaced by more pleasant thoughts and memories. And these, unfortunately, had a way of turning on him. For whenever his fondness caused him to lower his guard, he found his eyes and thoughts returned to the woman before him, rather than she who was an ocean away. Perhaps his response was only natural, but he wasn't going to allow himself that excuse. For how might he feel if Marisha were to do the same to him?

Nevertheless, time and again, he had to chide himself for his wandering gaze and force himself to look away. While Dyanne and Holly enjoyed each other's company, Torin brooded silently, welcoming an onslaught of darker contemplations, which seemed the surest way to keep all others in check. He thought of Darinor, the Illysp, and his own headstrong foolishness. He thought of those who had perished in the War of the Demon Queen, and of how many of them might have been saved had he made better decisions. He thought of the wizard, Soric, and wondered if it would not have been better to leave the kingdom to his elder brother while seeking his own purpose elsewhere.

Most especially, he thought of Arn and Ashwin and Cordan, who had died for him already on this trek, and of what little their sacrifices would mean should he fail to accomplish his objective. It left him to wonder how many others might be asked to lay down their lives before his task was finished.

Such grim reflections made fertile ground for the return of Necanicum—and return she did. Though he tried to brush them aside, the witch's riddles refused to go away: the mention of his fall, of finding less than what he needed, of the loss of his friends. What confused him as much as anything was how much she seemed to have known about him—or thought she did—even before her supposed divination. Either way, it was foolish to be troubled, for nothing of what she'd told him could be translated into a course of action. Short of that, he would be just as wise to dismiss the old woman's cryptic comments as elements of her own imaginary world.

He was still trying to convince himself of this when they emerged from the northern stretches of the Widowwood and onto the highland prairie of central Yawacor. The midday sun remained dominant in the sky, though Torin had ceased some time ago to take comfort in its warmth. Somehow, the incessant rains had seemed more in keeping with his grim presence upon these shores.

They traveled no road, but over a plain of rugged boulders and windswept grasses. Wild orchards grew here and there, stripped of their summer fruit. But there were no signs of human settlement—no farms, no crops, no cattle grazing in the fields. Some of that lay farther west, his guides told him, but most of it to the north—from what they'd been taught. Having been born and raised in the Fenwood, neither Dyanne nor Holly had ever been this far out herself. It was as much an adventure for them now as for him.

A few hours later, they reached a river labeled on their maps as the Tanir. Here they spotted what looked to be a small cluster of nomadic tradesmen, although they didn't get close enough to learn for certain. Instead, they veered eastward, upriver and closer to the edge of the mountains, searching for a shallows over which to cross.

They found it in a wide bend where the river flattened out over a distance of nearly a mile, diminishing its rush. The girls seemed to have no problem wading across the bed of slick stones, their breeches rolled to their knees and their soft leather boots in hand. Trailing behind them, Torin slipped more than once, but managed to keep his balance and stay relatively dry. He wasn't sure why he bothered, for he desperately needed a bath, and now, while the sun was up, seemed a good time. Once across, his companions agreed, and made their way along the shore to an area pooled deep enough for that purpose. Neither seemed to care if he should want to bathe with them, but Torin didn't feel right about doing so, and so sat ashore with his back to them, with a warning from Dyanne that he not be foolish enough to attempt to run off.

When the girls had finished, he took his turn at scrubbing away the grime and weariness from his journey, taking special care to wash the various cuts and scrapes suffered in his battles to get this far. The waters were numbingly cold, but that only served to invigorate him further. He took his time, so that when finally he emerged, he could scarcely stop his teeth from chattering.

Even so, he felt much better than before, until he climbed the secluded bank to where the girls should have been waiting, and found them missing.

He glanced around. Had they decided to abandon him after all? Not likely. Not without saying something, or attempting to take his talismans. Might some unforeseen ill have befallen them then? His stomach knotted at the thought, leading him into the tall grasses in search of signs.

He'd gone a dozen paces without seeing any indication of flight or struggle before it occurred to him that the girls might be playing some kind of game. Perhaps they were hidden somewhere nearby, observing him, waiting to see how he would react. It seemed a strange thing to do, and rather purposeless, but he knew well enough already not to put anything past them. Best that he turn around and head back to await their return.

He was about to do so when he heard a rustling in the grasses just ahead, from an area of massive boulders that must have tumbled down out of the mountains, but still seemed out of place in this grassy field. His pulse quickened, and he reached slowly for the Sword, drawing it quietly from its sheath. With a hunter's steps, he crept toward the disturbance indirectly along a peripheral line, so that he could approach the desired spot without setting off an alarm.

He had taken just a few strides with that plan in mind when there was a sudden flurry of motion to either side of the area he'd been focused on. The two movements converged in the center of the target zone, like a pair of predators working together to take down a larger prey. There was a grunt of surprise, a clash of arms, and a sound like a sack of grain being slammed to the earth.

Torin lunged ahead, forgoing any thought of stealth as he whipped past sawing blades of grass. Whatever the struggle, he didn't want to arrive too late to affect its outcome.

He should have known that where his guides were concerned, he would find things well in hand. Neither Dyanne nor Holly had been taken hostage; rather, it was they who had brought down the intruder. He couldn't see the other's face, for it was blocked by Dyanne's back as she sat upon the unfortunate man's chest, in an aggressive posture Torin recognized all too well. Holly, meanwhile, had kicked wide the victim's legs, and crouched now between them with one of her throwing knives in hand, its tip digging at the man's groin.

Holly glanced back at Torin's approach, her fierce grin seeming to mock his concern. For a moment he stayed where he was, listening to the labored breathing and muttered oaths of the apprehended trespasser. Then the victim seemed to gather himself, and the last sound Torin expected to hear carried above that of the nearby river, borne up by the afternoon wind.

The sound of laughter.

"I don't have me much time for this now, ladies," the man snickered. "But if you can hold the thought, I might be able to oblige you later."

Dyanne leaned forward. "Speak again without leave, and you'll lose such desires forever, my friend."

A prick from Holly's blade further dampened the other's amusement, cutting short his lingering chuckle. Torin, however, stepped forward curiously, coming around for a better view.

"Gavrin?"

The man was in a poor position to respond, what with Dyanne's blade at his throat, but managed to turn his head toward the sound of Torin's voice. When his eyes found the other, they squinted, then widened in surprise.

"Torin, was it? Shades of mercy. If that's you, my mother was a gnome."

Torin grunted. "It wouldn't surprise me."

Dyanne glanced up as he strode near. "You know this smelly lout?"

Torin nodded. "He was my guide through the Cleft, before I stumbled into your forest."

The woman eyed the rogue beneath her distastefully. "He can be trusted, then?"

"That depends. What are you doing here, Gavrin?"

"Moss," the big man reminded him, a marveling gaze fixed upon the blade of the Sword. "You still owe me for that day of travel, by the way."

"We'll see about that," Torin allowed. "Just now, I'm trying to decide whether or not to have my friend here slit your throat."

Moss chuckled, until he realized no one else was going to do so with him. "I heard noises," he said, "someone in the river. I'm guessing now it was you. I came to check it out."

"Slithering about like a snake in the grass?"

"Can't be too careful," Moss replied, with an obvious effort to hide the strain in his voice. "Thought you might be one of Lorre's scouts."

"Lorre?" Dyanne echoed dubiously. "Why would his scouts be this far south?"

"Have you not heard? Neak-Thur is fallen. The Bastion is his."

"What?" Dyanne balked, her alarm evident. "When?"

"More than a week ago, turns out. Even before I met our mutual friend here."

Dyanne looked again to Torin, her features grim.

Torin was also frowning, but gave a slight nod to one side. "Let him up."

"Actually, my friend," Moss offered, "it's grown quite comfortable down here all of a sudden."

It wasn't hard to imagine why. Dyanne had pinned the rogue's arms with her knees, so that her thighs all but cradled his neck. Once again, the Nymph leaned close, shifting her weight so that it pressed down upon the dagger gripped in her left hand.

"Just so you know, I don't need *his* permission to drain your filthy throat," she hissed.

She gave the man a chilling smile, teasing her blade across his flesh, then sprang up in a single lithe motion. Holly followed with another prick, drawing a stifled shout, before joining her kinmate. Both kept their weapons at the ready.

Moss sat up carefully, massaging the back of his head. "Ah, well, some other time then."

Torin shook his own weapon as it hung at his side—just enough to draw back the other's attention. "You haven't finished explaining yourself."

"Have I not?" the big man asked, rising slowly to his feet.

"What it is you're doing out here," Torin prompted, "other than lurking about."

"Ah, that," the other said, continuing to stare at the Sword as he brushed himself off. "Well, after the guilt of losing you in the mountains, I headed on to Sydwahr. There I heard about Neak-Thur from the garrison general himself. The man is in rally mode. He's taken on the role of prime commander of the so-called Southern Liberation Force. Offering a handsome sum to any who should survive the retaking of the keep."

"You signed on as a soldier?" Torin asked, his skepticism plain. "If that's so, where's your army?"

Moss shook his head. "Me? A soldier? Why, I'd have to be dumber than my old mule." He looked to the Nymphs, trying another grin on them. "Signed on as a flank scout. The army is to the west. A waste of my talents, to be honest. Ain't much chance Lorre intends to send a force farther south anytime soon. Makes far more sense to await our attack at Neak-Thur."

Torin glanced at the girls to gauge their reaction, then back to his former guide. It irritated him that Moss should be giving Dyanne such attentions. "Then why not serve at least as a point scout? Or didn't this general trust you?"

Moss seemed unfazed by the jab, returning Torin's sneer with a wily smirk. "I didn't wait to find out. Volunteered, you see. The share is less, but I've a much better chance of living to see it."

"And this army," Dyanne verified. "It's marching on Neak-Thur now?"

Moss bowed in what looked to Torin a pathetic attempt at chivalry. "As we speak. Aim is to lay siege before the warlord has a chance to entrench himself too deeply. Strike should come within a few days, no later than the outset of the new week."

"How many of you are there?" the woman pressed.

"Twelve thousand, give or take—mostly what's left of the city garrison. Plus whatever General Chamaar can roust along the way."

Again Torin searched the faces of his Nymph companions, wondering at the consequences these events might have regarding their quest.

"You're not by any chance still meaning to visit with the man," Moss prodded.

"Not that it's your business any longer, but yes, that's precisely where I'm headed."

Moss snorted and shook his head. "So that tumble down the mountain didn't knock any sense into you."

Torin glared at the rogue but soon turned back to Dyanne. He was no longer interested in what the other had to offer.

"If that's the case," Moss continued, "why not join up with the Resistance? General Chamaar ain't being picky. And even if he was, I'll wager he'd love to have that there blade of yours on our side." The rogue grinned at Torin's suspicious frown. "With any luck, by battle's end, Lorre will be our prisoner, and you can ask of him whatever you wish."

Torin hesitated, waiting for either Dyanne or Holly to reject the offer. Neither did.

"And what would be your stake in it?"

"Same as before. I lead you on for a fee—"

"I have the only guides I need," Torin said flatly. He looked to the girls for confirmation. "Unless they'd rather part ways with me here."

Dyanne shook her head. "Dynara would not approve. Nor do Holly and I have yet what we came here for."

"Are you their charge, or their prisoner?" Moss murmured.

Torin ignored him. "You prefer his plan, then?"

Dyanne and Holly shared one of their long, knowing looks, in which an entire debate seemed to pass between them in complete silence. When finished, Dyanne turned back to him.

"The rogue is right. You'll have a much better chance of getting from Lorre what you need if he is *your* prisoner, rather than the other way around. Besides, the Southland may not get another opportunity like this. If this siege should fail, and Lorre is allowed to fortify himself any further, the war will have all but ended."

Torin did not mistake the fire in her eyes, the burning desire she had to affect this struggle, rather than merely fall victim to it. It had been her primary goal all along.

"But we can get you to Neak-Thur," she insisted. "In fact, I have every intention of visiting the city myself, so that I can put together a firsthand account to deliver to my clan—should it not prove too late to convince them to join the Resistance. *His* help," she said, nodding toward Moss, "we don't need."

"Let me at least guide you back to the main force," Moss urged. "I can do so quickly, and introduce you to the general. It would entitle me to a bonus, should we not all end up dead."

Torin studied the big man. Greedy as ever, but making no secret of it. It was difficult to mistrust him in the face of such shameless honesty.

"Four is safer than three," the rogue added, leering openly at Dyanne.

Not necessarily, Torin thought. Nevertheless, in this case, the scoundrel was probably right. Although he had no doubt his current guides could deliver him safely, they had admittedly traveled beyond their principal element. Nor did he see any real risk. Whatever else Moss might be, he was no threat to the three of them.

But it was the girls' decision to make, even if he might like to pretend otherwise. He turned to Dyanne with a look that said as much.

"He's proven already how incapable he is," Dyanne observed bluntly, staring the rogue down. "At the same time, I don't suppose we can stop him from following us, unless you agree to let us empty his sails here and now."

The candid manner in which she uttered the threat stole a measure of the color from Moss's cheeks. Torin pretended to consider, sure that Dyanne was bluffing, but enjoying watching the rogue squirm.

"No," he said finally, sheathing the Sword. "Let's give him a chance to prove that my mishap in the mountains wasn't his fault. If he fails to convince me, you ladies can do with him what you will."

Moss chuckled, though he couldn't hide the sweat thickening upon his brow.

Holly sighed before sheathing her blade. Dyanne, however, brandished hers in final, unmistakable warning.

"Very well," the Nymph Hunter agreed. "But if he so much as coughs in my direction, I'll be taking his most prized parts back to my clan as a personal trophy."

Torin nodded. "You heard the woman," he said to Moss.

The rogue laughed, nervously this time, while rubbing his throat. "Well then, if you'll all follow me?"

"We should rewrap that first," Dyanne said, directing a look at Torin's wrist, which had started to bleed through its bandages.

When that was done, the three gathered their few belongings and fell into step behind the affable rogue, who had begun already to soothe his rattled nerves with a giant wad of tobacco grounds. Sluicing and spitting, he led them north, across the rolling plain, ambling now toward war.

NIGHT FELL SWIFT AND STEADY on the plains of northern Partha, closing round the little company come to camp at the edge of Llornel Lake. The clouds that had followed them throughout the day hunkered now as if to join their fellowship, their dark forms reflected in the lake's surface. Allion watched them churn and brood among themselves, sullen guests uninvited, wishing they would pass on.

His gaze shifted to find Darinor, who sat between him and Marisha upon this lakeside ridge selected by the Entient as theirs for the night. Like those haunting storm clouds, the petulant mystic had put a damper on this entire journey—even more so, Allion decided, for the weather had been just as foul in the days in which Marisha and he had been alone, and yet hadn't bothered him. With Darinor around, however, he couldn't help but be sour, his enthusiasm for this trek shrouded as surely as the moon and stars on this shadowy night.

Marisha appeared no less glum. Strange, given that this was what she had asked for in the beginning. But she, too, seemed perturbed by her father's behavior—gruff and irritable throughout the day, grown worse with the setting of the sun. The man spoke only when forced to, and then in a tone bitter and sharp. What had begun as an opportunity for hunter and healer to deepen their friendship had become like a blossoming tree felled too soon, with Darinor the wedge that had been driven through.

Allion did not believe for a moment that it was accidental either. Since daybreak, the Entient had shown a complete disinterest in partaking of the pair's camaraderie. Yet whenever he and Marisha happened to show signs of closeness, whether with words or physical contact, Darinor had been there to intervene. No matter how innocent the sentiment or gesture, the Entient acted as though it were his duty to see that nothing improper was shared between they who had sworn to protect each other. Once he had found a way to separate them, he would drop back once more, recusing himself from their ongoing conversations, only to continue eyeing them like a hawk.

This above all else frustrated Allion, for it made him feel as though he had done something wrong. Thinking back, he was sure he hadn't. And anyway, what business was it of Darinor's? As best Allion could tell, the man had no right, after all these years, to swoop in and start playing the role of protective father.

After watching her sulk more and more as the hours had worn on, Allion wondered if Marisha did not feel the same. Likely, it was his own imagination at work, but in some ways she seemed more annoyed by the interruptions than he. This suspicion was confirmed, he thought, when she looked back from the deepening night, turning upon her father with features angry and set.

"Tell me, Father," she demanded, shattering the leaden silence. "Tell me when it was you decided to accept your calling. At what point did it become clear to you that you had to abandon my mother? I've asked you before, and you've refused to answer. I've waited long enough."

For a long moment, Darinor still did not answer, choosing instead to stare down at the sweep of open grassland leading up to their camp. With the lake to their backs and nothing taller than a shrub within fifty paces, they had a clear view of anything that might approach. In addition, Darinor's mount had been hobbled at the bottom of the rise, to serve as unwilling sentry. Allion kept his bow close, even though he had spent his last arrow in the fight against the goblin Illychar. He gripped it now in anticipation of the mystic's response.

"Most are born," Darinor said finally, "with their life's scroll unwritten. For those, the future is filled with naught but possibility. Circumstances vary, of course, due to birth and condition. But as history has shown us, with the proper application of luck and determination, even the bastard son of a pauper can make himself into a king, the lowest-born daughter into whatever she wishes to be.

"That was not the case for me," he confided wistfully, peering beyond their present surroundings. "My future was set. I didn't know it at first, for I, like many children, was encouraged by my father not to limit my dreams, but to follow them, to accomplish whatever in my heart was the greatest of things. Nor was there anyone else to discourage me. We lived in isolation on the tiny island that Algorath had settled centuries before. Raemes, it was called, a crumb of earth surrounded by ocean far to the southeast. I was given to understand that it was my own private staging ground, that one day I would rejoin the larger world, in whatever manner I might choose."

A howl sounded miles away, low and mournful. Darinor waited for it to die out before proceeding.

"I was eighteen before I learned the truth, the history of my family and its function through the ages. At long last, it was revealed to me: the manner in which I was expected to serve. As my father had, and his father before him. All the way back to Algorath and beyond.

"It was too much. I had no intention of spending my entire life as a recluse. I had long before cultivated a desire to live among others, to experience that which I learned about from my father in tales and books. Though I had no practical basis for my yearnings, I'd grown weary of my sedentary life, consumed with the need to know companionship, shared laughter, love."

Allion's shoulder itched, but he refused to scratch it. He hesitated even to breathe, so scared was he of interrupting the man's reverie. Not because it spoke to him, or that he even found it interesting. But Marisha was hanging on every word, her stern features softening with that heartfelt empathy only she could feel, and he would not disturb her.

"So I rebelled. I refused the fate my father had determined for me and sailed from his island in order to make my own. For twelve years I explored the lands of this world, coming at last to these shores, where I met your mother. We settled in this very land of Partha, in the city to which we now travel, in fact, where we lived our quiet life and gave thought to raising a child. A more significant decision than you might imagine. For as I had learned, the Entients—even our splintered offshoot—were very particular in their system of procreation. Most do not produce child until their twilight years. At that time, they make use of a willing woman in order to give birth to a single son— manipulating the seed to make certain it is a boy—so as to replace themselves in the order. One of the best ways, it seemed to me, to sever ties with their kind was to break this tradition, to have a child early on, and to allow that child's gender to be determined naturally."

The mystic turned his head now to regard Marisha, whose eyes glistened. "You were my greatest achievement, the purpose I had long been seeking. One with whom to share my own knowledge and experience, with the freedom of choice that for me had been a lie. I had no regrets, and have none now."

He held her gaze for a moment, then looked away. "But my father's fate would not be so easy to escape. Six years after your birth, he found me, having spent a decade tracking me down. He was dying, and needed to bequeath to me the Pendant of Asahiel. Though I fought against it, his visit triggered in me a sense of responsibility—not necessarily to continue the legacy of my forebears, but to at least preserve that which they had accomplished over their long lives. I now had a reason, you see, to care about the fate of this world and its inhabitants, a need to see it remain safe, so that my daughter might know the joy and peace it seemed I was destined to be denied."

The man paused again. When he resumed, it was with a heavy sigh.

"I confessed all I had hidden of myself to your mother, who, as I've explained already, decided she could not bear to wither before my eyes while I should remain young and vital. After leaving the Pendant to you, I spent another year wandering these lands, seeing all that I had not yet seen, visiting remote regions like the village Diln, where it seems I first influenced your young husband-to-be."

The Entient turned eye to Allion as he said this—as if the hunter had forgotten even for a moment what Torin and Marisha had agreed to. He scowled, but bit his tongue, waiting for the other to move on.

"When my travels were completed, I boarded a ship that would drop me off where I had begun, a prodigal son returned home to preserve that which Algorath had started."

"And what was that, exactly?" Allion asked. His irritation and impatience was such that he could keep still no longer.

"Learning," the mystic snapped. "An exploration of life as you know it, and in ways you could scarcely comprehend. All in an effort to keep headstrong mortals like yourself from destroying one another. The curse of all Entients, since the inception of that order. Except that my studies have been as Algorath's, unfettered by the collective decisions of a guiding council, answering to none save my private curiosities. Which is why I'm not accustomed to the countless questions and demands you and others seem intent on badgering me with."

Allion shrank back on Marisha's look, which seemed to plead with him not to start an argument now. He realized then what it was that had him so agitated. It was not Darinor at all, but the story of the mystic's past and the unspoken implications it held for Marisha. Was she not his daughter? The child of an Entient? Entitled to a life span of centuries? Forced to bear the burden, perhaps, that Darinor himself had been cursed with?

They were matters that Marisha herself had been wrestling with for weeks, he now realized, ever since her father's return. He understood now that her private issues went far beyond those of abandonment—first by her father, and more recently by Torin. The despair and loneliness reflected in her eyes ran deeper than that. He wished suddenly that he might do something to help her find the answers she needed, but he did not even know which questions to ask.

A sense of hopelessness overcame him then, an inner wave so terrible and unrelenting that for a moment, he thought it might crush him where he sat. He really was in over his head. All of them were. He had failed to recognize the previous night's encounter for what it was: a foreshadowing not just of the conflict that lay ahead, but of the doom awaiting them all.

Perhaps they should simply flee now, while they could. Abandon these shores to its demons and head out across the seas, to make their home on some secluded isle as Algorath had done—and for all they knew, Torin as well.

The thought spawned another question, forcing him to regain control of his swollen tongue. "You've said before that many among the Finlorians wanted to flee across the oceans during the first Illysp invasion, and that the Illychar seemed content to let them go. Why is that?"

Darinor ignored him for quite some time, looking to Marisha instead. Allion couldn't tell if the other was dodging that question in particular, or had simply tired of the hunter's inquiries. Eventually, Marisha nodded, indicating that she, too, would have an answer.

"It is unknown for certain," Darinor grumbled, withdrawing into his cloak against a sudden gust of wind, "but some believe that water contains qualities that are anathema to the Illysp, whether in spirit or physical form. It does not harm them, mind you, in any obvious sense. But on an instinctual level, they show signs of wishing to avoid it."

Allion frowned, an internal sense of his own ringing a discordant tone. It was a feeling he got whenever one of his younger siblings attempted to lie to him. "Is that why you were so intent on reaching the lake before stopping for the evening?"

Darinor snorted. "If it were that simple, we would all of us have nothing to worry about, would we? A simple rain shower, and our trials would be ended." He shook his head. "No, my young man, this lake will not protect us. But neither is there an Illychar out there that would mistake this pathetic body for the great sea that cradles this land. It is this our enemies seem to fear—its vastness, perhaps, or its stormy unpredictability. What is it you really wish to know?"

"Can we escape them?" Marisha asked for him. "If we had to, could we simply vanish overseas?"

Again the scarecrow figure shook his head. "I don't know," he replied, and this time, Allion did not sense any dissembling. "Let us hope it doesn't come to that. For even if all the peoples of these lands were able to run as you suggest, we've no guarantee that the Illysp lack the will—or means—to follow."

It was a grim assessment, and suspicions aside, Allion was disheartened further. For if true, then the only hope for them was indeed to lock the Illysp away from this world as they once had been. Otherwise, they might as well be searching for a way for man to escape death itself.

"I don't understand," the hunter admitted dolefully, "how creatures as mindless as those that attacked us last night can possibly act with reason and intelligence, as you continue to suggest."

"They possess more cunning than you can imagine." A familiar refrain— one that the mystic had been exhorting from the beginning. "They have been trapped for millennia. One does not endure such a fate without learning patience and subtlety."

"Or madness," Allion claimed, taking in the other's gaze as the night's rains began to fall.

Like the man himself, Darinor's smile was mostly wild, and a little sad. "Perhaps a bit of both."

CHAPTER THIRTY-ONE

THE RAINS RETURNED DURING THE NIGHT, blowing out of the west. Dyanne had predicted as much, and thus sought a stand of tightly packed evergreens in which to settle until morning. As Torin stirred from a fitful slumber, awakened by the patter of rainfall and Gavrin's beastly snore, he was glad that she had succeeded.

His gaze slipped to where he had last seen the Nymph the previous evening. She lay there still, eyes closed, face calm. Her smooth hands were tucked beneath her head, as she rested sideways on a pillow of moss. An unidentifiable pang gripped him as he silently observed the rhythm of her breathing. Such fire and determination within, masked by such graceful beauty without. A rare combination. He might never forget the way she had first greeted him, her dagger to his throat. But neither could he dismiss her dazzling, carefree smile, or the tenderness she had shown in nursing his wounds. In the morning twilight, he decided there was little he wouldn't give simply to know her thoughts, that he might share in the serenity of her dreams.

He considered his own dreams, including those of Marisha, and was warmed within by a flush of guilt. The disorientation of a new day, he assured himself. That's all it was. Though it might seem otherwise in that waking moment, his was a harmless fascination, one that he remained convinced would pass. And yet, as he sat there in the crook of a twisting root formation, knowing that he should wake the others and be on his way, a second glance at Dyanne's tranquil form told him that he would sooner disturb a nest of infant doves.

Moss's continued snoring, however, knew no such restraint, eventually drawing a disgruntled Holly from her sentry position. Torin turned at her approach from the camp's fringe, and watched her place a sharp kick in the slumbering rogue's ribs. The big man lurched, but his scowl was no match for Holly's glare. Muttering about the subtlety of women with a barrage of grunts and heavy sighs, the guide-turned-scout rolled himself from the damp floor of the sheltered grove and set about making ready to leave.

Torin merely smiled.

They were on the road again shortly thereafter, following a series of bumpy trails and obscure paths across the rain-drenched wilds of northern Wylddeor. They traversed rugged foothills and wooded dells, passing over barren rangelands and windswept meadows. Moss led, jovial despite his rude awakening, and garrulous even when it was clear no one was listening. Torin followed, with the girls behind keeping a close eye. From time to time, he tried to eavesdrop on what it was Dyanne and Holly kept laughing about, but spent most of the morning, as he had the previous afternoon, dodging further questions from Moss about himself and his "wizard's" blade. He went as far as sharing with the rogue some of the ancient legends of the Swords of Asahiel, but refrained from elaborating on how he had come upon this particular talisman. The man seemed to believe little of what he was told anyway, scoffing occasionally and interrupting often. Though surprised that one so widely traveled was not already familiar with the myths of these weapons being used in the world's creation, Torin had little patience for the other's mockery, and lacked both the energy and the desire to overcome the rogue's pagan beliefs.

Around midmorning, their company was intercepted by a pair of mounted sentries riding the eastern perimeter of Moss's Southern Liberation Force. The patrolmen were stern in appearance and gruff in manner, suspicious of Moss—despite the token he carried that proclaimed his position—and mistrustful of those who accompanied him. In the end, the more senior of the two determined it best that he and his partner escort them personally along the last mile separating them from the main force.

They covered that distance swiftly, despite the winds that gusted against them and the intermittent showers that muddied the earth beneath their feet. When at last they came upon the army, they found it just then making preparations to break camp. It had marched throughout much of the night, the younger of their two escorts divulged, having wasted too much time in the west coast town of Myniah, updating the people there as to the state of affairs and fighting a mostly vain effort to rally more to their cause. A thousand or so had agreed—less than a tenth of the population. The rest had elected to wait out the storm, or else to gather their possessions and retreat farther south.

The elder patrolman interrupted his partner at that point, yet wary of revealing too much to this group of strangers.

It was not until they were delivered to the eastern checkpoint, where one of the registry clerks was able to confirm Moss's position within the army, that the senior sentry relaxed, grunting in farewell and leading his companion out once more.

Torin marked their departure through layered curtains of swirling mist. By the time the pair had disappeared entirely, Moss had secured authorization for the four of them that remained to enter the main encampment.

They followed the rogue down artificial lanes of trampled earth, weaving their way through a sea of men and artillery stores and supply wagons. Although it appeared to possess all of the requisite ingredients, this was not an army as Torin had come to understand them. The formations between regiments were too loose, lacking structure and discipline. Armor and weaponry and uniforms—among those who possessed them—did not match. Men jostled about, bumping and shoving one against the other. Arguments echoed from every direction, a few of which even came to blows. Commanders called for order, but fellow observers seemed as apt to encourage the combatants as wrestle them apart.

Surrounded by such chaos, Torin wondered what it was he had agreed to join. These were not soldiers, but a mass gathering of wild frontiersmen. If they could not co-exist among themselves or break camp in an orderly fashion, how in the Abyss did they expect to be able to storm a warlord's keep?

His assessment was made even less generous by the number of whistles and stares and lewd growls aimed by these mercenaries toward the pair of Nymphs who followed him. Torin found himself clenching his jaw and keeping a hand on the Sword's hilt, almost anxious for one of them to make a grab. Dyanne and Holly were taking it in stride, neither rejecting nor encouraging the many propositions come their way. But that didn't stop Torin from feeling embarrassed and protective.

"Ah, here we are," Moss said, glancing back to make sure his companions were still with him as he turned toward one of the few tents visible amid the army's sprawl. A black pennon, little more than a rag, snapped atop its central pole, the only potential marker Torin could see. Yet Moss hastened his pace, pushing past a swarm of rogues milling about in apparent confusion.

They were turned away, however, by first one, and then a trio of guardsmen posted among others outside the tent. General Chamaar was in council within, the sentinels reported, once they had confirmed Moss's rank and identification. Should he wish to visit with the prime commander, he would have to file a request; otherwise, he should deliver his report to the master of scouts, and his charges to the master of recruits. Moss haggled with the unit's commander, by turns companionable and bullying, but was denied in the end. When finally Torin's company turned away, with Dyanne and Holly declining an invitation to remain behind, Moss left the flock of guardsmen with a snide remark that turned one of them red with anger.

"I think you offended him," Torin observed, looking back as the young officer's commander dismissed the affront and herded the members of his group back to their stations.

Moss shrugged. "So?"

"Have you no concern about upsetting folks?" Holly asked.

"Only if they're bigger than me," Moss answered with a wink.

His shameless pride intact, the rogue led them to another nearby tent. Here, a lone sentry barely glanced at the token Moss wore before nodding the scout and his companions through.

Inside, amid cots and stores stacked beneath a canvas cover so riddled with leaks that Torin wondered why they had bothered to erect it, sat a folding chair and table. Towering over the latter was a balding man in leather armor, who looked to be all limbs and no torso. Lanky arms supported his spare weight as he leaned over a set of maps. In the chair to one side sat a red-haired scribe, who sketched and scribbled upon a parchment while a third man, his back to the tent opening, murmured gruffly.

All but the scribe glanced up as Moss entered, their furrowed brows smoothing with recognition. Moss, however, hesitated.

"Ah, Lieutenant Bohwens, I see you're busy. I'll come back."

The balding man waved a stick-thin arm. "Come. Just verifying a report. We're finished, are we not?"

He looked to the third man for confirmation, a rogue dressed much like Moss in layers of fur crisscrossed by leather belts and pouches. This man, too, had a retreating hairline, though his bushy eyebrows more than made up for it. As if to further compensate, he was heavily bearded, so much so that only his eyes and nose were visible amid the tangled thicket sprouted from chin and cheeks. The man glanced at Bohwens, and nodded.

The lieutenant turned his attention to the new arrivals. "What do you have for me?"

"The eastern flank is clear," Moss reported, returning a nod of familiarity from his fellow scout before casting upon Torin what seemed a nervous eye.

"Then why have you returned before schedule?"

"Found me some friends of the Resistance. Thought Chamaar might put 'em to good use."

The bearded stranger gave a snort, but bowed politely to the girls as he headed past them on his way out.

"If they're recruits, why bring them to me?" the lieutenant asked.

"Just checking in, sir. I only meant—"

"Hargenfeld," Bohwens called, stopping the other at the tent flaps. "Show Gavrin here to the master of recruits, if you would."

Again Moss looked to Torin expectantly, though the young king knew not why. He frowned, though, suspicious of his guide's behavior as he tried to recall where he had heard this other's name before.

"Friends call me Rags," the crusty old scout grunted. His gleaming eyes were fixed on Holly and Dyanne.

That triggered Torin's memory, and his gaze snapped around to Moss, who responded with a sheepish grin.

"I've heard tell of you," Torin remarked. "Rumor has it you were buried last winter."

"Bah! Some might wish." He, too, glared at Moss.

The big man did his best to look innocent.

"This way," Rags grumbled in a resonant voice. "Just delivered a team there myself."

Following a string of inquiries, Torin's party arrived at an area marked off for battle drills. On the edge of this training field, they were introduced to yet another team of clerks, who were busy poring over a sheaf of troop registries. After waiting in line behind a half-dozen fellow candidates who looked to Torin more like outlaws, they came at last to speak with a grizzled scribe charged with recording their qualifications—to be used in determining their assignments.

"Name?" the veteran droned, without looking up from his table.

"Torin."

"Fighter, scout, laborer, or craftsman?"

"Fighter."

"Veteran or novice?"

"Veteran."

"Weapon of choice?"

"Sword."

"Have you your own blade?"

"Yes."

"Command experience?"

"Some."

"Any special skills? Riding, healing, blacksmithing?"

"I can ride well enough. And fire a bow, if need be."

"Recruited by?"

Moss stepped forward. "Moss. Flank scout."

While finishing his notes, the scribe reached into a box and handed Torin a wooden token. "Keep this until given your commission. Next."

Torin moved aside, somewhat befuddled, making way for Dyanne.

"Name?"

"Dyanne."

Whether drawn by the name itself, or the silky sound of her voice, the clerk looked up, revealing a face squinted sharply on one side, as if trapped in a paralyzed grimace. The good half smirked, taking measure of the woman from head to toe. "Cook or nurse?"

"Fighter."

The scribe chuckled. "Now, miss, don't know if you've heard, but this force is headed into battle."

"And by the looks of it, needs every blade it can muster."

The scribe looked to Moss. "These yours too?"

Moss nodded. "Badgers, they are."

"So's me missus, but that don't mean she's cut out for combat."

"Says the man sitting behind a desk," Dyanne observed.

The clerk's lopsided grin vanished. "I've killed more men than you've winked at, lassie."

"I should hope so."

"Now, now," Moss intervened, "let's not get ourselves all flushed and agitated." Though it was the scribe who had lost his composure, the big man leered at Dyanne as he said this. "Perhaps we should leave it for the commander to decide."

As if on cue, a group of soldiers approached from the drilling field, their rain-streaked faces bathed with sweat. They were speaking to one another, and thus had not yet seen those at the scribe's table. Torin, however, did a double take when he recognized the squat, muscled mercenary among them.

"Arn!" he shouted, overcome with disbelief.

The stubble-cheeked warrior with the pale blue eyes and neck covered in blond curls glanced around until he had found the source of the voice. When he did, he gaped before excusing himself from his comrades and hastening over with a broad grin to clasp Torin's hand.

"Shades of mercy, but I never thought to see you again," Arn greeted, gripping his shoulder.

"Me?" Torin replied. "I thought you dead!"

"Captain Jorkin was kind enough to fish me out of the swells. He might have gone after you, too, were the *Folly* in any condition to do so."

"The ship survived, then?"

Arn nodded. "Took a couple of days to get moving again, and we were limping along for awhile after that. Were it any other vessel, or any other crew, I might still be out there, if alive at all."

"What of Bull and my companions?"

"They debated for some time as to what to do. When we ran across a supply ship sailing east, they took it as a sign to hitch a ride home to tell what had transpired. If conditions were bad, they might only now be reaching Pentanian shores."

"What about you?" Torin asked. "I was only delayed a few days. How did you manage to get ahead of me?"

Arn shrugged. "Favorable winds, I guess. Put in at Razorport within a week of our attack. By that time, I'd decided I'd had quite enough seafaring for awhile. Marched straight through the Cleft ahead of an advancing snowstorm. Ran into this here army in Sydwahr, and accepted an appointment as master of recruits. General Chamaar and I go back a ways."

Torin scarcely bothered to follow the account. All he knew was that this man who had saved him back in Gammelost was alive and well. Left for dead by Red Raven and his pirate crew, Arn had yet managed to survive—as had the remainder of those who had followed the young king from Krynwall. For Torin, it was a tremendous relief—both from the guilt he'd been carrying, and to know that not all of those he might find himself fighting alongside in the coming days would be complete and untrustworthy strangers.

"Master of recruits, huh?" he registered finally. "Is it true you're not accepting soldiers of the female variety?" He nodded over his shoulder toward Dyanne and Holly.

Arn frowned, but seemed at the same time to look past the soft skin and pretty faces to the way the pair held themselves and the weapons they carried. "A soldier must be strong enough for those around him. Would you entrust your life to them?"

"I already have," Torin replied earnestly.

Arn considered him a moment, as if waiting for him to back down from that claim. At last his sneering grin returned. "If they're willing and able, we'll take them."

Torin matched that grin, and both men looked to the girls for their approval. Holly's eyes glittered, and Dyanne folded her arms across her chest. Neither uttered a word.

"But tell me," Arn said, forcing Torin's gaze back to his. "How did you escape those pirates? And what brings you to join our war against the North? As I recall, yours was a much different objective."

"I've been led to believe the two go hand in hand," Torin answered, then looked to those around him: at Moss, Dyanne and Holly, and Hargenfeld, standing silent to one side. Finally, he came back to Arn. "Besides, it seems everyone I've met or heard tell of recently has found their way here. I'd hate to be the only one to miss out."

Arn clapped him again on the shoulder. "Hah! Come then, and introduce me to your companions. Let us learn whether any among us is not merely a fool."

With a nervous smile at that remark, Torin fell into step beside his friend. Dyanne and Holly followed. Moss remained behind to make sure the scribe made record of his referrals, while Hargenfeld gave another of his gruff nods and went on his way. Little had changed, Torin warned himself, but it was hard not to feel heartened by this string of unlikely reunions.

He could only hope that it was a sign of better fortunes to come.

BULLRUM, OF THE LEGION OF THE SWORD, better known as Bull, felt his anger rise as he delivered his report. Despite the passing days and having already done everything he could, he had yet to come to terms with the loss of his king—a loss for which he held himself directly accountable. Recounting it now, and thus reliving the experience, had the sting of salt in fresh wounds.

The surviving members of his expedition team stood alongside him on the floor of Krynwall's throne room, respectfully silent beneath the grim gazes of those before whom he testified. Strange as it was to see Thaddreus sitting the throne, and with none but Captain Evhan at his side, Bull had agreed to their request that his story be shared first with them alone. No reason to risk widespread panic with the ill tidings they had come to share.

"And you've no idea how our king fares now?" Thaddreus asked, when the tale of Torin's abduction at sea had been concluded.

"None, lord regent."

"This is fell news, soldier."

Bull lowered his head in silent admission, eyes scraping the floor. The granite tiles, polished recently to a brilliant shine in expectation of his lord's wedding ceremony, mirrored his shame.

"If it would please my lord regent," he offered finally, "I request permission to organize a search party and set forth at once."

Thaddreus's wrinkled face twisted. Word was, it was their return that had dragged the ailing regent out of bed that morning, the first any but Captain Evhan had seen of him in three days. Judging by the sallowness of his skin, the former speaker of the Circle was yet in need of rest.

"Search how?"

"We could commission a vessel, and sail back out again. A fleet of vessels, if necessary. If we were to follow the course and heading taken by the pirates after our encounter, we might be able to—"

"A fleet of vessels? At this time of year?"

"They're pirates. If we can offer them ransom, chances are they'll set him free."

"Chances are just as good they might refuse. And that's assuming we had the coin to offer, which we don't. Or to purchase the fleet you would require."

Bull scowled. "Surely you don't mean to abandon him."

Evhan bent to whisper in Thaddreus's ear, but the old man brushed him off like a bothersome fly. "I've seen the ocean that surrounds our lands. A thousand ships might search forever and still come up empty. It's much to risk, especially when you cannot even assure me that His Majesty still lives."

Bull held back his response. In truth, he had known all of these arguments going in. He and his men had discussed their predicament at length before ever boarding the ship headed for home. Slim as it was, this had been their best hope, to return to Krynwall with the news, in hopes of mustering a fully equipped rescue force. The reaction he was receiving was about what he had expected.

Still, it grated at the proud soldier to have to accept the truth of his failure. He glanced at his companions, at Ulric to his left, and the brothers Silas and Kallen to his right, the latter of whom now wore a patch over one eye. The loss of that eye, along with the deaths of Ashwin and Cordan, had been for nothing. The voyage had been an utter loss.

"Perhaps we should consult the Circle," Bull ventured in a last-ditch effort. "One of the Elders might think of another way."

But Thaddreus was already shaking his head, his silver mane rustling. "We have no choice, I think, but to await the return of he who suggested this course. Perhaps when Darinor is with us, or Allion, they will see things differently."

Bull shook his own head in protest. "That could take days, and he's been gone a fortnight already."

"You have done all you could," the regent offered. "You men should not feel guilty for the misfortune that befell you."

"But—"

"This kingdom is indebted to you for your loyal duty. However, the best for all concerned is that you should be returned or reassigned, each of you, to a position within the City Shield. Let us turn our eyes and efforts forward, to the defense of this city and nation, rather than looking back on those who chose to forsake it."

Bull glared, but gritted his teeth, not wishing to say something he might later regret.

Thaddreus rose. "See to it, Captain," he said to Evhan, then looked down again upon the others. "Dismissed."

BULLRUM WAS STILL FUMING AS HE MARCHED down the length of castle corridor, matching strides with the young captain of the City Shield. It was just the two of them now. The others already had positions within the Shield, to which Evhan had bade them return. He alone needed special attention, given that his regiment, his commanders, his entire legion were stationed some fifty leagues to the south, camped at the border of another's lands.

Bull didn't like it. He didn't like that Allion, Rogun, and the army were gone, leaving only the Shield behind. He didn't like that old man Thaddreus sat a throne to which he didn't belong—a throne that even Torin had eschewed until such time as he should be crowned. And while the arguments made sense, he didn't like how quickly the regent had dismissed the notion of a rescue.

All in all, the brief meeting had left a foul taste in his mouth. Though its outcome was not unexpected, he hadn't been prepared for the complete lack of concern exhibited by the city leaders. Perhaps he would be better off consulting one or more members of the Circle behind Thaddreus's back.

He glanced over at Evhan. Might he find in the younger man an ally to his cause? Or would the captain betray him to Thaddreus? With so much time piling up against them, would it even matter?

The entire affair dwelled like a sickness in his stomach. There was something more going on here; of that he felt certain. And yet there were too many issues to which he was blind, too many holes sapping his judgment, for him to unravel the truth. Besides, a soldier's task was to execute his assignments without question, and Bull had built himself a nice reputation doing just that. But never before had he been placed in a situation such as this, in which—for whatever reason—he did not feel he could trust those whose orders he was meant to follow.

"This way," Evhan said with a gesture as they came to a forked landing. As a matter of habit, Bull had started to climb the stairs toward the offices of the legion's staff commanders, which also housed those of the City Shield. The Fason, however, was bidding him follow to the lower wing. The soldier grunted in apology and altered his course.

Had he not been so preoccupied with his thoughts, he might have paid closer attention to where they were headed. Down past the armory and training grounds they veered, marching right on by the fitting rooms, ammunition closets, and strategy chambers. It was not until they reached and turned down a hall that led to the inner dungeons that he fell back with hesitation.

"Where are you taking me?" he asked.

Evhan stopped and cast about furtively, as if wary of being overheard. "You want to help the king, don't you?"

Bull felt his own forehead crease with suspicion. "What are you talking about?"

"Much has happened since you left, my friend. If you wish to survive, you'll come with me."

Bull wasn't sure if the words constituted a threat or a warning, but when Evhan hastened forward without him, he decided there was only one way to find out.

When they reached the dungeons, Evhan borrowed a torch from its sconce and proceeded down to the lower levels. Bull tried once more to question the secretive captain, but the younger man only signaled for silence.

At last they came upon a storeroom at the very end of the lowermost hall, well past the last of the cells, where the walls were no longer of blocks shaped square and smooth, but of packed earth and bedrock. Here, Bull accepted

Evhan's torch while the captain fished a key from a string tied round his neck. The latch released, the door opened, and with his heart beginning to drum, the big soldier followed the Fason through.

Despite the light of the torch, it took a moment for his eyes to adjust, so thickly layered were the shadows about the room. Crates and barrels filled it, along with lengths of chain, clamps and pins, tools of iron, and various other dungeon materials. Dust and webs lay thick over much of it, revealing those contents that had gone too long without use.

"You've heard of the tunnels beneath the city, have you not?" Evhan whispered.

Bull nodded. "Who hasn't?"

The captain did not answer, but moved toward the far wall, which was lined with wooden boards. Taking the torch with him, he knelt for a moment in the corner, groping along the hidden edge of an iron cask. There was a quiet click before a section of the boarded wall swung away, creaking softly on oiled hinges.

Bull approached it at once, crouching low to peer through the opening. A stale breeze, smelling faintly of mold and sulfur, blew inward against his bearded cheeks.

"This is but one of many passages throughout the palace grounds," Evhan revealed. "Follow the correct path, and it'll take you safely from the city."

"What's down this one?"

"Salvation."

Bull heard the rasp of a blade over the flickering of the torch and spun at once. Or tried to. Coming up too fast, he caught the back of his head on the crown of the secret doorway. It slowed him only momentarily, but in that moment, he felt the explosive thrust of a dagger plunging deep into his back.

He gave a howl, arching sharply, but still managed to stand and turn around. Evhan's expression was one of disbelief as Bull threw a punch that cracked against the traitor's jaw and sent the young captain flying. He then reached for the dagger, but brushing against its handle with his fingers only sent waves of pain shooting out from his spine.

With a roar, he threw himself instead upon his assailant, fists pummeling. The movements set his back afire, but he overcame it with sheer fury. Beneath his onslaught, Evhan thrashed defensively.

So intent was he on smashing the other into pulp that Bull did not hear the creak of hinges until it was too late. A cord wrapped round his throat, then yanked him to his feet. Hands of iron clamped about his wrists, pinning his arms behind him. A kick to his ribs dropped him to his knees.

A face came into view, blackened and shriveled, as if stricken with rot. It was a face not quite human, but rather gaunt and angular, like something out of legend.

Evhan was rising then, spitting blood and something more as he drew his rapier.

The Fason looked as though he was about to speak, then lunged without a word. His blade bit deep, clear into Bull's heart. The soldier growled and gritted his teeth, refusing this time to cry out. Then Evhan's blade yanked free, and a pulsing spray emptied out down the front of his leather vest.

Bull's last thought was to wonder if it would not have been better to join Ashwin and Cordan in death on the high seas.

CHAPTER THIRTY-TWO

THE WALLS OF ATHARVAN were etched with scars the adorning banners could not hide, pitted and worn by wind and time, mottled in patches and along crooked seams where the stone facing had been mended or rebuilt. Sprouting from the western foothills of the inimitable Skullmar Mountains like a cluster of growths at the base of a massive tree, the great city had been rattled and reshaped more than once throughout the centuries by tremor and landslide. True to their conquering nature, however, the men of Partha simply swept up the rubble, repaired their buildings and streets, and went on with their lives.

Despite its sometimes cobbled appearance, Allion was by no means unimpressed with the largest city he had ever witnessed. By any measure, the Parthan capital was among the greatest cities in all of Pentania. Not quite as old or as battle-hardened as Souaris, nor home to as many citizens or artificial wonders as Morethil had once been. But Allion had not yet seen either of those renowned cities, and though he'd heard both Marisha and Torin speak endlessly of each, it was difficult to imagine a more awesome array of towers and courtyards and roadways than that which climbed the broken slopes before him.

And this from his distant view well west of the outer wall.

They had been working their way for hours now along the switchback road that fronted the city's main entrance, caught in a crush of citizenry begging entry. Showing no concern for whom he might waylay or offend, Darinor had shoved forward through the grinding throng, fighting for headway like a fish climbing upriver to spawn. He had left their mount behind, knowing that at this juncture, the large animal would only slow them down. Still, the highway was hemmed in on all sides by ridges and escarpments, boulders and fault lines, fences and fortifications both natural and man-made. Even for the towering Entient, from whom the angriest and most imposing strangers fell away with scarcely a complaint, travel was slow and arduous.

Holding Marisha's hand protectively, Allion followed as best he could, offering apologies with every step. These crowds had a moblike quality to them, rife with bitterness and resentment and fear. Most had been dispossessed, either by Spithaera's minions or the same unnatural hosts that had been hunting Alson's countryside these past few weeks. Deprived of the most basic human needs—food, shelter, and a sense of security—they had come to demand it of he who ruled them.

Worse, it became clear to Allion from the threats and slurs and altercations all around him that there were Menzoans—"Menzoes" as they were less affectionately known—intermingled among the Parthan masses. Although the recent war against the Demon Queen had brought a halt to the age-old dispute between eastern nations north and south by severely gashing both sides, the pity and tolerance extended by the Parthans toward their northern neighbors—who'd been much harder hit—remained tenuous at best. Forcing a path through this volatile mix felt like marching through a giant tinderbox with a dripping torch to light the way.

Nevertheless, most simply grumbled or hurled epithets after the overbearing stranger, which Darinor disregarded. Only as they neared the heavily guarded city gates did the Entient's brusque behavior result in the hiss of drawn steel. Allion whirled instinctively, to find an old man whose cart of fruit jams had been toppled, with several of the small jars shattering upon impact.

"Where d'ya think you're going?" the elderly vendor snapped, reaching out to grab Marisha's wrist.

Darinor glared, and Marisha struggled, but the old man held her fast. It was likely not the first indignity the codger had suffered, but he appeared determined to make it the last.

"'Less you pay for these," he snarled, "I'll be taking one of her pretty fingers for each."

Allion searched for a way to appease the man, but couldn't hear himself think over the encouraging roar of the crowds. One woman gasped in fright, but the rest seemed incited toward reparations of their own. As his pulse quickened, the hunter looked to Darinor in desperation.

The Entient, however, was staring heatedly at the old man's dagger. In the gray light of overcast skies, his sapphire eyes seemed to glow.

All of a sudden, the old man shrieked and dropped his blade, its handle as red as a flaming poker. He let go of Marisha as well, coiling around his scorched hand. The surging throngs fell back, repelled by the stench of burned flesh and the discarded weapon that hissed and steamed upon the roadway of crushed gravel.

No one else tried to stop them as Darinor shouldered on and Allion and Marisha hurried in pursuit. Leaving behind a string of oaths and a common murmur of protest, they came at last to a line of clerks in official city regalia who, along with a phalanx of soldiers, were sorting through those seeking entry to the city beyond.

"Next," called a droopy-eyed youth near the center of the barricade.

Darinor breezed past the tradesman who had started forward, slipping between a pair of guardsmen who were otherwise engaged.

"Name and business," the clerk prompted, eyes rooted to a piece of parchment weighted by stones upon his drawing table.

"The name is Darinor," the Entient growled. "My business is with your king."

The young clerk was not intimidated. "Have you a writ of appearance?"

"A what?"

"General hearings for persons seeking admittance to the royal court have been restricted to those bearing a writ of appearance from their local governor or liege lord. Until you obtain such a writ, you'll have to take your petition elsewhere. Next."

Allion glanced up at the chipped outer wall, drawn by its looming mass and the roar of activity that resonated from within. His attention snapped back as Darinor gave a disgusted snort and started forward, triggering a rush of sentries even before the spurned clerk had shouted, "Guards!"

With a hedge of halberds and spears encircling them, Darinor came to another halt.

"Who is your commander?" he snapped, considering the pack of soldiers with disdain.

"Sir," one of them replied from beneath his studded helm, "you have not been permitted entry. If you insist upon your present course, I will be forced to take you into custody."

"Then be quick about it," Darinor spat. "I care not where I meet with your king, be it throne room or dungeon. But I've not come this far to be detained by feckless grunts such as yourself."

The ferocity of the Entient's retort put the guardsman on his heels. "Sir, His Majesty does not see anyone unannounced. If you wish to—"

"Then send word, confound it. Bear with you my name and that of Allion, regent of Krynwall. Assemble an armed escort, if you must. Just put an end to this delay!"

The guardsman hesitated, his face a battleground for what might have been a standoff between duty and self-preservation. "Have you a seal or signet to present?"

They didn't. Allion had left all of that behind with Thaddreus. He'd been in such a hurry to depart that he hadn't even considered having the Circle draw them up an official notice of their intent to meet with the Parthan king.

"I am known to Chief General Corathel," the hunter offered instead, "and to many of his commanding officers. If you wish, they can confirm my identity."

To Allion's surprise, the guardsman nodded, then excused himself for a whispered word with his senior officer. After a brief council between the two, a herald was dispatched, and an escort assembled. Within moments, they were headed beneath the shadowed enclave of the gatehouse.

On the other side, avenues wide and narrow were jammed with more of those they had left behind. Allion was grateful for the army escort, for it allowed them to pass unchallenged through the agitated swarm.

After awhile, everything began to look the same to the visiting hunter: an endless procession of walls and bridges and cramped alleyways, filled with the stink of man and his endeavors. At the base of towers and buildings piled one atop the other, there was no telling which way to turn. For Allion, it was a disconcerting feeling. Were he abandoned in the middle of the darkest wood or deepest jungle, he would yet be able to read the natural signs and follow them clear. Here, he was at the complete mercy of those who led him.

By his estimate, another hour had passed before they came at last to the palace, a sprawling compound raised upon a broad, jutting plateau, and whose area looked to be at least twice that of Krynwall's. In a region so prone to earthquake, it made sense, Allion supposed, to build out instead of up, thus mitigating the potential for a catastrophic collapse.

Once cleared by the gate guard, their company proceeded through a thick and heavily buttressed curtain wall topped with patrolling soldiers. On the other side, they attracted a second ring of guardsmen, forming now a double wall on all sides. Archers and crossbowmen tracked them from the rooftops, weapons ready.

Except for the wide, ornately sculpted grounds that fronted it, the squat building into which they were finally ushered bore little resemblance to the royal castles Allion had heard tell of. For a moment, he worried that they were indeed being led into a dungeon holding area, there to await their audience on the king's whim. But after another whispered conference and a series of stern looks aimed their way, Allion and his companions were given over to a fresh flock of soldiers prepped for their arrival, whose uniforms bore the falcon sigil of the Parthan royal family.

Through vaulted halls they marched, with Allion and Marisha stealing glances at many of the ornamental displays that decked the polished walls. For all of its crude, patchwork exterior, Atharvan was not without its comforts after all. Of the three newcomers, only Darinor appeared unmoved by the many tapestries, engravings, relief sculptures, and other adornments that brought warmth and majesty to an otherwise stark and weathered granite bunker.

Their trek ended belowground at an arched doorway—its keystone chiseled into the shape of a now-familiar falcon. Once again, word of their coming must have preceded them, for a steward awaited them, flanked by another pair of royal guard. The steward took a long, careful look at Darinor before turning to Allion.

"You are Allion?"

The hunter nodded.

"The same Allion who helped to slay Killangrathor?"

Allion was surprised, then emboldened to be granted such acclaim. Everywhere he went, people spoke of Torin and his Crimson Sword. Far fewer seemed to appreciate or even believe the critical role he had played alongside Kylac in bringing down the father of the dragonspawn.

"Yes, yes," Darinor grumbled impatiently. "Has your lord agreed to meet with us?"

The steward turned a slow eye back to the Entient. "I am to relieve you of your weapons and bid you take comfort within. His Majesty shall join you presently."

Allion watched the Entient's reaction guardedly. It was better than they might have hoped for, he wanted to say, but knew that his words would have no sway upon the other's outlook.

"I am unarmed," Darinor declared, then, much to Allion's amazement, lifted his arms in the air, inviting the steward's men to check for themselves.

When that was finished, the three of them were allowed inside what turned out to be a cozy sitting room, complete with food and drink. Half a dozen guardsmen kept watch within, while an equal measure remained posted without. The steward took his leave to notify King Galdric of their arrival.

Thankfully, they were not kept waiting long, else Darinor, Allion was sure, would have stormed the inner keep and in the process gotten them all killed. Allion was just beginning to feel the soothing effects of the strongest wine he had ever tasted when the steward reappeared with a pair of men surrounded by yet another ring of royal guard. One, he recognized.

"General Maltyk," he greeted, rising to his feet.

The lieutenant general looked much as Allion remembered him, with a knavish gleam to his eyes and a cropped, cornsilk beard.

"Master Allion," he said, striding forward to clasp the hunter's hand. "I imagined you taller by now, what with the tales that accompany your name." He turned to Marisha. "You, my lady, appear radiant as ever."

The woman blushed as he took her fingers in hand and placed them to his lips.

"I'm happy to see you, General," she replied. "And to see that your knee has healed properly."

"With much thanks to you, my lady," Maltyk said, smirking at his own forced propriety. The general turned then, giving a nod to the other who had accompanied him. "My lord, I present to you Allion and Marisha. This other," he added with an eye toward Darinor, "I'm afraid I cannot confirm."

"No need, General," King Galdric replied. "If he travels with the dragon-slayer, we shall count him a friend."

The king who had ruled Partha for more than thirty years stood proud and tall, as a monarch should. Stories held him to be a powerful man, a hunter and gamesman, said to have wrestled wild animals in his youth. By the looks of it, those days were behind him, but Allion saw plenty of evidence to suggest the rumors might be true. Although grown soft about the middle, his arms and torso remained as thick as trunks. His skin was worn and scarred in a healthy way, bearing testament to a life lived outdoors in a conquering fashion. In bearing and appearance, he had the aura of a man who had climbed every mountain, swum every river, bested every enemy that had dared rise before him—and rather than wage a senseless struggle against time, had learned in these later years to settle comfortably and be content with his past achievements.

He stepped forward, flocked by his personal guard, who mimicked his every move like a school of fish in flight. "Welcome to Atharvan," he said. His measured tone was smooth, yet forceful. "It's good to finally meet you in person."

Allion was about to drop to one knee when Galdric extended a hand. The king's warm eyes and encouraging smile convinced him to take it. "You honor me, Your Majesty."

"You've earned it," Galdric assured him. "Were it not for the deeds of you and your friends, I would not have a kingdom today." The hunter bowed graciously. "The same goes for you, my lady. Your reputation precedes you. As my general suggests, your very presence warms these halls."

"Have we finished with the pleasantries?" Darinor snapped.

"Darinor," the king acknowledged, though his voice seemed to tighten. "The prophet come to us in our hour of need. What brings you to Athar-van?"

The Entient scoffed. "A wiser man would not have to ask."

Allion cringed. He had dared hope the mystic might show a little more tact in dealing with Galdric than he had toward others. Apparently, that would not be the case.

But if the king felt slighted, he did nothing to show it, offering instead a nod and a smile. "Quite right. Clumsy of me to ask. You've come in response to my message, have you not?"

Darinor grunted.

"I can assume, then, that you do not care for my decision, and have come to persuade me to alter course."

"If you would save your people," the Entient agreed, "you will do as instructed. I believe our initial message made that clear."

Again the king showed remarkable restraint. "Have you had yourself a drink?" he asked.

The Entient declined with a shake of his head. Allion and Marisha nodded politely, showing the man their goblets. Galdric drifted toward the serving table, guardsmen darting out of his way, where he hefted and then drained a small flagon.

"A fine vintage," Galdric proclaimed, "although better when it has been decanted."

"As long as your soldiers engage the enemy in scattered groups, the Il-lychar will continue to fight that way," Darinor pressed while the other wiped his mouth. "Assemble, and they will have little choice but to come after the main army in search of the warrior coils their Illysp brethren crave."

"Your strategy is clear," the king assured him. "Curious, but then these are curious times. Do not mistake my hesitation for a misunderstanding of the circumstances."

The man's tone was steady, his conviction unmistakable. Allion's early sense was that Galdric was every bit a match for Darinor. Despite having come, in part, to lend his voice in support of their common cause, the hunter found himself wanting to hear out the dissenting king's arguments.

"What other reason could you have for being foolish enough to stand alone in this?" Darinor demanded.

The king settled into a chair across the room, taking with him another flagon. "As I'm sure you're aware, we lost more than two-thirds of our West Legion in this war against the so-called dragonspawn—a third of my forces overall. My people are starving, and driven to terror by the bands of savage races now ravaging our lands. On top of that, I've got Menzoes—whom I'm doing my best to help and not grind beneath my boot—accusing me of cavort-ing with demons. In short, my plate is full."

Allion had heard the whispers on his way in, how it was strange that Atharvan should be one of but a handful of eastern cities that had managed to escape the wrath of the Demon Queen, making its rulers the target of unfair rumor as to what sort of foul pact they had signed in order to be spared.

"I've been listening to the same arguments, in one form or another, ever since my arrival," Darinor countered, glaring at Allion.

"I'm sure you have," Galdric granted. "And to you, I must sound an old fool making excuses. But as I attempted to explain in my response, it is too late for us. The struggle you hope to avoid in the west has already begun here in the east. For every murderous elf or goblin your citizens have seen, my people have encountered tenfold. Can you imagine the outcry were I to send away the only protection they have?"

"Small indeed," Darinor argued, "compared to what you shall hear when all have been made into Illychar themselves."

The king shook his head dismissively. "We have long lived beneath a cloud of such threats. Our enemies may defeat us, but they will never intimidate us. Were it otherwise, we would have surrendered to Killangrathor's unholy spawn, I'm sure."

He took a deep drink, stopping short of draining the flagon as he had before. Allion looked to his own cup and managed another sip.

"Understand," Galdric continued, as Darinor stewed silently across from him, "that this has not been a unilateral decision. I've consulted heavily with my generals. As a matter of self-defense, we cannot give ourselves over to your proposed course."

Allion glanced at Maltyk, standing over his king's shoulder, then back to Galdric. It wasn't hard to appreciate their position. After all, his own people—himself included—had not been easily convinced, and they had yet to face anything approaching an open assault. Calm as he appeared, the king of Partha had to still be reeling from his war of survival against the Demon Queen. He was down to a single legion, units of the East having been fed into the decimated West, so that what had once been an army of twin halves was now a unified whole. Despite being short-manned, it had taken an act of great faith and mercy to let fall the northern front against those with whom his people had been waging a civil war off and on for centuries. Galdric had done so even before this new threat had emerged, giving ear to the entreaties of fellow rulers like Torin who had urged forbearance, when he might as easily have put a swift end to the Menzo rebellion once and for all. Clearly, the man was not unreasonable. Was it fair to ask more of these people than they already had?

But they had to, Allion knew. The course they had elected did not allow for exceptions. If Darinor was to be believed—and it still seemed they had little choice—then the hunter was going to have to help find a way to make these others agree.

"Is that General Corathel's position, then?" he asked.

A faint sparkle lit the corners of the king's eyes, while his lips compressed as if holding back a congratulatory smile. Only then did it occur to Allion that

Galdric might be taking their measure, given the calculated manner in which this interview was unfolding.

"Therein lies much of the problem," the king confessed. "You say we must gather the entire legion, is that not so?" He glanced at Darinor, who looked ready to explode. "But we cannot do so, even if we wished it. One of my divisions is missing."

Allion blinked. "Missing?"

"The Second Division, led by Lieutenant General Jasyn and Chief General Corathel himself. Upon last report, they were driving south into Vosges, hunting a sizable pack of these—what do you call them?—Illychar. A week ago, the reports stopped coming in. All attempts to reestablish lines of communication have failed."

Allion could not make himself believe what he was hearing. The Second Division, foremost among those of the newly unified Parthan Legion. The First no longer existed, except in memorial to those who had fought and given their lives, to a man, in the battle against the dragonspawn at Bane Draw and Kraagen Keep. Of the five active divisions, the Second was the head, comprised of the best and the brightest among Partha's soldiers. A fifth of the army in terms of raw numbers, but of even greater value as the unit that set the example and paved the course the others followed.

Galdric swished the wine remaining in his flagon. "I have already ordered their withdrawal, but that order goes unheeded. Since your plan requires that all our forces unite—and because I cannot afford to sacrifice an entire combat division—the Third is even now being prepped to go after the Second. If successful, perhaps we shall reconsider committing our armies to yours."

He hefted the flagon to his lips and chugged down the remainder of its contents. While he did so, Allion looked to Maltyk, searching for some sign of what the other might be feeling. From Corathel on down, the surviving commanders of the former West Legion had been rewarded for their efforts against the Demon Queen by retaining their positions—granted preference over their counterparts from the East—when the two legions were rolled together. Thus, Maltyk, as lieutenant general of the Third Division, would be the one to carry out the task the king had just described. Knowing this caused Allion to wonder what choice, if any, his friends had really been given in accepting their new appointments.

But that thought was swiftly eclipsed by the more ominous issue at hand. The entire Second Division. Some ten thousand soldiers. Guided by a pair of generals who had survived no fewer than four major battles against Spithaera's dragonspawn. How might they have simply disappeared? Even if they had been wiped out, signs would have remained, and word sent home. The matter as it stood suggested any number of foul possibilities that Allion didn't dare consider.

He felt Marisha take his hand, then looked past her to where her father brooded like a thunderhead.

"I don't like it," the Entient rumbled, as Galdric passed the empty flagon off to one of his guardsmen and signaled for another. "This is exactly what the

Illysp want, to suck our forces into combat in an area where superior numbers are all but meaningless."

"That may be," the king admitted, twisting at the braids of a yellow beard flecked with gray. "But if so, then they already have what they want."

"Sending in another division is not the answer. You would only feed their ranks."

"Easy it is to find flaw in another's thinking," Galdric conceded. "Harder by far to conceive a plan of one's own."

Darinor grunted, grinding his jaw as if testing a sore tooth. "Let me go," he said finally.

The king nearly dropped the flagon delivered by his guardsman. "Go where?"

"Into Vosges, in search of your wayward division."

Marisha gaped at her father in horrified fashion.

"Alone?" Galdric asked.

"If might were the answer, I should think that ten thousand Parthan soldiers, with a legion commander at the helm, would have matters well in hand."

The king was squinting now, as if trying to see in Darinor something he had overlooked before. "It may just be that our enemy is picking off my messengers, and that the battalions themselves are fine. If that's the case, a sizable regiment would be much better suited to the task."

"A force of any size would only slow me down. Besides, I have experience in dealing with these creatures," the Entient maintained, with a brief turn toward Allion and Marisha. "How to avoid them, or do battle if I must."

"And what of our natural enemies? The jungle itself and the savages who live there?"

The Mookla'ayans, Allion thought, and shuddered.

"The least of our concerns," Darinor assured them all. "What I must know is this: If I am able to find and return your division to you, will you agree to my plan to add your army to those assembled just south of the Gaperon?"

The king took another long drink, then climbed from his chair and to his feet. Given the quantity of wine the man had consumed, Allion half expected him to keel over then and there. But if the drink were to hold any influence, it had yet to take effect.

"I'll grant you this," Galdric countered. "Should you manage to locate General Corathel and convince him that yours is the course we must follow, I'll issue no order to the contrary."

Darinor considered the king's terms, then dipped his head in acknowledgment. "So be it."

A RED SUNSET LIT THE WESTERNMOST ROOM among those in which Allion had been left to wait while Darinor discussed with King Galdric the route he would be taking on the morrow. Though no one had said so, the hunter supposed this suite of chambers would belong to him and Marisha for some time—at least until the Entient returned from his foray into Vosges in order to guide his daughter safely home to Krynwall. It went without saying that he did not trust Allion to do so. And while the other was away, this was likely the safest place they could be.

None of which was of any consolation to Marisha. As soon as the assigned chamberlain had shown them their quarters and closed the outer door behind him, she had begun fuming at the unfairness of it all—that her father should run off alone, once again, while leaving her behind. He wouldn't be happy, it seemed, until he got himself killed, while she lay tucked away like some doll in a cupboard.

To make matters worse, there was no one to whom she could think to carry her appeal, no one who might understand her predicament and prevail upon Galdric—and in turn, her father—that they were mistaken to keep her stored away. For that, she needed someone with both clout and a woman's sensibility. But the king was unmarried—had been ever since his wife had died years earlier. And she had borne him only sons, which meant the only women to be found in the royal household were those she saw carrying scrub rags and feather dusters, food trays and watering spouts, fresh candles and soiled linens—none of whom looked likely to have the king's ear.

Allion had been quick to point out that he was not any happier about the situation than she. He had come, he reminded her, in part because he was tired of being shackled to a palace's grounds. Though the rooms Galdric had accorded them were nicer than his own back home, it didn't mean he would be comfortable occupying them.

When finished venting helplessly, they had gone their separate ways, Marisha to her quarters in the east, Allion to his in the west. If nothing else, the hunter was grateful for the ensuing silence, as he stood near the bank of open windows and watched the sun make its first appearance of the day—just in time to bleed away in a crimson streak across the evening sky. It had been too long, he thought, since he had experienced a moment of such simple peace.

Then the outer door to their suite opened. Allion turned to face his doorway, and spotted Marisha across the way in hers, as muffled steps dragged across the common room located between the two. By the frown on the woman's face, Allion knew who had come even before the lean shadow fell into view.

Darinor glanced at each of them before entering the hunter's room. Marisha followed hard upon his heels, her determined features set. Allion steeled himself, preparing for a repeat of all the arguments he'd so recently finished listening to.

Instead, a moment passed in which the three of them simply stared at one another—Darinor at Allion, Marisha at Darinor, and Allion alternating between the two.

"I've asked Galdric to provide mounts and supplies for the three of us," the Entient announced finally. "We journey south at first light."

Marisha's harsh expression crumbled at her surprise. "You don't intend to leave me behind?"

"And entrust your safety to Galdric?" Darinor huffed. "I think not. Not when it would mean leaving you here alone."

"I could stay with her," Allion offered hurriedly.

The Entient's stare seemed to burn through him, even as a rare smirk reshaped the corner of his mouth. "Except that I have need of you. From what my daughter has shared with me, you have traveled this jungle before—even encountered the natives who live there. That experience may prove useful."

Allion's mind raced, desperate for an excuse. A trek into Vosges was not what he'd had in mind when departing Krynwall. The very thought of returning to the southern peninsula—perhaps the most dangerous territory Pentania had to offer—sent a chill ratcheting up his spine.

"In any case," Darinor continued, "I must also persuade Corathel to reverse course, once we find him. For that, I need someone to whom he might respond favorably, since I'm told my demeanor does not necessarily agree with everyone."

An actual jape, Allion thought. The first he had heard the man utter. Its humor was lost on him, however, buried by the truth of his helplessness.

"We'll be ready," Marisha assured her father.

Allion looked to the woman, at her expression grown eager and solemn. It was for the best, he supposed. As perilous as this journey promised to be, it might be safer than leaving him and Marisha here alone.

The weight of her father's gaze caused him to break short his study. In marking the other's scowl, it occurred to him that this might have been yet another reason for taking them along, to avoid having to trust them on their own. If so, the man wasn't saying.

"At first light," Darinor reminded them.

Allion nodded, then watched the others leave his room. When alone, he blew forth a long, slow breath before turning toward the fallen sun.

CHAPTER THIRTY-THREE

THE PROMISE OF BATTLE CHILLED THE AIR.

They were less than a day out from Neak-Thur, and if Torin had harbored any delusions as to where they were headed, there was no denying it now. The musk of the army surrounded him—of wood and leather, of grease and oils, of men and horses and the earth tilled up by their tramping feet. Amazingly, the rogues that comprised its ranks continued to laugh and jest, each with his neighbors, as if marching to a festival rather than to war. But Torin would not be fooled. He felt the truth in his bones, enveloped by a biting cold within and without that not even the Sword could fully dispel.

They were not yet ready for this. That much had seemed obvious from the start. But time was working against them. The longer they took to muster a response to Lorre's takeover, the longer the warlord had to siphon reinforcements from the various outposts of his northern lands. This was their one chance, a counterstrike swift and sure, and, no matter the odds, General Chamaar was determined to make the most of it.

Torin had been introduced to the prime commander the night before, after a full day's march. By that time, Arn had already recounted for the man a loose recitation of the outlander's background. The master of recruits must have embellished quite a bit, Torin decided, for one of the first things the general had done was to ask that he assume command of one of the forward regiments—a company of some two hundred men. The young king had balked at the request, explaining that he lacked the tactical experience to maneuver a unit of that size. But Chamaar had insisted, reassuring him that what maneuvering might be required after the initial positioning would be determined and executed at the wedge and battalion levels. All he need do was charge in the direction indicated, redirect when commanded, and see to it that his men followed.

It remained a terrible responsibility in Torin's mind. He had led men to their deaths before, and was loath to do so again. Nevertheless, as he stood there matching the general's challenging stare, he had recognized the deep, inexplicable faith with which the other regarded him, as if seeing in him some quality of which Torin himself was unaware. A general's special talent, perhaps, to compel a man to believe in himself and take action he normally would not consider. Whatever, Torin found himself overwhelmed with the urge to show this Chamaar exactly what he was capable of.

Once that had been decided, he was introduced to each of the general's wedge commanders—Gilden, Jaik, and Bardik. Of the three, only Gilden made a significant first impression, wrapped in bands of muscle that put even Arn's to shame. Jaik was taller, and leaner, greeting Torin with a squared jaw and a look that suggested an intolerance toward foolishness. Smaller than either of the others, Bardik had grinned almost sheepishly from beneath an overgrown mop of mud-colored curls.

They had shared dinner there in the command tent, Chamaar and his chief lieutenants along with Arn, Torin, and the pair of Fenwa with whom he traveled. Torin had cringed when the general acknowledged the Nymph Hunters as "the women who would do battle alongside men," expecting Dyanne to introduce herself properly. Instead, she had surprised him by offering only a sardonic smile and a promise to stay out of the way.

Before daybreak, Torin was roused by Commander Gilden—or "Lancer," as he seemed better known—and presented to his unit. Soon after, the entire army was assembled and driving north once more across a rainswept plain. Torin marched at the head of his regiment as he had all that day. This placed him near the center of the overall formation, in the company of Chamaar and the three wedge commanders, which he quickly came to recognize as both a blessing and a curse. For while it meant that his troops held their lines and kept silent any murmurings against his freshly issued authority, it also made it more difficult to keep track of Dyanne and Holly, who time and again grew bored with the measured pace and ventured forth on their own, knowing where to find him upon their return. Though he understood better than to worry for their safety, the mere separation caused in him an unexpected anxiety, which he dared not confess.

Perhaps it was this and not the specter of looming battle that had so jangled his nerves. Wherever the pair went, stares followed, including his own. He felt as if he'd been made to share a treasure that should have remained his own—which was ridiculous, of course, for though he might wish otherwise, neither Dyanne nor her kinmate were his to protect.

Not that their movements or the attentions drawn should matter to him, regardless. Whatever his feelings, he could ill afford such a dangerous distraction.

But telling himself this did nothing to help, particularly as he watched Dyanne marching ahead of him, laughing and hanging on the every word of a lumbering Jaik—as she seemed far too inclined to do. While Torin received endless instruction from those around him, the commander of the East Wedge had taken it upon himself to see that Dyanne and her companion were properly entertained. An innocent courtesy, perhaps. But to Torin, there was nothing innocent about the way in which Dyanne held the other captive in her radiant gaze. The implications, subtle and unfounded as they were, left him feeling raw and irritable.

"They always take a fancy to those in uniform," a familiar voice moaned wistfully.

Torin turned, startled to find Moss at his elbow. Just a moment before, one of the other sergeants of his wedge had been teaching him the terms given to a series of formations and commands likely to be employed in the upcoming battle. So obsessed was he with Dyanne's responses toward Jaik that he hadn't even noticed the sergeant's departure or Moss's approach. A pointed reminder, it seemed, as to what could happen should he fail to keep his focus.

"Well," Torin said, "if it isn't my reliable mountain guide."

Moss grinned through his tobacco-stained teeth. "Been meaning to apologize about that. You must admit, it wasn't entirely my fault. Anyway, I left you in good hands, did I not?" The rogue winked, then nodded toward Dyanne.

Torin pretended not to notice, clenching his jaw as Dyanne gave another lilting laugh in response to something Jaik had said. He wondered what it was about the wedge commander she found so amusing. His awkward gait, perhaps, or his oversized head.

Moss leaned close, nudging him with an elbow. "What I wouldn't pay to stoke her fire, eh?"

Torin's sudden urge was to knock the brute senseless and grind his lewd smile into the earth. However he might choose to classify his own fascination, base desire wasn't it. Dyanne seemed too special, too unique, to be considered in such a manner. That Moss of all people would suggest otherwise put a sour taste in his mouth.

"How is it you charmed these Nymphs, anyway?" the big man pressed, oblivious to his offense. "Anything you can tell me that might help me win their favor?"

Recognizing that it was misdirected, Torin forced himself to swallow his fury. Still, he wished the rogue had the sense to back off.

"Why should I help you with anything?" he grumbled finally. "You lied to me."

"Lied?"

"About Hargenfeld."

Moss snorted, his hot breath clouding the air before his ruddy cheeks. "That? Come now. Rags was already out here, west of the Cleft, likely for the season. You never would have agreed to await his return. I did you a favor by offering to take his place."

"A favor that left me for dead in an avalanche," Torin recalled dryly.

The rogue shrugged, blowing into his hands in an effort to warm them. "Couldn't have been much colder than this."

Torin glanced at the roiling heavens. "Aren't you supposed to be scouting our flank?"

"We're reporting every six hours now. Just came in to see how you and your friends were getting along."

"How very noble of you," Torin mumbled. "I assure you we'll be fine."

"So long as those clouds hold," Moss allowed, turning eye toward the blackened skies. "Let's just hope this blows over before tomorrow."

With that, the rogue clapped him on the shoulder before swaggering off as suddenly as he had appeared. Torin glared after him a moment, then resumed his vigil over Jaik and Dyanne, his bitter thoughts echoing darkly Moss's sentiment.

Indeed.

Throughout the remainder of the afternoon and evening, his routine was the same, an endless string of mobile briefings with various colonels, lieutenants, and sergeants bearing impact upon his command. Between these and during, he did his best to mark Dyanne's whereabouts, to follow her comings and goings amid the army throng. When she was away, his gaze stole through the surrounding crowds in furtive search. When near, he fixated upon her, suffering a pang of envy for every word or smile aimed another's way. He felt ridiculous for doing so, but could not make himself stop.

Then, about the same time the sun had surrendered its vain attempt to ward off the night and a freezing sleet had begun to fall, Hargenfeld returned from the point. Once his report had been delivered to Chamaar, a ripple passed through the ranks as the entire army ground to a halt, with orders to settle in for what was sure to be a restless night.

"Nearly two to one against us," Chamaar shared with the rest of them some time later.

They were gathered in a loose circle in the command tent, the general and an assortment of officers. Torin wasn't certain that he should be there, given the number of those who outranked him who were not. But Dyanne and Holly had entered at Jaik's invitation, and Torin wasn't about to let them do so without him. So far, none had questioned his presence.

"From what the scouts could discern, a good many of these were orcs," the general amended, "so the disparity is not so great as it may seem."

This drew a harsh chuckle from the collective assembly, but caused Torin's stomach to squirm. He had never seen an orc. Except for the Mookla'ayans, the elves of Vosges, he had never encountered any of the elder races. By all accounts, they were mindless savages, the lot of them. Then again, the same had been said of Cwingen U'uyen and his Powaii people, and as Torin could attest—in their case at least—it simply wasn't true.

But even if it were, and he were set to fighting monsters on the morrow, could any monster be more horrifying than those he had faced during the War of the Demon Queen?

"It gets better," Chamaar assured them, kindling the anxious fire seen burning in the eyes of his listeners. "It appears he means to guard the city with his troops, rather than the other way around. Only a token garrison, maybe one in ten, hunkers within." He looked to Hargenfeld as he said this, and received the other's confirming nod.

A few of the rogues present began to grumble.

"So to him, men are more expendable than mortar," said one.

"I'll wager the warlord himself is one of those sheltering within," hissed another.

Chamaar raised his hands to quiet them. For the first time, Torin noticed the many scars that crisscrossed the general's meaty fingers. He looked like an old bear, hunched in the shoulders, but possessed of an intelligence and ferocity that seethed beneath the surface of his gleaming eyes. His shape and movements suggested aches and pains too numerous to count, and a strength that had long ago been used up. But as with that trundling old bear, Torin sensed that this was a deception. If nothing else, he could tell by the way others reacted that he would not want this man barreling down on him in the heat of a battle.

"Since it's to be a battle upon the plains, he'll be expecting us, with our smaller force, to hit him as far to the east as possible. He'll expect us to go straight for the city gate, where we would have the protection of the curtain wall at our backs as we seek to force his flank."

Torin nearly scoffed at the notion of "protecting" themselves by placing their backs to an enemy wall and its accompanying siege defenses. But given his limited knowledge of this particular city, he opted to hold his tongue for now.

"Knowing this, our adversary will position his strongest troops to defend against this course. Our next best option, then, would be to force instead the western flank. It would mean fighting through his entire army to reach our ultimate goal, but it would enable us to use the sea as our rear guard."

Several of the officers were nodding, although Torin wasn't one of them. He was busy watching Dyanne as she observed Jaik, while the stone-faced wedge commander rubbed his beardless chin in thought.

"Thus," Chamaar said, crouching down to point and sketch with a dagger in the dirt, "we can expect to find the second-strongest enemy contingent here, to the west. If he keeps his back to the Bastion, and we fail to flank him, we cannot win."

Torin was still concentrating on Dyanne when, without warning, her gaze whipped about to catch his uninvited stare. Before he could think to look away, the woman grinned so that a warm flush eddied through him, then turned her attentions aside. Too late, his own eyes shifted, only to find those of Chamaar.

"So then," the general asked, "where do we strike?"

A test, Torin realized. There was no reason to believe that it wasn't. The old bear had surprised him, and this after he'd been blinded as though by a cresting sun.

For a moment, he froze. He could feel the eyes of those assembled burning into him. He wondered if Dyanne's were among them, but was afraid to look.

His gaze slipped to the crude drawing in the center of their layered huddle. He could barely see it from his place amid the shadows, then recognized that he didn't need to.

"We hit them where their ranks are weakest, and the matchup favors us. We hit them where they least expect it."

Though he feared his voice might crack, it held strong, even under the general's appraising stare.

"And where is that?"

Torin wasn't entirely sure that he was on the right track, but it was too late to back down now. "In the center of their force."

A host of murmurs followed, some agreeable, others much less so.

"Then we save Lorre the trouble of surrounding us," someone protested.

"Outlanders," another muttered.

But Lancer was nodding approvingly, the shaved sides of his head reflecting the lamplight. And at the corner of Chamaar's mouth, beneath the overhanging end of his iron-gray moustache, Torin thought that he detected a smile.

"When striking an armored opponent, you aim for the weakest link," the general agreed, speaking again to all assembled. "We find and force the most likely seam. As our enemies surge ahead to flank us, we drive north until we hit the wall of the Bastion, displacing Lorre's troops with our own. We then veer east along its southern face toward the city gate, cutting our swath among his reserve units and supply stores. If we can do so quickly, his strongest troops, positioned out front and to either side, will not have a chance to engage us until it is too late."

Some of the men continued to express doubt as they studied the L-shaped path traced in the mud before them. It was a long shot, at best. At worst, suicide. So much depended on the speed and depth at which they were able to drive the initial wedge. If they were to stall, there in the middle of the enemy multitude, they would be hewn down from either side like stalks in a farmer's field.

"Lorre knows we're coming," Jaik reminded them all, his voice deep and contemplative. "His scouts are probably watching us even now. How do we position ourselves to execute this strike without revealing too soon our exact intentions?"

"Carefully," Chamaar admitted. "We'll make it appear that we mean to drive straight for the city by folding the Central Wedge alongside that of the East. The West will serve as our fishhook, so that it appears we mean to hold them off on that flank. At the last moment, Gilden's wedge will split off to lead the charge through the center. Bardik and the West will follow in order to help fill the gash. The true test will be in holding the thickness of our lines. We must not be severed. At the same time—Lancer, Bardik," he said, looking at each of the wedge commanders in turn, "we cannot afford to waste time engaging fronts east and west, but must focus on driving north until we hit the Bastion. Is that understood?"

The pair nodded, their youthful faces anxious, yet solemn.

"North to the wall, then east to the gate," the general reiterated. "Those pouring in from behind will prevent those in front from getting squeezed. Meanwhile, Jaik and I will keep the forward units on the eastern side engaged, so that they cannot double back to help with the rear. If all goes to plan, Lancer will complete his circle to meet back up with me, forming a ring around the eastern segment—from which we can choke the life while holding off the western counterassault."

And if all doesn't *go to plan?* Torin wanted to ask. Instead, he watched the brows of those harboring doubts straighten with grim resolve, their thinking coming into line with that of their general.

"Torin," Chamaar added suddenly. "I'd like your company to spearhead our assault alongside Lancer. From what Arn tells me, you're just the man we need."

In other words, Torin thought, his mercenary friend had told the prime commander of what had happened in their battle at sea against the *Raven's Squall*—what always seemed to happen when he wielded the Sword against an enemy. How he had charged ahead, unstoppable, yet caught up in his own euphoria, mindless as to the strategy and limitations of those around him. Driven by emotion. A reckless fool.

Exactly what was needed here.

He didn't trust himself to speak, and so nodded instead. After all, he wanted to be near the front, among the first to find Lorre when finally they forced their way into the city. Should another do so before him, he might not get a chance to obtain the answers he required.

The council disbanded soon after, with runners sent out to relay orders to the various regiments. There was no second-guessing, no study of the many pitfalls in the course laid out before them. They hadn't come this far just to dither over their chances of success. These men trusted in their leaders, who in turn trusted their troops to execute their assignments. At this point, that mutual trust was all they had.

Torin only wished he could say the same. The general he did not doubt. Chamaar had shown too much confidence in him to be denied the same courtesy. But as he exited the command tent, he could not deny a deep and troubling concern about the others—those who continued to behave as if unaware that tomorrow's dawn might be their last. In comparing this army to those of Partha, Kuuria, and even Krynwall, he could not imagine they had the discipline to pull off such a dangerous maneuver. Many were here only for the money, fighting not as a nation, but as individuals who—if successful—might go back to cheating and fighting one another before the week was out. More likely, he could expect them to collapse and flee at the first sign of turmoil, leaving him trapped in the middle of a hornet's nest that *they* had stirred up.

"Troubled thoughts?"

Torin spun, surprised and delighted to see that Dyanne and Holly had followed him from the assembly. "Where's Jaik?" he asked, casting about.

Holly smirked. "Why, did you need to speak with him?"

Torin felt himself redden. Though he tried, he could think of nothing more to say.

But Dyanne did not acknowledge his embarrassment. "It looks to be a good plan," she assured him.

"They always do," Torin grunted, "when scribbled in the dirt ahead of time."

"You don't believe it will work?"

No. But what else was he to do? Sneak ahead in the dead of night and ask the armies encamped at the city doorstep to deliver him to their lord? Odds were, it would then be Lorre who wielded the Sword of Asahiel in battle on the morrow.

"At some point," Dyanne allowed, "it becomes only natural to question those who would guide us."

"Like you and Dynara?"

Dyanne considered him closely, maple eyes glinting. "If you truly disagree with the general's plan, you should do so openly, here and now, rather than risk following a course you don't believe in."

Torin shook his head. "It's not the plan I don't believe in. It's the ability of these mercenaries to carry it out."

Dyanne glanced at Holly, who nodded. "If you hadn't noticed, we spent a good deal of time today working our way among those we're set to battle alongside. This general and his commanders, they're dedicated men—if there is such a thing. And these fighters, though not quite soldiers, are wild and headstrong. They will not be easily repelled."

Torin wondered how they could possibly have determined such a thing by simply passing from one conversation to the next; yet the bigger mystery was what she wanted out of this. A reassurance, it seemed, that he was up to the task. That when the time came, he would lay aside his doubts and do what he must. Hadn't he always?

"You won't see me back down," he promised her.

"Good. Although, just to be sure, we'll be at your side the entire time. If these rogues can't see you to victory, we will."

It was an absurd statement, outlandish in its boldness. And yet, Dyanne's smile was so wondrous, the gleam in her eye so reassuring, that the worries were wiped clean from Torin's mind, while a surge of confidence filled his chest.

A smile of his own warmed his face. But then a voice called his name, and Arn muscled past a cluster of rogues and into view.

"Lancer is looking for you," the man said, with a polite nod to the pair of Nymphs. "He says we've much to discuss."

Torin's smile faded as Dyanne and Holly stepped aside and went their own way, the latter with one of her mischievous winks. His sense of assurance followed, like sand drawn out by a retreating wave, leaving the sharp edges of his buried doubts exposed once more. Only this time, he felt no foreboding, only a curious sense of resignation. No matter whose instincts proved out—his or Dyanne's—they would suffer the consequences together. One way or another, they would have their answer on the morrow.

Resisting the urge to look to see where Dyanne was headed, he turned instead to follow Arn, glancing skyward in surprise as a drizzle of snowflakes began to fall.

CHAPTER THIRTY-FOUR

*T*HE SNOW FELL THROUGHOUT THE NIGHT. By daybreak, the land was covered, and men awoke within their blankets and lean-tos beneath an icy crust. Torin emerged, clinging to the Sword for warmth, to gaze upon the world with fresh wonder.

"Going to be rough footing in this," Moss grumbled.

Torin glanced back to find the big rogue huffing in the early dawn. "Moss," he greeted, genuinely comforted to see the other's face. It had not been a pleasant night. He put out his hand as if to catch a few of the windblown flakes. "I thought you said I'd never see it snow down here beneath the mountains."

Moss shrugged. "Looks like I was wrong. Won't be the last time I'm caught in a lie."

Torin's lips tightened with his amusement. Under better circumstances, he might have grinned.

"Where are the girls?" Moss asked.

"They were wise enough to accept the hospitality of Commander Jaik's tent," Torin muttered.

"The same offer wasn't extended to you, eh?"

"Arn offered to make room. I figured I could set a better example by roughing it alongside the men of my unit."

Moss came to a stop beside him. "I hear you're going to be out front."

Torin nodded, then turned back to look over the stirring encampment. "Come to say good-bye then, did you?"

"Thought maybe I could wrangle an embrace from those companions of yours."

This time, Torin could not help but laugh and shake his head. "I suppose you'll have to settle for one from me."

"Won't be necessary," Moss said hurriedly.

"Are you sure? You might not get another chance."

"I'll make do," the big man assured him.

"How about this, then?" Torin said, picking at the strings that held his coin purse and handing it over to the rogue.

"What's this?"

"Your payment. For seeing me as far along as you did."

Moss hefted the small sack. "There's more in here than we agreed on."

"If I survive this, you can pay back what you don't deserve."

The rogue gave a broad smile as he tucked the bag away. "If that's the measure, then you've not paid me enough by half."

Torin laughed again and clasped the big man's hand. "Farewell, Gavrin. Good luck to you, whatever happens today."

"If you get the chance, spit in old Lorre's face for me, would you?"

Torin nodded, endured a hearty clap on his shoulder, then watched the other flash a final grin and swagger on his way.

Though sorely tempted to seek out his Nymph companions, Torin turned his mind instead toward the preparations of his company, meeting with each of his platoon commanders to gauge their readiness. Most, it seemed, were prepped and eager for the day's fighting to begin. *Fools all,* Torin thought.

A light breakfast was consumed, cold and quick, after which Torin was summoned to a final briefing with the army's principal commanders. The reports brought in by Moss, Hargenfeld, and the other scouts had done nothing to change the day's strategy. They would go forward as planned.

En route back to his regiment, he finally caught brief sight of Dyanne and Holly. He might have asked how comfortably they had slept, but did not get a chance. Just as well, he decided, since he wasn't sure he wanted to know.

And then they were off, the entire force, one unit after the other. They left their tents and food stores and other nonessential supplies behind, carrying with them only what they would need in battle. A horse would have been nice, Torin thought, as he waded through snowdrifts that in some areas came clear to his knee. Marching at the head of his company, at the left hand of Lancer and the Central Wedge, he and those alongside were to forge the trail that others would follow. Of the mounts they had, most were toward the rear, hauling wagons of siege tools and carts for bearing off the wounded. The rest had been assigned to the runners and lookouts. In any case, as long as he was relegated to wishing for things he couldn't have, he could do much better than a mere steed.

A stinging wind lashed their faces, blowing from the northwest and bearing with it the scents of salt and sea. They were nearing the ocean, Torin realized, that of Yawacor's western shore, opposite the coast on which he had landed and farthest from his own home. Snowfall continued to blanket the region—even the beaches, the outriders reported. Something not seen in nearly twenty years. A good omen, the men whispered, though Torin couldn't see how.

It wasn't long before the smell of the ocean was followed by its sound—a deep, restless roar that underscored the wailing wind and seemed to Torin to resonate within him. He looked for the source, but caught only occasional glimpses through the fog and trees as the army proceeded north along a craggy shoreline. Limestone cliffs held it at bay, and even atop those bluffs, he could not see over their westward rise.

But as the land began to slope downward, and the line of trees tacked eastward, Torin's view to the west opened up, revealing a mist-shrouded vista of rocky beaches and churning waves, wheeling gulls and diving herons. A palette washed of color and detail, but which laid claim to the horizon and beyond. In gazing out over that expanse, Torin lost himself in its boundlessness, and before he knew it, he had reached his goal: the city of Neak-Thur.

The scene appeared suddenly before him, on the other side of a small ascent. Nearly a mile distant, at the eastern edge of a snowswept coastal plain, lay that which they had come to reclaim. Neak-Thur had been described as a sprawling assortment of streets and buildings, erected in a northerly line upon the west-facing slopes of a series of foothills belonging to the Dragontail Mountains. A meandering curtain wall was said to hug the city on its seaward side, snaking over and around ridgelines and hollows. Toward the north end he would find the Bastion, a battlement that extended from the city's outer wall and shot due westward, running the full half-mile trek to the reefs of the sea. It was this that made Neak-Thur the gateway between lands north and south, for the Bastion was an impassable tollway, like a giant arm reaching out to forbid progress. Its ramparts were heavily fortified, and it was pierced by only a single gateway. Unless by ship or grant of permission from the Council of Rogues, no one ventured farther north or south than Neak-Thur.

Until now.

While Torin recognized easily enough the city's layout as it had been mapped out for him, his attention was drawn more to those who now inhabited it. Through increasingly thick curtains of windblown snow, he peered down not upon a formation of towers and walls, but upon a dark mass of enemy soldiers perhaps twenty thousand strong. The earth was alive with them, like a hill swarming with ants. Torin could not discern which were human, but given their superior numbers and entrenched position it did not seem to matter. Whether stationed upon the hillside walls and rooftops of the city proper, or carpeting the southern plain with their backs to the Bastion, the armies of Lord Lorre had infested the Southland's only defensive fortress, and, from Torin's view, would not be relinquishing it anytime soon.

But if any he traveled with were daunted by the sight, they did nothing to show it. Looking from side to side, Torin heard nary a complaint as men shifted from their marching lines and into battle formation. Personal judgments aside, he admired their courage. Though they be cutthroats and vagabonds, there was an undeniable spirit that drove them. In that moment, Torin felt a part of something much larger than himself, and he welcomed the sensation.

He glanced up to find Lancer pacing the front lines. When he reached Torin's position, the commander of the Central Wedge stopped, regarding the outlander with a devious yet congenial smile clinging to his young face.

"Nervous?" Lancer asked him.

Strangely, he was not. Despite their untenable position, he was more curious than afraid. "I've seen battle before," he reminded the other.

"But never quite like this," Lancer promised, before grinning fiercely and heading on down the line.

While his troops continued their final preparations, and those far below rustled about as if doing the same, Torin revisited in his mind the strategy they would use. The initial feint on the eastern edge was crucial in hiding their true intent. Once the Central Wedge broke free of the main force, its charge would have to be fast and relentless. Chamaar and Jaik would keep the eastern edge of the south front occupied while the other battalions stretched after to widen the central breach. Most importantly, they could not allow the ring they formed to be broken.

The demands were hefty; the odds mounted against them. But success was conceivable if they executed properly and with unwavering savagery.

He could see now why Chamaar was not greatly concerned by the defenses of the city's curtain wall, which was not nearly as well equipped as the Bastion. It made sense, Torin supposed. The only anticipated threat of significant strength was that posed by Lorre's Northland armies. As he had seen for himself, the reefs and cliffs warding the western shoreline discouraged a sea landing. Ferrying troops to a southern location would require time and cost easily avoided by a more direct approach. The city had been constructed with that in mind, the bulk of its defenses given over to the Bastion. The bad news was that Lorre's armies had already proven strong enough to overcome that obstacle. The good news—if there was any—was that their liberation force would not be required to do the same.

And yet, if the first phase of their plan worked and they were able to scatter the larger force set down as battlefield fodder, they would still have to storm the city. From what Torin could see, that would be no simple task. For the outer wall, which looked to have been reconstructed several times to accommodate the city's haphazard expansion, was breached by only a single gate on its western side. This south-facing portal was set in a curving corridor formed by an exterior branch that ran alongside the curtain wall, so that one's approach to the city began with a westward march into this forbidding passageway, looped north through the gate, then continued to loop east and into the city. Not only were the battlements on either side of this corridor well defended, but its walls formed a vicious bottleneck.

The rogue to his left nudged him with an elbow. "It ain't too late to run and hide, if that's what you're thinking."

Torin glanced up at the man, a beefy brute with a sly smile and a mouthful of crooked teeth. "I was just wondering how long it took Lorre to ram the city gate."

"He didn't," came the smooth female response.

Torin whirled to find Dyanne and Holly striding toward him, with Dyanne speaking as though she had been at his side the entire time.

"Commander Jaik says that he used ropes and scaling ladders to swarm the walls, and a team of giants to force the gate from within."

Torin managed to hide his smile. He had begun to wonder if the girls had changed their minds about joining him. "And are we to do the same?"

"One thing at a time," Dyanne said, taking up a position to his left. Holly did likewise, shoving aside the leering rogue that had addressed Torin a moment before.

"Are you sure you want to go through with this?" he asked them.

"Are you?" Holly piped.

Torin smirked, and questioned them no more.

As their army stood there, jostling with a final inspection of blades and buckles, Torin closed his eyes. The wind intensified, whistling in shrill tones that overlaid the lamenting groans of an implacable sea. The air was singing, a mournful symphony that seemed to warn of destruction.

Then came the drums.

They began slowly, a soft, steady pulse buried beneath nature's tune. For just a moment, Torin thought he might be imagining them. But he could feel them as well, shuddering through the earth—individual beats that struck upon his heart before ebbing slowly, as if to sap him of strength after pounding him into submission.

Lancer came marching back then, wheeling into place at the head of his wedge. That put him on Torin's right, so that they stood shoulder to shoulder.

"Bastards think they can intimidate us," the commander said, grimacing with excitement.

Torin nodded. The sinister cadence echoed ominously on the wind. But to a reckless band such as this, the dreadful beat was merely fuel for their madness. A passion began to build within Torin as he tightened his grip on the hilt of the Sword. If death awaited him, then death he would greet, snarling and fighting, raving with the dauntless savagery of a man possessed.

"Tell me, why do they call you Lancer?"

The warrior did not look at him, his busy eyes darting across the battlefield as if memorizing every drop and rise. "Folks will tell you that a few years back, when I was only nineteen, I slew a giant with a single throw of a spear."

Torin considered the man, whose bulbous arms and rippled torso bulged beneath the seams of a black leather tunic. "Is it true?"

"No," the commander admitted. Finishing his survey, he glanced over, snow clinging to the sun-bleached tuft atop his otherwise shaven head. "I was seventeen."

The call to ready arms echoed down the lines. Most had already done so. Torin himself waited. *Not yet.*

The pace of the drums quickened—a piercing rhythm of three staccato beats pounded home by a longer, more menacing one. Torin felt it like a flurry of war hammers, a pummeling assault that left just enough time to draw breath before the next series was driven home. Shields and weapons rattled to the rhythm. Heels tamped the earth in time. Nerves throbbed with anticipation, screaming for release.

A frightful roar resounded from the east. Torin turned to find a horse and rider barreling along the front lines from that direction, waving a pennant and hollering a bestial cry. Behind him, Chamaar and his troops had begun the charge, shouting as they streamed down along the plain, an avalanche beginning its descent.

The signal rider swept past Torin's position, and the dam broke. Lancer led, bellowing a cry taken up by the thousands who followed. Torin jogged alongside, gritting his teeth. He did not look for Dyanne and Holly; he could feel them there beside him, their fire as radiant as that which burned at his fingertips. The Sword remained sheathed, his hand clenching its leather-wrapped hilt. Its strength coursed through him, billowing in waves.

The winds gusted, and the snowfall quickened. Torin squinted against the giant flakes that stung his eyes, focused on his assignment. Though strung out in a westerly line, the entire army was bearing northeast, where Chamaar had promised they would find the heaviest concentration of Lorre's troops. As Torin peered ahead, he saw that there was indeed a thicker assemblage in that area—thickening by the moment as the enemy re-formed to meet their attack. A grim smile etched its way across his features, his heaving chest warmed by a secret sense of triumph.

They had covered perhaps three-quarters of the distance when Lancer gave a whoop and broke suddenly off course, veering northwest into the very throat of the enemy. A chorus of barbaric howls rent the air as the entire Central Wedge peeled off in pursuit. Torin was among the first to follow, but soon found that he could not match the commander's sprinting pace. Lancer, his massive legs churning, was quickly outdistancing them all.

Out came the Crimson Sword from its sheath, the glow from its inner flames as bright as Torin had ever seen. The heat of their divine power flushed through him in a cascade, causing his muscles to swell with energy.

Even so, he could not match Lancer's unlikely blend of strength and speed. Ahead, the dark forms of the enemy threatened to devour the reckless soldier, but Torin could do nothing to slow him. All he could do was give chase, watching the wedge commander thunder like a madman toward his goal—the wet leather and metal scales of his armor glistening, exposed knots of muscle flexing, his body in perfect balance with the smoothness of his stride as he raised his shield, steadied his spear and . . .

Crack!

With the ear-wrenching crunch of a splitting tree, Lancer launched himself into and through the enemy phalanx set to receive him. Their wall crumpled as his spear punched through two of the tightly packed bodies and drew blood from a third. By then, his broadsword was free, hacking and thrusting, while his shield swept aside the tips of the polearms aimed his way. Bodies convulsed, enemies coughed blood from beneath plate armor visors, and the screams of the wounded blared like a trumpet.

In the next moment, Torin was there, sweeping through the ranks that had begun already to close about the driving Lancer, who continued to push forward into the enemy swarm. At his back came Dyanne and Holly and a deluge of frenzied rogues. He could sense them clearly, his awareness heightened by the waves of power emanating through him. Crimson flames ripped through the darkness that sought to devour them, lighting the way.

On they poured like a gushing river, flooding the breach. An eddy amid the wash, Torin twisted and swirled with uncanny instinct, giving himself over to the Sword's guidance and euphoria. The invincible blade arced and jabbed, angling flawlessly and without wasted motion. His foes scattered before him, squealing their inhuman cries.

For his enemies were not in fact human. As helms worn by the forward troops went flying, and as he dug past the more heavily armored front lines, Torin found that most of those arrayed before him bore the salamanderlike features attributed to a creature said to have long since been driven from his own shores: the orc. Though these were the first he had ever encountered, he recognized from the renderings of artists and storytellers the bulging eyes, froglike mouths, and slime-coated skins. An amphibious race, it was said, shorter than the average man, and lacking in tenacity. More at home in swamps and marshlands than anywhere else, most had nevertheless been forced to retreat over the years into pool-filled caverns and subterranean grottos, else risk being hunted to extinction by man.

How many of these, Torin wondered, might gladly return there now?

He had finally caught up with Lancer, around whom enemies continued to crumple. Many, it seemed, had already lost their zeal for this battle, falling back among their own. With each swipe, the Sword cleaved armor and flesh alike, its flames burning brightly against any stain. And as Torin pressed his advantage, fighting forward with Lancer on one side and the pair of Nymph Hunters on the other, he made room for even more of his allies to funnel after.

A moment later, he had taken the lead, driving ahead at his commander's urging. General Chamaar had been right. There would be no need for further maneuvering. He need only remember their plan. Cut north until he reached the Bastion, then turn east and carve his swath along its bulwark toward the city. He knew the goal, and by extension, so did the Sword. Nothing could oppose their singular will.

He had expected he might have to worry for Dyanne and Holly. At this point, he should have known better. The duo battled as they had in Necanicum's wood, like a pair of dancers whose routine had been honed to perfection. Holly slashed with her knives at the seams in her opponents' armor, severing veins and tendons, and when forced to throw one, she seldom missed her mark. Dyanne fought with a rapier in her left hand and a dagger in her right, while using various tumbling techniques to great effect. Back to back and side by side, so close that at times they seemed intertwined, it looked as if the girls were in no danger of falling behind.

So he forged ahead, tireless, a font of calculated rage. It was as if, at long last, he had found a release for all of the pain and fear and doubt he had suffered over the past weeks. That the enemies before him weren't the cause of that pain didn't matter. They had made themselves an easy target, and he would see them destroyed.

The cries of his company spurred him on. Glancing back, Torin was exhilarated by their success. With scarcely an effort, they had shredded the line of armor-shelled orcs set down as a blockade and sent the lighter, more mobile units behind them stumbling in retreat. His opponents were giving him a widening berth, and the shadow of the Bastion was looming ever nearer. Ghastly work, but thus far, child's play.

The thought lodged unexpectedly in Torin's mind. Indeed, up till now it had been *too* easy, almost as if they were being encouraged along this course. But Torin dismissed the notion and its unsettling implications. It was nothing more than their strategy fulfilled. As intended, they had struck along a vein of weaker troops, where Lorre would have least expected. For once, all was going according to plan.

Except for the trolls.

They appeared suddenly, revealed by the waves of enemies that parted before Torin and his companions, exposed like boulders beneath a retreating surf. Like those of the orc, the purported features of this legendary creature were unmistakable. Their hunchbacked bodies were dominated by massive, knotted shoulders and powerful, lengthy arms. Their heads were little more than protruding bumps, their faces a tight gathering of eyes, nostrils, and mouth over a low-slung jaw.

Unlike the orc, they did not give way, but held their line as Torin charged to meet them. On average, they were of human height, but of much thicker build. Their waists were like tree trunks, their legs like gnarled logs. Their skin was mottled, and hardened beyond the need for heavy armor. They wielded blunt weapons for the most part—hammers and clubs and cudgels—which were better suited to their slow, lumbering swipes.

But what struck Torin the most was what they would be doing here, positioned within the middle of the horde. He'd been told that given their strength and their impassive nature, trolls made for an excellent bulwark. Likely, they would be found among Lorre's most sensitive areas—east or west—and almost assuredly out front. To encounter them now, at this critical juncture, was something his commanders hadn't anticipated.

But Torin and his allies had come too far. Should they slow their charge or attempt to withdraw, their foes would close on either side and grind them into gruel.

The first of the trolls fell with an emotionless grunt, the fires of the Sword reflecting in its beady eyes. Before its body toppled, a spiked club wielded by its companion came whipping about in roundhouse fashion. Torin ducked the blow and came up with a strike that severed the second creature's arm. Rather than stand aside to let him pass, the remaining trolls pressed in.

For a fleeting moment, he wondered if he had made a mistake. But then Lancer was there, spattered in blood, using his shield to ram aside two of the beasts at a time. With the wedge commander at his back, Torin concentrated on sweeping clear the opposite flank, so that those coming behind could pour on through.

To his horror, Dyanne and Holly were the first to do so, and Torin nearly took a club to the head as he cried out for them to wait. Once again, he needn't have worried. While Dyanne feinted high, Holly slid beneath the squat legs of their assailant, using her knives to slash at knees and ankles. When the brute leaned forward to reach after her, Dyanne dropped low, and using the troll's weight against it, somehow sent it into a forward roll until it ended up on its back. A thrust to its throat by one of the trailing rogues put an end to its surprise.

It was rough going, for the unit of trolls was stacked almost as deep as it was wide. But after they'd hacked through a dozen lines, the path opened up once again, troll ranks giving way to those of humans, who seemed only too happy to part formation and allow the stream of maddened rogues through.

Directly into a wall of giants.

Torin spied them through a thickening veil of mist and snow, which lent a dreamlike quality to their shadowy forms. But there was no blinking away their sudden appearance. Though proportioned like humans, these savages ranged closer to ten feet in height, making them stronger and faster than their lesser cousins. Much like the trolls, they wore only patchwork armor, revealing a coarse, fur-covered hide shaggy around the calves and forearms. Their teeth were more like tusks, and their eyes, set deep above their bearded faces, burned bright and cold with advanced intelligence.

Torin's stomach lurched, and his mind reeled. According to Chamaar and his lieutenants, giants were the rarest and most prized of Lorre's soldiers—used predominantly as battlefield commanders, stationed in only the most vital areas. Only if Torin were extremely unlucky would he stumble across more than one at a time. Before him stood seven.

A barbed greatsword came at Torin in a rush. Somehow, he met its strike with one of his own. Flames gushed from the Crimson Sword as it cut the monstrous blade in half. Ducking and spinning, he took the giant's leg at the knee, dropping it with a howl that wracked the smaller man's bones.

Even as he fought, the truth sounded like a great brass bell in his head. Chamaar had been betrayed. Sold out by one of the scouts, perhaps. Hargenfeld maybe, or—Torin's gut tightened—Moss. It was the most likely explanation, far more feasible than the idea that Lorre had been able to guess and prepare for this strategy. To lure them into the heart of his force before clamping down like an iron trap.

Whichever, the trap was now sprung. The trolls had slowed them, but the giants had brought their progress to a sluggish, grinding halt. Lancer was doing his best to trade blows, but in this case even the mighty wedge commander was outmatched, and only his quickness and battered shield were keeping him alive. Dyanne and Holly were doing well just to keep clear, their weapons almost useless against these creatures. Meanwhile, enemy forces all around were closing from the sides—even the squalid orcs, become suddenly courageous.

Torin worked frantically to turn the rising tide. But the giants were simply too swift and too powerful, wading among them and slaughtering his troops in droves. And with its momentum stalled, their burrowing wedge had lost its only advantage.

His gaze slipped to the east, toward the foothills and the city nestled upon them. He wondered if the East Wedge fared any better. Perhaps with the defense set as it was, Commander Jaik and General Chamaar had been able to do more than merely occupy the attentions of those warding the city gate. But the stretch of ground between them was too great for him to tell. He could see nothing beyond the curtains of snowfall and the flaring wall of his adversary—the spray of blood, the snarling visages, the glint of a descending axe . . .

Torin leapt to the side just in time to avoid its deadly arc. But doing so put him in line with a second giant's charge. Instinct saved him, as he was somehow able to tuck and roll to avoid a wicked spear, then plant his free hand so that he was able to spin back with the Sword and score a deep gash along the giant's hip.

And yet, he found himself cornered, sandwiched between a wall of enemies at his back and another giant—the axe-wielder—looming over him. He might have been finished were it not for the pair of throwing knives that careened off the side of the giant's face. Though they did not stick, they distracted the beast long enough for Torin to regain his balance and sweep aside those converging on him from the rear. When he came back around, the giant was on one knee, Dyanne's dagger protruding from the back of the other. As she wrenched it free, the giant looked up, eyes wide as the Crimson Sword lopped off its head.

Torin cursed the poor creature, drawing Dyanne and Holly back the other way. He cursed the sky above for its brooding indifference. He cursed the land, slick with ice and blood. Most of all, he cursed the overlord, smug in his tower far above the melee, no doubt laughing as he watched his brutish forces throttle the enemy that had so foolishly entered his trap.

There was time for one more curse, and he saved it for the giant whose jarring blow caused Lancer's knees to buckle and sent the commander's weapon skidding from his grasp. Torin lunged ahead, ignoring the scrapes drawn from a pair of orc blades in passing. But he knew already there was nothing anyone could do. Kicking aside the fallen man's shield, the menacing giant arced its sword high.

Lancer, however, was not as helpless as he appeared, prying from its shallow bed a frozen stone that fit square in the palm of his hand. As the giant's blade fell, the wedge commander gathered his great legs beneath him and, with a furious grunt, launched himself to his feet, coming up inside the blade's arc and using the rock to deliver a crushing blow to the center of his opponent's face. The giant toppled over backward, dead before it hit the ground.

With Torin warding his back, Lancer cast aside the lucky stone and reclaimed his sword and shield. The pair then turned as one, Torin looking to repay the orcs who had gouged his flesh. He found one twitching, the other gurgling, the first with punctured eye sockets, and the second with a flayed throat.

Dyanne winked at him while using her blades as a shield so that Holly could retrieve her knives. Or perhaps she was merely clearing grit from her eye. Torin hadn't the chance to decide before the next group of enemies was upon them.

Lancer barked and shouted, fighting to rally his men. Three giants were down, while a fourth was mortally wounded. Torin was able to spill the entrails from another as it honed in on the wedge commander. That left only two, one of which wisely backed away and sent the lesser troops around it to die in its stead. Slowly, painstakingly, the wedge began to crawl forward once more.

But the enemy crush was cutting their trailing line into segments. While the head of their force inched northward, Torin and his companions found themselves racing back now and again to help shore up the collapsing walls. They remained together for the most part, an effective quartet—Dyanne and Holly weaving and slashing, Lancer bashing and cleaving, and Torin bearing the unquenchable flame that had quickly come to inspire them all.

Time lost all meaning, save for its withering effect upon the vigor and morale of those he battled alongside. Though the power of the Sword fueled him, the same could not be said for those who followed. Its aura aided them, but to a much lesser degree. That they continued to carry on as well as they did inspired him in turn.

Then again, they had no choice. They were fighting for their lives now, their line deteriorated to the point that in some places, there was nothing more than a chaotic mingling of friend and foe. Wherever possible, allies clung to one another in desperate pockets, but did so as helpless eddies in a raging torrent, at the mercy of the current's flow.

Or so Torin believed before a pair of familiar faces came crashing through a knot of soldiers from behind: Arn and Bardik, of the West Wedge. He did not dare question how they had made it all this way—past a Central Wedge buffer of some four thousand men. All he knew, all that truly mattered, was that they brought with them a renewal of the indomitable spirit that had begun to wane.

"To the wall!" Arn bellowed, pointing up at the looming hulk of the Bastion as if to remind Torin of their goal.

Though pressed from the east, Torin shifted focus as Arn barreled northward, hurling his hammer ahead of him and into the face of an openmouthed troll. The blow caved in its already blunt features, preempting its own strike. But its nearest comrade came stepping around without hesitation. Hefting a crude mallet of its own, it braced itself to intercept a now weaponless Arn.

That didn't slow the former swordhand and now master of recruits. He continued forward with a growl, legs pumping, to hurl himself at his newest challenger before it could draw a proper bead. With a thunderous crack, his helmeted head struck the troll square in its mammoth chest, after which both fighters collapsed in a heap.

Torin was unable to break away to go to the fallen man's aid. But Bardik was already there, wearing studded bucklers and wielding a pair of shortswords. He fought like a wrestler, low to the ground, virtually on all fours as he swept the earth of enemies around Arn's body. The enemy's thrusting assaults appeared clumsy and misdirected as the agile wedge commander scrambled and twisted, deflecting blows with his arm shields and lashing out like a serpent with his dual blades.

In a moment, a wall of rogues had helped to surround their embattled leader. Disengaging from his own front, Torin moved to check on Arn, who, after a slap from Bardik, was shaking his head. Though clearly dazed, the stout mercenary looked as if he would recover. The same could not be said of the fallen troll.

As Bardik helped Arn to his feet, Torin handed him his hammer. The mercenary considered it with a look of momentary confusion, then tightened his grip and brushed his comrades away.

"Fetch me a giant," he sneered.

Rejuvenated, those serving in the vanguard chopped and smashed and angled forward through the resisting hordes. Emboldened by the various feats of their commanders, rogues poured through in reckless waves, mad with a lust only battle could foster. They had nearly reached the Bastion. There they could spread out, putting the wall to their backs and turning their attentions to a single front. Depending on how well Chamaar and the East Wedge had held up after all this time, the day might yet be won.

But just as it appeared they had attained their first goal, Lorre's forces opened wide, revealing a bank of ballistae set in place before the giant wall. Bardik had to fall flat to avoid being riddled with missiles, while Torin found himself ducking behind Lancer's shield. From high atop the battlement, enemies rained down additional stones and arrows, into the face of the attackers. It was a full-scale barrage, and completely unexpected. Torin knew that if they did not react quickly, it would be the end of them.

As dozens fell, Torin yelled and gestured, ordering the men to fan out. While it meant abandoning their precious lines and dissolving further into chaotic melee, the only way to escape this new onslaught was to take cover among the enemy. Lancer and Bardik must have agreed, for they echoed his command swiftly among those pouring in behind them.

Within moments, the hailfire from above slowed to a trickle, and then ceased altogether. Hacking almost randomly now amid a milling throng, Torin clenched his jaw in bitter determination. It would take more than a few carefully concealed armaments to stop them.

But the surprise counter hadn't needed to stop them, only blunt their assault and shatter their formation. To that end, it had been a masterful success. Separated from his companions, alone amid a sea of thrashing bodies, he could do little more than raise his weapon in personal defense. And though scores had fallen before him, individual exploits were not going to win them this battle.

Casting about for Dyanne and Holly, he caught sight of Lancer, and began working his way toward the man. Perhaps if they could take out those who operated the ballistae, they might yet make their eastern rush along the Bastion, raising some form of cover from the archers stationed above.

Even as he considered this, another pack of giants came thundering into the fray, more than twice as many as he had encountered before. Torin blanched at the prospect, yet roared in to meet them. But before he could engage, the troop split, one half edging south of the other. Each group then planted itself in the shape of a ravelin, pointed westward, so as to further split and divide the attacking force.

The coordination of these movements struck Torin as rather extraordinary until he caught sight of the individual directing them. A human, given his size and shape, though his body was shrouded in black plate and his face masked by a sinister visor. Torin was unable to pause long enough to make a full study, but the more he saw of this man and the movements of those around him, the more convinced he became of his role in orchestrating the defense.

Lancer must have recognized this as well, for the tenacious wedge commander, bruised and sweating, was making a concerted charge in that direction. Acknowledging the threat, the man in black immediately sent forth a giant to dispatch him.

"Torin!" Lancer yelled, grimacing as his blade and the giant's clashed. "Lorre's general! Take him out!"

Torin whirled, disemboweling another foe in the process. Leaving the breathless Lancer to his private struggle, the young outlander did as ordered, taking aim at the enemy commander.

Orc and troll, human and giant—all rose to impede his progress, and all were cut down. With fresh focus and a divine strength undiminished by pain or fatigue, he barely broke stride. The Sword's power gushed through him, as if sensing that, yes, here was an undertaking that mattered, that might at last make a difference.

And yet, as he came upon his goal, a conflicting thought took root. Despite the efforts of those around him, his aim was not necessarily to eradicate this army, but to secure an audience with Lord Lorre. What better way than to hold the warlord's chief commander hostage? They were losing this battle—if they hadn't already. Perhaps taking the man alive would give them all something to bargain with.

These thoughts ripped through him in a flash of inspiration as his blade carved a flame-spitting arc through the general's sword. His opponent then lunged at him with a spiked shield, but Torin was so much swifter, hacking off the spike with a ready swipe while stepping aside and reaching out a foot to trip the man to the earth. A backswing swept through the midsection of a charging bodyguard, after which Torin turned to find the enemy commander on his back, clinging helplessly to but a shattered sword and a severed shield.

In desperation, the general tossed aside his blunted blade and tore a dagger from his boot. Torin smirked in warning as he placed the tip of the Sword against the other's chest.

In that same moment, in the corner of his eye, he saw Dyanne go down.

His reaction was instinctive. Like a whirlwind redirected by gusting winds, he abandoned the fallen general and bounded toward the woman. She had only slipped, it now appeared, and though sorely pressed, was holding her own—she and Holly—against a pair of snarling swordsmen twice their size. In a moment, the girls might have regained the upper hand. But Torin wasn't taking the chance. He ripped through both enemies with a single swipe, turning their torsos into bloody fountains before either could even turn at his approach.

He stood over them for a moment, heaving with fury, while beside him Holly pulled Dyanne to her feet.

"Our savior," Holly quipped.

Torin turned to look at them. Despite her wry comment, Holly nodded, as close to a show of gratitude, he suspected, as she might ever come. Their limbs were starting to droop, their faces streaked with dirt and blood. Even they were near the end of their strength.

His focus shifted back to the general, who had regained his feet with a swell of bodyguards closing ranks around him. Torin understood clearly the opposing leader's gestures, and, despite the din, could not mistake the ringing command: "Bring me that sword!"

All of a sudden, the ravelin-forming giants came at him in a stampede. Torin marked their approach, noting at the same time that Lancer had broken free and was mustering another charge at the general. The young king made a swift decision.

"Stay with Lancer," he begged his Nymph companions, then dove back into the fray.

Fearing that he might have already squandered their best opportunity to decapitate their enemy, he headed south, away from the Bastion. The best he could do now was to run a misdirection attack. Perhaps he could draw enough of the enemy to allow Lancer the chance to finish what he could not. He only hoped the commander would capture rather than kill the general, for the more he considered it, the more he believed that to be their best chance of escaping this bloodbath.

Many saw him coming and did their best to simply clear out of his way. Even so, he could not outrun the thundering giants. Sooner than he would have liked, he was forced to turn and confront them.

An image of Kylac Kronus flashed through his mind, the boy warrior who had seen him through in his quest to reclaim the Sword of Asahiel. Wielding a broadsword instead of those slender blades carried by the youth, and lacking the years of training, Torin could not begin to match the other's fighting style. But he did his best, lunging forward and back, ducking from side to side, letting the Sword take command. The giants quickly surrounded him, working together to bring him down. But the Sword tore through even the thickest and strongest of their weapons, leaving them with stubs and hafts. Some hurled these at him, only to strike one of their companions across the way. One opponent, overcome with frustration, dove at his back, thinking to simply tackle and smother him, and instead lost its own head. With the divine energy and awareness granted him by the Crimson Sword, Torin was as elusive as smoke, and would not be contained.

From beyond the circle of giant bodies, his situation must have appeared dire indeed. For he could hear Arn bellowing, rallying a pack of rogues to his defense. The boulder-shaped mercenary came rolling in a moment later, his war hammer crushing a giant's hip. Through the breach poured Bardik, slashing and skittering, and behind him, a dozen of his troops, howling as if possessed.

"Go!" Arn shouted to him, intercepting a giant's cudgel and knocking it aside with a growl. "Lancer needs you!"

Torin almost refused, fearing that Arn and his rescue party would be crushed in his stead. But Arn knew as well as he that if they did not secure the opposing general, they were all doomed.

Snarling, Torin cut his way free, leaving the rest to his companions. He trudged north once more, dripping sweat and the blood of his enemies, eviscerating any who came near. The ring of guards around the general was twice as thick as when he'd left it, but those in his direct path fell to either side like chaff. Within moments, he had cleared their ranks and come upon the center region, where a smattering of rogues fought a losing struggle, while Lancer and a handful of others were already on their knees, yielding to those holding blades to their throats.

Torin's blood boiled. He cast about for the general, but couldn't seem to find him. He turned toward the group holding Lancer when a booming voice stole his attention.

"Surrender or she dies!"

The outlander's head whipped around. There stood the general, flanked by towering giants, clenching Dyanne's hair in a gauntleted fist, raising her chin with his dagger in the other.

Torin did not pause to consider his options. The Sword fell from his hand with a sucking splash to the slushy earth, where its internal flames sprouted forth to lick the muck from its gleaming surface.

A trio of giants came forward. Torin continued to stare at Dyanne—at the hair matted against her forehead, at the fierce defiance flashing in her eyes. When the giants reached him, one of the brutish creatures claimed the Sword, while the other two pricked his rib cage with a blade from either side.

With a signal from the general, archers atop the Bastion began targeting anyone that approached the outside of his guard circle, friend and foe alike. The enemy commander would risk no further rushes on his position, Torin realized. Trapped in that protective pocket, Torin could do nothing but scowl as the giant delivered the Sword to its general, trading the weapon for Dyanne. As soon as she was handed over, the Nymph elbowed the creature in its stomach, but the giant didn't flinch, and the surrounding soldiers merely laughed.

For a moment, the general stood frozen, staring at the Sword, no doubt awed by the power pulsing at his fingertips.

"Offer them quarter," he commanded finally.

As criers and standard-bearers began to relay the order across the battlefield, the general surprised Torin by removing his helmet. A murmur of respect passed through the attending troops, several of whom dropped to one knee. Torin himself was further taken aback by the man's appearance—by chiseled, age-worn features; by white hair that clung with receding interest to a weathered brow; and, as the general came before him, by a pair of empty eyes the color of dull steel.

The general hefted the Sword, bathing Torin in its glow. "Your name."

Torin glared. The flanking giants pricked him deeper with their blades. "Torin," he grimaced.

The general's rugged face was an inscrutable mask. Amid the clangor of waning battle, the ocean roared.

"Mine is Lorre," the general replied finally. "And you, *Torin*, should have killed me when you had the chance."

CHAPTER THIRTY-FIVE

A LLION PEERED AHEAD through the tangled growth and saw only endless stretches of the same. Insects hummed, surrounding him in stinging swarms. The jungle was dark and sweaty, rife with foul scents and threatening shadows.

Just as he remembered it.

Even now, in the dead of winter, Vosges was a muggy place best left to the flies and spiders, serpents and bats, toads and leeches, and whatever other loathsome creatures made it their home. More than two hundred years ago, it had been recognized formally as one of the five realms of Pentania, set aside along with its native population as a kind of historical preserve by the now-defunct League of Man. Informally, the peoples of Pentania—then and now—had no use for either the savages or their uninhabitable lands.

That included Allion, who'd had more than his fill of the stinking marshlands when he had journeyed south previously with Torin and Kylac, in search of a Mookla'ayan guide who might lead them to the ruins of Thrak-Symbos— the fabled resting place of the last known Sword of Asahiel. He remembered having hoped to never again set foot within its borders. Alas, *never* had come far too soon.

It had taken them two days to reach the Kalmira Forest, which bordered the marshlands on their northern front, and another two and a half to slink their way through. Thus far, it had been a somber journey—for a variety of reasons. Some had to do with painful reminders: of Kylac, whose continued absence left a void not easily filled; of the dragonspawn, a scourge from which these lands had only scarcely begun to heal; and of the annihilation of Feverroot, the Lewellyn community that had for so long been Marisha's home. Others were a continuation of present concerns: the mysterious disappearance of the Parthan Legion's Second Division, for which they had come in search; the brooding presence of Darinor, who continued to exhibit signs of disapproval toward the slightest interactions between Allion and Marisha; and, of course, the constant threat of Illychar.

They had been lucky on the last count, at least. Though they had spied parties of Illysp-possessed creatures on more than one occasion, they had thus far been able to avoid attack. Most of those spotted had been elves—which stood to reason, since the Finlorians had been the prominent race upon these shores at the time of the Illysp's initial emergence. Once, however, Darinor had pointed out that of an ogre, a lumbering, misshapen monstrosity that looked more like a wandering hillock, lumpish and ragged and standing—even stooped—at over twelve feet. That sighting alone had been enough to remind Allion to keep his feet quiet and his head low.

If there was any good news, it was that the trail of the Second Division had been an easy one to follow. Never had a force this size traveled this far south into Mookla'ayan territory. While Partha had been trying for centuries to eradicate the cannibalistic natives, war to the north against the secessionist Menzoes had long prevented them from launching a full-scale onslaught. But that distraction no longer existed, and with most of the Illychar attacks having come from the Kalmira, Partha had been lured southward in full force. That much, King Galdric had admitted. What he hadn't told them was what Allion could now see for himself, that the Parthans' goal seemed to be to lay waste the entire region, if necessary, in order to drive forth their unwanted neighbors—the Mookla'ayans, along with the Illysp—once and for all.

Still, the terrain itself favored the smaller, scattered, more mobile parties in which the Mookla'ayans preferred to hunt and fight. The same held true for the Illychar. From what Allion could see, the grinding path of nearly ten thousand men had indeed cut a crude swath through the forest and beyond, but had come no closer to accomplishing that which hundreds of smaller incursions had failed to achieve in the past.

Fortunately, he and his companions had not come for conquest, only to find Chief General Corathel and persuade him to turn around and go home.

Then again, Corathel's position, at last report, had been leagues to the north of where Allion marched now, still within the confines of the Kalmira. He had hoped they would find the general and his troops in that vicinity and *not* have to set foot within the southern jungles. That hope, like so many others, had proven futile.

And so he carried on alongside the lovely Marisha and her overbearing father. Though focused on the land and its foreign signs, the hunter had lost count of the many stolen glances he and Marisha had shared. Each time she had caught his lingering gaze, he had felt a tiny shock, followed by a warm flush through his veins. He had tried to stop, but found that he was addicted to the feeling.

He was more impressed with her now than ever. He had always admired her grit and compassion—and having learned of her longtime possession of the Pendant of Asahiel, he understood better now how she had persevered, surviving the horrors of enslavement at the hands of the dragonspawn when no other members of her village had. Yet here she was, no longer blessed with the talisman's strength, pressing on as if she were. It seemed to Allion that once accustomed to such power, a person might be unable to function without it. But not Marisha. Though he could only imagine what it must have been like—losing her lungs, perhaps, or her still-beating heart—he was humbled by her fortitude.

A forbidding presence loomed suddenly over him—Darinor, come to interrupt his wayward thoughts, as if triggered to do so where Marisha was concerned. Too late, the hunter withdrew his furtive gaze from the woman beside him and braced for the inevitable reprimand.

"Keep moving," the Entient whispered instead. "But stay close. We've eyes upon us."

An inner chill washed away all feelings of warmth. In a heartbeat, Allion flashed back to that moment months ago, during his prior expedition, when Kylac had admitted to them that the A'awari, the more barbaric of the Mookla'ayan clans, were shadowing them. If he lived for a hundred years, the hunter would never forget how that encounter had ended. And he had no desire to relive it.

A cold sweat broke along his forehead. He pricked his ears, but could hear little over the snap and rustle of their movements through the brush—just the patter of afternoon rain streaming through the mesh of vines and branches and leaves. Before he even realized it, he was nervously thumbing the bowstring slung tight against his chest. His eyes swept back and forth, seeing nothing but the glistening greenery.

Somehow, he managed to edge forward despite his fears. If the danger was that great, he assured himself, Darinor would let them know.

Then, through the tapered edges of his vision, he detected movement, a subtle shifting of shadows that confirmed they were not alone. His stomach knotted. He had no way of knowing who tracked them, be it Illychar or Mookla'ayans—or both. But he feared that the longer they waited, the tighter the noose would become.

He hefted his quiver of arrows, hoping the simple movement might give his enemies pause. While it would be foolish to suggest an outright threat, he did not want to appear helpless. All of a sudden, Galdric's plan of sending the entire Third Division to rescue the Second seemed not such a bad idea.

He wished again that Kylac were here—he who knew the ways of the Mookla'ayans, and could speak with them if necessary. That the youth had not heard tell of the land's most recent plague and returned to his friends in their time of need troubled Allion more than he cared to admit. It caused him to wonder just where Kylac had gone, and what the lad might have gotten himself into.

"Halt and declare!"

Marisha gasped, while Allion did well not to jump from his skin. His hand was on the hilt of his hunting knife when he spied the speaker, camouflaged in a wrap of vines and leaves that made him all but invisible against the jungle backdrop. From there, the hunter's eyes narrowed upon the loaded crossbow the stranger carried, cranked and ready to fire.

A sharp rustle announced the emergence of a team of archers from the screen of foliage to either side, stepping forth with longbows drawn.

"Allion," the hunter managed before his voice croaked. "Of Alson. You are Parthan, are you not?"

"What business have you in these lands?" the leader demanded.

"We come from Atharvan, at the bidding of King Galdric himself."

"I see no messenger's sash."

Allion reached for a scroll tube hanging from his shoulder, then thought better of it as the surrounding bows flexed and tightened. "I carry a signed order," he said, his irritation lending him strength, "granting an audience with Chief General Corathel, legion commander. If you know where he is, we are to be taken to him, by writ of your king."

The leader seemed to consider, then snapped his fingers. One of the flanking bowmen came forward, and, though camouflaged like the rest of his team, was immediately recognizable as a Parthan soldier. Rear guardsmen, Allion realized, and relaxed considerably.

Still, he scowled as the other broke the leather thong by which the scroll tube was fastened and carried it to the squad commander. The corporal put away his crossbow in order to read the message. When he had finished, however, the man's frown only deepened. Again he signaled. The members of his unit put away their bows, only to draw their swords, filing down out of the brush to assume the stance and formation of a prisoner escort.

The corporal tucked away Galdric's note and produced again his crossbow. "If you are who you claim," he said, gesturing with the loaded weapon, "come with me."

BY THE TIME THEY REACHED the main encampment an hour later, Allion was furious. Furious at being herded south under armed guard like a common criminal. Furious at the corporal's refusal to permit them either questions or answers. When the hunter had tried, the corporal had threatened to have him bound and gagged. Ordinarily understanding of another's fears and suspicions, Allion was growing weary of such undeserved treatment—more for Marisha's sake than his own. He kept wondering why Darinor was tolerating it, almost wishing that the renegade Entient would summon one of his lightning streams and spare them this insult.

His best guess was that the petulant mystic was taking some form of grim pleasure in the hunter's frustrations.

The division was just now making camp at the edge of a bog, upon ground wet and spongy and alive with crawling things. The soldiers were everywhere—thousands of them—stowing their equipment carts, building fires, clearing the area of deadwood and brush in order to erect their tents and canvases for the night. To Allion, it didn't make sense. The men he passed, though wearing stern faces caked with mud, did not appear to be under duress. The division was well, it seemed. So why hadn't at least some of Galdric's messengers gotten through?

Their party continued on, drawing only minor attention from those it passed. They stopped occasionally to allow the corporal to confer with a sentry, then moved on. Their path skirted the slurping ground of the bog's rim. Beyond that, shrouded in mist, was a lake that reminded Allion of the one Torin had swum across, back when his friend went by the name of Jarom— just one in a series of challenges that seemed now a lifetime removed.

Eventually, they came upon the tent the corporal had been seeking—that of a high-ranking officer, judging by the number of guardsmen posted out front. The corporal moved ahead to deliver his hushed report, handing over Allion's message and gesturing back at the hunter and his companions. Leaving them to the guardsmen, the corporal and his soldiers marched away without a word of apology.

Allion, meanwhile, was ushered along with Marisha and Darinor inside the tent, where they were allowed to seat themselves under the watchful eye of a pair of sentinels. Before leaving, the commander of the guard unit encouraged them to relax. The general, he said, would be with them presently.

Though the hunter tried, he could coax not a word from the stone-faced sentinels. When he looked to Darinor for help, he found the Entient resting comfortably, eyes closed.

Another hour had passed before they next received visitors. Even then, it was not quite whom Allion had expected. For the trio who entered was led not by the legion commander, Chief General Corathel, but by the division commander, Lieutenant General Jasyn.

Allion was on his feet the moment they passed through the tent flap, and though this caused the sentinels to raise their crossbows, Jasyn motioned quickly for them to be put away.

"Allion, Marisha," the general said, turning back to his guests. "What a pleasant surprise."

He was clutching the note from Galdric, Allion noticed, shifting it to his left hand in order to extend the other in proper greeting.

Allion returned the gesture, and his frustration melted away. The Second General was not a large man, but his grip was fierce and strong. More than that, he exuded the most welcoming demeanor one could imagine. With but an armclasp and his crooked smile, he made it seem as though he were greeting his dearest friend in all the world. He might have been a jester as easily as a soldier, so filled was he with an irrepressible love of life.

When finished with Allion, he moved to accept Marisha's embrace.

"Now that's what I call a welcome," he said suggestively.

Marisha laughed and released his armored, mud-spattered frame. "You look well."

"As do you," Jasyn said, eyeing them over again. His dark hair was tousled, his cheeks lightly freckled, lending him a boyish charm. That look faded somewhat when he regarded the rising Darinor.

"You are General Corathel?" the Entient asked in his resonating voice.

"Jasyn," the other corrected, "lieutenant general, Second Division." He glanced down at the parchment rolled up in his left fist. "You must be Darinor."

"Where is Corathel?" the Entient asked, looking past the aides and sentinels and toward the tent flap.

Jasyn's features tightened—a little too quickly, Allion thought. "The chief general is not with us, at the moment. But if you will allow me, I'm certain I can be of some assistance to you in his stead."

Darinor tucked his chin into his beard, making what sounded like a low grumble, but kept his tongue to himself.

"You must forgive the rough treatment," Jasyn apologized, turning back to Marisha and then Allion. "We have learned the hard way that given the nature of our enemy, our trust cannot be afforded lightly."

His gaze shifted again to Darinor, who nodded. "The Illysp infest your ranks."

"More than once, our dead have risen against us," Jasyn confirmed, then seemed to realize the pall he had cast upon their proceedings. "But we need not talk of such things just now. Soldier," he said, speaking over his shoulder to one of his attendants, "bring supper, for myself and for my friends." Then to Allion, "Tell me instead, what brings you here?"

"The issues are one and the same, I'm afraid," Allion replied, his gaze trailing after the departing attendant.

"I see," Jasyn said, and seemed to lose a good measure of his enthusiasm toward this reunion. "In that case, if you would pardon me for but a moment?"

The general signaled to his remaining attendant, who stepped forward to unbuckle a spiked pauldron covering the general's left shoulder—an injury, Allion recalled, suffered in the Battle of Kraagen Keep. Without a trace of self-consciousness, Jasyn allowed the attendant to remove also his armored leather jerkin and the shirt beneath, revealing the thick wrap of bandages helping to keep that shoulder in its proper position, and more scars than Allion could count. Once those bandages had been removed, Jasyn flexed and stretched muscles and joints while the assisting soldier brought forth a basin of water and, with a soiled rag, began helping the general to wash himself down.

About halfway through this process, the general motioned to Allion to begin his account. The hunter obeyed, keeping silent his suspicion that Jasyn had been using this time for something more than making himself comfortable. Cordial reception aside, the general was contemplating matters of his own, as if trying to decide what he could—or could not—share with his unexpected guests.

Allion tried not to be troubled by these suspicions as he related the story of his visit to Atharvan and the concerns of King Galdric over the lack of communications from the legion's foremost division. When the lieutenant general did not respond right away, he went on to divulge their intent to speak with Corathel and persuade him to abandon this course for that which Darinor insisted they must take in order that all might survive this unnatural plague.

Once he had concluded, Jasyn considered them carefully—Darinor in particular—before tendering a reply.

"We have in fact been receiving messages from His Majesty, King Galdric," the general confessed, "the last not two days ago."

"And his order to withdraw?" Darinor asked pointedly.

Jasyn stared at the other, his eyes piercing. "Yes."

"Then why haven't you done so?" the Entient demanded.

"On my order," the commander declared, suddenly combative, "we've ignored these summonses and offered no response."

"Why would you do that?" Marisha asked. Unlike her father's, her voice held no accusation, merely gentle concern and a desire to understand.

Jasyn blew out a long, slow breath. He glared briefly at Darinor before turning back to Marisha. "We entered the Kalmira a little more than two weeks ago. At that point, General Corathel began leading an expeditionary force with which to chase down scattered groups of Illychar. A week later, they failed to return from one of their forays. Evidence suggests they were captured by the jungle savages."

Allion gulped. He had known that the Mookla'ayans would come into play here eventually. Though he'd been befriended by one of their kind, in many ways, he still feared them worse than he did the Illychar. Perhaps because he knew that death at their hands promised to be slower—and far more painful—than at the hands of some raving ogre or goblin.

"The division has continued to push southward ever since," Jasyn added, "while I myself have been spearheading a forward detachment in pursuit of the chief general, following the trail of him and his men."

"So why not report this to Galdric?" Allion asked. "Why leave him to guess as to the fate of an entire division?"

Jasyn shook his head. "His Majesty will not permit one man's disappearance to serve as an excuse not to return—not even Corathel's. He has replaced chief generals before; he will not hesitate to do so again." The commander leaned forward, eyes glittering in the light of candles used to illuminate the interior of the tent. "But I refuse to leave the man in the hands of those savages, to see him devoured like some wild animal. I will see him freed, or else slain with dignity—by my own hand, if necessary."

Allion wasn't sure whether to admire the commander for his loyalty, or be repulsed by the man's obvious hatred of the Mookla'ayan people—a feeling he knew to be born mostly of fear and misunderstanding. In this case, the hunter thought, both were understandable.

Darinor, however, did not seem to appreciate—or did not care about—the other's dilemma. "Are you not sworn to obey your king?" he challenged.

"I am not some lowly conscript," Jasyn argued. "As a lieutenant general, I am entitled—by oath—to use personal judgment where it concerns the lives of those I lead. I have consulted my battalion and company commanders, and they in turn have consulted their troops. All agree. Chief General Corathel will not be left behind."

Allion decided then to forgive the man his prejudices, and view this instead as an act of supreme devotion. After all, were the chief general to be abandoned, Jasyn himself might be next in line for the man's position. Yet here he was, risking his life and his professional future by shunning the orders of his supreme commander and electing instead to do what he could to save a personal friend. That the entire division had voted to support him in this spoke volumes as to *their* respect and admiration for the missing chief general. Given his own experience in fighting for the man, Allion was not about to suggest that they had made the wrong choice.

"So we find and rescue Corathel first," the hunter allowed, ignoring Darinor's heated stare. "How long can that take?"

Jasyn was quiet while seeming to take measure of Allion's sincerity. "Longer than I had hoped. The division moves slower every day as this cursed jungle gives way to wretched swampland. But sending smaller, advance patrols too far out from the main force makes them easy targets for the more nimble savages—and the Illychar skulking throughout this region. My own detachment numbers more than a hundred, and returns every night to the security of the division body. Each day we set out ahead, hoping to find and return Corathel to us. Each day we have failed."

Marisha reached out to the commander, but before she could say something that might comfort him, he spoke again through gritted teeth.

"But I swear to you this: We will press on for as long as it takes, forcing our enemy into the sea, if necessary, before tucking tail and turning for home."

Allion looked at Marisha, seeing in her ardent expression that she had already sided with the lieutenant general. He glanced then at Darinor, who fumed, but seemed to understand that in this situation, there wasn't much he could do. If ten thousand soldiers were willing to defy their own king, they sure as blazes weren't going to heed the wishes of a mad stranger.

"Your determination is well and good," Allion remarked finally. "Except that by the time we reach the ocean, it may be too late to save Corathel."

"What would you have us do?" Jasyn asked.

Allion didn't know. They might try to venture on ahead—just he and Marisha and Darinor—as they had in coming this far. But he wasn't sure the Entient would go for it, or that it even resembled a good idea. For up until now, they had been trying only to avoid their many enemies. In this instance, the goal would be to confront them.

"How many are we up against?" the hunter asked.

"It's difficult to tell. Our trackers' best guess is that the party we follow numbers more than forty. If they are making any attempt to hide their numbers, it might be twice that."

Allion's stomach plummeted. "Are they A'awari, or Powaii?"

The Second General's brow furrowed.

"Clan names," Allion explained. "To which do these belong?"

Jasyn spat. "Does it make any difference?"

Allion could only hope that it did. Based on his limited experience, they had a far better chance of bartering with the more peaceful Powaii than with the truly savage A'awari.

"Maybe not," he said. "But I am known to the chieftain of the Powaii clan."

The Second General raised an eyebrow, suggesting that this was a part of Allion's story he hadn't heard before—and that he did not necessarily approve of. "I couldn't tell you," he said finally, shaking his head. "But perhaps you can tell for yourself. For we are holding one of their party captive."

Allion nearly leapt from his seat. "A Mookla'ayan? Why didn't you say so?"

Just then, the missing attendant reappeared at the tent entrance, with a line of soldiers bearing trays of food. Jasyn considered the savory platters, but had taken note of the hunter's anxious stance. Grudgingly, he rose to his feet, signaling for his other aide to fetch him a fresh shirt.

"Perhaps because I did not want to spoil my supper," he muttered.

CHAPTER THIRTY-SIX

Upon the crest of an endlessly shifting wave, Torin rolled through the undulating darkness. Reality had abandoned him, leaving him adrift within a sea of images—haunting vestiges of a life he had once known. Faces swam before him, of allies, enemies, and those who would ask of him the impossible. But he could no longer seem to separate past from present, nor friend from foe.

A shrill grating echoed in his ears. All at once, the clouds of confusion parted, and though the darkness remained, his vision drew sharply into focus. Even so, it took him a moment to recognize where he was, and to recall how he had arrived there. His understanding did nothing to ease his concerns.

He was staring at the vague outline of an ironwood door, set securely in a stone wall. At the top was a tiny viewing window filled with rusted metal bars. Beyond lay a long, dark tunnel smelling of mold and brine. Though underground, he felt at times like he could still hear the ocean's roar.

The light of a lantern bobbed nearer, stinging in its brightness as it flooded the corridor and spilled through the barred opening in his prison door. Torin shied away, turning his gaze to the darkened corner where a chamber bucket lay. At the far end of the tunnel, the sharp squeal that had awakened him sounded again as the outer door to these dungeons slammed shut on rusted hinges.

Heavy footsteps scraped across the rough stone—sandaled and thick-bodied. He'd known few other sounds in this dank emptiness, and so recognized this one immediately.

Trolls.

One of them thrust its flat, shoulder-sunken face into view through the window bars, eclipsing much of the light. Torin glanced up out of the corner of one eye as its own beady orbs flicked about in study. A moment later, an iron locking bar slid free, and the door pushed open.

A pair of the brutes entered. They might have been the same ones that had checked on him before, but Torin couldn't tell for certain. One hefted its knotted club while the other inspected the cuffs by which he was chained to the back wall of the cell. When satisfied that he had done nothing to compromise the integrity of his shackles, the trolls filed out and ushered the third member of their party forward.

It was the girl, Saena.

She had first come to him shortly after he'd been led down here, deep within the city, following the fight for Neak-Thur. While acclimating himself to the darkness and wondering why all his battles seemed to end with him in irons, Torin had been surprised by her smiling introduction. As his prison attendant, she had announced, it would be both her duty and pleasure to see to his needs. If there was anything he required, so long as it was within her limited power to grant, he need but ask.

Torin hadn't known what to make of her then, and wasn't sure what to make of her now. She seemed far too cheerful to be trusted, given the situation. Friendly though she appeared, he wasn't going to fall victim to her charms.

And yet, for three days now, she had been his only human contact. Though he continued to anticipate an interrogation of some sort at the hands of Lord Lorre, thus far he had been left waiting. That isolation was beginning to exact its toll. Day by day, hour by hour, his moments of madness grew a shade deeper and lingered a little longer. In that regard, Saena had become a life-giving sun, visiting him regularly, bringing food and conversation—tending to his comforts, such as they were. It was quickly getting to be that he depended upon her more than he might care to admit.

"Hungry?" she asked, hefting her tray of meat and potatoes, bread and fruit.

"Any word of my friends?" Torin asked in turn, sidestepping as always even the most innocent of her questions.

Saena set the tray down upon the edge of the sleeping pallet on which he sat. She was near enough that he might have lashed out and caught her up in his chains, then threatened to strangle her unless her troll escort set him free. But would the impassive brutes even care? Would Lorre? Undoubtedly, the overlord's halls were filled with slave girls. One would not be missed. More than that, Torin lacked the will to harm the only companion he had—least of all a young woman who had treated him with such kindness. In all likelihood, Lorre knew this, and had selected her for just that reason.

"The girls are well," Saena assured him, having learned by now that it was Dyanne and Holly for whom he was most concerned. "I believe His Lordship means to decide what will become of you before he determines the fate of any of the others who attacked him."

Torin didn't know if this was good news or bad. He wanted to remind her that it was Lorre who had invaded Neak-Thur first. Instead, he glared at the open cell door, beyond which the trolls had taken post.

"They're not so bad," Saena said, "once you get used to the smell."

Torin scowled at her perpetual smile. No matter how surly his disposition, he could not seem to shake her unflappable good cheer. "I don't suppose you could dim that light," he grumbled.

The smile remained as she dropped lightly to the floor, seating herself cross-legged and setting the lantern behind her back. "How's that?"

"Better," Torin admitted, chewing already on a mouthful of food. He was no longer surprised by how warm his meals were, or how tasteful.

"Good," she said, practically beaming.

Torin examined her with a suspicious eye in the diminished light of the lantern's halo. Under better circumstances, he might have found her attractive, with reddish cheeks full and round, eyes bright and inquisitive, and a billowing fountain of long, black curls. Drab leather attire nevertheless revealed her womanly curves, though never did he get the feeling that she was trying to draw that kind of attention. In fact, she seemed not to even realize how pretty she really was.

She was his age, he had decided, or near enough to it. He wouldn't bring himself to ask, to show the slightest interest that might spark a friendship. Maddeningly enough, this, too, did not seem to bother her. A grunt here or there was usually enough to keep her talking throughout his entire meal, which generally determined the length of her stay.

"How are you feeling today?" she asked.

Torin's frown deepened. "How do you think?"

Saena ignored his barbed tone. "Those melons there, they came all the way from Billak Mar."

Billak Mar. The northern city nearest her home region. It was her favorite topic. With Torin's reluctance to contribute to their one-sided discussions, Saena had taken it upon herself to share with him longing memories of the fields and orchards to which she'd been born, the friends she had left behind, and her fear that she might never again see either. Lorre's intent was to press southward until all of Wylddeor—along with its plentiful natural resources— was under his control. Of that there was no secret. But how long it might take to subdue the lawless rogues that roamed this territory was anyone's guess.

"Delicious," Torin mumbled.

Saena's smile broadened with delight. He rarely made such concessions. But while he tried to hide it, he did feel sympathy for this girl whose life had been uprooted, become a pawn in the games of a tyrannical overlord and his dreams of conquest. She didn't speak of Lorre that way; she didn't speak of him much at all. Probably because she dared not. Mostly she shared childhood tales of happiness and whimsy—a shield, Torin supposed, against the realities of her life.

For a moment, she seemed to be waiting, as if believing she had cracked his shell and expecting him to say something more. When he didn't, she started in on one of her stories, this one having to do with the time she'd caught a cousin stealing melons from her father's patch in a misguided effort to win first prize at the local fair for the region's best-tasting jam.

But halfway through the meaningless reverie, while he sat there listening to the clank of his shackles as he ate, Torin decided that he could take no more of her unabashedly pleasant humor.

"How can you be so merry?" he growled, slapping his spoon against his plate and drawing a momentary look of interest from his troll guards.

"I'm alive, aren't I?"

"You're a slave," Torin said. "That isn't living."

Saena appeared confused. "I'm not a slave."

Torin hesitated. "You're not? But I thought—"

"My father was conscripted as a sergeant in His Lordship's army. Had I let him go alone, I might never have seen him again. So I asked for a position as well, and His Lordship granted my request."

"Allowing you to haul food and empty chamber buckets," Torin muttered dryly.

Saena shrugged. "Among other things. Better that than being shipped off to live with my uncle in Kasseri. Besides, this way, I get to meet interesting people like you."

Interesting? Torin coughed on a piece of bread. "You know nothing about me," he reminded her.

"I know more than you think," she said, and for just a moment her smile became mischievous.

Torin washed the food from his mouth with a swig of juice. "Like what?"

"I know that you do not belong here, fighting alongside rogues. I know that you are not just an outlander, but a king. Torin of Alson, the young man who braved the ruins of an ancient city to reclaim the legendary Sword of Asahiel. How's that?"

Torin simply stared, speechless. By the time he thought to deny her claim, it was too late.

"We of Lorrehaim are not as uncivilized as those you may have encountered in Wylddeor," she continued, flashing again that damnable smile. "Your story is well known—though I must admit, difficult to believe. I wasn't sure that I did, until I heard what had taken place on the battlefield. By that account, at least some of what I've heard about you must be true."

Again she gave him the chance to acknowledge or reject her declarations. Unsure which—if either—might benefit him, Torin kept to his silence.

"What remains unclear is what you would be doing here, taking part in a civil war so far from your own home."

Torin cleared his throat. He was going to have to say something, he realized. There was no point in trying to make himself invisible if so much about him was already known—or at least suspected. Better to divulge the truth before potentially disastrous assumptions were made.

Still, he wasn't sure what he could say that might paint him in a more favorable light. "I did not come to take part in any war."

"The soldiers say you had His Lordship himself at the tip of your blade. Is that not so?"

Torin tensed. All of a sudden, Saena seemed to him far more than an innocent servant girl. Then again, perhaps he could use that to his advantage, pleading his case to one who might be more willing than Lorre to hear him out.

But before he could prepare a response, Saena continued.

"They say you could have killed him," she said, "but stayed your hand. Why is that?"

"I didn't know who he was," Torin admitted.

"And had you known?"

"It would not have affected my decision. As I said, I did not come here to slay the man."

"Then what *did* you come here for?"

Torin took a deep breath. "I came here to speak with him."

Saena laughed. "Strange way to seek an audience."

"I was given to believe that should I knock on his front door, I might end up in irons." He hefted his manacles.

"Fine job you did avoiding that fate," she replied with a smirk.

Torin glowered. He was quickly beginning to wish that he hadn't opened up to her.

"I'm sorry," she said. "I only thought to make you smile. Your face looks as though it could use one."

Torin shook his head and scraped up another mouthful. What cause did she think he might have to smile?

"Tell me," she begged, leaning forward over her crossed legs. "What did you mean to speak with him about?"

Torin made her wait while he finished his food, though he had already decided to grant her request. "I came to speak with him about elves."

"Elves?"

"The Finlorians, specifically. I was told that if they still exist, Lorre might know where they are."

"Why would His Lordship know anything about elves?"

"Word is he has a fondness for butchery, especially when it comes to the older races—that he slaughters those who refuse to serve him." He nodded toward the troll sentries in emphasis. "Perhaps it is the same with the elves."

Saena's features tightened defensively. "What you've heard is only partly true. From what I've seen, His Lordship does not slaughter for slaughter's sake, but to protect his subjects from the often bestial urges of these animal races."

"A matter of perspective, perhaps," Torin allowed. "To be honest, I'm in no position to judge. Whichever, I'm at the end of my trail. If Lorre knows nothing of the Finlorians, then it may be true that no one does."

"And why must you find these Finlorians?"

"Because it would seem that in desecrating their city, I unearthed an evil best left buried—an evil that only they may vanquish."

He did not know that he could say it any plainer than that. Nor, he hoped, would he have to try. He stared at the woman, trying to impress upon her his shame and his need, hoping that she would accept the truth as he understood it.

By the look on her face, it seemed to be working. Her smile had been replaced by a thoughtful frown. "You make it sound so dire," she remarked, trying out a chuckle.

Torin continued to stare until her attempt at merriment had faded.

"In that case, I wish you luck. Rest assured, His Lordship will wish to speak with you about this and other matters." She got to her feet, taking from him the empty food tray. "I'll see you at supper," she promised, before snatching up her lantern and exiting through the doorway.

Torin watched her go, his only connection to the outside world, until the cell door was shut and the locking bar thrown into place. He tried to catch sight of her again through the window, but the bodies of the trolls—blocky and hunchbacked to the point of near headlessness—obscured her from view.

With her went the light and his meager hopes, and when the outer door had closed, he was left with nothing.

Almost nothing, he amended silently. He felt the Pendant, hanging from its chain, warm against his chest. Lorre's guards had been careless when stripping him of his weapons, and had not bothered to take it. Even so, he'd found the talisman to be of little solace, for he failed to see in it any short-term value. At best, it was a ward against his festering despair.

And a poor one at that. For the Stone could not guard against his own dark thoughts. Though he might try to deny it, this scene remained eerily similar to when he had wallowed in the Demon Queen's dungeons at Kraagen Keep. He was Lorre's prisoner and plaything, spared for reasons known only to the warlord. And without Kylac Kronus to spring him from this cell, his destiny seemed now in another's hands.

The sudden darkness blinded him. Since it made no difference, Torin closed his eyes, wondering how long he had before madness set in.

SAENA NEVER RETURNED WITH SUPPER. When next the trolls came for him, they came alone. With scarcely a grunt, they removed his shackles and seized him on either side by the meat of his arms, squeezing in unmistakable warning.

They hauled him from his cell and out from the dungeons, following a twisted line of halls and corridors. Torches lit the way, along with the occasional window through which the smothered light of moon and stars shone. Torin blinked and squinted while struggling to keep his bearings. From outside, he heard clearly the relentless thunder of rain.

For some time, they proceeded upward through the keep, climbing stairwells that traced the rise of the mountain ground. Despite his efforts, Torin was soon lost. Were he to manage to break loose, he still would not know which way to turn in order to find his freedom. Then again, he had no intention of leaving without first securing the Sword and his friends, making flight at this juncture a poor choice.

Doorways marched past with military precision, evenly spaced on either side of a featureless limestone corridor. When that passage intersected another, the trolls turned him to the left, through an empty doorway, and into the chamber beyond.

An audience hall, Torin decided, dominated by rows of benches facing a platform at the front of the room to his right. Probably used for the briefing of officers, since the wall above that platform was all but concealed behind scrolls and easels that held maps and military diagrams. The side wall straight ahead was lined with rain-streaked windows through which a training yard was visible, framed in the distance by another wing of the keep. At the back of the room where he had entered, to his left, sat a great table in front of a bank of cupboards built into the wall.

Like the rest of what Torin had seen of the keep, all was stark and unembellished, with an eye toward function and little else. The ceiling was high and flat, the floor tiles cracked and scraped and in need of polishing. Despite several brightly burning torches, the place had a martial feel to it, cold and rigid and thoroughly uninviting.

His troll escorts released him beside the table at the back of the room. They turned then, and lumbered from view.

Torin was momentarily at a loss. The trolls did not close the door behind them. Nor did they take up guard posts—he could still hear the reverberations of their heavy departure. Had they set him free? It seemed a strange place to do so. More than likely, someone was watching, awaiting his reaction.

So he waited in turn, savoring the non-darkness. He searched the chamber again, but saw no one and no place anyone might hide. As his gaze circled around to the entryway, it snagged upon a spiked club mounted above the lintel. The weapon was old and weathered, with a leather-wrapped haft and a dark stain of what was undoubtedly blood. An odd ornament, given the complete lack of decoration elsewhere throughout the room.

"That once belonged to an orc chieftain," said a crisp voice, and Torin whirled. Striding toward him from the front of the chamber, from a doorway hidden by a rack of giant maps, was Lord Lorre. "I find it a useful reminder that helps to keep their officers in line."

Torin held still as the overlord approached. Suddenly, the temperature in the room seemed to drop, and a burrowing dread writhed in the pit of his stomach. His feeling was that he was not worthy of this man's presence, a feeling brought on by the warlord's austere bearing.

"An unsightly trophy," Torin observed, refusing to be intimidated. "I can only imagine those that adorn your own walls back home."

Lorre stopped less than a pace away, staring down at him with a stern visage. The man seemed taller indoors, perhaps because he was no longer surrounded by giants. He was dressed in a black tunic and breeches, with a ruggedly athletic build and an air both imperial and indignant. By all appearances, he was unarmed.

"This *is* my home," the warlord said. "And for the time being, my new seat of power. Is that something you wish to challenge?"

Torin considered the man's face—its high, rigid cheekbones and pale, leathery skin, wrinkled with age and scarred with the wounds of battles untold. But it was the eyes that fascinated him, those hollow, steel-colored orbs that bored into Torin and left him feeling empty within.

Finally, he shook his head. "I only want to know what you intend to do with my friends."

"If by friends you mean that lawless rabble with which you assaulted this city, rest assured, they will be granted the same choice afforded all those who oppose me."

Torin frowned. "Which is?"

"To take up their arms in my service, or not at all."

"Then you would make them into slaves."

Lorre crossed his arms in front of his chest. "You have no doubt heard much about me, most of it ill-favored, else you would not have joined these rogues in their attack."

"You lead monsters in the slaughter of men," Torin accused.

"I find that the two are often inseparable, don't you? The fact remains, you are not of this land, and its struggles are not your concern. My interrogator tells me that you have come in search of something. Is this not so?"

Interrogator? Saena, Torin realized. Despite his earlier suspicions concerning the girl, the extent of her role surprised him.

"Skilled, is she not?" Lorre teased. "And with a memory like a spider's web. I know every word you have spoken to her. What I want to know now is which were truth, and which were lies."

The man stepped closer, bending near with those soulless eyes and his cropped white hair. His breath was like a mead hall hearth in need of sweeping, and Torin had to fight the urge to recoil.

"All I told her is true," Torin said. "If I am not allowed to find the Finlorians, a dark force will claim my lands, and may soon spread to yours."

Lorre waved the possibility aside. "I fear not whatever ghosts you unearthed in those elven tombs. But I, too, have interest in their descendants, they of the once-mighty Finlorian Empire."

"And why is that?"

"Because, long ago, they stole something from me, and if possible, I would have it back."

The glass-filled windows rattled. Outside, the rain fell in horizontal sheets, bent sideways by a strafing wind. Torin bit back his next retort, sensing it better to hear the man out.

"Few know what I am about to tell you. I was once married to one, you see—a Finlorian. In our selfishness, we gave birth to a daughter. A cruelty, I now understand, for nowhere were we accepted, among my wife's people, or mine."

Torin remained silent, stunned by what he was hearing. At the same time, his mind raced, trying to figure out what sort of game Lorre might be playing.

"We made our home as best we could," the warlord continued, "traveling from place to place. But there was no escaping man's intolerance, which finally took from me my wife."

Torin saw already where this was headed, and understood now the emptiness in the warlord's eyes. It was not pain, exactly, for that had long ago been buried beneath an avalanche of hate and vengeance. Feelings such as fear and compassion and remorse had since been stripped away. All that remained was a warrior's defiance, the need to fight because fighting was all he knew.

"I was not born a warrior," Lorre stated in the same clipped and measured tones. "But I became one to defend my daughter from a similar fate. My first recruits were fellow outcasts, those branded for one reason or another as undesirable to society. By virtue of our creed, we began to attract the scattered dregs of the older races, who knew better than most what it meant to suffer man's bigotry. Together, we began to fight back against any who would deny us our basic freedoms."

"By denying the freedoms of others."

"By securing for my daughter and my followers a region of our own, free from prejudice and ridicule, with strength enough to deter any who might take it from us."

Torin saw an opening for continued debate, but decided to ignore it. "And the Finlorians?"

The warlord's face darkened. "The Finlorians, who could have protected my wife but chose instead to view her marriage to me as an abomination, had the audacity to come to me with a proposal for peace. At the time, I had no intention of invading their domain or any other. But they feared the very possibility. For the wild region we had settled continued to grow, simply because more and more came to us, seeking to join our community. Up until then, we had shown no hostility beyond that required to defend ourselves. But our neighbors saw only our swelling ranks, and so began approaching us with their various entreaties. War did not begin until the Finlorians betrayed us."

"And what great treasure did they steal from you?" Torin asked flippantly.

Lorre growled. "My daughter."

Torin flinched in spite of himself. A backward step put him up against the edge of the table.

"For all my carefully laid defenses, I could not shield her from her own confusion, that of a young woman torn between two cultures. One of the Finlorian emissaries, a prince, became enamored with her, and before I knew it, had used his sorcerous wiles to seduce her, then whisk her away under my very nose. What's more, she was with child at the time, the seed of her husband, a human among our camp."

The warlord leaned back, recrossing his arms, which had slipped out to form fists on either side.

"So began my conquest, to rescue my daughter and to punish the Finlorians for their treachery. Instead of giving her up, or even fighting to save their lands, they elected to run and hide, sheltering her and the traitorous prince in a way refused my wife and me."

"You were unable to find them?" Torin asked, taking care this time to sound appropriately sympathetic.

"My hunt lasted only so long. As soon as my armies moved against the Finlorians, the human kingdoms of the north—fearing that they were next—moved against me. Foolishly so, for my anger at that time was such that I was desperate to exact vengeance upon someone—anyone—for what had befallen me. Unable to engage the Finlorians, I granted the humans their war. For I'd come to understand that those who practice cruelty know no other language. To ensure peace, I first had to establish a universal order—a cause to which I chose to dedicate my life. Since then, I have tamed or killed any who stood against me, be they orc or elf, dwarf or troll, man or giant—or something in between."

Torin shook his head. It should not have surprised him that even one as ruthless as Lorre should have his reasons. Nevertheless, he could not seem to reconcile the man's motives with the results. "It seems to me you've become the very thing you are so impassioned against."

"Oh? And what is that?"

"One who would bend the wills of others to his own," Torin answered, choosing his words carefully.

"A tyrant."

Torin clamped down on a useless denial.

"Call it what you will. I care not what you think of me. You see me as a leader of monsters. I say that I harbor not the blind prejudices by which men have driven such mighty creatures as the giant from your own land. You see them as slaves. I say that they follow me because I offer them conquest, the ultimate freedom from subjugation, a place in this world they would not otherwise have."

The man's demeanor was so proud and commanding, his words so brisk and authoritative, that Torin saw little room to argue. "And what would you have of me?"

Lorre regarded him silently for a moment, then stepped back and clapped his hands twice. "Only that you complete the quest you came here to fulfill, that you find the missing Finlorians. When you do, you will lead me to them."

A recollection flashed through Torin's mind—a phrase spoken by the witch Necanicum with regard to Lorre and his quest. Something to do with *him* leading the overlord, rather than the overlord leading him. He had only a moment to dwell on it, however, before a giant emerged from the same hidden doorway through which the warlord had entered. The beast strode forward, its shaggy head brushing the chamber's ceiling, cradling within its massive hands the Crimson Sword.

When the giant reached them, it offered the talisman to Lorre with bowed head. The warlord took it, studied it briefly, then extended it to Torin hilt first.

Torin resisted his urge to snatch it from the man's grasp. "You're returning this to me?"

"It is an elven talisman, is it not? Were it not the key to your quest, you would not have brought it."

Torin scowled. While he was loath to admit it, the warlord was right. He accepted the weapon, only briefly entertaining the idea of forcing Lorre to his knees. "With this, you would be the most powerful man in Yawacor."

"I am that already," the warlord said dismissively. He gestured to his giant, which took its leave, ducking through the nearest exit.

Torin continued to frown as he considered the blade. The weapon itself was genuine; he wasn't sure he could say the same for Lorre's purpose. "I've been told you are without mercy."

"Good. Nor should you mistake this as such. It so happens I want something that I believe only you might provide."

"And what makes you think I will find them where you could not?"

"For nearly two decades," Lorre explained, "I've had bounty hunters continue the search. But none of *them* ever recovered a lost Sword of Asahiel. Perhaps that talisman you wield, along with your tale of strife, will be enough to lure the Finlorians from their hole."

Torin forced himself to meet the man's gaze. "I've come to enlist their aid, not bring them war."

Lorre shook his head in resignation. Not even when on his back on the battlefield, pinned by the tip of the Sword, had the man exuded such a defeated air. "It has been nineteen years. It is likely too much to hope that my daughter or grandchild could be returned to me. Nor would I force it upon them. But I would know whether they are safe and content. I would know that if they live still among the elves, they do so of their own choice, and not under some faerie enchantment. That is all I ask."

Torin failed to hide his skepticism. "You said that you would have back what they stole from you."

"If held against their will, then yes, I would stop at nothing to set them free. Nor would you, I think, were we speaking of those most precious to you." The warlord paused, his steel eyes glinting in the firelight, and somehow Torin knew he was speaking of Dyanne. "Either way, I will not ask that you make that determination, nor assist in any way their rescue, should it come to that. Those I send with you will be assigned that task."

Torin snickered. "I'd wager that a brigade of trolls or giants wearing your insignia would hardly increase my chances of being welcomed into a Finlorian village."

"You'll need a guide, one who can lead you along their former trails, near enough for you to sniff out their current haunts. That is why you came to me, is it not?"

It was, and Torin saw no cause to deny it. "My companions go with me," he said instead.

Lorre's brows slanted sharply inward. "You are in a poor position to make demands."

Maybe so, Torin thought. Then again, he still had the Pendant. And as long as he—or Lorre—held on to it, Darinor might eventually find him. "Be that as it may, those are my terms. My companions join me, or I go nowhere."

"You mean the girls," Lorre said, and a cruel smile tugged at the corner of his mouth.

"And the rest go free, General Chamaar and his men."

"The rest will be used to bolster my ranks, taking the place of those they killed."

"The commanders, at least—"

"Will be treated fairly. Those who please me most will be granted their choice of rank and region."

Torin had not finished his protest, but the warlord raised a hand to stop him.

"Two of your companions shall accompany you, and you shall take also two of mine. A just offer. If you wish to barter further, then bring me back something more to barter with."

Torin glowered. As much as he hated the thought of leaving behind Chamaar, Arn, Lancer, Bardik, and whichever other of his known comrades had survived, he understood well enough the precarious ground he stood upon. That Lorre would grant him both the Sword and Dyanne—which the shrewd warlord knew well to be his two most valuable bargaining chips—was already more than the young outlander had any right to hope for.

"And the peoples of Wylddeor," Torin added finally. "What will happen to them?"

"Your assault has set those plans back a bit," the warlord replied candidly. "I have a kingdom up north to maintain. I'll not likely make a decision on the Southland before the spring."

"But in the end, you will impose your rule over all, will you not?"

Lorre stared at him, slow to answer. "I will offer them my protection. I cannot help those who refuse."

Once again, Torin considered slaying the warlord where he stood. Surely, Dyanne would want him to. For the sake of her homeland. For the future of her people. As he peered into the warlord's hollow eyes, he wondered if the man would even care.

"Come," Lorre suggested in that commanding way of his, "I will see you to your companions."

Though less excited, perhaps, than he should have been, Torin turned with the man, only to spy again the bloodied club hanging above the door. The sight gave him pause.

"If your men follow you so freely," he questioned, "what need have you for tokens such as this?"

Lorre grunted as he eyed the club. "More so than the other races, an orc's first loyalty is to its own fear. To balance those scales, it helps to impress upon them repeatedly that my retribution will be every bit as swift and painful as an enemy's blade."

"I would think a creature that cowardly would make a rather ineffective soldier."

"Even cowardice has its uses when staging troops, as you yourself recently learned."

The warlord was mocking him, but Torin let it go as he recalled their charge through the center of Lorre's force—a charge meant to divide and scatter those ranks. He remembered how weak the central front—comprised almost entirely of orcs—had seemed, and how quickly it had folded, luring them in. Suddenly, one of the many questions that had been haunting him for three long days rose to the fore.

"Tell me, who betrayed our assault plans to you?"

Lorre scoffed at the notion. "Young man, I've fought more battles than you've even heard tell of. I need no informants to tell me how to prepare a battlefield."

The man might have been lying, Torin knew. Yet he decided not to press the issue. It was the first piece of news since his capture that he truly felt good about—that Moss, a man he had befriended, had not betrayed him.

The warlord sneered. "If someone *had* sold you to me—you and the lives of your friends—would you not want revenge?"

"I might," Torin admitted, "if I understood better what purpose that revenge would serve."

"Perhaps one day you will," Lorre said, then flashed him a haunting look. "May that day never come."

CHAPTER THIRTY-SEVEN

"THROUGH HERE, SIR," the soldier beckoned.

Allion followed, a step behind Jasyn as their small company pursued the young guardsman through the nighttime jungle. The path they traveled wasn't much of one, just a twisted game trail covered over by endless varieties of weeds and brush. With the sun down, the air had turned cold and clammy. The hunter barely noticed, his thoughts on what lay ahead.

He turned where indicated, ducking beneath the toppled ruin of a splintered trunk before climbing over a mesh of gnarled roots. Leaves slapped at him, some filled with nettles and thorns, and he took care not to send them flinging back at Marisha. Behind her, a scowling Darinor matched pace.

Their guide cut sharply once more, veering left of a hidden streambed. A giant tree came into view, straddling the earth atop a sprawl of massive roots, leaving its underbelly exposed. A sentry stood post at its base, beside a curtain of hairlike vines that dangled from a high, crooked arch.

After trading signals with the outer sentry, the young guide stopped and pulled aside that curtain. Both soldiers held salute as first the lieutenant general and then Allion slipped past.

Inside, another pair of guardsmen snapped to attention.

"The prisoner?" Jasyn asked.

One of the guards pointed. Even then, it took Allion a moment to find the captive elf, so well did he blend in with the night. He was sitting upright, bound with his wrists behind him and his knees to his chest. His olive skin, clothed in leathery vines and painted with curling, decorative tattoos, made him virtually invisible against the shadowed foliage that crept up against the inner wall of roots beneath the leviathan tree. Animal eyes gleamed in the darkness.

Despite the ferocious glare leveled from those eyes, Allion felt a shock of relief. The native was Powaii.

"Did you send for Kae?" Jasyn asked of the guiding soldier, who shuffled in after Marisha and Darinor.

"Yes, sir. She should be here any moment."

Jasyn marched forward with torch in hand. Its light caused the defiant elf to recoil. "Well?" the lieutenant general asked of Allion.

The hunter nodded, his eyes on the Mookla'ayan. "We may be in luck."

He moved a step a closer, ahead of Jasyn. The elf grimaced fiercely, freezing him where he stood.

"So far, we've been unable to communicate with him," Jasyn admitted. "I've had a team of translators working on it, but they tell me that their speech patterns must be wrong. For the wretch does not appear to understand their words or gestures, and his own have come across as gibberish." He glanced over at the hunter. "They've confessed that their study of the savage tongue comes mostly from books, and not from actual conversation."

Seeing Allion's misgivings, the commander advanced to within spitting distance of the bound captive. He crouched down, bringing the torch close to the other's face.

"I suspect, however, that this is not the problem," Jasyn added, sneering as the elf looked past him to focus on some distant point across the enclosure. "I believe he understands well enough, but is simply refusing to answer their questions."

"Let me try," Allion said, willing himself forward until he had crouched down beside the general. The native's eyes came back to him. "Does he have a name?"

"Not that I'm aware of. Ask him."

Allion hesitated, making a quick study of the other's face. Like all Powaii, he was completely hairless, and the oil of his skin shone in the torchlight. Small, horn-shaped wood chips hung from his earlobes, and another, slightly larger, from his lower lip. Had he been standing, he would have been perhaps a head taller than Allion. Despite his brave mask, he did not look comfortable.

"Allion," the hunter said, prodding at his own chest. "And you are?" He reached toward the Powaii native, who snarled.

Before anyone could stop him, Jasyn belted the elf across the cheek. "Answer his questions, you filthy spoor."

Allion put a hand on the general's arm. "It's okay. Just, please, give me a moment."

The commander jerked free, flashing his teeth at the native in warning.

"Sir, the translators are here."

Jasyn turned. "Let them in."

Allion glanced back as a trio of soldiers—who had the look of anything but—filed past the curtain of root tendrils to join them under the natural canopy. His gaze lingered as it found Marisha's, then swung around to the cornered elf.

"Allion," he said again, and though the native refused to look at him, he thought he saw this time a curious twitch in the other's brow. "Cwingen U'uyen," he pressed, trying the name of the Powaii chieftain, and knew the elf had understood him when eye contact was made. With a surge of adrenaline, he continued. "Kylac Kronus. Thrak-Symbos. Asahiel."

The elf's face shot forward, bulging eyes fixed on Allion. It happened so swiftly that both hunter and general rolled back on their heels. All of a sudden, the imprisoned Mookla'ayan was raving like a madman, letting fly in a language coarse and guttural. Jasyn snapped his fingers, while the scrambling translators tripped all over one another, fumbling the scrolls and tablets and etching tools carried with them. In the shadow of the archway, the sentries drew their weapons, awaiting their general's command.

"Wait!" Jasyn barked. "Guards, as you were. Kae, get your scribes in order. Allion, have him slow down."

The hunter patted the air between him and the native, with no real idea of how the elf might interpret that placating gesture. Having recovered from their panic, the Parthan translators gathered round, taking their individual stations and organizing their materials.

"Unbind his hands," one of them shouted—a woman, Allion now noticed. Off the general's incredulous look, she explained, "We need to see his hand movements."

Jasyn reached out with a dagger and sawed through the ropes that bound the elf's wrists. As he withdrew, he kept the weapon between them. But the native did not even glance at him. Still tied at the ankles, and with ropes securing his legs to his chest, the Mookla'ayan was not going anywhere. He continued to focus his rant on Allion, chirping and grunting, hands weaving before him.

The team of translators could barely keep up. Their leader—the woman—listened intently to every utterance, while watching closely a flurry of gesticulations quick and harsh. Every now and then, she would say something to one or the other of her companions, who scribbled frantically in an effort to mark it all down.

Caught in the middle, Allion could only gape at the wild Mookla'ayan in helpless bewilderment. Though he wanted to step aside and let those who might make sense of this take over, he didn't dare, afraid that doing so might break the narration. He did not move—and only barely breathed—while for several moments, the elf stared at him, neck craning, the horn on his lip bobbing up and down as he spoke.

When at last it ended, the native slumped back, an accusing look marring his face. In the sudden silence, Allion could hear sounds from the division encampment filtering through the forest tangle.

It was Darinor's voice that broke the stillness. "What did he say?"

Allion blinked. The translators were already in a huddle, poring over their notes and referring every so often to a sheaf of pages that seemed to contain some sort of word key.

"Little of this makes sense," the woman replied, shaking her head. "He speaks of evil in their jungles, of the walking dead. We think he means the Illychar. After that, it seems to be no more than superstitious ravings."

"Concerning what, exactly?" Allion prodded.

The woman, Kae, was having a whispered argument with one of her partners, who kept pointing insistently to something on his tablet. Finally, she slapped his hand away.

"He mentions repeatedly the name 'Jarom.' It has been said that Jarom unleashed this evil, but that he would return to cleanse it. A veil of darkness, he speaks of, followed by some sort of light. His sense of time is muddled.

Past, present, future—it's all intertwined. But I think he's telling of a prophecy, long held by their people—a prophecy that he believes has or will soon come to pass."

Allion matched stares with Marisha and then Darinor. To them, he could tell, it all made sense enough.

"What's his name?" the hunter asked, turning back to their captive.

Kae turned with him. She cleared her throat before hacking up a sharp clucking sound, accompanied by a quick hand gesture.

The native remained silent for a moment before glancing in her direction and giving a reply. Though Allion could not begin to match the elf's pronunciation, it sounded something like "Wyvern Seas." Kae consulted briefly with her companions.

"Wyevesces," she said. "Jaquith Wyevesces."

Allion frowned. "Wivva . . . ?"

"We'll call him Weave," Jasyn declared impatiently. "What about Corathel?"

Kae wet her lips and once again cleared her throat. Her speech this time was longer and more animated, and to Allion's ears, only vaguely resembled the Mookla'ayan tongue. To make up for it, she spoke slowly, carefully. In contrast, Weave's blistering response seemed to express twice as much in half the time.

"He says mostly the same thing," Kae translated, after yet another hurried conference with her fellow interpreters. "More about swarms of the walking dead that must be made to lie down again. And he calls them something else—intruders, I think—that must be turned away."

"I want to know about the chief general," Jasyn growled, brandishing his dagger. "Tell him that if he doesn't start making sense, I'm going to feed his eyeballs to a swamp worm."

"Hold on," Allion begged, reaching out again to restrain the agitated commander. "Try this first. Tell him that I've come to lead both the Parthan armies and the Illysp far away from Mookla'ayan lands, but in order to do so, we must first have our men and our leader returned to us. Tell him that."

Kae looked to Jasyn, who scowled.

"Please, just try it," Allion urged.

Jasyn nodded, and the woman did as she was asked. Another lengthy and challenging dialogue ensued. Allion glanced back and forth between the speakers, trying in vain to follow along, to gain a sense from pitch or body language as to the elf's mood and tone. In the midst of it all, a single word jumped out at him, chilling his blood: *A'awari.*

He forced himself to wait until the round of conversation had ended before leaping to any conclusions.

"All right," Kae said slowly. "If I understand correctly, our friend here says that he does not belong with those who took the chief general's unit hostage."

"Of course not." Jasyn snorted.

"He claims to belong to a separate clan, the Powaii. Those who took the general were A'awari, a clan with which his own is at war. He says he is a scout and nothing more, that he was tracking the enemy's movements through Powaii territory when he was set upon and taken captive by our soldiers."

Allion closed his eyes as his hopes fell. It seemed this rescue would not be so easy after all.

Jasyn leaned into him. "We're no longer in luck, are we?"

The hunter shook his head, blowing a long, weary breath. "Ask him if Cwingen U'uyen can help us."

"Who?" Kae asked.

"The chieftain of his clan. Ask him if Cwingen U'uyen might help us assemble a rescue party."

After a few jumbled attempts, the question was delivered and an answer received. This time, Allion did not have to wait for the translation to know that it was not good.

"This U'uyen is far away to the southeast, leading their people and directing forays against the Illychar. Wyevesces says that he is too far removed to help us."

"Then we go it alone," Jasyn determined swiftly. "Ask him if he will agree to lead a unit of my men in pursuit. Tell him that when the chief general and his soldiers are returned to us, he goes free."

When the question had been asked, the elf looked to Allion. The hunter met that feral gaze, and nodded.

"He is not concerned for his own safety," Kae said a moment later, interpreting the native's response. "But for the sake of his people, and in tribute to he who fought alongside Cwingen U'uyen in the basilisk's lair, he will do his best to guide us in the pursuit of our captured chieftain."

Allion was surprised by the reference to his own heroism within the ruins of Thrak-Symbos, and was further moved by the respectful manner in which the elf stared at him while the words were being relayed. That his name had found a place of such honor in Mookla'ayan lore was humbling.

As might have been expected, Darinor was quick to spoil the moment. "This could be an Illysp trap."

"How so?" the hunter asked.

"How do we know the Mookla'ayans holding your precious general are not Illychar themselves?" the Entient asked, fixing him with a hawkish gaze. "To catch up to them, even with a guide, you will have to split off as a much smaller group. It might be that they are goading you into doing just that."

Jasyn shrugged. "A chance I have to take."

"And when *your* lieutenants come after *you*? They, too, will be picked off, one by one."

"It's the only option we have."

"It is foolishness," Darinor snapped. "Corathel's to begin with, now yours to follow."

Allion's own gaze narrowed. "Or perhaps there *is* another option, one you've not shared with us."

The Entient turned to him. "Such as?"

"Legends say the Entients can view men and their dealings from afar. Can you not do so here?"

"If I possessed such a skill, do you not think I would have made use of it before now?"

Allion's frown betrayed his doubts.

"That power belonged only to the original Ha'Rasha," the mystic explained, shaking his head gruffly. "The fools inside Whitlock have managed to approximate it to some extent, but only with a complex array of magical devices."

"And there's truly no way to exercise the ability without this equipment?"

Darinor scoffed. "If I were to strip you of your weapons, could you fell a wild boar with your will alone?"

Catching Marisha's look, the hunter decided to let the matter go.

"If that's the case," he said instead, "then it would seem we're stuck. To turn this army around, we must rescue Corathel. And to rescue Corathel, we must set forth with a group small enough—and swift enough—to make up the ground we've already lost. If anyone can follow a Mookla'ayan trail, it's another Mookla'ayan," he added, gesturing toward their prisoner.

He glanced around beneath the base of that giant tree, regarding each of those in attendance—the elf and his translators, Jasyn and his soldiers, Marisha and her father. All seemed to be waiting for him, so he took a deep breath to steady himself.

"I suggest we get to it."

TORIN STOOD BENEATH THE SHADOWED ARCH of the Bastion's solitary gatehouse, judging with suspicion the man before him. The fierce gaze and battered armor were those of a seasoned soldier, albeit one clinging desperately to a waning prime. His coal-black hair was scratched with gray, his large frame gone pudgy at its center. The pouches beneath his eyes were deep and sagging, while the orbs themselves were flat and cold. Nothing in the man's face suggested that he had ever known mirth.

"Warrlun," Lorre introduced. The overlord of Yawacor was standing a few paces back, ringed by giants. "Been with me from the beginning. Has even saved my life a few times."

Torin glanced in Lorre's direction, then back to Warrlun, who loomed over him by almost half a foot. The soldier was standing far too close, chin tucked into his chest, looking down in a manner meant to be intimidating.

"He knows everything there is to know," the warlord added. "His strength and experience will serve you well."

Torin swallowed his reservations and nodded. He wasn't comfortable with this arrangement, and Warrlun's presence did not put him any more at ease. Still, once they were out on the road, it would be easy enough to change matters. Best that he hide his true feelings for now.

He looked again to the warlord, waiting to see who else from among the man's entourage would be given over to theirs. He was quite certain it would be one of the attending giants. Not only would the formidability of these creatures dissuade against the double-cross Torin was already considering, but as natural mountain dwellers, they would be the most familiar with the distant reaches into which some believed the Finlorians had fled.

Instead, upon Lorre's gesture, it was Saena who stepped forward from amid the guard circle.

"This one, you already know," the warlord intoned.

Torin's grunt was more surprise than acknowledgment. His comely prison attendant—and, as he had later learned, one of Lorre's interrogators. What was the warlord thinking?

In the next breath, he was silently congratulating the man on his clever selection. The young girl was a perfect choice—not only because of her matchless memory, but as one whom Torin would be far less likely to kill or leave stranded on the open road.

Saena bowed in greeting—first to Torin, then to Dyanne and Holly. Torin turned with her, glancing back at the pair of Nymph Hunters and finding fresh comfort in the fact that they had decided to join him. After all, he'd had no real assurance that they would. He had bought them their freedom to do with as they chose. They had undertaken this mission at its outset to guide him, yes, to determine whether he was who he claimed to be and to punish him if he was lying. But more than that, they had come to see for themselves what progress Lorre was making in his conquest of the Southland, and to do what they could to thwart his advance. With the way things had ended up, Torin would not have blamed them had they elected to race home to warn their fellow Fenwa of the gathering storm.

But Dyanne had assured him that news of Neak-Thur's fall and of the rogues' devastating failure to recapture the city would find its way to the Nest soon enough. Though their family and friends might think them enslaved, tortured, or dead by now, both Hunters had agreed that they had invested too much in this quest to turn away from it now. He was no longer their hostage, and they could no longer force their company upon him. But if the choice was truly theirs, then they chose to see him through.

Looking at them now caused him to wonder if they already regretted that decision. Holly barely glanced at Saena. The smaller Nymph was too busy glaring at Lorre as if calculating the odds of getting one of her throwing knives past his retinue of giants. Dyanne managed a polite nod, her emotions locked away behind a dispassionate front.

He had felt strange at first, seeing her again. Though he'd had plenty of empty hours in which to ponder, he still wasn't certain what his hasty surrender on the battlefield said about him and his feelings for the woman—or Marisha, for that matter. For when the latter had been threatened in a similar fashion, he had refused to yield, willing to sacrifice even her life, if absolutely necessary, for the greater good. With Dyanne, he had submitted before such conflict could even manifest.

Regardless, all that mattered now was that he felt safer knowing she and Holly would still be with him.

The grooms arrived then, leading a team of horses fully outfitted. As each animal was assigned to a member of the party, Warrlun turned to confer privately with Lorre one last time. Torin marked their conversation with a persistent wariness. Though no longer certain Lorre was the monster he'd imagined, he remained unconvinced of the warlord's objective. Were they to find the Finlorians and meet up with the man's wayward progeny, would learning how they fared provide satisfaction enough? Or did the old warrior have a more sinister plan for retribution in mind?

Torin turned back to his mount, bending to check straps and fittings. It was too soon to tell. And without a guide, he would be lost, his hopes of locating the elusive Finlorians all but dashed. For the time being, he would have to trust the self-proclaimed overlord, and hope that the man's designs would not interfere with his own. Blazes, he had trusted Raven, a rampaging pirate, hadn't he? Was this so different?

"Your first stop will be Vagarbound," Lorre explained, while Warrlun moved away and climbed into the saddle of a sorrel gelding. "A two-day ride at most. From there, may fate cut you a favorable course."

Torin nodded as his left foot reached for the stirrup. A moment later, he sat astride the roan mare, which tossed its head and whickered, as if sharing his misgivings.

He looked ahead, peering northward as a massive portcullis was raised. The doors beyond had already been opened, revealing another unknown horizon awash in early shades of gray. The snow had melted, exposing windswept fields of trampled sword grass on either side of a wide and rutted highway. Farther west, the ocean raged against its rocky shore.

He tried to focus on this—the road ahead—and not the battlefield behind him, which after four days still stank of death and disappointment. Crews piled and sorted, while the smoke from communal pyres stung his eyes. It would be months, Torin thought, before evidence of battle was completely hidden. It would take much longer than that for the scars to heal.

Despite his best efforts, he found his gaze drifting back toward the city and the countless comrades still imprisoned there. They deserved better, Torin knew. And given the chance, he would make sure they received it.

"Should we meet again," Lorre offered, "may it be under better circumstances."

Torin considered the warlord and his ring of giants, and nodded once more. Then he kicked his heels, urging his steed forward alongside those of his company. Dyanne and Holly were to his right. To his left rode Warrlun and Saena, the handpicked agents of Lord Lorre.

His latest companions, for better or worse.

With a mix of hope and apprehension inspired by each, Torin trotted past the open gate and into the rain-drenched morn.

CHAPTER THIRTY-EIGHT

Aᴌᴌɪᴏɴ ᴛʜᴜᴍʙᴇᴅ ᴛʜᴇ ꜰʟᴇᴛᴄʜɪɴɢ of the arrow nocked loosely to his bow-string as he peered intently through the misty gloom. He cast his gaze this way and that, but could determine little, enshrouded as he was by jungle. Ears cocked, he strained for some further sign of that which had alerted him.

Second General Jasyn gave another signal, and the soldiers accompanying them fanned to either side of the hunter in spread formation. Allion crept forward at the point, hoping the warning he had just called wasn't merely another false alarm—before swiftly changing his mind and praying that it was.

To one side, the brush rustled. The hunter whipped about, nerves drawing as taut as his bowstring as he raised the weapon and took aim.

A swamp badger poked its masked face through the shiny foliage, eyes glittering as it took in the scene, then ducked away.

Jasyn motioned for his soldiers to stand down. "That's two now," he said, chuckling at Allion's expense. "On edge, are we?"

Allion just shook his head as he relaxed his bow. Better to deal with the embarrassment than be caught with his guard down.

Jasyn glanced at the lowered weapon as he moved forward to retake the point. "You know, in Partha, only those too weak or craven for close-quarter combat become bowmen." He clapped his friend on the shoulder. "Perhaps you just haven't the stomach."

"Until you've stared down a dragon, Commander, you don't know what craven is."

The general chuckled companionably and nodded in due deference. He then gritted his teeth and signaled to the soldier he'd put in charge of handling their guide. The brutish lad came forward, prodding the Powaii native dubbed "Weave" at the end of his leash. The elf uttered no complaint. Jasyn had made it quite clear before setting out that morning that should the savage attempt to escape or seek to betray them in any way, his armies would not stop until they had exterminated the entire Powaii clan.

But Allion had sensed that it wasn't the general's threats or handlers that would keep the elf in line, as much as the native's own word. He sensed it again as Weave loped past him now with those long, lean strides, eyes darting briefly in the hunter's direction. Once more, Allion felt a stab of shame to see the proud Mookla'ayan forced to endure such treatment, and wished there was something he could do.

He found Marisha, whose gaze was also trailing after the elf. No doubt, the kindhearted woman was having similar thoughts.

Darinor followed behind her, a long and sinister shadow, and, as always, Allion was forced to redirect quickly to avoid the Entient's glare. With twirling fingers, he returned his arrow to its quiver before shouldering his bow. He then fell into line among those of his company, resuming the southern march.

Despite their fears and skepticism, they had commenced before the sunrise, determined to overtake Corathel's abductors before it was too late. It was possible, Weave claimed through his team of translators. Unburdened, the Mookla'ayans they meant to catch would have long escaped them by now. But this same patrol, which according to Weave was comprised of roughly threescore A'awari, had been slowed by the unwieldy contingent of Parthan prisoners numbering an additional score—just half of those who had accompanied the chief general to begin with, Jasyn had noted bitterly. All signs suggested their enemy was not concerned with any pursuit numbering less than a hundred, and had pushed their pace accordingly.

Both good news and bad, given that Allion's party numbered only thirteen. With such a small group, and with Weave leading, they stood a reasonable chance of finding their quarry within a day or so. But subduing or even escaping that quarry would be another challenge altogether. Even if Jasyn and his men were able to free their comrades—and even if those comrades were in any condition to fight—their force would number half that of the elven captors. Having seen these A'awari in combat before, Allion would have shuddered to face those odds on an open battlefield, let alone here amid the tangled terrain of the natives' homeland.

But as he himself had agreed, it was their best—if not their only—chance to reunite the Parthan Legion and, ultimately, to fulfill Darinor's envisioned defense plan against the Illysp. Were it otherwise, Allion was certain the Entient would not have agreed to come.

The hunter could only hope that having the mystic with them would offset the enemy's advantage. It would have to, he reminded himself, for of their thirteen, only a portion were prepared to do any real fighting. Jasyn had refused to trust Weave with a weapon, and the soldier assigned to the elf as a handler would likely be too busy with that to contribute in any meaningful way. Marisha, though capable of defending herself, was no warrior, and neither, Allion suspected, was Kae. The division's lead interpreter—the only member of her team to join this mission—was becoming more confident, more adept, with her Mookla'ayan language skills as they went along. But the fact that she carried only a dagger and shortsword—while her fellow soldiers were strapped with weapons head to toe—suggested to Allion that she'd been brought along for the sole purpose of communication. As critical as that purpose was, the hunter doubted her words would be strong enough to save her from a Mookla'ayan spear.

That left only himself and Darinor in addition to Jasyn and a half-dozen handpicked soldiers. And while it wasn't Allion's place to doubt the skills of these elite fighters, each would have to prove the equal of Kylac Kronus himself before the hunter would believe that six could overcome sixty.

Of course, such thoughts did little to inspire confidence in an already dubious venture. So Allion fought instead to give full focus to his eyes and ears in an ongoing effort to attune himself to the unfamiliar jungle. It may have been that all he had detected this time was a harmless badger. But he took heart in that he, at least, had sensed the creature when it seemed no one else had.

Hours slipped past at a sluggish pace, matching that of the drifting trailers of fog. Their own was much more hurried. As foolish as it seemed to go crashing and splashing with abandon through the trees and marshes, there was no other way to make up time. They paused only when necessary for Weave to double-check the signs. The farther south they went, the softer the ground became. In many areas, this made tracking easy—not so much the barefoot A'awari as the Parthans, whose heavy boots left deep prints in the mud. But in other areas, the prints were swallowed up entirely by stagnant groundwater pooled up from below. When that happened, the native relied on marks Allion could see—broken reeds, bent sedges, torn leaves—and others he could not begin to discern: scents beyond human detection, subtle currents in the listless air, and, more than anything, an innate familiarity with the Mookla'ayans and their ways.

On such occasions, when unable to trust his own eyes or those of his men, Jasyn made certain to grumble his displeasure and reiterate his threats, ever fearful that the savage might simply be leading them around by a noose. And indeed, whenever he heard the call of a bird or animal he did not recognize, Allion half expected a band of Weave's own clansmen to come leaping out of the brush and put a swift end to this reckless pursuit.

Miles became leagues, and despite the arduous progression of time, the hours eventually formed a day. Misleading, Allion knew. For in the tightly woven jungle, dusk came early, stealing upon them with the swift assurance of a master thief. Nor was the close of their day to be marked by the theft of the sun. The members of the party simply drew in closer to avoid becoming separated in the dark. They lit no torch, but trusted once again in Weave, whose Mookla'ayan eyes functioned as well in darkness as in the light. Blinded and weary, they pressed on.

Nevertheless, at the onslaught of midnight, Allion found himself huddled among the party's leaders, ready to call a break in their search. The trail was yet half a day old, and they were simply too tired, too wet, too bedraggled to continue. The time had come to take some rest and resume their journey on the morrow.

Then they heard the scream.

It belted suddenly through the darkness, laced with terror and powered by agony—the bloodcurdling howl of a man who knew it to be the last sound he would ever make. In the trees above, birds scattered from their nests, while Allion looked to Jasyn with an expression of sudden horror. The others froze in place, sitting or leaning upon various stumps and logs, afraid to move.

The sound itself lasted but a moment before melting away. But its aftershocks were still in Allion's blood when the next sounded, this time shrill and quick before the issuer was able to clamp down and defy an unspeakable pain.

Crouched low beside the general and hunter, Weave gestured to Kae, whose words were but an unnecessary echo of Allion's thoughts.

"We had best hurry."

With their next breaths, they were tearing again through the jungle, thrashing and weaving headlong through a twisted, sucking, overgrown landscape. A continuing chain of screams ushered their progress, like whips against their backs. Though no one said it, they knew it was their men who were dying—those they had come looking for. Without regard for their own safety, forgoing any pretense at stealth, they barreled onward.

Before long, a glow arose to the south, red and angry like the morning sun. But dawn was yet hours away, and this glow smelled of smoke and burning flesh. It lit the sky ahead, growing brighter, built upon the flow of human screams.

There were other cries now, too, a sequence of yelps and squalls to which Allion soon detected an undeniable rhythm. A deep hum underscored the noise, a low rumble like that of the earth itself.

When at last Weave brought them all to a skidding halt, it became clear what had happened. Their quarry had come to a stop—hours ago, as the trail suggested. Long enough to prepare for the ceremony even now taking place. A ceremony that took the breath from Allion's lungs and filled them with dismay.

He stood with his companions atop the forested ridge of a wide and deep depression. The muddy hollow had been cleared of its larger brush and vegetation, all of it scraped and piled into the middle to form a central rise beside an earthen spur. The mound had then been set ablaze. Its flames roared skyward into the night, illuminating the figures of not just sixty, but hundreds of A'awari—an entire village of men, women, and children—all of whom danced and circled and chanted beneath the eruptive halo of bloody light.

Near the center of it all, a Parthan soldier was brought forth from a rapidly dwindling herd, trussed to a pole. The soldier tugged and squirmed against his bindings, but, like those before him, could only wail as his captors hurled him from the top of the jutting spur and into the deadly conflagration. A'awari viewers yelped with delight as the man shrieked his torment, glowing and thrashing until he blackened and lay still.

Feeding upon his flesh, the flames drew higher.

Allion recoiled from the wash of heat emanating from those flames. In all that commotion, it appeared their arrival had gone unnoticed. Standing uninvited upon the hollow's rim, he had a clear and unmolested view of the continuing slaughter.

Another prisoner was hauled forward, hefted by a pair of A'awari by the pole to which he was slung and carried like his companion to the top of the spur. Behind him, only seven were left. This one held bravely, clenched with anticipation. But he, too, arched and howled when his body hit the blaze.

Jasyn drew his sword. The sharp rasp woke Allion from his horrified trance. Reacting instinctively, he reached forth to restrain the maddened general.

His grip alone would not have been enough to stop the man. But others were there to help, grabbing the division commander about the arms and waist, holding him back.

"Fool!" Darinor hissed, standing aback of their gathering. "Would you give us all away?"

Jasyn whirled, reddened eyes flashing. "That's Corathel and his men out there!"

"Which makes you the only commander these other men have—those who might still be saved."

Jasyn growled and heaved, fighting to break free.

"Are you blind?" Darinor pressed. "You cannot kill them all."

"Watch me!" the lieutenant general snapped.

Allion felt himself tearing inside. Darinor was right. But there had to be some other way.

"Weave," the hunter asked, turning to their guide. "What can we do to make them stop?"

Kae forced her gaze from the terrible scene long enough to translate. As she finished, another scream ripped through the night.

Weave spoke hurriedly. Twice, Kae had to stop him and have him repeat something. When she turned to Allion, her face was sweaty and ashen.

"They are seeking to appease the Mookla'ayan deities," she said, "in hopes that the gods will see fit to lift this scourge from their lands."

Allion's mind raced. "If we can convince them that those prayers have been answered, might they let the rest go?"

Kae shook her head. "I don't—"

"Ask him!"

She did. While the two spoke, Jasyn seemed ready to explode. Another prisoner was sacrificed, leaving only five. They could not even tell, Allion realized, if Corathel was still among them.

"Either that, or they will kill us all," Kae answered.

At that moment, they were finally spotted. A disinterested youngster standing toward the back—who was unable to view much over the heads of the elven throng—yanked on his mother's arm, pointing them out. The woman ignored the child at first, but when at last she turned, her reaction was immediate. Allion watched it with a feeling of impending dread, as if watching a dragon draw a deep breath. Even as it occurred to him to warn the others, A'awari began to swing about, one by one, in response to the elf-woman's cries.

The alarm spread faster than the hunter had imagined, given the frenzy in which the A'awari were engulfed. What began with a few curious stares passed quickly through the rear ranks and toward the center. Before he could even appreciate the sudden danger in which he found himself, Allion was staring down at wave upon wave of angry Mookla'ayan warriors, all rushing toward his position.

He came to a decision in that instant—a decision born of instinct more than any rational thought. While those around him gasped or fumbled for their weapons or prepared to flee, the hunter stepped to the fore.

"Follow my lead," he said.

Useless as it would have been, he should have had them scatter into the woods. Instead, he strode down the hollow's embankment, reaching up to cross his wrists over his head, just as he remembered Kylac doing. The Mookla'ayans came at him in a swarming crush, but he forced himself to continue on.

A soldier ran past him, one of Jasyn's. Sword high, the bearded man thundered toward the enemy. Before he came within a dozen strides, he hit the earth—nerveless, Allion knew, from the poison contained in the many darts sticking from his body.

Still Allion moved toward that oncoming tide, using every ounce of will he could muster not to cower or close his eyes. His body went rigid with fear as the A'awari closed round, chirping and shrieking, brandishing their blowguns and spears and half-moon knives. They leapt and circled and clicked their teeth, baring wicked piercings and flashing cruel tattoos of barbed and serrated design. But for the moment, at least, it would appear they did not intend him harm.

Their countless numbers blocked the way forward, forcing him to a stop. Allion risked a backward glance. His comrades, he was relieved to find, were mimicking *his* movements rather than those of the unfortunate soldier ahead of him. Darinor, he could see, was furious. And Jasyn, he feared, might bite back at any moment against those gnashing all around him. Neither understood yet what Allion intended. And in truth, Allion himself was not yet sure. Their surrender had bought them time, nothing more.

He looked to the center of the clearing, where the fifth of those who remained of Corathel's company was being held up at the lip of the spur, his bearers just waiting to toss him over. Whatever the hunter was to do, he had only moments in which to do it, else that soldier—and all of the rest of them—would soon become casualties of the ongoing sacrifice.

From that forward direction, the crowds began to part. With obvious reluctance, A'awari viewers fell aside, making way for a string of ceremonial guardsmen driving toward the disturbance in arrow formation. With his attention focused along that course, Allion didn't notice what was going on behind him until he heard the unmistakable rumble of Darinor's voice.

"If you have some miracle to summon, you had best do so before I summon mine."

Allion spun. His companions had been ushered forward so that all stood now within the same pocket of thrashing natives. Darinor was considering some form of attack, one that he did not appear to have much faith in. Nor did Allion, should he allow it to come to that.

But the mystic's words gave shape to the vague idea that had been swirling in his head—and a shred of hope where none had lain before.

"Wait," he said. "Not yet."

The line of forward guardsmen reached them at last, their hairless flesh painted and scarred, their bodies riddled with bone piercings. Each wielded a spear much taller than himself, and wore upon his shoulders a mantle of tanned skin. Allion tried not to guess at what manner of animal such smooth skin might once have belonged to.

The warriors quickly formed a circle around the intruders, shoving aside the eager onlookers to surround the hunter and his companions three-deep. Though his arms were already growing heavy, Allion forced himself to keep them overhead, and his gaze fixed to the south, toward the fire and whoever led this grim service.

The crowds began to quiet expectantly.

"Kae," Allion dared, "tell them I will speak with their shaman."

The woman's voice was a tremulous squeak. "Shaman?"

"You know what I mean. Whatever they call the leader here. Have Weave explain it to them."

When one of the towering warriors stepped forward to glare down at Allion, Kae found her nerve, and began to relay to him—without the benefit of hand gestures—the hunter's intent. She had only barely begun when Weave brushed past her and came to stand beside Allion, croaking some demand of his own. The hunter could only hope it was the same message he intended. He thought about asking Kae, but the guardsman before him was so close now that he couldn't turn around.

When the Powaii finished speaking, that same guardsman, perhaps their leader, snarled before turning on a bare heel and opening his arms to the crowds that had closed behind him. His clansmen parted once more, clearing a path to the heart of the ravaged dell and that awful inferno. Prodded by the iron ring of A'awari spearmen, Allion and his companions followed.

His march was like that of a condemned man through an angry mob of those he had offended. He tried not to notice the looks of hatred and bloodlust, but it was impossible not to. Even with his eyes closed, he could feel their menacing stares, as surely as the intensifying waves of heat from the sacrificial blaze. It seemed as if their wrath alone might melt the skin from his bones.

His party was led to the base of the rise from which Corathel's men were being tossed—even the soldier who had been paralyzed, his limp form carried by a pair of A'awari guardsmen. The chief general, Allion noticed, was indeed there, last in line, bound in ritualistic fashion. The general and the three beside him gazed with incredulous stares as they saw who it was that had come.

Allion's attention, however, was drawn to the left of the Parthan captives, where the A'awari guard ring opened to reveal another of their clansmen, who wore an elaborate headdress made of elven skulls. He might have been a chieftain—the A'awari counterpart of Cwingen U'uyen. Or he might have been a priest of some sort, a shaman. Perhaps both. To Allion, it didn't matter, beyond the simple fact that this was the one he needed to address.

Weave did so first, lowering his arms and prostrating himself before the skull-wearer. Allion contemplated doing the same, but decided against it.

His recalcitrance drew an angry murmur from the crowd, and an even sterner grimace from Skull-wearer. The shaman—if that's what he was—pointed, and the leader of the guards raised his spear, aiming it down as if to skewer Allion where he stood.

The hunter held his breath, but managed not to flinch. He glared back at the warrior as he said, "Kae, tell Weave to stand up."

Kae stammered for a moment before collecting herself. When she had delivered the message, Weave glanced at Allion before bowing even deeper to Skull.

"I said get up!" Allion shouted, with a kick to Weave's ribs.

At the same time, the hunter uncrossed his wrists and lowered his hands. A gasp ran through the surrounding press. Both Skull and Spear wore looks of stunned incredulity. Before that disbelief could translate into punishment for his insult, Allion rushed to explain.

"Kae, tell them that we accept their humble sacrifice."

"What?"

Spear barked to his shaman, then drew back, preparing to throw.

"Tell them!"

Kae blurted something that might have been gibberish, but it was enough that Skull raised a hand to restrain his captain of the guard from punching a hole through the insolent hunter.

Spear protested—angrily. So, too, did a trio of lesser priests huddled beside their leader. When that huddle broke, the shaman spoke.

"He would know who we are to desecrate these proceedings," Kae said.

Allion looked to the fifth surviving member of Corathel's company, still held atop the ridge. The man's heart could not possibly be beating any faster than his own. "Tell them that I am he who unleashed the evil that plagues them. Tell them that I've come now in answer to their summons, guided by one who has heard their prayers."

The hunter watched carefully the expressions of his listeners as Kae translated his words to them. All around, the crowds had gone silent, straining to hear over the roar of flames. The features of those near enough to make out the woman's claim tightened with increased suspicion.

All this time, a confused Weave had continued to kneel, halfway between the bold stance Allion suggested and the posture of submission demanded by their enemies. As Kae finished, the hunter reached down to grasp the Powaii native by the arm and haul him boldly to his feet.

Again the crowds gasped and murmured, and the lead spearman grumbled. The attending priests conferred with one another, pointing often at Weave, then passed their judgment on to the shaman. When the shaman spoke, all listened.

"We are bearers of filth," Kae interpreted, using her hands now to gesture as needed. The others, Allion noticed, continued to hold theirs overhead. "Who among us is capable of hearing their sacred prayers?"

Without turning, the hunter addressed the only member of their group who at this point could help him. "Darinor?"

The Entient, it seemed, had been awaiting his cue. With a terrible swoosh, the flames of the A'awari bonfire doubled in height. Great streamers spewed forth, erupting skyward to form a blazing canopy that spanned the entire hollow. Hundreds of Mookla'ayans cried out. While warriors dropped to a crouch and mothers shielded their young, these streamers became arrows of fire that drew aim upon the base of the rise where Skull and the rest of them stood. The shaman remained erect as he stared down that barrage, while those around him began to cower nervously. The missiles came on.

Just when Allion began to fear that Darinor truly meant to impale them all, the fiery bolts veered in flight, screaming overhead, shrinking and coming together, forming a giant ball that coalesced directly above their startled faces. The Entient gathered that ball before him, drawing it into his outstretched arms. He then split it in two—one for each hand—where the flames of each twisted and swirled above cupped palms like a swarm of bees.

Allion worked hard to maintain the strict, authoritative grimace marking his own features. He had hoped for a display of thunder and lightning that would rattle the very heavens. What Darinor had given him was even better.

With the sound of those ready fireballs crackling in his ears, the hunter felt his confidence swell. "As their prophecy states, he who brought this pestilence upon them shall be the one to remove it. Grant me these remaining offerings," he said, gesturing toward Corathel, "and I will use their stink to draw the evil ones from these lands."

In the awed hush, his voice carried clearly. So too did Kae's translation, drowning out all but the continuing rumble of flames. Breathless, Allion awaited his enemies' response.

For a moment, he wasn't sure that his ruse—truthful as it was to some extent—would work. The lead guardsman lowered his spear, but snarled while the priests deliberated. Skull simply stared at him, glancing every so often toward Darinor and those still-churning fireballs. Allion dripped sweaty beads, roasting in the bonfire's warmth, fighting to appear confident.

Then, without clear cause or warning, the forward rows of onlookers began bowing flat against the earth. The movement swept back among their clustered lines, until the whole of the lower congregation was on its knees. Their hums and whispers sent a shiver through Allion despite the intense heat.

The priests took pause, by all appearances as surprised by the reaction as he. When their conversation resumed, it seemed to Allion that its pace had quickened.

At last, their discussion concluded. Hoping for the best, Allion braced for the worst.

"The human vermin go free," Kae translated.

The relief was evident in her voice, as it was in the grunts and sighs of Jasyn and his men. Following the Second General's lead, the rest of them finally lowered their arms, glancing cautiously at the surrounding A'awari guardsmen.

Skull signaled, and another set of guards carried Corathel and his men over to join them—including a much relieved soldier draped from his pole at the top of the spur. Throughout it all, Allion matched the shaman's gaze without a hint of gratitude, to make it seem as though this result was precisely what he had expected.

At the same time, something in the shaman's look tempered the hunter's barely bridled elation. The Mookla'ayan was releasing them, yes, but not necessarily because he'd been convinced by Allion's act or Darinor's display. The elf's eyes smoldered with mistrust, deep and feral. His granting of their request, the hunter suspected, had more to do with appeasing his superstitious followers than anything else.

With Corathel and his men cut free and leaning upon Jasyn and his comrades for support, Allion nodded to the shaman and his priests in stern acknowledgment. He turned to go when the shaman spoke again.

"One must remain," Kae said, and Allion's senses screamed an alarm.

He looked back to Skull, who smirked cruelly before thrusting his hands to the heavens and crying out in a voice loud and shrill.

It was a yell meant to be heard by all. And it was. Throughout the hollow, bowing natives leapt to their feet, shouting praises.

Allion turned to Kae.

"To glorify those above for answering their call."

Skull's smirk became a grin so savage it made Allion's toes curl. For their freedom, the barbarian meant to exact a price.

"And what is to become of he who remains?" the hunter asked darkly.

Kae relayed the question. The shaman answered and clicked his teeth. At his response, the roar of the congregation grew tenfold. Allion looked to his translator, but the woman could only shake her head.

"*Grindaya,*" she said. "A ritual of some sort. I don't know the word."

Together, both she and Allion turned to Weave. The Powaii native wore a haunted look.

As the cheers of the crowd settled into a single, frenzied chant, one of several acolytes brought forth a ceremonial spear. From the tip of this spear hung beaded strings—teeth, Allion saw, strung together on leather thongs. Bidding this acolyte forward, Skull turned a wicked eye in turn to each member of the hunter's party. When that eye found Marisha, the crooked smile slipped free, and a long, gnarled finger was leveled toward her.

"Grindaya," he said again.

The Mookla'ayan multitudes shrieked and bellowed, voicing their savage pleasure as the acolyte dangled and then shook the strings of teeth over Marisha's head.

Allion's heart plummeted, his eyes locking with those of his startled friend.

"No," he said, then whirled upon Skull. "No!"

The shaman pretended not to hear him. Or perhaps the elf really couldn't, given the tumult surrounding them.

He stalked right up to the shaman then—or would have, had Spear and another guardsman not intercepted him, using their weapons to block his path. The sudden and threatening movement brought a stunned hush to the unruly throng.

"Not her!" Allion yelled at Skull over crossed spear hafts. He then spun around to seize hold of the one dangling its tooth strings over Marisha's head. With a yank, he forced it away, screaming at the acolyte bearing it. "Not her!"

The spectators gasped. Skull's gaze narrowed. The shaman spat what sounded like a curse.

"Very well," Kae said. "You decide."

The acolyte pulled away, glaring at the hunter with hate-filled eyes. The pit in Allion's stomach only deepened. He turned to Marisha with a feeling of panic.

"It's okay," she said bravely. "I'll stay."

"You will not," Darinor growled immediately. He hefted one of his still-crackling fireballs. "Nor will I."

Allion looked away from them to the others. Despite his many trials in recent months, he could not recall having ever felt such despair. To cope with the death of a friend was one thing. To be the one to pass that sentence was not something he thought he could live with.

But his choice was plain. Either he condemned one of them, or he condemned them all. He considered each of his companions in utter helplessness. One of Corathel's soldiers, perhaps? Or Jasyn's? Any one of them might be willing to make the sacrifice in order to set the others free. And yet, he knew that neither commander would allow one of his men to die in his stead. When the arguments concluded, it would be Corathel who stayed behind, ordering Jasyn to depart. Even if the lieutenant general were to obey that order, they would be giving up what they had come here to accomplish.

All of which, Allion decided, was mostly irrelevant. The simple truth was that he could not ask any of those who had put their faith in him—not even those who were relative strangers—to now lay down their lives for him.

The multitudes were fast becoming restless. The hunter could hear and feel their growing agitation.

"I will stay," he said, forcing the words past a lump in his throat.

It was Marisha's turn to gasp, but Allion ignored her and turned back to Skull. Nothing happened. When he realized that Kae hadn't spoken, he moved again toward the acolyte bearing the ceremonial spear, to stand beneath its grisly strings.

He pointed to himself and repeated, "Grindaya."

The shaman's expression became devious.

"How can this be," Kae interpreted a moment later, "if you are truly the one meant to save us all?"

Many among the gathered masses were grumbling with renewed suspicion. Allion gulped as he realized his mistake. And yet he couldn't think of what else to do.

As the restive murmurings began to spread, Weave stepped toward him and bowed. Allion realized the native's intent even before Kae untangled the words.

"He asks that you permit *him* to make this sacrifice."

"Kae, no. I can't allow that."

Weave spoke again before the woman could even translate the obvious refusal.

"He says it is the only way. They will take one of us, or they will take us all. He is grateful that you would sacrifice your life before his. But it is you who will help to drive away the greater darkness from among his people."

By now, their friends had pressed close—Jasyn and Corathel, Marisha and Darinor—to take part, if necessary, in the whispered debate. Allion's gaze flew to the Entient.

"Can't you do something?"

"This is your plan, not mine. Would you risk unraveling it now?"

"It is the only way," Kae repeated. "Please. He says it will make his journey in the afterlife a short one."

The native knelt before him, but raised his head. The look he gave was of such courage and comfort that Allion had to fight back tears. He faced Marisha, unable to speak, yet pleading for help.

Her eyes glazing with tears of her own, Marisha grabbed him by the arm and pulled him aside.

Weave stood beneath the symbolic spear, and made a gesture of supplication to Skull and his priests. The viewing hordes raised a cheer.

The shaman gauged his people's ongoing reaction before coming to a decision. He strode forward, flanked by his retainers. Glancing warily at Darinor, he spoke again to Allion.

"He would send with us a blessing," Kae said.

Had he been thinking clearly, the hunter might have flinched as Skull reached out with one hand to grip his forehead. As it was, he paid it no mind, his eyes turned toward Weave as he searched frantically for another solution.

The crowds quieted. The shaman muttered for a time with bowed head, keeping his hand in place. Whatever he had to say, he did so quickly. By the time the A'awari withdrew his touch, Allion's mind was as barren and useless as before.

Skull gestured. The guard circle around the hunter and his company tightened. They were being dismissed. Allion resisted at first, as another set of guards closed about Weave. But the elf nodded to him encouragingly. Trapped in a daze, the hunter allowed Marisha and the others to pull him away.

Darinor led them this time, still bearing those swirling balls of fire. Escorted by the ring of warriors, they cut northward, back across the clearing through the gathered hosts. Some of the elves bowed or called to them, while others surged past without a glance, fighting anxiously toward the center. Every so often, Allion craned his neck, peering back with shock and worry, trying to catch a glimpse of the one he was leaving behind.

When deposited at the outer edge of the hollow, Allion followed his companions in climbing the embankment to reach the jungle fringe. There he stopped and spun about, refusing to be led farther, needing to see for himself what was to become of their Powaii guide.

From that elevated vantage, he gazed past the heads of his escorts, who were melting already back through the crowd. It took only a moment to discern what was happening. While those particular guards had been guiding him away, others had gone to work on the poles previously used to secure Corathel and his men. The poles had been lashed together, forming a triangular mesh to which Weave was bound with his arms and legs spread wide. The entire assembly was now being carried to the top of the spur, where it was planted like a standard into the ground.

The Grindaya spear was tied on so that the tooth strings hung over the doomed elf's head.

As Allion looked on from afar, the shaman called out to his congregation, working his way through a rhythmic invocation. A ceremonial knife was brought forward—a hatchet, really, with one of those Mookla'ayan half-moon blades. Skull took it, and with a line of acolytes standing by with torches, raised its glinting head high.

His stroke removed one of Weave's feet at the ankle. The Powaii elf wailed, calling out for strength, perhaps. Marisha threw her arms about Allion's neck, burying her face in his shoulder. The hunter wanted to do the same, but forced himself to watch.

Before Weave's cry had ended, acolytes rushed forward to close his wound with their fires. The shaman, meanwhile, retrieved the foot and cast it to another pack of attendants, who quickly carved it up with their own knives and began distributing the slices to a violent press of their clansmen.

The recipients devoured those slices raw.

The ritual seemed to last forever. Piece by piece, Jaquith Wyevesces was cut apart, his wounds closed to keep him alive, his severed scraps consumed by the bloodthirsty natives. Those farther out urged their clansmen on with lusty howls, singing cruel praises, delighted by the torture of a hated rival. For as long as he had strength, Weave continued to call out to the unmerciful heavens—cries that resounded in Allion's ears far louder than those of the vicious hordes.

Though the hunter's companions begged him to depart, he remained transfixed upon the heart of that hollow until Weave's head sagged and his body grew still. There wasn't much left of the elf by then—little more than a ruined torso. But the process continued, and Allion could not make himself avert his gaze.

"Come," he heard Darinor say.

Reality crept back slowly. In the brush behind him, Kae was sobbing. Marisha clung to him as if otherwise unable to stand. He could sense the others—Corathel, Jasyn, and their men—standing frozen with awe and reverence, like sentinels at post upon consecrated ground.

Corathel was the first to respond. With military stoicism, the chief general had his soldiers light torches from the flames Darinor still carried. When that was done, he sent them northward in pairs, side by side into a jungle dark and chill.

A moment later, Allion felt a hand upon his shoulder. It was Jasyn, still with him at the hollow's rim. The Second General wore a pallid expression that shone red and yellow in the fiery light. His eyes were those of a man beset by ghosts.

Without a word, the pair of them turned together, drawing Marisha with them. They followed Corathel, leaving Darinor to take up the rear. The Entient did so, releasing one of his fireballs into the ether, while bearing the other as a lantern at his daughter's back.

Spurred by the ringing clamor of hundreds of bloodthirsty A'awari, they pressed ahead through the darkness, while, behind them, smoke and fire and savage screams filled the night.

CHAPTER THIRTY-NINE

ToRIN ROCKED GENTLY IN HIS SADDLE, listening to the rain as it drummed relentlessly upon the sodden earth. As he had on the previous day, he rode behind the others, where he could keep watch on those in his company.

Where none would interrupt his thoughts and suspicions.

They plagued him now as before—as always. He had hoped that once removed from Neak-Thur, he would find a measure of peace. But the fresh air of the open road had done little to alleviate a host of nagging concerns. Nor would it, he now realized, as long as those who were the cause of his concerns rode with him.

They carried on as he did, bundled tightly unto themselves. Conversation thus far had been limited and lifeless—and not simply because of the disagreeable climate. Undoubtedly, his companions were as troubled as he by the nature of their forced camaraderie, wary of how this unlikely quest might unfold.

The tension began with Warrlun, Lorre's appointed captain. Riding atop his overburdened gelding, the old soldier had positioned himself well ahead of the rest of them, leading them along the bemired roadways of northern Yawacor at a distance that did not invite discussion. He had uttered barely a word since their departure, even when all had camped together the night before. Such aloofness did not necessarily make the man untrustworthy; and yet Torin could not deny the doubts that clawed within his stomach like a pack of rats. There was something in the old soldier's air, a dangerous intensity in his eyes, that unnerved him. The man had accepted this mission for personal reasons, and whatever those were, Torin could not make himself believe that they coincided with his own.

Despite these reservations, it was Saena who concerned him more. For as innocent as the young woman seemed, she was the one, he was sure, who had been sent to memorize the path to the hidden Finlorians—should they be able to find it—so that she might lead Lorre's armies to it later. Whatever else came about as a result of this search, Torin had no desire to bring harm upon those whose support he had come to beg. But how might he accomplish the one without risking the other?

As a matter of reflex, he had sought solace from such fears in the company of Dyanne. But the young Nymph posed perhaps the most discomfiting dilemma of all. For reasons he didn't dare examine too closely, he had found himself feeling less and less comfortable around her. Surely by now, he might safely consider her a friend. Why, then, did she cause him to feel so unsettled and inadequate? She did nothing to demean him; yet he felt like a child in her presence, unworthy of her attentions, awkward and fascinated all at the same time.

More and more, he wondered what she thought of him—as if it should matter. He thought constantly of asking her, of making some attempt to confess to her his uncertain feelings. Perhaps her reaction, whatever it was, might help him to better understand his own irrational state. But he could not bring himself to do so. He could no longer even speak to her without fighting a lump in his throat and a nervous pounding in his chest. The very notion of approaching her on such a topic made him dizzy with fear.

He did his best not to dwell on the matter. As with his reservations toward Warrlun and Saena, his inability to confront Dyanne had no tangible basis, and might have no relevance at all beyond the wilds of his own imagination. Perhaps he had merely grown weary from his trials. Perhaps he needed a crutch, yet understood that it was not fair of him to use her so. Perhaps he simply cared for her enough as a friend that he did not wish to say anything that might upset her.

Or perhaps he cared for her too much already.

As always, he shielded himself against that possibility with recollections of Marisha. But even these had taken on an increasingly darker cast. For he could no longer think of his betrothed except in relation to the Nymph Hunter, arousing feelings of both shame and guilt—particularly because those comparisons seldom favored the woman he had offered to wed. Physically, Dyanne held an unfair advantage in that she was here before him while Marisha was an ocean away. But appearances were less important than the way each made him feel. And in that regard, the Hunter was once again the clear winner. For thoughts of Dyanne and her kin generally inspired dreams for a hopeful future, while thoughts of Marisha invariably reminded him of a bitter, strife-ridden past.

Perhaps because, as difficult as it had been, his time here in Yawacor had been marked by one unexpected discovery after another, whereas so much of his time with Marisha had been marked by war. Whatever the reason, such associations were clearly unjust. But one did not feel differently simply by willing himself to do so.

A gust of wind ripped through him, carrying with it a sharp and sudden chill. It really didn't matter. He had sworn an oath, to himself if no one else. He needed no ceremony to make it official. He was pledged to Marisha, and as long as she felt the same toward him, he would do nothing to jeopardize their eventual union.

As he was making himself this promise, Saena pulled on her reins to fall back alongside him. Just as she had the day before, he noted, when she had started up front with Warrlun before dropping back among the girls, and now finally to him. She greeted him with a smile.

"You look lonely back here."

Torin shrugged and grunted. Though he would have preferred she left him alone, he couldn't bring himself to say so.

"Warrlun says that we should reach Vagarbound by midday," she offered. Torin made himself nod.

"It'll be good to sleep tonight in a real bed."

Torin's jaw clenched. Either she couldn't see or didn't care that he was trying to ignore her. He still didn't trust her, not after the way in which she had played herself off as an innocent prison attendant while he had suffered in Lorre's dungeons. Better that he keep his distance. If there was any chance she served again some secret agenda, he would rather not play into it.

And yet, her disposition beneath the gray and sodden skies of Lorrehaim was as carefree and disarming as it had been within the bowels of the overlord's newest city. Despite his evident lack of interest, she plied him with another of her one-sided conversations, carrying on about anything and everything and nothing. Try as he might, Torin could not be so rude as to disregard her completely.

"I think I know why Lorre sent you," he said finally, trying to steer the woman's chatter in a meaningful direction. "But why Warrlun?"

Saena's eyes shifted toward the front of their column, where the old soldier rode as if oblivious to those who followed.

"I know little about him," she replied. "Only that he is one of His Lordship's most trusted lieutenants."

"Isn't it your job to find out about people?" he asked, somewhat pointedly.

"Well, look at you, for instance. I've already spent more time in your company than I ever have in Warrlun's. Other than the stories concerning your reclamation of the Sword of Asahiel, and aside from the nature of your quest as you related it to me, what do I really know about you?"

"There's nothing more to know," he assured her.

Saena laughed. "There's *everything* to know. What is it that makes you smile? Do you have a favorite color? A favorite food? Who are your friends and family? Is there a queen of Alson?"

Torin's eyes flicked toward hers. All of a sudden, he felt a flush of embarrassment, fearing that somehow, the personal questions with which he wrestled had been exposed to her all along. "The answers to such trifles are hardly relevant to what we mean to accomplish here."

"Perhaps you're right," she agreed. "I use them merely as examples. A person is defined by many things—tastes and fears and passions—characteristics that are ever evolving. It takes a lifetime and more to truly get to know a person. We're lucky if we ever even get to know ourselves."

Torin couldn't help but chuckle. "Is that why you carry on the way you do?"

Saena gaped as if wounded.

"I only mean, you seem as if you intend to share everything there is to know about you with any who will listen."

"If others would share more, perhaps I wouldn't have to reveal so much."

He thought he might finally have succeeded in offending her, until he turned to find her grinning. "Well, you might consider doing us all a favor by starting with that friend of yours up there," he suggested, nodding to indicate their guide ahead.

"A badger would be more agreeable." She huffed. "I much prefer your company to his."

She smiled again. Torin could only shake his head.

He reverted to silence after that, grunting now and then as she rambled on. Whatever plans Lorre's chosen pair might be harboring, trying to uncover their plot now was clearly a waste of time. Especially when he could not even decide who was the more troublesome of the two.

While lending one ear to his companion's nattering, he went back to his own concerns, worrying now about distant friends—Allion in particular—as well as those nearer to him, like Moss, Arn, and Lancer. It disturbed him to have left one after another as he had. When all of this was ended, would he be able to make things right?

At midday, as predicted, the mists parted and the city of Vagarbound came into view. A thick and rain-lashed palisade bounded the city on three sides, with its back, like Neak-Thur's, built upon the mountain slopes. Guardsmen stood post atop various watchtowers, monitoring a light flow of traffic heading in and out the city gates along a narrow and rutted road. Just outside, wooden schilltrons kept visitors hemmed along a desired course. These, along with the giant wall of sharpened stakes, gave the city a bristling and hostile look.

They reined to a halt outside the gates, awaiting their turn with the outer guard. Ahead of them, inspectors examined the cargo carried by a small wagon caravan. When at last that team was cleared to enter, Warrlun spurred himself forward at the head of their column.

Torin was surprised not to be waved right on through. The city captain straightened noticeably upon viewing Warrlun's token of rank, but even then asked them to declare the nature of their business. Warrlun did so, presenting a small scroll bearing the seal of Lord Lorre himself. A series of follow-up questions was asked, and signals exchanged. All the while, a scribe took notes on his tablet, marking down names, anticipated length of stay, and more. As part of this interview, the guard asked them to present any weapons for inspection. Once again, Torin looked to his company's leader, as if to ask if this was truly necessary. But Warrlun himself complied with the request, and nodded gruffly at the outlander's hesitation.

Though reluctant to make himself and his belongings a matter of public record, Torin saw no reasonable way to refuse. Not surprisingly, the Crimson Sword drew openmouthed stares from both the guard and his scribe. They remembered their duty, though, and withheld comment, moving on to make note of the various blades carried by the others. When finished, the guard saluted Warrlun once more.

"If we can be of any service, Commander, let us know," he offered, motioning them on.

"I will, Captain," Warrlun assured him, then urged his mount forward through the wide-flung gates.

"A bit overzealous, aren't they?" Torin muttered as they left the patrol behind.

"This isn't the Southland," Warrlun scoffed. "His Lordship likes to maintain the peace, and the best way for a city to do so is to regulate who and what passes through its gates."

"And that doesn't bother you?" Torin asked, returning the stare of a gap-toothed street patron.

"I've nothing to hide," the soldier replied, facing forward again with a haughty air.

Torin left it at that, falling back among his more civil companions. Though it felt now as if the eye of every citizen were focused on him, it was too late to change matters. He could only hope that come nightfall, the list to which their names had just been added was not sold to a band of thieves—or worse.

From what he could see, calling Vagarbound a city made generous use of the term. As with most of the communities he had visited here in Yawacor, it was more an outpost, a collection of shops and homes and services catering to a wild rabble of huntsmen, tradesmen, and prospectors that roamed this northern region. The streets were unpaved, covered over with wood shavings in a vain attempt to help travelers against the mud. Buildings lined the rutted avenues, beaten by the near-ceaseless downpour. Despite the weather, activity abounded, with vendors hawking foods and garments and tools to an organized throng of haggling patrons. Wheels creaked, mules brayed, mud sloshed under hoof and foot. Soldiers wearing the insignia of Lord Lorre were everywhere, keeping watch.

The assorted smells caused Torin to grimace. But he kept his discomfort to himself, hunkering in his saddle, hood lowered against the rain. He considered asking Warrlun how exactly the old soldier intended to gather the information they had come here to collect, but decided he could wait to find out.

They ventured for a time down the principal roadway, paying no attention to those who stepped forth from booth and stall and storefront stoop to bid them look closer at various wares. The banners and signs were garish enough, fighting for prominence like forest trees in search of the sun. Torin quickly lost interest in them, for they all seemed to offer the same things—none of which he had come here to find.

Their first stop was at a small shack wedged back between a pair of competing taverns. After a quick survey, Warrlun bade his companions wait where they were, then hitched his steed and went marching down the narrow boardwalk.

Only after careful search did Torin find the pricing board that suggested this to be the headquarters of an expeditionary outfit. The place looked abandoned, but when Warrlun knocked, the door opened, and the old soldier disappeared inside.

"Don't worry about us," Holly quipped. "We'll just sit here and keep our saddles dry."

Torin snorted in agreement, looking to Dyanne to see if she might glance his way. She didn't.

Their guide left them mounted in the rain for several minutes. Torin was about to propose that they tether the horses and duck inside one of the taverns for a warm drink when the old soldier reappeared. The commander stood framed by the doorway a moment longer, shaking hands with whoever it was on the other side before making his way back to them.

He offered no apology. He did not even look at them as he climbed atop his horse, huffing with the effort.

"We're to find our man at the Giant's Tongue. This way."

The ordeal finally ceased after following a nearby crossroad up a steep hill and arriving at an angular, two-story building jutting forth at yet another intersection. White paint peeled in tiny strips from the outer walls, one of which held a plaque of wood with branded lettering: THE GIANT'S TONGUE.

Yet another inn and tavern, Torin decided, though judging by the smells wafting through the open doorway, this one was more meathouse than alehouse. His stomach growled, stirred by the aroma of roasted steaks, seasoned stews, and fresh-baked breads.

When all had dismounted, Warrlun handed Torin his reins. "Tether the horses on the north side," the soldier instructed. Without waiting for a reply, he then climbed the inn's stoop and strode into the murky depths beyond.

Torin had half a mind to abandon their guide then and there. Instead, he swallowed his pride and followed orders, leading his companions around to where a long line of steeds had been picketed beneath a sagging awning, watched over by a pair of young grooms. Torin balked at the requested holding fee, particularly since he was now penniless. But Saena came to his aid before he could cause a stir, with funds provided her by Lord Lorre. After paying for each of their mounts—including Warrlun's—the company shuffled quickly out of the rain.

They paused upon entering, allowing their eyes to adjust to the dim lighting and for their bodies to shudder through a series of escaping chills. Water dripped and pooled from their cloaks and onto the thick animal rug laid down across the entry. Directly ahead, a long serving bar split the lodge down its center, leading back toward the kitchens. Booths and tables filled the open areas to either side, along with staircases climbing to the upper levels. Antlers and pelts and other hunting trophies hung upon the walls, as well as from every rafter and corner and crude chandelier.

A serving girl strolled forward to greet them. "Need help finding a seat?"

Torin only barely acknowledged the woman, his gaze shifting about in search of Warrlun. "We're supposed to be meeting someone."

"Well, ya ain't likely to find him stood here. Come on in; take a look around. There's a cloakroom behind ya, should ya choose. Give a holler when you're ready for me."

Her suggestive tone finally drew his full attention—though by that time, he was able to catch just a sly smirk and a twitch of her hips as she spun about and headed off with a drink tray toward one of the nearby tables.

Saena started around the opposite side of the bar, giving him a nudge in that direction. Torin forgot about the serving girl and scooted after his companion, only to soon find himself again in the lead. With the girls on his heels, he proceeded deeper into the Tongue's smoky bowels, edging past stools and tables crammed with noontime patrons. Few bothered to take notice of him, involved as they were in their own affairs. Whistles rang out, but might as easily have been calls to the various serving girls as invitations to the lovely ladies who followed him.

At last he spotted Warrlun, down at the end of the bar, standing head and shoulders above those around him. The soldier was conversing with one of the barkeeps, who was pointing farther back toward a distant table. By the time Torin came upon them, the barkeep had gone back to work and Warrlun was starting off in the direction indicated.

"Secure that booth," the commander ordered.

Weary of being bossed around like some grunt in the other's army, Torin nevertheless did as instructed, veering toward a secluded corner in which server visibility gave way to customer privacy. As he did so, their guide strode toward the table pointed out by the barkeep, a table fighting to withstand a riotous brood in the midst of what appeared to be some manner of game. Six burly men were taking turns pounding their lidded tankards upon the table's surface. Suddenly, all stopped and bellowed in laughter before drinking heartily. The last to finish tossed a coin onto a growing pile in the center of the table, amid the jeers of his fellows. A server stood by with a cask, used to fill the empty mugs. The pounding began again.

Torin continued to watch as the girls slid into the bench seats of their own booth. Warrlun, he noticed, had stopped to observe from a distance, focusing on a dark-haired man who sat among the others but did not appear to be participating in their revelry. When another round had ended, the commander stepped forward, tapping this individual on the shoulder.

The stranger glanced at him, seeming more concerned with the mound of coins. A moment later, his head whipped back, eyes wide in startled recognition. The eyes narrowed, then widened again, and a greasy smirk slid forth. Warrlun said something, though Torin could not begin to hear the man's words over the surrounding clamor. Whatever it was caused the dark-haired stranger to excuse himself from the others and rise to his feet. Following the sweep of Warrlun's arm, he made his way over to the newcomers' booth.

For a moment, the stranger's gaze found Torin's. His expression was that of a man who had not only lost his way, but no longer recalled what he was looking for. Then he caught sight of the women—Saena and the pair of Nymphs. All of a sudden, he seemed to remember himself, and that greasy smirk widened into a cunning, almost predatory smile.

"These yours?" the stranger asked, turning to Warrlun as the soldier came up behind him.

"Have a seat."

The stranger bowed to Dyanne and Holly, who occupied one side of the booth. "With the ladies' leave?"

Before either could respond, he slid in next to them—putting Holly in the middle. Across the table, Torin found himself in much the same position, scooting closer to Saena to make room for Warrlun beside him.

"I'm surprised to see you here again, my friend," the stranger began, focusing on the broad-backed soldier across from him. "How many years has it been?"

Despite his obvious bravado, he seemed to Torin shifty and tentative. His dark eyes were hollow and red-rimmed, and darted continually to the open side of the booth—as if the man himself were contemplating escape. Warrlun's presence here had unnerved him, whatever else he would have them think.

"You look well, Traver," the old soldier responded.

Fitter than the commander, anyway, Torin agreed silently. This Traver's size and shape was not all that different from his own, though the man's age was no doubt much closer to Warrlun's.

"Mountain air," Traver said, winking at Saena. "Keeps a man young."

Warrlun leaned forward. "Ethric tells me you're heading up the hunts these days."

Again, that hint of buried nervousness from Traver. He was trying to determine, Torin thought, if Warrlun's visit here meant trouble for him. If that was the case, then it was reasonable to assume he had something to hide.

At that moment, one of the servers found them—the girl who had greeted them, Torin saw.

"What'll it be?"

Traver appeared much relieved by the interruption. "A rack of Jaecy would be delicious, right about now."

"Hands to yourself, Traver," the woman snapped, "else the next hide you tan will be your own."

Traver shrank back in apology. "Forgive me, my lady. I am not myself when enraptured by your beauty."

Jaecy scoffed. She would have been pretty, Torin decided, had she not looked as if she'd lived her entire life in this frontier environment. Her hair was brightly colored, yet dirty and tousled. Her skin was fair, though pitted in areas with rashlike scars. Her tavern rags and serving apron were patched and stained, though her body beneath was shapely enough.

"What'll you have, stranger?" she asked, fixing Torin with a judging eye.

Torin was embarrassed to have been caught scrutinizing her so carefully. "I don't . . . What's good?"

Jaecy scoffed again, though with more amusement than disgust this time. "Outlander, ain't ya? Place ain't named the Goblin's Ears, ya know."

"Lamb and potatoes for all," Warrlun resolved impatiently. "Ale to wash it down."

"You his father?" Jaecy asked.

"And some privacy," the soldier replied sternly.

Jaecy scowled, but managed another smile for Torin before striding away in her tight leather breeches. Traver stared after her before turning back, seeming now a little more at ease.

" 'Round here, a man doesn't buy another a meal unless he wants something." He sat back, trying to judge Warrlun's response. "So, to what do I owe this kindness?"

"If you're leading Ethric's team, that makes you His Lordship's foremost bounty hunter, does it not?"

Traver snickered. "Whatever keeps me out of the army."

"I need to know what you've seen."

"The Finlorians? Come, my friend, it's been twenty years. The elves are long gone, and His Lordship would do better to accept that."

"Mind your tongue, rogue."

"No disrespect intended," Traver assured the other. "I only mean, seems to me like a waste of good coin to keep funding our excursions."

"And yet you continue to accept those funds," Warrlun reminded him. "Time now to report."

Jaecy returned then, bearing a tray of mugs and a pitcher of ale. Torin managed to avoid her gaze as she filled those cups, catching only a sidelong glance as she spun the empty tray on her fingers and slipped away.

Traver was the first to drink. "Reports are what they have been for the past two decades. Not a sign. Not one that can be followed, anyway."

Warrlun studied the other carefully, as if measuring the veracity of his claim. "We mean to go up."

Traver nearly spat a mouthful of ale. "Bit late in the season, ain't it? After all this time, why the sudden urgency?"

"Ask this one here," Warrlun said, giving Torin a shove.

Traver's eyes narrowed. "Who is he?"

"Name's Torin," Warrlun replied before the young king could speak for himself.

"*The* Torin?" Traver asked, his interest piqued.

"You've heard of him?" Warrlun did not seem surprised.

"Of course. Been a favorite tale in the taverns of late. Figured it was just one of them meant to help while away the winter."

Torin didn't care for the way in which Traver was eyeing him. He was about to say so when the bounty hunter turned back to Warrlun.

"And what's he got to do with the elves?"

"It's a long story. But that talisman he recovered, the Sword of Asahiel, was once theirs. His Lordship believes it just might be the key we need to draw them forth."

Traver went back to staring at Torin, thoughts whirring behind those darkened eyes. Finally, he shook his head. "My friend, we had us some good hunts. But there ain't nothing to find up there. As long as His Lordship's payments keep coming, rest assured, I'll keep working toward that big score. But me and Ethric, we've got a legitimate business to run as trappers and furriers. I can't be spending every waking moment in the pursuit of ghosts."

Warrlun leaned in toward the center of the table, bearing down upon the shifty bounty hunter. "You speak as if you have a choice. I'm not some soft-skinned desk clerk asking to join one of your leisure excursions. I've come on behalf of His Lordship to commission your services, in collection of a debt."

Traver looked again as if he might flee. His smooth features showed neither fear nor anger, but Torin sensed it nonetheless. He might have trusted the stranger more, in fact, were he to display some sign of hostility or offense. Instead, the man just sat there, smooth as a lake at sunrise, taking it all in.

"Commission, you say?"

"Has cost ever been an object with regard to this venture?"

The bounty hunter took another drink. "Very well, you shall have your expedition—though I'll not have you say I didn't warn you. When were you thinking of leaving?"

"Today."

Traver laughed. "Come, my friend. It would normally take me three days to prepare my team for a trip into the Dragontails this time of year."

"We don't need your team," Warrlun argued. "Just you. A pair of stout hands, if you must, to help carry supplies. But no more."

"And am I to assume the ladies will be joining us?"

"This is our company," Warrlun confirmed. "Approved by His Lordship."

Traver's smirk slipped free. "You leave a man little room to bargain. But I do have one condition. Tonight, the city holds a dance to begin its celebration of the winter harvest. I would have the ladies attend as my guests." He gave them all a princely grin.

Torin looked immediately for Dyanne's reaction, but as usual could read nothing of what she might be feeling. Beside her, Holly scowled with suspicion.

"We do not have time for festivities," Warrlun grumbled.

"Oh but we do," Traver assured him. "I'll have Ethric begin preparations. But it'll take at least the rest of the day to make things ready for the morrow. An evening of merriment is all I ask. If that's too much, then you can drag me back to His Lordship in chains."

Torin could not have been more skeptical of what he was hearing. To his thinking, this bounty hunter had agreed to Warrlun's request far too easily. And to make use of the girls as some kind of bargaining chip set his teeth on edge. What was the man truly after?

"We leave at dawn," Warrlun insisted. "So long as everyone can agree to that, I care not how this evening is spent."

Torin wasn't so ready to concur. "I don't think—"

"The entire city will be there," Traver pressed, speaking only to the girls. "It will be great fun—perhaps the last you'll have for some time."

Holly turned to Dyanne, and Torin was horrified to see that they were actually considering the charlatan's proposal.

"Sure," the smaller Nymph said. "What can it hurt?"

Traver looked to Saena, who shrugged sheepishly. "Then it's settled," he declared, slithering from the booth and rising to his feet. "If you'll forgive me, I will see to all necessary arrangements at once. Warrlun, my friend, I thank you for the drink and the offer of food, but in truth, I have already eaten. I trust you'll have no great difficulty disposing of my portion. To the lovely ladies, I bid a good afternoon. I'll see you all tonight."

He bowed low, then spun away with a flourish, only to turn back with a neglected thought. "Pardon my haste. This dance tends to be a fancy occasion. If it should please you ladies, I will have a word with a tailor friend of mine, to see what he can do about fitting each of you with gowns for this evening."

Holly glanced at the other two women at the table, her own mischievous smile brightening her face. "Thank you, sir. That would be lovely."

Traver's grin nearly swallowed his ears, and he bowed again. "Name is Hopper. On the corner of Pick and Cammerlin. Just tell him I sent you."

"Go, knave," Warrlun growled. "See to it you don't forget the real business at hand."

Traver winked, glanced briefly back at the drinking brood he had been observing earlier, then sauntered toward the exit.

Torin watched him go, seething with mistrust. "What in the Abyss was that?"

Warrlun regarded him in annoyance. "Is there a problem?"

"You tell him we're hunting elves, he agrees, and we're off just like that? How do you know we can trust him?"

"Watch your tone, boy. As I said before, this isn't the Southland. Up here, we have ways of weeding out undesirables."

"So your lord explained to me," Torin sneered, refusing to back down. "Somehow, that doesn't put me at ease."

"I'm not interested in your sense of ease. If it helps, I've known Traver a long time. Bit of a rascal, but we'll not find a better guide. I'd sooner leave you behind than him."

Torin had by no measure finished his objection, but stopped short when he caught sight of Dyanne shaking her head. There was no need for this argument, she seemed to be saying. And she was right. It suddenly occurred to him why she might have agreed to attend this ridiculous festival. Just as she had spent time before among Commander Jaik and the other rogues with whom they had eventually done battle at Neak-Thur, so too would she take advantage of this opportunity to learn what she could of this Traver by more subtle means. At least, he hoped that was why she had agreed.

Even so, he might have said something more, but Jaecy chose that moment to reappear with six steaming platters.

"Lose one, did ya?"

Warrlun grunted, taking two helpings for himself and handing the woman a few coins, which she tucked into the pocket of her apron. This time, Torin was too agitated to be bothered by the undue attentions she lavished upon him.

"Just let me know if ya need anything else," she added. "Anything at all."

Warrlun dismissed her with another grunt, digging already into his first plate of food. Torin stowed his complaints and did likewise.

As he ate, however, he continued to reflect upon this newest addition to their troop. In all honesty, he had no reason to think any less of Traver than he did Warrlun. But at least Warrlun—whatever his secrets—made no pretense at being anything other than the gruff soldier that he was. Traver, on the other hand, was hiding something behind his genteel manners. And though uncertain of what that might be, Torin was troubled to think he might be the only one to sense it.

Despite his double portion, Warrlun was the first to finish both food and drink. Upon draining his mug, he shoved aside the empty platters and lurched to his feet.

"I'll secure us a set of rooms for the night." Glaring at Torin, he added, "Fetch our gear before it drowns out there."

Once again, he turned away before Torin could protest, leaving the disgruntled king of Alson to gnaw silently on a bitter retort.

CHAPTER FORTY

*H*E COULD NOT ESCAPE THE SCREAMS.

Even now, hours later, surrounded by the bustle of the Parthan Legion's Second Division, they were with him. Those of Corathel's men whom he had arrived too late to save. Those of the A'awari clansmen who had cheered the bloodshed. But most of all, those of Jaquith Wyevesces, the Powaii native who had surrendered his life bit by bit so that Allion wouldn't be made to forfeit his.

He had told himself that what he saw had not been real. None had spoken of it the night before, as they made their way northward from the Mookla'ayan gathering. When they were far enough removed that a pursuit seemed unlikely, Corathel had posted a guard and ordered the rest of them to sleep while they could. But whenever Allion closed his eyes, the echo of screams had intensified, and he saw in his mind Wyevesces, staked to that triangular mesh, thrashing and wailing against a torment the hunter—even after serving witness—could scarcely imagine.

He'd been almost thankful when it was realized that few others were sleeping either, and thus the whole company roused to continue its trek. Still, its members kept silent, as if by avoiding the topic they might pretend the ordeal had never taken place.

Eventually, however, Allion had come to understand the unfairness of doing so—to himself and to Weave. To simply bury the memory would be to dishonor the elf's sacrifice. And even if he were successful, hiding his pain deep within could only mean that it would be there to haunt him forever.

Instead, he had begun efforts to deal with it properly. While still en route through the jungle, he had sidled up to Kae, Mookla'ayan scholar and interpreter—she who stood the best chance of helping him to make sense of it all. He'd soon found that she was as scarred by the events as he. They had spoken in hushed and solemn tones for more than an hour, tentatively at first, before trusting one another with their deeper thoughts and feelings. Others, like Jasyn, had soon joined them. Even the embittered Second General was forced to admit that he no longer knew what to think of these Mookla'ayans, so wild and barbaric on the one hand, yet capable of such noble sacrifice on the other.

Among Allion's many questions to Kae was that regarding Weave's plea—specifically the part about making the native's afterlife journey a short one.

Kae, who by then had seemed more angered than saddened by the entire affair, had been kind enough to explain what the Powaii had meant. According to elven beliefs, when one died, he undertook a quest in death to undo the evil he had committed in life. Only after rectifying all of his misdeeds would the deceased find peace. Thus, the better he lived, the quicker and easier his afterlife's trial would be.

Superstitious nonsense, Kae had added with a huff, sniffing back tears. But Allion was not so certain. He was beginning to understand, he thought, Kylac's keen interest in this race—how the youth could claim that the better one got to know them, the less savage they seemed.

Since speaking of it helped, Kae went on to highlight some of the variations held with regard to this elven belief. To the ancient Finlorians, for instance, burial and preservation of the body had been very important, so that the individual would have strength for his posthumous journey. To others, like the Mookla'ayans, the strength granted the individual was that maintained by the living who consumed his flesh. Thus, as horridly sadistic as Wyevesces's fate had seemed, it was also an honor, for in devouring his flesh, his enemies had made certain that he would not lack for this much-needed strength.

Fire, on the other hand, while often used to cleanse impurities, was considered an insult to the dead, for it laid waste to the body and therefore hindered the departed's ability to complete his quest for redemption in the afterlife. While Weave's death seemed to expose certain inconsistencies, there could be no mistaking what the A'awari felt toward the Parthan soldiers they had condemned.

On past midday they had marched, discussing these and other topics, little of which had done anything to put Allion at ease. The same held true later on, when the hunter remembered the blessing Skull had bestowed upon him just before his departure, and had once again sought enlightenment on the matter from Kae. Unfortunately, the woman had been able to hear only portions of the shaman's benediction, and had paid little attention even to these. From what snippets she could recall, it had sounded to her more like a divination. Mostly, the A'awari had warned of betrayal. A dragon had been involved, something to the effect of: He would know his true enemy when he made his return to the creature's lair. Once again, nothing more than superstitious nonsense, Kae had claimed—and most assuredly nothing in which to take heart.

By midafternoon, they had finally reunited with the Second Division, which had been beating its way steadily southward after Jasyn's advance patrol. Though subdued by the decimation of Corathel's personal regiment, the Parthans hailed the lieutenant general's success and the legion commander's safe return. Against the murdering savages, they would soon have their revenge.

But that had yet to be decided. Despite Darinor's insistence, Corathel had flatly refused to discuss the Entient's proposed withdrawal to Atharvan—and from there, the redeployment of the entire legion to Kuuria—while straggling northward with their decimated band. The chief general had listened to the other's arguments, but would not be drawn into a debate without his more senior advisors, whom they would find along with the rest of the Second Division. Their council could wait until then.

And so it had, although not a moment longer. Once they had reached their main force, a halt was called to the division's southward march, and talks convened. While Darinor ducked into a tent with Jasyn, Corathel, and a select few others, Allion had slipped off to be by himself, alone with his torment.

Well, not completely—for Marisha had yet to leave his side. Nor had he asked her to. Even now, he only barely registered her presence, lost as he was to the chorus of continuing screams.

"You cannot go on blaming yourself," she said, imploring with both words and gaze. One arm hugged his shoulders as he sat against a moss-covered trunk. With the other, she used a finger to gently stroke his stubbled jawline.

"Words, Marisha," he replied, staring down at the nest of leaves and roots in which he was cradled. "Speaking them doesn't make them true."

"No," she agreed. "You must believe them. And that is what I need you to do."

He did not respond, refusing to be placated.

"Weave's sacrifice was just that: *his* sacrifice. To assume responsibility is to take from him that which he freely gave."

This time, Allion struck the woman with a withering scowl. When he tried to look away again, she caught his chin and held his face to hers.

"Let us do him justice instead, by embracing what he did for us. Let us remember him for his devotion to a cause much greater than himself—a cause that you and I must continue to fight for."

"I can't get his cries out of my head," Allion confessed. Indeed, it seemed as though they would never end.

"Nor should you try. Like so many others we have loved and lost, Weave will live on through our memories. In time, the pain and guilt will lessen, and we will find better ways in which to remember him. I, for one, am reminded of him simply by looking at you."

"Because I let him die."

"Because I saw in him a person of staunch and selfless dedication. Because I imagine he was one who found joy in simple pleasures, and in simple goals. Some live their entire lives in search of grandiose dreams, forsaking any and all who cannot carry on alongside. Then, there are those like you and Weave, who are content to play their part, however minuscule it might seem. I may be confused about many things, but I've come to believe that *that* is where true nobility lies."

Something in her voice, an underlying sullenness, caused a strange flutter in Allion's chest. All at once, he had the impression that she was speaking with a specific person in mind.

"Simple goals, huh?" he muttered dryly. "Is that what drew you to Torin?"

His pulse quickened. Despite his offhanded tone, deep down, he knew it to be a question he should not have asked.

Marisha stiffened and withdrew, confirming his fears and telling him that he had struck the right nerve.

"Looking back, I think it was events, more than anything, that bound us," she said finally. "That and the Pendant. I was so desperate to understand. With his yearning for the Sword, it just seemed . . . I don't know. That there had to be a reason."

Though looking away now, she fell back into him, laying her head atop his chest. Allion swallowed, feeling her heart as it beat against his side.

"He hasn't abandoned us, you know. He's coming back."

She peered up at him, and Allion was surprised by the intensity in her eyes. "More and more, I wonder if it would be so bad if he didn't."

Allion gaped in astonishment. "Marisha!"

Before he could say anything further, her lips were on his. Worse, he was kissing her in return. He knew he should break it off; his thoughts begged him to. But he couldn't make his body respond.

He knew not how long it lasted. He knew nothing beyond her taste, her scent, and the intense heat that washed through him in waves. She shifted in front of him. Her hands were on his face. His were in her hair. Nothing else mattered to him. Only that he had found his escape—from the sorrow and from the pain—and, in its place, a bliss that was frightening.

Too late, he heard the rustle of nearby brush. He forced himself to pull free, to separate his mouth from hers. Opening his eyes, he gazed past her to see who had come.

Framed in backdrop by the stark and looming branches of a disease-stricken swamp elm, was Darinor.

Allion froze, the risen warmth gushing from his veins. He felt Marisha turn, and heard her startled gasp.

For a long moment, the Entient stood his ground, glaring down on them, caught somewhere between fury and resignation. When at last he moved to cross his arms, Allion flinched, as certain as he'd ever been that his death was upon him.

"Corathel has agreed," the mystic rumbled. "We make for Atharvan within the hour."

"Father . . ." Marisha began.

But Darinor simply spun about and stormed off through the jungle brume, leaving them to the chill of a smothered passion.

TORIN HAD JUST ABOUT FALLEN ASLEEP when there came a knock at his room's door.

Uncertain of his bearings, he waited for it to sound again. When it did, he rolled up from the lumpy mattress on which he lay and padded toward the disturbance. Before he could think to be more cautious, he threw back the latch and swung the door wide.

There in the hallway of the inn's upper level stood Saena.

"I'm sorry," she said. "Were you napping?"

"I wish," he replied. Beset by his relentless doubts, he had spent most of the last hour or so simply staring at the ceiling.

"Where's Warrlun?" she asked, peering within.

"Making arrangements, I'd guess."

"May I come in?"

Torin yawned, but opened the door wider to allow her entry.

Saena sniffed. "Your room smells as good as ours."

Torin shrugged, only half closing the door behind them. The cramped chamber stank of must and mildew. But they had been lucky to acquire rooms at all. The innkeeper of the Giant's Tongue had laughed, at first, when Warrlun had inquired about space at this or any other inn in town. Only after acknowledging the commander's rank and accepting a good deal of extra coin had the man agreed to relocate a couple of parties to the common room in order to free up these—one for the men, and one for the girls.

"Shouldn't you be visiting Traver's tailor friend right about now?" Torin asked.

Saena did not miss the enmity in his tone. "You're not still worrying about *him*, are you?"

"Among other things," he confessed.

"Dyanne and Holly don't seem too concerned."

"From what I've seen, Dyanne and Holly aren't concerned by much of anything."

"Nevertheless," Saena argued, "in this case, I'd have to agree. Of what harm can he be to the five of us?"

Torin's count was a bit different, since he wasn't exactly considering Saena and Warrlun to be on his side. But he saw no benefit in admitting that just now. "I don't know," he said instead. "I guess I've grown weary of putting my faith in complete strangers."

"Perhaps you just need an opportunity to ease your mind," she suggested. She shifted from foot to foot, eyes wandering.

Torin regarded the woman suspiciously. She seemed unusually nervous. "Meaning what?"

"Would it trouble you to accompany me to that festival-opening dance tonight?"

Her gaze pinned his at last. Torin's thoughts switched suddenly to those of escape. "I'm fairly certain Traver's invite was for you girls alone."

"Nonsense. The whole region is invited, which would include you."

"I'm not exactly in a celebratory mood," he told her.

"Which is why you should go. It'll give you a chance to set your cares aside."

"Some sleep would do better."

"You tried that already, remember?"

He shook his head. "Saena—"

"Please? If not for yourself, do it for me. I don't wish to attend alone. Dyanne and Holly have each other. Without a companion, I fear I might seem to Traver like easy prey."

Torin fiddled with the door pull while peering into Saena's pleading brown eyes. The last thing he felt like doing was cavorting with a bunch of rowdy strangers. Then again, it might be better that he stay close in order to keep an eye on Traver, to make sure the ruffian didn't try anything untoward with any of his companions. Though quite sure each could take care of herself, how would he feel if something happened that he might have prevented?

He looked away, then back to Saena's anxious face. Holding back a sigh of defeat, he forced instead a meager smile.

"All right."

"Terrific," she replied, her familiar beam restored. "I'm off to the tailor, then. The festival is set to begin at dusk, so I'll meet you back here in a few hours. If you must, try to find your sleep between now and then."

Torin nodded, opening and then shutting the door behind her.

Once she had gone, he shuffled back to his feather-stuffed mattress and fell heavily upon it, wishing now that he had simply ignored the young woman's knock.

CHAPTER FORTY-ONE

THE NEXT TIME SAENA CAME rapping at his door, when the last of the meager daylight had faded, Torin was sorely tempted not to respond. Though wide awake, standing beside a poorly sealed window overlooking the rains outside, he continued to have second thoughts about what he had agreed to.

"Torin? Torin, are you in there?"

He closed his eyes. He had already told the woman yes. It was too late to ignore her now.

He moved to the door, and with a deep breath pulled it open. Saena looked radiant in a gown of black and red, woven of a thick material that hugged her frame. She appeared far too elegant, Torin immediately determined, to be accompanied by the likes of him, who had scarcely taken the time to bathe and shave before donning a clean tunic and breeches.

"You look lovely," he managed, and saw her eyes sparkle. "Are you sure you want to be seen with me?"

She curtsied before him. "I would be honored, milord."

For some reason, the gesture made him uncomfortable, and he found himself glancing back and forth down the hall.

"Where are Dyanne and Holly?" he asked, noting well their absence.

"Traver escorted them on ahead. We're to meet them at the pavilion, wherever that is."

Torin gritted his teeth before grabbing his cloak from a nearby hook and handing it to her. "It's still wet out there," he muttered.

Together, they made their way down to the street, taking advantage of a rear exit so as to avoid any jeers or stares from the tavern patrons below. From there, they simply followed the masses. Small wonder this frontier city had seemed so busy earlier. By the look and sound of it, everyone within a dozen leagues had come to take part in the celebration.

A light rain dripped from blackened skies, but could not dampen the spirit that had swept over the people of this city—resident and visitor alike. Fire hissed atop lampposts and torches and in the hands of juggling street performers, who sent it spinning and twirling to the delight of onlookers. Food and drink were everywhere, while music and laughter enlivened an already festive air.

Saena slowed continually, drawn to one happening or another with child-like enthusiasm. Torin, however, kept them moving along, anxious to catch up with his Nymph comrades. He wondered if he might run into Warrlun anywhere, and hoped that he didn't.

The crowds thickened as they neared an open-walled stage covered by a wooden roof erected high overhead. The structure was enormous, with risers and balconies built along the edges. Beneath the permanent awning, hundreds were in attendance, milling on and around a boarded dance floor, waiting for the festivities to begin in earnest. Minstrels sang and played in the background, but as of yet there was more talk than laughter, more eating than drinking, more mingling than dancing. Activity here was louder and more heavily concentrated than it had been in the streets, causing Torin to yearn for the quiet and privacy of his room.

His fears concerning his humble dress, at least, appeared unfounded. While most of the women wore gowns and jewelry, few of the men looked any more regal than he, with as many outfitted in tunics and jerkins as vests and doublets. More importantly, many were wearing their blades as ornamentation. A great relief, since he wasn't about to let the Sword—even masked by its leather wrappings—out of his sight. All in all, he felt he blended in nicely. With any luck, he would escape this insufferable night without notice.

A youthful attendant intercepted them, begging to hold the lady's cloak for a mere copper. Saena accepted his offer with one of her smiles, only barely remembering to check with Torin, whose cloak it really was. He shrugged. It was just a cloak. If lost, he could find another.

After that, with Saena clinging to his arm, he mounted a pair of steps to reach the pavilion floor, feeling as though he were wading into a churning ocean.

"Now what?" he asked of his companion.

"We meet people," Saena exclaimed, enraptured by the sights and sounds of merriment all around her.

He should have known. Alighting upon one conversation after another, the woman proceeded to make happy acquaintances of any who would have her. In a matter of moments, she had introduced him to no fewer than a dozen strangers, most of whom greeted him with an eager smile and a ready handclasp. Torin was hard-pressed to see a point to it all. It would be a miracle if, after tonight, he were to ever encounter any of these people again. If this quest had taught him nothing else, it was that he was liable to lose any friends that he made. So why seek to gain any here?

Still, he nodded politely and answered when spoken to, trying and for the most part failing to remember the names of those with whom he came in contact. He spent the majority of his time standing around awkwardly, searching for some sign of Dyanne, wondering how he was to ever find her amid this throng.

Saena, meanwhile, was never satisfied to remain in one place for long, always venturing off to engage someone new. At times, she would seem to simply disappear, abandoning him at the side of one he had only just met in order to greet another. Thus far, she had always returned. He wasn't sure what he might do if she didn't.

It was during one of these absences that he found himself looking abruptly at a familiar face.

"Hello, outlander," the woman greeted.

Jaecy, he recalled. From the Giant's Tongue. Only prettier than he remembered her, with braided hair, rouged cheeks, and a deep-cut dress that exposed more flesh than Torin was comfortable seeing.

"Having fun?" she asked, twisting her hair into curls with a restless finger.

As he searched for a response, his ears keyed to the music, which had grown much louder—generated now by a full orchestral troupe. "The tunes are lively enough," he replied.

Her smile turned lascivious. "You like this ballad, do you?"

Torin turned his attention to the bawdy lyrics. Too late, he wondered what he had gotten himself into.

"It has a fair melody," he answered finally.

"A fine rhythm to dance to," Jaecy agreed, moving close.

"There you are," a voice interrupted.

Torin turned as Saena reached up to seize him by the arm. With a brittle smile for the local serving girl, his companion pulled at him with a firm, energetic grasp. He glanced back to Jaecy with a look of helpless apology, but made no attempt to resist as Saena whisked him away through the writhing crowd.

"I think we're safe," he observed after several moments of pushing their way into the throng. The song had ended, and the dancers were applauding. A perfect time to make their next escape.

He turned to find the nearest egress when Saena spun him about and cast her arms about his neck. All around them, other dancers were pairing up, as musical pipes started off what promised to be a tender ballad. Torin resisted, at first, as Saena began swaying to the slow, smooth tempo, then finally relented, setting his arms loosely about her waist. It was pleasant enough, he had to admit, to feel a woman's embrace again—even if they were only forced together by circumstance.

She drew closer, and he fought the instinct to push away. Instead, he allowed his gaze to drift over her shoulder in survey of those around him.

Where he finally caught sight of Dyanne.

He was startled by the reaction just seeing her in that moment triggered: a warm rush deep in his breast that rolled quickly over his shoulders and down his spine. The Nymph was breathtaking in a woolen dress of similar style to Saena's—tight upon her torso and billowing slightly over her legs, where it ended several inches above her ankles. Its frills and highlights were the color of the emerald, set upon a background of deepest night. Its fit was less than perfect in certain areas—such as the plunging neckline that revealed more than it should have of the corset beneath. But that was to be expected of a garment for which she had been fitted at the last minute. And in a way, such tiny flaws served only to accentuate her own, natural beauty.

In turning with the music, he was about to lose her, and so he shifted his head, angling for a better view. Weaving couples clogged the dance floor between them—a distance of ten or more paces—but now that he had spied her, he was determined not to let her out of his sight.

With her, of course, was Holly, and Torin had never been so grateful for the pair's camaraderie. For even together, they faced no small task in warding off the packs of suitors surrounding them. Torin's jaw clenched when he saw Traver among those that circled like vultures. The man was hanging back, feigning aloofness as he spoke with another group of ladies, but his shifty gaze never strayed from Dyanne and Holly for long. That the girls appeared to be ignoring the scoundrel was Torin's only consolation.

He determined that he would make his way over to her just as soon as this dance with Saena ended. Even as the idea entered his head, however, he was struck by a sobering thought. What would be his reason for doing so—just to say hello? Perhaps he, too, might invite Dyanne to dance. But would she welcome him? Or would she turn him down as she had the rest?

That was it, he realized, the truth behind his inability to approach her over the past few days. He was afraid. Afraid of being rejected. Afraid of losing what bond they had. As small and inconsequential as their friendship must seem to her, it was already more than he was willing to risk.

The song came to a close. Partners bowed to one another and withdrew, or else moved off together in search of drink or rest or any number of social pursuits. As others took their place, Torin merely stood there in the center of the floor, paralyzed with indecision and self-doubt.

"Thank you," Saena said.

Torin nodded, but could not quite manage a return smile.

The music turned lively again, and Saena was off to mingle with the crowds. Torin followed her for a time, climbing the steps of an elevated platform at the pavilion's edge. There he stopped to lean against the railing—a comfortable position from which to keep his eye on Dyanne.

The entertainment lasted well into the night. Revelers came and went, singing and dancing and partaking of the festive atmosphere with all manner of mindless amusements. As much as possible, Torin kept to the side—like one of the city watchmen there to keep the peace. As tempted as he was at times, he could not bring himself to let go and join the excitement—not even when it seemed that Dyanne and Holly had chosen to do so. Throughout the hours he watched them as they frolicked from place to place upon the pavilion floor, offering pleasant smiles and good cheer to all while somehow evading the more serious overtures that surely came their way. They were like butterflies amid the throng, capturing attention wherever they flew, but never constrained to any single area—or any one person—for long.

For a time, Traver followed them everywhere they went. But even he, Torin noted, eventually moved on in search of those more likely to fall victim to his charms. Witnessing this brought a smile to the young king's face. And yet, as he watched Dyanne spurn the advances of one swain after another, he had to wonder just what a man might do to win her affections.

Every now and then, Saena would return to him, introducing him to another newfound friend, engaging him in conversation, or drawing him out for another dance. He tried to accommodate her, but he was never more content than when she let him be, allowing him to observe rather than participate, leaving him alone with his reflections.

Dyanne and Holly remained inseparable. On rare occasion, Torin caught one or the other's playful smile. Whenever he did, he felt that familiar tug, the need to confront Dyanne with his feelings—or at the very least, to engage in some lighthearted activity that might open a dialogue between them. But time and again, he failed to make himself do so. He could not take that chance without having at least some assurance that her reaction would be a positive one. And while he knew not what it might take to impress her, he felt certain it was something more than he possessed.

Even the most obvious opportunities passed him by, such as when Dyanne herself began swaying from side to side while skipping through the crowd to a fast-paced rhythm. Holly followed directly behind, clinging to Dyanne's hips, mimicking her friend's every lean and shift. Together, they pranced through the gathered masses as if they owned the entire floor. Others soon joined the chain, latching onto Holly in the same manner. Within moments, a string of no fewer than a dozen people was worming its way across the pavilion, a laughing procession that drew additional members with each winding pass.

More than once, the string of dancers slipped by Torin's position. Each time that it did, he had to resist the urge to grab on. It would be so easy, he told himself, to reach out, to free himself of all senseless concerns and to join the celebration. Yet with Dyanne at the head, he dared not, fearing that the string might break beneath his uninvited weight. The best he could do was to stand aside and admire the woman's cheerful inventiveness, basking in the delight she so easily brought to those around her.

Indeed, all but he appeared to be enjoying themselves—and even he no longer wished for the festivities to end. For he might never again be given a chance such as this, to study the more whimsical side of this woman he had come to hold in such high esteem. He followed her motions whenever possible, feeling as if he could watch her forever. There was something lyrical about her beauty—made all the more stunning by the joyfulness that went with it. Everything about her was compelling: her hair, strands so delicate they could only have been woven by Olirian hands; her skin, so bright and smooth in the gleaming lamplight; her smile, like the lustrous sparkle of a priceless gemstone . . .

Torin forced himself to look away. He did not know which was more absurd: his thoughts, or his helplessness to properly express them. The entire issue was ridiculous. He would simply march up to her and confess what he was feeling. If she cared for him in any measure, she would flash him that dazzling smile and admit as much. If not, he would continue on his way, reminding himself that it was her choice to make.

He had just about summoned the courage to do so when he saw Jaecy once more. The serving girl was clinging to some fashionable rogue out on the dance floor, doing nothing to discourage his hands as they slipped lower and lower about her waist. But unless Torin was mistaken, she was staring right past her partner, fixing her eyes on *him*. When she caught Torin looking at her, she sent him a wink.

His resolve crumbled—not because he was enticed by Jaecy's interest, but because it occurred to him that he might do all a favor by accepting his limitations, settling for someone who clearly fancied him, rather than pining for someone like Dyanne, whose matchless perfection would seem to place her forever beyond his undeserving reach.

At that moment, a bell mounted in a tower above the pavilion sounded the midnight hour. Almost at once, the music tapered off. Many in attendance groaned with disappointment.

"What's happening?" Torin asked of a stranger beside him at the rail.

"Curfew," the other replied, turning already for the exit.

Just like that, the evening had come to an end. City guardsmen stepped forward, urging the revelers to depart. Many seemed only too eager to comply, to head back to their inns and homes for sleep or else other, wilder forms of entertainment. Torin, however, felt his heart sink. Though he hadn't even wanted to attend, he felt cheated by the abrupt conclusion.

As the crowds began to disperse, he looked for his friends. Saena had left him only moments earlier, but might have been anywhere. He thought to stay at the rail so that *she* could find *him,* until an overzealous soldier prodded him along.

He was filing out with all the rest, head bowed with regret and frustration, when someone grabbed him unexpectedly by the arm. He glanced over, certain to find either Saena or Jaecy peering up at him.

It was Dyanne.

He blinked, so surprised that he nearly swooned. He looked down to where she held his arm, which tingled with the warmth of her touch. She glanced back and forth at the masses around them, then led him aside into the shadow of one of the pavilion's supports.

"What is it?" he asked. It was all he could squeeze past the lump in his throat.

She pulled him close, facing him squarely. "Did you learn anything tonight?"

Their escorts, Torin recalled with an effort. He shook his head. "Nothing useful. What about Traver?"

"A harmless lecher, from what I've gathered. Spent half the night trying to look down my bodice."

Torin could not tell if she was flattered by the notion, or embarrassed. All he could think of was how marvelous this woman was, how blessed he felt to be here and now the center of her attention. Even among so many people, it seemed to him that they were alone in all the world.

His stomach tightened. He could deny the truth no longer. Despite his quest, despite Marisha, he had to know what Dyanne might feel for him. Nor could he imagine a better opportunity to find out. The magic of this moment was unmistakable, like that in which he had first drawn the Sword of Asahiel.

"Where's Holly?" he asked, buying time as he fought for the right words.

Dyanne huffed. "Traver's trying to convince her to let him show her a *truly* good time."

"What's wrong? Are you feeling left out?" he remarked, and immediately cursed the day he'd been born. The words had been a reflex, laced with jealousy and sarcasm, born of the secret fear that, indeed, it was Traver's affection she desired. Regardless, that was not the message he had hoped to convey.

Dyanne scoffed, and punched him playfully, giving him a chance, perhaps, to redeem himself. Yet any other words he might offer were buried beneath their own weight. He couldn't simply blurt out how utterly enthralling he found her. He had to find a way to soften the blow.

In the meantime, he knew that he should at least apologize. But before he could even do that much, Saena found them.

"Are we ready?"

Torin thought to excuse himself and Dyanne for a moment longer, yet wasn't sure how to do so. When Holly and Traver sidled up to them, he knew his moment had passed.

"We're not spending the night out here, are we?" the smaller Nymph demanded. Though Traver hovered over her, it appeared clear that she had spurned his offer.

She continued past, dark threads of hair draped upon her tiny shoulders. Perhaps it was the energy of the night that lent such a bold spring to her step. Dyanne turned to follow. Saena led Torin after.

They paused in a long line of others to retrieve their cloaks, then huddled one last time beneath the pavilion awning.

"I suppose I'll see you all tomorrow, then," Traver said.

"Bright and early," Dyanne assured him.

The rogue spoke vaguely to Torin. "I trust you will see the ladies safely back to the Giant's Tongue?"

Torin glared in response. Traver wasn't even looking at him; rather, he was glancing about as the dregs of the crowd filtered past, no doubt searching for one who might yet accept his evening's proposal.

Damn you, was Torin's only manageable thought.

His curse was not directed toward Traver.

CHAPTER FORTY-TWO

HE WAS STILL BERATING HIMSELF THE NEXT MORNING, when he awoke to realize that the previous night had been more than just a dream. In a way, he was grateful, for it meant that the many images he had captured in the shadow of that central pavilion—images he had recounted time and again throughout his sleeping hours—were in fact real moments that he might cherish forever. By the same token, it meant the conclusion to that evening—that which had caused him such bittersweet torment—could not now be simply blinked away.

It seemed almost impossible that he could be so foolish. For all he knew, his quiet moment with Dyanne had been the only one she would ever offer him. And he had wasted it. Throughout the hours of restless slumber that had followed, he had fought to change the words that had escaped his mouth—those he had spoken to her when it would have been better to say nothing at all. Alas, only the darkness had been there to listen.

He closed his eyes with a silent groan, unsure which he should be more ashamed of: his inability to express his true feelings, or the fact that he should even want to do so, given his betrothal to Marisha. He'd been so quick to judge Traver, when he himself was no better than a faithless rogue. For what would he do if he were to discover that Dyanne cared for him? Would he be able to ignore her as he had Jaecy? Or would he forsake his private vows and betray the young Lewellyn who but a short time ago had been the measure of his entire world?

Bile filled Torin's mouth as a wave of self-loathing washed over him. Regardless of the answer, how could he continue to indulge this obsession? He had far too many pressing concerns to make matters of the heart a priority. He had a task to complete, and as soon as that goal was achieved, he would be leaving this land and all of its inhabitants behind.

And that was exactly as he wanted it.

He forced his eyes open again, waving aside the demons that picked like ravens at his heart. Predawn shadows blanketed the room's contents, like dust-covered linens draped over abandoned stores. His gaze shifted to the bed that lay empty beside his own. Its sheets remained tucked and folded, unused during the night. Warrlun had never returned, having opted to remain with Ethric, most likely, after their long evening of outfitting and preparation. While the history between Traver and Warrlun went way back, Torin had learned that it was old man Ethric, Traver's senior partner, who had led those Finlorian-hunting expeditions of long ago. No doubt, Lorre's chief commander and former lead bounty hunter had much about which to reminisce.

As if summoned by his musings, there came the scrape of a key in the outer door lock. The inner latch was already lifted free, left open in case Warrlun should decide to return in the middle of the night. Beneath his covers, Torin reached for the Crimson Sword, which lay sheathed on the mattress beside him.

As expected, it was Warrlun who shoved his way into the room. He appeared almost disappointed to find that Torin was already awake.

"Up," the old soldier barked. "It'll be daylight soon."

"Just getting my bearings," Torin grumbled.

"Wake the girls and meet me out back by the horses. We're on our way before the sun hits its first mark."

With one hand on the scabbard and the other on the hilt, Torin was fully prepared to draw his blade and run the commander through if it would appease his own simmering frustrations. But before he could even complete the thought, the old soldier turned and stomped away, leaving his key in the lock and the door open wide.

TIME DID NOT PERMIT FOR BREAKFAST, so they packed it for the road, adding fruits and cheeses and fresh-baked breads from the Giant's Tongue to the stores of nuts and vegetables and dried meats that would sustain the members of their company in the days ahead. The task was assigned to Saena, while Torin worked alongside Dyanne and Holly to saddle the horses. Warrlun stood by, contributing now and then with a snide comment or stern command. For once, however, Torin was grateful for the soldier's presence, as it provided a ready excuse for his own gruff silence as he fought to keep his eyes from Dyanne.

When all had been made ready, the five from Neak-Thur led their mounts to a set of stables attached to the rear of the tiny expeditioner's storefront at which they had first stopped on their way into town. There, they were greeted by a leering Traver, whose red-rimmed eyes had darkened from lack of sleep. They stood around for only a few moments while Warrlun and the wispy-haired Ethric engaged in private conference—barely long enough to be introduced to the pair of Traver's men who would be accompanying them. Trackers both, it was said, and accomplished mountain rangers. Torin forgot their names as soon as they were given, as disinterested in them as they seemed to be in him.

They set off together, picking their way down muddied streets toward Vagarbound's central gates. Dawn's rays had yet to break over the steep ridge of the Dragontails to the east, its arrival naught but a muted glow through drizzly skies. Nevertheless, the town was already astir. Last night had been just the beginning, Traver informed them, riding beside the girls. Starting today, the weeklong festival would commence in earnest, with events and contests and prizes that promised laughs and excitement for all. A pity, he claimed, that they could not remain but a few more days. For once, Torin did not completely disagree with the man. Perhaps if they were to stay even a little longer, he might find a chance to relive—and rewrite the ending to—last night's episode.

The gates had only just been opened when Torin's company reached them. Once again, they were compelled to wait in line while teams of clerks and watchmen cleared those coming and going. There were a great many more seeking entry than exit, Torin noted—thankfully so, as now that he could see the open road, he felt anxious to be upon it.

"Good speed, Commander," the gate guard bade Warrlun as the approval to leave was given.

The old soldier grunted, returning the other's salute as he spurred his mount out onto the downward-sloping roadway. Traver followed, accepting a nod from the guardsman that seemed to the suspicious Torin a little too familiar. The girls went next, with Torin on their heels and Traver's hounds trailing.

They had to ride west a fair ways before the road turned north again, skirting the line of the mountains. All the while, they rode in silence—except Traver, whose mouth never stopped moving. Torin's brow soon ached from glaring so hard. He had expected that once he was free of the city and the false sense of calm generated by its merrymakers, his wayward thoughts would be swept aside by a renewed urgency. But while the relative solitude did indeed sharpen his focus with regard to his quest, not even the chill northern winds could smother the coals glowing deep within his breast. Envy and longing burned constantly, as mile after mile, league after league, he watched Dyanne laugh and smile and respond with wonder to the various jests and compliments and tales with which Traver kept himself and the others entertained. She couldn't possibly be as amused as she pretended to be, but that didn't matter to Torin. All that mattered was that she should allow one such as Traver the enduring pleasure of her conversation, while he himself was left trailing behind like some baggage handler in a royal train.

Of course, that was more his fault than hers. Were he not so craven, he too might share her company, rather than merely serve witness to it. Dyanne had always seemed confident, fully content with just Holly's companionship. But never had she truly behaved in a manner he might brand haughty or disdainful. In essence, it was not *she* who was keeping this distance between them.

But moments of such clarity visited him seldom, and even then were quickly buried beneath irrational fears. He could deny it if he wished, but the truth was, Dyanne was developing an attachment to this rogue—moment by moment, hour by hour—leaving Torin at a loss to explain why. Traver was a tall man with thick bones and an athletic build. But he wasn't what Torin would allow as handsome, and was much too old for her in any case. His gracious smirk might have been wiped away by a wind gust. Perhaps it was the man's false charm, his invasive gaze, or the fact that his head, much like Wedge Commander Jaik's, appeared too large when compared to his body.

Whichever trait she found so endearing, Torin wished that he could borrow it for but a little while, just long enough to see if she might take a similar fancy to him.

Instead, he was forced to carry on behind the woman as he had from the beginning, an unnoticed observer, with no choice but to remind himself that despite all they'd been through, he barely knew her. Certainly her attentions were none of his affair.

"Are you feeling all right?" Saena asked him, and only then did he realize how unusually quiet she had been all day.

"Well enough," he muttered, watching his breath cloud the air. "Just looking forward to finishing this business."

Saena nodded, then slipped back into silence. All of a sudden, Torin felt a pang of guilt that had nothing to do with his heart's betrayal of Marisha. For it occurred to him in that moment just how much he had come to rely upon Saena's presence—and how he continued to take it for granted. His thankless manner should have driven her away long ago. Yet for some reason, she insisted on being the friend that he so desperately needed here in this strange land. Perhaps it was time to lay his suspicions to rest and do more to express his appreciation.

But he said nothing, turning both his gaze and his roiling thoughts back to Dyanne.

They spent the night in the shadow of the mountains, at the base of the pass known as Goblin Reach. Snow dusted the trail as it climbed into the rocks ahead, providing a glimpse of that which they could expect to find amid the higher elevations. Barring ill fortune, they would be through the pass in a day or two, beyond which lay the Splinterwood. While many of the signs discovered years ago suggested that the Finlorians had fled into the highest reaches of the Trollslay and Wyvern Spur Mountains, Traver was among those who believed that the elven folk would have eventually made their way down into what was commonly known as the Forgotten Forest, a vast stretch of ancient wilderness grown up between those twin prongs of the northern Dragontails. It was there that the search would begin.

Never mind that trackers and hunters and frontiersmen of every variety—himself included—had been scouring that forest for decades, Traver snickered, and found no traceable sign.

Torin kept waiting for Warrlun to order the rogue to be silent, but he never did. Instead, Traver prattled on while Torin consumed a relatively tasteless dinner without interest. Despite his best efforts to disappear within himself, he could not help but sneak an occasional glance in Dyanne's direction, hoping that she might acknowledge him in even the tiniest way. But she seemed to be genuinely absorbed in the rogue's blather, encouraging him with her ready responses and pressing for more with her many questions. Holly was no help, as she was behaving much the same. Torin wanted to suggest that if they were to stop feigning interest, the rogue might actually stop, but he did not want the kind of attention such an outburst might bring.

So he chewed his food and kept his tongue, ignoring—and for the most part ignored by—his companions. Once or twice he felt compelled to grunt or shrug in response to an aside from Saena, but in general, even she let him be. At last, with Traver's voice echoing in his ears, Torin crawled beneath his lean-to, burrowed into his bedroll, and bade silent riddance to the grueling day.

He awoke among a bed of misty tendrils sprouted forth from the sodden land. Once again, he had scarcely slept, haunted by fears and suspicions and desires and regrets too numerous to recount. Most troubling of all, perhaps, was the understanding that this might continue for weeks or months. Until they were able to drive the Finlorians from hiding, or until his current comrades tired of the search, he could expect to endure an intolerable string of days like the last.

His chest ached at the prospect.

He found no time to sulk, however, as Warrlun beat them all from their tents and into action before the break of dawn. As before, Saena was put in charge of breakfast, while Torin and the Nymphs and Traver's hounds—Brolin and Kifur—broke camp. Warrlun and Traver kept to one side, discussing the day's plans.

They started out beneath another light rain; by now, Torin was simply grateful that it was not a heavy one. He was far less pleased with their travel formation, which remained as before—with him stuck near the rear, watching Traver carry along beside his companions from the Fenwood. By midmorning, he was seething over Dyanne's refusal to simply dismiss Traver as the charlatan that he was. The man's tales had become ever more grandiose—and, to Torin's ears, increasingly absurd. But the girls, especially Dyanne, seemed to hang upon the charming rogue's every word, forcing Torin to swallow his skepticism and say nothing.

He was beginning to wonder if the problem lay with Traver at all. For all his scathing reservations, he alone seemed unable to trust the man. Saena had expressed empathy, at least, but that wasn't the same as having worries of her own. Might it be that only his fierce and senseless jealousy was fostering his mistrust?

But no allowances could lay his feelings to rest. Nor did it seem to matter that it was best he should keep his distance from Dyanne for the sake of Marisha. Despite a heavy cloak of guilt, his envy was a blade that would not be turned aside.

It continued to cut at him as the snow cover thickened and the temperatures dropped. They were well up into the mountains by now, surrounded by ice and rock and gusting winds. Torin was readily reminded of his trek through the Dragonscale Cleft much farther to the south, and followed carefully the path forged by his guides. His eyes drifted from peak to peak, searching for anything that might result in a rockfall or avalanche.

Even then, his overall focus remained on Dyanne. Foolish as it was, he could not seem to stop. He told himself that he was hoping for too much, yearning for something he could never have. A mortal did not ask for the hand of a goddess. But with the majesty of her presence shining consistently before him, it was too much to prevent himself from dreaming.

The thought had no sooner entered his head than she looked back at him suddenly. Her eyes gleamed mischievously, and that dazzling smile broke upon her lips. His entire body flushed with an unexpected warmth, and he forced himself to turn away in chagrin. Could it be that she suspected how he felt? His emotions had become so strong, it seemed entirely possible that they had taken tangible form. Had she felt the heat of their brush? Surely she had noticed by now his stares of obsessed admiration. Had she recognized them as such? If so, what did she think of him? Would she ever reveal to him her private feelings?

His eyes settled on Saena, who offered him a reassuring smile. He might have looked away again, but forced himself to return that smile instead, determined to avoid Dyanne's knowing gaze. Once again, he took comfort in she who kept nearest his side. Perhaps she did so because that had been the assignment given her by Lord Lorre. But Torin was no longer so sure. By all appearances, her friendship was genuine, and not merely that of a servant fulfilling her sworn duty.

Or perhaps that was what she wanted him to believe.

He dragged his eyes back to the road, tortured by his restless emotions and the doubts they fostered within him. His suspicions had become all-consuming. If only he could settle matters with Dyanne, he believed, then all the rest might lose their edge. But when and how was he to do so?

It wasn't long thereafter that Warrlun signaled Traver to the head of their column. The trail had begun to break apart, branching into a sudden maze of draws and defiles. The wrong path might lead to a dead end or worse. The time had come for Traver to stow his tongue and take the lead.

For a moment, Torin feared that Dyanne meant to ride ahead with him. But she did not, declining his princely invitation in order to stay back with Holly. Traver's bow could not mask his disappointment, causing Torin to sneer with satisfaction.

Now was his chance, Torin realized as they continued on. All he need do was sidle on ahead to where Traver had been. He doubted that anyone other than Holly would pay any attention to what he might have to say to Dyanne. And while it would in fact be nerve-wracking to have the smaller Nymph listening in, better that than waiting for a moment in which the two were apart.

But once again, he held his reins and himself in check. As frightened as he was of what the sardonic Holly's response might be, he still feared Dyanne herself more. Confessing himself to her would be like stepping out over one of the blind ledges that surrounded them. He could readily imagine the lifesaving thrill he would experience should he find solid footing on the other side. But if there was nothing there, how severe would be his fall?

Brisk winds swirled and gusted around them, bearing light flurries of snow that dusted their cloaks and piled atop the ever-deepening drifts that covered the trails. But their icy murmurings were nothing compared to the tempest that continued to build in Torin's heart. It was fast reaching the point where he would do anything to silence his own inner voice, even if it meant leaping—in fact—from the nearest mountain ridge.

The sun made a brief appearance, but failed to penetrate the leaden shield of the skies. Traver kept them moving at a steady pace, selecting from among the meandering pathways that snaked over and among various shelves and corridors of shattered stone. Dyanne and Holly followed behind Warrlun, just ahead of Torin and Saena. Brolin and Kifur remained at the rear, hauling the pack horses and keeping close watch on the many dangerous overhangs of ice and snow.

Come noon, they found themselves amid a rugged array of natural caves— openings that ranged from the narrowest fissure to a yawning breach through which their entire company could have ridden abreast. The terrain grew increasingly jagged, and the horses took turns slipping and stumbling upon a carpet of loose stone hidden beneath the snowy crust. Boulders lay everywhere, fallen from the ravaged slopes like crumbs from some giant table.

More than once, Torin detected flashes of movement among the rocks and deadwood and other mountain debris. Birds and other small animals, it seemed, venturing forth from their nests and dens to mark the passing of this strange company through these stark, windswept halls. Though it occurred to him that any number of larger, more dangerous creatures might have fashioned homes up here, he was too distracted to grant the matter more than a passing concern.

Up ahead, Warrlun mumbled something to Traver that Torin couldn't hear, casting about as if wondering where they were. Traver responded with a confident gesture and some words of assurance, then kicked his heels, urging his steed onward into the mouth of a slender defile. Lorre's chief commander glanced once more at the empty ridgelines, then followed the other in.

The last of their train had entered when the first missile struck, driving into the snow at the head of their column almost before its whistle had sounded. Traver's horse reared, and the clutching rogue was nearly dumped from his saddle. Warrlun reached for the sword strapped across his back.

"Ambush!"

Torin's own horse was rearing and stamping, startled by the sudden commotion. He, too, might have reached for his weapon, but it was all he could do to cling to his reins. While he wrestled with his mount, shadows emerged, springing forth from the crags and hollows all around. He saw now the pair perched on either side atop the cliffs that formed the defile into which Traver had guided them, and felt the rush of those who closed at each end to seal the members of his company within.

His thoughts raced. Brigands? Since starting through the passes that morning, they had encountered not another living soul. What fool of a brigand would attempt to earn his living up here in the dead of winter?

A moment later, the truth was revealed.

"Don't be foolish, my friend. Put the blade away."

Torin whirled toward the sound of Traver's voice, as he finally brought his edgy mount under control. Their guide had done the same, flanked now by a pair of frontiersmen armed with loaded crossbows. The attention of these ruffians, Torin noticed, was aimed not at Traver, but at Warrlun, farther in.

"What is this, Traver?" the commander hissed, like a cornered viper.

"Come now, don't ask as if surprised. You can't expect a man to make any real coin hunting something that doesn't exist."

"His Lordship pays—"

"Food and supplies," Traver responded dismissively, "little more."

Torin's arm itched, urging him to reach for his blade. But he dared not. Not with Brolin and Kifur glaring at him, their own swords already drawn. With them were two others, emerged from some cave or outcropping that he had overlooked on his way into this tight gulch. Up above, the two crossbowmen held aim squarely upon Warrlun, but from their elevated position, it would be a small matter to turn sight and bury a bolt or two in the outlander's hide. Nine against five, by his tally—and that was counting Warrlun and Saena as allies. Either way, their enemy held every advantage.

"And your fur trade?" Warrlun pressed. "Why risk that over a few stolen riches?"

The commander was stalling, Torin realized, which meant that he, too, understood the severity of their position.

Traver laughed. "I'll still be a furrier when this day is done—only a much wealthier one."

A few of his men snickered, their breath clouding in the frigid air. In that moment, Torin felt certain that he and his company were not the first to fall victim to this band.

Warrlun grunted in response. "His Lordship will have you hanging from a gallows before week's end. Mark my words."

"My dear friend, how is His Lordship to know?"

Torin continued to search for an escape. No matter how he looked at it, he and his friends remained trapped within this corridor of rock, pinched from above and on either side. At the same time, he felt a growing fury building within—not just at his captors, but himself as well. For if he hadn't been so self-absorbed, he might have sensed his enemies' presence before now.

Now that it was too late.

"Ethric," Warrlun declared, issuing the man's name in low warning. "Ethric will send word, once he learns what became of us."

Traver's smug grin slipped somewhat, his expression become almost pitying. "Who do you think sent my companions on ahead?"

That was why Traver had invited them to attend last night's festivities, Torin realized. The ruffian hadn't done so merely to ogle the women, but to give the rest of his band the chance to set the stage for this assault.

Warrlun was slow to respond. A crimson rage colored his cheeks, while his gloved fingers tightened about his sword hilt. Torin half expected him to simply explode.

"If that's true," the commander finally growled, "then why haven't you killed us already?"

"Because I'd rather not kill all of you," Traver admitted, glancing at the women. "Not at first, anyway. Nor do I wish to have to drag your carcass to where it won't be found. So I'll make you an offer: Surrender your arms and come with us, and I'll do what I can to make your death as painless as possible."

Warrlun looked around, marking again the positions held by Traver's men. "You leave a man little room to bargain," he said, echoing the rogue's earlier words from back at the Giant's Tongue. "But I do have one condition."

Traver's brow arched with amusement before curling in suspicion. "Drop your sword, and I'll consider your request."

The old soldier obeyed, letting his heavy blade fall to the earth, where it landed with a muffled crunch in the crusty snow. Torin shrieked a silent oath as the commander reached slowly to place his hands behind his head. What was the fool thinking?

"Well then, what shall it be, my friend?" Traver asked, dark eyes gleaming with triumph. "An amusement with one of the ladies, perhaps?"

A dreadful smile came to Warrlun's lips, the first that Torin had seen the man give. "Only that you and your vermin die first."

Even as the words registered, the soldier's hands whipped out from behind his head with a pair of concealed daggers. The blades went flying, hurtling end over end toward the crossbowmen perched atop the ridge. Neither hit its mark, but came near enough that both enemies missed theirs. One hastily fired bolt clattered against stone while the other struck the commander's saddle—empty now as Warrlun rolled to the ground to retrieve his sword.

That was all Torin saw before he, too, threw himself aside, using his horse as a shield. The Sword was in hand by the time his feet struck, and its power engulfed him as his passion was unleashed.

His first thrust took Kifur through the chest, spilling a wash of blood that set the horses to screaming. Brolin fell next, followed by one of the nameless brigands at his back. Torin spun then to guard against the chaos behind him. One of those above was using heavy coat and shield to fend off Holly's throwing knives, while his partner reloaded. Dyanne couldn't reach either, and so was dashing toward the front on Warrlun's heels. She, too, had forsaken her steed, which bucked feverishly but couldn't find the room to turn around.

The forward crossbowmen flanking Traver held their ground and took level aim. Warrlun barreled toward them with a growl. By that time, Torin was reengaged with the lone ruffian still in place at the rear of the passageway. He would have already brought the man down, but the horses continued to panic and scream, and his every instinct was required to dodge their flailing hooves.

He dipped a shoulder without knowing why—until a crossbow quarrel tore across his cloak and splintered against the mountain face. He spun and ducked, then fell in a loose tangle as Saena was thrown from her mount. After bracing her fall, he found himself charging toward the front, hurdling the tumbled body of one of the perched bowmen. Warrlun, he now realized, had killed one of the forward marauders and taken up the man's crossbow. It was his bolt that had felled the one from above.

Dyanne was even now finishing off the other that had stood beside Traver. Torin fought through another scramble of unknown limbs, turning himself around once more. He did so just in time to slice through the descending blade of the last remaining rear guardsman. There was a clutch and a scuffle, then a shriek from overhead. A crossbow landed at his feet, followed by a body with the handle of a throwing knife sticking from its eye.

His own horse shoved past, charging after those that had managed to clear out—either forward or to the rear. He tucked back against the rock to avoid its charge, only to be pinned there by the crushing bulk of his remaining adversary. The man took hold of his wrists, fighting to keep him from bringing the Sword to bear.

Up high the two went, with the larger man smashing Torin's hands against the stone, struggling to break his grip. Eyeing a dagger in the other's belt, Torin wrested his left hand free, leaving only his right to maintain hold of the Sword. While his opponent sneered in anticipation of taking the fiery blade for himself, Torin tore the man's dagger from its sheath and shoved it deep into the other's gut. The ruffian stiffened, thrashed in defiance, then fell back with a shove from Torin, staggering on unsteady feet.

Sensing no other immediate threat, Torin pushed himself away from the wall and tightened his grip upon the Sword. The stubborn marauder actually plucked the dagger from his own belly and snarled. But before Torin could finish the job, a crossbow bolt lanced through the rogue's neck, dropping him to his knees and then flat to the earth.

Torin knew without taking stock that all had been accounted for.

All but one.

"As you were, Your Highness."

He turned slowly toward the mouth of the defile as the last of the horses bolted through. Somehow in the confusion, Traver had managed to worm his way from one end to the other, past the knot of thrashing limbs and heaving bodies, dodging blades and quarrels, to reach the opening. There he stood with bloodied mouth and crazed eyes, clutching tight a human shield.

Saena.

"It's over, Traver," Warrlun spat, fitting another bolt to his stolen crossbow. He seemed not to notice that he had a pair of the shafts sticking from his shoulder, with another buried in his side. "I'll gladly kill her to get to you."

"You might find that difficult to explain to your precious Lordship."

Warrlun took aim. Traver's eyes widened.

"No!" Dyanne yelled, pushing aside the commander's weapon.

The old soldier looked like he might just swing around to put the bolt through Dyanne's face instead, until the tip of the Nymph's rapier snapped up between them to prick his chin.

Traver laughed, his smug smile making a triumphant return. "Well, then, it seems we have a dispute as to how we're to handle this."

"He's right," Torin said. "You can't escape us, Traver."

"I can if you wish to preserve the life of this young lady," the ruffian argued, teasing his knife against Saena's throat. His cheek was all but flush against hers, but he managed to press closer as he sniffed the veil of her hair.

"And where will you run?" Warrlun demanded, his finger still on the trigger of the lowered crossbow.

Traver shrugged. "The Southland is yet filled with men of opportunity." One of his fallen comrades gave a dying moan. "Might be some time before His Lordship lays claim to it all."

The commander shook his head. "A cutthroat like you would find a knife in his back ere seeing his first dawn. So why not save us both the trouble? Should you beg, I might even make it quick."

Torin looked to Saena, taking measure of the courage and fear that warred within her eyes, seeking some sign as to what she would have him do.

"Or perhaps instead I shall ransom this pretty thing back to Lord Lorre. Hmm?"

The rogue was desperate, Torin could tell. Despite his bluster, he had never imagined the odds could turn against him so quickly. And yet, desperate men were the hardest to bargain with, for a man with nothing more to lose could not be relied upon to make rational decisions.

"What about a trade?" Torin asked.

Traver snaked a glance in his direction. "A trade?"

"You know what this is, don't you?" Torin replied, shaking the Sword in emphasis. "I'll wager you asked your friends working the city gate if I carried it, and they gave you a good description. It's what you and your men came for, is it not?"

Traver's greedy eyes turned back to Warrlun, too late to hide the truth.

"You'll have it," Torin assured him, "if you agree to turn her loose."

Traver snorted. "So that our commander there can put an arrow through my back the moment I turn around?"

"You can take me instead," Torin offered. "My companions will make certain he doesn't harm you."

He wasn't sure the plan made sense. All he was looking for was a way to break the present stalemate, to remove Saena from harm's way—even though it required every ounce of willpower he could summon not to rush the brigand here and now. Which was more important: his quest, or the life of this lone woman?

Then again, his quest seemed hopeless. Without Traver to steer them, they'd be lucky to escape this maze their guide had led them down. His mission had failed, so why not salvage what he could?

His enemy, he could tell, was making his own calculations. The others awaited Traver's response with bated breath—all but Warrlun, who continued to huff and snort like a rampaging bull.

"Toss the blade over here," the outlaw commanded. His scowl suggested that he was not yet convinced of Torin's plan; but evidently he had decided to play it through.

Torin recalled again his face-off in Spithaera's lair, and that with Lorre on the battlefield of Neak-Thur. In both instances, luck had rewarded him: once for his defiance, and once for his willingness to admit defeat. He wondered suddenly how many times he would be forced to endure this scenario, and how much longer his luck could hold out.

Though it pained him to even imagine Traver's oily hands taking hold of the divine talisman, Torin capitulated. He did not toss the Sword, as Traver had asked, but thrust it like a battle standard into the earth. Crimson flames bubbled up like springwater as they enveloped the buried portion of the blade, melting the snow and causing the bedrock to glow.

"Step back," Traver snarled.

Again Torin paused, wondering if this was the right course. He could assume that his friends would not honor his hasty offer of safe passage. But even if he could rely on them not to permit Traver's escape, killing the rogue would become much more difficult once the man had taken possession of the Sword.

He took a reverse stride, comforted by the warmth of the Pendant, even as he ached at leaving the Sword behind.

Traver's wary eyes narrowed in warning, and he tightened his grip on Saena's throat. Her terror looked to be melting beneath the heat of a rising anger, leaving Torin to pray that she was not contemplating something foolish.

Despite all of his careful reasoning, what happened next was not something Torin could have foreseen. As Traver waited for him to continue his retreat, there came a sharp and violent crack from the mouth of the defile. The ruffian stood straight up, arched at the back, while Saena was thrown forward by a sudden momentum. Traver's clinching arm slipped from her like a length of loose rope, while at the same time, his dagger fell from his other hand, barely nicking the woman's throat as she pitched to her hands and knees.

Torin lunged ahead to catch her, snatching up the Sword as he went. Traver never moved. He simply stood there, eyes wide, mouth agape, as if mounted on a pole. A moment later, a stream of blood spilled over his tongue and teeth, and his body slapped down face-first at Torin's feet.

The young king looked up from the wicked gash that appeared to have severed the dead man's spine, and spied immediately the shadowy figure standing over him—holding an axe that dripped a line of fresh blood from its gleaming edge.

CHAPTER FORTY-THREE

BLOODY AXE OR NO, there was something odd about the figure standing there now in the mouth of the narrow defile, something more than his startling appearance and inexplicable actions. He had the height of a middling child, but with his broad shoulders and heavy coat seemed almost as square. In truth, Torin could not even confirm yet that it was a *he*—or even human—as the shadows of the mountain cleft prevented him from seeing into the depths of the other's cowl.

Torin held perfectly still, one knee upon the earth as he crouched over Saena, sword arm ready. It was too early to know if the stranger was a friend come to save them, or merely a rival come to claim Traver's unsecured spoils.

"Get her up, ya fool," the stranger rumbled in a husky voice. "She ain't got the skin to be lying in the snow."

Torin rose slowly to his feet, pulling Saena up with him. Together, they stood to one side of the defile. Her eyes went to Traver's corpse, while his remained fixed on the new arrival.

"We're indebted to you," Torin offered.

The stranger gave a snort. "You be the man who belongs to that blade?"

Torin glanced at the Sword before granting a wary nod.

"Torin, I'm guessing. Of Pentania."

The outlander's suspicions deepened. "And what do we call you?"

The stranger shifted, as if taking stock of those farther down the trail. He had yet to lower his axe. His squat form and bold stance reminded Torin suddenly of Arn—except that he was a good head or two shorter than that, even.

At last, their mysterious savior seemed to arrive at a decision. With one hand still gripping the handle of his weapon, the other reached up over the top of his head, pushing back his concealing hood.

Saena gasped, though she moved quickly to stifle it. Torin felt his own eyes widen. Before either could react further, Dyanne made a sound of indignation as Warrlun slapped her rapier away and, ignoring the line of blood drawn on his own chin, raised his crossbow, taking aim once again at the far mouth of the defile.

"What are you doing?" Holly demanded, crouched halfway between Dyanne and Warrlun at one end, and Torin and Saena at the other.

But Warrlun wasn't listening, his gaze squeezed in focus upon his target. "Clear aside!" he shouted to his companions.

"Wait!" Saena managed, overcoming her own surprise to step farther out into the shot's path.

Torin wasn't sure what to do; neither were his friends of the Fenwood. Holly was glaring at Warrlun, but Dyanne was casting back and forth between the soldier and the stranger, as if uncertain whom she should trust.

"Commander, I beg you," Saena implored, her hand raised as a shield. She then turned her plea upon Torin. "Don't let him shoot."

That was enough for Torin, though it took a moment for him to find his tongue. "Dyanne."

The Nymph was back on Warrlun in an instant. He tried to fend her off, but she ducked his swatting arm and seized hold of the crossbow quarrel buried in his side. With a twist of the shaft that made him cry out, she slid in close, positioning her blade this time below his belly.

"It'll hurt a good deal more if you pull that trigger," she promised.

Warrlun grimaced, but refused to drop his weapon. "Daft wenches. Can you not see he's a dwarf?"

Dwarf. That would explain it. The unnatural build, squarish and stout. The gravelly voice, like pebbles rolling downhill. The spiky beard, erupting outward like a tangle of roots. And the bony protuberances that covered his face and skull, like a cluster of bulbous mushroom caps seeking to sprout through his skin. Torin had never seen a dwarf before, but the descriptions he'd read as a child fit this individual like woven mittens.

"Bah, let him shoot," the dwarf gruffed. "Them darts ain't gonna hurt this skull." He tapped the flat of his axe blade against his forehead for emphasis, striking one of the spurs grown up like a blister on his brow.

"Dwarf or no, he saved my life," Saena reminded Warrlun.

"Yet hasn't told us why," the commander growled.

"You've not given him a chance," Holly snorted.

"Then let him do so now, the filthy mole, before I take the wind from his throat."

"You must be Warrlun," the stranger drawled. "Lorre's right hand, they said."

"You seem to know all about *us,* friend," Torin intervened. "Have *you* a name you would share?"

The dwarf seemed to grind his teeth. He looked to Torin, one eye pinched in judgment. He then lowered his axe, leaning forward upon its upended haft. "Call me Crag, if ya like."

"And to what do we owe the fortune of your visit, Crag?"

"Looked like the lady could use some help."

Warrlun was incensed. "Are we to stand here questioning him all afternoon? He's stalling. Probably waiting for his pack to catch up so that they can trap us all over again."

Torin took note of Crag's simmering reaction, even as he fought back against his own exasperation. "And what would you propose, Commander?"

"That you quench that fiery blade of yours in his belly so we can round up the horses and make our way out of here."

"Hardly a proper show of gratitude," Holly observed.

"Why should we be grateful?" Warrlun huffed. "How do we know he's not in league with Traver?"

Torin glanced down at the body of the ruffian leader, cooling upon the earth. To his own surprise, he felt little satisfaction in the other's demise. "A strange way to treat one's comrade."

"Treachery is what dwarves do best," the commander warned.

Crag bristled. But while Torin's overall sympathies remained with Saena and this stranger who had rescued her, he knew that Warrlun raised some valid concerns.

"Your timing would indeed appear Olirian-blessed."

The dwarf shrugged. "I might've shown sooner, but I saw no reason to trap myself with the rest of ya."

"Then you knew about the ambush?" Torin scowled. "Why not warn us?"

"I told you," Warrlun spat. "Ain't none more treacherous than a dwarf."

Crag's voice became a low growl. "'Cept for them that slaughtered 'em."

"Enough!" Torin shouted. "Dyanne, if our good commander speaks again, take his tongue." He looked then upon Crag with a heavy sigh. "This would go faster, friend, if I didn't have to beg your every word. So I'll ask once more: How is it you've come to be here?"

Crag continued to glare at Warrlun for a moment, before turning his stony gaze back to Torin. Even then, he seemed to be keeping watch upon the other out of the corner of his eye, as if anything less would be unwise.

"These here are *my* trails," the dwarf said finally. "Anything passes through, I know about it."

There came a huff from Warrlun, but Dyanne's ready response with the tip of her blade discouraged anything more.

"Go on," Torin urged.

"Last night, a handful of your friends spent the night in one of my caves." The dwarf gestured disdainfully at a couple of the bandits' bodies. "Spent hours wagging their tongues, flapping 'mong their selves 'bout the trap they'd come to lay. Spoke of a king from Pentania, man named Torin, rumored to wield a sword of elven myth. Said he done teamed up with Warrlun, chief commander to the villainous Lorre—that together, they was in search of the elves what went missing decades ago. Need I go on?"

"You learned of us from Traver's men," Torin repeated, making sure that he understood. "Meaning, again, that you could have warned us earlier."

Crag's huff might have been a laugh. "And which of ya would've believed me?" His eyes flicked round to the others. Even Saena, Torin noticed, was uncomfortable meeting his gaze.

"Seems clear your kind is not well liked here in the north," Torin acknowledged. "So why risk mixing in our business at all?"

"Got wax in your ears, lad? This is *my* land, and it's all I got. Whatever takes place here ain't just your business, but mine."

For a gruff old fellow, he seemed to Torin particularly sensitive. "What I mean is, why take part in our struggle, knowing this would be the thanks you'd receive?"

The dwarf seemed suddenly uncertain of himself. "I figured to stay clear, just keep an eye on things—till it came evident none of the rest of ya were gonna help the lass."

His disapproving frown softened, somewhat, as he looked to Saena. Torin, however, saw only that the dwarf had evaded the more obvious truth. As charitable as he might claim to be, Crag wanted something. It was the only reasonable explanation.

"Well, then," Torin decided, "perhaps it would be best for all if you were to accept our gratitude and allow us to be on our way." He took hold of Saena's arm, pulling her back as he gave a polite bow.

"And where do ya think you'll be headed?"

"As you heard, I came here in search of elves. Until I find them, my search continues." He turned away, marching back toward Holly and the others.

"Is it any ol' elf you're looking for? Or did ya come seeking the Vandari?"

Torin spun, breathless. "What did you say?"

"Did I misspeak the name?"

"You said *Vandari*."

"Ah, then ya *did* hear me."

"What do you know of them?"

"I knows my history, is all. Said to be the guardians of the talisman you now bear. That not right?"

"What do you want?" Torin asked.

"We ain't talking 'bout what *I* want. We're talking 'bout what *you* want."

"You know where they are."

Crag lifted a hand from the butt of his axe, holding it up as if to slow things down. "Don't be putting your words in another's mouth, lad. I ain't said any such thing. I'm only trying to draw bead on what it is you're doing here."

Judging by their continued silence, Torin's companions—even Warrlun—were as stunned as he by this odd turn of events. It was difficult to think clearly, here amid the rocks and the snow and the carnage. The sickly sweet smell of blood filled his nose, an odor to which he'd not yet become inured.

"Well why else would a man wielding a Sword of Asahiel be carrying out such a desperate search?" Crag pressed. "Hoping they can tell ya how to use it, I'm guessing. Or are ya merely looking to return it to its rightful owners?"

Torin frowned at the mockery in the other's tone. "Whatever it takes to warn them of the peril that came with it."

This time, Crag's laugh seemed forced. "Got a ghost story to tell, do ya, lad?"

"Let's see how good your history *really* is," Torin challenged. "Ever heard of the Illysp?"

The dwarf's brow furrowed. "Can't says I have."

"You soon will. You and those you care about. For when they're finished conquering my shores, I've no doubt they'll come to conquer yours."

Crag's smirk vanished, and his squint deepened. "You humans finally chased the wrong animal up the wrong tree, did ya?"

"The Illysp are not natural creatures," Torin continued, "but parasites from beyond this world. I won't claim to fully understand, as I've never actually seen one. But I'm told it was the Finlorians who first woke them, and that if we're to seal them away again, it won't be without the Finlorians' help."

"Then this threat is to *all* of Pentania?"

Torin nodded wearily. "Without prejudice."

The dwarf looked as if he were chewing on his thoughts—and didn't like the taste. "If this be true, what cause have ya to be traveling with one like him?" He nodded toward Warrlun, who clenched his jaw but remained still.

"An unfortunate encounter with the armies of Lord Lorre," Torin confessed. "But he knows this country better than I do. Without him, we're lost."

"And yet he'd have ya rely on one like this," Crag noted, kicking Traver's motionless foot. "Looks to me like you'd be better off without him."

"You know someone else who can help us, then?"

Again, Crag's expression soured. "Lorre and his kind chased off them Finlorians long ago. Ya know that, right?"

Torin nodded. "I've been told. I've also been told that the last of the dwarves were wiped out soon after."

Crag spat. "Ain't far from the truth, I'm afraid. Thanks to that one's master."

Torin winced and checked again on Warrlun. He wished the dwarf would stop testing the other's patience.

"We've not come for bloodshed," Saena promised. "I, too, come from His Lordship, merely to bear a message to his daughter and grandchild, whom he believes are being harbored by the same people Torin seeks."

This time, Crag's laugh was genuine. "I'll shave my beard and be a web-footed orc 'fore I believe that one, lassie."

"Either way, you can't refuse Torin for our sake. If you can help him, you must do so."

"Must I, now?" the dwarf asked, raising his brow. "Was it *him* saved one of *mine*, rather than the other way 'round?"

Saena pouted, but crossed her arms in defiance.

"We've told you what it is we want," Torin reminded the dwarf. "So tell me now, what is it we can do for you?"

For a moment, he thought the other meant to deny any such need or desire. Were he to do so, Torin had every intention of walking away, for it would be an obvious lie.

"I can tell you this," the dwarf offered. "It wasn't word of this elven talisman that piqued my interest, but mention of you and your homeland, a royal outlander from far-off Pentania. Not many of those come 'round here."

Torin nodded slowly, trying to guess where this was headed, but as of yet uncertain.

"My great-grandfather used to speak of your land—back when it was still called Tritos. Used to fill my head with the many wonders of the great dwarven nation of Hrothgar settled there. Himself lived upon one of the lesser isles, among the Tuthari dwarves, distant cousins to the proud Hrothgari."

Risking offense, Torin snuck a glance back toward Dyanne and Warrlun, just to make sure the Nymph still had things well in hand. To his surprise, the commander had lowered his crossbow, though his fierce scowl—and Dyanne's ready blade—remained.

"Sailed 'cross the great sea, he did," Crag continued. "No place for a dwarf, I tell ya, out there 'mid the wind and waves, where nothing is permanent and all is motion. But he did so, him and a few hearty clansmen, to help settle this virgin land and sow the seeds of a new nation of dwarves that would not be confined by the smallness of the isle upon which his forefathers had long lived."

A ragged gust whistled through the slanted walls of the narrow defile. Holly shivered. They had tarried for too long, Torin thought. They needed to be on the move again, and soon, before the skies soured. Of course, they also needed to know *where* to go.

The dwarf went on, oblivious to such concerns. "They were not alone. Other races came, to join those already here. The land was plentiful, but unforgiving, and competition fierce. Still, we dwarves are tougher than most, steadfast and determined. It took centuries of struggle, but in our own way, the Tuthari flourished."

"Until the coming of Lorre," Torin presumed.

"Until the coming of Lorre," Crag echoed. "His reign marked the end of ours. When my people would not stoop to his will, he sent forth his army of misfits to break our backs. Not only that, but he turned our other neighbors against us, trolls and giants. We was branded traitors and thieves and slaughtered without cause. Them Finlorians, they were the smart ones. They ran. Us Tuthari fought, and paid the price.

"Too late, we fled southward, those of us able to escape the noose Lorre had laid. Still he hunted, and so still we ran, down through northern Yawacor and into the southern wilds. His armies drove us from all but the most uninhabitable reaches, and even then, would not let us be."

The fire in the dwarf's eye was unmistakable. "You need not fear ambush from my friends, for I'm all there is—the last of the Tuthari of Yawacor. The last anywhere, from what I know, as it wasn't but a generation after my great-grandfather's voyage that our original ground south of Tritos was overrun by the endless waves of marauding humans come to claim the Finlorian Isles. Let your commander there kill me, and indeed the dwarves of this land will be no more."

Torin still wasn't certain what this dwarf—this Tuthari—was looking for. If it was pity, then he had found it, at least among the women, who had turned their collective glare upon an unapologetic Warrlun. But Torin didn't think that Crag was interested in their pity. Pity would not bring to life his loved ones. Pity would not reunite him with—

Torin caught himself. His gaze locked with that of the dwarf in sudden understanding.

"Might be that I'm able to help you," Crag said. "Might be that in return, you can help me leave this land behind and set sail for your own, so's I might live again with my own kind."

But Torin was already shaking his head. "The Proclamation of Man was ratified nearly four hundred years ago. Any dwarves living upon Pentanian shores disappeared even before then."

"Not the Hrothgari," Crag maintained stubbornly. "From what my great-grandfather used to tell me, had man driven them out, struggle would've been such that the whole world would know of it."

"Perhaps your great-grandfather was merely telling stories. For I'm advising you now, in fair warning, that there are no more dwarves living upon Pentanian shores."

Crag scoffed. "Precisely what the Hrothgari would have you humans believe."

Torin glanced helplessly at Saena. "So be it. If you're so certain, why not set sail on your own? What do you need *me* for?"

The dwarf eyed him with great disgust. "What am I to do, lash together a few limbs and just float away at the mercy of the waves? Think, lad. Ain't but a few out there what wouldn't run screaming at the mere sight of me—fewer still what wouldn't sell me to those who'd like to mount my head as a trophy. I'm trapped, make no mistake. Doomed to wander these trails as I begin my second century, my best hope that I can outlive the hatred what's claimed these lands.

"But you could help me now. I heard the awe with what these others spoke your name. Seeing for myself the blade you carry, I think I understand why. And a king, no less. Man like you got influence. With your protection, just might be I'm able to cross the sea safely and find a place 'mong my cousins to the east."

Torin was sorely tempted to laugh. If he had such sway as the dwarf suggested, would he be allowing a complete stranger to dictate to him the terms of their potential accord? Or perhaps he could relate to the other the truth of his own recent journey, so much of which had been spent at the mercy of others. He was lucky, certainly. But considering how far he had stretched that luck already, he doubted it would hold out for two.

He said nothing of that to Crag, however, biting back the threat of laughter. It would not help his cause to weaken himself in the dwarf's eyes.

"I'd be happy to serve as your guardian escort on such a voyage," he agreed instead, "though I'll not be held responsible for who or what you might find when we arrive. But the fact remains, I'll be going nowhere until I've accomplished what I came here to achieve."

With that, the pressure was shifted squarely onto Crag's knotted shoulders.

Though Torin's promise would no doubt prove easier to give than to keep, it was the best he could offer at this time. The dwarf scowled as if realizing this, as if weighing its worth against that which he was being asked to give.

Torin found himself holding his breath. By the sour look on the other's face, it wasn't going to be enough. Despite whatever soul-searching and effort had brought the dwarf to them in the first place, he was clearly having second thoughts about the entire affair.

"Just yourself," the Tuthari reasoned finally. "None of these others need go."

Holly cleared her throat. "Where he goes, we go."

Torin looked to the Nymph, then farther back to her kinmate. When Dyanne nodded, he found it hard not to smile.

Crag squinted sharply. "That how it is?"

"They're Wylddean," Torin replied. "Fenwa. *You* try telling them no."

"Nymphs," Crag snorted. "I heard of 'em." His smirk—if that's what it was—vanished as he turned eye to Saena. "And Lorre's lackeys? Now would seem a good time to be rid of 'em."

Saena looked at Torin plaintively.

"Rid how?" the young king asked.

"That'd be up to them. For the lass's sake, I'd say turn 'em loose, provided they foot it out in the opposite direction. Should they insist on following, might have to tie 'em up—though with the wolves 'round here, might be kinder to give 'em the blade of my axe."

"I told you," Saena insisted, "I bear a message, nothing more. The only knife I carry is for cooking."

"Shame 'bout that," Crag replied, his gaze slipping briefly to regard Traver's bleeding carcass. "Meat of it is, I serve them Finlorians as lookout, gatekeeper to their lands. It would be a betrayal of their trust to guide one such as him"—his eyes narrowed reflexively as they shifted toward Warrlun—"to their front doorstep."

So that was it, Torin realized, the reason for the dwarf's pained hesitation. The risks in all of this to his own life were easy enough to accept. Those to the safety of his friends were much harder to assume.

"I'm sworn to His Lordship to serve as guardian to the girl," Warrlun growled, breaking his long silence. "You'll have to kill me if you expect me to forsake my oath."

"Wolves will be pleased to hear it," Crag replied icily.

"What if we blindfolded him?" Torin suggested.

The Tuthari grunted—another harsh laugh. "You'll *all* be bound and blinded," he agreed. "Ain't no other way of it."

Torin swallowed against his own misgivings. "And if we can agree to that, what's the danger?"

"The worst there is," Crag snapped. "That which ain't readily seen. The Finlorians, they don't believe in fighting. Abolished all weapons years ago when they ran from Lorre. Don't have as much as a hunting bow among them, since they feed only on what the soil can grow. Should a fight find 'em, they have naught but cooking knives with which to defend themselves"—he looked purposefully at Saena—"and even so, would refuse to raise 'em."

"But you'll be there to watch over him," Torin reminded the leery dwarf. "As will I."

"You willing to vouch for him, then?"

Torin considered the old soldier, Warrlun, who glared back with a gaze full of fire. The man refused to be cowed, and had revealed himself already as a formidable opponent. While it was tempting indeed to leave him to the rats and the wolves, the commander had done nothing as of yet to deserve such a death sentence. So long as he was kept under close watch, and unable to mark the path by which Lorre might return with an army, what could be the harm?

"I'm willing to promise that if he threatens anyone in any way, I'll kill him myself," Torin answered finally, keeping his eyes locked on Warrlun's as he made this oath.

By the gnarled look on his face, the dwarf was nowhere near agreeing. But it would seem he'd run dry of alternatives. "As close as we'll come, I reckon, to a fair pact."

He stepped forward then, reaching out a gloved hand riddled with spurs and growths. Torin shook it firmly, though he nearly cried out within the crush of the other's grip. Crag stared him in the eye, then spat and shook his head, as if disgusted with himself for accepting the terms they had set.

"Fools," Warrlun snarled. "He'll kill us all in our sleep."

A legitimate possibility, Torin knew. But if Crag had wanted them dead, why would he have helped them against Traver? The dwarf was too blunt-spoken to strike Torin as the liar Warrlun claimed him to be. Either way, when the truth boiled free, the young king was willing to team with this stranger— as he had Lorre's commander—for only one reason: He didn't feel he had much of a choice.

"Crag will have to show the same trust later on," Torin observed, "if he is to give himself over to my protection."

"*If* you make it that far," Warrlun snapped.

"A concern that needn't worry you," Crag retorted, finally releasing Torin's hand, "unless ya rest your tongue long enough to tend to those wounds."

Warrlun glanced down at the array of crossbow bolts that had pierced his leather armor to become lodged in his flesh. While the damage to his shoulder appeared largely superficial, blood seeped from the one in his side.

"My wounds will keep," he decided. "I'll not trust any here to tend them—least of all some pox-ridden dwarf."

Torin wasn't going to waste time arguing. "We'll need to round up the horses."

"You'll just have to turn 'em loose again," Crag reasoned. "They ain't gonna be able to follow where we're going."

"What of our food and supplies?" asked Saena.

"Got plenty 'nough for the day or so we'll need."

Torin looked to each of his companions before turning back to Crag. "Well, then, how do you want to do this?"

The dwarf hefted his axe so that it leaned against his shoulder. "Come," he bade them. "We'll fetch some rope."

CHAPTER FORTY-FOUR

*F*OR TORIN, IT WAS LIKE MARCHING THROUGH A DREAM—scuffing along that dark and twisted trail to nowhere. The air was dank and stifling and stank of minerals. Water dripped, not from leaves and tree limbs, but from dagger-tipped rock formations. These drops echoed as they fell, slapping often into invisible pools, or else atop sister formations grown up beneath. There was the skitter of insects, the flap of bat wings, and the scrape of an occasional rodent. But mostly, there was only the huff of their own breathing, the pull of the ropes that bound them, and the insufferable repetition of stepping forward with a blind and trusting stride.

While backtracking through the defile in which Traver's company had ambushed them—leaving the bodies of the brigands as carrion for scavengers—Torin had expected Crag to lead them down some other trail. Instead, after blindfolding them as promised and tethering them together in a single line, the dwarf had guided them almost immediately down the gullet of some cave. Saena had quickly voiced Torin's own surprise that their trek should begin underground, but Crag refused them the slightest explanation.

For hours they had carried on, with no choice but to trust in the motives and competence of their guide. Only Warrlun gave protest—muttered warnings to his companions as to the foolishness of this course. Once Crag had threatened to gag him, even the commander's tongue grew still.

When according to their guide night had fallen outside, the Tuthari had removed their blindfolds, revealing a wondrous cavern. Its natural formations were like nothing Torin had ever seen—not even during his trek beneath the Tenstrock Mountains en route to the lair of the Demon Queen. The veins of luminous minerals embedded in its walls were so thick and so bright that Crag's torch became almost unnecessary. Their glitter and sheen had sparked a flurry of questions and comments, many of which the dwarf was agreeable enough to answer or respond to. While doing so, he had fed them a blend of meats and berries gathered from aboveground, along with shoots and mushrooms harvested from below. Feeling famished, Torin had accepted readily that which was offered. Of his comrades, only Warrlun had refused.

They had slept in their tether line, hands bound by a length of rope to the waist of the person in front. Torin had been placed near the rear, aback of Holly, Dyanne, and Saena, with only Warrlun behind him. If there was a method to the order Crag had chosen, Torin wasn't sure what it was.

They had suffered through just a few hours' rest before moving on again, their footing challenged at every step by the often jagged flooring. Though Crag served as the front of their tether, kicking aside loose stones and sending back warning of any trouble spots, they had spent a good amount of time tripping and stumbling over various humps and jags in the stone path. Oftentimes, a single member's fall had threatened to drag down the entire company—save for Crag at the head, whose strong and stocky body seemed capable of bearing the weight of all who followed with scarcely a grunt.

It was daybreak when they had stopped for another meal—though once again, Torin had only his guide's word to go by in this sunless underworld. During this respite, they had suggested again to Warrlun that the soldier allow them to treat his wounds—at the very least, to remove the crossbow bolts still buried in his flesh. But the commander had gritted his teeth and flatly refused any such proposals. Stubborn fool, Crag had grumbled. If that was what he wanted, so be it. It would serve the dolt right if he bled to death.

Continuing on, they had passed through a stretch of tunnels so tight that at times, the walls scraped at them from either side. Torin had felt as if he marched through a thicket of brambles, with sharp rocks tearing at him like thorns. How Warrlun was able to manage it—with his thicker body and those snagging quarrels—remained a mystery.

On occasion, Crag had removed their blindfolds, when necessary to prevent one of them from falling into a subterranean chasm, when climbing over boulder mounds, or when otherwise the terrain became simply too treacherous to navigate blindly. Though brief, these periods had afforded them continued glimpses of the territory through which they trekked, a stunning maze of channels and pockets hidden deep within the mountain core, full of sparkling deposits of minerals and gemstones seldom viewed by human eyes. That such a world could exist beyond that which he knew filled Torin with a humbling sense of awe.

A sharp pull from behind brought him back to the present, scrambling for balance as the rope cinched about his waist and threatened to haul him down. Warrlun had stumbled again. Turning sideways, Torin reached out with bound hands to help the other to his feet. They had only heartbeats in which to get moving again before the ropes tightened farther up the line and Crag became aware of the difficulty they were having. More than once, the dwarf had threatened to leave the headstrong soldier behind. For as the hours passed, weariness had aggravated the hunger and blood loss that the commander continued to suffer, making it ever more difficult for him to keep up.

Surprisingly, Warrlun found and then took his hands, struggling mightily to his feet. The length of rope between Torin and Saena drew taut, and she gasped worriedly. But the old soldier was up and moving again, and this time did not even snarl at Torin for helping him. Perhaps the man was truly waning toward death. This journey had taken its toll on all of them, but none more so than Warrlun. While much of this was indeed the warrior's own fault, Torin could not help but admire the man's tenacity, and hoped now that it would not prove his undoing.

"Everything all right?" Crag asked, his gruff voice echoing amid the cavern gloom.

"Is this the easiest way to get there?" Torin called forward in response, hoping to deflect the dwarf's attention.

Crag did not respond right away, but muttered finally, "It's the only way."

Not long after, the blindfolds were removed again as they passed through a wide cavern torn apart by bottomless fissures. Torin snuck a glance back at Warrlun to find the other's face pallid and dripping with sweat. Even in the feeble light of Crag's torch, there was no denying the commander's ragged state.

Torin said nothing about it, however, other than to offer the man some water, which, despite a scowl, he drank readily. They kept moving, winding around the many pitfalls and keeping a wary eye on the shadows that painted the cavern walls. Though it seemed unlikely—given the lack of sizable prey to sustain it—Torin kept expecting to run across some ogre or dragon living within these caves and tunnels. Maybe even a demon from another world, such as Spithaera. For however improbable such an encounter might seem, he need only look ahead to the dwarf leading their column to be reminded that anything was possible.

When they had cleared the splintered cavern, Torin fully expected that Crag would stop them in order to replace their blindfolds. Instead, the Tuthari delved without breaking stride into a tight-fitting corridor of dank stone, leaving the rest to plunge after. Perhaps their guide realized that at this point, after a day and a half of travel, there was no conceivable way that they could have memorized this path. Or perhaps another unnavigable stretch lay just ahead. Whichever, Torin wasn't about to offer a reminder.

As they continued down this most recent tunnel, there came a murmuring from somewhere ahead. Torin was only vaguely aware of it at first. But the sound grew, in volume and intensity, until its roar filled his ears, deep and resonant and unrelenting. By that time, he could feel it as well, beneath his feet and in his chest. The air in the tunnel became damp, and the walls slick, soaked by a thickening layer of mist. Footing became treacherous as the companions struggled onward over stones and depressions in pursuit of their guide.

The tunnel brightened, filling with natural light. Crag extinguished his torch, stuffing it into a sack along with the others he'd brought. As they rounded a bend, the light grew tenfold, forcing Torin and his friends—so accustomed to the darkness—to squint against the sudden glare.

Ahead lay the end of the tunnel, its mouth covered by a churning waterfall and the clouds of mist stirred up beneath. Despite the sting of afternoon daylight, the companions slipped anxiously forward, more than ready to leave the suffocating blindness of the inner earth behind them.

Before they could step free, however, their guide turned back, gathering them together at the edge of the cave mouth.

Over the din of the cascading waters, he shouted to them.

"This is it. The Finlorian dell lies just beyond this threshold. Aefengaard, they calls it." His eyebrows knotted sternly. "One false step from any of ya, I'll be carving ya up like a festival bird. Hear?"

Torin nodded solemnly, then turned toward Warrlun just in time to see the big man sway unsteadily. Before he could lend assistance, the commander crumpled, legs gone slack beneath him.

The soldier lay there for a moment, slumped against the algae-coated walls, as the others looked on.

"Go on," he managed between breaths. "I'll wait here."

Torin's gaze shifted from Warrlun to Crag.

"This some kind of game, Lorre's man?" the dwarf asked.

But it was clear that it wasn't. Warrlun's face had taken on the pasty gleam of candle wax. His breathing was shallow and labored, wheezing in and out. Peering down at the crossbow shaft in his side, they found his leathers soaked in blood. Though much of it had clotted, there was no telling how things looked on the inside.

"He's *my* guardian," Saena said. "I'll stay and look after him."

"Better would be to tote him 'long and let the Finlorians tend to him," Crag observed.

At that, Warrlun tensed, glaring up at them with bloodshot orbs. "I'll not be pawed by some greasy elf, any sooner than a filthy dwarf." He settled back, coughing from his exertion. "Go. Deliver His Lordship's message. By the time you've returned, I'll have regained my strength."

The companions glanced at one another, each waiting for someone else to speak the truth.

It was Crag who finally did so. "More likely, we'll find you dead."

"Better here than in an elven wood," Warrlun spat.

Harsh manner notwithstanding, Torin looked upon the soldier with a measure of compassion, wishing that such grit were not so misplaced.

"If that's your choice," Crag huffed, shaking his head. He bent forward, drawing a dagger with which he cut the tether line between Torin and Warrlun. Once severed, the extra length was used to truss the soldier's feet in a manner to match his wrists. It seemed a cruel thing to do, as it was obvious the man wasn't going anywhere. But Crag would take no chances, and Torin wasn't willing to fault him his precautions.

When satisfied, the dwarf unstoppered Saena's waterskin and offered the dying man a drink. Warrlun reluctantly accepted. Unfortunately, he appeared all but unable to swallow, leaving the majority of the water to wash down his chin.

Having made every effort, Crag snorted, looking upon the man with what seemed a cross between pity and disdain. He then shouldered the bundle containing the companions' weapons, making certain not to leave a single blade behind. Turning his back upon the doomed warrior, he stepped beyond the mouth of the tunnel, guiding the rest ahead.

From where they stood, the trail snaked out to the left of the plummeting waters, skirting the edge of the mountain bluff. The river into which the falls emptied lay far below—several hundred feet, by Torin's estimation. Rather than stare down that dizzying height, he forced his eyes back to the narrow path upon which he trod, shuffling dutifully after his companions at the end of their rope train.

After awhile, the cross slope became less precipitous, allowing the trail to widen and draw back from the edge of the cliff. When it did, Torin's gaze slipped out to the walls of the valley—emerald mountains striped with silver ribbons of meltwater runoff. It was a relatively small dale, not more than a couple of leagues running north and south, and perhaps half that in width. The sheer, towering peaks that surrounded it did indeed appear impassable save by flight, making somewhat more believable Crag's claim that the valley's only entrance was that which lay behind them.

There wasn't much to see below. If any had settled there, then they had done so beneath the forest canopy—a dense ceiling unbroken by glade or clearing. Even the river vanished as it entered that unforgiving thicket. Torin searched in vain for signs of humanoid life. Except for the colorful flash of birds winging from treetop to treetop, alighting carefully upon the surface, it appeared nothing that entered ever came out again.

Eventually, they too were swallowed by the lush tangle. More jungle than forest, Torin now realized, overgrown with varieties of trees and plants that even he, raised in a wood, had never seen before. As wild as it all seemed, however, he began to wonder if much of it wasn't cultivated. For it struck him that in an area so densely grown, there was precious little deadwood. Competition should have been fierce, for water and for sunlight; indeed, even the largest trunks were sheathed in smothering ivy. Yet all appeared healthy and verdant, as if woven together by a singular, guiding hand that had worked to ensure a cooperative and harmonious existence.

The more he saw, the more certain he became. There was magic at work here, a vivacity in the air. Everything around them was a perfect profusion of color and song. A watering rain trickled in glistening streams down trunks and stems to lie in pools that fed the earth. Butterflies flitted upon a gentle breeze, dancing overhead as if inviting him to play. Stranger still, Torin found himself wishing he could join them, that he and his friends might laugh away the remainder of this day while scampering through the forest in spirited delight.

At the same time, he was horrified by the thought. For his very presence seemed a blight upon this land. Marching along the narrow animal trails, they could not help but leave their mark upon this pristine wilderness. Every torn leaf was an insult; every boot print a scar upon the earth. He was ashamed to so defile this mystical region, and knew that the sooner they were away, the better.

But Crag led them onward, pushing past flowering shrubs and bushes laden with berries—now, in the dead of winter. They spied birds and insects, rabbits and deer, each of which, again, seemed at perfect ease among the others with whom it coexisted. And yet, no matter how hard he looked, there was still no sign of those Torin had come to find.

"Where are the Finlorians?" he asked finally. "You said this dell was their home."

Crag snickered. "All around us, lad. Safely out of sight. Or did ya expect 'em to come running out to shake your hand?"

Torin glanced about self-consciously. He hadn't known *what* to expect, though this would not have been it. Not after what he had glimpsed of the splendors and marvels that had marked Finlorian society at the height of their civilization. Temples and treasures and statuary would have been more in keeping with the onetime majesty of their greatest city, Thrak-Symbos. Then again, he could not imagine anything of that nature leaving a greater impression than that which the elven people had helped to create here.

When finally they came to a halt, they did so unexpectedly, beside no discernible marker. And yet it appeared they had reached at least a temporary destination, for Crag untied the rope that had tethered the Tuthari to his charges, and let it drop to the earth.

"Stay here," he ordered them, then wagged a crooked finger for emphasis. "Remember my warning."

With that, he trundled off around the base of an enormous tree, carrying their weapons with him. Torin's gaze shifted reflexively, climbing upward through the nest of boughs. He wondered if it was up inside the trees that the Finlorians had concealed their homes. But all he saw were dagger-shaped leaves and great, peeling strips of bark that hung down like withered vines. If anything lay therein, then it was well concealed from his wandering eye.

They waited in silence, listening carefully for any change in the forest's mellifluous sound. Despite the magnificence of his surroundings, Torin was soon distracted by Dyanne. Though he tried not to be obvious, he could not help but study her profile whenever he felt it safe to do so. In full thrall to whatever enchantment graced this land, he found her to be more radiant than ever. For too long now, his interactions with her had been limited to longing, unnoticed stares. He ached to know her thoughts, but could not bring himself to ask. Whatever she might be feeling—toward him and toward their current venture—remained a mystery.

It seemed almost cruel when Crag finally returned to them, reappearing from around the base of that giant tree. He did not look happy, his hanging expression like that of a scolded child. But then, Torin had absolutely no notion of what the dwarf might look like when pleased.

"Come," the Tuthari growled, taking up their tether line like a horse's lead rope.

The companions did not ask where he was taking them; they simply obeyed. Together, still bound and in single file, they started around the tree. A smile of amazement slowly gripped Torin's cheeks when he realized that the tree's roots formed a sort of staircase, spiraling downward as they rounded the great trunk. Had there been any question before about whether the Finlorians had manipulated this land through some magical means, there was no denying it now.

With each step, Torin's excitement grew. This was it, the culmination of a journey spanning weeks and events he could scarcely recall. From the moment he had bid farewell to his friends and passed through Krynwall's gates, this had been his sole objective: to find and meet with the last remnants of the elves of ancient Finloria. Even throughout all of the secondary conflicts—his escape from Soric, his battle against Lorre, and his inner turmoil regarding Dyanne and Marisha—he had never completely lost focus of what it was he had come to do. And though it seemed as unlikely now as before, he felt certain that his quest was about to come to a fruitful end.

For if a people could tell a tree how to grow, then surely they possessed magic enough to help thwart the Illysp scourge.

They stopped again when the staircase of roots leveled out, barely more than a quarter-turn around the mammoth tree. There, among the gnarled folds of the tree's bark, lay a narrow cleft, veiled by a curtain of ivy. Alone, Torin might never have seen it. Even after Crag had drawn back the dangling strands, he doubted it could be the opening they sought.

"Watch your step," the dwarf said, then disappeared within.

The cleft turned out to be much bigger than it looked, carved at an angle so as to disguise its width. No, Torin amended quickly, not carved, but shaped smoothly by natural—or supernatural—means. It opened not into a central hollow, but a corridor that sloped gently downward, spiraling deeper beneath the earth. Keeping step behind their guide, the companions followed it—a path illuminated not by fire or sunlight, but by hairlike roots dug down through the ceiling that glowed with a dim radiance.

"What causes them to shine like that?" Saena asked, unable to contain her wonder.

Crag glanced back as if to reprimand her, but answered instead. "Tree filters it down from leaves overhead. An elven trick."

"Magic?" she replied, speaking the word on everyone's mind.

The dwarf shrugged. "Something like that."

The tunnel wound on until leveling out at last within a large chamber—a foyer. Openings branched off in multiple directions, doorways to reaches unknown. Flowers grew in the center of the floor, beneath a heavier concentration of light from the glowing root tendrils. Other roots dripped water that had seeped from above, directing it into a spring pooled up from below and hemmed in by a wall of shale. Streams fed out from this pool by way of slender troughs dug along the walls, carrying water, Torin imagined, throughout the complex.

He was given little time to investigate further. Crag marched them ahead, around the central garden and to the left of the corner pool. They passed through one of the doorways and down a short hall. This one opened into a second chamber, larger than the first, and colored by a familiar red aura.

Only then did Torin realize that Crag no longer toted the fur wrap in which their weapons had been bundled. He found it instead lying against the wall, just inside the doorway of this second room. The covering lay open, but Torin barely glanced at its exposed contents. For he knew already that the one artifact that concerned him was no longer there.

He looked instead for the source of the red aura. A woman stood sideways in the center of the room, staring with wonder into the flaming depths of the Sword of Asahiel, held before her. The wrappings used to disguise the hilt hung from one arm, and she was even now stroking the naked heartstones with a mother's caress.

A moment passed before she could force herself to break away, and even then, she only scarcely considered them before turning back to the blade.

"I'm sorry," she said. "I'm afraid I did not believe Crag without taking a look for myself."

Her voice had a songlike quality to it, so that even these simple words sounded smooth and lyrical. Torin waited anxiously for her to say something more.

Again her gaze shifted to them, and this time, something made it stick. A scowl sharpened her already angled features.

"I should think you could unbind them, Crag."

The dwarf grunted. "I doubt that would please Eolin."

"Too late to worry about *that* now, isn't it?"

Crag huffed, but within moments, the companions were rubbing at the angry red welts raised upon their wrists.

"Seat yourselves," the woman bade them—a demand, not a request.

She gestured toward the circle of furniture that adorned the room, each piece woven from reeds and branches and tied together with strips of bark. Dyanne and Holly were the first to obey, stepping forward across a carpet of moss. Saena soon followed, and finally Torin. Of their party, only Crag still stood, planted in the chamber doorway with arms crossed.

Their host remained standing as well, facing the open circle of her guests. She held the Sword absently now, one hand on its hilt, the other near the blade's tip. "Which of you carries the message from my father?" she asked.

"You are Laressa?" Saena replied. "Daughter of Lorre?"

"I am Laressa Solymir, daughter of Shaundra and wife to Eolin Solymir—keifer of the elven nation of Finloria. Who are you?"

Her stern tone, Torin decided, could not mask her exotic beauty. Though lightly freckled, her skin had just a hint of the olive tone he had seen in the Mookla'ayans—the elves of his own shores. Cheeks, ears, eyes—all were prominent and high swept, angled at the outer edges. Her hair was blond and short, cropped close like her father's and tinged red by the light of the Sword—though the fact that she *had* hair was perhaps proof of her mixed heritage, as none of the Mookla'ayans Torin had met grew any at all.

Yet it wasn't her appearance that captivated him as much as her voice, her intense gaze, and the supple grace with which she moved. So delicate she seemed, dressed in a long, sleeveless tunic of pure gossamer. But that delicacy, Torin suspected, was a ruse, a natural defense against those who would mis-judge her a weak and fragile thing.

"I serve in your father's army," Saena admitted. "He asked that I come here to apologize on his behalf for any pain or confusion he may have caused you. He never wished for anything more than your happiness, and swears to this day that he will do anything to ensure it. If this is the home you have chosen, for you and your child, then rest assured for the remainder of your days that he will do nothing to violate it. He wants only to know that you are well, that you have chosen your own life, and that none other has chosen it for you."

Torin looked to Laressa, awaiting her reaction. The woman seemed at a loss for words.

"That's all?" she asked finally.

"His Lordship wasn't certain what else he might say, except that you are the one triumph he is truly proud of, a tribute to your mother—the only woman he has ever loved."

Laressa's eyes gleamed. Torin wanted to believe that she had been moved by Saena's words, but couldn't tell for sure.

"Then he did not send you in an effort to renew his hunt of my Finlorian brothers and sisters?" Laressa asked evenly, glancing in Crag's direction.

"Only if you were to ask that he do so," Saena revealed. "On his oath to your mother, he will sunder the earth if that's what it takes to deliver you from captivity."

Torin continued to study Laressa, even as a great weight lifted from his own shoulders. Saena's words reflected almost exactly what Lorre had expressed during his own interrogation. All this time, he had worried that the overlord was not being honest, that surely his agents—Saena and Warrlun—were the bearers of some secret plot against the Finlorian people, making Torin an unwilling facilitator of their designs. But now that Saena's story matched up with Lorre's own, it would seem he could finally lay his suspicions toward both the woman and her ruler to rest.

Laressa smiled sadly. "Captivity. He still assumes me to be the victim of an elf's enchantment, then, does he?"

Saena did not respond, allowing the elven woman to draw her own conclusions.

"My father never did understand," Laressa continued, her pointed gaze seeming to peer past her uninvited guests. "He never understood why his acceptance—and that which he would force others to share—wasn't enough."

"Acceptance?" Saena asked, bent forward in her seat by that natural curiosity of hers. "You were already married, were you not? And with child?"

"To a man my father selected—a man I did not love. Though it is true I carried his seed, theirs was not a culture to which I wanted that child to be born. I feared that she might feel as I did, like an outcast amid the human race."

"*She.* You bore a daughter, then?"

Laressa's countenance hardened in warning.

Saena pressed on anyway, though with a tone of carefully measured respect. "Except, with a human father and a half-elven mother, was she not likely to look more human than elf?"

"It was more than physical appearances that concerned me," Laressa confessed. "Her looks, like mine, might have made her an easy target for insensitive fools of both races. But a fool's ridicule is not all that hard to endure."

Her fingers began to rub idly against the Sword's polished blade. "No, my concern had more to do with culture and ideologies. My features may be predominantly elven, but it was more the beliefs and mannerisms of the Finlorians that I found so appealing. In a way, my father is right to believe that I was bespelled. For when Eolin welcomed me into their world, my own rapture made me helpless to refuse."

"You must have known it would mean war with your father," Torin interjected before he could think to check himself.

Laressa's gaze snapped around to find his.

"War was *his* choice, not ours. To avoid it, we left all that we knew behind. Eolin's father, keifer at the time, did so at his son's urging, refusing to fight out of respect for me and *my* father."

"And would you do so again?" It was Dyanne who spoke up now. "At what point would you take a stand to defend what is yours?"

There was a hint of frustration in the Nymph's tone—or indignation, perhaps. She was trying to be polite, Torin thought, to refrain from passing judgment. And yet this was the very question that had driven such a rift between her and her twin sister, Dynara.

"A home can be made anywhere," Laressa argued, "and is easily replaced. Lives are not."

"It doesn't bother you, then, to have been chased underground like animals?" Torin asked, thinking to defend Dyanne and her reasoning.

"How would you have us live?" Laressa asked sharply.

Torin glanced toward Dyanne, but saw no help coming from either her or Holly. "I only mean, it's a far cry from what I saw while trekking through the ruins of Thrak-Symbos."

Laressa laughed. "Thrak-Symbos? That was what, three thousand years ago?" Her gaze slipped briefly to the talisman in her hands. "Every people must evolve, both the individual and their society. Some whisper that it was the arrogance of our forebears in embracing material glories such as those you may have witnessed that led to our eventual downfall. Although I might argue that we are better off now than we ever were. Certainly, we are less obtrusive to those who would hunt us."

It was a useless debate, Torin saw. As long as the Finlorians were happy with their chosen existence—and judging by Laressa, it seemed clear they were—then he had no business trying to interfere.

He nodded gently, then lowered his eyes so that they fixed upon the Sword. "A people's choice, as you say. But as you know, those who find themselves in a position of authority have a responsibility to protect the lives of others as best they can. As Crag surely mentioned, that is why I've come to you."

Laressa shook her head. "I know not what to tell you in regard to your quest. Crag mentioned the Illysp—a term I've never heard—and the Vandari, who are but legend. I gather this enemy of yours is something you unleashed with the reclamation of this Sword. I understand as well that you feel my Finlorian ancestors are somewhat to blame. But I know not what you expect my people to do about it."

Torin gaped, then stiffened in denial. She had to be bluffing. He hadn't come all this way only to fail now.

Before he could articulate a better reply, they were interrupted by the snort of surprise Crag gave as another—an elf—entered the room from behind the dwarf, an arrival marked otherwise by not the slightest whisper of sound.

"*Noi mi, Eolin,*" Laressa greeted. "*Grin mai derrota anh Crag.*"

"So I see," the newcomer grumbled. "A blind gnome could follow the trail they left." Tall and slender, he, too, wore a long and lightweight tunic of some shimmering weave, cinched at the waist with a silken rope. "*Hym na decress a'i?*"

"*Ti thar Asahiel, noi mi, ugremme ti terrec Thrak-Symbos.*"

Eolin's bright eyes narrowed. "By whom?"

Laressa gestured smoothly in Torin's direction. "Torin, by name. A ruler of one of the human kingdoms occupying the isle of Tritos."

Eolin glanced back and forth between Torin and the Sword, with what looked to be a flurry of emotions vying for control. "Laressa, my sweet, perhaps our guests are ready for some fresh air."

"*Deh ta?*"

"We shall talk later," Eolin reassured her. Scowling at Crag, he added, "All of us. For now, I would speak with this Torin. Alone."

Laressa looked as though she might refuse, then bowed her head instead. "As you will, my love."

Without a word to anyone else, she rounded up the others. Torin stood, but remained behind as his companions were herded toward the exit, his feet kept rooted by Eolin's glare. Laressa passed her husband the Sword on her way out.

At the chamber doorway, Saena turned back, a look of concern painting her features. But Crag put a rugged hand to her back, moving her along.

For several moments thereafter, Torin stood silent, taut with anticipation while Eolin studied the Sword as his wife had earlier. Finally, the young man could wait no longer.

"What is it you would say to me, sir?" he asked.

Eolin's eyes lifted from the blade, his expression of awe becoming one of cruel mockery. "It is not what I have to say to you, but what you have to say to me."

Torin frowned, uncertain of the game being played.

"You have come to beg my audience, have you not? For I am Eolin Solymir, keifer of Finloria."

Torin was fast growing weary of the other's smug smile. "It is not necessarily your people's ruler with whom I came to confer."

"No," Eolin agreed. "You came to meet with the last of the Vandari."

CHAPTER FORTY-FIVE

"*H*ow do you know I seek the Vandari?" Torin asked. Unless he was mistaken, neither Crag nor Laressa had had a chance to relay that information to the elf standing before him.

Eolin's grim smirk tightened. "Because as keeper of their trust, I know full well the consequences befallen anyone fool enough to draw this key from the lock in which it was placed." He hefted the Sword—the key—for emphasis.

"The Illysp," Torin replied. His mind raced, struggling to keep step with that of the critical elf.

"A name you could not possibly know," Eolin countered, "unless given you by another."

"Darinor, scion of Algorath, gatekeeper of the Illysp seal. He told me—"

"He told you of the Vandari, they who created the seal and the only ones who might be able to do so again. He sent you to beg our aid in doing just that."

Torin wanted badly to correct the elf, to say something that might put a crack in the other's smug confidence. But, thus far, Eolin's assumptions had been completely accurate.

"Do you wish to hear my story?" he asked instead.

"On how and why you stole this talisman? For what purpose? So you can offer up excuse as to your actions?"

Torin's frown deepened.

"I care not whether you are an ignorant fool or a vain one. The truth will not change matters now, will it?"

"Perhaps not. But if we're to agree on a course of action against this enemy, we must consider—"

"*We?*"

"Those of us who must unite in order to thwart the Illysp rising."

"And pray tell," Eolin urged, seeming amused, "why should that include me?"

Torin was dumbfounded. "Are you not sworn to uphold the integrity of the barrier constructed by those of your order?"

"I am sworn to no such thing," Eolin claimed. "It was Algorath who agreed to keep watch over that which my forebears set in place. The Vandari have always served as keepers of the Swords. But that obligation ended when the last of the talismans was buried."

"It has now been unearthed," Torin reminded the other with a low growl.

"Through no fault of mine," Eolin snapped. "And as I will not be implicated in the Sword's removal, nor will I accept the burden of responsibility you seem so eager to displace."

"You are responsible for the lives of your people, are you not?"

"My people are safe enough," the elf asserted. Before Torin could object, he added, "That was the response your people gave when we Vandari sought their aid during the original Illysp War. I see no reason to sally forth to your rescue now that the tables have turned."

"That was different," Torin stammered in protest.

"Indeed it was. For *my* people had not hunted *yours* to near extinction. And yet they were refused anyway."

Torin recognized clearly now the morbid satisfaction that the elf was taking from all of this. It was a reaction he had not foreseen, and one he wasn't sure how to combat.

"I'm told it was your people, the Finlorians, who first unleashed this scourge."

"And we paid our price," Eolin remarked bitterly. "Now, it seems, it is your turn."

"How can that be your response?"

"You expect sympathy? I've watched my kind be butchered and harried for far too long to feel any pity for humans. Let mankind suffer the consequences of his own invasiveness—first, in having unleashed the Illysp, and second, in having eliminated those who might have been able to do something about it."

Torin's hands clenched into fists as he fought back the desperate fury rising within. It was not difficult to see the irony to which Eolin referred. But to take delight in it, to willfully stand back and watch a people fall victim to their own nearsightedness, was not something he was prepared to allow.

"Are you telling me you will do nothing to help?"

"What would you have me do? We are trapped, my people and I, here in this valley—by the armies of man. Were I to venture forth, I would be killed before given the chance to explain my purpose."

Torin leapt at the opening. "Lorre has made an offer of reconciliation to your wife. You need not fear his reprisals."

The elf's hairless brow lifted in surprise, but fell just as swiftly, weighted with distrust. "Only a fool would take that butcher or any who serve him at their word. And even if the warlord's offer were genuine, would he then send his armies to defend against the legions of huntsmen who would slay an elf merely for sport?" Eolin shook his head. "What you suggest is a preposterous risk no Finlorian would take."

"Yet no greater than the risk taken by Algorath in defying the will of his order to come to your aid."

Eolin scowled.

"Remember?" Torin pressed. "The Entients may have refused the Vandari, but Algorath did not. He delivered to them the Sword—the very talisman you now hold—even wielding it in their behalf. In doing so he risked his life—against the Illysp and against his own brethren—and sacrificed forever his position in their order, sentencing himself and his progeny to eternal exile."

"The Entients—"

"Are today as they were then," Torin finished, "blinded by an agenda the rest of us cannot comprehend. Nor should we care to try. That is their business. Ours should be doing what we feel is right, for ourselves and for those we care about. Do not ignore, as they did, a danger so easily seen."

Perhaps it was the Pendant, still hidden against his breast, that gave Torin the confidence to speak so boldly. Or perhaps it was the sheer magnitude of what was at stake. Either way, he was not about to relent.

"Let not the fate of your people—and mine—be determined by the many grudges you rightfully hold. What is past cannot be helped. So let us put that aside and give full attention to the future."

Eolin gazed momentarily into the fires of the Sword. But as Torin braved a step toward him, the proud elf raised his bald head in continued defiance.

"The animosity that mankind has shown—to my race, as well as others—is not merely a thing of the past. My people have accepted that, even buried the arms we would use against him. But he has done nothing to earn our forgiveness. Nor is he entitled to the kind of sacrifice you would ask us to make."

"Then consider not the faceless masses," Torin urged, "only, repay the kindness that Algorath showed you."

The elf's brow smoothed, his expression becoming impassive—an indication, perhaps, that Torin's words were making a difference. Nevertheless, the young king held his breath as he awaited the other's response.

"All your fancy pleas cannot change the truth of things," Eolin replied at last. "The Vandari and their powers are no more. What little knowledge I have would be of no use to you."

Torin took another step forward. "Tell me."

"And waste more time recounting what this Darinor has no doubt shared with you already?" The elf frowned reprovingly. "I know not how long you have traveled in search of my advice. Regardless, the best I can give is this: If you wish to defend your people, I would recommend you hurry home and do so."

"RAVENMOON LILY," LARESSA SAID, stopping to point out yet another rare and spectacular bloom.

The one called Saena bent close with admiration. "Smells of lavender," she said, smiling pleasantly. She stepped back then, affording her companions a better view. "But tell me, even with all of this around you, do you never feel trapped?"

Laressa withheld a sigh, already weary of the woman's relentless questioning. "Shelter and clothing, food and medicines—whatever we need, the land provides. Why should we desire to venture forth beyond the walls of this valley?"

"I was raised the daughter of farmers," Saena replied. "I know something about living off the land. But even the land has its limitations."

"The land supports us as long as we support it," Laressa argued. She gestured at the lush foliage surrounding her and her uninvited guests. "As you can see, this valley is well tended."

"But as your numbers grow—"

"Every child born is but another caretaker, devoted to the health of that which sustains us."

Saena swept their surroundings with a wondering gaze. "You make it sound so easy."

Laressa smiled. Though irritated at being asked to keep these others occupied while her husband questioned Torin privately within, she did feel a certain sense of gratification at their continued appreciation for her homeland. She had been suspicious of it, at first, but was fast coming to believe their interest genuine.

"Nothing worthwhile comes easy. But when you follow your passion, it often seems that way."

She turned down another trail, her movements a whisper as she passed through the undergrowth. The three women behind her followed respectfully, strolling along as gently as they could. The pair farther back—the Southlanders—had said not a word since emerging from Laressa's home. Saena, on the other hand—her father's messenger—seemed unable to sate her curiosity.

"Why do your people continue to hide from us? Can they not tell we pose them no threat?"

"You must understand what a shock it is for Crag to have brought you here," Laressa replied, glancing back at the surly dwarf who kept watch from the rear of their party. "It was his people, the Tuthari, who helped us to locate this valley. Aside from them, you are the first outsiders to visit Aefengaard since we settled it."

"Crag did everything possible to hide from us the route that brought us here," Saena assured her.

"So he told me. And I believe him. Nevertheless, my husband and I will have a fair amount of explaining to do on his behalf—especially once our people learn that you are emissaries sent by my father."

"Just her," came the reminder from the smaller of the two Southlanders.

Laressa paused again, this time to study Saena intently. "Indeed. The greatest surprise of all, I must say—that my father should entrust the safety of his messenger to a band of Southland strangers."

A confused look came over Saena's face. "He didn't. One of his most trusted lieutenants came as my guide."

Laressa turned a questioning gaze to Crag, coming up from behind the others.

"Left him bound at the cave mouth behind the Veil," the dwarf responded.

"And why is that?" Laressa asked him.

"Man could barely stand, much less hike any farther. Dolt was wounded back in the mountains, and refused treatment."

Laressa frowned. "Why did you not mention this earlier?"

"Ya hadn't finished scolding me 'bout these others I told ya was waiting outside."

Laressa's frown deepened. She started to say something more, but decided it would only prolong the argument. Instead, she spun about, setting course through the forest garden.

"Where are we going?" Saena asked, hurrying to keep pace.

"To help this man, of course. We can't just leave him to die."

"His choice," Crag huffed. "Not mine. Man has the head of a mule."

Laressa glared back at him. "Most do."

Though pained by the sound of whipping vines and tearing leaves resulting from the movements of those who followed, she continued to push ahead quickly. No good could come from any of this, she was certain. She was happy for Crag, hopeful that the bargain her friend had struck would indeed lead him back to Tritos and the kin he believed still resided there. And indeed, should the danger this Torin spoke of prove real, then the dwarf had done the right thing in trying to help.

But at what cost? It was not logic she wrestled with, but a feeling, deep in her heart and lungs. After twenty years, her people's haven had been breached by the outside world. As innocent as that might seem, she could not help but fear this intrusion to be the beginning of a larger series of events set to change her life forever. Even the greatest catastrophe grew from the smallest of seeds—like pebbles before a rockslide or raindrops before a flood.

She did her best to shake the feeling. Hopefully, Eolin would be able to tell the outsider what he needed to know and send him swiftly on his way. Hopefully, this unexpected visit need not have any effect upon her people after today. Though easier to hope than to believe, perhaps her worry was unfounded.

The roar of the Veil grew louder as they made their way up the path alongside the mountain precipice. Laressa seldom traveled the route. In all the years, she had found little cause to visit the caves serving as threshold to Aefengaard. Though it provided a decent view of the dell below, there were other trails leading up into the encircling bluffs that were just as wonderful. Her daughter was more the hiker than she, and more adventuresome. While Laressa was not as old as she sometimes felt, she had already seen more than her fill.

As they neared the stretch of waters that poured over the cave mouth and gave the falls their name, Crag hustled forward, taking the lead. It hadn't yet occurred to Laressa that this man they were about to visit might be dangerous—left bound and on the verge of death. No doubt her Tuthari friend was merely being cautious.

Then the dwarf halted abruptly, stooping to inspect a small depression in the rocky trail. The mark didn't seem like much to Laressa, but, whatever it was, Crag didn't like it. He half turned, muttering beneath his breath, though she couldn't hear him over the falls. Before she could ask him what was wrong, he drew his axe and dashed ahead.

The water-slicked path had become narrow and treacherous, but that didn't stop Laressa and the others from rushing after. A moment later, they stood together just inside the cave, where Crag glanced about in confusion. From what Laressa could see, mist alone filled the empty tunnel.

The dread feeling that had been bothering her tightened, constricting in her chest. Something was wrong. Braced upon his axe, Crag knelt to one side of the tunnel wall, there to inspect what appeared to be a set of torn bindings. She saw then that there was blood on the ropes and on the rocks upon which they lay.

The Tuthari reached down to pick up something else, and Laressa and the others leaned close to view what he had found.

A bloody quarrel.

Saena gasped. "Is that—"

"Clever rogue," the dwarf snarled. He snapped the bolt in disgust.

"Does this rogue have a name?" Laressa asked, struggling for breath. Deep down, she already knew.

"Warrlun, they called him," Crag grumbled, rising to his feet.

Laressa did not look to the girls for confirmation. She simply spun toward the trail, a sudden and certain panic chilling her to the core.

CHAPTER FORTY-SIX

TORIN CLAMPED DOWN against an impulsive flurry of brash denials. Though he could not afford to accept Eolin's response any more than he had Laressa's, it would do him little good to turn this into a confrontation.

Nevertheless, he had to find some means of convincing the elven king to reveal what he felt certain the other was hiding.

"And the Sword?" he asked, keeping his eyes level with those of his host.

Eolin considered the blade glowing brightly in his hands, mesmerized by the eternal dance of its inner flames.

"Take it," the elf said finally. He turned it around, laying it along his arm and presenting it to Torin hilt first. "You are certain to need it."

Torin continued to look only at the elf—he who claimed to be the last of the Vandari. "Is that not a violation of your oath? To entrust the last of the Swords of Asahiel to a fool human?"

"Do you not want it?" Eolin asked.

"I should think it would be better that you accompany me as its rightful wielder."

Eolin's stern expression relaxed finally into a cold smile. "A valiant effort. But I have sworn a greater oath. An oath of peace. A life free of hostility. I will not break that pledge in order to serve one my forefathers made ages ago—not even to a talisman as sacred as this."

"So why not keep the blade here with you? You would then be serving both vows."

Eolin's smile vanished. "Because while I will not be made to serve your kind, neither will I actively condemn them. This is your doing, and I will take no hand in it, one way or another."

Again he hefted the blade, urging Torin to take it. But Torin refused. Reaching for it now would be to admit defeat, to accept that no help was forthcoming. He couldn't do that. For the sake of his friends, he could not allow this elf to prove more stubborn than him.

"I am asking you to leave," Eolin said bluntly. "You may do so with or without the Sword. But do not think that you can bend my will in this. Doubtless, the Illysp grow stronger with every moment that you waste."

"You cannot hide from them forever," Torin agreed.

"Perhaps not. If that is the will of the Ceilhigh, so be it."

Torin clenched his fists in helpless anger. Easy enough to talk of peace when removed from any direct threat. He wondered, momentarily, what the elf might do were he to strike out at him. Would he stay true to his vow of pacifism? Or would he obey the more natural urge and use the Sword to defend himself?

But Torin abandoned such reckless thoughts almost at once. Becoming belligerent would only reinforce Eolin's judgments about him and his race. Nor would defeating the elf—itself a dubious proposition—guarantee the results he needed.

No, he decided, trying to coerce this people to join his fight was not the answer. For if they accompanied him under duress, how could he be assured of their loyalty when it mattered most? If they were to help him, they would have to do so willingly, eagerly even, with a strength of passion to see them through the worst—surely yet to come.

He took a deep breath, forcing himself to relax. Perhaps he would give the Finlorian time alone to think about it. Could another week or two make that much difference? Persistence, he believed, was a key to unlock almost any door.

Torin glanced down at the Sword. When he looked up again, he did so with one hand offered in parting.

"I *am* sorry," he said, "for any distress we may have caused you or your people."

The scowling Eolin returned his nod, but declined his outstretched hand. "May you reap a bountiful harvest of that which you have sown."

Torin bowed, as graciously as he could manage. As he came up, he reached for the Sword. Instead of taking it, however, he caught his breath, as a thick-framed figure suddenly filled the doorway at Eolin's back.

"Warrlun," he stammered. "What are you—"

The commander raised one arm. Too late, Torin realized what the man intended. As Eolin turned about, that arm came whipping forward, flinging a piece of shale taken from the pond they had passed in the foyer. The elf king spun just in time to catch the sharpened piece of stone square in the face.

Eolin fell back, blood spurting. Torin caught him, and both went stumbling. The Sword fell, bouncing off the arm of a wicker chair to lie upon the moss-covered floor.

When finally Torin regained his balance, he was in a low squat, with an unconscious Eolin cradled against him. The elf king's face was gashed deeply across the center. His nose was surely broken, his left eye a puddle of blood. The skin of his cheek was a loose flap beneath which blood pulsed in waves.

Torin didn't know where to begin. Nor was he given the chance. In the doorway, Warrlun had snatched up his broadsword from where it lay amid the loose bundle Crag had leaned against the wall.

"What have you done?" Torin demanded.

Warrlun regarded the fallen elf with a murderous rage. "Is he dead?"

"Near enough," Torin replied, eyeing the other's ready blade. He noticed then that the crossbow bolts that had punctured the commander's side and shoulder were no longer there.

Warrlun growled. "Then stand aside."

The soldier started forward, and there was no mistaking his intent. Torin had little choice but to drop the wounded elf and launch himself forward to meet the other's charge. He did so at the last possible moment, as Warrlun drew back that heavy blade, so that he could dive inside its arc. He heard the man grunt as he planted his shoulder in the commander's midsection, then kept his legs driving, snarling for added strength. Together, the pair surged across the floor, until Torin was able to slip his arms around the other's legs and trip them both to the earth.

A gloved fist cuffed him behind the ear, and his entire head started ringing. He pushed himself away, just in time to avoid the clumsy swipe of that giant broadsword. He staggered backward in a crouch, heart pumping, putting a hand to the side of his face, which felt afire.

Before he could do anything else, Warrlun was back to one knee, huffing for breath, pointing out with his free hand.

"This isn't your fight," the commander hissed. "Don't make it otherwise."

Torin looked to his own hand, but couldn't tell whose blood it was he found there. "Why are you doing this?" was all he could think to ask.

"To punish a traitor," Warrlun said. "To reclaim what was mine."

Torin's thoughts cleared with understanding—a realization that should never have eluded him. "You. You were Laressa's husband. The father of Lorre's grandchild."

"He stole them both," Warrlun spat, eyes going to the downed elf. "But after today, they'll be his no longer."

The soldier rose to his feet. Though not as helpless as he had made himself appear back at the valley entrance, he was still pale from hunger and blood loss. Indeed, it seemed as if his hatred alone gave him the will to stand.

"Is that why Lorre sent you?" Torin asked, disgusted with himself for not recognizing the truth much sooner.

Warrlun grimaced. "I don't need His Lordship's commission to settle this score. He'll thank me readily enough when I return with his daughter and grandchild. Now stand aside."

Torin might have mentioned the unlikelihood of any of them now being allowed to leave—let alone finding their way back through the maze of Crag's tunnels—but was too busy casting about for a weapon. His gaze fell quickly upon the Sword, yet in order to reach it he would have to surrender his place between Eolin and the man come to slay him. By then, it would be too late.

"I won't warn you again," Warrlun snarled.

Torin retreated another step, staggering as if dizzied. The commander started ahead in a slow rush. Torin baited him a moment longer, then flung a wicker chair at the oncoming soldier. Warrlun reacted swiftly to swat it away, its willow frame cracking beneath the weight of his blade. But it was all the time Torin needed to scramble sideways and retrieve the Sword from where it lay upon a blood-spattered floor. As Warrlun kicked away the last of the chair's debris, he found Torin crouched and ready.

"I'm afraid I can't allow this, Commander. Drop your blade."

Warrlun stopped, but made no move to obey. The soldier's eyes narrowed, and a low growl emitted from his throat.

Torin refused to back down. He was going to have to kill this man, he realized, if he wished to save Eolin—if the elf wasn't dead already. He might have checked, but didn't dare take his eyes off his adversary.

As if in response, there came a moan from behind him. Any thoughts Warrlun might have been having about leaving off—or at least pretending to—vanished in an instant. Both hands gripped tighter about the hilt of his broadsword, held before him.

"You can't defeat me," Torin stated boldly. "Lay down your sword before I cut it from your hand."

The man responded by sidestepping to Torin's left. Torin shifted with him, maintaining his defensive posture. Warrlun surprised him then by backing toward the doorway. His hopes for a truce, however, vanished when the commander stooped just long enough to fish one of his long daggers from the weapons bundle.

"Of what worth is he to you?" Warrlun demanded, brandishing both sword and dagger. "From what I heard, he would refuse your request. Perhaps with his death, the others of his clan will be better motivated to serve your cause."

To Torin, the soldier's voice barely sounded human. "I cannot force an army across the seas," he replied.

"Then you shall have one of mine. A legion, if that's what it takes, under my personal command. A small price to pay for one dead elf."

Torin shook his head. "I did not come to enlist men-at-arms, but for the secrets of Finlorian magic-users."

"So take them. One tongue at a time, if necessary. I can show you—"

"Drop your weapons, Commander, and I'll see to it that you are delivered back to your lordship for judgment rather than burial."

Warrlun's gaze narrowed dangerously. "I've waited too long to be denied my vengeance by a whelp like you. For the last time, stand aside!"

Torin knew that he should simply run the commander through. The longer he stood there, trading words, the more likely it was that Warrlun would get what he had come for. Eolin continued to moan, trying now to rise. Warrlun's fingers shifted about the hilts of his weapons, adjusting grip.

The soldier's lunge came much faster than before, his devastating broadsword sweeping down from overhead along an angled arc. Torin rushed to meet it, focusing on his opponent's wrist. Surely the loss of a hand would temper the man's bloodlust.

Warrlun howled as the flaming blade tore through leather and skin and bone. But he came on, spinning behind his dagger. The sword-strike, Torin realized suddenly, had been a feint. Overcommitted to thwarting it, he had opened his flank to the dagger's bite. He recognized it in a heartbeat, and pivoted instinctively, spinning sideways to evade the slashing tip.

He came about to reengage, but Warrlun did not. Seizing his opening, the commander dove toward Eolin, who had managed to sit up. Dagger leading, he threw himself upon the hated elf, smothering him.

Torin dashed toward the pair, and this time had no other choice. As Warrlun reared back upon his knees, bolt upright, Torin struck. The cut was so swift and clean that for an instant, nothing happened. Then blood began to spill from a ring around Warrlun's neck, and the severed head fell free.

The body slumped forward, but Torin gripped it by the shoulder and flung it to one side, so that it would not crush the elf beneath. In a near panic, he searched Eolin for fresh wounds. The Finlorian king was hunched forward upon the ground, his one good eye wide, his blood-filled mouth groping for air. His hands clutched desperately at his clenched stomach—

Only to grasp the protruding hilt of a buried dagger.

Torin bent to him at once, setting the Sword down beside him. "Don't touch it," he said, pushing past the dread that he felt. "Lie still."

Eolin coughed and sputtered, but lay back as commanded to gape at the ceiling. Torin pried the other's hands away so that he could take a closer look. Doing so caused him to feel as if the blade were buried in his own stomach. He might have cried out for help, but doubted anyone would hear him this far beneath the earth. Nor would that do anything to reassure Eolin. And yet he knew at once that he could not treat the elf alone.

"I'm going to remove the blade," he said in warning.

Eolin nodded, blood still pulsing from the flap of his torn cheek.

Torin took a deep breath and gripped the dagger's handle.

He hesitated when he heard the frantic patter of running footsteps. Still holding the dagger, he turned as Laressa came racing through.

The half-elven woman froze as she took in the scene: Warrlun's broadsword, still clutched by his dismembered hand; the headless body, seeping blood upon her chamber floor; her husband, lying amid the carnage, with Torin's hands upon the blade thrust deep within his gut.

Torin was too relieved to worry about how things must have looked, or to attempt an explanation. "Help me," he pleaded.

Laressa rushed forward with a wail. Torin felt certain she meant to strike him, but she skidded to a halt upon Eolin's opposite side instead, turning her back to Warrlun's remains as she settled in next to them. She moved at once to cradle her husband's head, gasping again upon inspection of his face.

"Laressa?" Eolin groaned.

"*Heh va, noi mi*," she cried, dabbing at his cheek. "*Heh va.*" She lashed suddenly at Torin. "Get away!"

Torin let go the dagger and leaned back. "The blade must come free."

Dyanne and Holly were in the doorway then, splitting up as they entered the room.

"*You* did this!" Laressa shouted. "All of you!"

Though wracked with guilt, Torin wasn't going to let that stop him from trying to save Eolin's life. He leaned forward again, and before Laressa could free herself to stop him, tore the dagger from the elf's stomach. Eolin grunted, but clenched his jaw and kept from screaming.

With that same weapon, Torin cut a strip from the elf's tunic and folded it over the wound, trying vainly to stanch the flow of blood. Laressa watched him for a moment, then let go her husband's head in order to shove Torin away.

"Leave him be!" she yelled.

A winded Crag came stumping in at that point, followed by a sweat-streaked Saena. The dwarf looked ready for battle, but after seeing that the battle had already taken place, his face turned ashen. Lowering his axe, he rushed forward.

"Stay where you are!" Laressa demanded, though her glare alone might have stopped the Tuthari in his tracks. "Do you see what you have done?" she cried, and this time, there were tears amid her fury. "Do you see?"

Crag stood motionless. "Laressa . . ."

"Take your murdering band and go. I want never to look upon your bearded face again."

"I didn't know—"

"Go!" Laressa wept, one hand tight over Eolin's stomach, the other reaching back again to support his neck.

"Let us help tend his wounds, at least," Torin begged.

"You have done enough!" Laressa spat.

She leaned over her husband's chest then, and began to sob gently. Eolin lay still—dead already, perhaps, or else slipped back into unconsciousness.

"We didn't mean for this to happen," Torin offered uselessly.

Laressa looked up at him with a blood-smeared cheek and stricken eyes. "Then leave, Torin of Alson. Leave and make certain that none set foot within this valley again." She aimed a final glare in Crag's direction, a clear expression of agony and betrayal.

The dwarf bit his lip. Then his shoulders crumpled, bowing forward with helpless resignation.

"Come," he said, his voice husky.

"As soon as his wounds have been tended," Torin maintained stubbornly.

"Now!" Crag barked. "Else you'll lie down beside him."

The dwarf hefted his axe, and Torin knew this wasn't a threat he wished to test. With leaden legs and a heavy heart, he reached almost absently for the Sword of Asahiel. For a moment, he considered leaving it as restitution for what had happened. At the same time, he understood what an insult that would be. Most likely, it would serve Laressa and her people only as a dark reminder of this day.

So he closed his fingers around its hilt, searching still for some further way to express his remorse. It was *his* fault, after all. This was all his fault. If only there were some way for him to set things aright. He would willingly give his own life, if necessary, to save Eolin's. Perhaps if he wished hard enough . . .

His blood began to tingle at the prospect. But before he could carry out the thought, Crag snorted gruffly. Dyanne and Holly, Torin saw, had already retrieved their weapons, and stood ready beside a stunned and heartsick Saena. All were waiting for him.

None had any words, and Torin understood how foolish he'd have to be to seek the right ones. With a stinging sense of shame, he backed toward his companions, his eyes still locked on the nightmarish scene.

Crag followed him, pushing him along, though the Tuthari stopped and turned upon reaching the exit. "On my oath, Laressa, your father will pay for this day's treachery."

Laressa lifted her head from Eolin's chest, though she did not even glance their way. "Look first to your own, dwarf, if you think blood will be washed away by blood."

She lowered her head, and her sobs resumed. Torin thought again to go to her, to see if anything might yet be done for the husband she was so quick to mourn. But the look Crag gave him caused him to turn and follow after the others.

They emerged moments later through the cleft in the base of that great tree. Torin was still replaying the events below in his mind, exploring the many ways in which he might have acted differently, when he heard Saena's gasp.

He looked up, startled to find a growing mob of Finlorians forming up around them. Their appearance should not have surprised him. Doubtless, the elven people had been observing the intruders carefully ever since their arrival. Perhaps an alarm had been sounded—maybe that which had sent Laressa racing back to check on him. Or perhaps word of what had happened to their keifer had somehow been passed up through the tree's roots the way light was passed down below. Torin wasn't in any mood to concern himself over how they'd been summoned, or why. If they had assembled now to break their vow of peace, they would certainly be justified in doing so.

But as he searched their stern faces, he found no signs of animosity. Fear and confusion, yes, alongside sorrow and resentment. But none carried weapons. None growled or snarled or otherwise suggested an overt threat. Only the looks remained, an army of brows pinched in accusation, cold stares from elves young and old that pierced Torin's heart.

In that moment, it seemed punishment enough.

"If ya hurry," Crag muttered, "he might still be saved."

The elf to which he had spoken responded only with a bitter glare.

So began their retreat from the valley known as Aefengaard, their route of departure marked by row upon row of Finlorians emerged from the surrounding wood, come to cast silent judgment. Crag bore the brunt of it, having taken the lead to show the rest of them the way out. In response, there was nothing the companions could do. Had it been permitted, Torin might have stopped and apologized to every single one of those he had frightened or offended. But his apologies were useless. So he kept his eyes on the path ahead, accepting the stares that riddled him like a volley of arrows, knowing each strike was well deserved.

Even when they had climbed free of the forest, Torin could feel their silent barbs like whips upon his back, and he dared not turn around. Not when he reached the falls. Not when he entered the caves. Not when he was engulfed by the welcoming darkness beyond.

◆ ◆ ◆

ONLY MOMENTS AFTER THE INTRUDERS HAD LEFT, Laressa looked up, drawn by the quiet rustle of those in a rush to lend aid.

"*Neren mi, thre tahlo huum.*" *The priests have come, my lady.*

Laressa sniffed, turning toward the others who filed then into the room, barely recognizing them through her tears.

"Please, my lady, stand aside now."

But Laressa refused. She knew there was nothing the priests could do. And she would not look on from afar while her beloved husband took his last breath.

"My lady, you must—"

Eolin coughed, grimacing and then clutching his stomach as blood pumped and spasms ripped across torn muscles. "Mind your tongue," he grunted harshly. "That is your queen you speak to."

"My lord, she must give us a chance—"

"Leave us," Eolin hissed.

"My lord?"

"I've only so many breaths to spare, and I would share them with my wife."

"But . . . my lord—"

"He is your keifer!" Laressa snapped. "Do as he says!"

The priests and their attendants hesitated a moment longer, then bowed and stole swiftly from the room.

"Have they gone?" Eolin asked, staring blindly at the ceiling.

Laressa bent to kiss his forehead. "Yes, my love. There is no one here but you and I."

"Torin?"

Laressa stiffened. "I sent him away, my love. All of them."

Eolin's spirits seemed to sag. His eye closed and his head settled deeper into her lap.

"My love? My love!" She shook him gently. One hand closed about his.

"Forgive me, sweet Laressa."

"Hush, my love. I am the one to beg forgiveness—for not asking Crag to dispose of the intruders the moment I learned of them."

The dying elf squeezed her hand. "I have erred, my sweet. I have been unfaithful to my charge. And swift indeed has been my punishment for doing so."

Laressa shook her head. "You have done nothing but good in your life. You have been a kind husband, and a noble servant to your people. Long will they praise your name."

He tensed suddenly, his entire body seized by convulsion. When it passed, he spoke with a renewed sense of urgency, and a weakened voice.

"Quiet now, my sweet, for there are things I must tell you, things you must know before I go. I know not if they will be of any use. Nor would I make them your burden. Should you find yourself unwilling—or unable—to act upon them, let the fault lie with me."

Laressa frowned. "What is this you speak of, my love? Has it anything to do with this . . . this Torin?"

"Not Torin," he whispered with increasingly shallow breaths, "but the talisman he carries. The history behind it. The legacy of those sworn to carry the truth, lest it be forgotten by all."

A sudden cold crept into the pit of Laressa's stomach, chilling the heat of her anguish. "The Vandari."

Eolin nodded. "A secret I should have shared with you long before now. For I am all that is left. All that stands between us and the great evil about which we have been warned."

The cold became a shiver that ran the length of Laressa's spine. "Evil," she repeated, and searched her memory for the name it had been given. "The Illysp?"

Her husband suffered another constricting spasm. But he gritted his teeth, and afterward his strength seemed to surge. "I should not have refused him, my sweet. I should have made certain he understood."

"Shall I send for him?"

"Listen first to what I have to say, as we may not have time for both. Listen, my sweet, and know the truth of how the Finlorian Empire crumbled."

CHAPTER FORTY-SEVEN

As the darkness of the deepening tunnel closed round, Crag lurched to a stop and whipped out his axe. Torin and the others held back, giving the dwarf room to bring that heavy blade down upon a knee-high rock that lay against the cavern wall. Crag roared, and sparks flew as the axe struck, cleaving the stone down its center.

For a moment thereafter, the Tuthari huffed quietly, one arm raised against his eyes as he leaned his forehead upon the wall, the other hand clenched about the butt of his lowered weapon.

The others left him to his pain and his fury, respectfully silent as they wrestled with feelings of their own. Torin had not the heart to look at the dwarf, or anyone else. He kept his gaze upon the floor, listening to the pounding sheets of the falls outside, searching within himself for a hole in which to bury his sorrow and his guilt.

"What now?" Holly asked finally.

Crag shoved free of the cavern wall. His face was sullen, though his eyes remained full of fire. "I care not," he said, "as long as we get moving."

"Did you learn what you needed?" Dyanne asked.

Torin looked to the sound of her voice, and found that her question was directed toward him. As their gazes met, an uncertain pang gripped him. "I have my answers," he mumbled, "though they are not what I'd hoped."

"I suppose you'll be heading home, then."

All at once, the source of his pang became clear. She was right. His quest had ended. The time had come to return to his own land as quickly as possible, to deliver unto Darinor the ill tidings he had found.

The time had come to say farewell to Dyanne.

He looked quickly to the others, half hoping one of them might have a better idea. Holly's dark eyes were inquisitive; Saena's were red and puffy. Doleful beneath his gnarled brow, even Crag kept silent, awaiting his response.

"Yes," Torin agreed. He turned his attention to the wall as he spoke, finding that to be much easier than facing Dyanne. "I suppose I must."

"You promised Crag," Holly reminded him, as if his hesitation were obvious.

"Do you still wish to accompany me?" Torin asked the dwarf.

Judging by his expression, the glum Tuthari would rather be dead. "I'm no longer needed here," he said. "Laressa made that much clear."

A *yes*, Torin decided, regardless of the other's grim tone.

"The sooner the better, I imagine," Dyanne added.

Torin made a quick study of the woman's face, his heart wringing in his chest. But he could not bring himself to refute her words.

"What of Lorre?" Saena demanded, and it struck Torin that this was the first time she had mentioned the warlord by name. "Is he to go unpunished?"

Torin shook his head. "From what I understood, Warrlun acted alone, not under orders from Lorre."

"If I'd known who he was . . ." Crag muttered, but when the others looked to him, it was clear he was speaking only to himself.

"Perhaps Holly and I will pay Lorre a visit anyway, just to be sure," Dyanne said.

"You mean to head south then?" Torin asked, as evenly as he could manage.

"We've done as my sister asked," Dyanne reminded him, "and seen you to the end of your road."

She turned to Holly, who nodded in agreement. "Much has happened that our sisters should be made aware of."

"You've held true to the story you shared with us in the beginning," Dyanne added, "so I see no reason to drag you with us back to the Nest."

She grinned as she said this. The best Torin could do was wince.

"You're welcome to accompany us," Holly offered, addressing Saena, "if you're interested in an escort on the southern road."

But Saena was studying Torin as if considering something else altogether. "How do you intend to get home?" she asked him.

Torin shrugged. "I'll need a ship, obviously." For some reason, she continued to stare at him. "Why? What are you thinking?"

"I'm thinking that my uncle in Kasseri might be able to help with that."

"Kasseri," Torin echoed, thinking aloud. "That's up here to the north, right?"

"On the eastern coast," Saena confirmed. "Through the passes of Serpent Reach."

Torin frowned. By his recollection, Autumn and the pirate Karulos had advised against that route. "I was led to believe those passes are snowbound this time of year."

"Probably so," Saena acknowledged, biting her cheek. "But our only other options would be a long sail around the southern horn, or else marching south as your friends suggest."

A tiny hope began to push aside some of the hollowness Torin had been feeling. Perhaps his time with Dyanne was not yet concluded after all.

"Serpent Reach?" Crag snorted, as if only now catching up to what they had been saying. "I can get us through that."

Both Torin and Saena asked at once. "How?"

"Passes are closed *above* ground, not below."

"You could lead us there from here?" Saena pressed. Torin could not tell if she sounded hopeful or skeptical.

"Direct route, more or less," the Tuthari assured her.

Saena looked back to Torin. "Well, then, perhaps we should do that."

Torin turned immediately to Dyanne. "We can't just abandon you here. You'd never escape these caves."

"They can come with us," Saena proposed. "Theirs would be a quick and easy sail down the coast."

"Except we'd then be bypassing Neak-Thur," Dyanne reminded them both. She shifted to share with Holly one of those silent conferences in which each appeared to read the other's mind. "I really think it best that we travel once more that way, to see what our good overlord is planning now that he has secured his position there. Besides, neither of us has sailed before."

"I'm sure you'd love it," Torin said, ignoring Crag's contrarian grunt.

"Whichever, we stick together for now," the dwarf grumbled decisively. "There's a course from here what will take us all down into the Splinterwood. The pass *you'd* need," he continued, nodding to Dyanne and Holly, "lies en route to the one *we'd* be taking. Overland trail should be easy enough to follow, should ya wish to chance it on your own."

"I don't like it," Torin blurted.

"Then argue it on the go," Crag gruffed, shouldering his axe. "Either way, we've a long track to follow, and I'm not for sullying this place any more than we have already. My friend down there asked us to leave, and it seems that's the least we're owing her."

The strain in his voice, as much as his words, put an end to any further discussion. As horrible as Torin felt about what had taken place in the valley below, he could scarcely imagine the sharpness of guilt Crag was feeling. While the dwarf retrieved the bundle of torches and foodstuffs left behind in the tunnel upon their arrival earlier, Torin looked to his remaining comrades, searching for any words of hope or comfort they might share. They ended up only shaking their heads.

Crag paid them no notice, but gathered his possessions, struck flame to torch, and trundled off into the cavern gloom.

THEY WENT THIS TIME WITHOUT ROPES AND BLINDFOLDS. Torin thought it odd that the protective Crag had not even tried to insist otherwise. Granted, there were several possible reasons for the dwarf's decision, based in varying degrees on trust and logistics. But one likelihood in particular kept returning to haunt Torin: The damage had already been done.

They marched throughout the evening and much of the night, wishing to put as much distance as possible between themselves and Aefengaard before settling down with the nightmares sure to follow. Despite Crag's earlier invitation, they did not speak further of their course. All knew their options, and seemed accepting enough of what had already been decided. From what Torin could tell, he alone was unsettled by the prospect of parting company with

Dyanne and Holly and leaving them to continue south on their own—the true reason for which was best suited to private debate.

So he, too, kept his mouth shut, head bowed in somber reflection of what had gone and what was yet to come. He didn't know which should trouble him more: the lasting harm his visit had brought upon the Finlorian people, or the fact that he was returning to Darinor empty-handed.

Either way, it seemed ridiculous that all he could think about was what would soon be left behind.

Yet he couldn't help it. The dim light of those subterranean caverns might mask her look, her movements, the hypnotic swish of her hair, but it did nothing to diminish her strength of spirit, the ease with which she found comfort and laughter in what seemed to him a dark and humorless world. How liberating might it feel if he could learn to share her outlook? Knowing that his time with her was swiftly coming to an end, he found it difficult to contemplate anything else.

It was well after midnight when finally they emerged from the tunnels and into the Splinterwood. At that point, Crag bade them all take a few hours' rest. While the dwarf did so among a pile of rocks within the mouth of the cave, Dyanne led the rest of them into the dense fringes of the aged forest and settled herself down upon a bed of leaves and moss. Torin watched her slip free of her soft leather boots, then covered himself with his cloak upon a mound of pine needles, his heart churning with secret emotions, his mind awhirl with words unspoken.

He awoke before the others, but did nothing to disturb their tranquil slumber. In the dawn's quiet, he could yet imagine that time might freeze this very moment. The daylight might never come, and he might spend an eternity free of death and demons, free of weakness and wrong choices, free to do nothing more than gaze upon Dyanne's beauty and experience the fullness of peace and passion that her mere presence somehow fostered within him.

But the day did break, of course, rays of sunlight spilling through the sieve of woodland boughs to eat away at blankets of shadow and tickle the flesh of those beneath. Before Torin could find a way to stop it, the girls were awakened, Crag stumped down from his bed of stone, and the five of them were on their way once more.

They covered ground much more swiftly out in the open, better able to navigate the trails and pathways of the forest than the cramped and jagged tunnels of the mountain underground. Torin, however, saw this as more of a curse than a blessing. With each step, hope gave way to inevitability. Not even the fires of Asahiel were able to comfort him, burning low within both Sword and Pendant, as if dampened by his despair.

He had fought for reassurance on several fronts. First, despite the lack of support to come from the Vandari, at least he knew now with cold certainty what he was up against. There would be no restoring of the Illysp seal, only a long and brutal war that somehow, he and Darinor would have to find a more conventional way to win. But by exhausting one of their primary options, they could now unite their focus in a single, concerted effort to find that answer, rather than spreading themselves and their resources across the breadth and span of two entirely separate lands.

Second, learning what little the Finlorians had to offer did not have to be considered a failure. By finding them at all, he had done what was asked of him, once again achieving something few thought possible. Having accomplished that, he had to believe that ultimate victory against the Illysp, however unlikely, was a goal that would prove similarly attainable.

And third, he was headed home. Rather than concentrate on what he stood to lose, he need only focus on what he would soon regain: Marisha and Allion, his friends and his castle, the land of his birth. That was how it should be, he told himself. It was what he had wanted all along.

Truthfully, however, he felt not the slightest sense of joy or expectation at the notion of his impending homecoming. Nor were his greatest concerns those stemming from the knowledge that he was on his own against the Illysp. No, despite all his pressing concerns, what worried him most was leaving a land he had never wanted to visit in the first place.

He measured his steps carefully, and with them, the passing of time. Yet it came as a complete shock when he found that the minutes had all disappeared. Ahead, Crag had come to a stop at what appeared to Torin little more than a game trail, which wound southward into the mountain foothills.

"This here will carry ya to the southern arm of Goblin Reach. For anyone heading south, this is the road ya want."

"Then this is where we say our good-byes," Dyanne agreed, peering down the narrow path.

"Are you sure about this?" Torin asked. When both Nymphs looked at him, he found himself rushing to explain. "We could accompany you south and just sail up from Razorport—especially if you've still a mind to report back to Lorre."

"We don't know for sure that Warrlun acted alone," Dyanne reminded him. "For you to pass through Neak-Thur with the Sword would seem a foolish risk."

"Then let us at least see you beyond the pass, so that we'll know you made it through safely."

"All they gots to do is stick to the main roadway," Crag insisted. He shook a finger at the Nymphs. "Don't go veering off as ya did with that rogue coming through."

Dyanne must have caught the glare that Torin let slip the dwarf's way, for she moved quickly to reassure him.

"Time for you is critical," she said. "We'll be fine."

"The fewer guard posts you have to pass through with Crag, the better," Holly added. "If you can make for the coast from here, you should do so."

Torin wished now that he had gone ahead and forced this discussion earlier, when he would have had more time to reason through and thus better present his arguments.

"Is it safe to begin heading up this close to dusk?" he asked, fighting to keep the desperation from his voice. "We could all camp here and set out fresh in the morning."

Heads turned to regard the position of the sun in the sky—the brightness of which mocked the squall that wracked him from within.

"It's barely midafternoon," Holly observed. "We've several hours of daylight yet to take advantage of."

"If we're going to split up," Crag grumbled, "we may as well do so now. Ain't much sense in one group or the other traveling half a day or more in the wrong direction."

Torin could not remove his gaze from Dyanne, his eyes drawn to the delicate strands of hair that flapped and swirled, tossed by woodland breezes. How could he admit to her the truth of his hesitation? How could he tell her that the only real reason for his protests was that he did not know how to say good-bye?

His chest tightened. His breathing quickened. He would tell her because he must. This was the moment he had long been waiting for—the moment in which he would confess all and beg for the honor of catering to her every need and desire. It had to be. For it might well be the last time he would ever see her.

"We'll be seeing you again, won't we?" she asked him, as if able to follow the torrent of his thoughts.

Her words raked his spine like a flash of lightning. The notion had not yet occurred to him. All along, he had assumed the only decision he might make was whether to leave her in the first place. In that regard, it seemed he had precious little choice. Was it possible that he might somehow, when this war was won, find his way back to her?

"I'd like that," he managed, his voice hoarse.

After that, he could only gape at the cherished face before him, veins pulsing to the frantic drumming of his heart. Though he searched, there seemed no words to properly convey his sudden sense of devotion. He wanted so badly to express a deeper commitment, to promise her that yes, she would see him again, no matter what that required of him. But he feared if he were to say anything more, the dam would burst, and he would be unable to control the sudden flood.

"Should anyone ask," Holly added, "I'll tell them we had quite the adventure." Torin turned to her, almost grateful for the interruption. "But it's clear you no longer need us. Seems as good a time as any to thank us and be on your way."

Torin swallowed the deeper feelings risen to his throat. "Thank you," he said. "I'd never have made it without you."

He bowed to the pair of them. When he came up, Dyanne was glancing at her kinmate with one of those knowing smirks. But when his eyes met hers, she flashed him a smile—that dazzling smile!—and nodded in return. "Good luck," she offered. "We'll look forward to your return, Torin of Alson."

She gazed at him a moment longer, but he had nothing more to say. So the

Nymphs bade their farewells to Crag and Saena, offering their apologies to the dwarf, and asking if the girl had any messages to be delivered to her lord and ruler. Only that she would report back herself, Saena had replied bitterly, just as soon as she had seen Torin on his way.

Then they turned, the two from the Fenwood, starting up the trail. They walked with the same confident gait with which they had first strolled into Torin's life, and did not look back. He stared after them, but the path took a sudden bend, and their forms were eclipsed all too swiftly by a shallow ridge.

Wait! Torin shouted, but the word went unspoken, unheard, unknown, echoing only within his mind.

Where all he had left were memories.

"They'll be fine," he heard Crag say. "Come."

Torin gulped, peering a moment longer down that empty trail. Then Saena tugged gently on his arm, and together they resumed their hike through the sun-filled wood.

CHAPTER FORTY-EIGHT

Allion closed his eyes and let the warmth of the water seep in, doing his best to dismiss all of the pain and tension carried with him throughout his journey. He hadn't bathed since setting forth from Atharvan nearly a fortnight ago—the latter half of which had been spent in slow, steady march alongside Chief General Corathel and the rest of the Second Division as it made its return. Though proud to have helped free the legion commander from the A'awari and turn the division homeward, he had done so at great cost—to himself and to others. Burdened for days by the weight of emotions too confusing and shameful to sort through, he was finding it difficult, even now, to grant them full release.

"More oil, milord?"

The hunter opened his eyes and looked to where one of his bath attendants—the king's own—stood beside the ornate tub, a pitcher upraised.

"No, thank you," he replied. The scent was strong enough as it was. "Some more petals, perhaps."

The girl obliged him, setting aside the pitcher and fetching a basket of rose petals, which she sprinkled liberally atop the water's surface. The other attendant stood behind him, arranging an assortment of rags and brushes. Except as a babe, Allion had never before been bathed by another, and he felt perfectly foolish now—especially with but a thin layer of oil and lye and petals to shield his nakedness. He had tried to refuse, of course, but a grateful Galdric had insisted, saying that it was the least the king owed him for returning to the Parthan people their army.

"That should do," he said, when the coverage of petals was thick enough to conceal him from any wandering eyes.

The girl set down her basket and came round to where Allion leaned back against the wall of the tub. He tensed as she began to rub his shoulders.

"Do my hands offend, milord?"

"No, no," Allion answered, having no desire to insult the girl or the king she served. "I'm not accustomed to such royal treatment, is all."

"His Majesty tells us you are well deserving, milord. Just relax."

Easily suggested, Allion thought. Not so easily done. For he was not so naive as to believe that the concerns troubling his heart would be washed away as readily as the dirt and grime that now clouded his bathwaters. What he needed was some time to himself, an opportunity to sort through the many emotions now warring within. He had expected that once he returned here, to Atharvan, that he would finally be able to break away from Marisha, Darinor, and all others who would disturb and muddle his thoughts. Alas, it seemed he would have to wait a little while longer.

The hunter could not remember a time in which he had felt so conflicted. Duty and respect had long been the tenets by which he defined his life. Seldom had personal dreams and desires been in opposition to the expectations of his elders, and, when so, had been easy enough to put aside. Certainly, he had never wanted anything so badly that he would consider defying king and country—or worse, betraying the trust of his closest friend.

One kiss had changed all that.

It was this that gnawed at him more than anything else—more than his ongoing fears concerning the Illysp, and more than his lingering guilt over the death of Jaquith Wyevesces. He'd even been unable to take heart in a report relayed by King Galdric that Evhan, captain of the City Shield, was once again in charge of Krynwall's home defenses, having escaped abduction by a gang of thieves within the city. No, Allion was much more concerned by what had happened between him and Marisha there in those southern jungles, and what it might mean—to all of them—in the weeks ahead.

He never should have allowed their relationship to progress as it had. He should have guarded his hidden feelings much more closely, for surely Marisha had sensed the truth of his heart and been lured accordingly. At the very least, he should never have returned her kiss, but should instead have made it clear right away that there could be nothing of that between them—not behind Torin's back, and not while so much of greater import lay at stake.

But it was too late. He could not put a stop to what had already happened. And in truth, he wasn't sure that he would even if it were within his power to do so. Riddled as he was with guilt, half his time was spent thinking not of how he might have avoided those brief moments in the jungle, but how he might continue them. The urgency of Marisha's kiss had filled him with a euphoria he had never before imagined. At times, he could think of nothing he wouldn't do to recapture that feeling and make it last forever.

Regardless, with everything else going on around him, this was a personal struggle he didn't need.

"This is supposed to *ease* your tensions, not increase them."

Recognizing the voice, Allion nearly jumped from the tub. As it was, he spun about, pulling away from the hands that gripped his shoulders, and sloshing water and rose petals onto the floor. He glanced toward the doorway as the king's bath attendants slipped from view, then turned a horrified gaze upon the woman before him.

"Marisha, what are you doing here?"

"The same thing those girls were doing," she responded, reaching again for his shoulders. "Why? Do you prefer them to me?"

Allion pushed himself beyond her reach, aghast at how quietly and effectively she had been able to dismiss the king's servants and take their place.

"This is hardly proper," he remarked, working to rearrange those petals that had been disturbed by his frantic movements.

"It might be too late to concern ourselves with propriety."

Allion disagreed. They had been extremely careful during their northward march not to exhibit obvious displays of their newfound affection. Aside from Darinor, who had happened upon them, no one else, Allion believed, had cause to suspect that anything untoward had taken place between Alson's queen-to-be and her sworn protector.

"The last thing I want is for Torin to hear about us from some rumormonger," he said, watching her carefully.

"That's *if* he even returns to us."

Allion gave her a sour look.

"I wish him to, of course. I don't mean otherwise. But how long must we be expected to wait?"

Once again, Allion wasn't certain what to feel. On the one hand, he was thrilled by the suggestion that she viewed their kiss not as a mistake, but as the birth of something more between them. On the other hand . . .

"What about your father?" he asked.

"What about him?"

"I doubt he would be pleased to find you here."

Marisha scowled. "My father walked freely from my life more than a dozen years ago. He hasn't the right to tell me how—or with whom—I should live it."

Allion gaped, both elated and terrified by the prospect her words conveyed.

"Nevertheless, I think you should send the girls back in before they—and I—have to explain to Galdric why they were dismissed."

"A wise choice," a thunderous voice echoed from the doorway.

Allion cringed, but forced his gaze to meet Darinor's as the Entient strode forward.

Marisha, though frozen for a moment, turned bravely to confront him. "Father, I thought you in council."

"The council proved brief," Darinor grunted. "This Galdric, it seems, is a man of his word. General Corathel gave his voice in support of our plan, and the king accepted it."

Our plan, Allion echoed derisively. The one to unite all major military forces in a single region of Pentania in an effort to draw forth the Illysp hungering for the bodies of soldiers. The one that would leave the majority of the civilian populace relatively defenseless. As if anyone other than Darinor—including they who had accepted his proposed course—truly believed it to be a good idea.

"We'll be departing soon, then?" Marisha asked.

Darinor's brow furrowed sharply. "Not before I have a word with our good regent," he said, turning his glare upon Allion.

"It's my fault, Father, not his."

"Go," the Entient commanded her.

"You'll not harm him," she declared stubbornly.

The look he gave made no such promise, but she must have taken some reassurance, for she finally acquiesced, stepping quietly from the chamber.

For a long moment after, Allion soaked silently while Darinor continued to glower.

"You do not approve of us," the hunter dared when the grim hush became unbearable.

"Is she not betrothed to your king?" the Entient asked.

"A man *you* sent away," Allion reminded him, "on a mission from which she fears he may never return."

"So you seek to comfort her in his stead."

Allion sulked. He wasn't sure whether he should defend himself, or take up a whip and have a hand in his own flogging.

"I wish for her to find happiness," he said at last. "As her father, I should think you would want the same."

"Happiness," Darinor snorted. "And have you no concern for that of your friend?"

Allion's gaze dipped helplessly to the waters beneath which he hid. "I didn't mean for this to happen. I only—"

"Spare me your excuses," the Entient rumbled. "I care not how you ply your fickle human emotions. Nor she hers. For if she is to embrace her legacy, she will outlive both of you by centuries."

Allion raised a confounded expression. "Then what *do* you care about?"

"I care about the potential for distraction and infighting at a time when we can ill afford either," Darinor growled. "I care about losing focus and inviting further disaster to join us."

The hunter met the other's stare, but had no response.

"Try to remember that," Darinor added, "as you take your rest in the coming days."

"Rest? Are we not returning to Krynwall?"

"I intend to wait and march forth when the legion is ready. I will not risk leaving those here to change their minds while we are away."

"How long?"

"That is for the army to determine. The sooner the better, obviously. In the meantime, whatever peace and solitude you might find is well deserved. Just bear in mind," Darinor pressed, upon catching Allion's look of surprise, "that your decisions, and those of my daughter, could have a far greater impact than either of you may have yet realized. If *she* cannot see that, I'm trusting *you* will."

It made sense then, Allion thought, that the Entient should come to him. No doubt, Darinor would have this talk with his daughter as well—if he hadn't already. But the Entient had likely learned by now that of the two, Marisha was the more bold and willful, while Allion . . .

The hunter exhaled slowly. Allion did as he was told, not as he wished.

Somehow, he managed to nod his understanding, hoping that Darinor would not demand of him some form of ironclad guarantee. For if that were the case, he had none to give.

Thankfully, his simple acknowledgment was enough. Darinor considered him a moment longer, then turned for the exit. As soon as he had left, the king's bath attendants reentered.

"Are you ready now, milord?"

Allion nodded absently, thinking of the prospect that his first kiss with Marisha might have been their last.

The attendants took up their rags and brushes. This time, the hunter offered no outward resistance—while, within, the war against his sense of duty raged on.

TORIN GAZED OUT UPON A WINDSWEPT SEA, bereft of the joy and freedom that had so enraptured him when first he had felt the ocean's caress. He stood not at the bow of the ship, but its stern, peering back at the forested bluffs marking Yawacor's northern shoreline—all but hidden by the closing curtains of mist. Overhead, midday skies held off the threat of rain, much as he refused to let slip what he was feeling inside.

He had said his last good-byes a short time ago, bidding thanks and farewell to Saena and her uncle, Braegen, who had been kind enough to arrange passage for both Torin and Crag upon one of his merchant vessels. So delighted was the man by the surprise visit from his niece that he had shown no distaste whatsoever toward Torin or his dwarven companion, and, much like Captain Jorkin during Torin's journey west, had bridled well his curiosity. He'd even gone so far as to push ahead the ship's scheduled launch by more than a week, in order to send them home as quickly as possible.

It had all seemed to Torin rather sudden, and he was not necessarily pleased. As important as it was that he hurry back to his own lands, it felt now as though he'd been denied the opportunity for a proper farewell. It had taken Saena's uncle less than two days to ready for their departure, and now, just like that, Yawacor was gone.

It hadn't really struck him until the ship had lurched away from the docks, leaving him to wave back at Saena and to wonder at the curious intensity with which she had wished him a safe journey. He could still feel the warmth of her parting embrace, the way she had looked at him as if aware of his inner torment. Both awkward and reassuring, she'd behaved as though she knew and understood his secret thoughts. In that final moment, he had considered opening up to her, so great was his need to express himself to *someone*. Instead, he had simply thanked the woman for all that she had done, apologized for not having done more of the same, and wished her well.

Of all those he had met, she was the only one with whom he had shared a heartfelt good-bye. With so many of the others—Dynara and the Fenwa, Arn and Moss, General Chamaar and his wedge commanders—he had simply slipped on to new horizons, like a cloud with no one to observe its passing.

The separation that pained him most, of course, was Dyanne's. In fact, he suspected that it was the grief he felt at leaving her behind that caused him to feel so strongly about the land and its inhabitants. Each and every person he had encountered was a part of his experience here, and, by extension, a reminder of she who had come to mean so much to him. Even Lorre, a onetime adversary, seemed now but another with whom he had unfinished business, another to whom he must find a way to return.

"Still stewing about Lorre?" grumbled a voice from behind.

Torin only half turned as Crag sauntered up to join him at the aft rail. He then looked past the Tuthari, glaring back at those whose scowls followed his companion. Though given strict orders by their employer that no harm was to come to either of their passengers, neither the ship's captain nor his crew had bothered to hide their displeasure at being accompanied on this voyage by a dwarf.

"I was, actually," Torin replied, finding that response to be honest enough. As of yet, he saw no reason to trouble his gnarled companion—or anyone else, for that matter—with the full truth of his anguish.

"Ya should let it go," Crag muttered. "That's what Laressa would want."

"Are those words meant to convince *me*, or *yourself*?"

The dwarf did not respond right away. Clearly, the treachery he had brought upon Laressa and Eolin was still eating at him. He had been friends with both for such a long time, the Tuthari had admitted during the trek to Kasseri—close enough that Laressa had shared with him years ago the story of how and why she had fled her father's kingdom to be with Eolin and the Finlorian people. But never had she mentioned Warrlun, her former husband, by name. Nevertheless, Crag was furious with himself for not having figured it out on his own, fearing that he'd been blinded by his own selfishness, insisting that he should have known.

With Saena's help, Torin had done everything he could to absolve the dwarf of such guilt. At the same time, he held himself every bit as responsible, and for the same reason. He, too, had been told the story—by Lorre—without names. He, too, had realized the truth only too late, when, had he stopped to think about it, he might have guessed. Had either of them done so, Warrlun would likely have perished much sooner, and Eolin's death been averted.

While each had forgiven the other, neither could forgive himself.

"We agreed," Crag muttered finally. "That's behind us now. At least until we settle matters on your own shores."

"I'm sorry I can't be more encouraging about that," Torin offered. During the past few days, he had finished relaying to the Tuthari everything he knew about the war that awaited them. Even if Crag's Hrothgari cousins were to be found, it was highly likely that they, too, would be hard-pressed at this point by the Illysp-bred swarm. Given Darinor's portrayal of the creatures, and the length of time that Torin had been away, it was quite possible that neither human nor dwarf would find much of a home to return to.

"Bah, perhaps we'll get lucky and get ourselves killed by pirates 'fore we ever set ground. If the waves don't swallow us, that is."

Torin nearly smirked at the thought, wondering suddenly about Red

Raven—Karulos—and his love, the enigmatic Autumn of the Rain. An unusual pair, those two. On the surface, they had no business being together. Remembering them now, Torin would have thought that Autumn might be better suited living among a people such as the Finlorians than storming the seas with a gang of rampaging pirates. She was like a princess; Raven, a common brigand. And yet that hadn't stopped them from forming a bond of adoration the likes of which Torin had seldom seen.

The sense of whimsy stealing over him vanished abruptly. Had he lost his own chance for such happiness by failing to tell Dyanne how he felt? Clearly, he was unworthy of her. Whenever he had seen or even thought of her, of how perfect she seemed, he'd been reminded of his own inadequacies. But could the same not have been said of Karulos? Might it be that the only thing separating him from the contentment the pirate now enjoyed was a willingness to confess his desires?

Of course not, he reminded himself quickly. Even if he'd had the other man's courage, he still had Marisha's feelings to consider. Given that, his decision not to say anything had been for the best.

So why was he continuing to torture himself over it?

"Either way, ain't much use in fussing," Crag said, looking to his taller companion.

Torin grunted, hoping that would be enough to send the other on his way. He wasn't trying to be rude; he just wasn't in a mood for company.

But Crag remained at his side, staring with him out upon that ocean. There weren't too many other places he could go, Torin realized. The ship upon which they sailed was about half the size of Jorkin's. And none of the crewmen wanted anything to do with the loathsome dwarf.

"Sailors—" Torin remarked finally, "a superstitious lot. If we do encounter any misfortune, they're as liable as not to blame you."

"And right they may be, the flat-faced dullards. Though they'll keep their distance if they want to keep their limbs."

Torin turned again to regard those who were at work nearby, whispering among themselves and casting guarded glances his way. "Doesn't appear we'll have much of a problem there."

Crag snorted, and Torin forced a smile. Perhaps he should be grateful for the Tuthari's company after all. For while it was Crag who traveled under *his* protection, having the dwarf beside him was probably the best way to maintain his privacy on what promised to be a long voyage home.

If only that was where he wished to be heading.

He closed his eyes, then, against his own wistfulness. The dwarf was right. Yawacor was behind them now, and there was nothing to do but let it go. If he wished for Crag to find peace, to begin looking forward rather than back, then perhaps *he* should do the same.

Even so, he was not yet ready. Not while he could still see those shores, faint as they might be. When they had faded, so, too, would his memories, and with them, he promised himself, the foolish reflections to which he so childishly clung.

Until then, he owed it to himself and to those whose lives he had affected, for better or worse, to remember, granting each of them the farewell they deserved.

With Crag grown silent at his side, Torin fixed his gaze upon the retreating horizon, and continued to wonder what might have been.

CHAPTER FORTY-NINE

RAIN FELL AND WINDS GUSTED, prompting Allion to pull the folds of his cloak tight about him. The day had started out promising enough. Then gray skies had closed about the sun, paving the way for thunderheads and frigid temperatures, and mocking the hopes of those who had been too quick to welcome the reprieve.

Much like their march from Atharvan had begun, Allion recalled grimly. After nearly two weeks of endless preparation, some fifty thousand soldiers—almost the whole of the Parthan Legion—had set forth from that capital city with the sun on their backs and a fire in their hearts. Though many within the ranks still doubted the wisdom of their course, it hadn't felt like that at the time. With dawn's crimson rays unfurled across the land like a royal carpet, with oiled blades and polished armor glinting, with the cheers of those who waved kerchiefs and blew kisses, the procession had felt more like a tournament parade than a march to war.

Allion was so anxious by then to be gone from that city that it hadn't even bothered him. Though first in line to volunteer for any task that needed doing, he'd found it hard to keep busy enough to prevent himself from spending time alone with Marisha. And even when he *had* been able to maintain proper distance, he'd been utterly helpless against the constant anguish of his thoughts. More than once, he had considered throwing decorum to the wind and surrendering to his passions. Darinor had ceased keeping an eye on them, after all. Having given his warnings, the Entient had left them to their own will. Together, hunter and healer had just barely managed to preserve the legitimate nature of their friendship.

Shortly after they had set out, however, the skies had blackened and storms had wrapped the world in a mantle of darkness. Spirits had swiftly dissolved beneath an onslaught of sleet and hail that had raged unabated for several days. More and more, men began to grumble, wondering why they had forsaken warm barracks for the open plain. Their commanding officers seldom had an answer to give.

Allion, too, had grown heartsick and weary. More than once, he had suggested to Darinor that they ride on ahead to Krynwall and leave the legion to its course. But Darinor, well aware of the soldiers' discontent, remained hesitant to do so. The men of Partha were as loyal as any to their leaders;

that much had already been proven. But in this case, even their leaders needed constant reassurances as to the necessity of abandoning their homes in order to lure their enemy to a ground of their choosing. As it was, Corathel was keeping a closer eye on the train of scouts that followed than on the road ahead, fully prepared to turn back at the first report of trouble. The Entient was unwilling to risk that they would hold course should he who had set it be the first to stray.

Where the mystic was now was anyone's guess. Allion lifted his head in quick survey. Before him, the army stretched out along its various lines and formations, marching rhythmically to an unbroken cadence. Most often, Darinor kept alongside Corathel, who made a point of riding back and forth among his troops. Better for morale, Allion supposed; although with the Entient in tow casting a stern pall wherever they went, the hunter could not help but think that in this case, Corathel would have been better advised to keep himself—and Darinor—out of sight.

Allion, meanwhile, marched beside Marisha near the rear of the procession, back among the loaded supply wagons that were most responsible for the legion's sluggish pace. It would not do to run ahead, though, for provisions were stretched thin in the lands to which they traveled. Nor would it pay to leave the wagons behind with a lesser guard and trust that they would not fall under Illychar attack.

Friend or foe, the army had encountered few travelers upon the road. Most of the former had long ago taken shelter within the nearest city or holdfast. Most of the latter were keeping their distance. There had been a few skirmishes along the outer edges, but nothing of high intensity or sustained duration. Exploratory strikes, Darinor had explained. The Illysp were tempted, and were urging their brethren forth to probe for weaknesses in the legion's iron shell—like wary scavengers come to pick at a dying body.

A positive sign that their plan was working.

None had yet struck deep enough for Allion to see. He could sense them, though, the heated stares that marked his every movement with feral hunger. Not only the Illychar, but the Illysp as well. From the corners of his mind, they would whisper to him—vague threats and wordless promises, haunting sensations without voice. Not quite there, and yet impossible to dispel.

So he endured them as best he could, just as he did the wet and the chill, keeping his imagination in check when the morning mists rose up about his feet like ghosts from the grave, or when a midnight howl struck a chord like that of the keening dead. He steeled his mind against their brush as he had so many other wayward thoughts, and focused mostly on the muddy path ahead, doing his best to trust where it might take him.

His only real solace was that this particular road was set soon to end. The northern mouth of the Gaperon yawned before them, that massive breach between the Tenstrock Mountains to the west, and the Aspandels to the east. From his vantage, it appeared as if the forward regiments were already slipping into its shadow, entering the long gateway into the lands of Kuuria. Within a day, they would reach the southern edge and unite this force with those already waiting—including those of his own kingdom, Alson, under the command of General Rogun. Perhaps then, Darinor would permit the three of them—Allion, Marisha, and the Entient himself—to return home to check on those left behind at Krynwall.

He glanced surreptitiously at Marisha. Despite the many words they had shared over the past several days, they had carefully avoided any talk of where they stood in terms of their feelings for one another. Each knew how the other felt, yet both understood that it was not something they could pursue at the present time. Marisha had made her preference plain that day in Galdric's bathchamber. Whether or not Darinor had spoken to her as he had Allion, she knew well enough to leave it at that. The hunter could only hope that when circumstances changed, her heart would remain the same.

With the hood of her travel cloak covering her face, she did not see him admiring her. Before she could turn and do so, Allion redirected his gaze upward along the sloping arm of the nearest mountain. Forested tufts clung to its rugged hide, sprouting amid crags and defiles and slides of loose stone. Halfway up, he spotted a lone sapling that had been all but buried by the scree tumbled down around it. While battered, it nevertheless reached forth with its broken limbs, straining for both water and sunlight, waging a stubborn war against its slow and certain death.

So intent was he on the sapling's struggle that he did not even see the horse and rider that stood upon a jutting overlook until the animal gave a whicker and started toward him. At about the same time, Marisha grabbed at him and pointed.

Darinor.

"Something has happened," Marisha presumed.

To Allion, her father's face appeared as grave and intractable as ever.

"Torin returns," the Entient declared.

Though he heard well the words, it took Allion a moment to grasp them. When he did, his eyes fell at once to the length of silver chain cupped in the Entient's open palm. A nervous shock flashed through his veins, and he felt his eyes go wide.

"Now?" the hunter rasped. "Where?"

"To the northwest. If he has not yet reached our shores, he will soon."

Allion looked again to Marisha. This time, her eyes found his, and she reached out to clasp his hand.

"I go now to meet him," Darinor said.

"Of . . . of course," Allion stammered. "Let us fetch some horses."

But as the hunter began casting about, Darinor raised a hand to stop him. "I go alone."

"What?" both Allion and Marisha echoed at once.

"No," Marisha added. "We're going with you."

"Are you so eager to confess to him your new association?" her father asked, staring pointedly at their clasped hands.

Marisha let go, but would not back down. "We travel together, remember?"

Darinor shook his head. "Not this time. I need you to remain with Co-rathel, to make sure he stays the course."

"We're only a day from the main force," Allion protested. "They won't turn around now."

"From there," Darinor pressed, as if the hunter had never spoken, "I want the pair of you to continue on to Souaris, there to await our arrival."

Marisha frowned. "You'll bring him to us?"

The Entient nodded.

"What about Krynwall?" Allion asked. "I thought our plan was to go back and see how she fares."

"You have the courier reports. Matters there are well in hand."

"But—"

"It is reasonable to assume that that is where Torin will head first. And it just may be that that is where I'll meet him. In any case, your city's soldiers are here, to the south. The greater danger is that which will come against them—against all of us—here."

Marisha glowered. "I won't be left behind, Father. I believe I made that clear."

"You also made clear an oath to obey me, should I permit you to continue on in my company. Would you put lives at risk by defying me again?"

The woman bit down on her next retort, her features both angry and sullen.

"This army we have assembled is our shield," the Entient went on, more softly this time. "I would have you stay behind it. I can escort Torin more swiftly—and quietly—if I travel alone."

"What if he brings with him another army?" Allion demanded. "Will that not attract attention? What if you are overmatched?"

"In that event, there is still precious little the two of you might do to favor us. The best you can do is to make sure our forces to the south are properly arrayed. Let me worry about Torin and any others that may be added to them."

Allion didn't like it, and it was plain that Marisha didn't either. But neither had forgotten their fight with the goblin Illychar, nor how that conflict would have ended had Darinor not been there to rescue them. Perhaps it was indeed best that they respect the man's wishes, and do as he said.

"Can you not tell if he bears some new power that might aid us?" the hunter asked.

Again Darinor shook his head, then drew his cowl as if warding off more than just the weather. "We will know where we stand soon enough."

Allion stared at the Entient, who in turn stared at his daughter.

"Do I have your oath that I will find you at Souaris?" Darinor asked.

Marisha reached out again to grip Allion's hand, then raised her head to face her father squarely. "Do not be gone long."

The Entient locked stares once more with each of them, as if to ensure himself of their compliance. "See to Corathel, then. Remind him, if you must, that only a fool mistrusts all of that which he does not understand."

With a slap of his reins, Darinor started north, weaving his way through the last of the supply wagons still rolling and creaking along, ignoring the many stray looks that followed.

Behind him, Allion gave Marisha's hand a squeeze, feeling every bit her father's fool.

"I RECKON THIS IS IT," Crag grunted.

With the lead rope tight in one hand, Torin reached up to rub his mount's forehead. "Are you sure you won't come with me?"

They had been over this already. With more than two weeks at sea, they'd had plenty of time to plot the paths they would take once they reached Pentanian shores. Much had depended on the state of affairs upon landing, of course—namely, to what extent Alson and her neighbors had been overrun. Even so, there were only so many options available, and their respective paths seemed clear.

Still, it was only courteous to ask.

"You've got your road," Crag said. "I've got mine."

Aside from the occasional squall, those weeks at sea had been largely uneventful. There had been no mishaps, no pirates, no sightings of any monsters of the deep. In fact, so consumed was he with other matters that they had been nearly halfway home before Torin even remembered the terrible leviathan encountered during his voyage west. By that time, Crag had begun to recover from a nasty seasickness—enough so that he'd been able to stay with Torin above deck and, little by little, redirect the young king's focus. As a result, Torin had finally put aside his lingering grief, and turned his eye to the future.

They had reached land just a few short hours ago. Amid shouts and furling sails and mooring ropes that sliced through the haze, they had docked along a pier very near to that from which the *Pirate's Folly* had set sail all those weeks previous. With its wharfside bustle and brume-filled streets, the town of Gammelost appeared just as Torin remembered it, unaffected by the chaos rumored to be sweeping the lands east. Nevertheless, he had emerged cautiously, having a long word with the harbormaster before taking his leave of the red-bearded Captain Gorum. With a cloaked Crag under wing, he had slipped slowly through town, from tavern to meathouse to livery stable, gathering news and supplies along the way. While word varied as to the state of the kingdoms and the nature of the enemy all faced, given what he already knew, Torin was able to sift through much of the baseless gossip and piece together what he thought might be an accurate portrayal of events since his departure. Both surprised and relieved to learn that the lands' armies were still positioning themselves for the greater war yet to begin, he had quickly resigned himself to what he must do.

"We don't have to part just yet," he maintained, standing now at the eastern edge of the seaport town. "We might share the road a while longer."

But Crag shook his head, a rustle within the shadow of his rainswept cowl. "Ya didn't spend the last of Braegen's coin on that beast only to tote it 'long foot beside ya. And I'll be sailing as Gorum's first mate 'fore ya have me sitting astride it."

The dwarf left little room for argument. Riding hard along the main roads, Torin might reach Krynwall by dusk on the morrow, and that was indeed his goal. Crag, on the other hand, was in no such hurry, and in fact meant to pick his way east through the thickest, most rugged wilderness stretches he could find, in hopes of avoiding any human inhabitants along the way. In any case, he'd made it plain that as far as he was concerned, the only good use for a horse was as a meal.

"It's a long hike to the Skullmars," Torin observed.

"I've got strong legs."

Indeed, misshapen as they appeared, the Tuthari's stout limbs could likely carry him up and down the slopes of Mount Krakken without breaking stride. But for some reason, Torin remained hesitant to turn the dwarf loose on his own.

"Ya done what ya promised," Crag reminded him, "and I ain't meaning to forget it. Time now to tend to your own business."

"You're sure you can find your people?" Torin asked, his skepticism no less than it had been when they'd started out.

"I'll find 'em. And when I do, I'll see if we can't do anything to help ya."

"And the same for you," Torin offered, as he had before. "If there's anything your people need, and it's within my power to grant, you need but ask."

Crag peered up at him with that discerning look of his, one eye pinched tight. He offered his hand, and Torin took it.

"I've a notion to return," Crag admitted, holding Torin fast within his crushing grip.

"To Yawacor?"

"To make things right. My people should be avenged, and a dwarven nation reestablished. And I owe it to Eolin and Laressa to see that the safety of their kind is guaranteed—forever."

"When this is done," Torin presumed.

"When this is done," Crag agreed, still staring at him as if in expectation.

"Call on me before you do," Torin said.

Crag nodded and pumped his fist, and Torin knew that that was what the dwarf had been searching for. "Until then, don't be giving up your fire."

Only after Torin returned the other's nod did Crag let go. As the dwarf hefted his pack of belongings, Torin realized what it was that so troubled him about this moment. This was it, the final separation. With Crag's departure, the last physical tie would be severed, and Yawacor would belong only to his past.

But there was no stopping it. Were it otherwise, he would have done so before saying good-bye to Dyanne. So he kept quiet as Crag considered his horse with a look of disgust, offered a grunt, and turned away, his back to the road as he headed south across the coastal plain.

For a long moment, Torin watched him go, thoughts of Dyanne coming unbidden. *We'll look forward to your return,* she had said. Perhaps. Until then, the mere hope—along with his memories—would have to sustain him.

His horse whickered and pawed at the earth, as if it, too, were anxious to be away. Torin did not keep it waiting, giving it one more pat before climbing into the saddle. After all, before he could give honest thought to any future involving distant lands, he knew that he must first confront and lay to rest the demons he had unleashed here.

With a kick of his heels, Torin started forward along the highway. He looked to Crag, who glanced back, and offered the dwarf a final wave. He then leaned over the head of his mount, riding west toward a break in the clouds and its gentle wash of midday sun.

ALLION'S HEAD ACHED AS HE RODE ALONGSIDE CORATHEL at the head of the Parthan Legion. While passing through the Gaperon, hemmed on both sides by mountains, the clamor of the army had grown tenfold. The creak of wheel and traces, the rattle of armor and weaponry, the thunder of booted feet—all had echoed so that now they seemed to throb from within his very skull.

Marisha, sensing his discomfort, had offered to brew him a tea that would deaden the pain, but Allion had politely refused. He would be well enough, he had assured her, once they cleared the pass and left the bulk of the army behind.

Their escort to Souaris was already being arranged. Last night, hours after Darinor had left, a pair of Kuurian heralds had ridden forth in welcome. Commander Troy himself would do so on the morrow, they had said. In the meantime, they'd been sent to inquire as to any particular needs or plans. As soon as Corathel had finished debriefing them, Allion had pulled one aside and asked about the condition of the western highway. The road to Souaris was well patrolled, the herald had assured him. But just to be safe, most were traveling by caravan, and accompanied by military escorts. If he should like, a special convoy would be prepared and awaiting their arrival.

At long last, that time was drawing near. The midmorning sun was just now cresting the eastern wall of the Aspandels, to shed light upon the highland range south of the Gaperon. The stretch they traveled was broken and boulder-strewn, the road lined by bluffs and freestanding rock formations that blocked his view. But already Allion thought he could hear the restless murmur of those who lay ahead, an allied force of close to eighty thousand, more than half again the number who trooped along behind him.

Likely, his head would hurt worse before it felt better.

He was distracted from its pounding, however, when finally the armies below came into view. Beside him, Marisha gasped, as awestruck as he to see so many assembled in one place. Their dark stain blanketed the land below like a quilt, each patch that of a different regiment. The whole of the Imperial Army, with garrisons from Souaris, Stralk, and every city in between—even the remnants of those from Morethil, the once-glorious capital that had been so ravaged during the War of the Demon Queen. And among them, somewhere, the armies of Alson, siphoned from their homeland per Darinor's instruction.

And now, Allion realized, the final piece of the Entient's puzzle: the Parthan Legion, come to fulfill Darinor's vision of a body united in Pentania's defense—a body the Illysp would be unable to resist. Seeing it here, for the first time, Allion could not deny the magnitude of what Darinor had managed to accomplish, summoning perhaps the greatest alliance of forces the land had ever known. A gathering of nations that had long regarded one another with cold shoulders and suspicious eyes, come together in common cause. Having played no small role in making it happen, Allion swelled with pride.

He was pulling forward then, the mount he'd been given keeping step with Corathel's as the chief general trotted ahead. A large welcoming contingent was riding northward to greet them, bearing a variety of standards. From behind, commands rang out for the legion to halt, allowing the parties space to confer.

As the delegations reached one another, Allion braced for another tedious session of overtures and formalities. Instead, the leader of the welcoming party, a tall man with hair so blond it might have been white, leapt from his mount and strode forward with helmet in hand. Corathel did so in turn, rushing ahead to clasp the other's arm and accept his embrace.

"Well met, General," the stranger greeted.

"And you, my friend," Corathel replied. "It does me good to see you."

"Circumstances might be better. But then, if all the world were at peace, we soldiers would find little respect, eh?"

Corathel smiled. "Never mind the respect. I just wouldn't want my men to grow bored." He turned back, then, to his line of lieutenant generals. "Some of them, I believe you already know."

But before the introductions could go forward, the other's eyes went to Marisha, whom he greeted with a deep bow. "On the front lines again, my lady?"

"To see that you bloody rapscallions keep your foolishness under control," she said.

The Kuurian smirked. "Just be careful, please. I doubt your lord would forgive me if you disappeared a second time while under my wing."

"Not to worry, Commander," Marisha replied. "I travel this time with a personal protector. You may have heard of him—Allion, by name."

The commander nodded. "The dragon-slayer. My herald made mention." He stepped forward. "An honor it is to finally meet you. I am Troy, high commander of the Imperial Garrison at Souari, and one of the joint chiefs of our little coalition here."

Allion, looking down from his mount, gripped the other's hand. "Troy, of course. I should have known. Both Marisha and Torin have told me much about you."

"And is it true that the bearer of the Crimson Sword makes his return?" the commander asked.

Transfixed by the man's piercing eyes and shrewd smile, Allion fought back a twinge of guilt, silently reminding himself that there was no way Troy could know of him and Marisha. "The word we gave your herald was received only yesterday. Torin is to meet us at Souaris—hopefully before the week is out."

"Fair news to a beleaguered regent, I'm sure."

Allion swallowed and nodded. "To all of us."

It took some time to finish introducing everyone, and to formalize the welcome of the Parthan Legion into Kuurian lands. King Thelin of Souaris, acting head of the Imperial Council, would have liked to have been here to do it himself, Troy said, but was pressed with matters of city and state. He had sent his high commander instead, as well as a pair of dignitaries, to beg his pardon.

Once all of the reunions and forced pleasantries had been exchanged, Corathel sent his lieutenants back to their posts to finish herding the legion southward. The chief general himself rode ahead with Troy, and invited Allion and Marisha to do the same. From what Allion had been told, the two commanders had forged a close bond while defending Souaris from Spithaera's dragonspawn. No doubt they were anxious to speak directly of this latest threat.

But the Souari commander surprised Allion by turning first to him and Marisha.

"Your escort is waiting," Troy informed them. "I've two squads of elite cavalry ready to accompany you."

"Is that not a shade excessive?" Marisha asked.

Troy grinned. "As I said, I'll take no chances. Intending no offense to your guardian, of course."

The commander turned to him, and Allion shook his head. "Of course not. Before we ride for Souaris, though, I suppose I should check in with General Rogun."

"General Rogun?" Troy asked, raising an eyebrow.

"Chief commander of Alson's forces, sent from Krynwall," Allion replied.

He'd been a little surprised that Rogun had not been among those to welcome their arrival. Perhaps he hadn't been invited. Or perhaps he had refused. Allion hoped that the general, ever the malcontent, was not proving troublesome to the other leaders of the coalition.

"General Rogun is not among us, sir."

"What? How do you mean?"

"Alsonian riders report that he remains at Krynwall."

Allion looked to Marisha, his stomach beginning to roil. "That's nonsense. He marched forth with both our legions more than a month ago."

Troy reined to a halt at the rear of his retinue. Allion, Marisha, and Corathel stopped alongside him. One of Troy's attendants, whose name Allion couldn't recall, looked back, but the commander waved him on.

"A single company from Krynwall arrived some six weeks ago, as you say," Troy reported, his face serious. "Their word was that the rest of Alson's armies, led by General Rogun himself, would be en route."

"I don't understand," Marisha said. "If they're not here, then where are they?"

"We thought it odd," Troy admitted, "given that the request for this alliance originated from Krynwall. But all reports from Alson are that the bulk of your forces have not yet been given the order to march."

"But we received word he had arrived here on schedule," Marisha insisted, turning to Allion with a look of fear.

The last of Allion's headache was replaced by a savage dread welling up from within. Rogun had never liked Darinor. In fact, the general had been opposed to this entire plan from the first. Allion recalled the surprise he had felt upon learning that Rogun had complied with the Circle's orders. Less surprising would be if the general had *not* obeyed those orders after all.

"Shall I arrange word with the Alsonian company commander?" Troy asked.

Allion's thoughts continued to race, mind aswirl with cruel possibilities. How could Rogun have manipulated the lines of communication running both north to Krynwall and south to the Gaperon? Most of Alson's southern couriers were in service to Drakmar, the barony of Nevik. To have taken control of the entire network meant one of two things: Either Nevik was somehow in collusion with the renegade general, or Drakmar had fallen.

The hunter's blood churned. He wasn't sure which notion angered him more. Either way, if Rogun had been bold enough to commit such open treachery against the will of the crown, it meant that Krynwall was next.

Both Darinor and Torin were riding into a trap.

Allion stared at Marisha, who gaped back in horror, having evidently arrived at the same conclusion.

"Father," she whispered.

"Your company commander—" Troy began.

"Likely knows only what he's told you," Allion interrupted. "Or else will no doubt resist revealing the rest." He gritted his teeth, still staring at Marisha. "We haven't time. Marisha and I must ride for Krynwall now."

Corathel shook his head. "Alone?"

"I'll fetch your escort," Troy determined at once. "Its riders shall accompany you."

"That's very kind of you, Commander," Allion said, "but we haven't a moment to delay."

"You'll need fresh horses," Troy insisted, "and stronger ones than these. Should you choose to head north, my riders will run you down within the hour."

Allion looked again to Marisha. "So be it. Have your men bring our remounts. They'll find us along the main road."

"Before the Illychar, I hope," Corathel grunted.

The hunter nodded, already wrenching on his reins to turn his steed about. "Send a team to Drakmar, as well, if you can spare them," Allion begged. "On full guard. Find out if Baron Nevik still lives."

"Go," Troy urged them. "I'll mobilize a division to follow. If your general has betrayed us, he'll soon be answering to Kuurian authority."

Allion put heel to flank to chase after Marisha, who charged northward as if meaning to split the trailing Parthan Legion in two. They were assuming the worst, the hunter knew, but if correct, then he could take little comfort in Troy's words. For the true question was not whether Rogun could be made to pay for his treachery.

The question was whether it would be too late.

CHAPTER FIFTY

DESPITE HIS HEAVY HEART, Torin could not deny the twinge of anticipation that began to build as he rode north across the land. *His* land. The land of Allion and Kylac, Baron Nevik and Chief General Corathel. The land of Marisha. Though it felt like ages had passed, his reunion with these and others was finally at hand. In a short time, he would be met by his true friends with open arms, and all would be well once more. That other, far-off land would be forgotten, and with time, when the ache regarding those left behind had vanished, he would be glad that it had.

When he reached Krynwall, however, that feeling fast began to dissipate, bullied aside by a sense of uneasiness. He wasn't certain from where it stemmed, but it prompted him to ride a distant circuit around the city before closing to a forested hillside a hundred yards to the northwest. He and his mount hid there for some time, studying the sparse traffic that filtered in and out through one of the rear gates. A storm brewed overhead, shrouding the dusky sky and threatening to break at any moment. Every now and then, an advance drop would strike his brow, but Torin only blinked these away, eyes locked on the walls before him.

Had he known where to go, he might have tried making his way in via the secret tunnels leading through the undercity to the palace proper. But it had been Allion who, as Fason, had acquainted himself best with those passages. Though Torin knew where a couple of the openings lay within, he knew not where to find the exit doors, or how to trigger them from the outside.

Finally, when it became clear that this distant vigil would do nothing to justify or refute his stubborn anxiety, the king of Alson slipped from his cover and led his mount down to the roadway. There he waited a while longer, until spotting a desirable position between two merchant wagons. Ordinarily, the watchmen and tariff collectors were more interested in companies bearing goods than lone travelers appearing empty-handed. From what Torin had witnessed so far, that much hadn't changed.

His hope proved true. As the inspectors closed in on the pair of wagons, one of the weary watchmen, clearly anxious for his shift to end, waved Torin onward with a grunt. Hood drawn against the impending rain, Torin nodded, and marched through.

He continued for a while on foot, keeping his gait casual and doing nothing to attract unwanted attention. At the same time, his eyes swept the buildings and streets, searching for some sign of that which haunted him. Throughout his trek, he'd heard nothing to suggest that Krynwall had been overrun. There were conflicting reports about the whereabouts of her armies, but nothing to suggest that they had been eradicated. Then again, information of any kind on the road from Gammelost had been scarce. Times being what they were, most of the land's populace had made for the nearest holdfast, abandoning winter plots and hunting grounds for the safety of wall and parapet. Few were those brave enough to be wandering the open range—fewer still who claimed to have wandered far.

Certainly, the dearth of patrolmen suggested that the army had been deployed elsewhere—perhaps to Kuuria, as most had said. While he found it alarming that Krynwall stood virtually undefended, she obviously still stood. Doubtless, Darinor and the Circle had had their reasons, and if the city could stand alone, then surely Torin had nothing to fear.

But he knew better than to dismiss his nervousness out of hand. Likely, it was nothing more than the unfamiliarity of a place from which he'd been gone for so long. It might even have something to do with his reluctance to have returned at all. But until he heard for himself a trustworthy account of all that had transpired in his absence, he could not be too careful.

Though anxious to reach the palace and his friends, he took a circuitous route through the city's districts, on guard against any spying eyes. Whenever he reached one of the more crowded plazas, he paused to listen to snatches of conversation, but stopped short of asking the kinds of questions that might draw notice.

The more he saw and heard, however, the more he knew his fears to be unfounded. As he neared the palace, his pace quickened. The sooner he carried through with this, the sooner he would find peace.

He hesitated again, though, when the gates of the palace grounds came into view, and he quickly turned off down a side avenue. Aside from a smattering of guildhouses, the surrounding area was reserved for gardens and shade trees, a poorly tended ground for picnics and the like. Picking his way through the overgrown tangle, glancing back constantly to check for pursuit, he pressed forward. When at last he reached a wall of bushes through which his horse could not pass, he tethered the animal to a nearby trunk, and proceeded alone.

His flesh itched by the time he reached the encircling iron fence, where he hunkered for several moments, peering inward upon the castle. All appeared as it should. And yet his entire body was taut with anticipation, his neck and shoulders tied up in knots. He took a deep breath, reconsidering his course. But where else was he to go?

He drew the Sword, and with a few effortless swipes, made a hole in the fence large enough to slip through.

Ducked low, he circled the grounds twice before finding his opening. Several of the entrances were warded by only a single guardsman, rather than the usual two. As luck would have it, he caught the lone man back by the kitchens taking pity on an overburdened scullery maid, and moving off with her toward the midden heaps. Before Torin could reassess the wisdom of his own actions, he dashed forward from the opposite direction, scooped up an empty barrel lying outside, and, trying to appear like any other servant, hauled it within.

He all but held his breath after that, his heart pounding as if a thief in his own castle. He wished, in fact, that he *were* a thief, so that he might know better what he was doing. As it was, he but scurried along as best he could, ducking aside whenever he heard voices, slinking from shadow to shadow.

His confidence grew as he found his way at last to the royal wing and set track for Allion's study. He hoped to find his friend before having to explain himself to any guardsmen—even though he'd heard rumor that Thaddreus, and not Allion, was now serving as regent. His next best hope was for a member of his inner circle—someone he knew he could trust. The odds of that were slim, but the closer he got to his former household, the better off he would be.

No sooner had he told himself this than his luck ran out. Turning a corner, he nearly trampled someone emerging from a side chamber. Torin tried to grumble an apology and continue on without allowing his face to be seen, but a voice called after him.

"My lord? My lord, is that you?"

Torin considered the voice before turning about.

"My lord!" Pagus exclaimed.

"Shh!" Torin hissed, drawing the young herald back into the chamber. It was a small storeroom, filled with racks of candles and holders. Pagus, he noticed, was clutching a bundle of each. Since there was no door, Torin pressed the boy quickly into the nearest corner, snorting against the smells of wax and tallow.

The youth's eyes were wide. "My lord, you're back!"

"Something I don't wish to proclaim just yet."

"Is something wrong, my lord?"

"You tell me. Is the city safe?"

"Safe enough, my lord, from what I'm told. The battle is to take place in the south."

"Battle?"

"Against the reavers, my lord."

"Reavers? You mean the Illysp?"

"Aye, my lord. 'Reavers' is what most of the common folk are calling them."

Torin remembered now having heard the term once or twice over the last few days. But he had thought the speakers to be talking of human brigands, not flesh-thieving spirits.

He leaned close. "Marisha—is she here?"

The spiky-haired Pagus shook his head. "She is with Lord Allion, my lord. At last report, they were marching with the Parthan Legion to Kuuria."

"And the Circle commands Krynwall?"

"Aye, my lord."

"What of Darinor? Is he—"

He cut short his own question at the sound of slippered feet rasping near, followed a moment later by a new voice.

"Master Pagus?" the voice called.

Torin searched, but saw no place to hide amid the narrow wall racks. Hurriedly, he tried to send Pagus out to answer the call.

But it was too late for that, as the caller had already reached the open doorway.

"Master Pagus, how long must you take to fetch—"

The speaker froze as he caught sight of them, jaw hanging open. Torin, however, felt a flood of relief at seeing his loyal seneschal, Stephan.

"Ceilhigh be praised," the steward whispered. "My lord, is it really you?"

Torin waved the man forward. When his shock had subsided, Stephan obeyed, charging the pair as if he meant to crush his lord in a feverish embrace. Thankfully, he remembered himself at the last moment, and bowed instead.

"My lord, I cannot say how greatly it pleases me to see you!"

"Enough, my friend. Quiet now. You'll stir the entire household."

"But, my lord, why weren't you announced?"

Torin patted his hands in the air to slow things down. "Because I do not wish to be. Not without knowing how matters stand." He managed a smile for the sake of his friend, whose features had twisted worriedly. "And you are just the person to tell me."

"Of course, my lord. I understand fully."

"Can you secure a more private chamber nearby?"

"Certainly, my lord."

"What about me?" Pagus asked.

"The chamberlains still need their candles," Stephan noted.

The boy looked to Torin in protest. "But—"

"Do as he says," Torin interrupted. "I don't wish to draw a crowd. The best thing you can do is return to your current tasks."

The youth frowned.

"I'll consult further with you later, I promise," Torin added. "In the meantime, I'll need you to make excuse for our chief seneschal here, in case anyone is to inquire."

Pagus continued to scowl, making clear that he would not be so easily pacified. Nevertheless, after glaring at his king a moment longer, he hung his head in defeat and, with his bundles in tow, marched toward the exit.

"And Pagus," Torin whispered after him, "be sure to tell no one else of my arrival."

The youth's head lifted, his eyes narrowing. But he gave a nod, and was gone.

"Is there not enough news to relay within the castle that you have him performing common chores?" Torin asked.

"He is worse now than before you left," Stephan replied. "Always under-foot, trying to take on some other task."

"The shadow of someone else I know, then."

The seneschal stiffened defensively. "My lord, you are well aware—"

"Indeed I am. Come, let us speak of things the other might *not* already know."

"Bring him in," Zain commanded, cinching a belt about his breeches.

His lieutenant nodded, opening the door and signaling to those outside. A second soldier appeared, this one escorting the young rat, Pagus.

Zain snapped his fingers. The door was closed, and his lieutenants took up post on either side of the boy, hands on their sword hilts.

"Well, then," Zain began, crossing his arms over his bare chest, "what have you brought for me, boy?"

The young rat was not looking at him, but staring into the candlelit room beyond, mouth agape. Zain followed that gaze to the pair of wenches lying in his bed.

"Cover yourselves, for mercy's sake."

The wenches smiled and made eyes at the boy, but did as the commander bade, pulling the blankets up about them.

"I'll ask again," Zain said. "For what purpose have you disturbed my rest this evening?"

Pagus blinked and cleared his throat. "I've brought news, Commander."

"Of course you have. Why else does a rat come calling?" He leaned forward. "What is it?"

The boy shifted nervously. "I'd like my payment *now*, sir."

Though he tried to bridle his surprise, Zain felt one of his eyebrows lift in response. "What's that, you say?"

"A gildron, sir."

One of his lieutenants snickered. Zain silenced the man with a scowl.

"Remember yourself, boy. This is not some hog-poke armorer you're reporting to now."

Pagus gulped, but matched his gaze. "I understand, sir. It's just that . . . I've been cheated before, sir."

Zain considered the youth a moment longer. "So be it." He turned to his snickering lieutenant. "Pay the rat."

The soldier did not protest, reaching at once to loosen the strings of his own purse.

"This had better be good, boy," Zain warned. "Else I'll be taking back that coin along with the hand that grips it."

Pagus gulped again as the coin was given. He examined it briefly before pocketing it. When he looked up, his smile took in his ears. "King Torin has returned, sir."

"What? When?"

"Just now, sir. In secret. He wishes no one to know."

Zain frowned. "Does he suspect danger, then?"

"He is wary of *something*, sir. What, I cannot say."

The commander-in-waiting of Krynwall's army reached up to trace his thin, jawline beard. "Are you certain about this?"

"Quite certain, sir. I intercepted him as he stole through the palace."

"And where did you leave him?"

"With Master Stephan, sir."

Zain controlled himself well enough to hide his smile. He'd had a hunch that taking on Faldron's palace informant as his own might prove worthwhile. But never had he expected to yield a windfall such as this.

"Fair enough," he replied finally. "You may keep your gildron—and your hand—for now. But say nothing of this to anyone else." He uncrossed his arms and bent close. "No one. Do you hear, rat?"

"I understand, sir. Is there to be a coup, sir?"

Zain was already turning to locate his boots, but spun back swiftly. "Another question such as that, and you'll be found in the sewers where you belong. Now go."

The boy opened his mouth, then closed it again, and twisted toward the door. Zain nodded, and the lieutenants set him free.

A clever boy, the commander thought. In need of some hard-fought experience, sure. But he might make a decent officer one day. Provided, of course, that he lived to see it.

When he had gone, the door was shut behind him.

"What now, sir?" one of his lieutenants asked.

Indeed. A question his troops had been asking themselves for weeks, ever since squirreling themselves away—one squad at a time—in and around the city. Only the general knew for sure. But Zain had his hunches. And his feeling in this case was that the time was fast coming to emerge from the stinking hole he'd too long been hiding in.

Not that it had been all bad, he reminded himself, glancing back at the wenches still warming his bedsheets. But the time had come for some fresh air.

"Relay word to General Rogun," he answered finally. "Let him know that our king is returned."

"I'VE MAINTAINED YOUR CHAMBERS PRECISELY AS YOU LEFT THEM," Stephan whispered as he shuffled down the corridor. "I even kept them guarded—until the army left and we no longer had the man to spare."

Torin nodded, unconcerned by the soft echo of the other's voice. Stephan had already made a sweep of these upper halls to ensure they were empty. Aside from that, it no longer seemed to matter should he be discovered. After his briefing with the seneschal, it appeared indeed that his intuition was mistuned, Krynwall secure. In the morning, he would meet with the Circle and announce his presence to the city. Following that, he would send messengers to Kuuria in search of Darinor, Allion, and Marisha, or else ride south himself.

As of now, the only thing at stake was a decent night's rest.

Still, his master chamberlain seemed determined that he get it. They lit no torches, moving by way of Stephan's solitary candle. Shadows clung to them like damp cloaks, cold and eerie. Torin could not remember a time in which he had walked this route without encountering any number of guards or servants or couriers. Rarely had he found such stillness to be so unsettling.

When they reached the door to his suite, Stephan drew a cord hung round his neck and selected from among a set of keys. Torin glanced back and forth down the hall as the chamberlain worked, feeling as if unwelcome eyes were upon him. When the door opened, he shook his head at his own paranoia, and followed his steward through.

His sitting chamber was as dark as the hall outside, its windows shuttered. As he crossed the threshold, Torin felt a pang of disappointment, rather than the thrill he had expected upon finally returning to his own room. It was like walking into a tomb, the stale air chill and oppressive. While Stephan stooped to light a second candle, Torin pushed ahead through the inky pool, searching for the far wall and the latch that would release the shutters.

"Would you care for a fire, my lord?"

"I'm liable to freeze to my sheets, otherwise," Torin agreed, tripping over the edge of a central rug.

Dodging a table and chair, he found his way at last to the window. After fumbling for a moment, he managed to release the catch and free the shutters. An eager breeze carried fresh air into the room, following a wash of cloudy starlight. Torin took a deep breath—in an effort to force the strange knot from his stomach—before turning to assist Stephan in building a fire.

The steward had set his candle down beside the hearth. In that very moment, the candle erupted, spewing forth a stream of flame into the depths of the fireplace. Stephan yelped and stumbled backward, while Torin himself jumped nearly out the window. His hand went to the hilt of the Sword, but by then the seasoned wood set already in the hearth had caught flame. As it did, the torrent of fire from the candle withdrew, to dance once more at the tip of the wick.

Torin searched the corners of the now brightly lit room. Crouched in a high-backed chair that appeared much too small for him, sat Darinor.

When Stephan gasped, Torin knew that the seneschal had seen him too. Still seated on the floor, his robes in disarray, the wide-eyed steward struggled to respond. "My lord . . . my lord, I didn't know . . . I didn't know he was here."

"Easy, Master Stephan," Torin said, waving a placating hand while still gripping his sheathed weapon with the other. "I doubt anyone does."

His gaze remained fixed on the not-so-unexpected intruder. The renegade Entient looked almost exactly as Torin remembered him, with his smoldering blue eyes, cadaverous skin, and craggy black beard tucked sharply against his dark robes.

"Welcome home," the Entient rumbled. When neither of his guests responded, he asked, "Where are your retainers?"

"They do not yet know I am here," Torin replied.

The flames in the hearth crackled.

"My lord," Stephan managed, "shall I fetch the Shield?"

Torin considered, his eyes still locked with those of Darinor. "That won't be necessary. I shall speak with our guest alone."

This certainly wasn't the way he had envisioned it. He had imagined for some reason revealing to Darinor that which he had learned before a council of others—the Circle, most likely, or at the very least, with Allion and Marisha present. But if this was what the Entient had in mind, so be it.

"But, my lord—"

"I require nothing else at this time, my friend. Please, leave me to my visitor."

Even now, he refused to shift his gaze, trusting that his steward would do as asked. It took another moment, but finally Stephan picked himself up off the floor, straightened his robes, and reached carefully for his volatile candle.

"I shall be waiting outside, should you need me."

"You shall return to your duties," Torin corrected. "You've spent too much time with me this evening already. I do not wish to raise suspicion." At last he risked a glance in the other's direction. "Agreed?"

Stephan glared at Darinor, looking perfectly miserable.

"Master Stephan?" Torin snapped.

"Yes, my lord. I shall see you in the morning, then?"

"Before dawn," Torin granted. "Please, go now."

He did so slowly, frowning all the way. When at last he shut the door behind him, Torin's head whipped back to Darinor.

"I heard that you were en route to Kuuria."

"I was," the Entient admitted.

"And the others?"

"Your friends?" Darinor asked, and there seemed a hint of cruel amusement in his tone. "They are well. At Souaris, by now. Or else tomorrow."

Torin forced himself to release his grip on the Sword.

"And you," the Entient pressed. "You travel alone, I see. Did you not find those I told you we must?"

His cold eyes, steeped in shadow, glinted in anticipation. All of a sudden, Torin realized just how unprepared he was to answer the questions Darinor had come to ask. He should not have returned, he recognized, not before he had better fulfilled his charge. He had told himself that he had done all he could, having learned the fate of the Vandari. But the scion of the renegade Entient Algorath had not dispatched him to Yawacor in search of hopeless truths.

"I found them," Torin said, his throat dry.

An expression of surprise flashed across the other's grim face, before raked brows restored to him a more demanding look. "So tell me, what did you learn?"

ROGUN LOOKED STERNLY UPON THE OFFICER stood before him. "This word comes direct from Commander Zain?"

"Yes, sir. From our line of palace runners, sir."

The general reached up to scratch at the itch crawling upon his neck, but of course could not reach it, so deep beneath the skin. "Have we word of movement on any other fronts?"

"Just this one, sir. All else appears calm."

"Appears," Rogun snorted.

He glanced up to the trapdoor of the cellar in which he and his personal regiment were stationed, not far from Krynwall's main gates. The waiting had been gnawing at him for some time, just as it had the rest of the men in this safe house and others throughout the city. It had taken weeks to smuggle his troops into position, but even afterward, there had been endless days left over in which to second-guess this course. Though none of his officers had dared to do so, Rogun himself had wondered constantly if this was the right move, and what the consequences might be once they executed it.

Perhaps the time had come to find out.

"Awake all eyes," he commanded, "and send forth full alert. Whistlers and standard-bearers to their ready positions. I want all troops standing by to attack on my signal."

His chief intelligence officer snapped a sharp salute. "Yes, sir."

CHAPTER FIFTY-ONE

The fire in the hearth hissed and crackled, its logs fast crumbling into embers.

"And that is all he would reveal?" Darinor asked, leaning forward in his chair.

"He refused to discuss with me that which you already know," Torin admitted, still standing before the Entient.

"Then we have learned nothing."

Torin's gaze slipped to the fireplace, in search of an answer, in search of escape. It had taken some time to relate to Darinor the events of his journey, even though much of it, thankfully, the Entient had hurried him through. In fact, there had seemed only two items in which the mystic held any interest: his encounter with the strange, ocean-dwelling leviathan; and his discussion with the Finlorian king, Eolin, the last of the Vandari. But after poring over each in great detail, an already weary Torin had become heartsick and exhausted, lacking the will with which to defend himself against Darinor's response.

"We've learned that the Vandari are no more," the young king said finally, "and that the once-proud Finlorians are powerless. We've learned that we can expect no aid against the Illysp."

The Entient's brow knitted sternly. "You would not seek to deceive me, would you, king of Alson? There is nothing more you may have forgotten to tell me?"

Torin might have laughed. If anyone was keeping secrets, it was Darinor. "What cause would I have to do so?" he asked instead.

The mystic glared at him a moment longer, those great eyes unblinking. "Very well," he decided, rising ominously to his feet. "Take some rest. On the morrow, we set forth for Kuuria to meet up with your comrades."

Torin scowled. Though that was exactly what he had wished for, he hadn't expected Darinor to grant it. "That is all you have to say?"

"You must give me time to think on this," the Entient said while brushing past him toward the open window. "On what comes next. If we are truly alone in this, as you suggest, we may have to rethink our current strategy."

A chill crept along Torin's spine. For some reason, it bothered him that Darinor did not seem more angry with him. He had anticipated many things:

fury, scorn—disappointment, at the very least. But not this stoic resignation, this odd sense that in some way, the Entient was almost relieved.

A violent wind gust filled the room, causing the flames in the hearth to rip and sputter. As Torin spun reflexively toward them, a scintillating light erupted behind him, accompanied by a deafening thunderclap. He dropped to a crouch, hand on hilt, and wheeled back to find Darinor facing out the window.

"What was that?" he asked the Entient.

Darinor shook his head. "Seems our brewing storm has decided to break at last."

Sure enough, as the peal of thunder rolled outward, rain began to fall in torrents. While Torin braced for another blast of lightning, Darinor reached up to close the room's shutters.

When the mystic turned around, he seemed almost surprised to find Torin still standing there. "Your efforts are not unappreciated. But there is nothing more you can do this night. Sleep now, while you can. I will see to your fire."

Torin continued to hesitate, still waiting for a reply to that initial thunderclap, before accepting that the Entient was right. He was doing himself no good by continuing to stand here, doubting everyone and everything going on around him. Perhaps the morning—and a fresh perspective—would give him something better to work with.

Suppressing the irrational urge not to, he turned toward his bedchamber. As he reached the inner doorway, however, there came a frantic pounding of footsteps from the hallway outside, a moment before the outer door burst open.

A breathless Allion came running through, dragging Marisha by the hand. Torin felt a rush of excitement. The hunter cast about, seeing Darinor first. When his eyes found Torin's, they widened as if caught unawares. He let go of Marisha, who rushed toward the hearth without a second glance.

"Father!" she cried. "You're alive!"

"What are you doing here?" Darinor snapped. "I told you—"

"My lord," heaved Stephan, having chased down the new arrivals. He gripped the edge of the doorframe, bent over his candle, fighting for breath. "They asked where Master Darinor was to be found. I tried to make them wait."

Torin's gaze swept back and forth, struggling to take it all in. Marisha looked around and spotted him at last, gasping with surprise. Allion continued to stare, but seemed frozen in place. Stephan appeared as if he might faint from exertion.

"Allion, my friend," Torin welcomed. "Help Stephan, would you?"

The hunter was slow to react, but when he did, seemed grateful for the distraction. Though Stephan tried feebly to brush him off, Allion helped him to the nearest chair. Torin, meanwhile, moved toward the outer door.

"Torin," Marisha said, "no one told us you were here."

"You didn't give me a chance," Stephan reminded her.

"I only recently arrived," Torin replied. "What's wrong?"

"Rogun," Allion said, finding his tongue at last. "We must flee the city at once."

"What?" Darinor asked. "Explain this madness."

Marisha spun back to him. "He wasn't in Kuuria, Father. The general, and Krynwall's armies, they have broken tether."

"We rode with all haste under Souari escort," Allion added. "Riders have been sent in search of any sign. Until then, I think it best that we leave, lest we be trapped."

"Trapped?" Torin asked. "You think Rogun means to invade his own city?"

"I'm surprised to find that he hasn't already," Allion answered. "So it may be we're wrong. But he has defied orders and intentionally deceived the Circle. He is waging his own campaign now, and that can't bode well for the rest of us."

"An ambush," Darinor stated plainly.

Marisha nodded. "Against you, and against Torin—his only voices of opposition."

The wind outside beat against the shutters, while the flames in the hearth flared suddenly, licking hungrily at the blackened walls of their stone cage.

"But no one knows that either of us is here," Torin argued.

"Which would make it that much easier to dispose of you," Allion observed. "Besides, if he *has* set a trap, the man would have spies. It may be that—"

"Enough!" Darinor roared, and again the flames jumped. He seemed much more disturbed by this news than he had by Torin's. "You do us no favor by whipping all into a panic. I will go and learn what I can. The rest of you wait here."

"Should we not alert the Shield?" Stephan asked.

"Why?" the Entient barked, and Stephan recoiled. "To send an even clearer signal to our general that something is amiss?" He loomed over the trembling seneschal like a bird of prey threatening to descend. "Remain here," he said. "Keep quiet until I return."

He swooped past a pallid Stephan then, veering toward the door. As Torin opened it, Darinor glared down at him.

"Open this for no man but me," the Entient commanded, then swept out into the darkened corridor.

Once again, Torin shut the door, this time bolting it from the inside.

As he placed his back to the portal, he looked again upon his dearest friends, Allion and Marisha. He found them glancing at each other—nervously, it seemed. When discovered, they swiftly turned their attention elsewhere. The hunter bent to check on Stephan. Marisha, after avoiding Torin's gaze, forced herself to meet it.

"Your voyage was a success, then?" she asked him.

Torin studied her, a peculiar feeling stirring in his gut. It struck him as odd that neither of his friends had yet rushed to welcome him. Then again, he wasn't exactly compelled to rush toward them, either. Not quite the reunion he had envisioned.

"It might have gone better."

"You've returned to us—alive. It might have gone worse."

Torin saw no reason to argue. "Which reminds me, I believe I have something that belongs to you."

He stepped forward, removing the Pendant of Asahiel and holding it up to her. For a moment, Marisha considered the talisman with clear hesitation. When Torin's expression became puzzled, she offered a wan smile and bowed her head, allowing him to drape the chain around her neck.

"Thank you," she said, tucking the heartstone down into the folds of her shirt.

Torin nodded. This was fast becoming awkward. Though his eyes were on Marisha, his heart and mind felt a thousand leagues away. The ensuing silence throbbed in his ears.

"I'm relieved to find you safe," he offered finally. "Both of you," he added, shifting toward Allion, who still knelt over Stephan. "You kept your oaths to each other, then."

Stephan was breathing easier now, but regarded the three of them with a frown, as if sensing that something was wrong.

"From what our chief seneschal tells me, it could not have been easy," Torin pressed, afraid to let the conversation die. "He claims to have received word of a journey into Vosges."

"General Corathel got himself into a bit of an entanglement with the natives," Marisha replied. "Allion helped to set him free."

"Don't," Allion said. His head twisted back to address her, but stopped halfway, his eyes on the floor.

"Don't what?" she asked him.

"Don't speak of me as some kind of hero."

Viewing the exchange, Torin felt even more uncomfortable. "Allion, is something else troubling you?"

It was a ridiculous question at this point. Clearly, there was much for the three of them to sort through. Were it left to him, they would do so at some other time, reacquainting themselves with one another when there wasn't so much going on around them, and once all had had a chance to rest. But he couldn't very well stand here and allow whatever wedge had come between them to deepen.

The hunter turned from Stephan to face the others at last, opening his mouth only to close it again. He shook his head, brushing aside whatever it was he'd been about to say, and asked instead, "What did you find in Yawacor?"

This time, it was Torin who was unsure how to respond. "A dead end," he muttered after a moment's thought.

An invisible pall thickened around them. Outside, the storm intensified, wind and rain rattling the shutters. Torin, his back to the hearth, looked mostly at Stephan, unsure what he could say to dispel this unnerving silence.

"My lord," Stephan offered, coming to his rescue, "perhaps we should—"

The blare of a horn cut him short, somewhere outside, but close. The seneschal's face formed an expression of shock and fright.

No one moved, listening again for the call of the horn. Just when Torin believed they must have been mistaken, it sounded again, clear and mournful. This time, the signal was taken up by others, and carried on through the palace grounds.

Torin dashed to the window, a step ahead of Allion. He threw back the shutters, and was slapped in the face by the gusting rains. From far below, in one of the royal courtyards, he heard the shouts of men and the clangor of arms.

He was still angling for a better look when the door to his chambers burst open, the cradle that held the locking bar torn from its housing. Torin spun, reaching for his weapon.

"We must go," Darinor ordered. "Now."

"What's happening?" Stephan demanded.

"An uprising," said Darinor, "here amid the palace grounds."

"Rogun?" Marisha asked.

"I don't know. I didn't ask to see their colors."

"Perhaps we should go and find out," Torin suggested, fingering the jeweled hilt of the Sword.

"Perhaps we should do as our regent first proposed and take flight while we can," Darinor snapped. " 'Tis seldom wise to examine a loaded trap from inside its teeth."

"Our escort awaits us," Marisha reminded them all.

But her father shook his head. "Anyone who saw you ride in will expect us to ride out the same way. It may be that your cavalrymen are already under attack."

"What would you suggest?" Torin asked.

"I would suggest *not* rushing out the front door and headlong into an ambush," came the Entient's retort. He turned to Allion. "What of the egress tunnels you spoke of in council? The ones beneath the city?"

"We'll have to hurry," the hunter said, "if the palace is already under siege."

"Then let us waste no more words here," Darinor replied, stepping out into the hall.

Marisha glanced back at Allion, who stood beside Torin at the window, before hurrying after. The hunter then passed that look on to Torin, as if deferring to his friend and king. But Torin motioned for the other to proceed, and, doing his best to shrug aside these curious interactions, peered out the window once more before shuttering it anew and giving chase to his friends.

In the hall outside, Allion finished lighting a torch. "Follow me."

Torin, however, took only a pair of steps before realizing that Stephan was hanging back, making no move to carry on.

"Stephan!" he hissed. "What is it?"

The seneschal stood there, gripping his candle by its holder, a sour look upon his face. "Go, my lord. I'll only slow you down."

"You will indeed if you continue standing there," Torin replied. "Come."

"Better that I stay here, my lord, where I can help to throw off any pursuit."

"Stephan—"

"Let him stay, if that is his wish," Darinor snarled. "We have no time to argue."

"It can't be that I'm in any real danger, my lord. I am a steward, nothing more."

Torin opened his mouth to protest, but Darinor cut him off.

"Go now, or give me the Sword. I'll not have you risk it a moment longer."

"I shall remain with the castle, my lord," Stephan assured him, "and keep her safe until your return."

"Whoever is coming," Allion spat back at them, "must do so now." The hunter reached out toward Marisha, seizing her hand as he had before. With his torch and the woman in tow, he sped off down the hall.

Torin's gaze whipped back to his chief seneschal, only to be blocked by Darinor, whose billowing robes seemed to fill the narrow corridor like a wind-blown curtain. Lest he be wrapped in their folds, Torin retreated a few steps, still straining for a final glimpse of the city's faithful steward. When finally he craned his neck at the right angle to find it, he caught sight of the other's determined nod.

Turning forward at last, he ran after his friends, leaving Stephan and his candle to hold back the encroaching darkness.

ROGUN'S BLOOD FELT AFIRE as he leapt into the saddle of his tamping stallion. All around him, his soldiers raced through the streets, spilling free of their bunkers and safe houses and forming up into battle companies. Horns wailed, bells rang, and whistles blew, spreading the call to arms. Tattered cloaks and beggars' rags were tossed aside, revealing the polish of armor and weapons hidden beneath. The very air crackled with tension and excitement.

There were others, as well—civilians darting this way and that, or standing gape-mouthed along gutters and walks. Many wanted nothing more than to clear a path. Others had emerged specifically to view the tumult unfolding around them. Some of his soldiers worked to beat them away, using loud voices and heavy clubs to send them scurrying back to their dens and hovels. But Rogun let them look. It had come time to free this people from incompetent rule. It had come time to prove himself, to demonstrate that he, and not Torin, Allion, or some misbegotten council, should be in command of the city. If ever he meant to stake such a claim, now was his chance, and he would not be denied.

"To the walls!" he shouted to a brigade of soldiers searching vainly for the rest of its unit.

He pointed with his sword, and the men raced on ahead, booted feet thundering against broken cobblestones. Beneath him, his horse bounced, anxious to follow. But Rogun continued to hold the animal in check, continued to make a spectacle of himself in that crowded plaza. When at last the number of civilian onlookers outnumbered those of his own regiment, the general put spurs to flanks and shot forth like an arrow through the street.

Wind and rain lashed at his open visor, but Rogun welcomed them as he had the latest reports—sneering in proud defiance. He could not have asked for a better opportunity. Unfortunate that Krynwall's citizens and collection of refugees should be made to feel threatened like this. But if this was what was required in order to make them see, so be it. By morning, the city would be his, secured from within, and he would see to it that all who opposed him—even Torin—fell to their knees to beseech *his* favor. While some might insist on vilifying the general for his deceit, or denouncing his brutal efficiency, the fact remained that without him, the city was headed for a fall.

And it was his duty to prevent it.

He slowed as he neared the closest rendezvous point, in a courtyard aback of the main gate. As he surveyed the ramparts, he could see that the feeble effort of the City Shield to resist his control was already crumbling. They understood the truth, he saw. Good of them to quickly accept it.

"Lord General, sir!" one of his aides shouted, signaling him as he churned to a halt. "Word from Commander Zain!"

"Let's have it, then," Rogun barked, flush with anticipation.

"He wishes to know, sir, if you require reinforcement."

The general shook his head. "Commander Zain's orders remain the same. He is to secure the palace. Tear down the gates, if necessary. I want none to leave the city this night. None!"

"Yes, sir."

"Relay at once, Lieutenant."

The officer obeyed, and was gone by the time Rogun dismounted. Handing his reins off to a wide-eyed groom, the general ran ahead and climbed the steps of the battlement, his personal guard in tow. Soldiers cleared aside, offering salute, which Rogun heartily returned.

When at last he reached the top of the wall, he gazed out upon his city, both within and without. For a moment, his chest tightened at what he saw. But it was too late for regrets or alternatives. His trap had been sprung. The only way to finish this was to follow through completely. Having concealed the bulk of his forces within the city walls, he was in good position to carry out his objective. Either way, he was determined to take back what was his—in such dominating fashion as to leave no doubt.

"Primary divisions are assembled and ready, sir," prompted the colonel at his side.

General Rogun smiled grimly. "Frontal sweep on my command. Inverse arch."

"Sir, the archers—"

"Are to provide cover only. Commence ground assault. This city will be liberated before dawn."

CHAPTER FIFTY-TWO

THEY RACED ONWARD IN A RAGGED LINE—Allion, Marisha, and Torin, with Darinor to usher them along. The flame of the hunter's torch whipped and guttered, riled by the bearer's swift and sudden movements. Its thrashing light cleaved the shadows of darkened hallways, sending them away like black spirits into the Abyss.

Though the maze of corridors bore Torin and his friends ever deeper within the royal complex, he could still hear the alarms echoing from outside the castle grounds. Before long, those calls had carried into the palace itself, reverberating throughout chambers and corridors, coming from every direction. Battle had clearly been joined, signaled by the clash of steel and the shouts of men. For the fighting to have breached his walls so quickly gave the young king pause, but hemmed as he was among his companions, he could do little more than run on.

Before long, the route they followed filled with servants, courtiers, guardsmen, and others, all rushing in a mad panic to one place or another. Torin thought it a chance to learn more about the chaos erupting all around them, but Darinor ordered the members of their company to keep their hoods drawn and their heads low. In this case, the Entient was probably right. Most of these people likely knew even less than they. The safest thing to do was escape while they could, then examine matters from afar.

The notion did not sit well with Torin, given the numbers of those he felt he was being asked to abandon. But he knew better than to argue, considering how long he'd been away. As unsettling as it might feel, he was no longer in charge here, and he did not want to endanger even more lives by trying to make some meaningless heroic stand.

Still, it became harder and harder not to draw the Sword as the resounding clamor continued to swell around them. But the talisman's telltale glow would surely give them all away. They had reached the ground level, and were shoving along an exterior wall, swimming upstream against a river of fleeing bodies. Through the adjacent windows poured the sounds of pitched battle in the courtyard beyond. But all was a writhing mass of moonlit shadow—black silhouettes of men and weapons come together in a grinding crush. He could match no faces to the horrid screams.

Allion cut suddenly down a stair to their right. The hall beyond was almost empty. At the next intersection, the hunter veered left, pausing briefly to bar the door behind them. The sounds of battle became muted and distant. Though his heart hammered in its cage, Torin felt his muscles begin to relax.

They tensed anew when he turned a corner and Marisha gave a startled shout. Bodies collided as his company ground to an abrupt halt, with Allion catching that of a frantic guardsman. The soldier looked up at them with haunted eyes.

"My lords!"

"Kien!" Torin responded, moving forward to greet the man who had often served as his private sentinel.

The young guardsman recoiled at first, forcing Torin to grip him about the arms.

"Kien, what has happened?"

The stricken soldier, a bearer of the City Shield, glanced from face to face. His own was sweat-streaked and smeared with blood. "My lord, we must escape! There are traitors, my lord, here within the castle!"

"Who are they?" Torin asked, still trying to calm the man.

"They turned against us in the armory, my lord. They—" He stopped and twisted at the sound of pursuit—the heavy footfalls of a sizable company coming apace. Immediately, he began to thrash and squirm in an effort to pull away. "My lord, we must flee!"

"We'll go around," Allion determined, and began pushing them all back the way they had come.

But he did not do so swiftly enough. A shout resonated from behind as they were spotted, a mad cry taken up by others. The pursuers' pace quickened, boots hammering against the stone floor, their stride lengthening. As he turned the corner, Torin looked back.

And froze.

"Bull?"

Sure enough, leading the charge of perhaps a dozen City Shield was Bullrum, the unofficial leader of his original expedition team to Yawacor. The man he'd met as a sparring partner—at that time a soldier in the Legion of the Sword—was clearly recognizable, despite his new uniform, sallow skin, and the hateful grimace upon his face.

That grimace changed somewhat as the soldier's eyes found those of his king, taut features loosening in surprise. His step slowed, and with it, those who accompanied him. All carried drawn weapons, Torin noted, including Bullrum, whose greatsword was stained with blood.

"Bull, what is this madness?" Torin asked. He knew not whether he should seek to embrace his old friend—whom he had assumed dead or lost at sea—or else draw his own blade.

Bullrum, too, seemed torn with indecision. His glare shifted to Darinor, who hovered over Torin's shoulder, and immediately his gaze narrowed.

Then Kien came back around the corner, just enough to peek at what was happening. "My lord, it's them!"

Bullrum's hesitation vanished. With a snarl, the brown-bearded soldier hefted his weapon and charged. Like boulders in a rockslide, the others came after.

Torin barely had time to free the Sword from its sheath. He might not have, were it not for the sudden whirlwind that formed in front of him and went shrieking down the corridor, blowing dust and grit into the faces of his enemies and forcing them all to cower in momentary surprise.

"Run!" Darinor commanded.

But it was too late for that. Already, the temporary gust summoned by the Entient was dying. Bullrum and his cohorts pressed forward, weapons weaving. Torin met them head-on. His intent was not to kill, but to frighten and disarm, hoping that the fury of the Sword would be enough to chase his city's former protectors away.

But their lust for battle was far greater than he could have expected. After severing a pair of blades nearly to the hilt, and then clearing a pocket with a great, spinning swipe, his opponents pressed in. A sword tip nicked his shoulder, while another slashed across his thigh. Torin was forced to maim three men in quick succession to even find room to breathe. Two lost their hands, the other his leg at the knee.

None backed away.

In the crowded corridor, there was nowhere for Torin to hide. Fortunately, his enemies were so reckless that they did as much damage to one another as to him. Blood spurted, painting the walls and the floor. Some wounds were so grievous that Torin could not believe the man who had sustained it was still standing. Nevertheless, not one of his adversaries surrendered the fight.

An arrow shot out of nowhere, whizzing over Torin's ducked head and lancing through the ear of one who stood over him. The man dropped his sword, and Torin made certain that he could not pick it up again, cutting him in half at the waist. The young king was out of options. If he did not kill these men, *they* would kill *him*.

Another arched stiffly as an arrowhead tore through his side and poked free, dripping blood and fluid from some vital organ. As desperate as Torin's situation felt, it must have *looked* even worse, for Allion to risk such shots. Putting the wounded man to his back, Torin whirled to stave off a more serious threat, then lowered his shoulder and twisted round to face yet another.

At that point, Kien charged in, taking up a fallen blade and adding his howl to the chorus of those that filled the hall. Torin continued to hack and dodge, his movements guiding—and at times guided by—the Sword. The weapon flared, its inner flames barely able to withdraw after one strike before being called upon for another. The press around him was starting to slacken, as the number of dead and mutilated began to mount. And still his remaining foes did not relent.

All of a sudden, he was free, having carved through the knot of guardsmen to the other side. He was down on one knee, arms extended, weapon thrust upward through the heart of his latest victim. There was very little blood, for while embedded in the other's chest, the Sword kept burning. Torin felt a flutter from the man's heart as it convulsed around the blade—as if suddenly brought to life. The old soldier gaped at him, lips curling in stubborn refusal, still struggling to bring his weapon to bear. But the man's muscles had stopped responding. For a moment longer, Torin peered into a pair of wild eyes, then tore free and let the man fall.

He spun about to check on the others. Kien was locked with what looked to be the last of their assailants. His blade was shoved deep through the front of the man's throat, but the fool continued to sputter, refusing to die. Despite a wash of blood, none of it seemed to be pulsing. The man grappled, clawing uselessly, but Kien held on.

Just as the enemy guardsman began failing at last, sliding down against the wall, one of the others who had appeared to be defeated rose up suddenly beside him. Bullrum, Torin realized. But before the young king could react, his onetime companion skewered poor Kien through the side with the length of that greatsword. Too late, an arrow struck him. Growling, Bullrum turned toward Allion and charged, driving Kien's openmouthed body before him like a shield. The hunter fired a second shot, which flew past Kien to catch Bullrum through the shoulder.

It drew no more than a grunt.

Torin launched himself in pursuit, knowing at once that he wouldn't reach the others in time. Bullrum barreled onward, gaining momentum. At the last moment, he threw Kien aside and unsheathed a dagger. Without the time he needed to nock another arrow, Allion reared back with his bow, as if meaning to whip the other across the face.

In the instant before that happened, Darinor stepped forward, seizing the crazed Bullrum about the neck. The dagger plunged upward, striking flesh somewhere within the folds of Darinor's robes. Ignoring the blow, the Entient gave a violent twist, spinning Bull's head halfway around on his shoulders. Bones shattered, and the soldier crumpled, facing backward, his limbs jerking uncontrollably. In a matter of heartbeats, the spasms ceased, and his body grew still.

Torin knelt at once beside Kien, examining the massive blade still buried through his side. The guardsman, slumped against the wall with blood bubbling from his mouth, offered a meager smile as their gazes locked. Then his eyes glazed, and his head sagged forward against his chest.

Torin looked to the others. Darinor was gritting his teeth, bent over as if ill. A moment later, he gave a yank, and cast aside Bullrum's bloody dagger.

Marisha gasped. "Father, you're hurt!"

She went to him without delay, bearing the torch that Allion must have handed to her. But Darinor straightened and swatted her away.

"Leave me be," he snarled.

Marisha fell back, her expression wounded. Torin studied her for only a moment before his eyes found Bullrum's ghastly stare.

"I've a feeling these weren't Rogun's," he declared.

Darinor nodded. "The Illychar have found us."

"And is that who we're fighting up there?" Torin gestured with the Sword

toward the upper levels of the castle, less certain than ever that they should be
fleeing this chaos rather than confronting it.

"Would you go and have a closer look after what you've seen here?" the
Entient growled. "Come, let us away before others discover us."

He started down the hall, past the pile of twitching corpses.

"Come!" he urged again when it became clear that no one was following.
"We shall sort it out later. Or do you intend that we surrender ourselves to
the enemy?"

A sudden and violent pounding within the tunnels behind them emphasized the danger. The door, Torin realized—the one they had barred. Though
oblivious as to who was fighting whom, he recognized well enough that the
noose was tightening around them.

He glanced at Allion, who, after looking over his shoulder at the sound,
grabbed the torch and Marisha and shuffled on to retake the lead.

Torin closed the lids to Kien's eyes before rising to his feet and hastening
after.

They raced first past the open doors of the armory, through which Torin
caught a glimpse of the massacre to which Kien had referred. A line of training grounds came next, complete with various closets and chambers used for
outfitting, storage, and planning. Most lay dark and open, leaving Torin to
wonder if anyone—friend or foe—hid within. He ran now with the Sword in
hand, numb to his wounds, fully alert for any sudden attack.

They scampered through halls and down flights of stairs, slowing only
when forced to fling aside doors of wood or iron. There was little point in
closing the portals, as most were not meant to be opened from the inside.
They had reached one of the central dungeons—built to house criminals of
noble standing, or whose offenses otherwise drew royal notice. Though filled
to capacity by Torin's father, King Sorl, they stood empty now. It was in these
prisons that Torin had found and pardoned Stephan and all others who had
displeased the prior king—and in whom he had found no fault. Of course, it
was also where the wizard Soric had kept Rogun while seeking to transform
the general into a loyal follower.

Looking back, perhaps Torin should have let that one rot.

He tried not to think of it, nor to breathe too deeply of the foul and stagnant air. If ever there had been a time to maintain focus, it was now.

At long last, they reached the end of their road—and in some sense, its
beginning. Before them stood a nondescript door at the end of a hall lined
with cells, beyond which lay an abandoned storeroom and the secret entrance
to the tunnel they sought.

Allion patted himself about the neck. "I don't have the key!" he exclaimed.
"I gave it to Evhan when I made him Fason!"

The hunter looked to Darinor as if expecting the Entient to do something.
But Torin pushed his friend aside, hefting the Sword. A moment later, a blackened gash had appeared at the edge of the jamb, and the door swung open.

They piled inside in a rush. While Allion moved at once to find the latch hidden behind an iron cask, Torin and the others shut the door and began stacking crates and barrels behind it.

"I've got it!" the hunter shouted.

Torin turned. A hinged section of the far wall hung open, revealing the dark crawl space beyond. "Lead the way," he said, huffing as he rolled another barrel into place.

At the same time, Darinor dropped a crate, then fell to one knee upon the floor beside it.

"Father!" Marisha cried. "Are you all right?"

The Entient put his back to the makeshift blockade, wincing as his daughter tried to search him for wounds. "I told you to leave me be!" he snarled, shoving her away as he had before.

"Father, you must let me have a look!"

"You have no time for that, and no time to be waiting on me. Go."

"Father—"

"Go! I will safeguard your retreat."

Torin glanced between the woman and her father, pained by her injured look. "*I* will stay," he offered instead. When the Entient glared at him, he held his ground. "You are the one who must lead us in this war. No one else has the knowledge to do so. I will stay, and fight as long as I must to give you the chance to get away."

"Don't be a fool," Allion chimed in at once. "The Sword cannot stay here, and without it, you may as well be weaponless. *I'll* stay."

"Give me your bow, then," Torin said as the hunter began to slip it off his shoulder. "Take the Sword and carry on."

But Allion shook his head. "If you think I'm leaving you to—"

"Silence!" Darinor roared, though it caused him to flinch and bend over his side. "My daughter is not staying here to die. If each of you insists on being the fool hero, *I* will take her and the Sword and leave you both behind."

The Entient turned to Marisha, who crossed her arms in refusal.

"Then again, I know not how long I can continue," said Darinor, his face and his tone softening, "and I would not risk leaving her alone. Moreover, neither of us knows the route through these tunnels. At least one of you must agree to guide her. The other can abandon her and risk death here alongside me, if he likes."

Torin looked to Allion. Together, they shifted their gazes to Marisha.

"No," she said. A crash resounded from back in the dungeons as an iron door was slammed wide. "No!"

Again she tried to go to the Entient, and again he fended her off with one hand while clutching his hidden wound with the other. This time, Torin and Allion both helped to restrain her.

"You must," Darinor said, "or you condemn us all—not just the four of us, but the rest of your kind throughout the land, maybe even the world entire."

"I don't care," Marisha replied, and began to sob. "I don't care!"

Torin felt the woman shudder, and was taken aback by the intensity of her passion. Never had he seen her like this—not even when he and Kylac had whisked her away from the slave pits of Kraagen Keep, leaving hundreds of others to their suffering. At that time, the young assassin had been able to appeal to her sense of greater good. It seemed they would not be able to do so here.

"I won't leave you, Father! I won't!"

And then it struck him. This wasn't the Marisha he knew. This was Marisha at six years of age, on the verge of losing the most important man in her life—again. Only, this time might be forever, and she wasn't prepared to let that happen.

"You will, my daughter, as I left you. For a time only. Because you must." The man reached out with one hand to take hold of hers. " 'Tis the natural order of things, for parent and child to say good-bye. We who are descended of the Ha'Rasha are no exception."

Marisha wept, gripping his hand and kissing it and washing it with her tears. She knew it had to be this way, Torin realized, else she would not have been so distraught.

"That it should happen now," Darinor added softly, "so soon after being given this second chance, pains me more than you know. But you have a legacy to carry on, and if I go to my grave this night, I do so knowing that it is a greater legacy by far for having you as its bearer."

"Father . . ."

"Go now," he pressed, and his tone hardened. "Do not dishonor your mother by lending greater weight to my passing than to hers. You bid *her* farewell. You must do so now to me."

He looked purposefully to Torin, then to Allion, and withdrew his hand. Marisha shook her head and tried to follow, but they held her by the arms, allowing Darinor to pull free.

"I love you, Father," she cried, sagging in their hands. "I love you."

The Entient turned his eye to Allion. "When you get clear, do not stop, but hurry south to Kuuria. If I can, I will meet you there. Otherwise, follow the plan we have set forth."

Allion nodded dumbly. The clamor of pursuit had reached the hall outside. Torin barely had time to meet the mystic's gaze one last time before their assault on the storeroom door began.

"Away!" Darinor snapped, rising boldly to his feet and putting his back to them.

"Father," Marisha whimpered. When Torin and Allion began dragging her toward the tunnel entrance, she wailed, "Father!"

Torin worried that they might have to render her unconscious in order to get her through the crawl space, to say nothing of hauling her through the secret maze of passes and trapdoors. But then Allion shook her arm, still holding their torch in his other, and forced her gaze to meet his.

"We'll see him again," the hunter assured her. "We'll see him again soon. Come now."

Torin couldn't tell what it was that finally persuaded her, but Marisha composed herself and nodded. Choking back tears, she shrugged free of their grasp and ducked through the opening before them. Allion followed, and, with a lingering glance back at Darinor and the pile of stores meant to barricade the door, Torin slipped through on the hunter's heels.

He shut the panel behind them, muffling the sounds of their enemies' assault, and leaving the renegade Entient to his fate.

He turned forward then, to find his friends. For their own fate lay somewhere in the darkness ahead.

CHAPTER FIFTY-THREE

TORIN HAD LEARNED AS A CHILD TO DISLIKE TIGHT SPACES. Once, when playing at moles and vipers, he had hidden in a burrow that had partially collapsed, leaving him trapped for hours until his friends had found him and been able to dig him free. Since then, he'd been prone to the occasional nightmare in which he was being buried alive or else forced to squeeze and writhe through a dark and twisted landscape while some vile creature—be it man or beast—hunted him from behind.

It felt like that now, and deep within, some voice kept urging him to stop struggling and simply wake up. But this was no dream, and the only way to escape would be to keep moving.

Yet the going was slow. The route they followed was not some singular access tunnel, but a patchwork string of chambers and passages—some used, others abandoned—stitched together by various false walls and secret openings. Part of a web, it was said, laid among the lower levels of the city. None knew its true origins, nor how widespread the entire network might be. There were maps to certain segments, but due to its secretive nature, most were left uncharted or incomplete. Most likely, it had come into being gradually, built in bits and pieces by smugglers and fugitives. From what Stephan had told him, this particular course had not been designed so much as discovered, one link at a time. At some point in history, when one of Torin's ancestors had decided he needed a bolt-hole from the city, he had evidently opted to save time and effort by simply tapping into what was already here.

A decision that might cost his progeny dear, Torin thought, choking on the dust-filled air beneath the floorboards of what was rumored to be a deserted charnel house. Time was slipping away from them. When they should have been running, they were instead forced to duck and crawl and search for hidden levers. Then again, for all he knew, their enemy was already outside, waiting for them to emerge—making this entire retreat a wasted endeavor.

But it did him no good to think like that. Better to take heart in the progress they had made. The most suffocating stretch was that which they navigated right now, and already, Allion was near the far end, triggering the panel that would allow them to spill free. From there, if Torin recalled correctly, it was in and out through a pair of false crates hidden in a cluttered cellar, and back into tunnels in which they could at least stand. They would be moving faster then, hoping that faster would be enough.

He watched his friends carefully—especially Marisha. She seemed to be holding up well. Every now and then, she would freeze momentarily at an unknown sound. No doubt, she continued to pray that her father might change his mind and manage somehow to catch up to them. The likelihood seemed unquestionably remote. But for her sake, if none other, Torin hoped she was right.

His memory proved true concerning the cellar and the tunnel beyond, though he'd forgotten there was yet another storeroom to duck into by way of secret opening before they could access the next set of corridors required. Fortunately, Allion remembered the path better than he. The city's former Fason led them without hesitation, moving urgently from marker to marker. Marisha followed close, clutching Allion's arm at times. Torin, wary of enemies, kept guard at their backs, eyes sweeping from side to side in the crimson glow of the Sword.

They exited the final storeroom through its main door, which placed them in a hall belonging to a metal foundry. Once again, they discovered all to be dark and quiet.

If only that meant they were safe.

Allion cut left, leading them to a metal door embedded in the rock wall. As he hauled open the heavy portal, a wash of heat swept inward, so intense that the air shimmered. With noses rankled by a sulfurous stench, they pressed through.

Despite the fiendish conditions, Torin felt a measure of relief. They had reached the smelter, the last major checkpoint of their journey. From here, they had but a few mine tunnels to run down, a cave to crawl through, and an air shaft to climb. A short jaunt through a private tract of woodland would bring them to a horse ranch whose possessor had long ago been friends with his royal grandfather, King Sirrus—and later with Torin's mother, Ellebe.

They were almost clear.

And yet, rather than hastening forward, Allion stopped suddenly to look around, clearly troubled.

"What is it?" Torin asked.

Already, however, he could see for himself. Blast furnaces scraped the cavern ceiling, belching smoke and gases through natural chimneys, doors wide to reveal the flames inside. Tools lay scattered—tongs cast aside, shovels left lying atop mounds of crushed ore and limestone. Molten slag flowed through troughs and piping, slowly filling a giant vat to Torin's left. The smelter was alive, yet there was not a single worker to tend it.

Allion turned to Torin with a telling look. Wherever these workers had fled, they had done so in a hurry.

"Suppose our tunnel is clear?" Torin asked, considering the several passages open before them. Though any number would carry them from the smelter, only one would do so beyond the city walls.

"We won't know until we try it."

"Then why are we lingering?" Marisha snapped. "Father might already be waiting."

Torin looked again to Allion, who slipped free of his bow. Handing Marisha their torch, he nocked an arrow to the string.

"I'll go first," Torin said.

They maintained their course, following a railway used to transport ore and other minerals in heavy carts. Torin set pace at a cautious jog, sweat pooling upon his brow, skin itching as invisible claws raked his neck.

The tunnel quickly swallowed the fiery glow of the smelter, leaving the aura of the Sword to stave off the darkness rushing headlong to meet them. But as they turned a bend, they were startled to find new light in the form of a lantern, gripped casually by a young soldier who carried an old scar upon his cheek.

"Evhan!" Allion exclaimed.

Torin drew up short, and placed a restraining hand on his friend's shoulder.

"Making our escape, are we?" Evhan asked, leaning against the cavern wall.

Torin held position at the front of their group, hackles raised in alarm. "What are you doing here, Captain?"

"Waiting for Your Majesty, of course. You promised to spar with us again, did you not?"

Allion tensed. "Evhan—"

"Now is hardly the time," Torin cut in, still gripping his friend's shoulder.

The Fason laughed. "Now may be the only chance we get."

There was a hint of movement from behind the young captain. Faces emerged from the shadows—haunting masks of shriveled skin and angled features. Faces that should have been dead.

But weren't.

"You've made us wait for quite some time," Evhan noted. "We were beginning to wonder if you meant to keep your promise."

"My promise was to a young man who is no longer with us," Torin replied, his gaze darting from face to face. They were elves, Finlorians, and seeing them immediately brought to mind his slow retreat from the valley of Aefengaard—moments he would have rather forgotten.

"Oh, he is with us," the Illychar purred. "I can feel him stirring. My guess is, he wants this as badly as I do."

"Then you are both fools," Torin replied, placing two hands upon the Sword as Allion fell back beside him. "His partners are gone, and this is no practice weapon I wield."

"He has acquired new partners, as you can see. Or do you think you can defeat us all?"

Torin wasn't sure. Not without knowing how many he faced. There were fewer than had accompanied Bull; that much he could sense. Of course, these were elves, who he knew from experience were swifter than humans—though perhaps weaker than . . .

The thought trailed off as the almost soundless movements of the elven

Illychar gave way to a deep huffing and the shuffle of lumbering footfalls. It resumed as a giant, lumpish head hove into view.

. . . An ogre.

The beast muscled past the puny Finlorians, stopping only when Evhan raised his hand. Its skin was as tough and wrinkled as a walnut, with knotted strands of black hair hanging about in seemingly random patches. It gave a snort at being restrained, blowing mucus from its bulbous, growth-encrusted snout. When rearing back, its head nearly scraped the ceiling, at more than twice the height of the average man.

He had not yet finished taking in the sheer bulk of the brute when a second shoved in beside the first, tipping a mine cart as though it were a wooden cup and fully blocking the way forward. Its vacant eyes fixed upon the talisman clutched in Torin's hands.

"The Sword will be ours," Evhan assured him, "one way or another. I can make it much less painful should you agree to simply hand it over."

"I'd sooner give it to one of them," Torin remarked, with a second glance at the ogres.

The Fason's eyes narrowed. He knew, Torin thought, that the surest way to survive this conflict—and to make certain *he* was the one to lay claim to the blade—was to resolve it without a fight.

"What if I were to guarantee your companions' freedom?" the villain offered.

It was the king's turn to snort—with mirthless laughter. "You would let them go?"

"In exchange for the Sword, yes."

Torin's thoughts raced. "Allow me to see them safely away, and I might consider it."

A quick motion from behind and to the side caused the pack before him to tense. Even without their reaction, Torin had felt that motion enough times to know exactly what it signaled.

"That's not going to happen," Allion declared, bow flexing.

Evhan turned to him with a cold smirk. "Loyalty, I suppose."

"I wouldn't expect your kind to understand," came the hunter's retort.

The Illychar's smirk broadened. "Perhaps you can explain it to us. Perhaps, while you do so, you'd care to share with your friend the secret you're hiding from him."

Allion scoffed. "Secret?"

"Is there more than one? Or perhaps you feel it is the lady's place to tell him."

Torin frowned, but kept his gaze upon his enemies. "What are you talking about?"

"*They* know what I speak of," Evhan hissed. "And unless they are blind, they will recognize this as an opportunity to take what they truly want—while at the same time protecting their friend from the harmful truth."

The ensuing silence fast grew uncomfortable.

"I've a better offer," Torin countered. "Make way, and you'll keep for now these mortal coils. Else you'll soon be yielding them to new hosts."

One of the ogres groaned restlessly, while the elves around it shifted with anticipation. Evhan held wide his lantern to rein them in. When next he spoke, his smirk had slipped.

"You cannot escape," he said. "Even now, a host of my kind lay siege to your walls. With but the pitiful few left here to guard your gates, they will soon be overrun. The greatest mercy would be to end this quickly."

"Done," Allion agreed.

His arrow ripped through the air, and Evhan, though he tried to dodge, caught it through the throat. His lantern crashed to the floor, and the tide of Illychar was unleashed.

"Run!" Marisha screamed.

Neither man had to ask where, or check to see if the other would follow. They spun together and bolted after her, back toward the smelter. Better that than trying to force their way past this knot of enemies—hoping there weren't more waiting behind. At least in the cavern, they would be able to see what they were up against.

The elves were the first to catch up to them. With the Sword in hand, Torin sensed where they were, though he hadn't turned to look. Thinking him unaware, they lunged at his back. Down swept the Sword, severing a leg. Torin then stopped and spun, slicing overhead to catch one that had scampered up and off the wall. As its blackened torso fell away, he pressed up close to the rock, making himself thin enough to escape the sweep of another's blade. The elf hissed in fury, but by the time it came back around, it was missing its sword arm.

Its head rolled after.

The others gave Torin a bit of room at that point, and he took it, sprinting out through the mouth of the tunnel. By then, the first of the ogres was nearly atop him, swatting aside one hesitant elf and grinding another between its foot and the iron rails upon the floor. It thundered on, moving not so much like a limbed creature as a rolling pile of boulders, great lumps of armored muscle looking for something to crush.

Torin veered suddenly as a fist came down—so hard that the ground cracked and rolled beneath his feet. He lost his balance and had to stoop to recover, losing precious seconds. Then came a familiar twang, followed by a sound like snapping twigs, as Allion's arrows ricocheted off the beast's bonelike skin. Still, it drew the ogre's attention, giving Torin the opening he needed.

He pivoted in reverse, coming back around the creature's flank. By the time the dimwitted brute had located the pesky archer, Torin had severed the tendon of one of its ankles and opened a gash in the back of its knee, eliciting a howl that seemed to shake the cavern walls.

He could do no further damage, however, for the elves were on him once more, springing out from around the massive ogre like fleas. They greeted him with withered faces and rictus grins, blades flashing with such speed and precision that he could barely track their movements. Fortunately, he didn't have to. Given the Sword, he knew instinctively which thrusts were feints and which posed real harm. Ignoring the former, he concentrated on the latter, chopping weapons and their wielders into pieces without a single wasted motion.

A good thing, since the elves didn't need to kill him, only pin him in place long enough for one of the ogres to finish the job. Too late, he felt the searing heat from one of the giant blast furnaces at his back. And while the first ogre was limping in place upon its wounded leg, the second was even now roaring in, the elves at its flanks.

Torin held his ground, backed up as close to the furnace as he could stand. At the last moment, he dove forward, slipping just inside the creature's lumbering reach. His momentum carried him directly between the ogre's legs, where he slid forward on his back, tearing at the skin beneath his jerkin.

The fleet-footed elves would have finished him then and there except for two things. One was the arrowhead that tore through the cheek of the first to reach him. The other was the smelting furnace into which the ogre had crashed—the same furnace before which he'd stood a moment earlier. Possessed of a savage fury, the beast had simply ripped it from its struts and seating, tearing it from the wall and flinging it down upon the floor in a twisted mash of iron and fire and metal tubing.

It may have been grace alone that saved him then. For as flaming debris spilled across the floor, crushing and burning and sending black smoke everywhere, Torin was miraculously unscathed—save for a rivulet of molten slag that swiftly burned a hole through the heel of his boot. He cried out and scampered away, still upon his back, thrashing with feet and elbows, until finally he was able to roll over and rise once more.

Most of his enemies were not so fortunate. Several of the elves had been squashed or set aflame. Those that had evaded more serious injury, like he, had done so more through luck than reaction or intent. The ogre that had caused the mess was clawing at its own face, having blinded itself, it would appear, with the blast of gaseous air released from the furnace upon separating from its chimney.

The same creature howled with fresh rage as its foot splashed down in a puddle of melted iron. That sight, along with the burn upon his own foot, gave Torin an idea as both he and his enemies began to regroup.

Sprinting from the wreckage, he looked first for his friends. He found them to one side, their backs together as they fended off a pair of elves. Marisha was doing so with torch and dagger, Allion with bow and hunting knife. At such close quarters, the archer's range weapon was no better than a lightweight staff. Neither, Torin feared, could hold out for long.

But then he spotted Evhan, emerging from the tunnel. The arrow had been broken and pulled from his throat, and though blood washed his chest, he appeared very much alive. Torin couldn't hear him over the crackle of flames and the keening of the wounded ogres, but saw well enough that he was trying to redirect his remaining troops in one last, concerted rush.

Torin resisted the urge to fly to his friends' aid, since doing so would only draw more enemies to them. Instead, he counted up those that had yet to be slain. There were more than he would have expected, given the gravity of the wounds that many bore. But as Darinor had warned, it took more than a ruptured lung or bleeding heart to convince an Illychar that it was dead.

Yet he could destroy them all, Torin reassured himself. He could make their bodies unusable and thus leave them no choice. He told himself this as he took his bearings without seeming to do so, and then faced his enemies squarely, daring them forward. They came on, many limping, some crawling—determined to finish him, lay claim to the Sword, and thus end this war before it truly began.

As they neared, Torin backed away slowly, letting them close rank, letting them tighten their own noose. They were taking no chances this time. The mad rush had failed. Now, they would cinch around him until he had nowhere to go.

He stopped at the edge of the trench, a sunken track along which wheeled crucibles were used to cart away molten materials. He didn't know that his plan would work, of course. If he was to miscalculate on any number of levels, he might very well be sealing the fate of all. But at this point, he was desperate enough to try.

"Are you ready to end this, then?" Evhan rasped, gurgling blood as he pushed to the fore of his ring.

Torin glanced back toward Allion and Marisha, but couldn't find them. Smoke and gases from the overturned furnace stung his eyes.

"You want the Sword?" Torin coughed, glaring from face to face. He was stalling, waiting for the second ogre to hobble near on its melted stump. The first, the one he had crippled, hovered over him, huffing its fetid breath.

Then Marisha cried out, and Torin knew his time was up.

"Let's see which of you wants it most."

He dropped his weapon then, into the spill trench—used to catch any overflow from the slag-bearing crucibles or the vat that supplied them. For a moment, no one moved, except to eye him with suspicion. But that suspicion was soon passed on to one another, as each of the Illychar came to realize that the Sword was its for the taking.

Like a pack of wolves, they descended, jostling one another to be the first to reach the discarded talisman. A crucible blocked the path of some, but was swatted clear by the ogre. As it crashed away, Torin sprang back to the other side of the trench, all but forgotten by his enemies. Evhan tried to call out a warning, but was ignored. He was too late, anyway. In the time it took for the Fason to realize what was about to happen, Torin tore free the safety pin and yanked down on the release chain, tipping the giant vat upon its hinges and letting its contents pour forth from its grooved lip.

An intense heat erupted over him, scalding his face and hands, but Torin held on, refusing to let the vat tip back. Already overfilled from having been abandoned for too long, the molten slag poured out like the runoff from a waterwheel, disintegrating anything it touched.

Piled together in a crush at the bottom of that trench, only a couple of the Illychar saw it coming—and still had no chance to escape. Even those upon the fringes let loose terrible wails as the slag rained down in gushing torrents, melting faces and flesh and bones. The ogre lasted the longest, but was soon eaten away down the center, falling in among the others and leaving only its burning limbs to poke free of the fiery river.

When those, too, had slipped beneath, Torin let go the pull ring and allowed the empty vat to settle back, wincing at the pain of his blistered hands. Covering his mouth against a horrid stench, he watched the molten flow as it drained off toward a recovery basin. Almost all of the Illychar were gone. Those that still lived had been reduced to flaming stumps, and were of no threat. Evhan was among the most whole, his body intact from the waist up, while his hips and legs had been melted away. Other than that, Torin saw only the blinded, footless ogre, which thrashed about near the center of the cavern, struggling to find its way.

He turned then, remembering his friends. He found them quickly this time, though the smoke had thickened and his eyes still burned. Marisha had not been hurt, as he'd feared. Her cry had been for Allion, held prostrate on the ground by a lone surviving elf. A curved blade of Finlorian design was pressed against the back of the hunter's neck, while his head was arched back sharply, hair gripped in the elf's fist.

All three stared in Torin's direction, as if frozen by the spectacle he had just produced. Marisha was the first to react, snatching up her fallen torch. The Illychar looked over in time to catch the flaming brand square in the face. With a terrible screech, it fell back, dropping its blade. Allion seized the weapon, and with Marisha's help, swiftly made sure the creature would never rise again.

As its hisses and screams died away, Torin looked back to the trench in which he had cast the Sword, a flutter of anxiety in his chest. But as the last of the slag drained free along the designated spill route, the blade was revealed, pure and pristine, unscarred by the superheated materials that had washed over it.

Torin smiled in spite of himself, though he waited a moment longer before retrieving the talisman with a pair of tongs from a nearby worktable. He inspected it for both residue and heat, but found no need to wipe it down or cool it off. The weapon had protected itself fully, as he'd hoped, and was as flawless as ever.

Armed once more, he found it but a small matter to finish off the handful of mutilated Illychar that remained. Even the blinded ogre fell swiftly. One on one, its sluggish movements and hardened skin were no match for the Sword; though, given its plaintive wails, Torin almost pitied the creature while putting it down.

Finally, he returned to Evhan, upon whom Allion was looking down with understandable sadness.

"Help me finish him," the hunter bade.

Torin nodded, and together, they carried the Fason's remains to the nearest furnace. Marisha moved on ahead, opening the door to the fire chamber used to preheat the blast air. Alerted, perhaps, by the grating of iron, the roaring of flames, or his imminent demise, Evhan jerked awake at the last moment, blinking unsteadily. Startled by his sudden movements, both men let go and fell back.

"This changes nothing," the Illychar sputtered, lying on the floor where they had dropped him. "You cannot stop what is already in motion. My kind will be free."

"As will Evhan," Allion growled. "Go now, and let him find peace."

The hunter moved forward, knife in hand. The legless Illychar reached out feebly to stop him, but could not prevent Allion from plunging that blade through his eye socket and digging around in his brain. After a moment of convulsions, his struggles ceased.

When finished, Allion withdrew slowly, wiping his blade on the other's tunic. Torin awaited his friend's signal, then bent to help him once more. This time, the ruined torso offered no resistance as they heaved it into the flames.

After watching it blacken and crumble, Marisha closed the door, leaving the three of them to gaze upon one another's soot-smeared faces.

"May we leave now?" she asked of Allion.

The hunter did not respond, so Torin placed a hand on his shoulder.

"Come," the king urged. "Let's go and see if any of what he told us is true."

At last, the hunter nodded, and the three of them turned away. Weapons in hand, they pushed on through the thickening haze, seeking their tunnel and an escape into the night.

CHAPTER FIFTY-FOUR

Sᴉᴅᴇ ʙʏ sɪᴅᴇ, the trio of friends staggered into the exit tunnel, stepping over and around the bodies of Illychar slain in the initial rush. Inside, the air cleared somewhat, while the temperatures cooled. Torin welcomed the change, taking a deeper breath and reaching up to wipe the sweat from his brow.

"Was that how it felt for you and Kylac in Killangrathor's lair?" he asked Allion.

The hunter ignored him at first, then stopped suddenly to stare at him strangely.

"What is it?"

Before answering, Allion peered back toward the cavern, a den of ash and smoke and unchecked blazes—complete with a river of molten stone. "The shaman," he whispered.

"The what?"

The hunter was not really speaking to him, but seemed to be wrestling with something in his own mind.

"What's wrong?" Marisha inquired with concern.

"The A'awari shaman," Allion repeated. "The one who slew Wyevesces. He told me I would know my enemy when I returned to the dragon's lair."

Torin could only look on helplessly as his closest friends faced each other, struggling to find meaning in a riddle he knew nothing about. Clearly, it had something to do with the foray into Vosges of which Stephan had made mention. But not even his seneschal had yet heard the story, other than the basic courier report of a Parthan division that had been lost and then saved.

"A prophecy?" the king asked.

Allion frowned. "A warning, I think."

"Well, it's behind us now," Torin offered reassuringly. "Time to move on." He took a couple of steps, but stopped when he realized that his friends had not followed. "Come," he urged again. "Those fires back there are still singeing my skin."

Marisha gave a gentle tug, and Allion started forward, a look of frustration creasing his brow.

Then, all of a sudden, as his gaze took in the emptiness of the path ahead, that look changed, overcome by an expression of absolute horror. Once again, the hunter stopped in his tracks.

"Allion," Marisha said, "you're worrying me."

The hunter seized the woman's shoulders, putting his face close to hers. "Darinor. The Illychar trapped him underground, did they not? When he went to check on the seal?"

Marisha stared back, eyes affright. "That's how he tells it. But why—"

"What would he have used to defend himself in those catacombs? Fire? Lightning?"

"Why not?"

The hunter shook her, trying to make her see. "Because he doesn't just conjure those elements. He summons them from the world around him. And if he had no source . . ."

"Allion," Marisha said, searching his face as if he were a stranger. "What are you saying?"

Torin's stomach writhed as a fresh dread seeped in like poison. It seemed quite obvious what his friend was suggesting. If weaponless, had the renegade Entient really escaped?

But the terrible consequences of that possibility, along with the utter dismay in Marisha's face, caused him to search for an alternative. "He would have carried a torch, would he not? A candle's flame was enough to set my hearth afire."

Allion glanced at him. "Maybe. Though I've never seen him use one."

"How can we know?"

"Stop this, both of you!" Marisha demanded. "My father is even now risking his life to save yours, while you stand here suggesting him to be some sort of villain!"

Torin's gaze drifted back toward the tunnel mouth, his thoughts returned to the slain Illychar. "Did he mean to save us, or deliver us?"

"My father is not a monster!"

"Marisha," Allion said, trying to make her meet his gaze. "The shaman spoke of betrayal."

"Of Evhan, then, if you must believe in such things. Evhan is the one who betrayed us."

The hunter did not respond right away, as if urging her to think it through. "If that is so," he said softly, "then tell me, how did Evhan know about us? Who could have possibly told him?"

The word *us* echoed in Torin's thoughts, and once again, he felt like an outsider. Only, this time, that which he was hearing sounded clear enough. He thought back to the secret Evhan had mentioned, and an odd warmth billowed through his veins.

Marisha glanced in his direction, and his suspicions were confirmed. Denial and understanding collided within, spawning emotions too confusing to sort through.

"Torin," he heard her say, from what seemed a great distance. "Torin, listen, we—"

"We have to go," Allion said. "We have to warn Galdric and Thelin—"

But *his* words, too, were cut short suddenly, though not because someone else's had trampled them. Rather, it appeared the hunter had simply run out of breath. His mouth was still moving, but it made no sound, like a fish groping for food.

"Allion?" Marisha asked. Then, as he dropped to his knees, she shrieked, "Allion!"

Torin sprang forward. At the same time, he felt a rush of heat from the Sword, gripped in his hand, and noted a deep glow from where the Pendant hung around Marisha's neck. He paid neither more than an instant's consideration, however, for Allion's face was red, veins standing out beneath his flesh. His chest heaved, and his throat strained, but still he made no sound. His eyes widened grotesquely a moment before the convulsions ceased and he fell back against the rough stone of the tunnel floor.

"Allion!" Marisha wailed again, cradling his neck and bending her ear to his mouth. His flesh was purple, his chest still. She began at once an attempt to revive him.

"He has overspoken himself, it seems."

They looked together toward the sound of the new voice. All at once, a shadow appeared. Though backlit by the red glow of the tunnel mouth, it had been invisible but a moment before. It came ahead now, growing in size and definition.

"Father," Marisha whispered, tears in her eyes.

"You already returned the Pendant to her, I see," Darinor grumbled, eyes ablaze as they fixed upon Torin. "You leave me no choice but to do this in crude fashion."

Before Torin could manage a response, there came a great swoosh and crackle. A torrent of flames gushed in from behind the renegade Entient, composed of molten materials summoned from the burning smelter. As the torrent neared, it split off into separate streams, each of which alighted upon one of Darinor's outstretched hands in the form of a swirling fireball.

Blazes in hand, the Entient took another step forward.

But so did Torin, brandishing the Sword as he stood over his friends. "What, no more ruse, then?" the king snarled.

"It would be wasted now, would it not?" Darinor growled in response. "In any case, I am out of patience. I had hoped this little snare sufficient to end matters between us, but it would appear I underestimated you. I will not do so again."

Torin's thoughts whirred, struggling to put the pieces in place. That was what the Entient had been doing when he'd left them there in the king's chambers, just before their retreat. He had set forth not to check on things, but to arrange Evhan's ambush.

"If you meant to kill us, why not help Bull finish us before?"

"Because I did not wish to give myself away by fighting openly against you. Bullrum's was a chance encounter, though I allowed him his opportunity. He failed."

"And those who came after? In the dungeons? Why send us on ahead?"

"Those were not mine, but yours—soldiers answering to General Rogun."

The Entient grimaced with savage defiance, teeth flashing amid the crags of his beard. "They will make fine Illychar."

"Then you were not as wounded as you appeared," Torin observed darkly. He glanced at Marisha, but the healer did not seem to be listening, too busy was she pumping on Allion's chest as if he were some sort of bellows.

In that moment of distraction, the first of the fireballs was unleashed. When Torin looked up, it was already upon him, leaving him no time but to raise his blade instinctively. As contact was made, crimson flames leapt forth to meet and then consume the offensive magic—though the intense heat of the blast caused the air to ripple around him.

"You must know your powers cannot harm me," Torin retorted, sounding much braver than he felt.

The remaining fireball split and spilled over into the Entient's empty hand, so that both were alight once more. "Not directly, perhaps. But how long can you afford to stand here while my armies surround you?"

"How long can *you*," Torin snapped, "knowing that Rogun's soldiers may find us first?"

The Entient's scowl deepened. "Whatever your general has come here to do, he is too late. Already, your dearest friend rots beneath you."

Torin had to clench his jaw to keep his lip from quivering. Beside him, Marisha began pounding Allion's chest, weeping in denial. She then kissed him, on the forehead and on the mouth, with tears and with passion. When Torin looked to her, another fireball came roaring. This one was not aimed at him, however, but went sailing past to strike the tunnel wall, hot enough to melt the very stone.

"You cannot save him," Darinor warned. "The only way to do so is to raise him as an Illychar."

"Never!" Marisha hissed, looking up at last. Her next utterance was a yell. "Never!"

Torin raised an arm to block her, but she brushed right past. With murder in her eyes, she lunged toward her father. Torin sprang after, but could not reach them before Darinor intercepted her with a backhand across the face. At the moment of contact, a burst of flames from the Pendant consumed those upon the Entient's hand and drew from him a sharp cry. Yet the blow itself sent her reeling. As Torin reached them, Darinor hurriedly stepped aside, keeping his distance from the Sword, while Marisha sprawled into a jag upon the wall, beneath which she crumpled.

Rather than chase after his enemy, Torin stopped to check on his friend. The Entient's flames had done no damage to her skin. But there was a gash from where she had struck her head, and she did not stir at his touch.

"You would destroy your own daughter, as well?" Torin demanded, feeling for a pulse.

"She is a coil," the Illychar corrected, shaking his hand as if stung by the Pendant's defenses. "Nothing more."

Torin rose from his crouch, his rage boiling.

"And what is she to *you* but a faithless harlot?"

"My friend," Torin snarled, starting forward slowly.

The Entient did not back off, but rather shifted to one side. He did so in the blink of an eye, so quick that he seemed to simply vanish and reappear. A third fireball was launched, once again skimming Torin's shoulder before blasting against the tunnel wall.

Startled by the sudden movement, Torin ceased his approach and instead stepped round the other way, keeping his adversary in front of him, measuring carefully the distance between them. It seemed Darinor was doing the same. Mirroring each other's pace and stride, the pair began to circle like cats at bay.

"Tonight would have been much easier without her interference," Darinor lamented, hurling yet another fireball. This one ignited a mine cart farther down the tunnel, filling the air with even more smoke and heat. "I would have taken the Sword as you slept. By the time you awoke, you would have done so as an Illychar."

"The Sword could have been yours from the very beginning," Torin reminded him. "If it's the blade you covet, why did you refuse it when it was offered?"

"Because I did not care to repeat the same strategy that failed my kind before," Darinor admitted, flinging a fireball that landed at Torin's feet. "Remember Sabaoth? What would your Sword have won me if the Vandari were to return with another, or an army, or a way to restore the seal? Your quest was not a lie. Securing your trust seemed a far better way to achieve control of whatever forces and talismans you—or they—happened to return with."

Torin tried closing the gap between them, but again his enemy flickered and speed-stepped, leaving only a fireball in the king's path.

"You could have made the journey yourself," he observed. "You could have found the Finlorians and pretended to befriend them as you did me. What if I had lost the blade?"

"Had you lost the blade, then it would have posed no threat to me. The more likely danger was that it would fall into another's hands, which is why you were given the Pendant to carry along with it, remember?"

Reacting to each other's movements, they continued to circle, back and forth between the tunnel walls. All the while, Darinor threw his molten balls of fire—haphazardly, it seemed—as Torin searched for a hole in the Entient's defenses.

"There were risks involved, to be sure," Darinor allowed. "But necessary that I might have the opportunity to carry out my designs here, where the real battle will now take place. In truth, you succeeded too soon for me to complete my web. Had I anticipated that, or believed for a moment you might succeed *without* carrying the Sword, I might have sent you on your errand with the Pendant alone."

Though the answer made some sense, it didn't feel right to Torin. Not a lie, exactly, but an incomplete truth. Either way, Darinor had used him. His quest had been little more than an elaborate scheme to steal or subvert for the Illychar any powers or plans that might be used against them. An unwitting pawn, he had done just that, playing the game as the renegade Entient had designed it.

So that in the end, the Illysp would possess all.

"But there are no additional armies," Torin said. "No more talismans, no other forces of magic for you to seize as your own. You have nothing save that which you started with."

"I have enough," the Illychar argued. "And without fear of retribution, I will now take the Sword, and move on to the next phase of conquest."

That was why the Entient had seemed almost relieved, Torin thought, upon listening to the king's report. And the lightning bolt—the one that had rocked his tower without spawning any others—that had been a signal to the Illychar troops. He still didn't know for sure where Rogun fit in, but was now willing to believe that the general had sprung his trap upon realizing that the Illychar were springing theirs. It was the most reasonable way to explain why Darinor had sent them off into the tunnels, away from a madness he could not fully control, and into an ambush that he did.

"For all your cunning, your traps have failed," Torin said. "The city is not yet yours, and never will you have the Sword."

Even as he extended this challenge, he felt a scalding heat beneath his foot. Glancing down in pain and shock, he saw that the toes of his boot had come in contact with a stream of molten rock, left in the wake of one of the Entient's fire blasts. He moved away quickly, looking up in time to drive his approaching adversary back a step.

Darinor gritted his teeth—a menacing smile.

To his sudden horror, Torin recognized what the Entient intended in prolonging this confrontation. While the fires themselves were shaped by a magic the Sword could dispel, the resulting damage—while difficult to fathom—was natural enough. All around, holes in the walls and floor sizzled, stone and minerals dripping to form rivers and pools. Farther back, the flaming mine cart had melted and crumbled into a molten slag like that he'd used against Evhan. Smoke and fumes and searing heat permeated the tunnel air.

"It can still end well for you," Darinor offered. "Surrender the Sword, and I will grant you a painless death and long life as an Illychar. Together, you and your friends can be reborn. Otherwise, I will burn your corpses, and let that be the end of you."

Torin growled and pressed the attack, desperate now to find an opening. But the Entient continued to stall, moving about, quick-shifting every now and then and throwing those fireballs to keep him off balance. Worse, Torin was forced to monitor the ground almost as closely as he did his enemy, in order to avoid contact with any of the melted areas laid as traps beneath his feet. There were holes in the ceiling now, as well, raining drops upon the floor. Little by little, he was being hemmed in, while Darinor, with his ability to flash from one spot of clear ground to the next, seemed able to avoid the flaming pitfalls with relative ease.

As despair closed round, Torin checked on his friends. Neither was yet threatened by the ring of fire, but both *would* be soon. Allion remained motionless, eyes wide, mouth agape, his color already fading. Marisha, on the other hand, was now stirring, moaning softly as she struggled for consciousness.

Torin looked away from her in a hurry, hoping that Darinor hadn't noticed. But the Entient had. No doubt sensing the young king's concern, he hefted one of his fireballs as if to take aim at the near-helpless woman.

"Burn them," Torin bluffed. "Burn them both. I'd rather say good-bye now than see them become agents in your service."

The Entient hesitated, his expression of savage delight slipping.

"Go on," Torin urged, stepping back deeper into the tunnel. "Destroy them now, and save me the trouble later. I can do nothing more to save them, as you say. But the path to my freedom lies open, and I mean to take it. Only, know that I'll be coming for you, Darinor, when and where you least expect it."

The Entient scoffed, though his eyes narrowed as Torin continued to retreat. Withdrawing step by step through the curtains of smoke and waves of heat, striding carefully around the puddles and rivulets of molten rock, the young king was steadily drawing the Illychar's attention away from Marisha. Whether or not he could actually make himself flee with the Sword to fight another day, he meant to buy the healer time to make her own escape.

"Until then," he added, jumping back over the last of the lava streams, "know that I'll be thinking of nothing more than how I shall take vengeance against you."

Darinor glanced back at Marisha, who was shaking her head, having risen to her knees. Torin gambled, at that point, by spinning suddenly and bolting for the exit, praying that his sudden movement would force the Entient to follow.

It did.

With a rabid growl, Darinor sprang after. Torin raced on without turning, trusting the Sword to mark for him the other's approach. But in this instance, it was difficult to do so. The Entient came forward in zigzag flashes of quicksilver movement. To his right, to his left, and suddenly, on top of him. Torin whirled in time to catch the enraged Illychar, but not before the other had dispelled his now-useless fireballs and seized the king's wrists in a ferocious grip.

From side to side they wrestled, with Torin twisting and grunting, struggling to free himself for a strike. The mystic's hands, however, were like iron cuffs, and would not be made to release. Though Torin battled with all the strength he could summon, Darinor was by far the taller and stronger, and in a matter of heartbeats, it was his own grip that weakened.

He continued to strain, gritting his teeth, refusing to let go. The Illychar bore down on him, reeking of decay and torment. From behind, Torin could feel the growing rush of heat as their bitter scuffle carried them along the railway toward the melted mine cart. In desperation, he tried to redirect their course, to drag his foe aside or to turn him the other way. But the Entient had found his target, and was pressing relentlessly toward that goal.

Torin let loose a howl and dropped to the ground, seeking to use the En-tient's own momentum against him. But Darinor only bent over, a smothering shroud. Torin knew in that moment that he was finished, that there was no more denying his own end.

Then came the sound of a bowstring, and the thwack as an arrow struck flesh. A bloody tip popped free through Darinor's stomach. The Entient snarled, but otherwise ignored it. He then doubled his efforts, pinching at the nerves in Torin's wrists, trying to force the king's hands to open.

His frail hope renewed, Torin cried out and held on.

Another arrow went flying, but missed, skittering off a nearby wall. Torin felt his hopes sag, and his grip upon the Sword failed.

A third arrow sang, and this one struck home. Darinor stiffened, spitting blood from a punctured lung, yet still made a lunge for the Sword. As soon as the other's hands let go his wrists, Torin reached up to snatch the Entient by his collar. At the same time, he tucked his knees in close. When the weight of Darinor's body shifted forward, Torin yanked down and kicked out, forcing his opponent into an overhead roll.

The Entient's hand brushed the gem-studded hilt a moment before he splashed down in the molten slag of the melted mine cart. His back arched sharply, but it was too late. He only barely had a chance to scream before the heat worked its course, engulfing his robes and then his body in metallic flame.

CHAPTER FIFTY-FIVE

Torin LOOKED ON UNTIL IT WAS FINISHED, mesmerized by the horrific display. After a moment, the bulk of Darinor's body had been reduced to nothing more than a black stain in the center of the slag pool, with flaming limbs sprawled out upon the edges. The renegade Entient—and his Illysp parasite—were gone.

Nevertheless, Torin had to force himself to look away, to turn his head and redirect his gaze back toward the mouth of the tunnel. Through smoke-filled air and veils of shimmering heat, he spied Marisha, standing over Allion, the hunter's bow in her hand. She stared back at him—past him really—as if peering down the tunnel's throat at something only she could see. Her weapon lowered, and her body sagged, as though it were about to fall.

Torin barely remembered to retrieve the Sword in his haste to reach her. Regardless, she dropped before he could catch her, settling to her knees beside the fallen Allion, dangerously close to a puddle of molten rock. Though the puddle simmered and steamed, she hung her head, and did not seem to notice.

The young king slowed as he came upon her, fearful of doing anything to interrupt her grieving. He was not yet certain of his own feelings. The fire of battle still pumped through his veins, allowing little room for reflection. There was still so much to be done. They were not yet safe.

He reached out slowly, but hesitated and withdrew as she began to sob. She bent low, closing Allion's eyes and kissing him once more. If there was cause to be angry, Torin did not feel it. On the contrary, recognizing that she had found with his friend something that he himself had been unable to give her filled him with a prevailing sense of peace. Aside from that, who was he to denounce either when, deep down, he had already given *his* heart to another?

She stopped to look up at him, tears of anguish streaming down her face. "I'm sorry," she said. "You should know that it was I who . . . He never meant—"

"Shh," Torin quieted, crouching beside her. His hand found her shoulder, and beneath his touch, she shook and sobbed anew. As he tried to think of what else to say, his eyes went again to the slow-moving rivulets of lava closing round. "Can you help me carry him?"

Marisha let loose a little wail.

"Marisha, we must move. Will you help me?"

With a noticeable effort, the woman toughened. "Where?"

Torin cast about. There was no way they'd be able to carry the hunter with them up through the exit shaft. But he wasn't going to simply leave his friend's body here, nor dispose of it without the proper rites.

"Back through the tunnel," he decided.

He sheathed the Sword and, with some gentle promptings, helped Marisha to gather her legs beneath her. Together, they hoisted the body of their friend up onto their shoulders, with an arm around the neck of each. Leaning forward so that the hunter's feet didn't drag, and with Torin supporting most of the weight, the pair began a return journey toward the tunnel mouth.

Between the two of them, they were able to maintain balance as they stepped over and around the various flaming pitfalls, few of which showed any sign yet of beginning to cool. They coughed and grunted, choking on the poisoned air and struggling with the weight of their burden. Marisha continued to cry, and Torin wished that *he* would, that he might wash away some of the ash and grit clawing at his eyes.

Back through the smelter they bore their friend, assailed by smoke and heat, sweat dripping from their limbs and faces. Marisha, Torin noticed, was having particular difficulty, slowing and staggering with every step, and his concern for her grew. As they neared the iron door through which they had first entered the cavern, she finally collapsed. Lowering Allion to the ground, he bent to check on her. Her breathing was ragged and shallow, her skin blistering to the touch.

He moved quickly to open the door. Smoke from the cavern spilled into the corridor beyond. There was no help for it. As swiftly as he could manage, he hoisted Marisha and then Allion through, then shut the door behind him.

He drew the Sword again for light, then leaned back against the stone wall, sucking breath and closing his eyes against his dizziness. He couldn't risk just waiting here to be found, for it might be their enemies that did so first. He had to keep going, had to get help.

But as his eyes opened upon the limp forms laid out before him, his resolve crumbled. What did he hope to accomplish with all this struggle? As Darinor had said, he was too late. The battle was over. No matter how hard he fought, his best friend was dead.

Reality fell like a crushing wave upon his chest, and Torin felt himself slumping, then sliding to his seat. His eyes seemed to swell as they fixed upon the hunter's face, filling with sorrow and desolation—emotions that even now could find no release. Their sweeping torrents assailed him from within, and Torin succumbed to the assault.

The games were ended. Darinor was slain, the truth known. At long last, there would be no more lies. But none of that made a difference. None of that could fill the terrible void that had opened within him. Split wide like a fissure in the earth, he would never find meaning enough to make him whole.

He tried to deny it. That's what he'd been doing before, was it not?

Throughout his confrontation with Darinor, he'd believed that somehow he could win this struggle as he had so many others. Dispose of his enemy, then see to his friend. Now he had, only to discover that all the denial in the world could not reroute this flood of truth. Its waters continued to pummel him, driving the breath from his lungs, the blood from his veins, the very life from his being. He could not blink. He could not cry. He could only sit there, waiting to be swept away.

Why him? It was not Allion who had unleashed this scourge. Nor was it Allion who had so readily run off to carry out Darinor's deception. How much better would everything be had Torin even once listened to the advice of his friend? If anyone deserved to die as a result of these failures, it was Torin, who had committed them, not he whose only crime was standing faithful to the end.

Shame wrenched Torin's stomach and would not let go. The inevitability of this moment should have been clear from the first. Even as children, Allion had been his protector. While both had had grandiose dreams, Allion had been the steady one, the one to temper those aspirations with the reality of his limitations. Torin had always refused such boundaries, pressing on despite any warnings and consequences. And yet, no matter how foolish the venture, Allion would insist on carrying on alongside, to see that no harm came to him. He should have known that eventually, his recklessness would catch up with him, and that when it did, Allion would be there to shield him—that Allion would pay the price, not he.

In the crimson dark of that near lightless corridor, Torin cried out. He did so without words or voice, but need alone. The need to put things right. The need to free himself of this despair. He had seen too many suffer already as a result of *his* choices. Time and again, he had accepted those sufferings because there was nothing to do but soldier on. But he could not accept this. He could not accept that after all they had been through together, after all the trials they had faced as one, that Allion should be made to forfeit his life, while here sat Torin, so much less worthy.

Please, he begged, a prayer without destination. *Please.* He would give whatever was required—the Sword, his life, every feeling of warmth and contentment he had ever known. Should it cost him all of this and more, he would see his friend's life restored. The Ceilhigh could take it all back—every pleasant sensation, every sweet sound, every dazzling image to have touched his heart. If need be, he would forget forever his journey to Yawacor: Dyanne's smile, Saena's friendship, Autumn's voice—

If ever you have need, of anything, call upon me, and I shall see it granted.

The words shot like sparks from a smith's anvil, and for a moment, Torin knew not where they might have come from. Then came a memory, gliding forth from his past—an image of the sea, a ship, and a striking young maiden's curious farewell.

Autumn.

Anything you wish . . .

Her words. Her promise.

. . . I am but a longing away.

Torin's blood began to tingle—as it had before, he recalled, back in Aefengaard, when he had wondered if it might be possible to save Eolin. Like then, he had nothing more than an impossible wish. But if he were to wish hard enough . . .

Without quite knowing why, he narrowed his focus, sending his pleas out to one who could not possibly hear them, to that captivating woman, Autumn of the Rain. Never mind that he had left her weeks ago, and an ocean away. Never mind that when first meeting her, he had wondered if she might be some kind of simpleton, incapable of understanding the world around her. He knew only what she had offered, and that he had never felt such dire need.

Help me, Autumn. Please.

It occurred to him that he might be giving way to madness, but it didn't seem to matter. Somehow, he found the strength to crawl forward. Setting the Sword down beside him, he knelt over the body of his friend. His lungs tightened, his chest burned, and still he called forth, beseeching the woman's aid, imploring the heavens to carry to her his silent voice.

His head grew light, and the world began to spin. He shut his eyes—not to ground himself, but to let himself be carried away. Be it a maelstrom of insanity or death, he would gladly relent if only it would strip him of his pain.

The darkness deepened, engulfing him. Around and around he went, a form without shape or mass, a consciousness caught in an endless vortex. He lost all senses—sight and smell, hearing and touch. He forgot who he was, and where he'd been. He clung to one thing only: his need for Autumn to hear him.

Then, amid the darkness, he perceived a light. A sliver of glory, it beckoned him. Strength, rapture, love—it promised all of these things, a whisper in the night to usher the passing of nightmare. He need but grasp it, catch hold of its majesty, and his horrors would be dispelled, his fears forgotten.

Torin stretched forth.

Responding to his need, the light continued to grow. A welcome warmth spread through him as its brightness intensified. It spread outward and around, chasing away the shadows, then drew near enough to coddle him, enfolding him with the softness of a cloud.

"Torin," a voice sang. "Open your eyes."

Though delicate in tone, never had a more compelling sound been uttered. Torin immediately obeyed, and found himself surrounded by a radiance greater than any he had ever imagined. Somehow, its brilliant intensity soothed rather than pierced his eyes, shining through to fill his heart with bliss. Gone was the chiseled stone of the corridor. Gone was the smoky air. All that remained was the light and the woman standing before him.

"Am I dead?" he asked her.

Autumn's eyes sparkled, glinting with their hint of amethyst. "If among the dead, what would I be doing here?"

"Then I'm dreaming."

"Oh? Am I the one you dream about now?" Her brow arched, and her mouth twisted, smiling as she had before—as if considering some private jape.

Torin wavered, not knowing what else to say. If he had found her strangely captivating before, then she was utterly enthralling now. Stunned by her mere presence, he couldn't seem to recall what she was doing here.

Her gaze dipped, and Torin's slipped after. He gasped then, his heart lurching. For he was not alone after all, but had been accompanied, as always, by his dearest friend—or in this case, the man's breathless body.

His nightmare had been real.

He cast about, finding nothing and no one else. It was just the two of them, as if they had passed together to some other realm. But nothing had changed. Allion was dead.

He looked back to Autumn, whose expression of amusement seemed to soften. "Your friend fought bravely. A shame it is to see his light dim so soon."

"It should have been me," Torin said.

"It is not for the children to decide such things," Autumn replied, smiling sadly.

Torin peered up at her from where he knelt amid the brightness. "Who are you?"

"If you know not who I am, what cause have you to believe that I can help you?"

He studied her face, her gaze, in search of hope. "Because there is no one else," he said finally, and his head fell.

Autumn kept silent for a moment before responding. In the interim, Torin thought he heard the distant crashing of waves. "Over the course of my life, I have been thought a witch crawled forth from the sea. Others have deemed me a star fallen from the heavens before fully matured. Were I to describe myself, you would not understand. *You* must provide the terms that to your mind would have meaning. So tell me, who am I?"

Torin looked up, and stared into her eyes. "Ha'Rasha," he whispered breathlessly. "An avatar—a true avatar—of the Ceilhigh."

The woman's hair glimmered, its colors dancing in the wash of light. "As fair a description as any. Cianellen, I am known, to those you speak of, those born of the Maelstrom to preside over all creation. Charged alongside my brothers and sisters with the care of this world and its inhabitants."

"But that was ages ago. After all this time, how is it possible that—"

"Few of us remain," the woman acknowledged. "Those who do have lived for countless lives of men, fortunate enough to have avoided the struggles of gods, avatars, and mortals alike—savoring life, rather than seeking to dictate it."

Torin's gaze fell again upon his friend. So peaceful the hunter seemed, the struggle and anguish sapped from his face. Torin, on the other hand, was beginning to feel something new, the stirrings of a bitter frustration.

"Is that not your duty?" he asked, looking upon her with a measure of accusation. "To have a hand in shaping this world? To look after those who reside within?"

Again she offered him a sad smile, as if pitying his inability to understand. Torin's frustration grew.

"We—each of us—see to our duties in our own way. 'Tis easy to second-guess that which is past, but senseless to do so. Do you not regret some of the decisions of your own life? And if so, what has that regret won you?" The pointedness of her gaze cut down his defiance before it could take root. "I live my life from one fancy to the next, ignoring as best I can the various conflicts by which this world is governed. I prefer to spend my time alone, surrounded by birds and animals—the most innocent creations of the Ceilhigh. Only occasionally do I take interest in the lives of those who deal most often in death and strife."

As he continued to look upon her, he remembered thinking of her as a child, though one for whom the entire world was a toy. An impossible dichotomy, but one which now might be explained.

"So why me?" he asked. "Why should *my* life interest you?"

"More than three thousand years have passed since anyone wielded a Sword of Asahiel. Not so great a time to some of us, but long enough that even I had supposed the talismans forever gone. You proved me wrong. I wished to congratulate you, in my own way, while taking a firsthand look at the Sword itself."

"You chose a strange guise in which to do so," Torin dared.

Cianellen's smile became mischievous. "Not so simple a matter as you might think. Foresight can be an inconstant trickster, and there were plenty of opportunities for my plan to go awry. I first had to draw to my shores the pirate that would be recruited to abduct you, and convince him to take me aboard. I then had to ensure that we were in port when Soric's mercenary captain came calling. When Karulos refused the assignment, I had to allow myself to be kidnapped, in order to convince him to do your brother's bidding. After that, I had to wait and trust that you would arrive safely."

"A lot of trouble," Torin agreed. "Why not simply appear to me? Or come upon me as a beggar in the street?"

"Would a beggar have seen you or the Sword under duress? Would a beggar have been witness to—or able to lend assistance in—your struggle against the wizard? Would you have listened to a beggar who told you to seek Lord Lorre in regard to the missing Finlorians?"

It made sense now, Torin thought—not all of it, but much that hadn't before. Her rare blend of innocence and wisdom; her scream after Soric had been carried away—which he now believed had closed the breakaway rift the wizard had left open; her prior knowledge of his quest . . .

"If you meant to help," he replied, his bitterness rising once more, "why not do so outright?"

The warmth of her expression never slipped, as if immune to his prodding. "The way of the Ha'Rasha is not to do things *for* the children of the Ceilhigh. Nor has it ever been. Though it may seem otherwise, all are bound—even our creators—by rules and consequences, only some of which a mortal would understand."

Torin scowled. "You sound like the Entients."

"Do not be too critical of your people's shepherds. The Entients have done much good, given their limitations."

"They used me. As Darinor used me. As *you* used me."

The real reason for his bitterness, he realized. For once again, it seemed he had been little more than an unwitting pawn in another's grand scheme.

"You underestimate the value of your own efforts."

"Do I? What difference do they make, if I am forever acting under the influence of another?"

"Are we not all affected by those around us? Do we not affect these others in turn? I may do so to a greater degree, for that is my power and my calling. But that does not make you a helpless victim, nor excuse you of the responsibility for your own choices."

"Then let *me* pay the price for it," he said, gripping his friend's cold hand. "Let not others suffer the consequences of *my* deeds."

"Is it your friend who suffers? Or you?"

But Torin would not be misdirected again. "Anything I wish, you told me. You know what it is I ask for. Will you grant it?"

A deepening sadness seemed to shade some of the luster upon Cianellen's face. "Death will not be cheated. Know you what is required?"

Torin's stomach tightened, but he kept his gaze steady. "Yes."

"And are you certain this to be your one and final desire? To turn these tables? To leave it to your friend and others to suffer the pain of your passing as you have suffered his?"

As she said this, he immediately thought of Marisha, of the anguish she had shown upon Allion's death. It led him to wonder if she would truly grieve for him as she had for the other. She would be saddened, he was sure. But if given a choice, this was what she would want. And he alone could give it to her.

"I would not deny them whatever happiness they have found."

"Even though that happiness was once yours?"

Torin nodded. Even so. Without reservation.

"And when you are gone, who will lead your people in the fight against your enemies?"

Torin looked purposefully upon Allion. "Someone who has already proven more capable than I."

It was not a burden he passed on lightly. But all would have to make concessions, it seemed, in order to gain what they most desired. Regardless, none could afford any more mistakes of the kind Torin had already made. He had rid the Illysp of their champion. Now seemed as good a time as any to bequeath the Sword and its responsibility to someone else.

"Very well, Torin of Alson," Cianellen agreed softly. "As this is your fervent longing, I will see it done, in payment of the favor you granted me. When your friends awake, they will remember not that Allion was slain, only rendered unconscious. Your own fall will be attributed to smoke in the tunnels. None will have any memory of this journey you have made. None but I will know the truth."

Again Torin nodded, and, as he did so, Cianellen stepped forward with enchanting grace, bending to kiss his forehead. When she pulled away, he found her beaming. Once again, they were going to wed and have a thousand children.

"So," he said, smiling back, "how do we do this?"

The woman knelt and kissed Allion's forehead as she had his own. When finished, she reached up to brush Torin's cheek. "My dear child, it is already done."

As she stepped away, a warm rush began to spread throughout Torin's body. The sensation did not frighten him, for it felt very much like the power of the Sword. And yet, while the Sword's strength often surged and roiled until given release, Cianellen's remained tranquil and soothing, lulling him quickly to sleep. The weight upon his eyelids increased, and he found the brilliant light receding. The sound of ocean waves grew louder as, little by little, he was wrapped in gossamer layers of darkness. As dreams of blissful serenity permeated his soul, a pair of amethyst eyes flashed once, the radiance disappeared, and Torin felt himself drifting . . .

. . . fading . . .

. . . into the ever black.

CHAPTER FIFTY-SIX

THE SUN SLIPPED SLOW AND SULLEN from the bedding of night, dismissing predawn shadows and illuminating the sky with a dull reddish hue. Allion felt it upon his shoulder, its delicate warmth like a gentle nudge. A new day was breaking, and it was time to carry on.

Nevertheless, he remained where he was, knelt at the side of Torin's death-bed, paralyzed with inconsolable grief. For hours he had sat there, ever since he had awakened and demanded of his attendants a recounting of all that had happened. Ever since he had come to know the agonizing truth.

They had told him first of the assault upon the city by a horde of Illychar, its members arisen from both within and without. The fighting had been con-tained, however, due to the equally stunning emergence of General Rogun and his legions, scattered in secret throughout the city. While battle yet raged upon the slopes beyond their battlements, it appeared Krynwall itself had been made safe.

They had explained then how the hunter and his friends had been dis-covered in a smoke-filled corridor far from the palace, by a contingent of soldiers led by Commander Zain in a sweep of the city's underbelly. He, the Lady Marisha, and His Majesty, King Torin, had been found together, sooty and sweat-streaked, their breathing challenged by the poisoned air. They had been carried back to the castle and treated at once. The lady had yet to regain consciousness, but was alive.

His Majesty had been found dead, and would not be revived.

Allion had refused to believe it, and, despite the protests of his nurses and physicians, had set forth at once. After stopping by to check on Marisha, he had hastened on to Torin's chambers in order to reassure these fools that the king was very much alive, only resting, recovering from his wounds and his weariness, mustering his inner strength for the battle that lay ahead.

But the hunter had learned all too soon that the rumors were true. He had seen it in the stance of the guards posted outside the king's door. He had seen it in the somber faces of the healers and attendants that he shoved aside. After pushing past a tearful Stephan and seeing for himself his friend's calm and bloodless countenance, Allion could deny it no longer.

Torin was dead.

He had fallen to his knees beside the other, shaking off all who came to him, ordering them to leave. When alone, he had gripped his friend's hand—pulling it from the hilt around which both were clasped—and wept.

For some time, his vigil had gone undisturbed, during which he had wrestled with emotions of sorrow, fury, and disbelief. Where one ended, another began, repeating in what promised to be an endless cycle. Unable to even recall how it had happened, he knew only that it did not seem real.

At some point during the night, Marisha had come to him, and together, they had begun the process anew. Even then, they could make no sense of it. There was too much they did not remember, too much that had gone unseen. The last thing Allion could recall, following the deaths of Evhan and his Illychar brood, was recognizing the truth about Darinor and then finding himself unable to breathe. Her father, Marisha had explained, had used magic to steal his breath until he had fainted. She was able to add to that certain details of Torin's ensuing battle. She herself had assisted by taking up the archer's bow. Unable to wake him afterward, she had helped Torin to carry him away from the burning battleground, during which point, she, too, had blacked out. That Torin was the only one to perish from the air they had all breathed did not seem likely, but that was the account both had been given.

In the end, such reflections had provided no sense of closure. All they really did was add fuel to the fire, reminding them that not only Torin, but Darinor had been lost. In addition to the feelings of devastation wrought upon Marisha as a result, came the terrible understanding that everything the Entient had urged them to do had been meant to serve the enemy's goals, and not their own.

Somehow remembering his duty, Allion had called for a courier, dispatching him to Kuuria with all haste. Commander Troy was to be advised to disband their gathered forces, to send them home to their women and children—who now sat alone in unguarded cities. If the attack on Krynwall was any indication, it was reasonable to assume that Darinor's true plan had been to siphon off their defenders in order to gain a stranglehold upon their homes and loved ones—if not to make them into Illychar, then to make sure the lands' men-at-arms didn't dare resist.

Merely a guess, of course, and likely only the beginning of what Darinor had planned. They couldn't know, for if the mystic had revealed his intentions, or the reasons behind his various machinations, neither Allion nor Marisha had been conscious at the time. But they had too much to worry about going forward to waste time on revisiting what was past. If they meant to undo the Entient's treachery, they had to act fast.

Save for that initial message, however, Allion knew not what to do. Nor did he have the heart to try and figure it out. Let Pentania's kings and councils decide. For him, so much of this struggle had lost meaning with the passing of his friend.

Marisha had stayed with him as long as she could, but after a fit of coughing caused her to relapse into unconsciousness, he'd seen to it that her attendants carried her away again, with orders to keep her bedridden at least until morning.

He had turned his attention back to Torin, then, thinking that together, they might yet awake from this nightmare. He still could not understand how he was better off than both Torin, wielder of the Sword, *and* Marisha, who possessed the Pendant. Granted, laboring upright, where the air was thickest, would have caused them to inhale more of the harmful smoke than had found its way into his own lungs. And by the sound of it, Torin had done more of that than Marisha. But could lying low in a comatose state truly have made all the difference?

Perhaps someone or something else had been involved. Might Zain and his patrolmen have found the young king unconscious and decided to finish him off? It was a sinister suspicion, darker, perhaps, than the commander deserved. But Zain was Rogun's man, and Rogun wished to be king. And yet, had he resorted to such treachery, would it not have been safer to smother all three of them? What good would it have done the general and his designs to leave Allion and Marisha alive?

These questions and others tore through his mind as part of a relentless whirlwind. If only he could find a few answers, then perhaps he could assign to all of this madness some sort of meaning. Perhaps, if he understood how and why, he could accept that his childhood friend was gone, and discover strength and reason enough within himself to go on.

But the answers did not come. Only memories, in a long and unbroken string—even the most meaningless of which had become suddenly sacred in light of Torin's unexpected demise. Until recently, they had never been apart. It seemed impossible that the Ceilhigh should separate them now.

Hence the reason he could not bring himself to begin this day. To do so would be to allow his nightmares into the light and admit that they were real. To do so would be to accept that his life must continue, while his best friend's would not.

The outer door opened, and Allion cringed. He thought to turn and yell at whoever had been admitted to leave him be, but held his tongue, knowing already who it was. Sure enough, the door closed quietly, and Marisha's scent filled the room as she padded near on slippered feet.

He spoke without turning. "I told them you were to stay abed."

"And I told them to step aside and let me be." She paused, holding still and silent, allowing the air between them to soften. "Have you slept?"

"No."

She came forward then, though refrained from kneeling. "I've spoken to Commander Zain."

Allion turned.

"I asked him to explain himself—his intentions. I was trying to figure out if he had anything to do with . . ." She trailed off, her gaze slipping toward Torin.

"And?"

"He insists that General Rogun disobeyed orders for the good of Alson—as this night proves. They used Drakmar, as you suspected, as a base for their operations. I know not whether Nevik was coerced, but Zain swears that he has come to no harm."

"We'll know soon enough," Allion muttered, having decided that he preferred coercion to the idea that Nevik had willingly betrayed them.

"The baron must have had his reasons," Marisha added, as if reading his thoughts. "For it was he who ordered his couriers to ferry false reports on Rogun's whereabouts between Krynwall and the Gaperon, leading each to believe that our armies were stationed with the other."

"And providing cover for our general to begin smuggling his troops back into the city."

Marisha nodded. "A secret defense against what he and others saw as my father's foolishness." She hesitated, lowering her eyes. "I've not told anyone the truth. Regardless, it seems they were right."

While loath to admit it, Allion was thinking along similar lines, having already surmised much of what Marisha had sought to confirm with Zain. For the moment, at least, it would seem he had misjudged his land's highest-ranking general. Though right about the trap the other had set, he'd been wrong about the man's reasons for doing so.

Not that any of it mattered now. Rogun, Zain, Nevik—there were questions everywhere as to who could be trusted. And that was without taking into account those such as Bullrum, Evhan, Darinor—the scores who had fallen prey to Illysp possession. With Torin gone, and no one to turn to for help, this seemed a war already near its bitter end.

"You believe his story, then?" Allion asked, and was forced to choke back tears. "About how he found us?"

"I don't believe he had any reason to see Torin eliminated. He could have killed us all and taken the Sword for himself or for Rogun, yet did not. Had he done so, he might have even been allowed to keep it."

It was something Allion had not yet considered: the fate of the Crimson Sword. The royal will stated that it should be bequeathed to Marisha, should the king become unable to wield it. Allion was listed behind her. After that, Torin had desired that it belong to whomever the Circle of City Elders should select as Krynwall's new king. With all three of them gone, Rogun might indeed have been the ultimate beneficiary.

The hunter lifted his gaze to regard the divine talisman resting upon his friend's body, where its radiance had dimmed. "He can have it, for all I care."

"Don't say that," Marisha said, and dropped to her knees beside him. She turned his shoulders, forcing him to look into her glimmering eyes. "Don't you do this to me. I need you now, more than ever. We all do. Don't ask me to carry on this fight alone."

"The fight is over, Marisha. All is lost. Can't you see?"

"All is *not* lost, unless you throw away what remains to us. Our city is safe. He who led our enemy is slain. We have each other, and the Sword. But you suggested it yourself when you sent your message to Commander Troy: If we are to recover from what has happened here, we must attempt to do so swiftly."

He tried to look away, but she seized his chin and kissed him hard on the mouth.

"I need you to take up that blade," she said. "I need you to do as Torin would have wanted, and lead us forward where he cannot."

The hunter looked again at the weapon, but shook his head. "It's too soon, Marisha. How can you even ask that I—"

"I ask because your grief and mine are a luxury we cannot afford. I ask because we are either moving forward or falling behind. I'm not certain where these events leave us—any more than you are. I know only that we cannot sit around and wait to find out."

He had no answer for that, and so just stared at her, at this remarkable woman who had lost not only the man who might have been her husband, but her father as well. Knowing *that,* how could he possibly deny her this urgent request?

He was still marveling at her strength of will when a knock sounded and the outer door to Torin's suite cracked open.

"Pardon the intrusion, my lord. You've a young herald here with a message from the Circle."

Allion stiffened, compelled to dismiss the guardsman under threat of torture should he permit any more callers. But as he turned to do so, Marisha's magnificent blue orbs fixed upon him, their yearning plain.

"You may admit him, Sergeant."

The door opened wider, and a somber Pagus stepped through. "I'm sorry to disturb you, my lord, my lady," he said, nodding to each in acknowledgment. He then looked upon the bed where Torin lay, his young eyes red and puffy.

"What news do you bear, Pagus?"

"My lord, General Rogun has returned. The enemy has been sent away in full retreat. The general has demanded that the Circle convene, that he might address the city's leadership."

Allion shared another look with Marisha. He should have expected nothing less. Rogun's ambush had saved them all this night. But for what purpose going forward remained to be seen.

"Has Elder Thaddreus agreed?"

"He has, my lord. He wishes that you would attend, to shed light on . . . on other matters, my lord. Provided you are well enough."

Allion turned away, from both the young herald and Marisha, back to Torin.

"What message shall I bear him, my lord?"

The hunter did not respond right away, but gripped his friend's cold hand once more. He then set it back atop the other, lifting both long enough to grab the Crimson Sword and pull it free. With the talisman's warmth gushing through his veins, he drew his cramped legs beneath him and rose slowly to his feet.

"Never mind, my young friend," he said, looking past the Sword to Marisha as she stood beside him. "I shall deliver it myself."

Look, they told her. *Do you see?*

Necanicum dug her chin into her shoulder, ready with her retort, but stopped as the red rim of the sun cleared the wooded horizon, spilling blood through the trees.

It has happened.

"I'm not a fool," she muttered. "I know what it means."

Then why do you tarry?

She had seen them before, these blood-suns. But never one like this. With a mother's instinct, her hand went to the phial hung around her neck, its inner heart beating to the rhythm of her own.

Have you forgotten what we are doing out here?

"I've forgotten nothing," she snapped, so suddenly that she felt a crick in her neck. "The only surprise would have been if it *didn't* happen, remember?"

But so soon. The Leviathan's hunger grows, and we still have a long way to go.

"Yes, we do. And if you quit pestering me, I could finish my breakfast, and we could be on our way."

To her surprise, the Teldara did not respond. Their silence alarmed her, momentarily. So seldom did they allow her the final word. She could almost feel their awe, and it was not like them to be awed by anything. It did not bode well.

"Oh, have it your way, then," she said, emptying her small bowl of mashed roots-and-berries in disgust. "I'm not all that hungry anyway."

You will need your strength.

"I have all that I need, and more, and never you forget it," she grumbled, gathering up her things. "You'd just better be right about this."

But of course, they always were.

They could have reminded her, but didn't, as she shouldered her skins and pouches and stamped upon the ground where she had slept, muttering a cleansing rite. When that was finished, she wasted no time, but shuffled onward, north through the trees.

While from the east, the dawning sun rained blood upon her back.